Summer of the Brilliant

By

Hank Burroughs

with Tony Burroughs

To Bobbie
Don't get caught reading this in church!
Hank

© 2002 by Hank Burroughs. All rights reserved.

No part of this book may be reproduced, stored in a retrieval system, or transmitted by any means, electronic, mechanical, photocopying, recording, or otherwise, without written permission from the author.

ISBN: 0-7596-6636-9

Cover illustration © Mystic Seaport, Rosenfeld Collection, Mystic, Connecticut

This book is printed on acid free paper.

1stBooks – rev. 4/13/02

Dedication

This book is dedicated to the late Arthur Knapp, Jr. Sailors everywhere remember Arthur but few have been fortunate enough to know him for as many years or in as many roles as I have.

When I came to Larchmont, NY, as a 16 year old from the middle of North Carolina, we became neighbors. He took us under his wing and soon my whole family was sailing on Long Island Sound from the Larchmont Yacht Club. He was free in his criticism of both my sailing and social behavior.

One afternoon just before sunset I was towing my 110 across Long island Sound for Manhasset Bay Race Week. I was under power with my Dad's 30 foot sloop when I spotted Arthur becalmed in his International, *Bumblebee*. When I offered him a tow, he said, "You damn well better, Willie Henry, or I'll tell your parents about the party you had last weekend when they were out of town." We both survived my teen years, and my life long love of sailing and respect for Arthur grew.

While I was in college, Arthur paid me the highest compliment by asking me to do the drawings for his book, *Race Your Boat Right*. In his third edition, he thanked me for the drawings, which were made and updated over a period of twenty years. "Matter of fact, he and his family moved in across the street from us when he was a kid, and doggone it, if we didn't make sailors out of that whole family of four cotton-picking Southerners—and damned good sailors at that!"

When my wife, Nancy, and I took our first long cruise in 1958, Arthur was on hand to personally survey the old boat we were investing our life savings in. The day we left he sent us on our way with a ship's clock, a bottle of good scotch and a jib from *Bumblebee*. When we left on our last cruise in 1987, he was also there to see us off (and to check out our latest boat).

I miss Arthur. He's in Fiddler's Green now. When he reads the book he will laugh – but I *know* that if he sees any mistakes in the sailing parts, I'll hear from him..

Acknowledgements

It is unlikely that anyone has ever had as much fun writing a book as I did. When I had written about a thousand pages I sent copies to some friends. I had been told that friends would not be objective, they would be polite and not criticize. Not true. Those people who actually read the book kept me busy making changes for several years. At one point I wiped out 200 pages and killed off 15 characters. I will always be grateful for the encouragement and the serious constructive criticism from all the people who helped me.

My wife Nancy should be listed with me on the cover. Her contribution was enormous. After the first year we started talking about the characters as if they were real. I got used to being told that "Gus would never do that" or "Rocket would do it this way." She has sailed with me on 8 of the 9 boats I've owned and been with me to every place that Devlin goes. While Rocket is a combination of several people she is mostly my wife.

After working with five different proofreaders I decided to use my professional judgement and picked the prettiest one. Fortunately for me Traci Martineau turned out to be far more than I hoped for. She became a copy editor, story consultant, severe critic and good friend. She made the book much better and the work a lot more fun.

The Sketch charts of the Bahams are used through the kindness and courtesy of Thomas Daly, the owner of Tropical Island Publishers. The *Yachtsman's Guide to the Bahamas*, which has hundreds of sketch charts like these, is not only an excellent book for anyone cruising this area – it is a real work of art.

The cover photograph is Carleton Mitchell's famous *Finisterre,* winner, of three Bermuda Races. It is used with permission of the Mystic Seaport, Rosenfeld Collection, Mystic, CT. My thanks to Peggy Tate Smith for her help and support in planning this cover.

My first reader was my mother-in-law, the late Zoa Dreyer. When I was a teenager I used to climb up on her roof at night to see Nancy. I had to crawl past her window. She would always catch me and tell me to go home. I was used to Zoa telling me where to go and what to do so I was pleased when she said go home and finish the book.

Barbara Anderson read an early version. She said she laughed at the serious parts because she couldn't imagine me writing a book but she liked it and encouraged me to finish it.

After Eric Benson read the book we went to lunch and I asked him what he thought. He told me. Then he said his daughters read it and told me what they thought about the book, then his wife and then his dog. I didn't believe his dog actually read it but Eric said the dog liked it. Encouragement helps and I never argue with my dentist.

My brother, Jim Burroughs, read several versions and made good suggestions. Jim sailed for many years with the late Arthur Knapp so he knows about the sailing stuff. He reminded me that some of the things he pointed out in the first version were still wrong in the fifth. Hard headed-ness runs in our family but I did make the changes. Jim also recruited readers for me – risking his friendship with a number of people.

Dr. Henry Leon is a famous clinical psychologist. He read an early version, psychoanalyzed Devlin, and pointed out that he was nuts. He also suggested that Devlin might be a little like me. After several versions of the book, and a lot of changes, Devlin is a little more normal but I haven't changed.

My son, Tony Burroughs, carried manuscripts on business trips all over the country. He called from Dallas one day to confess that he had lost a huge three ring binder with a lot of chapters and a lot of people. We were both relieved to find out that I had already killed all those people. He is responsible for Dr. Laufenberg and his part in the story. Tony will be even more involved in writing the next book. Look out.

My cousin, Jack Burroughs, read an early version and pointed out that Devlin was too mean so I made some changes. A few years later his son Justin (who was playing professional football at the time) read it and said Devlin wasn't mean enough. Readers have asked when the next book is coming out...when Jack and Justin get together and decide how nasty Devlin is going to be!

Nancy's sister Linda Brooks read the next to last version and pointed out that Dr. Henry Leon had normalized Devlin too much. She is personally responsible for what happened to Mr. Whittaker and his Mercedes-Benz.

I talked to Nancy's niece, Leslie Sylvetsky, right after she read the section on the Billy Goat and she wasn't too friendly. It was as if she had discovered a dark side to her uncle. After she read about art smuggling and craniofacial surgery I was O. K. again.

Peggy Gilbert read five different versions and suggested some way to make each version better than the one before. Peggy read the last version aboard our boat during a short cruise to Coconut Grove where we visited Monty's and Green Street. Like Nancy and Traci she refers to the characters by their first names. While we were having lunch at Green Street Peggy mentioned that Lisa was a really nice person. Nancy nearly choked on her sandwich because she and Traci had conspired to get Lisa Winter out of the book.

Caroline Lancaster was our waitress that day and asked if I was William S. Burroughs who wrote *Naked Lunch*. I explained that I was William HENRY Burroughs and write as "Hank Burroughs" so that there is no confusion.

Nancy's cousin, The Rev Canon Matthew Borden, an Episcopal priest, insisted that Sidney Fontaine is not realistic. He says that no Episcopal priest would ever have time to build both a model railroad and an airplane.

Les Woodcock is the only professional fiction writer who read the book. His comments, criticism and encouragement meant a lot to me.

Bob Hobson, my brother's brother-in-law pointed out that Devlin was an existentialist. I didn't know that and it sounded pretty bad so I went back and made him an Episcopal. A lot of Bob's ideas will be put in the second book.

I wanted the erotic parts to be interesting. I wasn't sure I knew how until Tony O'Callaghan read the book. He claims it took six months to read. He said that he would start reading at night, get interested in the sex and have to stop reading. At least I didn't put him to sleep. Tony now speaks fluent Spanish.

Sonia Peña is not an ordinary run-of-the-mill extremely beautiful Puerto Rican root canal dentist. She is unusual. In addition to helpful suggestions about priests, she pointed out that manuscripts that are double spaced and printed on one side in huge three-ring binders are hard to read on airplanes. Up until then I couldn't figure out why so few people finished the book. Sonia will appear again in the second book in the role of a psychiatrist.

Julia White was my expert on Hispanic people, their language and culture. We spent several mornings at Lester's Diner in Fort Lauderdale working on the Spanish phrases (and laughing hysterically.)

One day my brother Jim called and said Bill Wynn would be willing to read the book. He said to mail it to Bill in Destin, Florida where he was on vacation from being retired. I happened to be going to Destin a few days later so early one morning I knocked on Bill's door and surprised him with two huge three-ring binders. It rained the next two days and Bill couldn't play golf so he is the only reader to read from start to finish straight through. He pointed out to me that readers really like sailboat races — but not when Devlin and Rocket are about to be killed.

One day Chris Rennie called up and said he was my new agent and could get my book published. Before he could go any further I interrupted and asked him what he knew about boats. He said he was a sailor, owned a boat and had just read a book called *Sopranino*. Since Patrick Ellam's book is my all time favorite I knew Chris had good judgement. Eventually I learned that Chris works for 1st Books Library.

Authors Note: Important

Summer of the Brilliant is the first book of a trilogy. All three books involve a religious organization named **Prostates Tou Christu**. This is Greek for *Bodyguards of the Christ*, which is the title of the third book. Although it is total fiction, and only fiction, there are some real people in the story. Carlos Lehder Rivas who liked to be called Joe is a real person who owned a house on Norman's Cay in the Bahamas. It was called Volcano because of the conical roof. He was involved in some way in the drug trade. At the time the book was written he was serving time in an undisclosed Federal Prison. He testified during the 1991 trial of Manuel Noriega. Lehder says that the U.S. reneged on a promise to him of a reduced sentence to be served in a German prison. Lehder has never been accused of any sex crime and no implication was intended. A few of the people at the party are real but none of the real ones are actually involved in the story.

Five of the bars and restaurants, Monty Trainer's, The Taurus, Green Street, The Hungry Sailor and the Café Europa were real and doing well at the time this book was written. All of them serve great food and drinks. All are favorites of ours. The Horny Frog and Café de Rat Mort are pure fiction. The famous Fontainebleau is, of course, real.

Saint Stephens Episcopal Church in Coconut Grove is real but there has never been a priest there like Sidney Fontaine. Probably there has never been a priest anywhere like Sidney. Let's hope not.

The story of the robbery in December 1971 from the Tours Museum told by Ricardo Salazar is essentially true. The paintings were real and all the people were real. The story was taken from the files of the organizations mentioned.

The organization called the **Prostates Tou Christu** might be real. In the Fall of 1951 I frequently hitch-hiked up to Skidmore College in Sarasota Springs. My girlfriend had to be in at midnight while the girlfriend of my fraternity brother and traveling companion could stay out until one. I had an hour to wait so I found a convenient bar that stayed open late. It was always filled with immigrants from Europe, especially Russians. One of them, an Orthodox Russian priest, told me about the **Bodyguards of the Christ**. I was fascinated and talked to him many times that year to learn more. The following year he was gone. Several times since then I have spoken to other people who have heard of it but nobody has any written proof. I do not know if it ever existed but I believe it did. Maybe it still does.

Prologue

New Haven, Connecticut

Laufenberg pressed the button and the tiny machine stopped rewinding. He pushed the play button and listened once again to the critical part of the audiotape.

Dr.Laufenberg - Mr. Devlin, how did you feel right after you threw Milo Carter out the window?

Devlin - I don't know. I don't think I felt anything.

Dr.Laufenberg - That *is* a serious problem and it *is* something that concerns me. You had just thrown a person out of a second-story window and you felt nothing. He might have been killed, didn't that bother you?

Devlin - It was only the second-story and the snow was two or three feet deep.

Dr.Laufenberg - He could have been seriously injured.

Devlin - Do you think I should have hit him in the mouth instead? I could have hurt my hand.

Dr. Laufenberg (in a whisper) - Holy Shit!

The psychiatrist switched off his tape recorder, laughing again at himself for his last comment. Then he left his office to meet with his strange client in Guido's Bar and Grill. "Holy Shit!" wasn't the kind of thing that a professional said out loud during a session with a patient but it *was* the first thing that Otto Laufenberg could say after hearing how his patient had thrown a student out of a classroom window during a mid-year history exam.

Laufenberg was a very good psychiatrist. In addition to a first class mind, excellent training and extensive experience, he had an intangible quality that made people trust him immediately and completely. He also had a sense of humor. An unprofessional comment like this was rare but the story was startling and the way it was described was totally without emotion. His patient, Winfield Scott Devlin, had told it the same way he would have described a trip to the grocery store. He knew that Devlin could be dangerous – even capable of killing.

The case itself was simple. Milo Carter had been cheating by copying from his patient in tests and exams. He cheated from other people too, but Devlin didn't care about that. Carter had been doing it since freshman year but not in every exam, only once in a while. Devlin had told him to quit but he didn't. Devlin also told two instructors, who had done nothing. One day, during a history exam, Carter started doing it again so Devlin opened a window and threw him out.

While the dean conducted an investigation, Devlin was temporarily suspended from classes and required to see Dr. Laufenberg. The dean had made it clear that Devlin would be permanently expelled unless Laufenberg could provide sufficient reason for reinstatement. They had met twice a week for over a month and today was the final session.

"I don't think there is any reason for you to come back to see me again. From our sessions I have concluded that your condition and attitude are not mental problems. You do have a highly developed sense of right and wrong. That is admirable. You made a number of sincere efforts to put a stop to what was happening and consciously decided to do what you did. You made real efforts to get this person to stop cheating, you were patient in trying to solve the problem, and I know your actions were *not* taken in the heat of the moment. Actually, you were far more reasonable, I believe, than most people. You were methodical, objective, careful, thoughtful, mature, and completely unemotional handling the problem.

"There was a point Mr. Devlin, when you crossed the line into a mental state which I find to be very disturbing. You were faced with a situation which other people failed to solve for you. You were left to deal with the problem on your own. To use an old and trite expression, you took matters into your own hands. You appointed yourself judge and jury, you pronounced the verdict and carried out the sentence. Would you do the same thing again?"

Devlin looked very hard at the man knowing his answer would play a big part in allowing him to return to school in the fall. With a bad recommendation he would never return.

"Probably," he answered.

They were silent for a few minutes and just stared at each other. The doctor opened a drawer in his desk and took out a copy of a letter addressed to the dean with a copy to the parents. He allowed Devlin to read the letter. It was several pages long and described the visits to him and what they had talked about. It was completely accurate in describing how Carter had started cheating and copying test answers at the beginning of freshman year. It pointed out how Devlin had asked him to stop and had warned him on several occasions. It also mentioned his final warning to Carter but did *not* say that he had been very specific when he said he would "throw him out the fucking window." It also named the two faculty members to whom Devlin had spoken after the warning. This was a surprise. If the dean believed him, as Laufenberg did, those two would be in trouble. Dr. Laufenberg concluded the letter by saying that Devlin had lost control and became emotional when he realized that Carter was cheating again. He was not telling the truth but he was probably telling the dean what he needed to hear. His recommendations were strong and unqualified. He strongly recommended that Devlin be allowed to return to classes in the fall.

Devlin was surprised at the letter for two reasons. One, that he pushed so hard for him to get back to school, but even more surprising, was his statement that his actions were emotional and impulsive. Most of the last two or three sessions had actually centered around the knowledge that what he did was *neither impulsive nor emotional*. In his letter Laufenberg had told the dean the opposite of what Devlin had revealed to him. When he finished reading the letter, he didn't know what to say.

"Thank you."

"Mr. Devlin, there is a postscript to the letter which I do not want to put in writing. I don't want to put it in any record of my sessions with you. There is no reason for you to see me again professionally and the letter has already been mailed to the dean. Unless he insists on further action, the matter is closed and within a few days you will be informed that you can go back to school in the Fall. You are free to leave and I will send your parents a copy of the letter. I have nothing more to say to you officially but I would like to talk to you privately.

"When you walk out the door of the building, take a right turn. There is a tavern two blocks down on the left-hand side of the street next to a dry-cleaning place. Stop there and I will meet you. I will tell you a few things that are not in my official letter or even in my records. Some of the audio tapes will be destroyed. What I tell you will be unofficial."

After Devlin left the office Laufenberg turned on the tape recorder and listened several more times to what he considered to be the most important part.

While he was walking toward the bar Devlin couldn't help wondering what the doctor had left out of the letter. He was very relieved to find out that Laufenberg recommended he be allowed back in school. It was a beautiful day with a touch of spring in the air. The sky was a hard steely *bleu de cobalt*, with white puffy clouds in the east but over in the west some black ones were grouping for mischief. He didn't know the dean very well but felt confident he would do what the doctor suggested. He *did* think it was pretty strange for a psychiatrist to want to meet a patient in a bar but Devlin knew it was pretty strange for *anyone* to throw people out of windows. But then Carter had really pissed him off.

By the time he got to the bar the sky started to cloud up. Most of it was still a hard brittle blue but the ominous black clouds were beginning to move. Guido's bar was nothing special. It was only a little after four o'clock when he walked in so the after-work crowd hadn't started to fill up the place. He ordered a beer and sat down in a corner booth. Dr. Laufenberg came in immediately after. He looked quite different in an old beat-up maroon sweater he had worn so that he wouldn't look out of place in a blue collar bar. Around his eyes his skin was fishy white while the rest of his face was a dark tan. He had a small nose and huge eyes, wore big horn-rimmed glasses, and the combination made him look funny—like a cartoon owl. In the semi-darkness the white around his eyes made them stand out even more than before. He got a drink and joined Devlin in the booth, stared for a few minutes without saying a word and then took a big sip of whiskey. Devlin knew, somehow, that he could be trusted.

"Devlin, I'm afraid that you are going to kill somebody."

Devlin didn't know *how* to respond so he didn't say anything. Laufenberg waited a few minutes and took another sip of whiskey, finished it off while staring at Devlin, and motioned the waiter for another. When his drink arrived, he took another sip and started talking.

"A few years ago I worked as a psychiatrist in Attica Prison in upstate New York. In a place like that, there are all kinds of men. The variety of crimes they had committed was incredible and our long range goal was to try to rehabilitate them. I don't think we ever really did this but we *did* try. These men fell into groups more or less along the lines of the crimes they had committed. The burglars had similar characteristics, the sex offenders had their own, and so on. However, there was one small group of men that didn't fall into any distinct criminal pattern. In other words, they didn't have a history like the other inmates. They weren't part of any other psychological group. Basically, they didn't have enough things in common to make up a category. The similarity was that they all had committed crimes of violence without passion or emotion. I became very interested in these men and spent extra time with them. I even wrote a paper about them. It was eventually published but I realized later that it wasn't any good because of the final conclusions.

"Actually, the real problem was the *lack* of meaningful conclusions. We psychiatrists like to think we are scientists. We like to present facts that come to a conclusion or form a hypothesis. These men were all forced into situations beyond their control trying to solve their own problems. When they couldn't, they had gone to the appropriate place to ask for help. The help that they sought was not forthcoming. The authority in power failed to help them or never even tried.

"In every case I studied the men dealt with their problems intelligently, logically, and with great patience. They had all been very careful about not breaking the law. When they met with defeat, they kept trying to solve the problem and I believe they each had exhausted all legal means to do so. I am not speaking as a lawyer now. Perhaps in some cases there was a legal angle or something that could have made a difference. I don't know about that. Anyway, each of these men had tried everything he knew and asked help from every source that he could think of. Now, listen carefully, Mr. Devlin.

"At a certain point each of these men had been screwed by the system. This happens in life. It happens all the time. A lot more than we would like to believe. A normal person gives up and quits trying. Sometimes the person is bitter, at other times philosophical. It doesn't matter. What does matter, is that a normal person tries to go on and with life and forget what happened. He accepts the fact that life, or the system, or whatever has beaten him this time and he goes on to the next thing. He is sometimes ashamed of himself for giving up but knows he has to go on living.

"This group of men that I studied were not like that. They didn't give up or stop. They did what, to them, was the next logical step. They took over the situation, took one more step, and somebody got hurt. In some cases they even killed people.

"They didn't *plan* to kill, but they took the risk and it didn't work. They were put in jail for killing people. You have done something similar to what these men did and you might have been thrown out of school as a result. It could be worse."

"Do you really think I could kill somebody?" Devlin asked.

"I don't know. But I *do* believe you might go one step too far if you felt that there was an injustice that needed to be righted or a wrong that needed to be corrected. If the situation was extreme, then your dealing with it would be just as extreme. The way you would deal with it *could* go too far and *could* lead to a catastrophe. *If certain conditions were totally intolerable to you I do believe you could commit a murder.*"

Devlin sat back and looked at the doctor. In the darkness of the bar Laufenberg's black, oversized, horn-rimmed glasses with the white skin around his eyes made him look really weird. He did not know what to say or what to do so he just sat and stared. After what seemed like a very long time, Laufenberg excused himself and went to the men's room.

"Get me another whiskey," he asked as he left and this time Devlin ordered one for himself as well. He *needed* it.

When the doctor came back a few minutes later, he started talking almost before he sat down. Nobody in the bar was paying any attention to them. Guido's was beginning to fill up with people getting off from work and starting to get noisy.

"My report to the university was mailed yesterday. If I had included in it the things I am saying to you now, it would have confused the dean and I don't believe he would let you back into school. What I'm trying to explain to you is complex. It is also highly *speculative* on my part. I also want you to know that I am trying to prepare you and to warn you. This warning is for a moment that might never happen. But it could be an incident that could change your whole life if you do the wrong thing.

"Professionally, I am on very thin ice. As a psychiatrist I should *not* try to predict or forecast anything. I would certainly *not* put it in a report to the dean of the University. If I did, he would probably throw you out of school permanently and never use my services again."

Although two beers and the whiskey were affecting Devlin, his head was clear. The doctor had taken off his sweater. The whiskey had also affected him but he was tense because what he had to say was very important. During the entire time they had been there Devlin had hardly said anything. In the office Laufenberg had mostly asked questions and Devlin had done most of the talking.

Here in the bar, the doctor was doing all the talking. He was summing up everything he had been told and putting it together with his past experience and training. Devlin also had a strong feeling of trust. Laufenberg certainly didn't have to be telling him these things.

"I'm going to warn you that sometime in your life you are going to have a situation that you cannot accept. I believe that you will go much further than most people to try to make things right. You're going to try to change things and do everything possible to see that justice is done. I am not being facetious. This justice that you are seeking will be real, it will *not* be a mixed-up version that criminal minds think up. It will not be warped.

"At that point you will have done everything correctly and legally. But when the authorities fail, the sources that you look to for help, you will then try to do it yourself. But, when you have been unable to make things right, you will take an unpredictable course of action. You may not intend to commit a criminal act because you are not a criminal and do not think like one. What you do, however, will not be the action that a *normal* person would take. I am afraid that you will do something that will get you in a great deal of trouble, perhaps even prison. This is a warning to you. When that time comes, *do not trust your instincts.*"

Laufenberg was staring at Devlin intensely. His hand was wrapped tightly around the glass. He was not calm and collected like he had been during the sessions in his office. Devlin did not doubt one bit that he was right.

By this time it had started to grow dark outside and was starting to rain. A waiter looked at them and they both nodded. Somehow he knew not to interrupt.

"When I was asking you about getting into fights as a boy, you said you never got into fights. I don't believe that. Every boy gets into fights at one time or another. I stopped asking you questions about this in the office fearing what your answers would be, but I want to talk about it now. Was there ever an incident when you were forced to fight someone? Some incident when you had to use your fists to defend yourself?"

Laufenberg knew there was something left out. Devlin would not have understood it a few weeks ago. That afternoon in the bar in New Haven, with the rain coming down and two whiskeys in him, he knew and understood. He told Laufenberg about sixth grade.

Devlin had grown up in a nice town and in a nice neighborhood, the kind of place where bad things didn't happen. At least not very often. There were a few fights in school but not too many and he never got into them. He stayed out of them because he was afraid someone would get hurt. It wasn't fear that kept him out of fights, he just couldn't see any point to it. He wasn't frightened at the prospect of a fight when he was a kid and he never got excited or upset. He tried to avoid them if he could, which was most of the time. If somebody actually started one and he couldn't get away from it, he would turn it into a wrestling match.

He would go after the other guy but not with his fists. He would grab him up close where he couldn't hit back. He got in trouble a few times for being in fights but never for starting one. He got hit a few times and got some black eyes and bloody noses but he never hit anybody with his fist. He was embarrassed a few times when he avoided fights and sometimes somebody would call him chicken or something, but not too often.

In the fall when he was in the sixth grade he did have a problem. There was a guy in his class named Charley Crawford who started beating him up. Charley was a little older and a lot bigger. He probably failed a grade or two at some time. He started beating up Devlin after school. At first it wasn't every day, maybe three times a week. Sometimes he would use his fists but most of the time they would just wrestle and roll around on the ground. He would ask Devlin if he gave up and Dev would say yes and they would go home. If Devlin gave up too soon Charley didn't like it so he learned to time it. At this point the doctor interrupted.

"How long did this go on?"

"A month or two."

"What did you do?"

"Nothing."

"Why not?"

"I got used to it."

"You mean he would wait for you after school every day and beat you up?"

"That's right."

"Did you ever tell one of your teachers or your mother?"

"Not until later. I thought he would get tired of it after a while."

"Did he?"

"No."

"What happened next?"

Devlin told him about Mrs. Anderson. She was an art teacher in the high school, a tall, skinny woman with red hair. There was an art exhibit at the library one Saturday and he went down to see it. He had always liked to paint and draw and he really liked to look at pictures in books. His parents had all sorts of books about art and he spent a lot of time looking at them. That day he spent all afternoon looking at the exhibits. There were oils and watercolors and pastels and even some sculpture. He learned that most of the work was by Mrs. Anderson's students and that she had done some paintings herself. She was there all day talking to people, serving coffee and bragging about her students. She noticed him hanging around but she didn't try to run him off or anything.

Late in the afternoon the crowd thinned out and she came over and started talking to him. She asked him if he was an artist. She meant to be cute like when somebody asks a little kid if he is a fireman because he's wearing a fireman's hat. When she asked him if he was an artist, he said he was only twelve years old and how could he be an artist. After that she talked to him differently.

They talked about pictures and he asked her a lot of questions. She was very nice and didn't act like the questions were dumb. She told him that one particular group of pictures was by a girl student from a high school in the next town who took private lessons from her. He had never heard of private art lessons and didn't know there was such a thing. Devlin asked her how much she charged for private lessons and she told him they were expensive and that when he got a little older maybe he could afford them. He asked her exactly how much and when she told him he decided to call home because he didn't know whether it was a lot or not. He didn't have any money for the telephone but didn't want to make a bad impression so he didn't try to borrow from her. He found an empty office in the library and went in when nobody was looking. He called his mother and asked her if he could take art lessons. She said it was all right so he went back to find Mrs. Anderson. She was busy so he waited until people started leaving. When she was free, he told her he could take lessons.

"My mom says it's okay and I can take art lessons. I just called her on the telephone."

"What did she say?" she asked, looking surprised.

"It's all right. I can take art lessons if it's okay with you."

"When did you talk to her?"

"I just called from the coin telephone booth," he lied.

"What did she say exactly?"

"She said to find out if we pay by the week or the month, and if you would take a check on a local bank."

She was startled but she did agree to do it. She told him that he could come directly to the high school when his last class got out and use the room where she taught art class during the day. Because his school got out before her last class was over he could be there just as it ended. She said that they would try it for a while and see how it went, but only if he could be there on time and if he had some talent.

The first week was terrific. By not losing any time when his school let out and practically running, he could get to the high school about five minutes early. Mrs. Anderson said she thought he had talent so he started really looking forward to the lessons. Charley Crawford was out that week with the measles or the chicken pox or something.

That first week everything went perfectly but the next one was a mess. He ran out of school when the bell rang, just like the week before, and started for the high school. There was Charley waiting for him. He made up for lost time and really worked on Devlin. He tried to break away and run but this didn't work because Charley kept hitting him with his fists. He showed up for his art lesson twenty minutes late with blood all over his shirt. Mrs. Anderson was really upset. He told her another boy had beaten him up and that it wasn't his fault. She worked with him twenty minutes extra to make up for the time he had missed but she made it obvious that she didn't like it one bit.

The next day he went out a different door of the school and slipped past Charley. He did this for two days but Charley caught on to what he was doing and started following him. He would follow him out of the school door and then, when he was off of the school grounds, he would grab Devlin and start fighting. He showed up three days in a row late for art lessons. He decided that he had to do something.

He found Charley in the school cafeteria one day and told him what was happening, hoping he would understand. Devlin even offered to come back after the art lessons so they could fight. Charley thought the art lessons were the funniest thing he had ever heard of and started calling him Rembrandt in school. Before he learned about the art lessons he would sometimes skip a day. After that it seemed to be the biggest thing in his life to make sure he missed art lessons or at least be late. The whole thing seemed crazy. Talking to Charley was pointless. It just seemed to give him more incentive. Devlin told his mother about it and for a few days she picked him up after school and drove him to the lessons. This worked out fine but after a week she had to stop because she had too many other things to do.

After a week she thought Charley would forget about Devlin but as soon as she stopped picking him up at school, he started the beatings again. The doctor interrupted with a question.

"Why didn't you go to your teacher or the principal?"

"I did. I went to the principal and told him the whole story. I was afraid that I might get Charley in trouble and that would make it worse for me but I really didn't want to miss the art lessons. The principal said he couldn't do anything because it was after school hours and off the school grounds. My mother believed me but not completely. Anyway, I didn't want to keep bothering her."

"Couldn't you make your lessons at a different time?"

"The only available time was after her last class. She taught a few students at home but she lived too far away for me to walk or even ride a bike. We had to do it at the high school or not at all."

Laufenberg knew the details were very important. The twelve year old Devlin was in a situation where he had tried all the things he could think of and nothing changed. Nothing changed except Charley. He stopped hitting Devlin as much with his fists and started holding him down so he couldn't get away. What became important to him was to make sure he was late for the art class. Maybe he figured that a bloody nose or a black eye would scare Mrs. Anderson and get him into trouble or spoil his fun. Devlin realized that he had tried everything and had to do something about it himself. He had to do it quickly or Mrs. Anderson would get fed up with him being late which would be the end of the lessons, so he came up with a plan.

In his room he had a baseball bat. It wasn't a full size bat it was a souvenir he had gotten at a Yankee game. It was as big as a regular bat would be for a kid his size. The day after he came up with his plan he carried a poster chart he was working on in the school art class when he left school. When it was rolled up it was large enough to hide the baseball bat and he practiced in his room carrying the rolled up poster with the bat inside. He wanted it to look like nothing but art work. He carried the poster with him to school for three days in a row with nothing inside. Each time Charley would see him with the poster in the morning. Then in the afternoon, when he grabbed Devlin, the poster would fall on the ground empty. After the beating, he would pick up the torn poster and run to his art class so Charley got used to seeing him with the poster. He also started going out of a different door each day.

The day he picked to execute his plan, he went out a door that led to a courtyard which was the center of the whole school. There was an archway between two parts of the building which led outside but to go that way was longer than using an outside door. He picked that door because it was never used and nobody would be around when Charley followed. As soon as a person went out they turned around a corner of the building. He wanted to have a minute when Charley couldn't see him so he could get the bat out of the poster and get ready. He carried the rolled up poster with the bat in it to school in the morning and put it in his locker.

Charley saw him do it just like the other mornings and Devlin was sure he didn't know there was anything inside the rolled up paper. At the end of the school day he went to his locker and got the bat. He didn't carry any books with him because he wanted both hands free. He started down the hall toward the door he had picked while most of the kids were headed in the opposite direction since that was the shortest way out of school. When he got to the door he glanced back and there was Charley about twenty feet behind. He walked normally, but as soon as he got to the corner he turned it quickly so he couldn't be seen. He dropped the poster and took the bat in both hands, waiting like a baseball player in his stance at the plate, with the bat back and ready to swing. When Charley came around the corner Devlin waited two seconds to make sure it was him and then swung the bat as hard as he could. His aim was perfect and the fat part of bat hit Charley right in the mouth. It made a really terrible sound when the bat hit his lips and a loud cracking noise when his teeth shattered. There was a lot of blood and Charley screamed and fell down backwards. After he had heard the whole story Laufenberg just sat and stared. Finally he took a big swallow of his whiskey.

"Jesus Christ," he said.

Devlin didn't say anything.

"What happened next?"

"I grabbed the poster and took off running down the courtyard and out through the archway. I was only about two minutes late for my art lesson. Mrs. Anderson thanked me for being on time and we went ahead with the lesson. Afterwards, just when I was getting ready to leave, my mother came rushing in. She was very upset. She said there had been a terrible accident at school and that Charley Crawford had been taken to the hospital. She wanted to know if I knew anything about it and I told her I had hit him with a baseball bat. Her eyes got big and she started crying, then she got sick. She went into the next room and threw up in a sink. Mrs. Anderson didn't say anything but "My God!" or something like that. After a while my mom calmed down enough to drive me home. My dad was there and he had to hear the whole story.

"What did you tell your father?"

"I told him everything. That night my parents went to the hospital to see what had happened to Charley."

"What *did* happen to Charley?"

"His jaw was broken in six places and about half his teeth were knocked out and his lips needed hundreds of stitches. He didn't ever come back to our school again. It cost a lot of money to get him fixed – I think about five thousand dollars. His dad and my dad got together with some lawyers and insurance people and worked out who paid for it. Of course, my dad paid for a lot of the expenses."

"What about you?"

"What do you mean?"

"Were you punished or what?"

"Dad said that I needed to be punished but that he didn't know what to do. For the rest of that year my mother picked me up at school and I had to go straight home. Mrs. Anderson cancelled my art classes. They also had me talk to a psychiatrist."

"What did he tell you?" Laufenberg asked.

"The psychiatrist believed that I lost my temper when I hit Charley. Even when I told him I brought the bat to school and hit him on purpose he wouldn't believe me. He convinced himself that I just happened to be carrying the bat and what I did was out of fear. That's what he told my parents."

"What did you think about the psychiatrist?" he asked. Laufenberg was hunched over the table and looking at his former patient as if the answer were the key to some deep, dark mystery. By then Guido's was full of smoke and was also pretty noisy but neither of them paid any attention. It was raining hard outside. Very hard.

"You want the truth?" Devlin finally asked.

"Yes. What did you think of what the psychiatrist told you and your parents?"

"I thought he was full of shit. Charley Crawford was a pain in the ass to everybody. The teachers didn't like him because he was always disrupting the class making wise cracks. He wasn't too bright. They liked me because I worked hard, got good grades and stayed out of trouble. The only people that actually saw Charley after I hit him were two janitors and the people in the ambulance. The doctors saw him too but they were used to seeing people that were hurt."

Dr. Laufenberg drank some more whiskey.

"If the psychiatrist had seen him right after I hit him, he would have felt differently about what I did. I think he told people what they wanted to hear. A lot of the teachers were probably happy to be rid of Charley."

"Did you become a hero to the other kids?" Laufenberg asked.

"No, I wouldn't talk to the other kids about it. Everything they heard was second-hand. I don't know what the kids believed, but it was a long time before anybody wanted to fight with me again."

Devlin was aware, sitting there that day, that he was telling Dr. Laufenberg things that he had never told anyone else. Actually, he had tried to tell his parents and the psychiatrist but couldn't make them understand. This guy did understand and he had figured out some things that Devlin had not. The beer and whiskey made some difference, and the fact that he was a very skillful questioner was also important, but the other people just didn't believe what they were told. Laufenberg *did* believe it and he did *understand.*

"Mr. Devlin, do you believe that I told the dean what he wanted to hear?"

"Yes. You're telling me the truth but not to the dean."

"Are you proud of the fact that you hit Charley Crawford with a baseball bat and threw Milo Carter out the window?"

"No."

"Are you ashamed of it?"

"No."

"That's what I thought." He paused and took a sip of whiskey. "Let me summarize my thoughts and my fears. Most normal men have situations when an injustice is done. They try to fix it but can't. They keep trying and nothing works. The system just fails and they give up. They all know lawyers who are crooked, politicians who lie, doctors that charge too much and kill too many people. They do but they can't do anything about it. They give up because they know they can't win. They accept defeat and injustice because they don't know what else to do. Some people can't handle it and lose control and hurt somebody. Mostly, though, normal people just give up. On the other hand there are the criminal types. There are all kinds of true criminals. You are not normal and you are not abnormal like most criminals."

He stopped talking and just looked at Devlin.

"What am I?"

He looked at his empty glass for a few seconds and then looked up. He stared in Devlin's eyes.

"There is no formal psychiatric term for your condition but enigma would be appropriate. Mind-boggler could be the current vernacular," Laufenberg said.

"What about you? What do you call people like me?" Devlin said.

"I think you're fucking weird!"

The doctor kept staring for a few seconds and then started laughing. Devlin was startled for a moment but then he started laughing, too. He didn't know why they were laughing but he knew there wasn't anything really funny.

They sat for a few minutes without speaking. It was raining harder now, a driving, pounding rain that was drumming hard on the window beside the booth where they were sitting. Dr. Laufenberg got them another drink and then he started talking again.

"It is my feeling that there is a great deal of repressed anger inside you. When the other boy was beating you up every day and no one would help you, I believe you became very angry at your parents and the school. I don't think you are aware of it but the anger and resentment are still there. It would take long term therapy to deal with it and you don't have time now but I suggest you talk to your parents and consider it. Right now the letter I wrote is the only way we can get you back in school.

"I have to base what I say on the little bit I do know. I'm a highly qualified psychiatrist and many of my patients are very important people. Some have complex problems. I help them because I have the knowledge and training to understand them. I have also worked with criminals. I don't know if I really understand *any of them* but I do have the skill to work with them. You don't fall into either class. You are neither normal nor abnormal, and there are no other classifications. You fall into a special class with the guys in Attica. It has no name."

The juke box was playing a Polish polka very loudly and the rain was making a real noise on the window. They had to lean forward to hear each other.

"If I ever put down on paper what I have said and submitted it to people in my profession, I would be regarded as some kind of nut. What I am saying does not come out of a textbook. You have to understand that. My advice to you is not the kind I normally give.

"You seem to feel that there is some sort of *higher justice* in the world and that you personally have a responsibility to seek that justice when others fail. This is very dangerous. What you need is a Rabbi. A Rabbi, of course, is a Jewish minister or priest but the word Rabbi is also a sort of nickname for counselor or adviser. You need one badly. You need somebody you can talk to when you have a situation or conflict where you might choose a different course of action than normal people. Someone who will talk you into giving up when it is time to give up. While you are at Yale, you can call me – if you want to. You can use me as a Rabbi temporarily. When the time comes again, you must have someone to talk you out of dispensing your own brand of higher justice. Throwing people out of a window or smashing their mouths with a baseball bat is not an answer to the problem. If you can let someone stop you when the time comes you will make it. You will be all right."

He stood up and started for the door. Devlin followed him and they stood for a minute outside the bar. They were in the shelter of the building but they were getting rained on. Laufenberg didn't seem to realize it was raining. He put his hand out to say goodbye. The neon light from Guido's sign over the door gave a funny color to his face. The white skin around his eyes and his cartoon owl face were pale blue.

"There's one more thing, Mr. Devlin. I believe you have been honest with me in explaining that your acts were deliberate and not a temporary loss of control. They were not a case of overwhelming emotion. But there is something else. When you told me about throwing Carter out the window you explained that the windows were large with no screens, that you opened the bottom of one completely, that the sills were low and that you grabbed him suddenly and unexpectedly from behind. You also said you were an athlete in excellent shape. But that doesn't really explain what happened. *It's not enough!*

"We have all read or heard about cases where people in extreme cases have exhibited almost superhuman strength. Some people have even lifted overturned cars to free a trapped family member. In the thought process leading up to what you did to Crawford and Carter there was no emotion. There was just cold, rational thought. But with Carter especially, you performed, for just a few seconds, as if you were possessed of a strength and fury that goes far beyond the normal. *That fury is to be feared. It is to be deeply and seriously feared.*"

He stood there staring at the boy for a minute.

"You know, Devlin," he said, the water dripping off his face, *"I really wish I could have seen the expression on that son of a bitch's face when you threw him out the window!"*

Laufenberg turned and walked off into the rain.

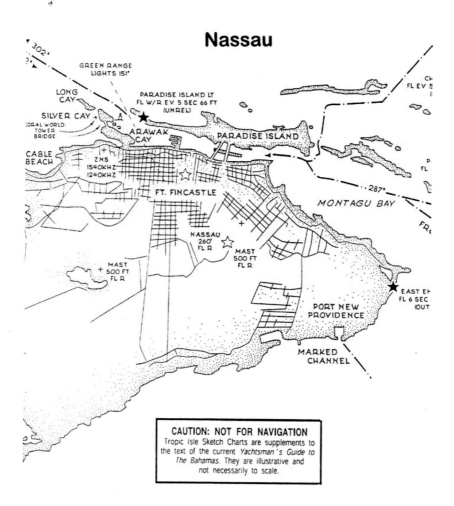

Copyright© 2001 by Tropical Island Publishers Inc., PO Box 8010 Red Bank, NJ 07701-8010 – All rights reserved. Reproduction in any form, including office copy machines, in whole or part, without written permission is prohibited by law.

Chapter One

The Bahamas - Wednesday, 10 May
I had not changed much in the years since college. I still looked as if I needed a shave most of the time, weighed the same one hundred and eighty pounds, and was still a little over six feet tall. My face had not filled in much so I still had high cheek-bones and looked as if I wasn't getting enough to eat. Most of the time I was a pretty nice guy, but I looked a little nasty. My full name is Winfield Scott Devlin and I have no nickname unless you count "Devlin" or "Dev."

Because of what Dr. Laufenberg told me that rainy day in New Haven, I did find a psychiatrist. I was too busy when I returned to college but the year after I graduated I found a man in Boston. I told the Boston man everything I had told Laufenberg except the things we talked about in Guido's bar. I did tell him about the suppressed anger but I pretended that Laufenberg told me this in his office. I remembered his exact words and repeated them to the Boston shrink.

"It is my feeling that there is a great deal of repressed anger inside you. When the other boy was beating you up every day and no one would help you, I believe you became very angry at your parents and the school. I don't think you are aware of it but the anger and resentment are still there. It would take long term therapy to deal with it. I suggest you talk to your parents."

I told him that this was the reason I was seeking counseling and went to him for nearly a year. He listened a lot but he didn't say much. He agreed that I had repressed anger. He said that I didn't consciously resent my parents lack of help when Charley Crawford was kicking my ass every day because I loved and respected them too much. He said the resentment was there in my sub-conscious though and that I needed to talk about it. I told him about Charley several times but I got tired of the story and I think he did too. Eventually I stopped going to him because I got tired of listening to myself talk.

I worked hard at staying out of trouble, and I learned how to accept defeat occasionally, but I had grown no wiser. I did get into a few rough situations which no rational actions could solve. Laufenberg had provided me with a set of guidelines but I didn't always follow his instructions. Sometimes I would get to the critical point and know that it was time to stop, but I just wouldn't and it usually turned out badly for me.

There was one time, however, when I got into a real mess, a situation where anyone in his right mind would have done things differently. Nobody except me, and maybe some of those guys that Laufenberg knew at Attica Prison, would have done what I did. He was right about me, though, maybe I was a little weird.

There was a big IF about the trouble I got into. Like a lot of things in life, there was a point when if this didn't happen, then this wouldn't happen, and that wouldn't happen, and so on. People can get very philosophical about the big IF. Joseph Conrad wrote a great novel about it and called it *Chance*. Some things are inevitable and some things depend on the big IF. My own feelings are summed up in the old saying by Confucius, "If the dog hadn't stopped to shit he would have caught the rabbit."

The point where things started going in the wrong direction for me was the night I ran into a friend called Snake. If I hadn't run into Sean Moran in the bar at the Pilot House in Nassau that night, I wouldn't have gotten drunk and I would have left Yacht Haven Marina early the next morning. I never would have met the people on the big motor-sailer.

I was bringing my boat, *Brilliant*, a forty-foot yawl, back to Miami in stages, after having kept it in the Bahamas for several months. By flying over for some long weekends and three weeks of straight vacation I had managed to get in a lot of cruising, most of it in the Abacos. I took various friends with me on the other trips, but this time it was a female friend. Her name was Sylvia and she was a really good sailing buddy. We had gone out on dates a few times and for a while it looked like a real romance might come along, but it didn't work out. We did become close friends. I think she had liked the idea of being in love with me and wanted to be in love with me, but it never really happened. I felt the same about her.

Sylvia had grown up on the Eastern Shore of the Chesapeake and had learned to sail before she could barely walk. She could sail with me for hours without saying anything. I liked this because I don't do much talking when I'm sailing. Actually, I don't do much talking anytime. With this girl you could have companionship and solitude at the same time. Nobody knew her as "Sylvia" because she had been called "Rocket" for years. She got the nickname when she was eight years old, during a cruise with her parents in a fifty-foot ketch, anchored in a place called Trappe Creek, over on the Eastern Shore. It was a hot August night without any breeze at all. Sylvia was asleep in the fore-peak with the forward hatch open and her father had moved out to the cockpit in search of relief from the heat. There was a sudden crack of lightning and a tremendous bolt of thunder. Her father, who was awake at the time, claimed that she ran from the forward bunk all the way into his arms in the time between the lightning and the thunder, which was about half a split second. He said that she was as fast as a rocket and from then on started calling her that.

Rocket could navigate, steer, trim sails and cook. She thought that an afternoon spent putting bottom paint on a boat was more fun than going to the movies. I was truly fond of Rocket and would have liked it if we had gotten serious. It just hadn't worked out that way.

I had a problem with women. I was too much attracted to very beautiful faces. I also liked cute ones and pretty ones and handsome ones, but not in the same way. For me to describe a woman as beautiful means she has a strikingly attractive and desirable face, with complete symmetry of her features. Also the proportions have to be totally perfect. Sometimes I use the word beautiful to describe a boat, but never anything else, only women and boats. Pretty is a good word, but it means more superficial, less elevated, and a more common appeal than beautiful. A truly beautiful woman is very rare, while merely pretty women are fairly common. To me pretty can mean sweetness and vivacity, but beautiful means elegance and nobility. Rocket was certainly vivacious, sometimes sweet, occasionally elegant but never quite noble. A character in a movie I saw right after I first met her had used the word bonny to describe his lady love. I liked the word and began to use it, particularly in my own imagination. It isn't popular now so I can elaborate and define the meaning my own way, in my own heart.

Rocket had big eyes that were a shade of light brown, kind of a golden butterscotch, smiling eyes. Her hair was also light brown and a little bit curly. The things I remembered most in the nice part of my brain where I keep my scrapbook, were her smiles, all the different ones. She could smile sweetly or impishly or sometimes just pleasantly with a grin that could light up a room or the cabin of a sailboat. She was truly a bonny young woman but she wasn't quite beautiful. If her nose was about one eighth of an inch longer she would have been beautiful. I know about things like that.

My fixation about very beautiful women caused me a lot of problems because there were not very many *truly* beautiful women in the world, and I had never found one who was not a pain in the ass. Being born with really great beauty is no harder than being born ugly, but it seemed to me that the women who were designed with perfect faces had been fussed over so much they couldn't behave like regular people. I worked very hard at trying to find beautiful women but I spent more of my time with the ones I really liked, the ones that were cute, and attractive but not quite beautiful. A lot of people had told me I would never find what I was looking for, a truly beautiful woman who was also fun to be with.

Anyway, the night when the big IF happened, I was sitting in the bar at the Pilot House Hotel in Nassau with Sylvia the Rocket. We had dinner downtown, and were walking back along Bay Street to help get over the affects of too much conch salad and New York sirloin. We stopped for a nightcap and were about to go back to the boat when a friend of mine named Snake Moran walked in. I had known him for several years but I was never quite sure of anything about him. I thought he was involved in illegal things, but I never knew which ones. He started crewing for me when I first bought my Star Class racing boat. Later on, when I bought the Hinckley, the boat I was cruising on, he became a fairly regular racing crew. We kept bumping into each other in strange places and he always insisted on buying me a drink. Sometimes a lot of drinks.

A person who knew Snake once described him as a maniac disguised as a crazy nut. Pretty accurate. To say that he was strange is like saying the Pacific Ocean is large. Once I ran into him on a back street in downtown Miami. He hadn't shaved for weeks and had a long, scraggly beard. The clothes he wore looked like they had been passed around at a derelict convention, with each guy living in them until his three-day shift was over. He smelled terrible and his breath was pure Thunderbird. I have an incredible memory for faces and recognized him immediately, in spite of the beard, long hair and the clothes.

When I stopped him on the street I offered to get him to a hospital, asked what had happened and *was it really him*. He started talking as if there was nothing strange going on and after five minutes I was startled, realizing that he was completely sober. He never explained what was going on, then or any other time he did something weird. He was unusual but very likeable. Once he told me his father was a gunrunner for the IRA, and that his mother was a French whore. At the time I believed him, but later he changed the story and his father became a diplomat and his mother a ballerina. Snake was like that.

That night in Nassau he came into the bar looking like something out of Gentlemen's Quarterly, with white shoes and slacks, a pale blue sport coat, a white shirt, and a pale blue tie that matched the coat. When I asked what he was doing in Nassau, he said he just returned from Venezuela, as if that explained everything. I complimented him on how nice he looked and introduced him to Rocket. Although both of them sailed with me quite a bit, they had never met until then.

"Rocket, this is Snake," I said. "Snake, this is Rocket."

"You look like a snake," Rocket said. Is that why you got the name?"

"I got the name because I'm sneaky and slippery, I strike quickly and speak with a forked tongue."

"You mean you lie a lot?"

"Certainly. Very smoothly, too. Why did you get the name Rocket? Do you streak naked across the sky like a rocket?"

"I don't streak at all. I just move too quickly to be seen. Do you want to see the fastest draw in the West?"

Snake nodded. Rocket didn't move.

"Do you want to see it again?" she asked.

"Do it with the left hand this time."

Rocket started laughing and we joined her. The rest of the night was like that and we stayed at the bar until closing time, which was about three hours longer than planned. When Snake didn't have a beard, he looked as if he never needed to shave. His skin was extremely smooth and seemed to be hairless. I had asked him on a number of occasions how got the name Snake and got a new version each time. Sometimes, racing the Star in Biscayne Bay we would sail in a bathing suit and tee shirt. He had a full head of hair, but he didn't seem to have any hair on the rest of his body, which was strong and very sinewy. He was a little shorter than I was but very powerful. I had seen his muscles moving under his very smooth skin and it *did* remind me of a snake.

We had a few more drinks and the two of them decided that I didn't have a nickname because I was totally colorless. They concluded that I didn't even have enough personality for people to use my first name or middle name, Winfield and Scott. They decided that just plain Devlin was the best name for me. The three of us got somewhat drunk and the conversation about names might have been the most logical of the whole night. We consumed a lot of booze and had a good time. Once, when Rocket went to the ladies' room, Snake asked me if I had seen Lisa Winter recently. I told him I had seen her in church a month ago. He said he had seen her not too long ago and had something he wanted to tell me about her when we got back to the U.S. Lisa was a very beautiful woman who refused to go out on dates with me, so when he mentioned her, I got a little uptight. Lisa could make me feel like that. We stayed at the bar in the Pilot House until they closed down and threw us out.

If I hadn't run into Snake that night and started drinking, we would have left Nassau much earlier than we did. I knew we would be hung over, so I set the alarm for two hours later than planned.

The next morning I had a hangover, but it was not as bad as I expected. I figured that it would last until about noon. Rocket was already up and bouncing around like she hadn't had a thing to drink. We decided to have breakfast up at the clubhouse beside the pool, instead of messing up the galley. On the way, when we were walking up the dock, she stopped me to point out a boat that she thought was interesting. It was a motor-sailer, which looked about fifty-five or sixty feet, but it was long enough to look more like a sailboat than a motorboat. The teak decks and trim were unbelievably clean, and the brass was polished and shined. The parts of the trim that were varnished were perfect, without a scratch or flaw anywhere. The boat was finished in fisherman colors, green topsides with a red waterline and trim, and cream colored spars and cabin top. The topsides looked like they had been waxed and polished every morning since the boat was built. All of the running rigging looked new and shiny white. Although it had larger cabin ports than are usually found on a sailboat, the proportions were right. Two young men were washing the glass and polishing the brass as we walked by. The boat was tied up with her bow facing us so we couldn't see her name or home port. After we walked further, and turned at the end of that section of dock, Rocket turned and looked back at the boat.

"Hey!" she said, "they named her after you. Look at the life ring."

On the yellow horseshoe in green letters were the two words *Ojos Verdes*, which means green eyes in Spanish. My eyes are a peculiar shade of green, kind of a brilliant emerald green. They are so green that people sometimes call me "green eyes," but according to Rocket and Snake, this does not qualify as a nickname.

The boat was magnificent, and I stopped to look because I like beautiful things. I can sit and stare at a painting or sculpture for hours. Once in the Louvre, I spent a whole afternoon staring at Gainsborough's *Blue Boy*. I can spend just as long looking at boats, if they have classic lines, and not the new strange ones. Most boats today look terrible. Part of this ugliness is caused by racing rules, and part by fiberglass, which is more tolerant of complex shapes than wood. The biggest problem, though, is greed. Some of the builders who sell boats have learned that fitting as many bunks as possible into a boat is appealing to the ignorant. The first question that most people ask a broker is, "how many people will the boat sleep?" I once owned a schooner that was over forty feet long and had only two bunks. She was a very fast boat and extremely beautiful. She was named *Vanitie*.

Before breakfast we had Bloody Marys right beside the pool at the Pilot House Club, and laughed about the night before. Our table was close to the water and shaded by three huge palm trees. Their fronds rubbed together gently in the soft sea-breeze, and filtered the early morning sun, creating shadow patterns on the white tablecloth. The drinks were in large frosted mugs, with crushed ice, celery stalks for stirring, and Tabasco sauce and horse radish on the side, for "fine-tuning" the taste.

"I wonder if I can get an order of conch fritters this early?" I said. Rocket was horrified.

"Nobody has conch fritters for breakfast! I'll get an order of runny grits and drizzle them all over your plate, if you order conch," she threatened. She knows I don't like grits.

We settled on bacon, eggs, hash browns and orange juice, with some freshly baked Bahamian coconut bread, toasted and buttered to perfection. I wanted four scrambled eggs on the dry side, and Rocket ordered her three poached eggs done with the whites cooked through, and the yolks "runny" so she could dip her toast. She was so serious in ordering, that I snickered at her while hiding behind my Bloody Mary. I don't mess with Rocket and her food.

The smoky, salty, bacon smell reached our table before the waiter, who was theatrically and precariously carrying our tray over his head. The aroma made me realize how hungry I was and I hoped breakfast arrived at the table and not on my lap. It did and it was excellent.

While we were eating, I told Rocket all about the different backgrounds, costumes, and occupations of my friend Sean Moran, but I didn't tell her about my suspicions that Snake might not always be exactly on the right side of the law, nor did I mention that I suspected a deeper, and perhaps darker side to his personality. He was more fun when you didn't take him too seriously.

On the way back from breakfast we stopped again to admire the *Ojos Verdes*. There were more people aboard now, and it seemed like they were about ready to leave. We could tell they knew what they were doing by the way they were handling their assignments with no wasted motion. While we were standing there, I started thinking about how to get some lobsters. We had originally planned to leave Nassau around dawn. We were going to get to the Berry Islands early enough to take the dinghy and look for some lobsters along the reef on the east side of Chub Cay, where the water goes from shallow to very deep. I didn't particularly like diving for lobsters, and don't even consider the specimens from Florida and the Bahamas to be real ones. Having spent my early childhood in Nova Scotia, I was used to the big lobsters with huge claws that came from the deep, frigid waters Down East. I considered them to be the real thing. The ones without claws were just big crawfish. I started thinking about how good a lobster would taste, and how we would not have time to go diving. By then, breakfast had settled my stomach, and I was already thinking about dinner. I finally talked myself into grabbing a taxi, going to the open air market, and getting six big ones at an exorbitant price. I rationalized the price by thinking of it as punishment for drinking so much the night before.

When I got back to the boat, Rocket had everything ready to go. The boat was aimed in the right direction, so we could go out against the current, and not get carried into the dock. The *Ojos Verdes* had moved around to the fuel dock, and it seemed they were ready to leave. After we turned west, the current was with us, so I throttled down the engine.

Going out of a major harbor like Nassau is interesting because there is so much activity, and I watched everything as we moved past the Hurricane Hole and Potter's Cay. There were some huge cruise ships at the Prince George wharf, with passengers lining the rails and waving at boats as they passed by. I waved back and looked for the buoys near Paradise Island Light. We passed the breakwater at Silver Cay and went out past the light.

After we cleared the harbor entrance, I steered a course of 310° for Chub Cay. The wind was out of the southeast at ten to twelve knots, just the right direction and speed for a short sail. I was still at the helm, preferring to be there going in and out of harbors. I knew that my negotiations with Rocket about how the boat was going to be sailed would start soon. I was ready and knew what my terms would be. In a few minutes she started to fidget. She played with the genoa sheet for a while, then walked back and looked at the speedometer. She played with the main for a while and I enjoyed watching her. Although she fell into the bonny category instead of beautiful she was still great to look at. She had a terrific body that bulged and curved in the right places and a pair of neat white shorts helped the package. Compact was a good description. Just enough but not too much. More female than female athlete. The cause of her fidgeting was the wind, both the direction and the strength. Because the speed and direction varied a little, it was driving her crazy.

When the wind came a little bit aft, the genoa would collapse completely. After a few minutes it would go forward a little and the genoa would fill, the boat would pick up speed, apparent wind would go a little further forward, the genoa would be trimmed a little, and for a few minutes everything would be perfect. Then the wind goddess would change her mind. *Aeolus* is depicted as a male, but no male could be so capricious. He, or she, seemed to wait until we had the sails trimmed perfectly, and then messed us up with a quick change.

Many years ago racing sailors had developed a sail for this downwind sailing. It was called a Sphinx's Acre. Nobody could pronounce it properly, so it became a spinnaker. This is the sail that Rocket would want to put up. She was right, of course, for these wind conditions it was the correct sail, if you were racing or in a hurry to get some place. Rocket was in a hurry whenever she went sailing, and always wanted the boat to go as fast as we could. I was like that when I was younger. Although I was really a racing sailor at heart, a cruise in the Florida Keys taught me to relax and even slow down, at least when I was cruising. Rocket hadn't quite made the adjustment. I knew if I held out long enough she would want to put up the spinnaker so badly she would do all the work herself. After another ten or fifteen minutes of fooling around, she came back to the cockpit.

"Do you mind if I set the spinnaker?" she asked me, with an intent look on her face.

"Can't you just relax a little?"

"The wind direction is perfect for the spinnaker."

"It's a lot of work."

"I'll do all the work."

"I'll make a deal with you," I said. "You fix me a Bloody Mary and you set the chute. I'll trim the sheets."

"That's very nice of you," she said sarcastically.

She moved fast. In just a few minutes she had the chute hoisted, topping lift and down-haul adjusted and the sheet in her hands. I got the after-guy on a winch and cranked back until the pole was perpendicular to the wind. When she had it trimmed properly, she went below and fixed me a jumbo sized Bloody Mary. Then, when she was satisfied that the boat was sailing the way she wanted, Rocket laid down in the cockpit and promptly went to sleep.

For the next few hours we had a beautiful sail. There was a moderate chop that made the sunlight sparkle on the water. The wind was still shifting back and forth, but only a few degrees, so I kept the spinnaker sheet cleated. With a small turn of the wheel I could keep the spinnaker full, and still stay on course. After sleeping for about an hour Rocket took the wheel. I sat down with my back against the cabin and read a copy of the *Miami Herald*.

My boat, the *Brilliant*, is a Bermuda Forty Mark Three. She was two years old at the time and as beautiful as they get. She is a keel centerboard boat designed by Bill Tripp and built by the Henry Hinckley Yard in Southwest Harbor, Maine. More than fifty years experience had gone into the construction and they don't build boats any better. Anywhere. She had powder blue topsides, a dark blue waterline and a white bottom. I had this color combination on every boat I had ever owned. My spinnaker was also light blue, dark blue and white.

Around two I went below and fixed some sandwiches. When I came back on deck and sat down I noticed a sail astern on the horizon. I watched it for a while, and then got the binoculars. From years of ocean racing I had learned something about how to judge the size of a boat in the distance, a skill which takes some time and patience to learn. I had also learned fairly quickly to tell if it is catching you. If you are racing big boats with handicaps, it is not too bad if the boat catching you is larger and has a higher rating. Getting caught by a smaller boat, with a lower rating, however, calls for screaming and hair pulling at a minimum. With the binoculars I could tell that the boat astern was larger and it was gradually overtaking us. It was also carrying a huge green and white spinnaker. Within an hour, the other boat had come up even with us, apparently on the same course but about a quarter of a mile northeast of us. It was the motor-sailer that we had seen in Nassau, the *Ojos Verdes*. She was a beautiful sight. The boat was ketch rigged and not only did it have a big spinnaker up, it had a mizzen spinnaker as well, quite an unusual combination for a boat just cruising. With the wind this far aft a mizzen staysail would not have been as effective. I was a little bit surprised that they had so much sail up, since people who ride around in sixty foot motor-sailers, with all the brass polished, usually don't carry racing sails. Gradually it pulled ahead of us, but not before Rocket brought her camera on deck for a few pictures. She used a really good telephoto lens and took nearly a dozen shots. She was a superb photographer, particularly when the subject was boats and I had some terrific pictures of my boat taken by her.

As the *Ojos Verdes* pulled ahead of us we began to approach the Berry Islands. At first they had been just a little smudge on the horizon which appeared to the right of our course. Coming from Nassau, you steer about 310° toward Chub Cay. You see Whale Cay and Bird Cay first and then as you get in closer you pick up Mama Rhoda Rock and a forty-four foot beacon on Chub Point. As you approach the Point from the southeast there is an area of shoals on your starboard side. After you pass the point, there is a good place to anchor in the curve formed by the point itself. If you anchor there you can get good protection in winds from north to east. You can find the entrance to the Chub Cay Club by finding a range maintained by the Club which will take you right in.

By the time we got abreast of the light, Rocket had taken down the chute and stowed it below. I turned up into the wind and we dropped the main, started the engine, and continued on in. The *Ojos Verdes* was in sight ahead of us, apparently headed for the same place we were.

After you've passed the point and gone a little further you go into a narrow cut that leads into the Chub Cay Club. The inside harbor is completely man-made, cut out of the coral island. The Club itself is on the west side, which is private. On the other side of the docks there's a small hotel with a swimming pool, a restaurant with a bar, and a small grocery store. Because the private part of the club is separate, and the public part is so nice, there is no feeling of being treated second class as it happens at Cat Cay. The narrow cut leading into the harbor is hard to find the first time going in. When I'm entering any harbor, particularly in shallow water, I go very slowly and carefully. The happy hour is just not as happy when you're sitting around waiting for a falling tide to stop falling. Going aground can ruin your whole day.

The *Ojos Verdes* was still up ahead. She looked like she was going into Chub but she was a little to the northeast of where she was supposed to be. Just as I noticed she was getting into shallow water, I realized she was already aground. We continued on our course, which was in the same direction but a little to the left and west of where they were. As we got closer it looked as if they were already trying to get free. I watched closely as the skipper of the boat was trying to get back into deeper water by turning his bow to the left and going forward. After a few minutes it became obvious that this wasn't working and that he was still aground. As we got closer, I could see that they had gotten into some shallow water, but were still not far from the channel. There wasn't any real channel, but there is a right way to go in. It's explained in the *Yachtsman's Guide to the Bahamas*, an indispensable little book that almost everyone carries. Anybody who owns a sixty-foot boat can afford one. The *Ojos Verdes* was in no danger, except that of missing drinks and dinner, but I thought I might as well offer to help them. Getting help and offering help at sea or in coastal waters can be touchy. To get help from a legitimate towing operation the price is exorbitant, but you know that in advance. Towing is their business and they have to charge the price to stay in it. I have helped people get unstuck and towed people plenty of times and, like most yachtsmen, I have never attempted to charge a penny. Only once, in the Florida Keys, did someone charge me for towing.

I was towed in by an ordinary yachtsman, a man with a wife and kids. There was absolutely no wind and I had stupidly run out of diesel fuel. No danger at all except boredom. The man actually told me there would be no charge and I don't believe he intended to charge me. However, a few days after helping me he bumped into a greedy lawyer and it ended up costing me several thousand dollars. The man claimed he had injured his back when he was helping me and the lawyer claimed my boat was in danger. The judge was an ass-hole and I ended up on the losing end.

After the settlement, the man apologized as we came out of the courthouse. He said his lawyer had told him he had to file the claim in order to protect himself. He wanted to shake hands. I told him to stick it up his ass and refused to shake his hand. About a year after the incident I noticed the man's name on the list of proposed new members for the yacht club where I belonged. I wrote a letter to the membership committee and the little rat was turned down. I also sent a copy of the letter to him and wrote "fuck you" at the bottom. After thinking it over I sent a fresh copy without the comment but the original expressed my feelings. I had thought about Laufenberg and my need to set things straight, so I congratulated myself for not strangling the man. I learned later that he had sold his boat.

I continued directly for the opening into the harbor but when I got fairly close I asked Rocket to get on the radio. I told her what to say to them and she understood immediately what I intended to do. I wanted to get a line from my boat to them and have them tie it to their main halyard. By hauling on it and pulling on the top of the mast I could heel them over. As they heeled over, the buoyancy would lift the bottom of the keel a few inches and that would be enough.

In trying to get free they had turned the boat sideways from their previous course so I had to turn him back before I could free him. If I could get his keel to lift a little with his stern pointed toward deep water, he could put the engine in reverse and back out of trouble. We needed to turn the big ketch first before we could heel it over. This part of the operation was simple. They would take my line and attach it to their stern. I would pull it with my boat and turn them until they were pointed in the same direction they were when she hit. Then they would attach the same line to their main halyard. The skipper of the ketch would have to put his engine in reverse at the same time I heeled his boat over. No great skill or luck was needed if he understood what I was doing. Rocket understood immediately what I was planning to do. She went below and called them on the radio. I couldn't hear what she said but I wasn't worried about her since she probably knew more about seamanship and boat handling than the guy at the wheel of *Ojos Verdes*.

While she was below I watched the ketch, particularly the helmsman. They didn't seem to be doing much. There were four men on deck and one woman, all watching me. The helmsman had gone below. After about five minutes Rocket came back on deck.

"I got them on the radio," she said.
"What did he say?"
"*Si.*"
"What?"

"He said *Si*. You know, 'yes' in Spanish."
"Did you explain everything?"
"Yes. Their draft is six feet, four inches."

She handed me a piece of paper with the draft written on it. This was important and she had written it down so there would be no chance of an error. Good girl. Good seamanship. My draft was only four feet, nine inches, so I could come close to the ketch and probably not go aground. I put the engine in gear and approached the other boat very slowly, watching the fathometer constantly.

With the centerboard down *Brilliant* draws 9'3", but with the board up she draws only 4'6". I got Rocket to lower the board until it was down to 5'6". I had marked a place on the cable and used this whenever I entered a harbor I didn't know. If the board hits bottom, I still had 12" between my keel and the bottom. I called it "the bronze fathometer".

Rocket got my towline out of the locker, a one hundred fifty foot line of three-quarter-inch nylon. She laid it out in the cockpit and arranged it so she could throw the end properly. When I got in close, I still had almost a foot between the bottom of my centerboard and the sand bottom. I turned sharply to port with the gear in neutral, putting it in reverse before completing the turn. I was trying to turn in as small a circle as possible. When I had the stern pointed toward the ketch I backed up until I was about ten feet away. I was positioned so that my stern was pointed toward the middle of the other boat. Rocket got the line to them on the first throw and they took it back to the stern. I guessed that the man at the wheel was a professional captain and ran the boat for an owner who didn't appear to be on deck. The two men that had been polishing brass and cleaning windows earlier at Yacht Haven were now on deck and following his instructions. I could hear them talking in Spanish.

The captain was talking quietly, loud enough to be heard but not shouting. Perhaps he was competent and had just gotten a little careless. When the line was cleated Rocket sat down in the cockpit. I moved my boat forward slowly until there was a strain on the line, then gradually gave it more power. After a few seconds the big boat began to swing just a little. I put it in neutral and then back in forward when the big ketch stopped turning. I did this two or three times until *Ojos Verdes* was turned in the direction she had been when she first went aground. I yelled across to the helmsman to go below again. I yelled in Spanish and he responded immediately. I sent Rocket below to make sure he was going to be giving it full power at the same time I had him heeled over the furthest. His boat would stay in the right position for only a few seconds at a time. She also told him to back up in the same direction he had come in and to put the gear in neutral and just sit there when he was floating again. I would then find the best way for him to get back into deeper water and into Chub Cay cut. I could explore with my fathometer since I had much less draft and a centerboard that could be pulled up if I did hit bottom. When she came back after calling again she was smiling and before I could ask she told me what he said.

"He says *'Si'*."

"Did he really understand what you said?"

"I don't know. He just listened and said *"Si"*."

I thought about going below myself but I didn't want to waste time and I trusted Rocket. The tide was going out but if we were quick enough it should be easy. When the captain came on deck he told the two young crew to attach the line from my stern to his halyard. He seemed to be pretty calm and I guessed he understood everything. He hadn't been aground very long and unless he was moving very fast when he hit, we should have no trouble. I had figured out what I would do next if the big boat wouldn't move but right now that didn't matter. It was important that the captain of the ketch accept my instructions. In a rescue situation, even a minor one like this, the rescuer usually ends up being in charge because the other guy doesn't have much choice. Sometimes the rescuer doesn't know what he's doing and the guy in trouble has to take charge or decline to be rescued. This time the other guy seemed willing to follow instructions so it might be easy.

I had my boat moved now to where I could pull the top of his mast over sideways. When I gave full power to my engine and the big ketch heeled way over he responded perfectly by gunning his engine. She hesitated for a second, shuddered and then came unstuck. Rocket was watching carefully, as I had asked.

"Neutral!" she yelled a few seconds before I realized the big boat was moving. I throttled down and slipped it into neutral. The second he was free I wanted to take the pressure off his mast and let him control his own boat. *Ojos Verdes* came off the bottom easily, backed a little way and then straightened up as the pull from my towline eased up on her halyard. She had not been very hard aground. Gradually, I backed up toward them until they could detach my line from their halyard. When the lines were separated, we pulled in ours. I moved the *Brilliant* around directly behind him, and started leading him away from the shallow water. Another fifty feet and there was enough depth for them to turn the boat around. I started back toward Mama Rhoda Rock, made a gradual turn and carefully checked my position. When I was lined up on the range, I headed very slowly toward the cut. My desire to lead them back carefully and then into the cut was not the Good Samaritan in me, I just didn't want to have to pull them off a second time. After they followed me safely into the cut, Rocket came back and sat down in the cockpit.

"Let's talk about dinner."

"What's there to talk about. We've got lobsters. We eat them tonight or tomorrow night."

"How will you cook 'em?"

"Steam."

"Will we melt butter?"

"Sure. Why not?"

"What about bread?"

"Maybe we can get some at the commissary," I said. "There's a small one right beside the restaurant."

"We should get some good bread so we can dip it in the melted butter. Bahama bread is good but it isn't crusty enough. To be good for dipping, a roll should be crusty on the outside and soft inside."

"Are you an expert on dipping bread?" I asked.

"Yes. What about salad. Have we got things for salad?"

"Yeah, I've got some stuff."

"Are we going to cook the lobster tonight or go to the restaurant?"

"Doesn't matter. We can decide later."

"I want to decide now so I can think about it."

"Why do you spend so much time talking about food?"

"I like to talk about food. I also like to read about it and look at pictures. My most favorite word is 'succulent'."

Rocket didn't really eat very much but I think she enjoyed the anticipation. When we went out to dinner she liked to know where we were going in advance so she could daydream about what she was going to order.

Chapter Two

Later that afternoon
Once we entered the narrow cut into the Chub Cay Club I forgot about *Ojos Verdes* and started to think about the next day. There was a tropical wave developing out over the Atlantic that would probably come through the Bahamas tomorrow. I needed to decide whether or not to stay in Chub for two nights or risk getting caught out on the banks. The cut into the harbor is only about a quarter of a mile long and curves a little to give protection to the inner harbor. When we got inside, I pulled alongside the empty fuel dock and went to the end so that *Ojos Verdes* could come in behind me if they wanted to. This was normal for me, having been brought up in New England where there is a long maritime history and tradition of courtesy.

There was no current at the dock and complete protection from the wind so docking was easy. I left Rocket to put out the fenders and went into the small dock office. My friend Jimmy Lightbourne was on duty there. He was a native Bahamian whom I had met years ago at Norman's Cay. He was a great guy and one of the best racing sailors in the islands. We swapped lies for a while and each of us told the other one how old and ugly he was getting to be. I asked for a slip close to the swimming pool which was not a problem since the harbor wasn't crowded. I told Jimmy to come by my boat for a drink after work, and went back outside to help Rocket with the diesel. I also checked the transmission oil, crankcase oil and batteries. My engine was a forty-six horsepower Westerbeke.

Engines were a mystery to me. I tried to maintain my engine as carefully as I could because I was very much afraid of it. I was scared that I would offend it and it would quit on me just to get revenge when I needed it the most. Neville Shute, who wrote *On The Beach* and a lot of other great books, also wrote one about a guy who starts a small airline in India and the Far East. All the mechanics belong to mystical Eastern religions. They talk to the engines, and pray to the engines, and treat them as if they were living things. Naturally, the engines always work perfectly. Since I mostly curse at my engine, I figure that some day it's going to get me.

While I was pulling the long diesel hose back up to the pump, I saw a man coming down the dock from *Ojos Verdes*. The big boat had pulled in astern of me. A boat that size has fuel capacity for many hundreds of miles and she had taken some fuel at Nassau but all arrivals must check in with the harbor master. The man who approached me was large, about six-four and maybe two fifty or two sixty. I knew he was coming to talk to me and I was glad he had no reason to be mad at me. I wouldn't like to have a guy that big for an enemy.

"I am Ricardo Salazar from the *Ojos Verdes*," he said with a Spanish accent. "I would like to thank you for helping us out in our very embarrassing situation."

"No problem. I'm glad I could help. I go aground myself more times than I like to talk about. You can pull me off next time. I was just glad that you understood what I wanted to do."

"I have used that particular method myself a few times," he replied.

Since he had on a khaki uniform and a captain's hat I assumed that he was the paid captain. A boat that size would require a full time captain and one or two crew just to do maintenance work. As we stood there talking I was amazed at the presence of the man. He was huge and obviously powerful, but there was more to it. There was an aura about him that was almost tangible. His head was huge and magnificent. He looked like he should have been a Roman general or an emperor with a toga or king of some country. His hair was coal black as were his eyes, the blackest eyes I had ever seen. His skin was dark, partly from the sun and partly natural coloring, perhaps Mediterranean. His nose was big with a slight beak to it but otherwise perfectly shaped. His teeth were very straight and very white.

"Your boat is in beautiful shape," I said. "Where was she built?"

"She is a Rhodes design, built by Abeking and Rasmussen. And your boat is a Hinckley built in Southwest Harbor. Correct?"

"You're right," I said. He took it for granted that I knew who Phil Rhodes was and that I knew Abeking and Rasmussen was in Germany. There may be a few owners of Hinckley boats that are not good sailors but I doubt it. It takes a really good sailor to understand quality. Anybody can appreciate a Hinckley like good art, but it takes knowledge to understand it. I was standing there holding the diesel pump in my hand while we were talking.

"Do you want to take on some fuel?" I asked, offering him the pump.

"No, thank you," he said. "But I would like to compensate you for helping me this afternoon. Would a check be acceptable?"

"No, not at all," I laughed. "I'm an amateur yachtsman of the old school." Actually I was a tiny bit annoyed but I wanted to be polite. The captain seemed like a nice guy and he was probably just following the owner's instructions.

"The owner of *Ojos Verdes* would feel more comfortable if you could accept some compensation. He feels that we were negligent and not careful enough. If you had not come along with expert help, we would have experienced some annoying delays."

The captain looked a little uncomfortable and I didn't want to make it any worse. Actually, the son of a bitch looked noble standing there and I really didn't like what was happening. I don't like to see anybody grovel.

"Suppose it had been me instead of you. I've gone aground plenty of times. Suppose you had helped me. Would you expect me to pay you?" I asked. "I mean, what if the owner wasn't aboard? Would you charge me for the help?"

"No."

"Look, I'll tell you what. I'll make you a proposition. You just say yes or no but don't argue. O.K.?"

He looked at me and nodded.

"The owner of your boat probably doesn't know much about boats or sailing or courtesy among yachtsmen or any of that. He probably comes from some place like Indianapolis or Philadelphia. Maybe he's a jerk. Maybe he's embarrassed and pissed off at you. Maybe he wants to get back at you a little by putting a price on it so you will feel bad. If you go back without paying me something he might get mad at you. There's no point in that. So I want you to give me a check. The last time I got pulled off was down at Islamorada in the Keys. Different boat than I have now. Deeper draft. That night I bought the guy who helped me a vodka and tonic in a bar. It was a nice bar so let's say I spent five dollars on that drink. Your boat is bigger, and we have to account for inflation so let's say twenty bucks. I don't want any money, but to keep peace on the *Ojos Verdes* you write me a check for twenty dollars. Your owner will feel that you have paid the price for your careless act and he can go back to Cleveland and tell his friends. You and I will have put the proper value on the rescue. You and I know that one six-pack would have been more than enough but your owner doesn't know that. Since the debt will have been settled he can't be mad at you and twenty dollars will put the whole thing in perspective." I finished what I was saying without cracking a smile but Rocket had come up from behind the captain and had heard the whole thing. She burst out laughing and started shaking her head. Her lips made three silent words. The syllables were, "you–ass–hole."

The captain had a straight face but his eyes started to crinkle and I knew he understood. It was me and him against the ass-holes of the world. The good guys against the bad. The poor against the rich. We understood each other.

"I appreciate your understanding," he said and pulled out his wallet. He gave me twenty dollars.

"Actually, the owner of your boat is probably a jolly fat guy with ten kids and twenty grandchildren," I said, accepting the check. He smiled and thanked me.

"Ricardo Salazar," he said, offering me his hand and repeating his name. His hand was huge but he made no attempt to show me how strong he was.

"Devlin." I said, "And this is Rocket."

"I am pleased to meet you Miss Rocket. I congratulate you on your seamanship. Please excuse me, but now I must be getting back to the *Ojos Verdes*."

When he had walked away Rocket looked at me.

"That guy looks like he ought to be a king," she said. "Maybe a noble emperor of Spain or something."

"He did seem like a nice guy. Impressive."

"You know, Dev," Rocket said, "for a guy who works hard at saying as few words as possible, that was some speech."

After he walked back to his boat, Rocket and I started the engine again and moved away from the fuel dock. We found our slip and pulled in with the port side toward the swimming pool. When we had the *Brilliant* tied up, we spent a few minutes cleaning up below. It was still the middle of the afternoon so we decided to sit by the pool and do nothing for an hour or two. I pulled out the charts and turned on the radio. After hearing a lot of weather that I wasn't interested in I got an update on the tropical wave that was moving into our area. I decided to stay two nights at Chub and let it pass through. Rocket said that was fine with her.

Getting our swim suits on was a little bit awkward. Rocket and I had established the fact that we were friends and no longer lovers. It made for a great sailing relationship but my hormones didn't always recognize the finer points. A forty-foot boat with two people aboard is pretty intimate no matter how careful you are. Rocket sometimes made it worse. She seemed to think she was fully dressed when she had on a tee-shirt and underpants. The shirt did come down to her knees but it still stirred up my glands. Anyway, we got changed that day without incident or accident and spent the next couple of hours at the pool. After a swim I read about five pages of Byron's *Childe Harold* and fell asleep. I woke up feeling slightly depressed, thinking the weather was part of the feeling. It was hot and muggy with a lot of activity in the sky. I found a note from Rocket saying she was gone to the beach for a walk and would be back at exactly five o'clock for the beginning of the happy hour.

Clouds at varying altitudes were moving in different directions at the same time, so the sky would get dark for a few minutes, and then the sun would come through. Out over the banks there were mountains of cumulonimbus clouds, towering high with some ragged cloudlets underneath. It was not a colorful sky, just odd shades of grey with occasional patches of white where the sun slipped through.

I jumped in the pool and tried to wake up. It was nice and cool enough to be refreshing so I swam a few slow laps but nothing serious. Because of my profession I stayed in good physical shape, running a lot, and working out at a gym three or four times a week but on vacation I make a point of letting down as much as I can. I drink a lot and eat a lot and really work at being dissipated. Constant clean living can get very tedious. After I dried off I went back aboard.

Rocket's note also said that she would like a Margarita with plenty of ice but not a frozen one. She was very specific. When on a vacation and cruising it is always wise to pay attention to such things as the amount of ice in a drink. It puts things in perspective. With an hour to go I put a bottle of tequila right on top of the ice.

The Hinckley boats are built in Maine but they are used all over the world, so they have a standard type ice chest. They are very well insulated, but not quite enough for a man who likes ice in the hot part of the world so I asked for extra insulation. I didn't want electrical or mechanical, both of which were available, but I did want a cold box. The yard got a little carried away and I probably had the best insulated ice box in South Florida. I had ten cubic feet and the whole interior was lined with stainless steel. I wedged the tequila between two chunks of ice.

By five o'clock I had changed clothes, combed my hair and shaved. I looked at my eyes in the mirror. Ojos Verdes. Green eyes. They look like the GO signal on a stoplight. I decided to dress up for the cocktail hour so I put on a clean pair of shorts and a blue knit Outer Banks shirt that had *Brilliant* embroidered in script on the front. I have about twenty powder blue shirts that are all alike. Some of them have my current boat's name and some have old boats I used to sail. Names like *Vanitie*, *Radiant*, *Foam* and *Starfire*.

When I worked out the details of my boat, before they even started laying up the hull, I decided that I wanted the interior finish to be white ash. The other options, cherry and mahogany, are probably even more beautiful, but the white ash gives the whole cabin a light and airy feeling. The exception is my cherry cabin table.

I fussed around in the galley and fixed some hors d'oeuvres and a pitcher of Margaritas. We had been drinking rum for the last few weeks and a change sounded good. My galley is very efficient. I have a stainless steel gimballed three-burner Force 10 propane stove with an oven. The whole stove compartment is lined with stainless steel. It is a beautiful galley, very basic, without a lot of silly stuff.

I put a white cloth over the little folding table that attaches to the steering column and sat down to wait for the Rocket. At exactly five o'clock she returned. She was so cute it was painful to keep my hands off of her. Her big golden brown eyes were incredibly expressive and they signaled "Margarita." We sat in the cockpit for a while, enjoying the drinks and the snacks, and watching the sunset begin. At times like that we didn't seem to need to talk very much. Some couples don't talk to each other because they really don't have anything to say, but that wasn't the case with us. If we had been in a restaurant, we would have had plenty to say. Sometimes, especially on a boat, it is shut-up time. I wondered why we weren't in love and I know she did, too. Neither of us could understand it.

About six o'clock Jimmy Lightbourne came walking along the dock. I welcomed him aboard and fixed him a Myer's Rum and water and we started catching up. I introduced him to Rocket and we talked about his wife and family. He told us about his new boat, a thirty-six foot sloop which he was planning to race all over the islands. The Bahamian racing boats are descendants of the work boats and have developed over the years into very fast and graceful looking craft. Watching them race at events such as the Out Island Regatta was a splendid sight. He was having his new boat built up at Man O' War in the Abacos by the Albury family. While he was talking, I went below and made a note in my notebook to check with Charley Fowler, a sailmaker friend, about buying a sail for Jimmy's new boat. I could set it up with Charley so Jimmy wouldn't know it was an outright gift. Charley could tell him that he wanted to promote his sails in the Bahamas.

When I came back to the cockpit I noticed Ricardo Salazar from the *Ojos Verdes* walking alone toward the bar, probably trying to get away from the owner's party. Poor bastard was probably lonely and the two young guys didn't seem like his type of people to hang around with. At that point I was "two drinks friendly." I hardly drink at all except on vacation and I am not very good at it. After two drinks I become exceedingly friendly. After four drinks I go to sleep. I am usually polite about it but I do go to sleep. Having had exactly two drinks I yelled at Salazar.

"Hey, Salazar, come on over and have a drink."

He heard me and walked over.

"Come on aboard and have a drink."

"Thank you," he said as he stepped into the cockpit and sat down. I got him a Scotch and water and introduced him to Jimmy Lightbourne, explaining to him what Jimmy told us about his new boat. Then Jimmy started into a detailed description of the types of wood he was using, the size of the frames and fastenings. Rocket listened intently. She would rather talk about boats than anything else except food. I glanced at Ricardo several times, particularly when he asked questions, and I was impressed. His queries were intelligent and pertinent and I was amazed at how much he knew about small boat construction. As he talked I studied his face, an extremely strong one with black eyes set wide apart. Although his head was large, his neck and shoulders were so powerful looking that all was in proportion. He looked Spanish but he could have passed for a number of nationalities. I wondered about him. He looked so patrician that it seemed he should have several servants in attendance, but his manner, although it had a touch of an imperial quality, was open and friendly. He talked to Jimmy, a black Bahamian with large ears and one pair of shoes, as if they were old friends. It was obvious that he knew what he was talking about and it was also clear that he respected Jimmy's knowledge.

It was pleasant sitting there in the cockpit. The sunset was magnificent. Darkish cumulus clouds had been building up in the southwest. They would mean business in the not-so-distant future, but now the last of the sun filtered through them, and outlined their still fluffy tops in bright cadmium yellow orange. *Jaune de cadmium orange vérit.* The breeze was cool, the drinks were cold and the conversation interesting. At one point Jimmy mentioned my old boat *Vanitie*. He knew all about the boat but Rocket and Ricardo didn't, so I gave them a complete description.

My ol' *Vanitie* was one of the least practical boats ever built or designed. She was a forty-four foot schooner but from a short distance she looked like a hundred-foot schooner. I bought her in Nova Scotia, lived aboard her in several places and finally brought her to Dinner Key in Coconut Grove. I stayed there aboard the *Vanitie* for several more years and finally sold her when I decided to buy the Hinckley. She was truly beautiful but totally impractical. One day looking through an old book on sailing yachts called *Sailing Craft*, by a guy named Edwin Schoettle, I came across something familiar. There was a picture and a sail plan of a boat called *Vanitie*. Since the name was the same, I bought the book and read the section about the original *Vanitie*. I came to the conclusion that somebody had taken the profile and sail plan to a designer and said something like this–

"I want a boat that looks just like this, only I want it to be forty-four feet long. I also want the same schooner rig that is shown on page 314 of the book."

Of course a competent designer would have quickly pointed out that you can't take a boat with a ninety-foot waterline, reduce everything down to a waterline of less than thirty feet and not change every critical measurement drastically. You can't, of course, but it appears that he did keep the sail plan and profile. From fifty feet away she looked like the original and many people thought the first *Vanitie* was the most beautiful yacht ever built. Low freeboard and long overhangs. Big sail-plan. My small version was slightly ridiculous but incredibly beautiful and very, very fast.

Down below she was what you would expect with no space at all. She had two pilot berths and two settees done in genuine crimson leather, real leather of the type you would find in a Jaguar sports car, very soft with a wonderful smell. The woodwork was light-colored teak, well varnished and waxed. The galley was tiny and the toilet in the fore-peak was not even enclosed but the bronze base for the commode was polished. She was really fun to sail, about as much over-rigged as a Star Class racing boat. The towering main mast set almost in the middle of the boat but her foremast was relatively short. She was supposed to be a staysail schooner when I bought her but she was really a cutter disguised as a schooner. If you started at the top of the main mast and drew a line down the triatic stay to the top of the foremast and then to the tip of the bowsprit it was close to being a straight line. Ricardo and Rocket asked all kinds of questions about the boat and I showed them some photocopies I had made from the book. I even had the plans of the *Vanitie* that I had owned.

After a while we got around to *Ojos Verdes* and he described her and the construction in great detail. I made a point of not asking any questions about him or the owner. He spoke perfect English with a slight accent and I wondered why he had spoken only Spanish when Rocket called him on the radio.

After we heard about *Ojos Verdes*, Rocket told us about her father's boat, a Howard Chapelle design named *Black Swan* that her family had sailed for years all over the Chesapeake. Most women would be out of place in a rum and whiskey conversation about types of wood and kinds of sails and winches but she was not. She was pleasantly high, which seemed to color and enhance the description and her charm and grace added to it.

As she started to describe the galley on the *Black Swan*, I got a sudden urge to cook dinner. I told the three people in the cockpit with me that I was going to give them a special treat, an Oriental dish called *Phoenix and Dragon*. I have a very, very short list of things that I can cook and almost all of them are Oriental. The reason for this is that I love exotic food but I also love cruising where there aren't any Chinese, Japanese, Thai or Indian restaurants. Usually no restaurants at all.

I despise cooking and I have no talent for it. I first tried a recipe book and the results were almost poisonous. Next I went to an oriental cooking school where I rarely prepared anything edible. Finally, in real desperation, I picked out eight dishes that I particularly liked. In several special sessions with the teacher I got him to rewrite the recipes so that I could understand and follow them. I always forgot which was a teaspoon and which was a tablespoon so I translated all measurements to the metric system, which I did understand. When I prepared one of my dishes I did it from a set of instructions that looked like they were written for a Heathkit Radio. I had no flair, no imagination and no creativity in cooking, at all.

It was as painful to watch me cook a meal as it was to see a watchmaker build a watch with gloves on so I always tried to do it without an audience. That night they were all too wrapped up in the details of boats to care what I was doing. Hull shape, sheer, rig, weather, and anchors were the topics of interest. Rum was popular that night. I was making a dish of chicken and lobster, the chicken being the Phoenix and the lobster was the Dragon. I cut up four large chicken breasts and put them in the marinade. I had measured out each of the ingredients in cubic centimeters. My marinade consisted of a little oil, sugar, cornstarch, soy sauce and sherry. I timed each step with a stopwatch so that everything would finish at the same time. While the chicken and some button mushrooms were soaking in the marinade, I cooked the lobsters. I like the subtle salty, sweet smell of the marinade, but the briny, shellfish aroma soon took over and that was probably what was reaching them topsides. Soon the more complex smells wafting up would really get their taste buds working into high gear.

I put on a cassette of tinkly Oriental music that I thought sounded like Thailand or maybe something from the King of Siam. Little bells and strange flutes and things. The three in the cockpit were talking about Twelve Meters and the America's Cup. I didn't participate because cooking was so hard for me that I couldn't talk while I did it. With five minutes to go I got them all below and seated. I had already set the table with everything, including chopsticks. When I had any guests aboard I liked to get fancy with dinner.

My dining table was somewhat unique for a boat because it was designed and built by the great artist George Nakashima. This puzzled the folks at Hinckley because they are fabulous wood-workers themselves but when they saw the table they understood. George is an artist who was interned during the Second World War in California, but now works with wood in a studio in New Hope, Pennsylvania. Each piece that he makes must be ordered directly from him and cannot be bought in any other place. He does not use any varnish or veneer. He had me pick the wood myself from a huge selection because he wanted to make sure the grain was just right. I picked cherry because it would look good with the white ash of the interior. Dark wood against light.

I always use white linen place-mats and real silver. My steak knives are engraved with the name *Brilliant* and I always use crystal wine glasses. Even my chopsticks are first class, really good ones from Shanghai. I don't know why I like to get so fancy on a boat but I think it is the same reason people like to do it at football games. When I go to a game I always like to walk around and look at the tailgate parties. It seems like there is a contest to see who can have the fanciest table and food. It's just fun. My beautiful cherry table and white ash cabin deserved real silver and crystal and Belgian linen.

While we were eating I looked at Ricardo from time to time. Sometimes, for reasons I can't explain, very large men do not look very intelligent. This was not the case with him. He appeared to be both intelligent and well educated. Although the conversation was in English, I asked him a few questions in my limited Spanish. I learned that he was born in Spain but little else except that his Spanish was Castilian. He never once mentioned the grounding or the speech I made when he tried to pay me. It was a wonderful dinner, the special kind that seems to take place only in the cabins of small boats. The enforced intimacy together with the soft lights on the different lustrous woods in the cabin and the faint rocking give a special aura to a dinner aboard. After dinner we had coffee and brandy. Ricardo started asking questions about my boat.

"I know that your boat has a centerboard and that it is a development from a boat called *Finisterre* but I know very little about that boat. Do you?"

"Actually I know quite a bit about the boat," I said. "A friend of mine, Arthur Knapp, sometimes crewed for the owner. It has an unusual history. Although it was clearly the hottest ocean racer in the late 1950s it was actually planned as a cruising boat. Carleton Mitchell had already won the Southern Ocean Racing Conference twice when he decided to build an ideal cruising boat for two people. When I was a kid guys like Carleton Mitchell, Corny Shields and Bus Mosbacher were our big heros. Sometimes we would sail over to where *Mustang* and *Revonoc* were moored in Larchmont Harbor just to look at the boats. Mitchell was a guy who liked cruising. The Bahamas and Chesapeake

Bay are two of the best places to cruise and centerboard boats are the best for shallow water. *Revonoc* was a centerboard boat."

The four people in the cabin that night were boat people. Sailors. We were still feeling the earlier drinks a little and sipping brandy. Some people would call our conversation a lot of bullshit. Some people would call it swapping yarns. *Finisterre* was a legend and they all wanted to know the details. I knew a few of them.

"Mitchell picked Sparkman and Stephens to design the boat because of his friendship and experience sailing with Rod on *Mustang*. And Rod had sailed on *Caribee*. Rod knew sails, rigging and seamanship better than almost anyone. Olin Stephens was the top yacht designer at the time. Their boat *Dorade* had revolutionized ocean racing. He had been the co-designer of the J-Boat *Ranger* with Starling Burgess.

"*Finisterre* was built by one of the masters, a guy named Seth Persson up in Old Saybrook, Connecticut and Carleton Mitchell was deeply involved in every step of the construction. They even built a plywood mock-up of the cabin to make sure that everything was in the right place."

"Was she built of fiberglass?" Ricardo asked.

"No. People were still learning to use glass. It was built of the best wood by guys who knew how to use it. Connecticut white oak for the frames, African mahogany and teak for the interior. The hull was 3/4 inch Honduras mahogany over 3/8 inch Port Orford Cedar. Double planked."

Jimmy was intrigued by the construction. His new boat would only be a little smaller.

"Later on," I continued, "When *Finisterre* was raced so succesfully, people claimed she was designed to be a rule beater, but that's not true. She was never designed to take advantage of any loop-holes."

Ricardo said, "I think it is amazing that a boat which was the most successful ocean racer ever built was actually planned to be a comfortable cruising boat. Of course most boats designed to a rating rule are hoped to be a rule beater. Most of the boats in Europe were designed to the rule of the Royal Ocean Racing Club. That too was a good rule. What was the racing record of *Finisterre?*"

"Mitchell started with the Southern Ocean Racing Circuit in 1955. At that time the 'circuit' included St. Petersburg to Havana as well as Miami to Nassau. He'd won the SORC in 1952 and 1953 with Caribee so he knew the route. He won the Miami-Nassau and got a second for the series.

"Then in the 1956 Bermuda Race she started really making history. Racing to Bermuda you can go from dead calms to real gear-busters in a very short time. Mitchell's crews were far more experienced than most. They were older and always included some of the top helmsmen. Guys like Dick Bertram, "Bunny" Rigg and Bobby Symonette. The crews weren't exactly the same each race but there was always a nucleus of the same very experienced guys.

"The Bermuda Race that year started slowly. By noon on Sunday the barometer started down and a day later a front passed through. A line squall hit really hard and knocked her over but the crew just changed jibs, and hauled ass for Bermuda. They won the whole thing, of course.

"In 1958 *Finisterre* had a tougher rating. It was adjusted up more than any in the fleet. Also by that time people realized that centerboard boats could go fast. Similar boats were being designed and built."

"Give us an example," asked Rocket. "There were always a lot of centerboard boats where I lived on the Chesapeake."

"Colin Ratsey's *Golliwog*. It was a City Island boat. Built at Nevins. Sails by Ratsey and Lapthorn. I used to go down to City Island sometimes after school. We would sneak into Nevins and look at the boats under construction. I think *Golliwog* was called a Series A. It was very similar to *Finisterre*. Colin Ratsey would also get great crews. Guys like Vinny Monte Sano and Arthur Wullschleger from the Larchmont Frostbite Dinghy fleet. My boat is an example. It is slightly larger and designed with six bunks instead of four but it is the same type." I continued.

"O.K. Back to racing. At the beginning of the 58 race, the wind favored the big boats but by Tuesday, the wind had died, and a horizon full of boats sat off Bermuda. While the big boats drifted along at two knots the small boats were sailing up on every little zephyr of breeze. The big boats got screwed. Carleton Mitchell and a few others sailed right up into Class A.

"On Wednesday morning, with most of the fleet still becalmed within 100 miles of Bermuda the wind started to blow like hell. It was big boat weather again but they were too close to the island to salvage anything on corrected time. *Finisterre* crossed the finish line only four hours after the first Class A finisher. They won again! Bermuda Race victory number two.

"The Bermuda Race is sailed every two years. *Finisterre* won a lot of races in between but everybody was waiting to see what would happen in 1960. By then her rating had been moved up again. By this time there were a lot of boats built in both wood and fiberglass that were very similar.

"*Finisterre* was designed to the Cruising Club of America Rule which produced fast cruising boats not fast day-racers. People complained about the rating but *Finisterre* was a fast boat period. The 1960 race proved just how fast she was.

"It was foggy as hell at the start and stayed that way for three days. Light air reaching and running. On the other side of the Gulf stream there was a lot of wind. By the time Mitchell reached the heavy weather, the bigger boats had suffered knockdowns, were hove to in Force 8 to 9 conditions, or were running off under bare poles. When the wind hit she took off with a No. 3 jib, a deeply reefed main and a full mizzen.

"I was on a forty foot boat called *Sitzmark* in that race. It was well designed and built but really fast only in heavy weather. We never stopped racing but we were out of balance for a few hours with just a jib. After that we really got her going. It was our kind of weather and we really sailed the boat well. We got a third in our class. Just as we crossed the finish line some guy in a motor boat is yelling '*Finisterre* has won the ocean race! *Finisterre* has won the ocean race! They were smaller than *Sitzmark* and in the class behind us but they had already finished. I think the newspaper article had already been written. *Finisterre* beat 109 out of 135 starters *boat for boat*. For the third time she got the Lighthouse Trophy for best corrected time!"

"What happened after that?" Rocket demanded.

"Carleton Mitchell let the record stand at three victories. It still does. Well before the next Bermuda Race he wrote to each of his crew explaining that Finisterre would not be racing."

We sat there in the cabin telling stories until after midnight. Everybody talked and everybody listened. Ricardo and Jimmy were still talking about construction details when they left. Within a few minutes Rocket and I were both sound asleep in separate bunks. I woke up briefly around three o'clock and noticed that *Ojos Verdes* had all of her lights turned on. I watched the big ketch for a few minutes to see if there was some sort of problem or emergency but I couldn't see anything.

Later on a rain squall passed through the harbor and I had to close the ports. It ran off the cabin top, over the deck and gurgled out the scuppers, clattered on the palm fronds and banana trees and spun like a vortex of wet light over the dock and the grass beside the pool. Streaks of lightning cracked across the sky, thunder rattled the hatches, and it was noisy for a while but after that I went back to sleep.

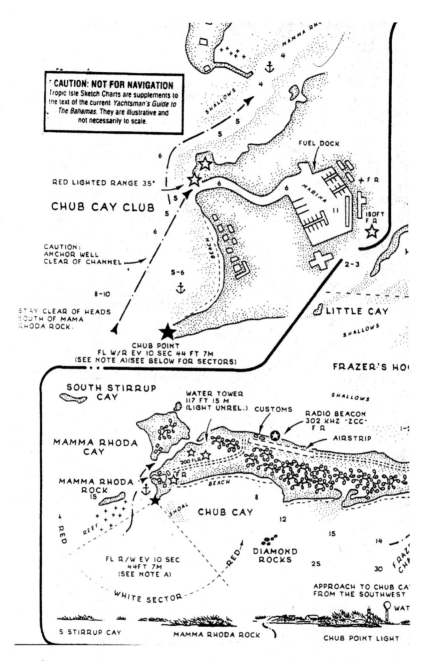

Copyright© 2001 by Tropical Island Publishers Inc., PO Box 8010 Red Bank, NJ 07701-8010 – All rights reserved. Reproduction in any form, including office copy machines, in whole or part, without written permission is prohibited by law.

Chapter Three

Thursday, 11 May

I woke up around seven the next morning and the first thing I noticed was the wonderful smell of coffee. The smell is nice so I closed my eyes and inhaled. Then I looked past the hanging lockers and into the forward cabin. I could see Rocket was still asleep and there was nobody in the galley.

Who made the coffee? I looked out the companionway and sitting there in my cockpit with a cup on the little folding table was Snake Moran. He grinned at me when I saw him. Somehow he had brewed a pot without making any noise. I quietly poured some into a styrofoam cup and went outside to sit with him. I talked softly to avoid waking Rocket.

"What the hell are you doing here? It's too early for happy hour. Why aren't you in Nassau or back in Miami?"

"I came to invite you to breakfast, I need to talk to you."

"What about?"

"I'll tell you while we eat."

I pulled on some pants and a shirt and wrote a note for Rocket telling her to come up to the restaurant if I wasn't back when she woke up.

"I thought you were going back to Miami?" I asked after we had walked thirty yards to the restaurant and ordered breakfast.

"I am but a friend offered me a ride in his little boat and I thought it would be nicer than flying."

"Anybody I know?"

"Guy named Don Aronow. Do you know him?"

"I've met him a couple of times at parties and yacht club things. Doesn't he race power boats?"

"Yeah," he said. "He builds them, races them, crashes them and then builds new ones. Boat called a Cigarette. Goes like hell."

That morning Snake looked like he was fresh in from the Med. He had on a long-sleeved blue and white striped knit shirt and a red kerchief around his neck. If I hadn't seen him with a beard on several occasions in the past, I would have believed he didn't need to shave. His skin was smooth, extremely smooth and flawless – smooth like a snake.

"I need a favor," he said. "I want you to take this back to Miami for me."

He opened a canvas duffel bag and pulled out a Sperry Topsider shoe box.

"What's in it? Anything illegal?"

"What's in here is not illegal but it is very personal. I don't want the U.S. Coast Guard to go through my stuff. With the boat we're riding in, we are sure to be stopped by the Coast Guard or Customs, or both. In that rocket ship of a boat we look like drug smugglers. We're so obvious that if we don't get stopped

I will complain personally to the government about their negligence. When we *do* get stopped and searched, they're sure enough going to want to see what's in my shoe box. When they see a bunch of letters they're going to get very suspicious and won't believe the letters are from my family. *Who would believe it?*"

"Next, they'll read the letters," he continued. "They aren't important, or illegal, or pornographic but they are very personal. Besides, I don't want to have to waste an hour sitting on my ass while they read them."

I didn't ask him to open the box. That would have been an insult of some kind. I believe there's some sort of code or something between men who aren't really legal. I don't understand it but I do know it exists. I have always believed that Snake was slightly illegal. The first time I asked him what he did for a living, he said he was an agent. The next time he said he was an exporter, and the time after that he had become a representative of foreign nationals, whatever that is. I really didn't know what the hell he did, or didn't do, and I'd stopped asking.

"All right. I'll take the letters for you but if I get into any trouble I'll read every damn one of them and if I'm really pissed, I'll send them to the *National Enquirer*. Now tell me about Lisa Winter. When we were talking in the bar at the Pilot House Tuesday night, you said you had something to tell me."

"Just that I've seen her several times with a man who looks about fifty. Nice looking guy. Grey hair. Expensive suits. I don't know who he is but they look very friendly. She's probably the best looking woman north of the South Pole, but I think she dates corpses."

About that time Rocket came in and ordered breakfast. As soon as she sat down Snake stopped discussing Lisa and started talking about art. I knew a fair amount about it since I'd been an art major for three years in college, but I didn't know much about what he was telling us. I had been surprised by him enough times so I was used to his unusual topics of conversation. A discourse on pre-Columbian art was no more startling than a comparison of jet propulsion engines or concert cellists. I was a little surprised, however, at how much he seemed to know about stolen art. One part of the conversation really made an impression on me.

"The art of the world is being looted. It's been going on for a long time but in the last few years it's become much more serious and confusing."

"Why has it become more confusing?"

"Philosophy."

"What do you mean?" Rocket asked.

"Some of the people involved in art stealing are not your ordinary run-of-the mill crooks. I don't mean their rank in the system, it's their motivation. Let me give you a hypothetical example, an imaginary made-up story.

"Imagine a little farmer out plowing his land a few hundred years ago." Snake held up his hands as if he were guiding a plow. "The farmer is in Turkey and lives there in the old Anatolian Peninsula. The Anatolian Peninsula is not your ordinary piece of geography, it used to be a regular crossroads of conquering armies and conquered people. More different civilizations fooled around there than almost any other place in the world. Before there ever was a country named Turkey there were at least thirty-five different cultures and civilizations. I can't name them all but I know there were at least that many. With all that action going on in the old days, the old Anatolian is like a giant museum today."

Snake's dark eyes were shining and darting back and forth between Rocket and me as he got excited. "It's common knowledge that this part of the country has at least twenty thousand monuments and ten thousand tombs. There could be as many as five thousand villages buried underground. Anyway, let's say we have this ordinary, basically honest farmer and one day he's out plowing away and he finds something that looks like a very small statue maybe six inches high. It was obviously made by a man. The farmer doesn't know what the hell it is and he doesn't know if it was made ten years or ten thousand years ago. What he *does* know is that if he takes his little statue to the proper authorities they will confiscate it. Take it away from him. If the piece is really valuable, the government might confiscate his whole goddamn farm so they can look for more items. Our honest farmer isn't too bright but he does know that he better turn crooked pretty quick or he'll get nothing for what he found. He doesn't show it to his wife because it's obscene."

"How could a statue be obscene?" Rocket wanted to know.

"It's a male statue with no pants on."

"Most of the old statues of men don't have pants."

"This one is in a state of extreme sexual excitement and is super endowed. O.K.?" She shut up and he went on. Rocket was like a little kid when she heard or read a story. She got very impatient and couldn't wait to find out how things came out.

"The farmer checks around and finds out his cousin knows a guy, who knows another guy, who says he knows where to sell little obscene statues. The same guy sells "feelthy peektures." Snake rolled his eyes and put on a lascivious leer. "The cousin puts him in touch with the guy who can sell it. The farmer sells the little objets d'art, illegally of course, to the man whom the friend of the cousin sent him. Got it?" He continued.

"Neither of them know what the statue is really worth. *Remember that!* It's important. Somewhere in the world today there are people who can tell approximately when it was made and what civilization made it and that would establish an estimated value. What it's worth is what somebody will pay for it.

That's true today and it was true when the farmer first found it. Art has no real value. It never has had any value. It's worth only what somebody will pay."

Snake Moran was telling his story like it happened just yesterday. I had never heard him mention art before.

"Let's say the farmer sells it for an amount equal to what he would earn in about three months. Not much, really, but to the farmer it's a wonderful deal."

We ordered more coffee. Both Rocket and I were intrigued and sat there intently listening to Snake tell his story.

"Now, the guy who bought it first sells it to another guy in Istanbul who is both an expert and a crook. He knows how to get in touch with a guy who does business with a museum. So far the man from the museum knows more than anybody else. He knows what age and what civilization the statue came from. He also knows something that the crook, who was also an expert, doesn't know. He knows that the funny-looking little statue with the huge sexual organ is part of a trio and he understands how numbers affect the value."

"What do you mean by numbers?" Rocket interrupted. "He only has one statue."

"The value of something like rare coins or stamps or little statues depends on a lot of things but the two most important ones are condition and rarity. If there aren't too many of a thing, it's price can go way up. There is a coin called a Stella, which is very valuable because there are only five of them in the whole world. A Kennedy half dollar, on the other hand, isn't worth much at all. A 1986S in proof condition might be worth fifteen or twenty dollars but most of the other years they made so many of them they just aren't worth too much.

"There's another thing. Pairs or sets. The Mona Lisa is worth a lot of money. But suppose it was discovered that the painting was part of a set of three. Let's pretend that old Leonardo had painted Mona and her two sisters at the same time. Three separate pictures but done at the same time, in the same room, by the same artist."

"Are you making all this up?" Rocket asked seriously.

"Of course I made up the examples but not the reality of the art market. Let me go ahead. Now *if* Mona was a part of a set of three, each picture would be worth more if the set were complete. Each one would be worth more as a part of a set, and the set would be worth far more than three times the value of each picture alone."

At that point one of the dock boys came in and told Snake that Don Aronow and the people with him were ready to leave. The Cigarette was refueled and they had finished everything.

"I'll be there in a minute," Snake said. "Let me finish. O.K. now let's say that the guy in the museum wants certification of some kind, so the seller gets some. He comes up with something in writing that describes the object and what period it came from and all sorts of things. The certification is sort of real and sort of fake but at least it's in writing. It turns out to be good enough. Not really good but good enough. Like when a teenager uses a library card to get served in a bar. If it's dark and business is slow the bartender might decide it's good enough.

The guy in the museum is an honest man in most things. He reads the Koran and prays a lot and doesn't beat his wife too much. He would never steal for himself but he knows the little statue is worth far more than he'll have to pay. *He also knows that the statue is part of a set of three all made by the same artist at the same time. All designed to be together.* He knows the set complete is worth an incredible amount. He knows that all three are in excellent condition because his museum already has the other two. Now here is when he turns philosophical."

Rocket interrupted again. "Where did he get the other two statues to make the set?"

Snake looked at her with a serious face and whispered. "He got them at the K-Mart."

Rocket looked startled for a second, then started laughing. Snake continued.

"O.K. The museum guy goes philosophical, he tells himself that he's going to rescue the little statue from an uncertain fate. He believes that his museum is better equipped to protect and display the statue than if he lets it go somewhere else. He knows this and he also believes that the Turkish Government doesn't have an automatic right to the property even though it was made there a million years ago. Although he hates the government, he believes himself to be a loyal patriot and doesn't want this piece of art to leave Turkey and end up in London or New York. Remember, he's honest, he's religious, he's a patriot and he knows that it would be an act of evil if he didn't buy the statue illegally.

"He also knows that he has the other two statues, that are part of the set, and that if the three are not put together now, they may never be. He knows in his heart that the only honest thing to do is to be a crook so he buys the little statue at a fraction of what it's worth. Now he's relieved that he has saved the three little idols and they can be together forever. He has a legitimate bill of sale and quasi-legal documentation and he has the complete set."

"Is that the end of the story?" I asked, laughing more at Rocket for taking it seriously, than at the story itself.

"No. Two years later the museum is robbed. Then the statue is sold by the robber through a fence. It's sold by the fence to another guy who puts it up for auction at Sotheby's where it is bought by a man who works for a very successful drug dealer. He paid five million dollars or something like that. The drug smuggler is killed by another drug guy in a fight over territories. The second drug guy also stole the car of the first drug dealer who happened to have the set of little statues in the trunk. The second guy doesn't know what the set is, or where it came from, or what it is worth, but he likes them. He bought a bronze bowl and put it on top of the statues, like a bowl with three legs."

"Where is it?" Rocket asked.

"It's in his office in Jersey City. It's worth millions but he uses it for an ashtray."

Snake stood up suddenly and said goodbye while we were still laughing at his story.

Just before he walked out he whispered, "Be careful with my box. I don't want you to damage the statue."

Rocket stared at him as he walked out and then turned to me. "Is he for real?"

"I don't know."

"Tell me about him."

"Some other time. We've got to get our flippers and masks off the *Brilliant* and get over to the dive boat."

I've been diving for years and used to spend a lot of time shooting fish with a Hawaiian sling and then got interested in just identifying the different species. After that I tried a little underwater photography but eventually reached a point where I just enjoyed the sensation of being underwater and looking at the marine life. I still had scuba gear at home but I no longer kept it on the boat. We had brought our fins, masks and snorkels for the cruise and had gone out on dive boats several times. We had signed up to go out again this morning for a couple of hours and would use their equipment.

There were two young guys working the dive boat, both very muscular and tanned. They were friendly and seemed to know what they were doing. We went out and around the point and headed north. We got out into deep water and opened up the boat to about thirty knots. Before we left the dock, they said they wanted to go to a spot they knew up near Little Whale Cay. After twenty minutes we turned in toward shallow water and anchored in about ten to fifteen feet. There were two other couples that morning, nice people who had come down together from South Carolina. One of the professionals went down with us and the other stayed with the boat. It was very pleasant down there and we just enjoyed it without trying to catch or shoot anything. Hawaiian slings were allowed in the Bahamas but we didn't even carry them with us. The other two couples were not beginners and managed to be very enthusiastic without acting silly. Everyone knew what to do and followed directions so it turned out to be a pleasant morning.

We got back to the dock just before lunch time and decided to eat in the restaurant instead of cooking aboard the boat. On a cruise I go out to eat whenever I have a chance. I love to eat but I hate to cook. If somebody else fixed the meal, then I got stuck cleaning up and I hated that even worse.

We ordered two Heinekens, conch chowder and the catch of the day which was grouper. I was about to take my first bite of the fish when I saw Rocket look up toward the door. I was facing away from it so I couldn't see what she was looking at.

"There's a really good looking couple. They look like movie stars."

I glanced over my shoulder and saw a couple come in the door and walk over to the bar. They were both dark-haired and tanned. From where we sat they did look attractive but I was busy with my fish and didn't pay much attention. I tend to do only one thing at a time and concentrate on that one thing. Sometimes at parties I would be amazed at people who would stand there talking and be looking over your shoulder. I wasn't offended by people like that but I was always curious as to why they would talk to one person while they were looking for someone else. I was designed differently or something. I did one thing at a time and I was busy eating. All my concentration was on the fish. I was always a poor conversationalist at a meal until the food was gone. About the time I finished my last bite, I felt someone behind me.

"Excuse me sir. I believe you are the man who rescued us yesterday."

I looked up and standing there was the most beautiful man I had ever seen.

"My name is Butch," he said. "I was aboard *Ojos Verdes*. If it had not been for you, we would have missed our dinner last night. If not dinner, at least the happy hour."

"My name is Devlin," I said. I stood up and shook his hand. "This is Rocket. Would you like to sit down?"

"Thank you. May I ask my companion to join us?" He motioned to the lady at the bar. They were the couple that Rocket had noticed coming in. He introduced us to his friend, a very attractive girl who appeared to be in her early twenties. Her name was Antonia. He introduced himself as Butch and the girl as Antonia, so I only used our first names. Butch asked if he could buy us a drink which I accepted without argument, remembering the professional captain.

Our conversation was a little weird. Rocket spoke only English, Antonia only Spanish, and Butch and I spoke both. For some reason, Rocket and Antonia seemed more interested in talking to each other than in talking to the men so Butch and I took turns translating. They used first names but somehow I figured out that they were both from Spain. I made a point of not asking questions about *Ojos Verdes*. Sometimes owners of large yachts and their friends considered paid captains on a lower social level. I didn't know if they were aware that the captain had dinner aboard my boat the night before and it didn't come up in our conversation.

The two girls were a real contrast. Rocket was a bonny girl, her face was very cute and very animated. She had huge golden-brown eyes that seemed to be able to say things. She could call me a jerk, as she often did with just her eyes or let me know she thought I was terrific. If she wasn't called Rocket, I might have called her Bambi.

Antonia was more of a classic beauty with little expression on her face. Her eyes were an unusual grey color with a tint of green, a little like the crest of an ocean wave on a cold winter day. Her eyebrows were as black as her hair and although they were well defined, I was sure they had never been plucked. Looking at her hair I felt a quick erotic desire to see if her armpits were shaved but instinctively knew they were untouched.

In spite of the contrasting elegance of the two girls it wasn't them that interested me most. I tried hard not to stare but I couldn't keep my eyes off Butch. His features were perfect, as if they had been designed by a computer. It seemed as if a group of sculptors had all agreed on a set of specifications for a perfect male head and put them into a computer graphics program. After they got the results in the form of a three-dimensional printout, they changed the nose just a tiny fraction.   This, and the slightly darkened skin made him look Mediterranean. His skin was flawless but not like porcelain because of the shadow of a freshly shaved beard. His hair was dark, almost black with a slight wave. I had looked carefully and closely at a lot of men's faces but I had never seen one that *perfect*.

Occasionally, the conversation jumped all over the place with all four of us talking at the same time. I asked about his nickname and he told us about his first day of college at Amherst in Massachusetts. He had never been to America before and didn't speak or understand English very well. He needed a haircut and wanted to get it over with before classes started.   Some boys in the dormitory, who were sitting around when he found his new room, gave him directions to the barber shop. He didn't know the word for haircut and tried to learn it from the boys.

One guy, who turned out to be his new roommate, told him to point to his head and say "butch." When he did that the barber took him at his word and cut off everything but a half inch. When he got back to the dorm he found out he had a new name as well as a new haircut and the name stuck with him. His family, who liked everything American, still called him that.

"Weren't you mad?" asked Rocket when he finished the story.

"No. I thought it was really funny. I knew it would grow back and I also knew I would eventually get even with him."

"How did you get even with him?" Rocket asked.

"You don't want to know." he replied.

Butch was still smiling and laughing at what had happened. I don't know if I had an image of Spanish men before that day but I think I did. Probably I had fixed in my mind a composite from movies like "Captain from Castile". I knew Cubans and Puerto Ricans and people from Argentina and other South American countries, but he was the first pure Castilian I had ever met. His English was excellent with a trace of an accent. His Spanish probably was too but mine wasn't good enough to know. The thing about him that impressed me the most, though, was that he was natural, completely open and friendly. His stories about himself were not egotistical. At one point he told us he had played end on the football team but said he wasn't much good because he wasn't mean enough.

I don't have much of a personality but I get along well with most people because I'm a good listener. I'm not very animated and don't tell stories well, but I grew up around people who had charm and personality, so I could get by. People think that I'm cold but not unfriendly. I'm not envious of people who are prepossessing and I never try to copy or imitate them but I am always interested when I meet someone like that.

Butch was a delightful person who seemed to be completely relaxed telling stories or listening. We sat for more than an hour talking mostly about the schools we had attended. Just as Butch finished a very funny story about his initiation into a fraternity, there was a huge clap of thunder so loud that it rattled the silver on the table. Rocket, who was allergic to thunder, jumped straight up.

"It's going to rain like hell! Let's run for the boat!" She was up and out the door so fast I was startled. Suddenly the sky outside was completely lit up by lightning. The three of us left at the table were laughing at Rocket and her quick exit but I decided to go with her. I thanked Butch for the drinks and said goodbye. The tropical wave which we had been expecting had arrived and the heavy rain was already pounding down, the palm fronds scraping noisily against each other. A tropical wave is not a major weather occurrence like a hurricane. It is fairly predictable, however, and there is no point in being out sailing when they come through. By the time I got back to the boat it was bouncing around on its lines and all over the small harbor people were running around closing hatches and tying things down. The wind had blown one of the tables and several chairs into the swimming pool.

The cockpit was well protected from both wind and rain with a combination of dodger and Bimini awning made of a heavy acrylic similar to canvas on stainless steel rods. I have a large dodger which protects the forward end of the cockpit and is designed so that you can leave the hatch open and the boards out for good ventilation in any kind of weather. It's low cut for visibility and it folds forward when you want it out of the way. The Bimini covers the whole cockpit for protection from the sun as well as rain, with pieces that attach in front, back and on the sides. Because we happened to be tied to the dock facing into the wind only the forward panel, which Rocket had just zippered into place was necessary to completely protect the cockpit. Rocket was too much of a skilled seaman not to do the correct things in spite of fear. She also seemed to have moved even faster than the pelting rain because she was completely dry. Sometimes the little girl was really amazing.

According to the indicator on the wheel pedestal the wind was gusting up over thirty and occasionally forty knots. We sat for a while in the cockpit waiting to see if the docklines would keep the boat from banging the dock. Although the boat was jumping around a little, the lines were absorbing the shock. Once at Dinner Key I watched a boat jerk so hard when the dockline came tight that it nearly threw a guy overboard. After it was over I talked to the owner and, as I expected, he had used some old Dacron jib sheets, which have no stretch, instead of nylon which is partially elastic. Rocket made a pot of coffee while I changed into dry clothes and we sat in the cockpit with hot mugs watching the storm.
    A gale at sea is exciting, sometimes frightening and always wet and uncomfortable. Sitting at the dock we were dry and comfortable but it was a funny feeling having the rain pouring down all around us and drumming on the canvas top but not getting us wet. From bright sunlight the sky had changed to darkness while the rain became a steady companion to the low moan of the wind. We sat for a while without saying anything. We both enjoyed being there and didn't need conversation. A little later Rocket slid over closer to me, apparently moving so that she could be heard without trying to shout above the noise of the storm.
    "Can I ask you a personal question?" Rocket had such an animated and expressive face that she looked like it was the most important question ever asked of anybody. At one time I used to start laughing when she got a very serious look and then asked where the beans were stowed or something equally trivial.
    "Sure."
    "Are you a switch hitter?"
    "What do you mean?"
    "You know. AC-DC."
    I was puzzled. Rocket and I had agreed that there would be no sex on the cruise since we knew that we would be friends and nothing else. It had been hard. I had some exciting memories and one of them flashed through my mind. I used to tease her until she would get so excited she would take her own panties off and not wait for me to do it. She knew I did it on purpose and tried to wait but she never could. It became a game and we both enjoyed it.
    "I thought we agreed to be just friends and no screwing. I think my behavior has been exactly right. I haven't tried to lay a hand on you the whole trip because we had an understanding, and now you call me a queer because I haven't tried to take your pants off." I said, a little annoyed and puzzled.
    "You never took my pants off. You always made me do it. Besides, that's not what I mean."
    "What do you mean?"

"That gorgeous girl in the restaurant, Antonia. She was a raving beauty, right? A first-class exotic piece that any normal man would get glassy-eyed looking at, right?"

"She was attractive," I agreed. "So what? I talked to all three of you."

"Wrong! You spent the whole time in there staring at the guy, at Butch! You hardly looked at her! It was so obvious that it would have been embarrassing except that the conversation was so mixed up. What the hell is with you anyway? Tell me the truth! I know you're not *completely* queer because of the things you did to me but I want to know if you're bisexual!"

Rocket looked so worried that I almost started laughing but couldn't because her cute little face looked like she was about to cry. I knew she was serious. People had only used the word bisexual for a few years now and nobody knew much about it.

"My appreciation of his face was totally professional. I am not bisexual."

"What the hell profession are you in? I thought you were a doctor."

"I am."

"I asked you one day when we were getting ready for the Columbus Day Race what you did for a living and you said you were a doctor. When I said what kind, you said you were a rear admiral and I assumed you meant a proctologist. I knew that they worked on people's behinds so I was embarrassed and stopped asking any questions. Now what the hell does operating on somebody's keester have to do with staring at a guy with a pretty face? Are you a pervert or something?" She looked absolutely fierce.

I couldn't keep from laughing and after a few minutes Rocket started laughing, too, but I'm sure she didn't know why. We sat there in *Brilliant's* cockpit for nearly an hour while I told her the whole story about Paris. She really seemed to want to hear about my life.

The rain was pounding down around us but it had settled down to a steady, heavy sound. We sat close together in the corner of the coaming and the cabin. It was not yet twilight but the storm made it partially dark under the shelter. The combination of the low moan of the wind, the rain and the partial darkness was strange, somewhat ethereal and it was easy to imagine that I was back in Paris that spring.

I could almost see Notre Dame, the Rue Montparnasse and the bridges of the Seine. I could smell the paint at the art school and the perfume of the whores. I told Rocket the whole story, including my getting suspended from college and getting the idea to go to Paris.

I wanted to be an artist all my life, ever since I was old enough to hold a crayon in my hand. I was always fascinated by pictures in books, not just kid's stories but all types of books. My dad encouraged me although he wasn't much interested in art. My mother, who painted both watercolors and oil, did even more. She didn't paint professionally but she was good. She also arranged flowers competitively and won all sorts of Blue Ribbons and other prizes. Her name is Glorious.

I was born in Canada, in Lunenburg, Nova Scotia, but we left when I was ten years old. My dad had been a hockey player and had gone to college on a scholarship. He married my mother when they were both in college. We lived in Lunenburg after they graduated, but my father wanted a city with better business opportunities and got a job in New York City through friends he had made in college. We bought a house in Rye, New York so my father could ice skate and play hockey at the famous ice rink at Playland. Rye was also on the water, Long Island Sound, and he could sail.

My mother bought all kinds of books about the great artists and I spent most of my spare time looking at them. I built a few model airplanes and trains and other stuff but I mainly liked art. I could recognize pictures and sculptures by the great artists even before we left Nova Scotia. Art was my favorite class at school and sometimes I even took private lessons, even after Charley Crawford. I didn't tell Rocket about the baseball bat and hitting Charley. My mother started me out with her watercolors and I would spend hours trying to copy Winslow Homer. I was fascinated by the Hudson River School. This was a group of men that painted spectacular outdoor scenery inspired by the cliffs and canyons of the Hudson River Valley.

By the time I got to college I was an accomplished artist or at least a damn good one. When I got to New Haven I majored in art and, of course, I found out that there were a lot of other guys that were also very good. I enjoyed history and literature and most of the other courses but my main interest was art. I tried almost every medium but the thing that I liked best was doing oil paintings of faces and doing life-size sculptures of heads. I was fascinated by the shapes and expressions of people's faces.

Most portraits are painted with very little expression on people's faces, maybe a slight smile or a little bit of a grim look. I liked to paint a face with a real expression, a total look of joy or sadness. I wasn't sure I could make a career out of painting portraits that didn't look like the usual ones, but I intended to try.

In February of my junior year, when I got thrown out of school for one semester, I talked my parents into letting me go to Paris to study art for five months until I had to be back for the fall term and football practice. It was spring and I found a place to live, a place to study and paint, and I was very happy. I loved every sight and sound and smell. It was a special time.

One of the people I met was a photographer, a guy from Idaho named Herb, just a few years older than I. He was a commercial photographer who earned money doing routine stuff like buildings for sale and office interiors, but he also liked to do portraits so we shared an interest in people's faces. One afternoon we went up to his flat. It was a Saturday and there was no school or work for either of us. He had one room fixed up as a darkroom and another was a workroom and office. There was no living room or bedroom so we sat on his couch which doubled as his bed. We drank some cheap wine and pretended to argue about noses or cheekbones or something. Just like in "*La Boheme*". He had to leave on an errand to pick up some pictures, and since he wasn't going to be long I decided to wait there until we'd go for dinner. He invited me to look through his pictures while he was gone so I shuffled through piles and piles of prints. There was one large pile of prints that really aroused my curiosity as the pictures were all front and side views of heads up-close. They looked like police files and some of the people were so ugly that they probably were. The prints were technically excellent, at least the lighting and focus, but there had been no attempt to make them interesting or different. When Herb came back, I asked him about this group.

He told me that he did the pictures for a doctor, a plastic surgeon for whom he worked on a regular basis. The doctor always wanted pictures before the surgery and then again after the scars had healed. He told me there were four pictures in each set and asked if I thought I could match them up. I thought he was just kidding but he said that most people couldn't do it. Since I painted faces he thought I might do better. I separated the men and women and then the sides and fronts. I spread them out on the floor and then started to match the fronts to the sides. Because I had studied bone structure, proportion and other things for portrait painting and sculpture, I could see things that most people probably couldn't, but it was still very hard. A few were easy, ones with small or subtle changes but most were surprisingly difficult. My friend Herb watched with a smile on his face not offering to help. He told me that I was doing better than most of his friends.

After almost an hour and several glasses of wine I had matched each face and put them in groups of four, except four pictures that didn't make sense. The "before" profile was a picture of an ugly woman about thirty years old with a huge beak of a nose, no chin at all, protruding teeth and bulging pop-eyes. The other profile obviously had to be an "after" since nobody would ever make a change in a face so attractive, but there was too much difference for them to be the same person. The second was a woman of about twenty with every feature right, a lovely woman. I pointed out the error to my friend and he laughed and explained that the pictures were indeed the same person. I had trouble believing him and looked at the front views. These were not quite as hard to believe but still startling.

I had studied the anatomy of the human face to paint and sculpt it better and I knew the names of the parts and bones and how they fit together, but could not believe what was in the pictures. One thought kept running through my mind and finally I said it. I told my friend that the doctor that did the operation was a true magician. He said that the doctor was no magician but was indeed a brilliant surgeon. He told me that he was using a very new technique, which in English was called craniofacial surgery. It was highly complex and it involved making actual changes in the skull. He had begged the doctor to arrange for him to meet the girl, which he did after first checking it out with her. He told me that I could also meet her if I wanted to see for myself and said that she was nice and was not offended by people who were curious about her operations and the changes.

He telephoned her where she was employed and she agreed to meet us after she finished work that day. We met her at a sidewalk cafe up on the Champs Elysses, near the Pan American office where she worked as a secretary.

She was even lovelier than the pictures showed, and very candid about the surgery and what she looked like before. She described the many operations in as much detail as she could remember and even talked about the teasing from her fellow employees at the airline office. The teasing had stopped rather quickly when the surgery was completed. She had taken a few weeks off from work after the last operation and when she walked into the office with her new face nobody recognized her. By the end of her first day back at work she had received separate invitations from seven men and two from women for private dinners to celebrate her new looks. I apologized to her several times for staring but I couldn't help it. She confessed that she had previously gotten a lot of stares because she was so unattractive.

Sitting there at the cafe in Paris I realized that something in *me* had changed. It began when I realized that a picture of an ugly girl had changed to a picture of a lovely girl. Somehow I knew that oil paint would not be the medium in which I would work in the future. Instead I would become an artist in human flesh. I was almost in a trance, staring at the girl, drinking wine and dreaming of the great surgeon-artist I would become. I would be the "King of the Cosmetic Surgeons". After a while, I started laughing at my daydreams. If I couldn't become the king, at least I would become a prince, the "Prince of Beauty".

We decided to stay there for dinner. I told them that I was going home and going to medical school. I was going to become a plastic surgeon and make people beautiful. They smiled when I told them and said they were happy for me, but neither of them laughed. They didn't question the suddenness either. The miracle of her face was there with all three of us.

Chapter Four

Later that day

Except my parents I had never told anybody what had happened to me in Paris. I don't know why I hadn't told Rocket the story before, when we were lovers, and I don't understand why I told her that night. By the time I got to the part where I decided to become a cosmetic surgeon it had become completely dark. We were still sitting huddled against the cabin and the rain was still coming down hard. We had finished a second drink before I started the story about Paris and we weren't high but there was a strange feeling of intimacy that I had never felt with anyone before. Rocket didn't move or say anything but I knew she wanted to hear the rest of it. I told her what I had done next. I remembered it all and told her all of it.

When we finished dinner at the sidewalk café in Paris, I went to the Pan Am office which was only a block away, on the right hand side as you walk toward the Arch of Triumph. It was late June. I made reservations for a flight home in the middle of July, which gave me about three weeks at home before I had to face another season of football. This time it would be mixed with Qualitative and Quantitative Analysis. I allowed myself time in France to see the doctor who was pioneering the development of craniofacial surgery. Doctor Tessier was there in France, performing miracles and I did meet him and have an hour with him. I was totally inspired.

When I finished my story about spring in Paris and deciding to become a plastic surgeon, the rain was still pounding down on the canvas over us and the wind was still blowing. We sat there in silence for a few minutes and then Rocket went below to read and take a nap.

"Thank you for telling me," she said, as she went down the companionway ladder.

A few hours later our dinner was a bit tense. We had been on the boat together for almost three weeks and sometimes it had been awkward. I tried to remember which of us had first backed off months ago, and in fairness to Rocket, I think I did when another woman entered the picture. However, it seemed to me that Rocket was nearly as relieved as I was when we stopped being lovers. Now, we wanted to be friends, or at the very least, wanted to prove that we could act like friends. We were like two people who had agreed to give up smoking and neither wanted to be the first to fail at the agreement. It had not been easy and, in fact, I had told myself several times that I would never again go on a cruise with another attractive woman. Next time I would sail with a man or a very ugly woman or, better yet, with several people. Never again with a woman I had once made love to. There were several of them in that category. Up until that night it had worked and we had been friends, had fun together and slept in separate bunks.

That night there was something different. The change was not in me, but in Rocket. She got fixed up for dinner. When you're cruising, you don't get dressed up unless you are going out, but now I noticed small things that were different. She had on a tiny bit of eye shadow, a little lipstick and a blue ribbon in her hair. She even put on a dab of perfume. This was a surprise. Rocket never used perfume. She had a very nice smell of healthy young girl and perfume was almost a waste. In nearly three weeks of cruising she had not done any of these things, even when we went out to a restaurant.

I have never had any interest in psychology, either male or female. I'm a very simple person and my motives for doing anything are never complex – even hitting people with a baseball bat. I don't analyze myself or other people and, since I had no idea why females think the way they do, I could only guess that Rocket had "prettied" herself up because she wanted me to try to make love to her. It made her seem very vulnerable if she were just trying to please me. On the other hand, her lipstick and perfume might have no meaning at all.

The cabin of a boat can be very romantic. In addition to the white linen and real polished silver, Rocket had put out two candles in hurricane glasses. She had also put on a cassette tape of Ella singing Cole Porter songs, not the jumpy ones but the romantic ones. My favorite was *"In The Still of the Night"*. For a while we didn't talk much and concentrated on eating. We had some left-over lobster, so I had fixed lobster salad and spiked it with some Key lime juice. We also had she-crab soup, salad and garlic bread. Rocket didn't cook much, she'd rather just eat and think about eating.

As long as we didn't talk, it was a beautiful, romantic dinner, but I guess I was waiting to hear what Rocket was going to want to talk about. When we finished dessert and were having coffee she surprised me by asking about my last year of college and medical school. She obviously was interested so I told her about it. I think I was both relieved and disappointed that it was nothing romantic or sexy. Rocket had never seemed so appealing.

After I got back from Paris, I changed all my courses and had to take physics, organic chemistry and biology, all at the same time. In a way this helped me get ready for medical school. My senior year was so bad that medical school was a relief. I spent weekends, nights and even Christmas vacation studying. That year I even gave up Frostbite Dinghy Racing at Larchmont. I would drive home on Friday night and spend all day Saturday at the Rye Free Reading Room. That's what they call a library if the town is wealthy enough and old enough to continue the name it used before the American Revolution. On Sundays I would go to an early service at Christ's Church, and then study at home all day. I didn't have any Saturday classes and there were too many temptations if I stayed at school. Late on Sunday I would go down to Larchmont Yacht Club and have a couple of drinks with the winter sailing crowd. Except for a few beers at the Club on Sunday afternoons, I even gave up drinking. I would talk to Clint Bell, the Chairman of the Race Committee, and Arthur Knapp who usually won the Class Championship. Both were old friends of mine and my parents. By nine o'clock on Sunday nights I would be back in the Yale Library.

My parents were in shock when I decided to give up art for medicine but they never tried to change my mind. I told them about the pictures and the girl in Paris and talking with Doctor Tessier, the craniofacial surgeon pioneer, and I think they understood. When I finished my last exam that year, I went on a three-day splurge and almost got thrown out of school again.

"You mean you almost didn't graduate after all that studying and everything?" Rocket interrupted. She was really upset, as if it were all happening today.

"What did you do that was so bad?"

"It's a long story. I'll tell you about it some other time."

"Tell me! Tell me! I won't be able to sleep!"

Sometimes Rocket seemed like a little kid in her enthusiasm for things. It was part of her personality, a very appealing part. Her face matched her psyche. A cool classic face just wouldn't have been appropriate for the variety of animated expressions which were so much a part of her.

We had folded down the dining table and were sitting on the port berth. I had gotten a small snifter of brandy for each of us. Sitting there would have been too close and intimate to be safe with the sexual tension between us, but I felt that telling stories about college or medical school was very safe, and certainly not an aphrodisiac. So I told her the story.

That night, because of a mix-up about cars when it suddenly started raining at a beach party in New London, my roommate and I got stuck without a ride back to New Haven. We had finished all our exams and were just waiting to graduate. We broke into the field house at the Coast Guard Academy looking for a place to sleep and got caught. The dean told us there would be a faculty meeting to decide if we could graduate. We had to wait for four days. I told Rocket the whole story while she listened intently.

"Were you scared? I would have been terrified."

"Yes, I was really scared. Deep down I didn't think they would stop us from graduating. I had already been accepted at Tufts Medical School but even the possibility of not graduating was an awful thought." I went on with the story.

"After I left the dean's office, I found Dave in a bar just off campus and told him the story. He was really upset. His Dad was an Episcopal Bishop from Hawaii and was already on his way to New Haven for the graduation. Dave and I got very drunk that night. I went home the next day but didn't tell my parents about it. When I went back to see the dean he told me that we would have been put on probation any other time, but that he would let us graduate. When I got up to the Cape and told Dave, he was one happy guy."

"Tell me some more stories. Tell me about Tufts and after that. Where did you intern? I want to know *everything*! Tell me about it."

I was tired of talking about myself. I guess I really don't like to talk much about anything but I like to listen. I don't mind a two-way conversation but I don't like this kind of thing about the past. For some reason Rocket was really pushing me. She seemed to want to hear about everything I had ever done.

"Why don't we go up to the bar and have a drink? I'll tell you anything you want to know, but some other time."

"Why don't you go on up and have a drink by yourself? I'm going to jump in the pool and cool off and then go to bed. I'm just too hot!"

There was no one else at the bar. I sat alone and watched the eleven o'clock news on the television behind the bottles. While I was sitting there, I suddenly realized Rocket wasn't talking about the weather when she said she was too hot. She meant she had hot pants. The tropical wave had passed through and it was much cooler than before, actually a little bit chilly. She was going to jump in the pool instead of taking a cold shower.

I sat there at the bar drinking rum and water and thinking about how strange women were. The more I thought the more I wondered about myself and why I felt so little emotion. I just do not feel the same things as most people. I think pretty much like other people, but I do not feel the same things. I am not without emotions but I do come pretty close. I don't get excited about most things and I don't know why. After two drinks I got tired of my thoughts and went back to the boat. Rocket was asleep in the forward bunk so I read for a while and then went to sleep myself.

I woke up early the next morning and turned on the radio for a weather forecast. It sounded good for the next few days. The winter weather pattern begins between November and January with a Norther, which is a sort of outbreak of cold continental high pressure air. It interrupts the normal easterly flow of air. The wind from the east has been blowing over the ocean which warms it up. Northers come all through the winter. They usually start with the wind coming around to the south and southwest. When the cold front arrives the wind suddenly shifts to the northwest, then works through north and finally it goes northeast and blows itself out. In the middle of winter this cycle takes several days but in the spring it only takes twenty four hours. Since it was now May, the weather was pretty stable and we had enjoyed good sailing for most of the cruise.

We had an early breakfast at the restaurant and got away from the dock around eight o'clock. We said goodbye to Jimmy and I told him I would write about the sails for his new boat. As usual, we didn't talk while we were getting started. Rocket knew exactly what to do without any instructions and we were able to get going without much commotion. I noticed that the *Ojos Verdes* was gone and wondered if they had left in the dark. We went out the cut and down past Mama Rhoda Rock and set a course for the Northwest Channel Light. The crossing from the Berry Islands to Gun Cay is a total of 75 nautical miles and just too far for one day. It's 14 miles to Northwest Channel Light on a course of 290° then 61 across the bank at 279°. I've crossed the Bank many times and gone the same route many different ways. This time I planned to go as far as we could in daylight and anchor on the banks. This would get us within ten or fifteen miles of Gun Cay. The next morning we would start at first light or a little before and get to Gun Cay Cut around eight or nine. It gets shallow over there and I like to go through in daylight. Anchoring on the banks is a little weird because there's nothing in sight but water and you still have the anchor down and you aren't going anywhere.

As we cleared Mama Rhoda and got on our course, Rocket went down below and hauled out the spinnaker. The sheets were all set up and the set went very smoothly. It was fun to watch Rocket move around on deck. I think they call it fluid grace or something like that and she knew exactly in what order to do things. She was deliberate and thorough and didn't make mistakes and yet she still moved fast. She told me how to trim the after-guy and when the chute went up I didn't have to adjust it more than a couple of inches. At times during the last two weeks I had watched her move around and all I could think about was what a great little sailor she was. There were other times when I watched her move and all I could think about was what a cute little ass she had and how much I would like to take her pants off and mess around. That day I admired her skill as a sailor. Actually there was no other option.

When you pass Northwest Channel Light going west, you pass from water which is hundreds of fathoms deep to water which is only ten or fifteen feet. From a deep beautiful blue to various shades of green and turquoise and azure. Sometimes the art lessons came to mind and I identified the colors. *Blue de Cobalt Verit* and *Laque d' Alizarine Bleu* and *Vert de Cobalt Clair Verit.* Sometimes I did this with sunsets and sunrises.

Rocket was at the wheel when we passed the light so I trimmed the main to where I thought it would be on the new course. She turned very gradually and out of habit we kept the spinnaker from breaking. Since we were cruising and not racing I over trimmed the spinnaker sheet first and then eased the after-guy. When I got the pole in the correct position about a foot-and-a-half off the head stay, the sheet required very little adjustment. When we were settled on our course of 279°, I adjusted the main sheet and boom-vang and then the fore-guy. As usual, when conditions were ideal we took turns at the wheel for an hour each. I was too lazy to set the spinnaker staysail while Rocket was steering but as soon as I got back on the wheel she took it forward and hoisted it. It seemed to add a quarter of a knot to our speed.

Gradually, the wind strengthened and became steadier. After about a half hour I realized that the strength and direction were perfect for the mizzen staysail. I got Rocket to steer and set it myself. As we increased our speed the apparent wind came forward. I went below and adjusted the centerboard, bringing it up and moving the center of lateral resistance aft to balance the weather helm. The spinnaker pole was about a foot off of the head-stay.

We sailed all day like that, making small adjustments in each of the five sails as they were needed. I don't usually work that hard except when I'm racing, but the Bermuda Forty is a fast boat and we had perfect conditions. It was great sailing.

Once, when Rocket was steering, my mind started wandering. I thought about another afternoon when Rocket and I were sailing down Biscayne Bay toward Featherbed Shoals. We had known each other about three months. We had made love for the first time only two weeks earlier and I was hoping we would do it again.

It had been a soft afternoon with a warm southeast breeze, not a wind but a gentle zepherette that felt good on your skin. There was a thin white layer of clouds with no shading but a sort of ripple pattern. They were too high and too thin to cause shadows below, the type that were called "mackerel clouds."

Rocket was letting the boat steer herself by touching the wheel only occasionally. In a race we would be using the light weather genoa, a full cut sail of very light weight cloth, but this day we had an old number two that I used for cruising. We had adjusted the center board so the boat balanced perfectly. I was sort of slouching in the corner of the cockpit, about half asleep, half daydreaming. I was actually thinking of my old boat, *Vanitie*, and how she would probably outsail us in this breeze.

"A dollar for your thoughts," Rocket said.

"Why not a penny?"

"I'm a big spender."

"I was thinking of my old schooner and how fast she was in this kind of weather."

"I don't believe you. I think you were ogling me. I could tell by the look on your face. You were thinking about getting me to go up in the forward bunk with you as soon as we drop the anchor. You had a look of intense lust and a lecherous grin on your face." I went along with her teasing.

"I apologize. I was wondering if you always wore pink underwear and planning on how to dispose of it. I'm guilty as accused."

"You can't be blamed for wishing. I *want* you to dream about me. Night dreams and daydreams both. How do you dream? In Technicolor or black and white?"

"Usually Technicolor. Sometimes black and white."

"When do you dream black and white?"

"Boat plans. Engineering drawings."

"You dream about engineering drawings? That sounds crazy. You must not have much imagination."

"I daydream about details. Like the shape of a centerboard or the way a bilge pump is installed." This was before Rocket knew I was a cosmetic surgeon. "I dream about boats a lot — past, present and future."

"You can daydream about me some more if you want to, but don't get too excited. We won't be at Elliott Key for another hour."

"I daydreamed about this Hinckley for years before I actually bought it. I had raced on them and against them for years. Once, in an overnight race from Larchmont around Stratford Shoals, I was steering a Loki yawl at the turn. In the light air down-wind we had stayed with a Hinckley *Bermuda 40* and I was the inside boat, close to the light. I wouldn't let them get inside me so they drove off a little to get clear air to leeward of us and then took off. With her beam and extra stability the *B-40* went into a freshening southerly, standing up, while we laid over on our ear and bounced up and down. I dreamed about owning a boat like that."

I dreamed about the boat before I bought it and now I could still dream about it while I sailed it. On top of the forward end of my cabin between the hatch and the mast is a double teak Dorade box with 5" chrome cowl ventilators. I can get excited thinking about something like that.

After we had passed through the markers at Featherbed we did anchor at Elliott Key. We did make the pink panties disappear and it was almost sunset when we left the forward bunk and had drinks in the cockpit.

"What's your favorite boat?" Rocket asked.

"It's always a toss-up between my last one, my next one, and the one I have now."

"Seriously. What was your favorite? Not counting this one."

"An *Owens Cutter*. My dad was back from the war. We had moved from Lunenberg, Nova Scotia to Rye and joined Larchmont Yacht Club. Other than dinghies it was his first boat after the war. He was the captain of a Corvette during the war. Do you know what a Corvette is?"

"Sure. It's a sailing warship larger than a sloop and smaller than a frigate. It has one tier of guns. Your father must have been very brave to go to war in a sailboat."

Rocket was slightly high from the lovemaking and the rum but it was nevertheless a Rocket type comment. She was right about the *original* definition but I wasn't sure she knew what a World War II Corvette was so I explained it to her.

"It was a fast warship that was smaller than a destroyer and used mainly for convoy duty by the Royal Canadian Navy. They also rolled worse than any other ship ever invented. The *Owens Cutter* was the most exciting boat because he let me come with him everywhere when he had it built. We made a trip to the yard while they were building her. I went to City Island with him to buy the sails. After the war when he wasn't working he had me or my mother or both of us with him every minute. It was like he was trying to make up for time lost during convoy duty."

"I'll bet you don't know why the *Owens Cutter* was designed?"

"You're right," I answered. "Owens was a power boat company. Why did they go into the sailboat business?"

"Some guys from Owens were sailing a New York 32 in the Annapolis Fall Series. It was blowing hard and they were tying in reefs and shaking out reefs and putting 'em back and then back in again. They kept cussing the main like it was created just to torture them. By the end of the series they had invented the *Owens Cutter* in their imaginations."

"They should have had Rod Stephens with them."

"They didn't," she said.

"Is that a true story?"

Rocket paused for a few seconds and then said, "I think so but my dad told me and sometimes he colorized a story."

"The cutter has a special look. Not just the rig. I think the topsides are just a little high and the cabin just a little low. What do you think?"

We had talked boats all through three drinks and dinner. It wasn't until later when she asked about my dad and what he was like.

"Responsible. Because he knew so much about the sea he got command of a Corvette before he was old enough to shave. When his ship was sunk by a submarine he managed to keep his men together in lifeboats until they could be rescued. There is a story that he yelled at his men and told them if they quit and died he would tell the government and their families that they were cowards."

"That's awful. Do you believe it?"

"After the war, many years later, I talked to one of the men who was there. He said it was true. They were torpedoed in the Western Approaches to England. My father was smart and he knew that rescue was going to be quick if he could just keep the men alive. The problem was hypothermia. The will to live was important. He forced them to eat constantly and never stopped yelling. The Royal Navy gave him a medal but they never mentioned his threat to report the men as cowards. He said he believed what my father said. He said he was mean enough to do it."

"Was he really mean?"

"No, but he was tough. By that time everybody knew about the incident when General Patton slapped the soldier. The man said that my dad would have felt the same way as Patton but would have handled it differently. He said that my father would have whispered in the man's ear. He would have said 'If you don't go back and fight like a man I'll tell your mother you were a coward.' He said the man would have gone back and fought."

"That's some story."

"My dad told me that really good men are more afraid of their mother's disapproval than anything else on earth."

I remembered that weekend because it was the only time I ever told Rocket much about myself until yesterday afternoon when I told her about how I decided to become a cosmetic surgeon.

Crossing the bank could be an exciting experience even if there's no wind. If the sea is fairly calm, it is like sailing in a giant aquarium. The water is very clear and you can see all sorts of marine life but with the strong breeze we had, it was a little too choppy to see much. We sailed right up until dark and dropped the hook. As soon as we had the sails put away we both went below.

When I'm cruising, I like to sit in the cockpit at twilight for a happy hour drink or a Sundowner or whatever, but anchored on the banks I preferred to go below. I enjoyed the open sea when the boat was under way but for some reason I found it depressing when I was anchored on the banks. The cabin seemed a lot more pleasant and cozy. Part of it was the banging around. If there is any chop at all the boat bounces around all night and you notice it less down below. You are also closer to the center of gravity there. We were both exhilarated from the fabulous sailing that day but our moods were tempered by the knowledge that the vacation was over.

We had a couple of drinks and Rocket talked for a while about her job and some of the people she worked with while I started broiling some blackened dolphin. She was a buyer of Women's Junior Sportswear at one of the big department stores in downtown Miami. I didn't know anything at all about merchandising and I could never understand why styles had to change so often. I owned three or four very nice and very expensive suits, custom made at Brooks Brothers and a couple from Seville Row in London, but I hardly ever wore them. I had four navy blazers, five pairs of grey flannel slacks and five pairs of tan poplin slacks. In winter I wore the flannels and in summer I wore the poplin. Whenever something wore out, I took it to Brooks and told them to make me another one just like the other one. Occasionally one of my friends would needle me and ask if I ever changed clothes.

While Rocket watched me cook dinner she told me some things about her work. She explained about the seasons and how store buyers looked at the new designs long before each one.

"Why don't you become a sportswear designer? You know all about sportswear, I mean about fashion and fabric and colors and models. Do you know anything about patterns and size scales?"

"Of course. You have to know to be a buyer. Especially with Junior Sportswear because you are in between girls and women and they have to fit right or you lose business to the other two departments."

"Do you know anything about drawing or sketching?"

"Actually I can draw a little. When I was in high school, I drew cartoons. I was pretty good at it."

"Hey, that's terrific," I said. "I didn't know you were an artist."

"I didn't know you were either. I thought you were just an asshole" - she paused - "specialist."

"Aw c'mon Rocket. I just don't like to talk about myself."

"Probably 'cause you're half queer."

"Get off my back. When I studied art, the human head was my favorite subject. Now I'm an artist in human flesh. I do some wondrous things. Butch was a beautiful man and I just appreciate beauty. Just because I've acted like a friend, which we both agreed that we would do, just because I haven't come after you like a sex maniac you call me a queer!" I said, laughing.

"You've enjoyed acting like a friend! Besides, I said you were half-queer. If I remember correctly, the other half was pretty good! Not quite up to superior but at least acceptable."

By now we were both laughing, but three weeks of being horny with no relief were about to get to both of us.

"One more smart-ass remark and I'll pull off your drawers and screw your brains out!"

"Don't you wish! You switch-hitter half-faggot!" she said and stuck out her tongue at me. "You wouldn't know what to do with a woman any more."

I put my drink down on the cabin table and stood up slowly. I started toward her with the intention of getting all I wanted of exactly what I had been wanting all week. Suddenly she yelled.

"The fish is on fire!"

She grabbed the fire extinguisher, which was mounted on the bulkhead in the galley and put out the fire. It took only a few seconds to end the little fire but it was enough to settle us both. By the time the fire was out and we had cleaned up the small mess it had made, we were calmed down and cooled off. We had another quick drink and I finished cooking the fish.

We didn't talk for a while and when we did it was not about sex. We talked about the possibility of her designing career during dinner. She told me how she started out tracing the comics and how she learned to draw a lot of the characters without tracing. Her favorite people were Li'l Abner and Daisy Mae and all the people in Dog patch. When I offered to help her with the art work she gave me a long look and I think we both wondered if we would see each other again. We went to sleep early and I slept pretty well, right up until the alarm clock went off at four.

We started while it was still dark and hoisted the chute as soon as we were under way. The wind was still in the same direction, and between ten and fifteen so we had breakfast under way and got to Gun Cay while it was still very early. We dropped the spinnaker before going through Gun Cay Cut because you have to make some sharp turns near the light to stay in deep water. I had decided earlier to keep going if the weather was good instead of staying over at Cat Cay or Bimini.

We put up a large reaching sail instead of the chute so we could head south of the rhumb line to Miami and allow for the northward set of the Gulfstream. The breeze held steady all day and we had another fabulous sail. We carried the stay-sails for most of the day, until late afternoon, when the wind came a little too far forward. I decided to go south of Cape Florida instead of going through Government Cut and we were tied up at my slip at the Yacht Club dock in Coconut Grove before dark. Rocket had left her car at the yacht club so we said goodbye there. It was awkward since neither of us knew what would happen next. The sexual tension between us had been a problem for the whole trip, something we had both expected and tried to handle with a little humor. At the end of the trip, though, something had changed and I didn't understand it.

When Rocket had jumped into the swimming pool instead of going to the bar with me, she said she had to cool off. Her comment could have been because of the weather but I didn't think so. I think she meant that she had hot pants but didn't want me to do anything about it but she also could have been concerned that with another couple of drinks she would have come after me. I usually understood her double meanings since I knew that she liked to tease. What I didn't understand was what had excited her in the first place. The dinner was kind of romantic but my stories should have cooled her off. I enjoyed being with Rocket as much as anyone I knew but there was too much sexual attraction between us to be comfortable as friends. Other than the fact that I didn't get laid on the cruise, it was almost perfect, but I would never again, *deliberately*, endure the same kind of abstinent misery.

Chapter Five

Coconut Grove, Monday, 15 May

The first day at work after a vacation is no fun whether you are a doctor or a bookkeeper. My partner had not scheduled any surgery for me on Monday or Tuesday so that I would have a little time to get back into a routine. This had also given me some flexibility in case the weather had turned out bad and we had to wait in Bimini before crossing the Stream. Since we got back to Coconut Grove on Saturday, I felt no pressure to start. On Wednesday morning I had a rhino-plasty and some eyelid surgery scheduled, an easy way to get back into it.

I was in a practice with another doctor in Coral Gables. We both did some surgery at our little clinic and some at a private hospital. To call our office a clinic is stretching things a little but it is very well equipped. Our operating room had just about everything you would find in a major hospital, at least for the type of operations that we do. One of our biggest luxuries was our staff of people. Except for our receptionist, our people were registered nurses so they really knew what they were doing and worked well together. They were all very flexible and would do menial tasks without bitching.

My partner, Bill Gaines, was the main reason why the office ran smoothly. He was slightly overweight, slightly bald and almost always happy except when he was complaining about the exorbitant bills from the golf club where he belonged. That was a constant source of irritation to him and he was very vocal about it. The chits from his club that came in each month were about the only things that could take the smile off his face. He was in his middle thirties with three kids and a very nice wife who didn't trust me because I was still single. The first year or two that Bill and I worked together she tried to fix me up with dates but she had stopped that. Bill had been a good choice as a partner.

When I decided to build a small office I chose to finish the building first and then select a partner. Since my family was fairly wealthy and very generous I had no problem getting the money I needed. I was still living aboard my schooner at the Dinner Key Marina and the *Vanitie* was collateral. For graduation I got a brand new Star Class boat along with a trailer and that was additional collateral. Without a partner at the start, I didn't have to worry about getting someone else's opinion on things. This was important for me. I have no trouble accepting instructions from another person and I don't have trouble telling other people what to do but on committees of any kind I am a big problem. If I agree with what the group is doing I don't say anything and don't make any contribution. If I don't agree with a group I try to take over and dominate. I don't have much patience and I become a pain in the ass. I can lead or follow but not much else.

I found an architect who knew Coral Gables and he helped me pick out the area and then a plot of land. It was in a part of town that was mostly residential but zoned so I could have an office building if it looked like a house. It was a section where the houses were fairly large and very well kept, with neat lawns and shrubbery. My contractor was someone I knew from the Yacht Club who was supposed to be reasonably honest, and the whole project was completed with very few problems. I had the office designed with enough space for three doctors, although I wanted only one partner. In the back of my mind I planned on renting the place some time in the future to three doctors. Then I would take a long ocean cruise.

When the office was complete, I decided to ask Bill Gaines to move in with me. I had been thinking about several people but he seemed to be the best choice. We were about the same age. He had gone to a good medical school and had done his internship and residency at an excellent hospital. I knew he was having trouble financially because he had a lot of debt from way back in college. He got married during his senior year and his wife got pregnant while he was still in medical school so she couldn't work after the baby was born. I knew about Bill's problems but they were not a factor in my choosing him and suggesting a partnership.

He was a skilled surgeon first of all, but beyond that, there were a number of things that made me want him. He had a warm, friendly personality and a lot of charm where I was a little cold and lacking in both. He talked a great deal, almost all of the time, even in an operating room. The other doctors and surgical nurses who worked with him were used to it and knew it didn't affect his work at all.

I didn't know it before we became partners but he had a tremendous ability to organize our business. This was great for me because I didn't like paper work and wasn't good at it. Bill wasn't quite as good as I was at complex facial surgery. He had the knowledge and skill but I also had the eye of an artist. I'm not really sure that my art background helped me at all but I liked to think that it did. Sometimes, when there was a complex and difficult case that involved several operations over a long period of time, he would ask me to do the job. This didn't cause a problem for either of us. Nor did it bother us that he really ran the office, overlooking our billing and management of the girls and every other part that wasn't medical.

When I asked him to join me I was pretty sure he would accept and even thought that he would be flattered, not because of me, but because the place was so nice. I asked him to set aside part of an afternoon to look at an office I was moving into. I think he agreed out of curiosity and, perhaps, a little envy since he knew I belonged to a yacht club and owned two boats. I had not mentioned to anyone at the hospital that I was building an office or looking for a partner. I told him that we would look at the office first and then I would buy him lunch.

When we pulled up to the front of the new building, Bill was a little startled. The landscape people had put in new grass and shrubbery and of course some palm trees. The architect and I had decided to put the building a little further back on the property than other houses on the street. I didn't need a back yard, just a small parking lot for the patients and staff. This made the front yard huge and it looked like a small park. There was even a large fish pond.

I got an interior decorator since I didn't know much about picking colors or even buying furniture. She had done an excellent job. All the colors were nice subdued pastels and the carpet colors tied in with the walls. It looked expensive and it was. The medical equipment had been installed and it was all very bright and shiny.

Bill hadn't said a word as he went from room to room looking at everything. After he had seen it all, he walked back to the reception area and said, "Well, Devlin, your new place is absolutely first class. It looks like something out of the movies. When do you move in?"

I knew he was envious as hell but he was perfectly graceful and didn't ask any questions about where the money came from or make any wise-guy comments. At that point, I believe he was just happy for me. He was that kind of a guy.

"In about two weeks," I said. "Why don't you move in with me? You can start paying rent when you get your debts paid off." He stared at me, obviously startled at my proposal.

"Are you shitting me?"

"No. Not at all. My parents are pretty well off and I was able to borrow quite a bit of money from them. I was able to get financing from the bank for the rest." I didn't tell him that my parents had given me more than half the cost of the building.

"Let's go to lunch," I said. "I'm getting very hungry," I knew he was really moved by my offer but I'm uncomfortable when people are emotional or sentimental. After making sure he understood correctly that we would both be equal partners in a practice but that he paid nothing in rent until he could afford it, I shook his hand and we became partners.

"Which office do I take?"

"Take your choice," I said, knowing it would mean something to him and nothing to me. After he picked out his office and practiced sitting at the desk, he asked if he could tell his wife. Although it was a somewhat touching moment, I was getting hungry.

"Why don't we pick up Anne and go to lunch? I'm really starved."

I wanted him to tell her in private and I was afraid he might get a little maudlin. It *was* exciting for me as well to have a partner and a new office but I didn't want to talk about it. I told him I would wait in the car while he called and asked him to just close the front door when he came out. As soon as he walked out and got in the car, I said I had forgotten something and went back inside. I went to the back of one of the closets and pulled out a large package wrapped in brown paper. I took the paper off and hung the picture behind the desk which Bill had picked out.

It was a huge color photograph of the sixteenth green at Augusta National Golf Club, taken during a Master's Tournament, and Arnold Palmer was putting. Bill was crazy about playing golf and anxious to join a country club. Any golfer would love the picture. When I was sure it was hanging straight I went back out to the car knowing he would have a pleasant surprise.

We had to pick up Anne since they had only the one car which we were driving. At lunch he told her that we were going to become partners but he didn't tell her about the new office until she asked where we were going to practice. He told her we had something picked out and he would show her after lunch. When we left the yacht club, I got him to drop me off at the hospital where my car was parked. Just before they drove away, I handed him a set of keys to the office. I'm sure it was something special for him to show Anne the new place. I can still remember that day, wondering if I would ever care enough about a woman to feel the way that Bill did. I didn't think so.

Although Bill and I were different in many ways there were a few similarities. We both had a total lack of interest in cars. When we became partners, we had two of the ugliest cars in town, maybe in all of Florida. Once, at a medical meeting, a doctor we both knew asked me what kind of car I drove and I really couldn't remember. My mother had bought it for me as a gift one time on a visit and I really didn't know. Our friend was truly astonished and turned to Bill with the same question, but Bill couldn't remember what kind of car he owned either. The guy was aching to tell somebody about his wonderful new car and he tried to tell us. We meant to be nice but neither of us even knew what questions to ask. He gave up on us pretty quickly and hurried away to find somebody who shared his love for automobiles.

For the first few months in the new building we parked out back in the small lot which we had for patients and our staff of four. There was plenty of room as our type of practice didn't cause crowded waiting rooms, but since no other people used the parking, a lot of patients started asking about the wrecks outside. We decided we had to get new cars because the beautiful new building required it. Since Bill was not paying rent, and would not be for a few years, it was a little awkward to be talking about new cars so I decided to make it easy and help him. I suggested that we buy them on time payments from our practice. Doctors usually don't have trouble getting credit because people think that their bills are exorbitant and that all doctors are rich. We set aside an afternoon when we could go together and buy two new cars. Bill decided he wanted a station wagon because it would look good at the country club he was planning to join someday. When the buying day came there was a minor emergency as we were leaving. A boy had taken a tumble on his bicycle and cut up his face. It was nothing serious but he did need some patching and a few stitches. We usually didn't get emergencies at the office, but the people were neighbors and we wanted to make friends with everyone in the area.

We agreed that Bill would go to a dealer and buy cars for both of us while I fixed the kid. Since Bill was getting a station wagon, I told him to get one just like it for me. I was always hauling sail-bags around and the extra room would make it easier. He was going to keep his old car for Anne and drive the new one to work so that our patients could see that we were respectable.

"What color do you want?" he asked as he walked out the door.

"It doesn't matter. Whatever they have."

The color didn't seem very important to me. Since I had not been interested in cars as a kid, I had never learned or cared much about them. My father gave me a car when I was sixteen and I used it but I never learned anything about how it worked. I was interested in art and sailing in high school and not much else. Because I played football and hung around with some nice kids it was O.K. not to care about cars.

Bill's car was ready in about a week – a maroon Pontiac, I think. A few days later the dealer picked up my old car and delivered the new one. Our receptionist, Lori, took care of the dealer and the paper work since I was examining a patient. She came back inside after seeing the car, walking into the examining room where I had a patient sitting up on one of the tables.

"Here's the keys to your new car. It's parked out back."

"What color is it?"

"Pig vomit green," she said, without changing expression. I had gone from having the ugliest old car in town to the ugliest new car. Cars I didn't care about, but I was an artist and knew color. Lori was right. Now, four years later, I'm still driving the same car. Since I haven't washed it much in all that time, the dirt hides the color a little.

By that time, at the end of May when I got back from the cruise with Rocket, Bill and I had been together more than four years and had become very close friends. He was easy to be friends with because of his warm personality and consistent attitude about everything. He had only one real mood and that was pleasant. When he went crazy every month over his expenses at the golf club, I thought he actually enjoyed the bitching. He had struggled from college through residency and, according to Anne, he had never gotten discouraged or depressed.

That Monday morning, right after the cruise with Rocket, he had already arrived at the office and fixed coffee. We each got a cup and sat down in my office. Bill had a list of what had happened since I left which was typical of his well-organized way of doing things. He also had a profit-and-loss statement for the month and year-to-date. He was meticulous about doing this every month and I did read and understand them. Actually, neither of us was very money-conscious but Bill had struggled for so many years that he really enjoyed seeing the numbers. By this time he had paid back his loans and we were both doing well.

Bill had me scheduled for a simple rhinoplasty at eight o'clock on Wednesday morning and some eyelid surgery in the afternoon. On Thursday, I was set up to start on a case that would require some craniofacial surgery. This would be very complicated and my kind of case, a big part of why I became a cosmetic surgeon instead of a painter.

Craniofacial surgery makes it possible to correct major congenital or acquired defects of the face and skull. The techniques, which are still new, give us surgeons wide access to the bony skeleton of the skull so that we can literally sculpt the bone. This type of surgery is highly complicated and requires teams of orthodontists, radiologists, one or more plastic surgeons, ophthalmologists, neurosurgeons, psychologists, anesthesiologists, and others. I was suddenly excited. There were only a few places in the world where it could be done. I had spent a whole year at New York University learning the skills. Only recently we had gotten a hospital and teams that could do the job in South Florida. I looked at the pictures with Bill and asked a few questions. I would take them home tonight to study them.

We went over the schedule for the next two weeks and I was pleased to see that there were several interesting cases as well as the routine ones. My mind was still partly in the islands and I wasn't quite with it yet.

Bill had scheduled our monthly luncheon for that day. We had gotten into a routine of having lunch together at his golf club or my yacht club and charging it to the business. Although it was our only questionable expense, we made it a point to talk about personal things only and never about surgery or the business part of the practice. It was sort of backwards but we both enjoyed the lunches. Because we were so busy, we needed the time together outside the clinic to keep track of each other personally. When we finished getting our schedule straight, I went into my office and left the door open so that all of the ladies could come in and ask about my vacation. Each one asked about Rocket, of course, some of them circumspectly and one directly. There was no one in the office in whom I had any romantic interest. When he hired people, Bill had made sure of that, at my request. The receptionist was the only single girl in the office and she was twenty-two years old. She had started with us part time when she was a freshman at the University of Miami and we couldn't afford a full-time girl. She was a terrific girl and very efficient but very liberal according to my ideas and Bill had to keep after her to watch her language. When she came in, she asked about the weather and the islands and the food and then asked what she really wanted to know.

"Did you sleep together?"

"No."

"Not even once or twice?"

"Lori, don't you think that's a pretty personal thing to ask an older person? Particularly a doctor you work for?"

"I'm sorry. It seemed like a perfectly normal thing to ask since both of you are single. Besides, I think Rocket is a terrific lady. I think you should marry her."

Bill and I had decided in the beginning that we would have an informal office. All the women were very formal and polite in front of the patients but when no one was around they called us Bill and Dev, or Devlin. Nobody ever called me Win or Winfield although that was my name. All the women took their problems to Bill as I think they felt I was a little aloof and he was easier to talk to, but they all seemed to know about my social life. This wasn't too surprising since I kept all my dates and social activities on the same calendar. I think Lori filled in the spaces with what else she knew and if she didn't know something she used her imagination. She went over a list of my personal calls which she had taken while I was away.

"Snake called. He wants his thing."

"What thing?" I asked wondering what he had told her.

"The thing you smuggled in for him."

"I didn't smuggle in anything. He was just kidding you."

"I don't think so. He sounded very serious and very sinister, as if it were really dangerous or something. He wants you to call him when you have a chance."

"What else?"

"I think sinister men are really sexy. Can you fix me up with Snake?"

"No."

"Gus Draper called and he wants you to come to dinner on the boat on Friday night. He said to bring a date if you wanted and he is going to have Frogmore Stew. He got the shrimp himself down by Jewfish Creek, really huge, giant shrimp. He has tons of them. Why don't you let me come with you? I love shrimp."

"Lori, you know I don't date girls your age. Besides, Gus and his wife are old enough to be your grandparents. You wouldn't enjoy the conversation. Who else called?"

"Who were you expecting?"

"Nobody."

"Then nobody called."

Sometimes Lori nearly drove me nuts with the things she said, but I don't have much sense of humor and I appreciate it in other people. I couldn't get mad at her because she always made me laugh. When I got tired of her talking so much, I had a sure way of getting her to shut up so I used it then.

"Lori, why don't you let me operate on your breasts? I might be able to reduce them down to large." This always worked so she got peeved and left the office.

The day passed pretty slowly and I couldn't reach Snake. After I hung up the phone I started thinking that maybe Snake had smuggled in some Goddamn statue or something, and maybe my ass was in a sling. Snake was a fabulous crew, probably a better sailor than I was. He was also very dependable. If he said he would do something it got done. If he said he'd be somewhere, he would be one minute early. On an ocean race in heavy weather he was worth two men. But he was also crazy as hell, showed up in strange places at strange times and didn't seem to work at a regular job.

On Wednesday I spent most of my time in the operating room. Most of the operations were routine but none were boring. I was always conscious of how I could change a person's life by changing his face. I thought that what I did was important and I felt that each operation was an opportunity to help somebody.

On Thursday morning at eight o'clock I had an appointment with a young girl and her mother. The girl had been in a terrible accident when a gondola car at a ski resort had fallen over fifty feet. From the brief description of the accident that Bill had taken on their initial visit it was a disaster. Seventeen people had been killed and everyone in the car was seriously hurt. I think she was lucky to be alive. I had studied the records from the surgeons who had attended her immediately after the crash. They were experts at fixing broken legs but not much at facial surgery. Fortunately, they hadn't made any major errors. Her name was Joan and her skull had been partially damaged. Bill had not put anything in the place where we noted referrals.

"Mrs. Pegram, Dr. Gaines probably told you that today we would just talk and try to work out a tentative schedule. Then I'll take a few X-ray pictures. Mainly we have to have a sort of plan. Each operation depends a lot on the one before it so we can't be completely specific but we will make some plans. By the way, were you referred to us by someone?"

"Mrs. Lisa Winter."

My heart practically stopped just hearing her name. I finished up with Joan Pegram and her mother by making an appointment for the following week and asking for all of her medical records from the family doctor. After they left, I sat in my office and thought for a few minutes about Lisa.

I first met Lisa Winter because of an accident that happened to her son Bobby. It was a terribly messy thing that occurred one Wednesday afternoon while I was still living at Dinner Key Marina aboard my old schooner *Vanitie*. I had been practicing medicine in South Miami for several years and sometimes got involved in accidents immediately after they happened. This was rare, however, and usually doctors allowed the paramedics to do what they had been trained for and get the patient to a hospital. As a cosmetic surgeon, part of my work is putting people back together after the accident and damage has been done.

This is both the best and worst of what I do. It is the worst because I am frequently working with someone who, in the few milliseconds of an automobile crash, has had his face change from being attractive to being very ugly, sometimes from one extreme to another.

The transformation can be exceedingly grotesque.

Good reconstructive surgery can sometimes make a badly damaged face almost normal and, once in a thousand times, even better than before.

Modern technology has produced some incredibly efficient machinery and some of these inventions are good at more than one task. The modern lightweight outboard motor is one of those machines. It has become popular all over the world because of its ability to provide propulsion to small and medium sized boats in a compact unit. It is also one of the most effective things ever designed for tearing up a human face. The blades of the prop are short and do not always kill a person, whereas the larger blades of an inboard would do that. Perhaps mercifully.

Bobby Winter was the victim of just such an outboard motor. It was an ten-horsepower Evinrude owned by a man named Whittaker from Key Biscayne who lost his grip on a slippery beer can. In trying to keep the beer from spilling, he lost control of his boat which proceeded to attack Bobby. Bobby had been sailing back to the club, which was conducting his sailing class, and was alone in an Optimist Pram concentrating hard on the trim of his sails. When the small runabout crashed into his pram, Bobby was thrown overboard and as his head came up out of the water the blades of the outboard did some work on his face.

Other than his face, he was uninjured, although he was knocked unconscious by the collision. Bobby was picked up almost immediately by the sailing class instructors who had been close by in a launch. They took him directly to the club dock. I would not have been there on a weekday except that I was racing in a Star Class Regatta and happened to be sailing into the Dinner Key Channel on my way home. Snake Moran was my crew that day and from thirty yards away we could see every detail of the accident. I'm an ambulance chaser, anyway, and whenever I see an accident I go and find out if there's a need for a doctor. I always knew the risk of legal trouble but sometimes my early work has been of critical assistance to people. In these situations I have never charged a fee and I have rarely been thanked.

When I saw the accident, I was headed for the Sailing Club dock anyway to haul my boat out. I knew a pram was involved and guessed they would end up there. Snake took our boat and I transferred to a club launch about a hundred feet from the dock, getting there a couple of minutes after the sailing instructors pulled Bobby out on the dock. The ambulance had not arrived yet and there were no doctors around so I took over the first aid immediately. Although he was in shock and barely conscious, it appeared that there were no wounds other than the ones to his face. These were extensive.

Cosmetic surgery is not usually performed on accident victims right away because it does not have exactly the same priority as keeping a person alive. Damage to the brain, any internal bleeding, or anything life threatening are the first and correct priorities. Once a victim is stabilized, and more or less safe, then the long process of correcting "superficial" damage can begin. In a perfect world, our trauma centers would be far more advanced than they are today, and each one would have a highly skilled cosmetic surgeon available for those few times when the injuries to the face are so great and the injuries to the rest of the body so minor, that cosmetic surgery becomes primary.

The first thing I did was to get one of the sailing instructors to run over and get my medical bag out of my car. He had no trouble finding the car with the strange green color. In addition to the things that most doctors carry I had a lot of additional equipment that would only be used by a plastic surgeon and I wanted to start immediately.

I cleared the dock completely by literally snarling at the people who had gathered around. I'm not physically intimidating, being only slightly over six feet, but in anger, for some reason, I'm frightening. I've been told that my green eyes, my "*ojos verdes*," become a strange shade of green and actually light up like some kind of weird creature. I told one of the sailing instructors who I was and what we had to do. I used one of them to help me with the boy, one to keep the dock clear, and another to clear a lane for the ambulance to come through the club gate and out onto the lawn.

I started working on the boy's face as soon as I had stopped most of the bleeding. It was important for me to do certain things immediately and put in stitches that would lay the foundation to eventually restore him to his normal looks. There was no way on earth that anyone could make him look anything but awful until a series of operations could replace the flesh. When the ambulance arrived, I explained to the paramedics who I was and what I was doing. They reminded me that I had no legal right to interfere and administer aid to the kid.

Fortunately, they were experienced men and understood right away when I explained that the child needed work on his face immediately but that everything else seemed all right. Once they had covered themselves legally they did everything they could to help and cooperate. One of them took over as my helper, replacing the sailing instructor and stayed with me right to the emergency room. I stopped work on Bobby temporarily while they loaded him in the ambulance and then did a few more things on the way to the hospital. Using a combination of a few critical sutures and some compresses held in place, I was able to do a temporary holding job until we got to the hospital. When we rolled him into the ER, I insisted on talking to the Resident in Charge and told him we needed a cosmetic surgeon *immediately*. The resident was a young guy named Ross who took one look at the boy and excused himself for a minute. I think he went out and threw up. There is something much worse about the appearance of facial injuries than other forms of damage. No matter how ugly a broken leg looks, or a crushed pelvis, it doesn't evoke the same outright horror as a cruelly smashed face.

A few minutes later I was advised that there were no plastic surgeons available. On checking further, I learned that the hospital had made calls to every cosmetic surgeon on their staff. I also knew that Dr. Ross had taken the boy's wallet from his pocket and called his home. A servant told him that Mr. and Mrs. Winter were out for the afternoon and would be picking Bobby up at six o'clock at the Sailing Club where they had dropped him that morning. When I found this out it was only a little after four. When they came to pick him up, they would still have to drive to the hospital. That was too much time to be lost.

I asked Dr. Ross if he could get the chief of surgery down to the ER, and when he arrived I told him who I was and that the boy should be worked on immediately. I described in the most technical terms possible what I wanted to do and why losing time would seriously jeopardize the outcome. What I said was a little bit of a con job because several times I threw in the name of New York University Medical Center where I got my training. I also used some terms that a man who operated on internal organs would recognize but not know quite how to evaluate. The Chief of Surgery was an intelligent and experienced man. Legally, he could not give me authorization to operate in his hospital but he did verbally tell me to continue administering appropriate first aid until a cosmetic surgeon on his staff arrived. I wasn't at all protected, but at least I thought he was neutral.

We got Bobby Winter into an operating room and I went to work on him. The primary surgical nurse who was assigned to help me was a tough looking woman of about fifty. I explained to her that I was not on the staff of the hospital and that some legal action might be directed at me later. Her feelings were clear.

"*Fuck the lawyers. Fix the kid!*"

We did that all right. It took several hours but it was as beautiful a job of surgery as I have ever performed. The things that I did could not have been done later as well or as easily as I did them then. The nurse had never worked with me before and I doubt if she had ever worked so quickly after an accident, but she was superb. Absolutely superb. We did an incredible job.

It had been several years since that operation but I could remember every detail. Partly because it was so messy and partly because of my confrontation with Bobby Winter's mother. While I was doing the surgery, I made a point of asking about every thirty minutes whether or not one of the staff surgeons had arrived. I did this in case of legal action later. I didn't believe it would make sense for someone else to take over at this point but I might have to prove later that I was doing the work because there was nobody else to do it. I had gotten an anesthesiologist to help and he was very good. I had used local anesthesia at the dock and again when we reached the operating room, but as he came out of shock I had to be able to keep him under long enough to do the work. While his face was laid open in so many places, I had to get the stitches in the right places to lay the foundation for future work. A human is not a piece of clay or granite and I had to be careful of every nerve and muscle and blood vessel. When I finished, I knew that he would look terrible until future operations, but I also knew that I had done things that had to be done before the healing process started, things that could not be accomplished as well later. At some point I had been told that the boy's mother had arrived but it was far too late to get permission for my work.

When we had finished, the surgical nurse introduced herself as Margaret Lindsey.

"I've never seen anything like that. If you get any grief from the lawyers, call me and I'll testify for you. If you ever need a surgical nurse to work for you, I'm available." I thanked her for the support and told her that her own work was excellent. I explained that nurses usually have a hard time working with me in an emergency, because I work much faster than I do in a regular case. She had not had any problems.

When they took Bobby to the recovery room, I went into a locker room to take a leak and to clean up. I had been supplied with a gown and mask but I looked more like a bum than a surgeon. I hadn't shaved in the morning because I wasn't working that day. There was a party that night at the Yacht Club. Either Myers or Bacardi Rum was going to sponsor it and I planned to shave just before the party.

I changed back into my shorts and knit shirt. I knew the boy would be waking up and wanted to be there so I started to look for the recovery room when Dr. Lazar, the Chief of Surgery, came in and told me that the boy's mother was outside. I went out to a small reception area where there was a lady waiting. She looked up at me as I walked toward her. Instinctively I knew that this woman was going to be a pain in the ass because she was in a "category of beautiful" where no one else had ever belonged. As a portrait painter and cosmetic surgeon I considered myself to be an expert on beauty. I even thought of myself as the *Prince of Beauty*, although I had never used those words with anyone but my mother. In my entire life I had never seen a woman so beautiful, not a painting, a picture, a movie or a real person.

Dr. Lazar introduced us and Mrs. Carl Winter started to ask me questions about what had happened. I interrupted her.

"Mrs. Winter, your son is going to be waking up in just a few minutes. I want you to be there with me to talk to him. I'm going to tell him that he had an accident and cut his face. Nothing more than that at this time. I want you to talk to him first so that he knows you're here. He has bandages over his eyes and he's going to be very scared. You tell him that I'm a doctor and that I bandaged him up right after it happened. It's very important that he *hears your voice immediately* and that you act calm and reassuring. Don't let him know you're frightened.

"Don't mention the operating room. He was in shock but came out with no problems. There does not appear to be any damage except to his face. We have plenty of time to explain everything before the bandages come off. Do you understand me?"

"Dr. Devlin," she said, "you are not going to handle Bobby's case. Dr. Lazar has assigned Dr. Montgomery to our case and he will make the decisions about what to tell Bobby."

I looked at Lazar and he confirmed what she said.

"Dr. Montgomery is on our staff here. One of our finest surgeons," he said smoothly.

"Fine," I said. "Let's talk to him right now. I want to explain what happened and what Bobby's condition is."

"Dr. Montgomery is not available today. He will want to examine your son tomorrow, Mrs. Winter." Just as he said it a nurse came in and told us that the boy was starting to wake up.

"Let's go in and talk to him, Mrs. Winter. I think it will go much better if a doctor is with you. Dr. Montgomery can talk to him when he examines him tomorrow," I suggested.

Mrs. Winter looked to Lazar for guidance.

"I don't believe there will be any harm in that," Lazar said condescendingly.

"Dr. Devlin, have you been drinking?" Mrs. Winter cut in.

"Budweiser," I said and stared at her. "Let's go in."

After the race was over that afternoon, I had calculated the scores in my mind and figured I was ahead by one point. I always carried a cold six-pack aboard and I drank two beers while we watched the others finish, and then sailed in. Although that was more than a few hours ago, it was still on my breath.

We had gone in and talked to Bobby, just as he was waking up, and it went well. He seemed reassured that his mother was there and seemed to accept what I said. There had been no damage to his eyes or to his vision but there were a number of cuts around the eyes that required bandages, so he couldn't see anything. I explained this to him. There had also been extensive damage to his teeth and jaw so he couldn't talk. He seemed to accept this too and nodded when I needed a response.

When we finished with him, I asked his mother if she wanted me to explain how the accident had happened and how I got involved. She said that she could learn all about that later. She also said that the matter of my participation would be reviewed by her lawyers and that I would hear from them. She asked a nurse where she could find Dr. Lazar and I asked the same nurse to call me a taxi.

Inappropriate response was a term that Laufenberg had used a few years back when he was trying to figure out why I hit people with baseball bats and threw people out of windows. I still had that problem because all I could think of riding in the taxi back to the sailing club was what a beautiful woman Mrs. Winter was. Absolutely spectacular. I should have been thinking about how she might sue me and put me out of surgery, but all I could think about was how beautiful her face looked. Her eyes were a dark shade of blue, almost purple. Her nose was simply perfect and her mouth was also. It was not wide but the lips were slightly full and they looked as if they had been designed to be admired. I was fascinated.

Two weeks after the accident I was asked to come down with an attorney to the offices of a law firm that had five names. I got a guy named Bellamy Craddock, who I knew from the Yacht Club. We sat down in a big conference room and everybody was introduced. Bobby's father was there and I was surprised at how old he was. Lisa Winter looked about thirty but her husband was at least fifty, a distinguished silver-haired man. I kept staring at his wife and lost track several times of what was being said. I should have been listening but I couldn't take my eyes away from her face.

One of the lawyers from the firm with five names explained that this meeting was informal and a professional courtesy so that we could fully understand the Winters' position. He made it clear that they were very wealthy and were not suing me for financial gain but because I had put myself above the law and operated on Bobby Winter when I had no legal authority. It was a matter of principle but they did plan to *sue for the maximum*. I heard words like malpractice, illegal, unauthorized, and drinking. During the recital of the events I half-listened and mostly stared at Mrs. Winter.

When Bellamy made his speech I didn't pay much attention but some guy came in and whispered to Mr. Winter, who then interrupted to tell us that Dr. Montgomery was outside. Winter had asked him to come down and say a few words. After my side of the thing had been presented, Montgomery came in.

I had never seen him or met him before and I was astonished at how tiny he was. He could not have been more than five feet or five feet one inch, or something like that, and probably had on elevator shoes. He had a mouth that was about as big as the opening of a coke bottle and talked like it was hard to get words out. I've never seen a ferret or weasel up close, but he was probably a cousin. He was the kind of guy who would make you start laughing if he wasn't so nasty looking.

He was introduced and asked to comment informally. He sat there and stared at each person for a few seconds then he looked at me like he was about to bite my leg. He said he had a copy of the operation report which I sent him and that he was going to read it. His voice was so contemptuous that I was amazed.

He read the report very carefully, stopping numerous times to explain the technical medical details so that everyone could understand. The report that he read was eleven typewritten pages of descriptions of everything I had done, starting at the dock. I do them on every procedure by dictating to a machine in my own office or in the hospital where I usually operate. When I worked on Bobby Winter, I got somebody to record for me. I carry a small dictating machine with me on races and summarize each one to try to improve. I used that machine. I had also included some recommendations for the next two operations with sketches and diagrams.

When he finished reading, he stared at me again and then explained that he had also talked to the surgical nurse and had made some phone calls to people he considered to be the best in the field.

I can remember almost word for word what he said. He stared at Lisa and Carl Winter the whole time and never looked at me again. I listened carefully to every word. Although I did not feel much emotion at the time, I knew that it was important and that I could be in serious trouble.

"There is no possible way that I would have done what Dr. Devlin did to the patient." He paused for a long time.

"I have been practicing for a number of years and consider myself to be a first-class surgeon. However, my experience has been almost entirely with cosmetic surgery performed on people with inborn defects or problems caused by aging. I have worked on some patients who were accident victims but whose wounds had healed prior to the surgery. I have had no experience working on patients still in shock from an accident. None whatsoever.

"I have learned that Dr. Devlin spent two years at the Institute for Reconstructive Surgery at New York University working under the famous Dr. Joseph McCarthy. I also learned that Dr. Devlin worked in the Department of Plastic Surgery at the Manhattan Eye, Ear and Throat Hospital working under the equally famous Dr. Thomas D. Rees. Dr. Rees is a professor of plastic surgery at New York University Medical Center.

"It would be the high point of my life just to meet and talk with either of these men. Devlin has worked for both of them. I have been told that Dr. Devlin has operated literally on hundreds of accident victims, putting the pieces back together, and using some techniques that have only been read about in South Florida. Miami is a nasty place but it is nothing like the battlefield that is New York.

"I also spoke at great length to Dr. Meyer Koblenz who was an attending surgeon at Bellevue. After his internship, Dr. Devlin went to New York University to concentrate on facial surgery. Koblenz told me that the Emergency Room at Bellevue had a deal with Devlin where they would call him any time there was severe facial damage. Devlin lived on a sailboat in the East River close to both New York University and Bellevue. He used a motorcycle in order to be able to get through traffic jams and would sometimes ride on the sidewalk when he became impatient with traffic.

"Dr. Koblenz called him an ambulance chaser. This is a very derogatory term when applied to a lawyer, I believe, but he meant it as a humorous and unusual compliment. Koblenz said that it was his own term for Devlin because of his impatience to begin work before the healing process started. He described an incident that took place after Devlin left Bellevue, but was still responding to emergencies at both places. It was during a snowstorm when an ambulance got stuck in a mess caused by the snow and too many cars. The ER got the location of the ambulance by radio and called Dr. Devlin who found the stranded ambulance on his motorcycle. He determined that the first priority was keeping the patient alive and did not start any facial surgery until the next day. The point is that he did have his priorities in the correct order. He saved the patient's life because it took three hours to get to the hospital in the snow. I am absolutely sure that keeping the little boy alive was Devlin's top priority and had there been any danger of hurting his chances of survival he would have made sure of that first.

"I asked about his character and was told that he was an eccentric with a cold personality. I was told that he would not talk if it was avoidable but that he could make patients feel totally confident.

"I was told that he was an artist with both a brush and a scalpel who could not balance a check book. I was also told that he kept meticulous records of operations. The recommendations which Devlin gave me for future operations could go right into a textbook on surgery without editing. The sketches and diagrams are flawless."

At that point I was listening to what the little rat-like creature was saying but I was staring at Lisa Winter. Her cool serene beauty was about to crumble into little pieces. He was looking at her alone when he said, "for me to replace Devlin on this case is an absurdity of the worst kind. I will not do it. I am taking myself off of the case. If you persist in this evil lawsuit, I will testify on behalf of Dr. Devlin. If he institutes a countersuit, I will then testify on his behalf.

"What you are trying to do, Mrs. Winter, is vicious and ugly. If you persist there will be no decent surgeon in the country who will touch the case. That is all I have to say and I will not answer any questions."

The tiny little man got up and walked out of the room on his elevator shoes. In my eyes he had become about seven feet tall. Lisa Winter had collapsed with her face down on the table. She was making some terrible noises and her husband was trying to console her. Bellamy Craddock grabbed my arm and pulled me away from the table and we left. As we walked out, I realized that the lawyer, who spoke for the Winters, was staring at me. I guess he was upset at losing a big fee. I could see his point since my career certainly meant nothing to him so I gave him the finger.

Early the next morning Bellamy called to tell me there would be no lawsuit. I wrote Montgomery a letter thanking him. I didn't want to thank him in person because I wasn't sure whether he would be gracious or bite my leg. I did eventually get together with him and got to know him. He was hard as hell to like, though, and it took me a long time.

Dealing with Whittaker, however, was another matter. Snake had watched the accident just as I did but while I concentrated on sailing to the dock as quickly as possible Snake used the binoculars to identify Whittaker's boat. I had told Bellamy that we knew who was responsible but he said that the accident itself had nothing to do with the case against me. He said we would wait until charges were brought against me and if necessary use it as a bargaining tool. When Bellamy called to tell me that charges had been dropped I instructed him to contact the Winters and tell them that we knew the identity of the man who had been driving the boat that cut up Bobby. The next day Bellamy called to say that the Winters did not want to pursue the case.

I told him I thought that the legal system was corrupt and that all lawyers were blood-sucking leeches. He agreed but he told me to forget about it. The Winters didn't need money and Bobby was getting the best medical treatment. I did forget about it – completely – until I got home that night.

I knew I was getting really pissed off so I called Otto Laufenberg and told him the whole story. Articles about the accident had been in all the newspapers but described the runabout as unidentified. Whittaker was a very wealthy developer. He had plenty of time to come forward and offer help or apologize or something. He didn't do anything.

When I finished, Dr. Laufenberg was very specific. Do absolutely nothing and accept what happened. He said that I had done a courageous thing and pointed out that I had already risked my right to practice medicine. He said it was time for me to act like an adult and that anything further would only make things worse for the Winters. They and their lawyers had made the decision to drop it. He was insistent and said that I could make no case against Whittaker.

I promised that I would do nothing but I lied. The system was fucked up and Whittaker was going to get away completely after doing what he did to Bobby Winter. Screw Laufenberg.

A few days later when Mr. Whittaker stepped out of the elevator into the underground parking garage of the building he owned, a bearded man asked to speak to him. Whittaker was dressed in a three-piece suit and sneered in disgust at the other man who looked like a tramp. But then Snake hit him in the mouth and we threw him into a nearby dumpster. Somehow Snake had arranged to have forty gallons of raw sewage put into the dumpster an hour earlier. Whittaker was in deep shit for only about fifteen minutes, however, because a television reporter and camera-man just happened to be walking by and heard his yells. They removed the bar that locked the top of the dumpster. There was extensive coverage on TV that night and in both Miami papers the next day. The newspapers seemed to think it was very funny and slipped in some very rude comments about Whittaker. Snake and I were described as "unknown assailants." No mention was made of the boating accident. They did mention, however, that Whittaker's new Mercedes-Benz convertible had been filled with as much shit as it would hold.

I sent clippings from the newspaper to Dr. Laufenberg with a note. It said, "Apparently I am not the only one to dislike Mr. Whittaker. The unknown assailants must have acted because of repressed anger from lack of parental support when they were children."

Chapter Six

Thursday Night, 18 May

On Thursday at six o'clock I met Snake at Monty Trainer's in Coconut Grove. It's on Bayside Avenue just north of the Merrill Stevens Boatyard and has a very nice restaurant inside the main building. Outside, right on the water, there's a huge deck area with tables covered by thatched roofs, like Tiki-huts. It's a colorful place that serves seafood, Mexican food and all kinds of tropical drinks. The waitresses are all cute and have tan shorts, tan legs and nice behinds. On weekends there's live Calypso music. It's supposed to be a tourist place but it's a favorite of mine and I see local people there.

I looked around and found Snake at a table with two bottles of Pauli Girl in front of him. He also had a platter of seafood and a platter of Mexican things. I don't like Mexican as much as my Oriental favorites but it is a close second. When he waved me over, I was a little surprised to see him with a full-grown beard. At Chub Cay, a few days earlier, he had been clean shaven.

"Did you bring my statue?" he asked with a semi-smirk on his face. I handed him the Topsider box.

"The statue is worthless. I tried to sell it to a pawnbroker and the best offer I could get was an even trade for a picture of Barry Manilow." Sometimes I tried to talk like Snake.

"The pawnbroker didn't know his art. The statue is worth millions. You should have gone to the Metropolitan Museum in New York. They would have swapped you even for Yankee Stadium. If I hadn't had an accident and broken his prick off it would be worth even more," he said with a semi-straight face.

"Seriously, Snake, what's in the box?"

"Only letters."

"I should have read them."

"Dev, I've got a real problem and I need some big time help." Now he actually seemed serious.

"I'll listen to your problem and I might be able to help but first you've got to tell me some other things. Like, who the hell are you and what's your profession? Where do you get those Goddamn disguises? I brought the box in for you not knowing anything. How about giving me some straight answers."

"I'm an international sleuth on the track of international crooks and gangsters and I made the beard myself. Didn't you open the box?" Sometimes Snake was a pain in the ass.

"I didn't open the box because I assumed that you were a small-time smuggler or something worse. I was afraid the box would explode if I opened it. Something like that."

A conversation with Snake was usually a series of smart-ass remarks. I don't usually talk like that, but he had a way of getting me to try to imitate him.

"Open the box," he said.

I opened it up and it was full of letters.

"The letters are personal. Nothing important except to me. They're mostly from my sister and a few from my parents."

I drank some of the cold Pauli Girl and nibbled on chips and salsa. For a while we ate Mexican food and raw oysters while we listened to Caribbean music. It was nice but I had to get things straight.

"Snake, we've been friends for nearly four years. You've been a good friend and a good guy to sail with, but you confuse me. When you're not wearing some sort of disguise or pretending to be somebody else, I start to think I know you a little bit. Other times you act downright crazy. I accepted your story about the letters in the box and didn't open it. I've asked you a lot of times what your profession is, but I never get a straight answer. You seem to be in some sort of disguise about half the time and you turn up in strange places looking weird. Remember the time I ran into you in Miami? You looked like a derelict and smelled like shit but you were dead sober. If you won't tell me what you do I'll keep on thinking it's something illegal. Every time I ask what you do you give me a different answer. If it's none of my business, O.K., but don't expect me to carry illegal boxes into the country. I'm not even sure I want to keep on being friends." I wanted him to know exactly how I felt.

"You could be involved in drugs for all I know. As a cosmetic surgeon, I don't have anything to do with drugs or drug addicts, but when I was a resident at Bellevue I saw what they can do to people. If you're involved in that shit in any way at all, I don't want to know you or ever see you again."

Snake listened, looked around and said, "Let's take a walk outside where we can talk."

We paid the check and started walking south in the direction of Dinner Key Marina. When we were clearly out of earshot of anybody he said, "You've probably heard of the International Police. It's called Interpol and I work in a department that doesn't officially exist. Interpol is really a network of policemen from many different countries who have an extensive communications system. The headquarters is in a suburb of Paris called St. Cloud. I don't work for the American part of it because J. Edgar Hoover fucked that up beyond belief. The country I work for doesn't matter."

"If you checked the records of Interpol, and had access to all details of every record, you'd never find my name. Only two people at Interpol even know I exist. I don't know if there are any other operatives who do the same thing as I do. There could be many of us or there might be none. I've met my contact *only* once and he's the *only* one I've ever seen. I get paid by deposits in a bank in Nassau, and I *think* the money comes from Zurich, but I'm not even sure of that.

I also communicate in ways that you wouldn't understand and don't need to know about." He was serious now, very serious.

"If anyone learned that I work for Interpol I'd become obsolete and useless. Because of the secret stuff I do, it's sometimes necessary for me to wear disguises and assume roles. I put on my make-up and disguises three different ways. Many times I *want* people to realize that the beard or hair piece, or whatever is fake. At other times I need my disguise to be good enough to fool anyone *except* an expert who is following me and watching me very closely. When I really need to, though, I can fool anyone, no matter how close they're watching. Because you're an expert on faces, you can recognize me when other people can't.

"You can't *ever* repeat or reveal what I've just told you about my job or the secrecy. Don't ever ask me again anything about what I do for a living. I've already told you too much, but I did it because I need help."

By the time Snake finished telling me the story, we were in front of the old Pan Am hangers where Merrill Stevens boatyard is now operating. We stopped walking and I looked him in the eye.

"If it's actually dangerous for me to know about your job then why did you tell me? I just kept asking because you change the story every time. Why don't you just pick out one cover story and stick to it? Every time I ask what you do, you come up with some bullshit story, and it's always different from the story you told before." I laughed at him wondering what would come next.

"There's no way I could stick to one story. People think I'm a flake and that's part of my cover. They learn pretty quickly that I'm a little screwy. Then they forget about it and take it for granted that I'm a real weirdo or a crazy eccentric. Sometimes when I'm in disguise I want people who know me to think — 'Hey, there goes that crazy Snake character in disguise again.' It's a double cover. I can do almost anything and people take it for granted that I'm crazy as hell. They don't even wonder what I'm doing or why. I'm a little like the village idiot. People already know I'm crazy so nobody thinks about it."

"You mean that all the strange stuff that you do is an act?"

"Not exactly. Let's just say that acting weird is easy for me because I really am slightly crazy, but I use it to my advantage." Sometimes talking to Snake gave me a headache. Even when he was supposed to be telling the truth he put on an act. Actually he was a consummate actor.

"If you bump into me somewhere, don't ever try to cover up or act any differently. I always have the same names, either Snake or Sean. My real full name is Sean Shannon Moran. If you're ever surprised to see me some strange place, just act surprised."

We were walking along the water, past the auditorium.

"O.K. I insisted, and it seems like I forced you to tell me, but I still don't understand. If your job is so secret you could have just kept it that way and not told me about Interpol. Now I'm scared I'm going to get my ass shot off just because I'm a friend of yours. Why did you finally decide to tell me everything anyway?"

"I need a big favor, a *really* big one."

"Is it dangerous? For me, I mean. I don't care what *you* do as long as it's legal. I'm a doctor, not a spy or a cop. What do you need me for? Why do I have to get involved?"

"I need your help with something personal, not business. If you weren't sure I was on the right side of the law you probably wouldn't help me. It's a big thing and also a little dangerous."

"Let's walk down to the Sailing Club and see if the bar's open. I need a Scotch or two." Cloak and dagger shit is not my thing. "Tell me what I have to do so I can make a decision."

"Do you operate on anybody tomorrow?"

"I have a couple of simple things in the morning. Why?"

"I need your help because you're a doctor and I know I can trust you."

I stared at him and waited. He told me an incredible story.

"I've got a sister whose name is Sharon Heather Moran. She was a student at the University and started dating a rich kid who thought it was cool to snort a little cocaine. He talked her into trying it and she got hooked. They went to some parties where they met some people who weren't very nice – parties with a lot of older people. The rich kid liked to hang out with a crowd like that. He was a real asshole but his father had become rich in a legitimate business. He is a much respected man and the kid is tolerated because of the father. The party people were very rich also but some of them were not so legitimate. One of the men they met was a big time drug dealer." Now Snake had my attention.

"I was in Europe at the time or I would have been able to stop it. Anyway, one of the leading citizens of the Miami drug business got the hots for my little sister. He asked the rich kid and Sharon to spend a weekend in the Keys with him and some of his friends. The kid persuaded my sister to go, even though she didn't like the man or his friends.

"My sister was apparently unhappy with the trip but she couldn't stay away from the drugs. The dealer gave them both plenty, whatever they wanted. Even a new drug called rock or crack or something like that. By the second day they were both totally stoned. The unconscious kid was driven back to Miami in his own car, and left in the middle of the night. He woke up in the car in front of his home.

"When my sister didn't show up for classes the next day, or the one after, he knew she hadn't come back from the Keys, but he was gutless and scared. He pretended they had a fight. When her friends in the dormitory asked him where she was, he said he didn't know. The dealer got her to call the college and say she was withdrawing from school.

"The drug dealer, whose name is Emile Hogge, had access to any drug you ever heard of, used them all on my sister. He kept her a little bit stoned all the time. He brought her back to his house, a huge place in Bal Harbor. He gave her exotic mixtures of drugs, combinations that had never even been tried before. He experimented on her. Naturally she would do anything to be able to get more drugs, so she became his sex slave and he used her for his own amusement. He made her do vile, degrading things that no woman would do with a clear brain. The worst whore in the world wouldn't do what my sister was forced to do, not for any amount of money. After a while the dealer got tired of using her himself so he kept her around for the amusement of his friends. Of course, by this time she would do anything for more drugs. They would hold back on the drugs until she would start into withdrawal. Then he would make her perform unspeakable acts, sometimes with a man or woman and sometimes with animals.

"She became inhuman, of course, you know how it goes. She is a very beautiful girl, Devlin. She was also beautiful inside, very kind and sensitive and deeply religious. She was a virgin when she met the drug dealer." Snake was talking in a level tone of voice but I could see that he was trembling with emotion.

We were standing in the park beside the water between Dinner Key Marina and the Sailing Club. It was a beautiful night with a three-quarter moon. There was a soft breeze rustling the palm fronds and the small waves were making a gentle slapping noise against the seawall. The story Snake was telling was in sharp contrast to the pleasant evening.

"I was in Spain when these things happened. When I got back I found out Sharon had disappeared. It took me two weeks to find out what had happened and to learn that she was still alive. I learned the things I have told you but I did not know if they were true. I had to find out. A few days ago I confirmed these things and found out where they're keeping her."

I was shocked at what he was saying. As a physician at Bellevue I had worked with drug addicts going through withdrawal. I knew that more people died of alcohol withdrawal than from drugs, but both were terrible and dangerous. I didn't know much about addiction – neither the mental or the physical part. Very little is taught in medical school about addiction. Many doctors pretend they understand it, but they don't. Psychiatrists who are specially trained *do* understand. To me it was shocking to find out drugs could take over a person's mind and body so quickly.

We learned in the emergency room how to treat an overdose and keep the addict alive. We knew how to handle withdrawal but we didn't learn anything but the physical part. Nothing at all about addiction itself. Once I had helped a close friend, who was an alcoholic, dry out another alcoholic, but that was nothing compared to what could be expected with Sharon. Hearing about a person who had been brought to the state of Sean's sister would upset anybody, but it was bothering me *too* much. I didn't really want to hear any more but I knew I needed to get the story all at once, and then perhaps get a little drunk. Maybe a lot drunk.

"Tell me the rest. How did you find where they're keeping her? What are you going to do and where do I fit in? Tell me the rest and get it over with, for Christ sake."

Snake Moran told me a story like I'd never heard before.

"It took me a while to find out who had done these things and of course I couldn't let the drug dealer find out that I was looking. I had brought Sharon to Miami to watch out for her, but none of her friends knew about me, nor my friends about her. Nobody except you knows that Sharon has a brother and that I have a sister."

"When I found out about the kid who had introduced my sister to narcotics, I interrogated him. I used an identity that was a fake and, of course, I was in disguise. I asked questions about the dealer by pretending that I was an agent from the D.E.A. I told him we were only interested in the big man, who he worked for, and where he lived. I told him that we had no interest in him personally and would protect him completely. I also asked him the name of the young slut who lived with the dealer." Sean kept on talking in a level monotone.

"Quickly and willingly he told me that the name of the drug dealer was Emile Hogge and that he had a house on Miami Beach in the section called Bal Harbor. He also told me that the girl was a slut named Sharon Moran. I told the boy that we would cover him and not tell his father. I asked if he knew the girl personally and he said he had met her only once. I will deal with the boy eventually, when I have time to spend on him." Snake was very intent now and even in the twilight I could see something in his eyes that was very cold.

"I had to confirm what I had learned and to get enough information to figure out a plan to get her back, so I watched the Bal Harbor house and the people who went in and out. I picked out one man and followed him for a week until I learned his habits. His nickname was Billy Goat. His preference was sodomy. He liked it with men or women or boys or girls. I learned later from the Billy Goat that they would hold back on drugs until Sharon was half crazy. Then they would give her permission to suck. While she was bent over or kneeling they would use a hypodermic needle and fill her up with some new mixture of narcotics. When the drugs took effect and she started to feel good they would make her beg to be sodomized. Billy Goat had a huge penis at the time and enjoyed the pain he could inflict when he forced it into someone's ass." Snake still had that ice cold look in his eyes but I could also see pain and a few tears.

"There were usually several men watching these performances with Sharon and sometimes women. They would cheer and applaud. Billy Goat never got enough, though, and he went to some places that his friends didn't know about, places in Little Havana and Overtown where young boys and girls are available.

The neighborhoods are not the best but they are ideal for capturing an enemy without anyone noticing. I followed him several times, waiting for the right time and place. One dark night when he came out of one of those dives where they sell children, I captured him. I had been lurking in the shadows where he couldn't see me.

"Some men are good at computers and some at sports. Every man has a thing at which he excels. My special talent is lurking. There is probably no one better at lurking in the shadows."

Even in pain, Sean Moran was a consummate put-on artist. It was part of his strange personality.

"Billy Goat was a powerful man but I hit him with a blackjack. I hit him very hard and put handcuffs on his wrists and wired his ankles together. As a precaution I chloroformed him, the way I had been trained to do, put him in the trunk of his car, and drove most of the night to an old shack in the Everglades. When I first came to Miami, I knew I needed a place that was completely secret, so I found this place. At first I thought I might take my sister there to have her dry out, but when I learned the extent of her addiction and degradation, I realized that she would have to undergo detoxification under the supervision of a doctor." I stared silently at him as he told me the story. For a few minutes, at least, he wasn't acting.

"There are two things that are essential when only one man is guarding a prisoner. First, you must kill him instantly if he tries to escape and never try to recapture him. Secondly he *must* know for certain that you are going to do this. The small cabin where I took the Billy Goat is almost impossible to find and there are no roads leading to it. You go many miles by car and the rest of the way on foot or by boat.

"When we reached the place where I left the car, I waited for him to regain consciousness. I cut the wires from around his ankles so he could walk. Before I told him to walk ahead of me through the swamp, I removed enough tape so he could see. I had a gun in one hand and an extremely sharp machete in the other. I explained to the Billy Goat that if he did anything at all that made me the least bit nervous, I would split his skull with the machete and shoot him six times. He understood, of course. He was a professional criminal and relied on lawyers, but also knew the raw laws of the city jungle.

"We went several miles by foot and then arrived at a place where I had a small boat hidden. I wired his feet together again and attached some weights so he would sink if he tried to escape. By the time we got to the boat, the sun was coming up and I could find my way through the little islands. We traveled five more miles in the boat to a small island and finally reached the cabin. When I got him inside, I wired him to the wooden wall with heavy gauge wire. I wrapped the wires around his wrists and arms five times in each place and then through small holes in the wall. I cut the wires off short and twisted them tight with pliers after they had passed through the wall and into the next room. I did this in fourteen places. His feet were also wired so he couldn't kick at me. I wanted him permanently fastened to the strong wooden wall. When he was in a position where he couldn't move, I took the tape off his mouth and we had a long discussion. It lasted several days. In the end he agreed to tell me everything.

"I told him I was D.E.A. and that we were going to hold him for questioning. I showed him my identification and explained that if he would cooperate we would give him immunity and let him leave the country and go to South America or Europe. An arrest by the D.E.A. is not too frightening to these men. Usually the lawyers will have them out on bail very quickly and then after a few postponements they'll be tried, but rarely convicted. It's an inconvenience to them but not much more.

"After several hours I realized that my pretense of being an agent for the Drug Enforcement Agency was not going to work. He refused to talk and demanded to see his lawyer. I then switched tactics and said that I was Ku Klux Klan and I thought he had nigger blood. I explained to him that I was going to light him on fire if he didn't tell me all about his boss and his group."

"Jesus Christ, Snake. This is the most disgusting story I ever heard of. It makes me sick. Why did he finally agree to tell you the story? What did you do to him?"

"I thought the best way to learn about Sharon was to wait until he was ready to tell me anything I wanted to know. I didn't want him to know that learning about her was my purpose so I questioned him about drug dealing and the people he worked for. I did, of course, learn a great deal about the dealer whose name is Emile Hogge. He's a South African and a racist."

"Why did the Billy Goat agree to talk? What did you do to him to make him talk about Sharon?"

"He told me everything because I agreed to kill him."

"What the fuck does that mean? Did you torture him?"

"Devlin, you've got to try to understand. What they did to my sister was barbarous."

"Fuck you, Snake. Tell me every Goddamn thing you did or I won't help you at all."

"Can you take it?"

"I'm a doctor. I've seen some pretty gory things. I want to know what you did to the Billy Goat and I want to know right now."

"Billy Goat decided he wanted to die sooner rather than later. Once he knew that quick death and slow death were his only choices, I made progress, but it took me four days to get what I wanted. He was standing up with his arms spread and couldn't move, wired permanently to the wall. First I convinced him that he had no chance to get away and that he was there to stay. The only way he could improve his situation was to die. After he had been there two days he shit all over the place. After that he didn't do it anymore because he didn't eat. I did give him some water. The stink was awful."

From the Sailing Club fifty yards away I could hear people talking and laughing, and also some music. Out of the corner of my eye I could see clouds moving past the moon. It was a beautiful night but I was out in the cabin with Snake and the Billy Goat.

"During my conversations with him I used a variation of the good-cop, bad-cop routine. It's called bad-cop, worse-cop. At times I was Ku Klux Klan and was going to burn him. Other times I told him I was a preacher and that he was going to burn in hell for his sins. In either role, I spent five or six hours each day burning him up with a cigarette lighter, a little bit at a time. I had a zippo and plenty of fluid and wicks and flints. I used a helluva lot of lighter fluid before I got the information I wanted. I had two cases of it and showed it to Billy Goat. I explained to him that he was large, and somewhat fat, so it would take a lot of fluid."

Snake was talking as if he were in a trance.

"During the four days we were in the cabin, I went into a different room frequently to make telephone calls, and he could hear only my side of the conversation. Of course there was no telephone, but he didn't know that. I talked to the Grand Dragon of the Klan, to the C.I.A., to the A.C.L.U. and many others. During the last few hours of his life, when his brain was messed up, I spoke with both Jesus and Satan. My purpose, of course, was to convince him that I was totally insane.

"Naturally he screamed a lot, but I was prepared. I had the cabin fixed up so that little sound could get out and there was nothing around anyway. I had a gas mask for the stink and some ear covers for the screams. I cut his clothes off on the second day and threw buckets of water on him so he wouldn't smell so bad and gave him water to keep him alive. On the third day I cut off his balls. I had most of the flesh of his right leg burned off up to the knee when he decided to die. After I cut off his nuts, I told him who I really was, and explained that I would kill him quickly if I was convinced that I had the complete story about my sister."

Snake was staring at me while he talked.

"When he agreed to tell me everything, I gave him morphine. Not enough to knock him out but enough that he could think about something other than the pain. I explained that as soon as I had the whole story I would kill him quickly. I had taken notes and wrote down names of everyone who was present when my sister was brutalized. I had a tape recorder going but he screamed so much that the recording isn't too good."

While Sean Moran was talking I was aware that he was a very different person than the man I thought I knew. He was a lot of fun when we were racing on a boat or going out for a few drinks, even when he was wearing crazy disguises. I had been aware from the first time I met him, however, that there was a strange and dark side to his personality. My receptionist, Lori, said he was sinister. I also knew that if I were seeing the real Sean Shannon Moran, he must be at least partially insane.

"The Billy Goat was very mixed up by this time. He knew he would be killed one way or the other, and I had convinced him that telling the truth would speed it up. He told me all he knew about how drugs are brought into this country, all about his boss and the men who work for him. He told me everything about my sister and confessed to every sin he had ever committed. He told me a lot about his boss, Emile Hogge, a name I had never heard of.

"When I started hearing the same things for the third time I decided it was the truth. He was near death and I was exhausted. It's very hard work burning a big man alive with just a cigarette lighter. I gave him another shot of morphine and asked if he could understand what I was saying. He nodded yes and I told him I was going to call a priest on the telephone in the other room and ask the priest to give him last rites. I went in the next room and pretended to talk to a priest. Then I came back and told him that I had described him to the priest and the priest said he would pray that the Billy Goat fried in hell. I think this hurt the Billy Goat's feelings but he believed my story and he was ready to die."

Snake stopped talking for a few minutes and then whispered as if he were taking a solemn vow.

"I'm going to get my sister, Devlin. Her brain is probably destroyed but I'm going to do it anyway. After I've taken care of my sister as best I can, I'll deal with the kid who got her hooked on drugs and all the people who watched and helped in her degradation and humiliation. They, too, will welcome death. I will search the history books for a proper way to deal with Emile Hogge." He stopped for a minute and then continued.

"What I did to the Billy Goat will be nothing compared to my revenge on Hogge. I have another source of information now. A guy who's in one of the Federal prisons has a relative who works for Hogge. Another man, who owes me a great debt, is in a position to either do some favors for the prisoner or have him killed. Although communication is awkward, I can keep track of my sister. I'm going to find a way to get her back but I need you, and your clinic, to detox what is left of her after I do it. Will you help me? Will you detox her in your clinic?"

"Yes," I answered without thinking. I knew I had no choice.

We went inside the Sailing Club. Snake went to the bar and I went to the telephone. I called Bill Gaines at home and told him I was getting drunk and asked if he could handle the surgery I was supposed to do the next day. I said I had gone to dinner with Snake and we had run into a couple of interesting women. Bill said it would be no problem, and that he could do one case himself and move the other.

I went over and sat down with Snake and a young couple named Herman who raced a J-24. They had just come back from Tampa where they had placed first in a big regatta. They were very excited and wanted to tell us all the details of the race. I talked a little and drank a lot of Scotch. Snake was drinking gin and tonic and they were having beer. By the time I left the Sailing Club I was pretty drunk. The Hermans dropped us off at the parking lot outside Monty Trainer's where we had left our cars. I made it home all right, and fell asleep immediately.

At 4:45 a.m. I woke up. The effects of the alcohol were wearing off and I felt strung out and shaky. My first thoughts were about Snake cutting the balls off the man called Billy Goat. I got up and went into the kitchen. I poured two shots of vodka in a glass, put some orange juice in with it, and let my mind wander. Sean Moran had been a friend and frequent crew for three or four years. He was strange, I certainly knew that, but it was a shock to find out he was involved with Interpol. And the kidnapped sister business was bizarre. I knew any young girl could be seduced into drug use. That had nothing to do with Interpol or Snake, but she was being held as a prisoner. I also knew that Sean had to learn where she was being kept and to learn that, he had to torture the man. I could accept that. It was ugly but necessary. He had done it and now he knew.

The *way* he had done it was the most horrible thing I had ever heard of. The fake telephone calls were insane, sick. But what he did had worked. Billy Goat had told him everything. Would I have been able to do what Sean did if I had a sister who was taken by drug dealers? I knew I would be able to die for a sister – or even a friend – but I didn't know if I would be able to kill.

I poured another drink when I finished the first one and sat on the couch trying to figure things out. The light was on in the kitchen but only a little came through to the living room. I was half awake and half drunk. My mind was racing.

I knew there was latent violence in me. I did not really understand why, but I knew I had to control it. Three times I had been to psychiatrists – when I hit Charley Crawford, when I threw Milo Carter out the window and then, when I was older, the one in Boston. Laufenberg had helped after Carter but not the other two.

I knew I had to detox Snake's sister. I had no choice. She needed a doctor for that and going to a hospital would be impossible. I would have to learn more about addiction and I'd start by writing the letter to Laufenberg. He was an expert on all forms of addiction.

As the sun was just beginning to penetrate the darkness outside, I asked myself how I would answer if Snake asked me to help him rescue Sharon. He hadn't asked but he might. Surely he could get friends of his who were experienced at that sort of thing. But then, why would he have friends who were experienced at kidnapping people from drug dealers? From anybody? Why would anyone have such friends?

I wondered what I would say in my letter to Laufenberg and how he would respond. Would he advise me not to help with the detox? Probably not. I had to do that much, but I was certain he would tell me not to help with the rescue. He would say that trying to rescue Sharon would be dangerous...it would be crossing the line...it would be going too far but...*but how much is too far?*

When I woke up it was a little after ten o'clock and the light was streaming through the Venetian blinds. It was Friday morning. Since I'd gotten drunk twice the night before I didn't feel very good. I needed to dry out and sober up, and I wanted to be able to enjoy dinner with Gus Draper and his wife, who were two of my closest friends and favorite people. I knew I needed to taper off a little so I had one shot of vodka in some tomato juice and a pile of scrambled eggs on toast.

There's a swimming pool at the apartment, so I went out and spent the day sitting beside it, baking in the sun and jumping in occasionally. I brought a cooler out with me and drank about a gallon of orange juice and a gallon of ginger ale. When the sun got too hot I moved into the shade of the palm trees that surrounded the pool. The entire day was spent recovering and planning.

By one o'clock I felt good enough to start reading to prepare for the detox. I'm not sure of the exact moment I made my decision, but I started planning as if I'd known all along that I would help Snake and his sister. I brought some medical books from my apartment and started making notes on what we would need and what I would have to do if things didn't go right. All of the emotion I had felt in learning about Sharon had disappeared. I was getting back to normal, and normal for me included little emotion. I knew I would take Sean's sister into the clinic and try to detox her and that we couldn't use a hospital or another doctor. Once she was taken away, the bastards who had been holding her would be checking every hospital detox unit in the state of Florida. They couldn't afford to have someone like her running around free and the cops couldn't protect her. I knew that the detoxification procedure might kill her and that I'd be in serious trouble if she died, but there was no other choice. We had to try to save her life and what was left of her brain.

After detox she would have to go into some kind of mental hospital for a while, anyway. I also knew, without his telling me, that Snake would need my help in getting Sharon away from the people who were holding her. Strangely, I found myself wondering what the word was for recapturing a kidnapped person. For some reason I was beginning to think of it as the snatch but I was sure that Snake would know a better name for it.

As I studied the medical textbook, I started thinking about the people who held Sharon and what they had done to her. I tried to think of words to describe them and what they had done, but the English language didn't have any. Perhaps the guys who ran the Nazi death camps knew the words. I knew they had done similar things. I think the Allies really screwed up at the Nuremburg Trials. They should have been able to come up with something more appropriate than hanging. I knew I could come up with something.

I thought about Laufenberg and his concern that I would go too far someday in trying to set things straight. This was the kind of situation he had described when the authorities wouldn't be able to help, and I would want to take the law into my own hands. I had learned that Sean Shannon Moran was a professional cop or spy or something, but I personally knew nothing about kidnapping or killing. I had no idea where he would get help if I didn't go along with him.

As the sun baked the booze out of my system and I started to feel better, I thought some more about Dr. Otto Laufenberg. I had sent him an invitation to my graduation to let him know I made it and had been surprised when he showed up. He knew a secret about me that nobody else knew. I once tried to explain it to my father before I left for Paris that Spring. Dad tried hard to understand, but he really didn't. Rage was something he could understand well, but not hitting a person with a bat and having no feelings about it.

When I introduced Dr. Laufenberg to my parents, they invited him to have dinner with us. I reminded them that he was the psychiatrist who had counseled me when I threw Milo Carter out the window. Glorious, my mother, was thoroughly charming and acted as though everyone invited his shrink to graduation and wasn't it sweet of him to come. I think he had been a little startled at my mother's friendliness and acceptance, but very quickly he started acting like an old friend. My mother does that to people.

I do believe that Otto Laufenberg had a sincere interest in me, but I think the real reason he accepted my invitation was an intense curiosity about when I would next use a baseball bat on somebody's teeth. I got a Christmas card from him six months later and we started exchanging letters. He'd invited me to come up to his ski house and I'd gone up several times while I was at Tufts. I started thinking that I might get Laufenberg to help me figure out where to put Snake's sister, if she lived through the detox. I spent more than an hour writing a letter to him.

After I had finished the letter, I went back to the pool and swam a few laps, and then started to figure out a way to learn more about drug detox. The medical books that I owned had some information, but not nearly enough. I needed a cover story to use if I went to question the doctors in a dry-out unit. For a cosmetic surgeon to suddenly develop an interest in drug withdrawal would arouse suspicion. I sat at a table that was under a group of palm trees where the condominium has a barbecue grill, and started formulating a plan. Since I no longer felt much emotion about what we were going to do, my mind moved swiftly.

On Monday I would call Alcoholics Anonymous and get some information about the whole recovery scene and find out if there were any groups like A.A. for drug addicts. I had read about an organization called Synanon that started in California. Its purpose is drug rehabilitation and it had become famous because it was successful. If I could find some organization in Miami that used volunteers, I might be able to associate myself with that organization. I could talk to a doctor who worked with a detox unit at one of the big hospitals and represent myself as a volunteer member of the recovery group. If, for some reason, the detox doctor checked me out I would prove to be legitimate. The recovery group might check my credentials but they wouldn't question my motivation. I was sure a legitimate group would welcome volunteer help from a doctor. Maybe I could invent a whole program. My mind was moving fast.

The story would be that I wanted to teach recovering addicts some basic first aid in dealing with other addicts who were in withdrawal or had overdosed. Addiction is simply not taught in medical schools but I knew that a person starting withdrawal from alcohol sometimes needed another drink or two before going to a hospital. With a drug overdose I knew getting to a hospital was important.

By two o'clock I was functioning at normal speed, thinking clearly, making plans and writing them down. I was back to what Rocket called my pointed-ears personality.

Rocket had a colorful way of expressing herself. Sometimes she put some color into something blunt that she wanted to say. Once when we were out on a date and she was giving me a hard time about my cold personality, she said, "You're just like that guy with the pointed ears. The one on T.V. from some other planet or something. He doesn't feel any emotion about anything. His rocket ship could be on the verge of being exploded all over the universe and he isn't nervous. Just keeps going in a monotone."

She had paused and looked at me intently. "Except for your pointed ears you don't look much like him. You're a lot uglier than he is. Your eyes are so green they look like something from outer space." I was not what you would call an animated personality.

While I was working on my notes, I thought about the clinic and what we would do there. I'd have to tell Bill what I was doing but keep him out of the detox part completely. If the girl died, I would have to get the police into it, but I had to make sure that no one else was involved. Bill would have to help me figure out a way to keep everybody out of the building for a few days. If Sharon lived through the first few days, we could take her somewhere else.

We had to figure out a false identity for her if we used an institution, and a plan in case her body lived but her brain died. I needed to talk to Bellamy, my lawyer, so he could be there with the corpse when the police arrived. I thought I'd tell Bill I was going to dry out a friend of mine, a prominent person who could not take the chance of going to a hospital or a private clinic. I would say it was a man. I could tell Bill that Snake was involved, but I didn't want him to know the addict was his sister. Bill knew Snake, of course, but just thought of him as a weird friend of mine who crewed for me in sailboat races. I'd never told him how strange Sean really was.

We also had to have a plan in case Hogge found out and came to try to kill us. Snake would have to figure out something for that part. I didn't even know how to shoot a gun. I made a list of the things I needed to do in case Sharon died and in case she lived without a brain. I also had a list of what to do if she came out all right.

When I thought about Gus, and that I was having dinner with him, I decided on an impulse to call Lori and take her to dinner with me. I realized that I must still be a little drunk, because I thought of her as a crazy teenager, but I decided to do it anyway.

On the way back from the pool to my apartment I stopped off at the mailbox. Since I got most of my personal mail as well as business mail at the clinic, I only check the box once a week. There were seven or eight envelopes and one that was obviously an invitation to something. While I was showering, I wondered who could be getting married and came up with nobody. As soon as I dried off, I called the clinic and asked Lori if she wanted to have dinner on Gus Draper's boat. She was excited and assured me she wanted to go. As soon as I hung up I started to regret the call. Taking her on a date, even one like this, made no sense.

After I had shaved and dressed I started to open a beer and then thought better of it, so I got myself a diet coke and opened the mail. It was mostly junk, some sale flyers and the formal invitation. When I opened it, I saw that it was for a sixtieth birthday party for a man I had never heard of. The man's name was Don Ricardo Guillermo Ochoa de Salazar. Sixty. The invitation specified cocktails and hors d'oeuvres, dinner and dancing. Black tie. It sounded very fancy. The address was in Miami Beach and the invitation itself, the paper part, seemed more appropriate for the coronation of a king. The card was almost an eighth of an inch thick with some kind of lettering that appeared to be gold leaf. I thought as I looked at it, that only somebody who was trying to appear important would send out something that fancy. Either that, or somebody so rich and so important, he didn't care *what* people thought. I wondered if there was anybody so rich he didn't care what people thought. Nobody I ever met. It was R.S.V.P. and the party was two weeks from tomorrow, Saturday night, June 3. I put the invitation and return card back in the envelope and decided to check it out on Monday. By late afternoon I recovered enough to look forward to having dinner with Gus Draper.

Chapter Seven

Friday night, 19 May

I thought about Gus Draper while I was driving down to have dinner with him. He would be a good man to help with the rescue but I couldn't mention it to him until I knew we would need help. I had met Gus a few years earlier up in Fort Pierce when I was bringing my schooner down from New York. I had lived aboard the *Vanitie* in the East River while I was learning my profession at the Institute for Reconstructive Surgery. The boat Gus owned back then was a Tahiti ketch that was about forty years old, a John Hanna design built by an unknown home builder. He had bought it a few months before in Cape May, New Jersey from a retired Delaware River pilot. He had been told by his surveyor that the boat needed a lot of work, but it was available for just about nothing, so he took it anyway and planned to fix it up. It was named the *Nancy B*.

He started down offshore from Cape May even though he didn't know much about sailing. He got himself caught in a northeast gale and almost lost his life as well as his boat. After four days of getting banged around he barely made it into the entrance of Chesapeake Bay. From there he went on down the Intra-coastal and made it to Elizabeth City, North Carolina, without any trouble. Then a big squall caught him crossing Albemarle Sound. The boat was doing O.K. for a while, even though it was leaking, but the shallow water and the wind kicked up a wicked set of short-spaced waves and really started throwing the old ketch around. The bouncing and shaking snapped the mizzen mast and it went over the side. The engine wasn't in any better shape than the rest of the boat but he kept it running. He was a superb mechanic and made it as far as Fort Pierce. I was already there when he arrived.

I had left New York about two weeks before he left Cape May, and I got to the Cracker Boy yard about a week before he did. I planned a stop there to work on the boat before I got to the expensive yards in South Florida. I had just put the pretty old schooner back in the water when Gus got towed in by a fishing boat. His engine had given up about halfway down from Vero Beach. I helped him tie up and offered him a beer. He refused the beer but took a coke and we sat in my cockpit while he told me the story of his trip south.

Some of the nice people at the Cracker Boy yard had offered me the use of a truck for occasional trips so I invited Gus to go with me to pick up some groceries and stop at a seafood place I had heard a lot about. He said he would like to get off his "pile of shit" ketch for a few hours so we went off together. The place we went to was called Theo Thudpuckers and it was out on the South Beach less than a hundred yards from the jetty and the beach. When we went inside, the waiter looked at Gus the same way I would look at a Doberman Pinscher whose foot I had just stepped on. Gus wasn't dressed very well and he was very tough looking, the kind of guy that mothers would keep their children away from. When the waiter offered us a table by the window where we could see the inlet, Gus said he was tired of looking at the Goddamn water. His mood was real deep indigo.

We started with steamed clams and raw oysters and then had something called Stuffed Mushrooms ala Michael. This turned out to be mushroom caps baked in a ramekin with a different kind of seafood in each one with cheese on top. The whole dinner was superb even though Gus wasn't pretty to look at. We drank coffee and talked until closing time. We were very different people but we liked each other right from the start. After learning that his engine had to be rebuilt, I got carried away and offered to tow his boat with *Vanitie*. Coconut Grove was his goal and he wanted to get there pretty badly. The idea of completely rebuilding his engine this far north was not appealing to him.

He had planned to spend a year at Dinner Key rebuilding the whole boat. Staying in Fort Pierce meant defeat and disappointment for him. Towing him with my boat was a really crazy plan but I was sober when I thought it up. Although my boat was over forty feet, it was seriously under-powered. I had a Universal Atomic Four, a wonderful little engine, but not nearly enough power for my boat alone. We decided to do it anyway and planned to start down outside. By the time we finished dinner and got back to the yard we had a plan.

We spent the next day getting ready and then left the yard and went out through the inlet at seven o'clock in the morning. We had a fair current going out as planned, but once we settled on a course going south it seemed the best we could do was a little under three knots. When we cleared the outer buoys and turned right we had a northwest breeze of about seven or eight knots. After a few minutes I realized I could carry the mainsail. We had to stop and head into the wind to get it up but it was worth it. *Vanitie* was under-powered with just the engine, but she was way over-rigged, and my main was a monster. I put up a jib for balance and off we went. With my engine running at cruising speed and the huge sail up we got above five knots. Then Gus put up his main and we went almost six. The sea was completely flat, and we were in close to the beach, so we wouldn't be hurt by the north-flowing Gulfstream. We had a little problem that night getting into Lake Worth Inlet at Palm Beach because we came in on an outgoing tide. At one point we were able to make good only one knot over the bottom even with a favorable breeze and the engine at high speed. It was dawn leaving Fort Pierce and dark coming into Palm Beach. We found a place to anchor and slept the rest of the night. The next two days were a pain in the ass because the weather was bad and we had to go down the Intra-coastal. We couldn't use the sails and we had to stop for bridges. We anchored one night in Lake Santa Barbara, just north of Fort Lauderdale, and then made it all the way to Dinner Key the next day.

When we passed through Rickenbacker Causeway and came out into lower Biscayne Bay I felt like I had reached the promised land. It's one of the greatest places in the world to race one-design boats and one of the big reasons I decided to live in Coconut Grove. Gus and I had become friends by then, so we got slips next to each other. We kept our boats together for several years, until I sold the *Vanitie* and bought the *Brilliant*.

Gus was a lot like the "Hairy Ape" in Eugene O'Neill's play. At one time he had actually shoveled coal on a merchant ship. His chest and arms were massive and covered with hair. He had a very interesting face – ugly, but strangely attractive. He looked rugged and tough but he was even tougher than his looks. He confided in me one time that his nickname when he was young had been "Beast." When he was in old clothes, he looked like someone to be avoided.

That first year Gus and I were together a lot since neither of us knew anybody else. I started setting up a medical practice right away and Gus started working on his boat. We ate together three or four times a week and we were truly a strange pair.

Our boats were also an odd pair. *Vanitie* was maintained so well she was like a model boat, with every detail just right. I kept the boat in perfect shape and enjoyed working on it. The topsides were waxed and polished to perfection and the teak decks looked like new. Even the brass was shined and polished. The *Vanitie* had light blue topsides, a dark blue waterline and a white bottom, which was beautiful, but truly a bitch to maintain.

Gus's boat, the *Nancy B.*, looked like a garbage scow. He did wash the dirt off and paint the cabin top but it was a very serious contender for worst boat at the dock.

We even looked funny going somewhere together. I found that Gus was a fairly clean and neat person, but he always dressed like a hobo. I looked very sporty when I got dressed up, not because I cared anything about clothes, but because my mother did. Actually, she still bought most of my clothes.

About a week after Gus and I arrived at Dinner Key Marina my mother came to visit. She got a room at The Grand Bay Hotel and proceeded to get me organized. She found a place for me to stow some of my gear and extra sails on a nearby houseboat and then filled up my sail-bins with new clothes. She made sure Brooks Brothers had all my measurements so she could order for me by telephone. When she wasn't buying me more clothes she put on a bathing suit and scrubbed my teak decks. She went out and bought me a new car, and took Gus and me out to dinner every night. Although Gus was almost fifty, she treated him like he was a college classmate I had brought home for the weekend.

My mother was a very elegant woman and she had a way of treating everyone – even a scruffy looking guy like Gus – as if he were also very elegant. She bossed him around and charmed him and she even went out and bought him some clothes. This could have been offensive but Gus seemed to appreciate it.

Just like everyone else, he was awed by my mother. My father used to tease her and say that with a name like Glorious, she had to be either a great lady or a strip tease artist. When she felt she had me a little better organized, she went to the priest at the Episcopal Church and signed me up as a member, made a large donation and went back home to Rye, New York.

Gus didn't like to talk much, especially about himself, so when we were together there were some long periods of silence. The cafés and restaurants in and around Coconut Grove got used to us and we got to know a lot of the regular customers as well as the waiters. Gus kept on looking like he bought his clothes from a Salvation Army sale and I looked like I shouldn't be seen with him. I got to know a lot about Gus but virtually nothing about his past. He was honest, dependable and very intelligent. He loved classical music but didn't seem to know anything about it, except how to listen. I got to know Gus pretty well but I never learned anything about his past.

For very different reasons, Gus and I had both decided we wanted our boats at Dinner Key Marina in Coconut Grove. During the first few months there Gus did only superficial work on his boat. One night when we were talking, he pulled out some plans he had gotten for a larger boat. He was going to buy an unfinished hull from a builder named Creekmore down in the Keys, and finish the rest himself. The new hull was going to be delivered with the outside finished and the engine installed but nothing below. It was going to be ready in a couple of weeks. The builder had produced the hull on speculation during a slow period, and put in the mast and rigging when Gus signed the contract.

When the time came, I got a friend to drive us down in my car to pick up the boat. Gus had never bought a car. He rode around on a motorcycle and used my car when he needed one. We brought the boat up Hawk Channel in a two day trip and he put it in the slip next to mine. We took the *Nancy B.* and moved it over to a slip on A Dock, and he sold it six weeks later. I didn't ask how much money he got for the old boat or how much he paid for the new one. We never talked about money and I had no idea where he got it or how well off he was. He lived cheaply and seemed careful with every penny, but he picked up every other check when we went out to eat, and he never complained.

When Gus got settled in on his new boat the first thing he did was to go out and buy a video cassette player. They were still a fairly new thing and there surely were not many on sailboats. Gus said he liked to watch movies but after he got it hooked up he never seemed to use it, at least while I was around. One day an operation was canceled, and I came back to the boat at three in the afternoon. I got aboard *Vanitie* and happened to glance over at the new boat and saw the T.V. screen lit up. I figured that old Gus must be watching a dirty movie on his new machine.

A few weeks later he asked me if I had ever heard of a movie star named Paulette Peters. I vaguely remembered her name. I didn't like movies very much and hadn't watched many since high school. Gus invited me over to watch one of her old movies and told me she was a favorite of his. While we watched it that night, Gus told me about her. She had been a very popular star for a few years and made eleven pictures. She was really something special with a unique quality that no other woman shared. Over a period of time I watched all of her movies with Gus, and Paulette Peters was amazing. She was impossible to forget, a beautiful woman with a special quality. She played the same type of girl in every picture, sweet and innocent, and completely without a trace of nastiness.

After her last movie, about two years ago, she disappeared completely from the public eye. The film, one of her best, was called *"Autumn of Innocence"*. Gus had fallen in love with her image way back when her first movie was made. He had seen all of her films countless times in theaters and on television. Now he had his VCR and he was beginning to put together a collection of cassettes of her pictures. The grizzly old bastard had turned out to be a secret romantic!

After he got used to the idea that I knew about his secret obsession, he talked about her all the time. I watched all the movies he had, one time through, and I also became fascinated. She could play a scene that was so sweet and sugary that any other actress would have been comical. With Paulette as the woman it seemed completely normal and quite believable. In her third picture the character she portrayed died at the end. Her fans were enraged. Letters poured in from all over insisting that Paulette *never* be allowed to die again. She was just too nice.

There was also a problem with leading men, and the studio had to cast a new man opposite her in each film. They had done some checking of audiences leaving the theaters and found that none of the men were thought to be nice enough to win her. At the end of the movies when the hero kissed Paulette the people really didn't like it because she was just too nice. She was everybody's sweetheart but just too special for one man. Gus had old movie magazines aboard and they, too, were fascinating.

In the beginning, I watched some tapes because Gus was a good friend and he wanted company. As I learned more and watched more I really became interested in her strange short career. Gus was like an encyclopedia and knew all the details including her childhood. He knew everything about Paulette and her movies except why and how she disappeared. He tried to find out why she had stopped making films by writing to her at every address and place he could find, but the letters came back unopened.

One day, when I realized I was watching and enjoying a film for the third time, I knew that I was getting to be as crazy as Gus. He was putting in ten hours a day on his new boat which he called *Pauletta*, but he was also spending two hours on his tapes. I talked to a psychiatrist friend one day in the cafeteria at the hospital. I used an imaginary friend instead of Gus, but I told him the truth about my own fascination.

"It sounds like your buddy is a little wacko," he said. "I'll bring you a book called *The Sixty Minute Hour*. It's a true story about a shrink treating a patient and how he starts to participate in the patient's fantasy. The patient thinks he can travel to an imaginary planet and he's in the process of getting it organized. The doctor works with him awhile and then he starts to help his patient make plans. Read the book and make sure that you aren't in love with Paulette yourself. If you can't talk him out of spending so much time on it, get back to me and we'll figure out something."

I read the book, and of course I realized the best thing for Gus would be finding out what happened to Paulette. If he knew the answer, it might end his obsession, or at least reduce it to a part-time thing. It was really none of my business but I seemed to have some kind of compulsion to make wrong things right.

I called my mother and told her the whole story. She acted as if it was perfectly normal for people to spend hours worshiping old movie stars and she said she would find out about Paulette. My mother, Glorious, has a way of getting almost anything accomplished, and her method is simple. She just tells a man what she wants done, and when she wants it done. In this case she told my dad the information she wanted. She didn't mention Gus, but she did say that she needed to know by the following Wednesday, because she was having some ladies in for lunch. It took my dad about two hours to find a person and an address. There was a man named Bernie Lambretti, who said that a letter sent to Paulette in his care, at his box number, would be delivered to her. I lied to Gus and told him my father got the address for me without asking why I wanted it.

Gus asked me to help him write the letter. When I asked why he needed me, he said he was going to ask her to marry him. I already knew he was nuts so I didn't argue and said I thought it was a good idea. I told him that the whole thing about Paulette and her movies was bad, and that he had to find out what was going on and end it. I helped him write the letter, and it was really a strange one but I felt that an intelligent letter might at least get a kind response. I found in helping Gus that he was quite literate, although he seemed to want to write it like a business letter. I can both speak and write adequately but my talents are in my hands and eyes. When we finally finished the letter, it was a little businesslike because of Gus, and a little *Byronesque* because Lord Byron was my favorite poet.

When we finally agreed on the wording, I typed the letter at the hospital. It was a totally honest letter that included the story of how he had watched her films for years, a description and picture of him and his boat, a proposal of marriage, and a suggestion of how they would live. It took us almost two weeks to write the letter.

Gus told me after he mailed it that he had put a round trip airplane ticket in the envelope. It was for flight #481 that came in on a Saturday afternoon in three weeks. He said he knew she was a wealthy woman and could buy her own ticket, but he felt that sending it would show her how serious he was. He also told me that writing the letter made him realize that he needed to get over her and concentrate on his new life in Coconut Grove. If she refused his offer he was going to try to stop watching the movies and forget.

After three weeks of hearing nothing, and with two days before the scheduled flight, he got an answer. I wasn't surprised because I expected a polite note, refusing the offer and thanking him. It was hard to imagine the sweet girl in the films ever hurting anybody. It was easy to imagine her married and impossible to think of her alone. She was too full of life for that. On a Friday afternoon he called me at the hospital and when I picked up the telephone he just whispered two words.

"She's coming."

I talked Gus into a haircut and some nice new clothes, but he wouldn't go for a suit. I don't think he'd been sleeping too well since he wrote the letter, and after he got the reply he was really nervous. Her letter was strange. It was hand written but sounded like a telegram. It said, "I will be on flight #481. Meet me at the airport. Paulette Peters." That was all it said, nothing else. I was amazed that she was coming.

Gus insisted I go to the airport with him. I wasn't too surprised because I would have been scared, too. We waited at the gate in the Miami terminal in a position where we could see all passengers as they came through the door. The plane was apparently a large one as a huge number of people got off. Finally the stragglers stopped and a man in an airline suit came over to close the door. Just before he closed it, two more people came through, a stewardess and an older woman she was helping.

We looked at each other and then back at the old woman. She looked maybe fifty or older, and she had makeup piled all over her face. Her mouth was a ridiculous red gash that must have taken a whole tube of lipstick. I knew it was Paulette, an old and ugly version of Paulette. She was also staggering drunk. Really stinko. Before Gus recognized her I walked up and took her arm.

"Miss Peters, Gus and I are here to pick you up. I'm Winfield Devlin, a friend of his. I hope you had a nice trip."

"Paulette Peters," she said, slurring the words.

When Gus introduced himself, she just repeated her name. The stewardess looked at us with a puzzled expression so I assured her that everything was O.K. With one of us on each side we managed to walk her through the airport and out to where we could get her in a car. Gus kept her from falling on her face while I got the car, and then we put her in the back seat. We decided to worry about her luggage later. I did look in her purse to make sure her identification really said

"Paulette Peters", and to find the claim check for the luggage. Both were there. Gus's letter was there, too.

Driving back to Coconut Grove we talked about whether to take her to a hospital or down to the boat. Gus told me right then that he was an alcoholic and that he hadn't had a drink for seventeen years. He also explained that he had gone on numerous Twelfth Step calls, which is A.A. terminology for helping another drunk sober up. The critical thing he said was to get her sobered up enough to talk, so we could find out how much she had been drinking, and how long. We couldn't stop the booze suddenly without knowing, and had to keep her a little drunk until we had a plan. When I suggested we take her to a hospital Gus said, "No way. Doctors don't know diddly-shit about alcohol addiction."

We stopped at the liquor store on 39th, which is part of the Laughing Loggerhead Sports Bar, and got a gallon of vodka. While Gus was inside, Paulette vomited all over the back seat. I couldn't do anything except to make sure she didn't choke.

When we got down to the dock, I watched her while Gus got a cart. Dinner Key docks have these little carts that are used to haul groceries so Gus pulled her out of the car and gently laid her in a cart. She was still passed out. He said he would have just carried her but he didn't want to get puke all over his new clothes. He picked up the handles of the cart as easily as if she was a sail-bag. I carried her handbag and the big bottle of vodka. When he got to where our boats were tied up, he put the cart down and hooked up the hose. He turned it on full force, waking her up and soaking her completely while he washed her off. I found a big old mop in a dock box and scrubbed the mess off the dock into the water.

After the shock wore off she passed out again. Gus slowed the water to a trickle and gently washed the vomit and makeup off her face. Este Lauder would have died at the waste of makeup. Then he took off the rest of her clothes. He didn't unbutton anything, he just ripped. There were some small boys fishing at the end of the dock and they stopped and came over when Gus started tearing her clothes off. Gus didn't say anything, he just looked at them and scowled. His look scared them and they took off running. When she had nothing left but her panties and brassiere, he hosed her off again. Her body looked a lot better than her face. Gus picked her up easily and carried her out on the finger pier beside the boat. Then he sort of handed her to me on the deck of the boat and I held her until Gus could go down the companionway. I handed her back to him and he dumped her on the bunk.

Gus was building the interior of his new boat, which he had named *Pauletta*, very carefully and was doing a fantastic job of carpentry, but he had finished only one bunk. He got a towel and dried her off and then we sat down and made a plan. When we figured out what we wanted to do, I went over to *Vanitie* and called the airline. I told them I was a physician, and that one of their passengers had become sick on flight #481, probably from the food. I said the person was under my care and asked if there were any other sick passengers. When they found out that all I wanted was to get them to deliver the baggage to Dinner Key, they were so relieved they agreed immediately. I gave them the claim check number and told them to bring the bag to the marina office where the manager would have the other half. It was something my mother might have done.

After that I drove to a pharmacy in Coconut Grove and got some Dilantin that I could use to prevent convulsions. When I got back to the *Vanitie* I called Los Angeles and tried to reach Bernie Lambretti. I did find somebody who said they would give him a message. We needed to know how much and how long she had been drinking. My message said to call Doctor W.S. Devlin and that it was urgent, and involved Miss Paulette Peters. I tried to scare the woman on the phone. Since it was a Saturday afternoon I felt lucky to reach anybody.

We decided that one of us had to be with her all the time until she was O.K. At eight o'clock that night, Gus took my car and went out and got a pizza and then we talked until midnight. I slept on my own boat until about two, when Gus called me over because Paulette had woken up. As soon as she opened her eyes Gus asked if she wanted a drink. She nodded "yes" and he gave her two shots.

She looked at him and asked, "Are you Gus Draper?"

He told her he was.

"I'm so ashamed I could kill myself."

"Don't worry about it. I'm in Alcoholics Anonymous myself. I need to know how much you had to drink, so I can figure out how to dry you out." Luckily she hadn't been drinking enough to need a hospital.

I didn't learn Paulette's whole story for almost a year. She had been in a private sanitarium when she got the letter from Gus and hadn't been drinking for over six months. Some deep, basic, instinct told her she had to take a chance and go to Gus no matter what. She knew she was getting worse mentally in the sanitarium even though she wasn't drinking. She had signed out of the sanitarium and gone to the apartment of a friend, where she started drinking again. The friend had helped her write the note to Gus, taken her to the airport, and helped her on the plane.

Bernie Lambretti had called me on the Sunday after we got her, and told me she had signed out of the sanitarium "A.M.A." It means "Against Medical Advice." We figured she had been very drunk for about ten days, but since she had been dry for a long time before that, there was no need for a hospital. After about three days of cutting down slowly, Gus stopped her completely. She had finished about a gallon of vodka. I made a point of being with her early in case she had the DTs. The scientific name is *delirium tremens* and it's a violent delirium from excessive alcohol, characterized by sweating, trembling, anxiety and frightening hallucinations. We had gotten her beyond the first critical point.

Another critical point comes about five or six hours after a person has stopped drinking and all the alcohol has been metabolized. I had some Dilantin for this part, in case she had convulsions, but she was O.K.

Gus kept her aboard for a week without letting her even get on the dock. He wouldn't let her off the boat and he wouldn't let her out of his sight. I don't know what he did when he needed sleep but I know he didn't give her a chance to drink again.

At the end of the week Gus decided to go down to the Keys and give her some time to get her brain working again. We got him loaded up with groceries and they left. He anchored at a place called Sunset Harbor on Key Largo for a month. When he needed water or food he took her with him in the dinghy in to shore. When she got better, he took her up on U.S. 1, and made her walk with him. They started with a mile and worked up to five and did it every morning when it was cool.

It was seven months before they came back. They had taken *Pauletta* all over the Keys and even out to the Dry Tortugas. The day they got back I was out sailing my Star boat. I had been racing and just crossed the finish line when I recognized the *Pauletta*. Snake Moran had been crewing for me that day and we sailed down and met them.

When we got near, I saw a woman on the bow and thought for a minute that Gus had found somebody new. Then I recognized her. Snake and I went aboard and we towed my boat. When we sat down in the cockpit and I saw the beautiful woman up close, I knew it was Paulette Peters, the movie star.

After spending the seven months in the Keys, they got the marina office to shuffle boats around, and moved into Gus's old slip beside my *Vanitie*. The first year they worked on the cutter during the day and went to A.A. meetings at night. After a lot of exercise and work and eating good food, Paulette had become beautiful again. At thirty-seven she looked twenty-seven and acted like the girl in the movies. Her personality turned out to be exactly like the characters she played. Since Gus didn't talk much about anything, I got my insight about their life together from her. She considered me a close friend, and told me that one day while they were in the Keys she had decided she had to be honest with Gus because she was totally dependent on him emotionally. That night, sitting in the cockpit in Boot Key Harbor, she had confessed to Gus that she was penniless.

"So what," he said.

That was the end of all conversations about money.

Supposedly the membership of A.A. in Miami doubled when people found out she was attending meetings. Of course, the big question that everybody asked was, would she stay with Gus, and would she marry him. A lot of the men around the docks found a way to get to meet her and many had propositions. Of course she had plenty of opportunities to leave Gus and go off with younger, better looking guys, but they didn't seem to interest her.

One night Paulette and I had gone out to get some dinner in the Grove. Gus had gone up to Palm Beach to speak at an A.A. meeting and she didn't go with him because of a dentist appointment. We had an outside table at the Green Street café and she brought up the subject of money.

"Dev, I wondered the whole time we were in the Keys whether Gus would keep me. You know what I mean – showing up at the airport drunk and looking like I did. I was really afraid he would just throw me overboard or something. All my life I had men worshiping me because I was so pretty and so sweet and so nice. When Gus saw me at my very worst, he really didn't seem to notice. I was so afraid that he was in love with just my movie image. I was also worried about having no money."

"Paulette, I have no idea where Gus gets money or how much he has. I know he doesn't attach any importance to it."

"I'm really in love with him, Dev. It's not gratitude or anything else. I had handsome men chasing after me for fifteen years and none of them was good enough to wash his socks."

This all happened several years ago and since then I had become very close to both of them. Gus was really almost like an older brother and Paulette like a sister.

That night, taking Lori with me to their boat for dinner was like bringing a new girl to meet the family. I locked up my car and walked over to the end of C Dock, where I had told Lori to meet me when I called to invite her. Although I was a few minutes early, she was there waiting. I told her to come straight to the dock from the clinic, and not to bother changing clothes, but she had obviously gone home and fixed herself up. She looked terrific, which was a little bit of a surprise, since I had never seen her in anything but a uniform at the clinic. She had even done something to her hair because there seemed to be more of it. I never noticed before that she had a lot of curls.

Lori had an interesting face with a nose that was a tiny bit small and a mouth that was a tiny bit large. Both her mouth and nose were well shaped, though, and the total effect was very attractive. I complimented her as we walked down the dock.

After we got aboard *Pauletta* and I introduced Lori, Gus showed us around the boat, while Paulette stayed in the galley. I had seen them a number of times in the last year, but always in restaurants or my apartment and once or twice racing on my boat. Gus had completed the interior of the boat himself and had done an incredible job. Everything was finished off like fine furniture. The dinette table was made of cherry and all the seats and cushions were wine-colored leather. Real leather that smelled good.

The thing that amazed me the most was the engine compartment which was clean and polished. All the surfaces were gel-coat and as smooth as the outside hull. The engine had been chromed. Gus had installed a permanent light fixture in every possible place. Each pump, fitting and fixture was shiny and even polished.

In the main cabin everything made out of metal was stainless or chrome. Even the backs of the doors on his cabinets were varnished to perfection. It was a long way from the days when we first came to Dinner Key. Gus's old boat used to be an eyesore, but *Pauletta* was close to perfection.

After he showed us both around below, he took Lori up on deck to show her the whole layout. As soon as they went up the companionway, Paulette started asking questions.

"How was your cruise?"

"The weather was good the whole time. We met a lot of nice people and ate like pigs. Good trip."

"That's not what I mean. What about you and Rocket?"

"We came back friends. No big fights. No sex either if that's what you're getting at. We are good friends, nothing more."

"I don't believe it. Three weeks on a romantic cruise and no excitement?"

I told her about the afternoon when it rained and we talked in the cockpit about how I became a cosmetic surgeon and about how Rocket put on perfume and a hair ribbon that night. I told her I didn't understand Rocket.

"Dev, I know you well and I love you dearly, but you are a bit of a jack-ass. You work hard at acting like a zombie most of the time and try to hide any bit of personality you have. What happened to Rocket seems simple to me. She learned that you are actually a romantic character and not an undertaker. You went to Paris to study art and learned the meaning of beauty through an ugly duckling who became a swan. It's a beautiful story but you never tell anybody. The first time I met you I was drunk but you were kind and helped take care of me. I learned about you inside out. I learned about the soft inside before I ever saw the hard outside. Now she knows about you and she's in love. So are you."

"I don't think Rocket's in love with me. She's a real flirt sometimes but I don't think it's love."

"She is a tease but only with you. That's probably just to see if you're still alive."

Before I had a chance to think about what she said, Gus and Lori came back down below and we started in on some appetizers. The whole night was very nice and a little bit different because of Lori being there. They had picked up some huge shrimp down near Jewfish Creek and served what is called a Frogmore Stew. Outside the Low Country, it's sometimes called Beaufort Stew for the town in South Carolina, although it really came from the crossroads community of Frogmore on the ocean side of St. Helena Island. In the town of Beaufort it is always *Frogmore* Stew. It's made of shrimp, crab, sausage, corn and potatoes all boiled up together and it's delicious. Since neither of them ever drank, I had brought a bottle of white wine for Lori and myself.

What made the night more interesting and different from when we usually got together was the conversation. Because the three of us were so involved in boats and sailing, we usually talked about related things, but Paulette started getting Lori into the conversation by asking her questions. Lori usually acted like a teenager at the clinic and I was surprised at her poise and her knowledge of some of the topics we talked about. Gus and I were not talkers but I was good at getting other people to do it. Paulette was expert at both. We found out that Lori had majored in English Literature at the University of Miami and was taking graduate level courses at night. After Paulette got Lori started, she pulled Gus and me into it and we spent the night talking about books. Gus turned out to be an expert on science fiction and John D. MacDonald's Travis McGee.

A friend of mine from Rye had gone to Worcester Polytech, a superb engineering school in Massachusetts. Because W.P.I. wants their graduates to know something about Liberal Arts, they have a special approach. They concentrate on depth and not breadth. I remembered this and when I got so deeply into medicine that I had little time for other things, I specialized on two writers. I could talk like an expert about the works of Joseph Conrad or George Gordon, Lord Byron, the poet. I had read many biographies and autobiographies and criticisms and most of the works of both, but I had read little else since high school except for those two.

Lori not only fit in, she really made the night a lot more interesting. I was proud of her. She was pretty funny when we were having coffee and dessert. She pulled out an eight by ten photograph of Paulette taken a few years back and asked for an autograph. Paulette acted as if that were perfectly natural and signed it. While we were having coffee I asked Gus what he was going to do now that his boat was finished.

"I'm going to build an airplane."

"You're going to do what?" I asked again, startled at his unusual but very specific answer.

"I'm going to build an airplane that I read about in a new aviation magazine."

He got up and went to a magazine rack up forward. He brought back a thin magazine opened up to an article.

"Read the article," he suggested.

I read the story which was about an airplane kit that was put together so a person could build it himself. Some guy named Frank Christensen had retired after making a bunch of money in the electronics business. He had tried to buy the rights to a classic plane called the Curtis Pitts. When they wouldn't sell he decided to design his own. He was now selling the airplanes in kit form with all the parts, instructions and everything.

There were several pictures of complete planes and they were beautiful. Two wings, bubble canopy, fixed wheels with streamlined covers—designed for aerobatics. It was the dream of every kid who tried to build a model airplane. My thing is boats but I could get excited just looking at the pictures.

"Have you bought it yet?"

"Not yet. I have to find a place to build it. I've been talking to Merrill-Stevens about renting space in one of the hangers."

Merrill-Stevens is a boatyard right next to Dinner Key and the shops are inside some old Pan-American hangars. They are huge old structures built in the thirties for the Clippers. Except for the fact that they are kind of gloomy inside, they would be perfect. I knew that Gus was a fantastic mechanic and an equally good carpenter. If anyone could build an airplane from a kit, it would be Gus Draper.

"Do you know how to fly?" Lori asked.

"I can get somebody to show me later," Gus said. "I've sent away for some brochures."

When we left to go home, Paulette made a point of telling us that I had to bring Lori back again. I didn't argue. I would have been polite, anyway, but Lori was a really pleasant addition and surprisingly good company.

Lori had her own car so I told her I would see her on Monday and we went home. She had been tactful and didn't ask me if I was sick earlier that day. For a date with someone I thought of as little more than a kid, it had turned out very well.

Chapter Eight

Saturday, 20 May
In the afternoon I went to the medical library at the hospital where I operated, and got everything I could find about drugs, even articles about the history of drug use and the Opium Wars. It was a complex topic but the key element seemed to be the drug dealer, the man who sells it for a profit. Kill all of them and the problem goes away. I wondered if I would actually get involved in something beyond the detox part. Drug dealers and drug dealing seemed to me to be the problem of the government or the police and not my problem. I didn't want to get involved, but I also knew that if it became necessary I wouldn't refuse to help Snake get his sister.

On Sunday mornings, when I'm not off some place cruising, I have breakfast at one of the sidewalk cafés in Coconut Grove. If I'm racing on Biscayne Bay I do it every morning so I wont have to clean up at home. I stop and pick up a copy of a New York paper or the *Miami Herald* or both. I'm from New York and I'm a Jet fan so during the season I always get two papers. On a nice day I'll sit for a couple of hours. I move around in a regular sequence to three different places and have a certain thing at each one. I have Eggs Benedict with mango slices and Jimmy Dean sausages on the side at *The Horny Frog*. This bothers Rocket and she never fails to point out that Benedict and Jimmy Dean *do not* go together. She does take her food seriously. Another one of my favorites is *Le Café de Rat Mort* which is really a second class night club that serves breakfast. Four scrambled eggs, hickory smoked ham, home fried potatoes with ham gravy at the Rat. Special things at each café. My routine drove Rocket crazy. She liked to think about Sunday breakfast all week long and day-dream about all the different things she could eat.

I come early and I leave quickly if things are crowded, so I don't keep other people waiting. I know most of the waiters and waitresses and I tip too much so I'm treated pretty well. The café section of Coconut Grove is somewhat European in character or maybe like Greenwich Village in the old days. Small shops, sidewalk cafés, trees and, more than anything else, an exciting atmosphere.

On Sunday mornings I try to catch up with the world. I read the paper thoroughly. I study the Book Reviews and Drama Section and I even read the editorials, although I don't believe much of what newspapers write. Once, in a course at Yale, the professor had given my class an inspired monologue on how wonderful our newspapers were and how they protected the rest of us. They were the watchdogs of democracy, he said. I was unconsciously moving my head from side to side and the lecturer noticed.

"You don't seem to agree with me, Mr. Devlin. What seems to be the problem?" he asked.

"After your last lecture I went to the library and got some old issues of newspapers written in 1938 and 1939. It seemed as if nobody heard about what was happening in Germany. I think that if the newspapers and magazines had done their job and had written the truth about the Nazis back then we wouldn't have been so totally unprepared. Maybe no war."

Nobody had ever blamed the whole Second World War on newspaper journalists before so he didn't know what to say. Anyway, I read the newspapers but I don't believe them.

Sometimes I have a girl with me, but usually I eat alone. If I ever decide to get married I'll bring the lady for breakfast a few times. If she can't sit and read and eat for two hours without talking, I will get rid of her. At quarter to eleven I usually go down to Saint Stephen's Episcopal Church, but during the last year I had been going to the Catholic Church for mass. My friend, Sidney Fontaine, who was the Curate at the Anglican Church, got on my back about it. He knew I went because of a woman but he didn't know who the woman was. Snake knew because of an accident and Gus knew because I told him, but Sidney didn't know. I went there to see Lisa Winter.

I had started doing it right after her husband died. I went to the funeral even though I had only talked with him a few times before the heart attack. It was not necessary for me to go but it was the right thing to do. I had to keep on seeing her some way and, as silly as it was, I became a regular at the Catholic Church and pretended that I belonged there. When I went to the funeral service I found out the times of the masses and came back the next Sunday. For several weeks I went to all of the services on Sundays and a few during the week until I found out which ones Lisa went to. Then gradually I started to go to the same ones.

I wrote out checks for the collection and eventually Father Pulvermacher, the priest, called me. I said I had been brought up in the Catholic Church but avoided the subject of actually joining. The church had coffee available after most of the Sunday services and I usually talked with Lisa briefly when we met. She was always pleasant and polite. I would ask about her son, Bobby, and she would bring me up to date. It was a natural thing for us to talk about, since I knew more about Bobby than I did about her. Sometimes she would show me pictures. I always studied them carefully, and tried to remember what she told me each time, so I could ask questions. He was fifteen now and in a school called Choate up in Connecticut. After a few months, our meetings got to be sort of a habit and I sometimes thought she looked for me.

Each time I saw her was an astonishing experience. I have as much appreciation for a beautiful face as anyone could. I know how a tiny change in bone structure or cartilage could make the difference between an ordinary face and a rare beauty. Lisa Winter was a rare beauty, there was no question about it, but that wasn't what I found so fascinating. I had known a lot of rare beauties and seldom found them to be anything special, except for their looks.

My fascination with Mrs. Winter had started right after the accident, when Bobby got so cut up. By the time I went cruising with Rocket, and then found out about Snake's sister, almost a year had passed. I had gotten a little older but probably no wiser and I still felt the same way about Lisa Winter.

Almost immediately after I had gotten the telephone call from my lawyer, Bellamy Craddock, saying the Winters were not going to sue me for malpractice, I got another call from Mrs. Winter. She asked me if I could have lunch with her so she could apologize for what she had done. It was direct and she didn't try to make the apology over the telephone. I started to say that no apology was necessary, but I decided very quickly that I would like very much to see her again. I felt I could put up with an apology if she kept it very short. If she had simply told me over the telephone that she was sorry and hadn't understood, it would have been enough for me since I don't like emotional conversations – probably because I know that the other person is feeling things that I don't feel.

Anyway, she had asked me to meet her at *Alfredo's*, a place in Coral Gables near the clinic, and suggested a time. I got my green car and drove there. When I arrived, she was waiting at a table and already had a drink. I sat down and ordered a Spritzer and realized again before we started talking that she was someone very special. I don't know why I felt it, but as soon as she started talking, my normal coolness or lack of feelings or whatever, disappeared.

When small boys are around very pretty girls they sometimes act silly and have a hard time talking. I had never had that problem before but now I thought about it. I didn't like to talk so I didn't. It had nothing to do with shyness or discomfort, neither of which I had ever felt, but there was something about her that made me feel funny.

Lisa's eyes were a deep, dark blue, almost purple. Her hair was a sandy blonde color, soft and shiny, with a slight wave. She had a perfectly sculptured mouth with the upper lip and lower lip in balance. Actually, *almost* in balance, since her lower lip had a slight plumpness or ripeness to it. Her upper lip had all its curves in the right places. I was fascinated by her mouth when she bit an olive from a toothpick and licked a dribble of juice from it, just before she started to make her speech. We had given the waiter our orders and she hadn't mentioned anything about what had happened at the hospital or the lawyer's office.

Then she started her formal apology. She told me how much she loved Bobby and how terrified she had been when they got the phone call. She and her husband had both been at his office and were getting ready to leave to pick up Bobby. Her husband, who had already had two minor heart attacks, started feeling chest pains and she made him go with one of his associates to another hospital downtown. She had to come alone to find Bobby. She told me of her terror when the accident was described to her and her abject fear when she found out from Lazar that it wasn't legal for me to have operated on Bobby.

It was a magnificent speech. Although I was sure she had rehearsed it, I also knew that it was totally honest and that her desire to word it correctly was not false. The restaurant was a little dark and what she was saying was emotional. The feelings she described were real and I was nearly hypnotized. Her charm and emotion and eloquence were more than I could handle.

I made the timeout signal, the T-signal referees use. Everybody knows the signal. It means stop talking and let me talk for a minute. When she stopped, I made my speech.

"Everybody fucks up occasionally. Why don't you stop your apology and let's eat lunch. I know what happened."

She stared at me like I was crazy. Then she started to cry and then she started laughing and then she started crying again. I didn't know what to do or say, so I started eating my sandwich. For some reason I liked it that she didn't run to the ladies' room. Finally she pulled herself together. For a while she just didn't say anything and then nibbled on her sandwich.

"Do you hate me?" she asked.

"Of course not. If I had a kid, and something happened, I'd be upset, too."

"I could have ruined your career."

"I don't think so. Legally you had a case but you would have dropped it as soon as you really found out about me."

"Are you really as good as Dr. Montgomery said you were?"

"When it comes to performing facial surgery on people who have just had a traumatic accident, I'm very good. I learned in New York City where there's plenty of opportunity. The need for that type of surgery is rare, actually, because there is plenty of time later."

She stopped talking for a few minutes and gave me one of those looks that good looking women do, and then whispered.

"Do you think there is any possibility that you could take Bobby's case again?"

"Sure, I'll be glad to. Actually Dr. Montgomery would be just fine, but I'll be happy to do it."

"Why would Dr. Montgomery be just fine? He took himself off the case."

"Montgomery took himself off the case to make a point. It was only during the time immediately following the accident that I was unusually valuable. I've simply spent so much time with accident victims that I've become good at it. Bobby needs to be told a little more about what's going to happen, though. He hasn't been told much and it's scaring him."

"How do you know what he's been told?"

"I've got a spy who's checking and calling me every day. I'll tell you if you won't squeal."

"Who is it? Not Dr. Montgomery?"

"No, Montgomery wouldn't do anything like that. My spy is the surgical nurse, Maggie Lindsey. After we got Bobby in the operating room, I told her I was not on the staff and that there might be some legal problems. I said there wouldn't be action against her but she might have to testify. I told her she didn't have to assist me if she didn't want to."

"What did she say?"

"Fuck the lawyers. Fix the kid."

Lisa burst out laughing and that's when I knew I might be in love. She had a serenity about her, a kind of grace that was just part of her. It was there, even when I first met her in the hospital, and it was there even at the lawyer's, but when she started laughing some things happened. Her deep blue eyes started to crinkle and some tiny dimples actually appeared. Her whole face changed to something different, not worse or better, just different. I am so conscious of faces that I can see things like this, but I wasn't prepared for the emotions it aroused in me. I was so fascinated that it was almost three o'clock before I realized I had lost track of time. I called Bill and lied about what happened. I said I had been telling Lisa about the need for a series of operations and why they were necessary.

Actually, I really had explained to her that he would look pretty bad for a long time. I was sure that I could make him look good again and I told her so. I don't know if she believed me or not but I knew she wanted to. It had been very late when we left *Alfredo's*.

From that day until I finished the series of operations on Bobby, we had seen a lot of each other. It had been strange, because at times we seemed to be like lovers discovering each other. At other times it was very professional. She called me "Dr. Devlin" and I called her "Mrs. Winter", but I think we knew there was something going on. I thought it was the same thing that happened when a man and a woman first start getting romantic feelings about each other but it didn't turn out that way. After Carl died, I thought it was my time so I waited a while and then started asking her out on dates. She always refused so I started the church business.

That particular Sunday morning, when I had just returned from my cruise with Rocket and just learned about Snake's sister, I went to the *Green Street* for Belgian waffles with Canadian bacon. My waitress there was always a young girl from Alabama named Caroline Lancaster. The first time I met her I had complimented her on her fantastic complexion without explaining that I was a cosmetic surgeon. Since I'm not very outgoing I didn't realize that I was flirting. She did though and we started teasing each other until she told me that I was a really good looking man but that she just couldn't go out on a date with me because her mother had warned her about older men. Afer a few more visits to

Green Street I explained that I was a cosmetic surgeon and that I really hadn't been flirting. By that time I had learned that she was pretty serious about wanting to be a writer. This morning I explained about how I had time to read only one poet in depth so I read only Byron. Between coffee and the check Caroline and I cover a lot of territory. After breakfast I decided to go look for Lisa.

I went to the Catholic Church and sat in the same place on the right hand side a few rows back from her usual place. She was there and I noticed several times during the service that she was glancing back. I hoped that it was because she had seen me. While I should have been listening to the Mass, I thought about her and decided that I would ask her to have lunch with me. I knew she would refuse but I wanted to do it anyway. I sat off to the side and not directly behind her so that I could see her face. She looked so beautiful I could hardly stand it and I felt the same excitement I always had felt, even though some time had passed. I looked for her after the Mass that day but she was gone and I stopped going to the Catholic Church after that.

When I got to the clinic Monday morning, I told Bill I had been with Snake on Friday night. I explained that we'd met two girls at Monty Trainer's and partied all night. Bill didn't ask any questions. He never missed a day of work himself and I usually didn't either so I said I just wasn't adjusted to being back from vacation yet. Lori was quiet all day and didn't say anything about the dinner on Gus's boat. I had half expected she would have told everyone in the office. Most of the day was spent in the operating room with fairly routine stuff.

I had a facelift at nine o'clock for a woman who was forty-three years old. The medical term for facelift is *rhytidectomy* and the procedure is defined as the "excision of skin wrinkles, particularly of the face and neck." This is not quite accurate since a facelift will not always remove small wrinkles or lines of the upper lip, the cheeks or the forehead. There is another procedure, called a brow and forehead lift, that can elevate fallen brows as well as improve some of the fine lines and deep frown grooves. What I did to the lady, whose name was Estelle Sondeman, was to remove redundant skin from her face, especially from her jawline and neck, as well as the excess fat located right beneath her jaw and chin. The procedure is called a facelift but it actually involves lifting her neck as well as her face. I was also going to do Estelle's brow, forehead and temples. The term "facelift" has been adopted by the public so doctors use it also.

The changes that I made in her neck, jaw-line and lower face would actually be more dramatic than what I did to her temples and forehead. Her facelift would make her look younger but would not really change her appearance. Estelle Sondeman had decided on general anesthesia so I worked with Jim Castell who comes in for operations like this. Jim is a first rate anesthesiologist and, of course, a fully trained M.D. We did local anesthesia ourselves. For an operation of this type we could use either one, so we generally left it up to the patient. The operation would take about four hours since I also planned to do eyelid surgery. In addition to Jimmy Castell, I had Margaret Lindsey, whom I had stolen away from the hospital, and Polly Pitino helping me.

When she was completely prepped and unconscious, I made an incision inside the hairline at the temple and then extended it down in front of her ear to the point where the bottom of her ear joined her head. I then extended the incision around under her earlobe, up behind the back of her ear, across the bare hairless area of skin over the temporal bone behind the ear and just above the hairline. The reason I cut above the hairline was so Estelle could comb her hair over the scar. This was a long incision but quite normal. The idea that there is such a thing as a hidden or secret incision is strictly baloney. It just doesn't exist. There are also stories that certain surgeons can perform a face-lift operation through incisions located only behind the ears. No way. More bullshit.

I made a small cut just under her chin to provide me with access so that I could trim away excessive accumulations of fat under her jaw-line and upper neck. I would do what is called "sculpting" or repositioning of the platysma muscle. This is the muscle in the neck that extends from the face down to the clavicle. After I made the first incision, I separated the skin from the fat and muscle underneath. This is called undermining and creates a flap of skin. Since Mrs. Sondeman had quite a bit of sagging skin, I needed to do a lot of undermining.

Working in areas like this which have muscles, nerves and blood vessels is not easy. It requires tremendous patience, skill, judgement, experience and artistry. I felt that I was as good as anybody in every area except artistry, where I honestly believed that I had a little extra talent and skill.

In doing the undermining I was careful to disturb the small nerve endings as little as possible. Some disturbance was going to be inevitable. This creates a feeling of numbness for several months, or even longer, after the surgery. This numbness, which is similar to the feeling produced by novocaine, eventually disappears.

After I had undermined her skin, I rotated it and reshaped it over the new contour. Then I put in temporary sutures to hold the skin layer in place while I trimmed off the excess. Finally I sutured the incision.

Because Estelle Sondeman had fat accumulations, it was necessary to use lipectomy. This is a technique that was originally developed in Europe, that literally sucks away the excessive fat. I inserted cannulas, which are different sized pipes, through a very small cut in the skin and then used a very high vacuum to suck away the fat deposits.

I had decided to perform surgery on the platysma and the S.M.A.S. The platysma is the most superficial muscle covering the lower face and neck. Close to this muscle is the superficial *musculoaponeurotic system*. Even though this has an impressive name, it has become somewhat useless because of evolution.

I tightened the deepest layers of her facial tissues so that I could perform what is a two-layer facelift, one on the platysma and the S.M.A.S. and one on the skin. When you do an operation like this, you really have to have your act together. You have to have a good knowledge of anatomy because the platysma and the S.M.A.S. are intimately involved with nerves, blood vessels and glands, and all of them have to be preserved and protected during the operation.

The front part of the platysma muscle was responsible for the cordlike structure in the front of her neck extending from beneath her chin toward her collarbone. I tightened bands of platysma or eliminated them. She would have a cleaner, younger looking neck and jaw-line when she recovered.

I worked on her platysma so I could create a sharp angle between her neck and her chin, since I wanted to eliminate any strong vertical neck folds. I draped the skin flap over the new contour and put in some temporary sutures. This whole procedure was very new and required great skill. After you do the sculpting and you reshape the skin flap you have to fill in every crevice. I felt that I was particularly good at this special thing, because at this point cosmetic surgery was both science and art. I'm somewhat arrogant about my skill in this area, feeling that my knowledge and talent as an artist gave me something extra that most surgeons don't have. Maybe it was just confidence.

After three hours and fifty minutes, I was finished with the operation on Estelle Sondeman. All extra skin had been trimmed away and all the final sutures put in. She would look good in a month or two. We took her into the recovery room.

During the whole operation I was extremely careful to try to minimize the chances of nerve damage. There would be some small trauma, of course, but it would wear off in a few months. Although I talked to Jimmy Castell, Claire and Polly during the operation, our conversation was strictly medical. Bill Gaines, on the other hand, could do a complete rhytidectomy with suction lipectomy, platysma surgery and the whole works while talking constantly about his latest game of golf, and the great chip shot he made. This was a difference in personality and not surgical technique. My concentration was so great during surgery that nothing else entered my mind. Bill's concentration was equally great, but in his case, he wasn't really even aware that he was talking. After an operation both of us could remember every detail but Bill could never remember talking or what he had said.

About 3:30 that afternoon, after the operation, I sat down at my desk and looked at the fancy invitation I had only glanced at on Friday when I was sobering up. On the right-hand corner at the bottom was a note that I hadn't noticed. Just the word "over," which was circled. On the back of the card was a note from the guy named Butch we had met at Chub Cay which said –

"We're having a party to celebrate my Father's sixtieth birthday. It should be a good one. Hope you can make it. Bring Rocket - or another girl if you prefer. Butch."

I was a little surprised at the invitation but I thought about it a while and then it didn't seem too strange. Many times I had followed up and called people I met cruising. I wondered for a few seconds who actually owned *Ojos Verdes,* and tried to remember if I had said anything insulting to him about the owner. Maybe Butch was the owner. I remembered that I had suggested to the paid captain a few things that were not too complimentary but I hadn't said anything to Butch or Antonia. I read the invitation again, wrote the date on my calendar and made a mental note to make sure my tuxedo was clean and pressed. I put the R.S.V.P. card in the box for outgoing mail. I thought about Rocket and wondered if I should ask her to go with me since I wanted to take a date. I had no way of knowing if there would be any unattached ladies there and doubted it, unless they were older women. Rocket seemed to be the girl to call in spite of our strained relationship. It would be a spectacular party if the invitation was any indication and she would enjoy it. Down inside I knew I wanted to see her again anyway.

That night I did call her, asked if she wanted to go, and told her she would be doing me a big favor if she'd come. She asked a few questions about what to wear and then said she'd like to go. I hoped we could enjoy ourselves together the way we had on our cruise without our sexual attraction becoming a problem.

Rocket was just not the type of person to sleep with someone just for the fun of it. Sex with her had to mean love, or at least the immediate prospect of it. After a few dates, when we first started seeing each other, we had enjoyed some very erotic times. After a while, when we realized that we were really going to be just friends, the screwing began to seem cheap, and we had stopped by mutual agreement. There had been quite a few times on our cruise when a tiny bit of encouragement from her would have been more than I could handle. I also knew that several times she had been in heat, but I had cooled it. When I was growing up, I never had friends who were girls. A girl was either a sweetheart type, in whom you had a romantic interest, or one you had a lust for. There were plenty of both, so I never developed a friendship with a girl. Young people had started having friends of the opposite sex, but I don't think I could have handled it as an adolescent. I also knew I shouldn't be seeing Rocket again so soon but I couldn't think of anyone else to ask and couldn't get her out of my mind.

I'd been trying to reach Snake for several days. When I finally talked to him I asked when we'd be going after his sister and he said he wasn't sure. There was a good chance that she had been moved. He said it was a problem but he seemed sure she was still alive. I told Snake that when he was ready, we could probably get Gus to help. They knew each other and Snake agreed he would be good, but told me not to say anything to him until he learned more about where his sister had been taken.

That night, after I left the clinic for the day, I went down to the Yacht Club where I kept the *Brilliant*. I went out to the dock where she was tied up and went aboard. I opened up the hatches and fixed myself a drink called a Rusty Nail, which is Scotch and Drambuie, a liqueur with a Scotch whisky base. It was a sort of ritual with me, when I wanted to think about the future, to sit in the cockpit of my boat with a notepad, a pencil and a Rusty Nail. My habit of concentrating completely on what I was doing at the moment kept me from thinking much about anything that required planning. With the kidnapping of Snake's sister and our rescue, or whatever, coming up I wanted to think and plan. Also I loved the Hinckley so much that I just enjoyed sitting on it.

It was a pleasant evening with a soft southeast breeze making it cooler by the water and rustling the palm fronds of the trees up by the swimming pool. Some people were coming out of the dining room while other people were having drinks and waiting to go in. For some reason I enjoyed watching dressed-up people after I had changed into shorts and a knit shirt.

The first thing on my list was a question. Do I trust Snake Moran? I thought back on how I met him, and what I knew about him, and after awhile I realized that I *did* believe what he told me. I didn't know of any way to check his story so my trust was strictly instinctive. Until he actually asked me to help him, and told me what my part would be, there was nothing else I could do anyway. In some ways Sean and I were opposites.

With me things were usually black or white. The difference between right and wrong, good and bad was always clear. My problem was not in knowing or recognizing when something was wrong. My problem was knowing when to use "do it yourself" justice.

I thought about all the possibilities for nearly an hour and then wrote down two more things – make sure that Snake explored every possible legal way of getting Sharon back – and buy a gun. I'd never owned one and didn't know the first thing about how to select it.

On Tuesday I managed to catch up on all my paperwork and spent some time reviewing my surgery schedule for the next few weeks. I was scheduled solidly with a few interesting things but nothing too complex or demanding. At about five thirty Lori asked if she could talk with me for a minute. When she closed the door I figured it was something important.

"Dev, I really appreciate you and Bill paying me for the overtime the way you did. I didn't expect it and certainly not that much. You guys didn't have to do it, but I need the money for something special so I won't argue. Thank you very much."

Bill had suggested that we pay Lori off the books because she had stayed late every night to change to a new record keeping system. She did the whole job after hours. We had split it and written her checks for twice the amount she was usually paid, but with no tax taken out. We had both written personal checks so that it wouldn't show up on the records. I told her again how much we appreciated her coming in and helping out.

"I'd like to ask you a favor," she said. I waited for her to tell me what it was, wondering why she was asking me instead of Bill, since he was the guy that the girls looked to for help and advice.

"I've decided to buy a sailboat and I want you to come and look at the boat I've found. It's a real piece of junk and it's in bad shape but I can get it for very little money and I think I could fix it up. I know that I should have it surveyed but I want somebody to look at it before I even make an offer."

"Do you know anything about boats? Do you even know how to sail?"

"I've been going to Dinner Key for about two months and taking lessons. There's some places that teach sailing over near the auditorium and I tried two of them. Now I know enough to take a boat out and sail around without hitting too many things. I'd never even been on a boat with a cabin until you let me come to dinner with you on Gus and Paulette's boat."

"What kind of boat is it? And where is it?"

"It's out of the water, laid up at one of those yards way up the Miami River. I think it's been there forever. It really looks bad and it stinks inside. It's also very old."

"Why do you like this particular boat?"

"Partly because I like the way it looks and partly because I could sleep aboard. Mainly just because I like the way it looks. If I got it fixed up I could even live there. It would be a lot cheaper than my apartment."

We looked at the calendar and decided that my surgery would probably be finished before five o'clock on Wednesday and that we could go to the boatyard straight from the clinic.

As soon as I finished seeing patients on Wednesday, I went into the bathroom that Bill and I reserved for ourselves and took a shower. I knew I would need another one after crawling around the boat but I needed it now anyway. I put on a pair of jeans, a long sleeved shirt and a pair of Timberland deck shoes. Lori had changed in the ladies room and she had on jeans and a blouse that was too large. I think she was self-conscious and trying to cover her large breasts.

She'd made arrangements for somebody to let us in the gate of the boatyard and wait while I looked at the boat. I followed her to what must have been the most run down crummy boatyard on the whole Miami River. The character that let us in the gate was as sorry looking as the yard itself. We parked inside the gate for safety because the whole neighborhood was so bad.

The boat was under a shed with a roof over it but no sides. It had a poorly constructed wooden frame and a rotten looking cover made from some kind of plastic material. We pulled the cover off so I could get a look at the deck while it was still light. The boat was supposed to be twenty six feet long and that looked about right. Sometimes people lie. It was made of wood and the paint was worn away in places. There was a wooden spar stowed next to the boat. It was gaff-rigged and the gaff and boom seemed to be with the mast.

I was somewhat surprised that the boat had bulwarks and rail-caps. I figured it must be quite old as the rail-caps were badly damaged and about half gone. The decks were teak. They were extremely dirty and the seams were in terrible shape. I took a knife and scraped away the grime and found clean wood underneath. The cabin sides were painted a cream color but I scraped away some paint and found more good wood. The cabin top was covered with rotten canvas that peeled away if you touched it. The forward end of the cabin was round, a design feature that seemed very, very old. I asked Lori when the boat was built but she didn't know.

I went below and started with the bilge, which was a mess. I had brought a huge electric lantern with me as well as a three-battery flashlight and some tools. The boat had inside ballast as well as an outside iron keel and also fixed ballast in the deepest part of the bilge in the form of cement. I assumed the whole thing would be rotten. I found that the cement was as hard as stone but I had brought a hammer and I chipped away a considerable amount of it. I saw that both the wood and the iron floor timbers beneath it were in good shape. The concrete was a mixture of cement, sand and BB shot. This was a really old-fashioned way of doing things but it was in excellent shape. At least it seemed like it to me. If Lori made an offer on this boat it would probably cost as much to have it surveyed as the boat was worth.

I spent an hour crawling around inside the boat sticking a knife or an ice pick into every place I could. I had never actually learned how to survey a boat but I had a pretty good idea where to look for dry rot. Since I had lived on *Vanitie* and done all the maintenance on her myself for several years I knew wooden boats pretty well.

The yellow pine used in her construction had kept as well as the oak, and apparently even a little better than the white cedar. She was framed with double bent oak frames. There were two pieces 5/8 inches by 1 1/8 inches finished together at 1 1/8 by 1 1/4. She had a white oak keel and deadwood, yellow pine planking above the waterline and white cedar below. She had black iron floor timbers, iron keel fastenings and copper rivets in the planking. Also black iron rudder post and a wooden well.

The stuffing box, shaft and propeller were all bronze. She also had an iron fitting at the heel of the rudder. I was amazed at the fact that she was not totally rusted and rotten. After a while I came up with an idea. I spent another hour checking the planking from the outside and then suggested we go someplace and talk.

Lori followed me back to Coconut Grove and we parked outside Monty Trainer's. We found a table far enough from the band where we could talk without going deaf. We both ordered steamed shrimp, conch chowder, and iced tea. I had some more surgery early the next morning and didn't want to drink any alcohol. After we had ordered, Lori apologized.

"Dev, I'm sorry it took so much time. I had no idea what I was asking you to do. I thought you would spend fifteen minutes looking at it and just tell me to forget it. I didn't think you'd spend nearly three hours examining everything. I thought that's what a surveyor would do after I made an offer. Is it that bad, or that good, or what?" Lori had not opened her mouth from the time we walked under the boat shed until now. I had been amazed at her restraint.

"How much do they want for the boat?"

"The yard owns the boat now because some guy left it there and just took off. There are storage charges of $4,600 on the boat and they say they will sell it for half that. I could afford that much but not a whole lot more."

It was just getting dark and I was enjoying myself. We were outside under one of the thatch roofs and the band was playing some soft Calypso, the kind that didn't blow out your ear drums. I was very much aware of Lori because she was so intense. I was used to the kid who made smart remarks. She looked pretty and with the oversize shirt I wasn't even aware of her breasts. Mostly, though, I was enjoying myself because of the splendid old boat.

"Lori, I don't know what you've got with this boat. It's very, very old. The materials and construction are so old I've never seen them before. I've read about them in books but I've never actually seen a boat built that way."

"I don't understand."

"The boat has concrete in the bilges. It's full of BB shot that's used for inside ballast. They used to do that back in the twenties and possibly in the early thirties but not since."

"Is it bad?" She looked depressed.

"There are a lot of things that would be considered bad today but they were O.K. back then if they were done right. The main thing is that I can't find dry rot. Hardly any. It's going to cost you a lot more than $2,300 to fix the boat up, though. Can you do some of the work yourself?"

"I don't know much about it, but I don't mind work."

"I have a suggestion. Make them an offer of $2,000. Or make it $1,800 and come up to $2,000. Find out if you can leave the boat there while you work on it. Ask them to make you a deal on renting the space so you can fix up the hull enough so it won't sink. Maybe if you come up with cash they'll let you use the shed free for a few months."

"What about the boat itself?"

"Frankly I was amazed at how old the construction seemed to be but what good shape the hull was in. If they accept your offer, which, of course, will be subject to survey, then I'll get Gus and maybe another guy I know and go over every inch of the boat. If the boat looks bad you can call that a survey and cancel. If it still looks good you can decide whether or not to spend money on a professional surveyor. If you spend some time and money on it you'll have a nice boat. It won't be worth a lot of money but it will be worth a lot more than $2,000. Even with the flashlights I couldn't do a thorough job in that short a time but I think you might have something special. She seems to be in very good shape. The wood has dried out so it will leak like a sieve for a while when you put it in the water."

"Do you think they'll accept $2,000?"

"I have no idea, but don't let on to them that you think you have anything special."

We finished our dinner and each drove off in separate cars. I loved boats of any kind, but particularly old wooden boats. I had enjoyed the whole thing. The old hulk was very interesting.

Chapter Nine

Saturday, 3 June
On Saturday I picked up Rocket at five o'clock. The party was supposed to start at six. We took the MacArthur Causeway over to Miami Beach and she gave me directions that were with the invitation. The address was on an island in Biscayne Bay up toward Baker's Haulover. On the way up, Rocket told me about her latest attempts to design sportswear and how much fun she was having. I had showed her the invitation and we made a few jokes about what we expected to find at the party. Neither Butch nor Antonia had said anything about the owner of *Ojos Verdes,* so we had no way of knowing if they were guests aboard or part of the family. It was a beautiful night, perfect for a party outdoors.

We drove across a small bridge and showed the invitation to a guard at a gatehouse who waved us through. The directions said *Casa del Malecón* and I thought it might be a private club. When we pulled up in front of the house, there were cars everywhere and most of them looked both new and expensive. Some policemen were directing the parking. We were told to park on the front lawn, on the grass. I was amazed at the number of cars and even more surprised at the size of the house. Having grown up in a wealthy town like Rye, I was used to huge houses but this place looked more like a country club than a residence. We followed several other people around one side of the house and through a garden out onto a large terrace. The landscaping was like the Fontainebleau or the Eden Roc with palm trees, bushes, and exotic flowers. Several huge banyan trees with their tangled and twisted roots were near the house. We learned later that there was a huge, irregular-shaped pool that resembled a small lake. It was surrounded by trees and even had several sand beaches. It was somewhat like the Venetian Pool in Coral Gables except with flower gardens everywhere—right on the edge between looking natural and looking perfect. Out on the big terrace, which was landscaped in several different levels, there were about ten tents in a row, with a band at each end. There were several bars and huge buffet tables that were spectacular, even from a distance. The place even smelled good, a combination of salt-water air and gardenias.

When we came out of one of the gardens through some trees and onto a terrace, we were at the end of a short receiving line. As soon as we took our place, waiters appeared with champagne, lots of fancy hors d'oeuvres and a variety of both exotic drinks and highballs. It would have been easy to get smashed in a hurry. After we got drinks and a few small nibble things, we started looking around.

"Well, Dr. Devlin," Rocket said with a big smile. "This is where I'm going to live when I get to be rich and famous?"

"Why not rent it for awhile to see if you like it."

"Seriously, Dev, have you ever seen anything like this place? It looks almost too nice to be real. It could look tacky or phony or something but it doesn't look that way at all. Do you know what *Casa del Malecón means*?"

"In Spanish, *Malecón* means breakwater or seawall. There's a famous highway that runs around Havana harbor called the *Malecón*. It's very beautiful at night."

"I'm really impressed," she said.

"It's certainly beautiful. I've been to a few places in Newport that are much larger but this is as pretty as anything I've ever seen. I bet the lighting is spectacular when it gets dark." Neither of us made comments about the place being ostentatious. It was simply spectacular. Period.

"The water is over there," said Rocket, pointing. "See the masts sticking up above the palm trees."

"The water is all around us. This is an island."

Off in the opposite direction from the swimming pool I could see what looked like the main and mizzen masts of a large boat. I turned back to Rocket.

"Rocket, you look gorgeous tonight. Why didn't you wear that dress in Nassau?"

"It's terrific, isn't it? I got it at the J.C. Penney for thirty-nine ninety-five."

"I'd guess Lord and Taylor for at least five hundred."

"The correct answer is that I borrowed it for the night from a buddy who is the buyer for Evening Wear at Nieman Marcus. She owes me three more favors than I owe her."

It was an Oriental dress, a simple sleeveless black silk sheath with a mandarin collar, much more sophisticated than I would have expected from Rocket. She looked gorgeous and very sexy. We had moved up quickly and I could see Butch introducing someone to an older woman who was probably his mother. Antonia was standing beside him. When he finished, he turned and looked at Rocket and me.

"Rocket! Devlin!" he said. "I'm really glad you could make it. It's good to see you again!"

Antonia greeted us both in Spanish with a warm smile and a little twinkle in her eyes as if she was about to laugh.

"Let me introduce you to my mother," said Butch. "You already know my father."

"Hello, Dev. Hello, Rocket," said the huge noble-looking man, who had been the professional captain of *Ojos Verdes* when he was sitting in the cabin of *Brilliant* eating *Phoenix and Dragon*. He was as just as imperial looking as I had remembered and in a tuxedo he looked like royalty. I figured out very quickly that the captain of *Ojos Verdes* was really the owner. I guess when I started talking about what a jerk the owner was he decided to play a little joke on me.

"Forgive me for pretending I was the professional captain. I may be a real jackass but I can assure you that I am not from Indianapolis," he laughed, and shook my hand. Then he introduced me to his wife, a tall elegant woman who managed to look extremely attractive in a terribly severe dress that seemed European. We talked for a few minutes in Spanish and it became obvious that either Butch or his father had told her about meeting us in the Bahamas. She was very nice and appeared really pleased that we had come to the party.

My parents used to call people like her "gracious." Another woman might have appeared phony. With her it was probably real and I realized that it didn't matter. Her manner was perfect and if it was not real it was a really good act. This was a bit of a revelation to me. I was not a student of human nature and insights like this were rare. Although I had excellent manners and most of the social graces, I had learned everything by rote and never wondered much why people were supposed to act polite. My mother had, at times, appeared a little phony, but I always knew why she was doing it and what she did always seemed right. I hoped I would have a chance to talk to Ricardo's wife again. Her name was Carmela.

Ricardo was talking to Rocket as if he was very happy to see her. "Miss Rocket, my son Butch has told me that you are capable of moving at a most incredible rate of speed when thunder is used as the starting gun. I am told that you made it from the restaurant at Chub Cay to your boat in less than two seconds!" He seemed really amused at Rocket's quick exit.

I felt a little foolish knowing what I had said to Ricardo about the owner but I remembered that I had pulled him off the sand bank and fed him a damn good dinner. In the short space of time that we talked to Ricardo Salazar, my impression was one of a very friendly outgoing man, apparently happy to be sixty years old. His wife spoke briefly to Rocket, just a few words in Spanish, apologizing for her lack of English. She had called me Dr. Devlin, although Butch had introduced me as Devlin. I didn't remember either Rocket or me telling the story about how she got her nickname, but we were drinking a lot that night and one of us probably had told it. Obviously Butch had told his father about meeting us in the restaurant and about us leaving in a big hurry when the tropical wave passed through. When we were about to move away from them Ricardo said, "Look for me later. I want to talk some more about boats!"

"Well, Dr. Devlin," Rocket said. "The professional captain didn't seem to hold it against you that you called his owner a few names." We moved out onto the terrace.

"Should we find a table or would you like to dance with me first?"

There were two bands, each one set up at opposite ends of the terrace. We danced for a while near a band that was playing slow music. The tents were striped green and white and the green was the same shade as *Ojos Verdes*. I also noticed some sort of insignia at the ends that looked like a Coat of Arms.

Somebody had worked out the acoustics so that either band could be heard all over the grounds but neither one too loudly. One band played South American and Spanish music while the other one played typical American songs. I am not a good dancer, and except for opera, I don't even like music very much, but this was different. Both bands were extremely good and made the switch from one to the other without a pause.

Rocket was a very good dancer and managed to keep me from stepping all over her feet. The sun was beginning to set over in the west across Biscayne Bay and lights were beginning to go on in Miami. Rocket looked good and smelled good and moved as gracefully as she did sliding around the boat. We danced without talking for a while and then she said, "Dev, could you do me a big favor and introduce both of us to a few people tonight. Sometimes you wait for other people to speak first and sometimes they don't ever speak and it doesn't bother you. You just stare back as if the person was an ass-hole for not introducing himself. I get butterflies when I'm with a big bunch of strange people but I don't think you care enough to get nervous about much of anything."

I said I would be friendly and we danced for a while. I was a little surprised that I was enjoying the dancing. Perhaps I was getting over the trauma that I had experienced as a ten-year-old being forced to put on white gloves and dance with fat girls. Probably not. Rocket was something special. Although it had been only two weeks since we got back from the cruise, I found it unbelievable that I could have spent twenty one days on a small boat without ravishing her. She started talking again.

"At a normal party I wouldn't mind introducing myself but somehow these seem to be kind of old world people or something. They seem to be very gracious and polite and I feel compelled to act very ladylike. Actually, I never had anybody kiss my hand before."

"I'll be a perfect gentleman. But don't become impressed too fast. Butch and his family and his girlfriend really do seem nice, but there is something about this party that you may not have noticed."

"What?" she looked up at me.

"There are no ladies between the ages of thirty and fifty."

"What's that supposed to mean?"

"The women over fifty are wives. The women under thirty are girlfriends or mistresses. There's no in-between."

Rocket looked startled, but she started looking around. After a few minutes she said, "You're right. How did you notice something like that?"

"I look at women's faces. That's my business and I can't help it."

"Most men stare at breasts and behinds. I'm not sure I can get used to a man who looks at every other woman's face. Just doesn't seem normal."

"Do you think it's nicer to stare at a woman's breasts and her behind?" I laughed at her.

"It may not be nicer but it's more normal. I'm going to feel self conscious knowing that you're going to be staring at my face." She looked serious. "Sometimes on the boat you would be ogling me and I would have to look down to make sure I had on my underpants."

"Sometimes you didn't have any underpants on. Just the Tee-shirt."

"You weren't supposed to know. If you were really looking at my face you wouldn't have."

We were having this conversation while the band was playing a fairly subtle fox trot. It would have been a very tough conversation doing a waltz or a rhumba.

"Are you disappointed to find out that I've been staring at your pretty face all this time instead of your bottom?"

"Yeah, I guess so. My face is cute but not quite all-world. On the other hand, as you well know, my entire body is really quite nice. I also think you're lying. Don't tell me you haven't spent a lot of time staring at my gorgeous derriere. I've seen you ogle. I mean really *ogle*. A few times you stared so hard I thought you were staking me out for a hemorrhoidectomy or whatever it's called."

"You shouldn't talk dirty when you're all dressed up." A man who I didn't recognize tapped me on the shoulder to cut in and dance with Rocket. She didn't seem to recognize him either, but I remembered dancing school and said the polite things. I walked over to the buffet table to take a look at the spread. There was an incredible number of things on the table, mostly things I didn't recognize.

"Excuse me," I said to one of the men in a white suit and chef's hat. "What is that dish?"

"It is *Salpicón de Mariscos* – different kinds of shellfish, boiled and served cold in *Salpicón* sauce. There are clams and shrimp and oysters and crayfish and lobster. The sauce is made with olive oil, capers and hard boiled eggs and parsley. Try some. It's delicious!"

I filled up a small plate.

"What's that?" I asked, pointing to another strange looking dish.

"*Gambas al Jerez*. Big shrimp cooked Andalusian style. The shrimps are sauteed with diced ham and fino sherry. And of course, the white sauce. Try some of these, too."

As I started to move away from the buffet table, I saw one more thing that looked interesting.

"*Mariscada a la Plancha con Salsa Romesco*," the man said. "It is a dish from Cataluna. It's an assortment of fresh shellfish grilled in the shell on a hot plate griddle and brushed with olive oil while they are cooking. The famous sauce gets its spice from very hot, dried peppers. Just like you get at Burger King."

I piled all three of my Spanish seafood specialties on two full-sized plates and left my empty glass on the table. I had lost track of Rocket while I was selecting food so I looked around the dance floor. I didn't see her for a few minutes and then spotted her in front of one of the canopied bars. She was with four other people standing and talking. I found an empty spot on the buffet table and put one plate down. I kept my eye on Rocket and stuffed down about half my total pile of food. All of it was delicious but I lost track of what each thing was named. When my pile of food was reduced to just one plate, I walked over to see who was in the group.

When I got closer, I recognized one of the women as Patricia Rivera, a gorgeous young girl who was quickly becoming popular as a television news analyst. I had watched her a few times and formed a theory about women on television news. I'm convinced that the T.V. stations start their selection process with a huge group of bright, articulate ladies who all have terrific voices. They pick the best looking 10 percent and then they analyze the mouths. All of the mouths are pretty, actually they are all very pretty, but that's not enough. They find a mouth that moves in unusual ways. In the old movie, *"Singin' in the Rain"*, Donald O'Connor does a scene where he moves his mouth in fifteen different directions at one time, or at least in rapid sequence. The ladies don't move their mouths as much but they do a modified version. It's fascinating to watch. A beautiful woman becomes a beautiful unique woman by moving her mouth in unusual ways. I decided to ask Patricia about my theory.

I realized the man with Pat was Snake Moran. The full beard he'd grown when I was with him a week ago had disappeared. He was absolutely clean shaven except for long sideburns and a pencil-thin mustache. When he didn't have on fake hair, his skin was so smooth it was like porcelain. I wondered what the hell he was doing at the birthday party of a Spanish gentleman. The man who had cut in and danced with Rocket was a congressman, one of our chosen representatives from South Florida. Rocket introduced me to everyone, even Snake. I felt sure she had just been introduced to him as Sean by the congressman and had forgotten getting drunk with him at the Pilot House. She referred to him as a dealer in antiquities. I wondered if she made that up because of the bullshit story he had told us about the little statue with his dick broken off. What a crazy bastard he was. She was a little crazy, too.

After I got us a drink, we found a table and sat down. I was next to Patricia and I couldn't help staring at her. Up close, her face was very interesting. She had big eyes that seemed to smile all the time. As a cosmetic surgeon I should be able to describe a pair of eyes better than smiling, but it's a poetic or artistic description and not scientific. Her hair was a dark reddish brown, slightly wavy and sun-bleached blond in places.

Rocket noticed that I was staring at Patricia, so she pointed it out, explaining that I was a pervert who looked at women's faces instead of their figures. She explained to Patricia and to the whole table that I was both an artist and a plastic surgeon so I went around staring at people's faces all the time. People seemed to think it was funny.

The congressman, whose name was H. Walker Griffeth, started telling us about his efforts on Capital Hill to save Lake Okeechobee and the Everglades from developers. Snake explained to H. Walker that the problem was the dairy industry and the sugar cane people. Pretty soon he started quoting statistics on chemical pollution of the air and water. Snake either was extremely well informed or making up a lot of things in a hurry. I knew it could be either. Rocket always got excited about environmental problems and causes and this was her chance to dump on a politician so she jumped in with Snake. H. Walker's wife was named Helen and she looked a little drunk but she was smart enough to not say much.

Patricia, who was sitting beside me, seemed to lose interest in the swamps and started asking me questions about faces. I told her my theory about news-ladies' lips. She was amused but she thought it made sense so she started talking without making any sound so I could watch her mouth up close. It was fascinating to watch. Her teeth were very white and even and her lips were slightly full. When they were closed, it was a very pretty mouth but when she started talking her mouth took off in different directions. It was fabulous to watch. She told me that the T.V. people had been pushing her to stop moving her mouth so much and to practice in front of a mirror. She leaned over and whispered in my ear that she was going to tell the studio that she had consulted a professional and they could "go piss up a waterfall." Several times during the rest of the night when I happened to catch her eye she would wiggle her mouth and wink. I liked her.

The conversation bounced all over the place like it usually does when six slightly drunk people are sitting at a table with a band playing in the background. I did learn that Ricardo Guillermo had a title, Duke of Spain or something like that, and that his wife was a distant cousin of the King. I also learned that he was extremely wealthy and owned many vineyards as well as a ranch on which he raised bulls for the *Corrida*.

H. Walker Griffeth seemed to know a great deal about Ricardo and his family. He also seemed to be a very close friend, or at least he claimed to be. At one point, Rocket asked if Butch and Antonia were engaged. According to H. Walker's wife they were very close friends and had grown up together. She said that Antonia's family was also very wealthy and that she was like part of the family. She said that Antonia and Carlotta, who was Butch's sister, had been in convent school together since they were five or six years old. H. Walker Griffeth's wife told a story about Antonia and Carlotta being allowed to take a trip together to France with only one bodyguard or chaperone, when they were about fourteen. Apparently they nearly drove the *duenna* lady half crazy sneaking out of hotels and smoking cigarettes and things. The woman threatened to commit suicide and Don Ricardo had to come and get the girls. After a while everyone including me went to the buffet table for food. When we got back to the table, we compared what we had chosen with everyone else.

Helen told us she was a paté freak. Her plate had brown things like everybody else but she also had a lot of pink and green things. They looked like pistachio nuts along with olives and truffles. Rocket had a huge assortment of seafood piled up on her plate. She had Maine Lobster, Pacific sockeye salmon, cracked Conch, Abalone, Little Neck Clams, Chesapeake oysters and Alaskan King Crab. She also had a small portion of *Gambas al Jerez*, the huge Andalusian shrimp and one of *Salpicón de Mariscos*, the mixed shellfish.

Snake had two huge slabs that looked like tenderloin of beef American style and nothing else. H. Walker had a huge lobster and a small steak with a salad on the side. I didn't mention that I had already eaten two piles of seafood when I described my own small dishes.

A little while later Butch and Antonia came over and sat with us. Butch told us how much his father was enjoying the party. Ricardo, we learned, was a very outgoing man who had started off with a fortune and increased it to a massive fortune. Apparently he had made very few enemies in accumulating wealth.

Antonia made a point of sitting down beside me. She said she needed an interpreter because she didn't speak English. I was conscious of Rocket looking at me from time to time and I knew she was watching to see whether I looked at Antonia or at Butch. I was very much aware of Antonia and tried to keep her in the conversation. Several times she said things to me in English as if she was trying it out. At one point Butch started telling a story about how his Father gave him his first big assignment in the export company that the family owned. Butch was supposed to have several hundred cases of wine from one of their vineyards shipped to one of the sheiks in an Arab country. Because of the ban on alcoholic beverages of any kind, the shipment was supposed to go to the French Embassy where they would pretend it was something else and then make sure that it got to the sheik unofficially. Butch got the shipment mixed up and it went to the Saudi Arabian Embassy in cartons marked bananas. It was a very funny story and Butch told it well. I had noticed that in all his stories he was the person he made fun of. I wondered if he did this deliberately to somehow offset his good looks. An arrogant man who was as good looking as Butch could make enemies quickly and easily. I had learned to ask questions and to be interested in other people to make up for the fact that I didn't have much personality. It seemed to work for me and other people seemed to like to talk more than listen.

While Butch was talking, Antonia listened and laughed when everyone else did. Maybe she had heard the story before. Butch and H. Walker did most of the talking for a while and H. Walker started asking about who had been invited to the party. It seemed that Ricardo was friendly with many of the top businessmen in Miami as well as people in high-level government jobs. Butch seemed to know all of them. At times the women seemed to be having one conversation and the men another. I was half listening to Helen Griffeth and half listening to H. Walker when Butch interrupted.

"Dev, I have to take Sean Moran up to the house to get an appraisal and evaluation of a small work of art that my father is planning to sell. It's actually a tiny statue of a monster or devil. Would you and Rocket like to come up with us? It'll only take a few minutes."

Rocket immediately said that she wanted to go with them but I think she wanted to see the house and not the statue. I thought about it for a few seconds and decided I really didn't want to see either one. The grounds and gardens and trees and flowers were really incredible but I had no desire to see the inside of the house.

"How about if I just wander down to the dock and take a look at *Ojos Verdes*. Your father told us all about her when he pretended to be the professional captain. I don't need to go below but I would like to look around on deck. Would that be O.K.? I can meet you back here when you're finished."

He stood up to go inside and then had a suggestion.

"Toni, why don't you go with Dev. You can show him the boat down below. In case the cabin is locked, you know where the key is."

"Certainly," she said in Spanish. "I'll be happy to show Dr. Devlin the boat. Let me get us both another drink."

I followed her over to the bar and got myself a rum and tonic. She asked for something I had never heard of called a *Horchata Valenciana*, which she told me was a Valencian summer drink made from *chufas*, which are tigernuts.

When we had our drinks I followed her. We went over past the swimming pool which I had only seen from a distance. It was amazing closer up with several white sand beaches and a waterfall coming from a group of palm trees. The lighting had been set up to accentuate the flowers.

We walked down a path through a whole group of banyan trees and finally out onto the docks. I looked around and counted the boats. There was the *Ojos Verdes*, of course, and down at the other end of the dock there was a long boat that looked like a Donzi or Cigarette, a launch and a Soling. Up on the dock was a Star on a trailer and several Lasers. Ricardo seemed to have his own little yacht club. I also noticed a guy in a khaki uniform who had some kind of handgun in a holster strapped around his waist.

The main part of the dock was concrete but the boats were all attached to floating docks. We went aboard *Ojos Verdes* and I walked around examining everything. I was amazed at the condition of the boat. The varnished areas looked as if the last coat had been put on a few hours ago and the teak deck had obviously been scrubbed recently. I looked at some of the running rigging up close out of curiosity and I think they probably replaced it every time it got dirty.

The whole dock area was lit up and had that funny feeling of a night football game played under lights, where you can see darkness in the distance.

After I had finished looking around the deck, I went back to the main companionway. Antonia had opened it up and stood aside while I went down the steps. She told me where the light switch was and I flipped on the cabin lights.

After I flipped the switch I turned and looked up at Antonia, who was trying to come down the steps. She suddenly slipped on one of the steps and slid down part way, stopping on one heel. Her dress was split in front and the sides overlapped. When she slipped, the sides pulled open and I found myself staring up at her underpants. For a few seconds I just stared, and then helped her down. The headroom in the cabin was probably seven feet and it could be a long fall.

"Bueno, ya que terminó de inspeccionar el encaje de mis pantaletas, le gustaría ver el yate?" she said when she was on her feet. What this means in Spanish is - "Now that you have examined the details of my panties would you like to see the boat?"

I didn't know whether to apologize or just act as if it had never happened, so I acted just as if it had never happened. She showed me around the boat and it was magnificent. So often wealthy people who own large boats decorate the interiors like a French whorehouse. Not this boat. It was totally seamanlike. The cabin sole was teak with holly strips and the bulkheads seemed to be teak with rubbed-effect varnish and wax. As on deck the metal was highly polished, some of it brass and some of it chrome. No carpets anywhere. It was the way that a commercial fisherman would expect a yacht to be. It was a man's boat, a seaman's boat.

I was surprised at how much Antonia knew about the basic construction of the boat. I was also impressed with how she described the details of the electronics. She obviously knew how to operate each piece of equipment and how it worked. She told me she had started sailing on the *Ojos Verdes* when she was only ten years old and had made several offshore passages. I had been surprised when H. Walker Griffeth told us that Antonia and Butch were old friends. Personally I knew I would have a hard time being just friends with a girl as beautiful as Antonia. When she finished showing me everything on the boat we went back up to the party and found the table we had left. We sat and talked for a few minutes before Butch and the others came back.

During the last hour I had seen Antonia in different lighting and from different angles. Since I was obsessed with people's faces, I had strong feelings about what I saw and I decided that if there was an opportunity I would ask Ricardo about painting her.

Whenever I meet new people, I always look at their faces and make an unconscious judgement that either they need cosmetic surgery or that they don't. Most people really don't. The next thing that happens is that I look and I decide if I want to paint the face. It is rare that I meet a new person socially who needs surgery and even more rare when I see a face that I want to paint but without conscious thought the decisions are made.

I want to paint when a woman is extremely beautiful or when a man has an unusually interesting face. With women it's beauty and with men it's character or unusual features or even ugliness. I don't paint ugly women and I don't paint handsome men. Actually, I seldom paint anyone any more but I still make the decision. I knew after meeting Butch and Antonia that I would like to paint both of them. Or either one. With Antonia the reason was obviously her great beauty. With Butch I wasn't quite sure as I had never wanted to paint a beautiful man before. I wasn't even sure I had ever seen one that I would actually call beautiful.

After a while Butch and Rocket came back and we talked for a while about *Ojos Verdes*. Then Butch and Antonia excused themselves to move around and talk to friends and guests. Before he left, he said he would call me and that perhaps I would like to go sailing on the big ketch. I said that I would.

We sat at the table for a while and I danced with Helen and Rocket a few times. I also danced with Patricia who talked while we were dancing, with exaggerated movements of her mouth, which I thought were extremely funny. We decided that I would write a professional looking letter to her, stating that she should do mouth exercises so she could excel at unusual ways of talking. She would show the letter to her bosses and have fun pretending it was real.

Later, I slipped away and went back to the buffet table where I caught Rocket piling up another plate of seafood. We laughed at each other and went back to the table for fifteen minutes of high concentration, no talking, just gorging. I tried five new things and liked them all. While we were having some coffee, Snake said he wanted to take me away for a few minutes to introduce me to someone. As we walked away from the table he whispered.

"I think I've found out where Hogge is holding my sister. It's in the Bahamas. A place called Norman's Cay in the Exumas. Ever hear of it?"

"Sure. I've been there a lot of times. Do you know Jimmy Lightbourne, the guy who works at the dock at Chub? He races his boat all over the Islands. Jimmy's from Highbourne Cay or Staniel, somewhere in that area. What the hell is she doing there?"

"I don't know but I am sure that she *is* there. What I've heard is that Norman's Cay has become a sort of hangout for some people who might be involved in a little drug smuggling."

"When you find out more, let me know."

Snake then introduced me to a man named Don Aronow who was famous in the world of offshore powerboat racing. Don was a big, good looking guy who was very friendly. He had a way of looking you right in the eye when he talked to you, as if what you had to say was the only thing he was interested in. I did the same thing when I talked to people but with me it was an acquired skill. We looked at each other as we talked and it was very friendly. I knew very little about power boats of any kind but I did read the sports pages and there were frequent articles about him. He built the boats in a section of Miami that had been nicknamed Thunderboat Row. He raced his own boats and frequently won.

Snake apparently knew Don pretty well and had been on some of the races. We talked about offshore sailboat racing as well and he said he would like to try it some time. He was a likeable guy, with a face that looked like he was having a good time. I remembered that it was Don who gave Snake a ride back from Nassau in one of his Cigarette boats.

While I was standing there talking to them, Butch came up and asked if he could talk to me for a second. He told me that Toni, who I figured out was Antonia, had asked him to ask Rocket if I could dance with her. Now, Butch was supposed to tell me to go ask Toni. I was confused and wondered why Toni just hadn't asked me directly. Butch explained that a Spanish lady of her class didn't ask a man to dance. It got sort of arranged by other people. Now I was supposed to go over to the table and ask Antonia to dance, as if it was all my idea. I said O.K. knowing that Rocket wouldn't care anyway, even if she hadn't been asked. I couldn't dance worth a damn and avoided it whenever possible out of courtesy to the ladies.

I walked back to the table and asked Antonia if she would like to dance. I asked as formally as I knew how in Spanish, then asked Rocket if she would mind. She granted her permission very politely but I thought she was going to burst out laughing at the formality.

I was a little over six feet but with heels Antonia was only a few inches shorter. She danced gracefully, and without effort she made me almost seem graceful. She didn't speak at all and her face was impassive, without expression. We danced several dances, a waltz, a fox trot, graceful dances without a lot of jumping around. Out of habit I studied her face as we danced.

Her nose was slightly long and very straight as if her pure Spanish blood had not been diluted. Her lips were stained and glossed but actually it wasn't necessary. Her generous upper lip and full lower lip didn't need to be painted. As I stared at her, I knew that the surgeon in me was seeing the shape and sculpture of her face, while the artist was seeing something else. Her mouth, with no makeup, would call attention to the lovely shape. With lipstick gloss it became a frame for her very straight and very white teeth.

Because I had been so startled to see a man as beautiful as Butch in the restaurant on Chub Cay, I had not really paid much attention to Antonia. Rocket had been right when she accused me of staring at Butch and not looking at Toni.

I found myself thinking about what a great looking couple they were and realized that Antonia, as beautiful as she was, did not arouse me. We were finishing a rhumba when the band took a break. She startled me a little. Instead of just thanking me she started talking.

"*Dr. Devlin, estoy terriblemente avergonzada por lo que pasó en el barco, yo no lo hice a propósito. Es muy importante para mi que usted piense bien de mi. Muy importante.*"

She was saying that she was terribly embarrassed by what happened on the boat. Also, that it was very important that I think well of her.

"Hey, Toni, don't worry about it. I'm sorry I looked up your dress. I should have looked the other way."

"*Gracias,*" she said, looking a little relieved, but not smiling.

We went back to the table and sat down. There was another couple there and H. Walker was still talking. Helen had sobered up and was talking to Rocket. After awhile Rocket leaned over and whispered to me.

"Butch told me that we should come down to the sand beach by the pool when the party starts to break up. He said that some of the younger people were going to go there and sing songs."

I looked at Rocket to see what else he had told her but that seemed to be all he had said. I danced with Rocket several times after that and actually enjoyed the dancing. The slow ones anyway.

"Dev, you've just *got* to see the house sometime. At one time this island was a beach and tennis club. Ricardo bought it, tore down everything and started from scratch. He even brought in a lot of huge rocks and sunk pilings all over the place. He thinks a hurricane is going to hit Miami one of these days and he wants the house to be wind-proof and waterproof."

"Why is he so obsessed? Did you find that out, too?"

"Yeah, Butch talks openly and teases him about it. I'm sure you realize that the house is worth millions. Apparently the paintings and artifacts are worth far more than the house. Maybe ten or twenty times as much as the house. Apparently, Ricardo is an expert and a real collector. He loans his stuff to museums for exhibits all over the world."

"I can see why he would want to protect his stuff. It *is* an amazing house."

Rocket described steel shutters on windows with triple panes and even said she was told that a twenty foot wave couldn't get into the house. I was impressed.

Later, I went back to the buffet tables several times and really made a pig of myself on things I had never tasted before and probably never would again. Although I had a lot to drink I stayed pretty sober because of the food and the dancing. I had never been to a party quite like this and I really enjoyed myself. Rocket seemed to feel the same way as I did, constantly talking about what a great party it was.

Sometime after midnight, we realized the party was going to break up so we went down to the pool. Although it was about the size of a small lake it wasn't hard to find the group. There was a section of sand beach that was cut off from the rest and very secluded. There were rocks and flowers and palm trees all in a sort of U-shape around a section of beach. To get to this part of the pool you walked down some steps that had either been cut out of a rock or man-made out of stones and mortar. I couldn't tell which one in the dark. At one end of the little beach I found out you could walk in the shallow water around a corner of the rocks and see a wooden deck with men's and ladies' bathrooms. At the deepest part of the U-shape, the furthest from the water, there was a small Tiki bar with a thatched roof and every kind of drink you could want. A bartender was taking orders and handing out beach towels and blankets. For some reason everybody seemed to be whispering or talking in a low voice. There was a lot of laughing but that, too, was low key. I was really curious.

I had no idea what to expect. I would not have been at all surprised if people started taking off their clothes and started a huge sex orgy. There seemed to be a lot of people in their late twenties or thirties that I had not seen when we first arrived. Butch and Toni seemed like the international jet set to me and there sure as hell was enough money involved for anything. I was also expecting somebody to offer me some cocaine or at least some marijuana. I had never tried either one, and had no intention of starting that night, but I had been offered both before.

I looked around for Snake Moran and Patricia Rivera but I didn't see them anywhere. I didn't see anybody whom we had met earlier. We took off our shoes and went around to the bathrooms and I figured that if the party started to get raunchy I could grab Rocket and walk past the doors to the bathrooms and around to an open place where the beach ran up to the grass and back to the terraced part of the lawn. I had our exit planned. We wouldn't have to walk through the crowd and past the Tiki bar up the stairs.

We each used the bathroom and then went back and sat down on our beach towel. I took off my tuxedo jacket and my necktie. She took off her shoes and whispered that she hoped she could keep her friend's dress from getting messed up. The bartender had suggested we have some kind of concoction with rum and coffee and whipped cream so we tried it and found it to be very good.

The whole section of the beach was fairly dark except for some torches and some hidden lights in the palm trees and flowers. Very softly I heard the sound of a guitar and a voice. It was Butch.

"I want to thank you all for coming to honor my Father on his sixtieth birthday. I would like to sing his favorite song for you."

Butch sang a song in Spanish very softly while he played the guitar. It was a beautiful song, a sad song that reminded me of *"I'll take you home again, Kathleen"* although neither the tune nor the words were similar. Then he sang another song in Spanish and I realized it was *Lord Jeffrey Amherst*, the college song. When he finished, he got everybody singing the same song in English.

We all sang some songs and then Butch sang alone again. He was the leader and he named the tunes. We did all the college songs, even the Notre Dame Fight song. Toni contributed with three haunting melodies in Spanish I had never heard before, very beautiful ones. Some woman sang a few in French that sounded a little like Edith Piaf.

Rocket and I had picked a spot where we could sit with our backs against a rock wall. I went back to the Tiki bar for more drinks. Butch saw me and gave me a blanket without interrupting what he was singing. It was very late and a tiny bit chilly, so I wrapped the blanket around us and put my arm around Rocket. She put her head on my shoulder. It was very romantic and I was a little surprised, and very much relieved, at what was happening on the beach. Couples were sitting together and singing all the old American favorites mixed in with other songs in many languages.

Occasionally a pair would kiss but nobody seemed drunk and there was no sign of drugs. It seemed like a beach party back when I was at Yale or in the summer at the Larchmont Yacht Club. It was very nostalgic. The whole surroundings were as beautiful as a movie, with the palm trees up against the sky, and the flowers accentuated by hidden lights. The torches made it seem like the South Sea islands. I thought Rocket was falling asleep with her head on my shoulder when she whispered.

"I'm falling asleep. I'll allow you to kiss me goodnight one time very quickly because the party is very romantic, but if you so much as squeeze one breast I'll break your arm."

I leaned over and gave her a small kiss on the mouth but as soon as our lips touched it very quickly became a wet juicy kiss and we were suddenly clinging to each other. All of the desire and lust we had held back on the cruise had gotten hold of us. We had a blanket around us, and covering us. It was dark and nobody could see what we were doing. I put my hand under her dress then up between her legs.

She spread her legs to make it easy. I put my hand between her thighs. The narrow strip of her nylon panties was wet. I rubbed and squeezed and it became much wetter, very slick and slippery. I worked my finger under the edge of her panties and between the lips, then up inside her. After a few seconds she pulled her mouth away from mine and whispered.

"Bath house."

I knew what she meant. We got up off the blanket and walked around the corner of the rocks to the wooden deck platform and the doors to the bathrooms. There were lights on in both of them and both the men's and ladies' were in use. We stood there for what seemed like forever waiting, almost in pain, afraid to touch each other. Finally a toilet flushed and a woman came out of one door. It was empty. We looked around. There was nobody in sight so we went inside and locked the door. It was a small room with a stall shower, a lavatory and a toilet stall. There was a bench against the wall and some bathing suits hanging on hangers.

It had been more than six months since we had touched each other, but we knew what we wanted, and didn't hesitate. Rocket reached under her dress, pulled down her pink panties and stepped out of them. She left them on the floor. Then she pulled the end of the bench away from the wall and put one foot up on the bench. I stood close in front of her and dropped my pants and shorts. She used both hands to guide me between her lips and up inside her. When I was all the way in, I sat down on the end of the bench and she sat on top of me. Her legs were straddling mine and her mouth was fastened to mine.

We stayed there with me thrusting and Rocket bouncing until we were exhausted. We didn't say anything and when we finished we went back out to the beach. Everyone was still singing. I went up to the Tiki bar and got us another drink and we sat back down on the beach and sang some more and drank some more. After awhile, we both fell asleep.

I woke up a few hours later and looked at my watch. It was getting close to sunrise but it was still very dark. Suddenly I realized that there was nobody beside me. Rocket was gone. I walked up to where Butch had been sitting and he wasn't there. Nobody was there but the bartender. I had to pee so I walked around the rocks to the bathrooms. I thought she might be there but both bathrooms were empty. I suddenly realized that she might be with Butch. The idea made me feel funny. We were supposed to be just friends in spite of what we had done sitting on the bench a few hours ago. I went into the same room and used the toilet. I looked around and her pink panties were there on the floor where she had dropped them. I picked them up and put them in my pocket. They were still wet and slippery.

I couldn't blame Rocket and I couldn't blame Butch. They had spent time together earlier tonight. Rocket and I were supposed to be just friends and Butch was something special.

It was still very dark when I got back to the beach, but as I turned the corner of the rock I could see the bartender doing something in the Tiki Bar. A few candles and torches were still flickering. I decided to get myself a cold beer and go home. When I got close I could smell something good and realized that it was bacon and eggs cooking. The man behind the Tiki bar was bent over but then he raised up and it was Butch.

"Good morning, Dev. How about some champagne and eggs and bacon?" He looked completely fresh, as if he had slept for ten hours. "I'm going to eat and then go for a swim. After that I think I will hit the sack."

"It was a terrific party," I said. He handed me a plate and a Styrofoam cup of champagne. On the plate was a pile of hot steaming scrambled eggs, bacon, sausage, ham, home fries and hot buttered biscuits. Butch had fixed them himself. We talked for a few minutes about the songs and how we both remembered college and missed New England. If Butch had been with Rocket he certainly wasn't acting like it. I wasn't sure what to do, so I went back to where we had been sitting to get my tuxedo jacket and tie. The sun was starting to come up and there was some light. Over against the wall there was a blanket rolled up a few feet from where we had been. It was Rocket wrapped up and sound asleep. I woke her up and told her about the eggs and bacon. That got her attention. Nothing would wake up Rocket faster than the thought of food. After we finished our breakfast, Butch said he would call me about going sailing and gave us a full bottle of champagne to take with us.

When we were crossing the Julia Tuttle Causeway, I told her about thinking she had gone off with Butch. She laughed about it and said it would have served me right for attacking her when she was vulnerable. It was a beautiful dawn with a light warm breeze. The sky was blue with wispy white clouds and the sun was just coming up. We were both a little bit drunk and I was still very hot and horny. Rocket was, too.

"When is the last time you had a woman, Devlin?"

"Six months ago. You were the woman. It was the last day we were lovers and the day before we became friends."

"That was the last time for me, too, but early this morning we had a little accident in the bath house at Butch's pool and now I'm in a bad way. I'm in major heat and you've got to fix me. You've got to take me to my apartment and screw my brains out until I cool off and after that we can be friends again. You shouldn't have kissed me on the beach even if I asked you to. It was all your fault. You should have known how excited you get when you start messing around in my underwear."

"I've got your underpants in my coat pocket. You left them on the floor of the beach house. They're all gooey."

"I don't want them now. I don't need them and they would get in the way." She squirmed and wiggled and pulled the tight black sheath dress up above her waist. "Give me your hand."

She still had on the black stockings. I drove with my left hand while she helped me and told me what to do. She giggled and drank champagne out of the bottle all the way to her apartment in Coral Gables. She also described in detail the incredible things she was going to let me do to her.

When we got inside her apartment, we ravished each other. The quick fucking in the dressing room beside the pool at Ricardo's party was barely a start, and the fingering in the car driving home just made the trip more fun. Rocket couldn't wait to get into the bedroom so she started taking her clothes off in the living room. She pushed me down on the couch and teased me while she took off her slinky silk dress. When she had the dress off she started pulling up her black slip very slowly. I was taking my clothes off while I watched. Rocket had on the black stockings with a garter belt and when she reached the point where the lacy bottom edge of her slip was an inch or so above the top of the stockings she started to wiggle. I could see the skin above her stockings and then as she slowly pulled it higher, the triangle of curly brown hair.

Then she turned around and did the same thing with her back toward me. She had a boyish figure with slim hips but when she pulled the black slip above her waist and wiggled her plump little butt at me there was no question that it was one of the very best of female behinds.

"*Ogle* my behind, rear admiral Devlin. Don't think about pretty faces, think about gorgeous behinds. Mine, of course."

Rocket almost always acted very ladylike. Although she referred to me as an ass-hole pretty often, she never used any other words you wouldn't use in front of a priest or minister. When she was hot, it was different. She almost always got out of control and not only used all the lewd words and expressions, she made up a lot of new ones. She was still an imp, though, and when she turned around facing me again she had a huge grin on her face and in spite of my excitement I couldn't help thinking how cute she was. Her body was all woman but her face was part sweet little girl with dimples and part pure mischief.

She finished the playful strip tease and stood in front of me naked. She was well tanned except for the strips of white, which were larger than most girls because Rocket didn't ever wear bikini bathing suits. She insisted that her shape was so great she didn't need to show any skin.

"Don't you think I've got a fabulous *derriere*?"

By the time she got all her clothes off I was also naked and ready. I stood up to go after her when she stopped me.

"Give me my panties."

I found my coat and got the pink panties out of my pocket. They were sticky. Rocket stepped into them and pulled them up.

"This time you're going to have to take them off yourself, Devlin. That is if you want any of what's inside."

When Rocket got hot she was totally uninhibited. Sometimes she seemed like she was half crazy. She said I was technically very skillful as a lover but much too restrained.

"You fuck like a mortician," she told me once. Maybe she said mummy. I can't remember.

I started toward her, trying to look menacing.

She started backing away, trying to look like she was very frightened. She backed all the way into the bedroom where she let me catch her and put her down on the bed. I kissed her and licked her and squeezed and felt everything. I even kissed her nipples, which I didn't usually do because of her impatience.

Rocket never stopped talking except when I was kissing her. She alternated between telling me how good things felt and how hot she was, with instructions of what to do next. She also slipped in a few comments.

"When I squeeze it gently like this it makes your eyes turn green. *La pinga con ojos verdes*," she giggled.

After squeezing, kissing, and licking every part of her body, I put my hand between her legs. The narrow strip of her nylon panties was even more wet and slippery. I rubbed it and squeezed it and she got wetter. When Rocket was hot, she got very wet and pungent. This time she was a mess from what we did in the bath house and getting fingered all the way home. Her juice was all over both of us and the smell filled up the room. I loved the smell and the wetness and this time I took off her panties. There were only two of us but it was an orgy just the same. It was frantic and we didn't stop until we both were exhausted.

Chapter Ten

Sunday, 4 June

On the Sunday morning after the party at Ricardo Salazar's, I woke up at nine o'clock. Even though I'd slept for only a few hours I felt surprisingly good considering the party the night before. Maybe the combination of Spanish food and a few hours in bed with Rocket was some kind of health cure. I decided to go out for breakfast and a church service. I woke up Rocket and asked if she wanted to go with me. She said she wanted to sleep for a few hours so I told her I was leaving and kissed her goodbye.

I changed clothes at my apartment, drove the short distance to the café section of Coconut Grove, and parked my car. The parking lot attendant recognized me with the green car and made a few remarks. I was used to it. This was my day for having breakfast at the Horny Frog. That meant Eggs Benedict with a side order of Jimmy Dean sausages, sometimes at a sidewalk table and sometimes inside. The eggs were maybe the best in the world because of the superb Canadian bacon in them, but the coffee was second class, and I always teased them about it. I missed Rocket's snide comments about my choice of breakfast here. I had almost offered to bring her back a plate of Eggs Benedict, since she loved them so, but she sure didn't like me to order sausage with them. My waiter didn't need to ask what I wanted. I was lucky to get an outside table because the weather was just like the evening before with a clear sky and a few white cirrus clouds.

Everything was the same as usual with the people at other tables chattering away and the regulars all engrossed in their newspapers. I decided to think about Norman's Cay later on in the day and concentrate on the newspaper. I could put the raid out of my mind in spite of the potential problems, but I couldn't get Lisa Winter to stop intruding on my thoughts. I was still upset that she hadn't shown up at the last church coffee hour and wondered if she had left because of me. Then I found myself thinking about Patricia Rivera. Lisa Winter refused to go out with me and I had to stop seeing Rocket. Maybe Pat could be my new girlfriend.

I decided I'd go to the service at the Episcopal Church and grab Sidney Fontaine for a late lunch or dinner. Sidney was the Curate at the church, and a close friend, who I used as a counselor. He had been educated at Oxford in England and knew an incredible amount of History and Theology. He was also a black man in a mostly white congregation who lived in a very lavish apartment and drove a Mercedes. He dated white women and some Orientals in addition to many black women. I decided to ask Sidney what he knew about drugs and how he felt about them. Although he was brilliant in many things, he was probably the worst person I could think of to talk with about problems with ladies. In addition to going out with women of all sizes, shapes and colors he also dated women much older and much younger.

When I got to the church that day, I found out that Sidney was going to do the sermon. It was a real adventure when he preached and the congregation always listened intently. Part of this was his verbal and intellectual skill and part was the fact that he had a tendency to forget where he was and to stop completely. The congregation would hold its breath and there would be complete silence while they mentally rooted for him to remember. When he got his thoughts back together and started again, the whole audience would breathe a collective sigh of relief. He also had another problem that was completely separate from his tendency to forget. He would occasionally stutter or stammer. I wasn't sure he didn't do this on purpose, although he denied it.

That particular day he was terrific except for three long pauses that seemed forever. He was very popular with the people in the church and everybody enjoyed the adventure. On the way out I asked him if we could get together and we made plans to cook a steak by the pool at my apartment that night. I also told him I wanted to find out what he knew about drugs and drug smuggling.

Sidney came over around five, bringing a bottle of Burgundy with him. It was a perfect choice, but far too good to drink with a half-burnt steak. We sat outside at the little barbecue area beside the swimming pool. It was surrounded by palm trees and flowers that shaded the area from late afternoon sun. With a propane grill and a big round table, it was very nice for cooking outside.

We started talking about drugs almost as soon as he got there. I wasn't ready yet to mention that I was going to be involved in trying to rescue Sharon from a drug dealer, but I did know that if we needed people to help, Sidney would be a good one. I knew I could trust him. He was a good sailor and knew his way around boats. If we were going to take her from Norman's Cay we would need some boat people. I did need to know how he felt about drugs and drug dealers. Although I knew very little about the drug scene, I did have strong feelings about anyone who would sell drugs. I asked him what he knew and got one of those answers that would really piss you off if you didn't know Sidney.

"Yes, of course. I'm an expert on the subject. What would you like to know? I'm n-not in favor of drugs."

"Nobody is in favor of drugs. Why do you even say something like that? Are you trying to be cute?"

"My d-d-dear Devlin. I think I need to educate you somewhat on the current state of drug use in the United States. Why don't you let me finish this delicious piece of sirloin while it's hot, and then I will enlighten you?"

I had grilled the huge piece of beef and fixed a salad. It really didn't make sense to talk until we had finished it. The wine was excellent, of course, but too delicate. I only had one glass because I had surgery the next morning. I knew that Sidney was going to give me a lecture. It would be good and I knew I would learn a lot, but I sometimes got irritated at Sidney for acting like a fop. I had told him several times that I thought he was full of shit and that I thought he tried to act like people he met when he was at Oxford.

One night, about two years earlier, I had been at a dinner party at Sidney's apartment. Gus and Paulette, who also went to the Episcopal Church in Coconut Grove, were there and I had brought a date with me. Sidney had invited a beautiful Oriental woman named Lea Kahn. After we finished dinner, Sidney started a long discourse on King Arthur and the Knights of the Round Table. He pointed out that the real historical Round Table was on display in Winchester, England. Then he explained how the manners and mores of our modern day culture came from the knights and their ladies. It was very interesting but Sidney got carried away and talked too long. Gus and I don't talk very much so we just listened. At one point Gus got tired of it and when Sidney paused for breath he interrupted.

"Sidney, I don't know why you're so interested in knights. I've seen a lot of pictures and I never once saw a black guy in a suit of armor."

Sidney didn't slow down.

"Gus, you didn't examine the p-pictures carefully. There were hundreds of us. My p-p-p-people just had the face masks pulled down. Didn't you ever hear of the famous Black Knight. He was a Moor from Spain. B-black as the Ace of Spades."

Tonight, after I fixed coffee, he started in on drugs.

"First you have to understand that our Government is in favor of d-drug use – at the highest levels. If you can't accept that, then nothing I tell you will make sense."

"Bullshit, every politician I have ever heard of has denounced drugs."

"It's more subtle than that. Our President is a decent man but he knows far more about p-p-peanut farming than he does about narcotics. He has helped the drug people enormously. Now listen to me carefully and don't conclude that I am full of excrement until you learn some n-nasty f-facts."

"The President's sons are casual drug users. One of them was thrown out of the Navy for using drugs. The biggest problem, though, is that his key advisor on drugs is a man named Peter Bourne, a psychiatrist who finally got kicked out of his job in Washington for writing an illegal prescription for one of his aides. Before he was even p-p-picked for the job he made his feelings on drugs quite clear."

"This morning at Church, when you invited me over, you mentioned that you wanted to talk about drugs so I brought something with me that I want to read. This is an article called "The Great C-c-c-cocaine Myth" which was published in August 1974 in a publication called "Drugs and Drug Abuse Education Newsletter." It was written by P-peter G. Bourne, the same advisor to the White

House on drugs. Let me read it and then I'll leave it with you." He read from the paper but I couldn't believe it.

"At least as strong a case could probably be made for legalizing c-cocaine as for legalizing marijuana. Short acting, about 15 minutes, not physically addicting, and acutely pleasurable, cocaine has found increasing favor at all socioeconomic levels in the last year. Although it is capable of producing psychosis with heavy, repeated use, and chronic inhalers can suffer eventual erosion of the nasal membrane and cartilage, the number of p-people seeking treatment as a result of cocaine use is, for all p-practical purposes, zero. One must ask what possible justification there can be for the obsession which DEA officials have with it, and what criteria they use to determine the interdiction of a drug, if it is not the degree of harm which it causes the user."

"As you know, Dr. Devlin, I am somewhat cynical about our government anyway, but I would bet that Peter Bourne has possibly sampled a marijuana cigarette. P-perhaps even two. Possibly two or three thousand. Certainly lots of coke."

Sidney was all wound up. He was wearing a shirt that actually had lace on the front and he was gesturing with his arms and hands like someone from the theater. I knew him well enough to know that he enjoyed acting like a dilettante. He was probably the most intelligent and well educated person I knew, but he liked to act like a fairy.

"Dev," he said, shifting to a serious mood without the arm waving. "Our Congress is filled with bright young liberals who grew up with marijuana. The Democrats are not very much against drugs, but the Republicans are very much against heroin because they don't think Republican voters use it.

"Our President doesn't use drugs. Rosalind wouldn't allow it. But when it comes to drugs he doesn't *know* anything. Take a hard look at the Democratic platform. They consider drugs to be about as b-big a threat as Wrigley's Spearmint.

"The p-p-people who sell drugs in the United States have an opportunity right now like they have never had before to expand their business and grow fabulously rich. And they will do it. There is a rumor, and it is only rumor, that there is a new drug being merchandised called c-crack. I don't know much about it but it is supposed to be a cocaine derivative. It is supposed to b-b-b-be extremely addicting and very cheap."

"Do you think drug use will increase?"

"Rapidly."

"Where will it come from?"

"Colombia. Medellin. I'm sure of that."

"Jesus!" I said, amazed as much at his total conviction as in the scene he projected.

"No, n-not Jesus. He doesn't approve of drugs. I'm sure of that as well."

We spent another hour talking about it. Actually it was mostly me asking questions and Sidney giving me answers. I did explain a little to him about the medical aspect of the problem. The whole conversation was grim and depressing. I could only feel a total contempt for our Government for making it so easy for drug dealers.

I think we were both tired of the subject when Sidney suddenly switched the conversation to women. I hadn't planned to tell him what had happened with Lisa unless he brought it up. We had just poured ourselves a little bit of Amaretto when he looked at me intently.

"Dev, I've got an idea that will double your p-profits."

"Are you going to give me some extra prayers during the week?"

"B-b-b-better than that, I'm going to bring a young lady to your office and let you make a mold of her head. Then you can make an exact replica in plaster of Paris. You can buy some wigs if you want. You can p-put the head in your office with a sign on it that says ten thousand dollars. When a new customer comes in you give her your usual sales pitch and regular prices, but you never mention the head. If the ladies don't ask about it you don't say anything, but if they do ask you just say that's the deluxe model. N-now instead of hearing your schpiel about how good looking you're going to make them, they can see this full-size fabulous head. Naturally they will all want to look like the head. You can pull out a red wig for a red-headed lady and a b-blonde wig for a blonde."

"N-now anybody who is getting her head rebuilt is going to naturally want the deluxe job, so you never mention money because you already have a sign. You only need one thing you don't have now."

I had been listening to Sidney and trying to keep a straight face while I sipped my Amaretto. He loved to tell preposterous stories as if they were fact. I was doing O.K. with my straight face until he told me what I had to add to the clinic.

"You've g-got to get credit cards, Dev. Even your rich ladies don't carry ten thousand cash."

An evening spent with Sidney was always fun. Sidney's father was an English Lord who had married a Negro woman from South Carolina. I had seen a picture of her and had no trouble understanding why. He had taken her back to England and they lived in his ancestral estate. My friend had grown up with the combination of respect paid to a wealthy Lord and the contempt that some people felt for a man of mixed color. Sidney did not fit the image of a priest in anybody's religion and yet when it came to the important things he had to be one of the best. The best description of Sidney is the old Mark Twain expression. Sidney was a pisser.

"Sidney, your idea for a model head is perfect, but I already have a lady in mind."

I told Sidney all about Lisa Winter. I told him how I had fallen in love when I was treating Bobby, how we had met often for lunch and dinner without any screwing and how I had attended mass at the Catholic Church to be able to keep on seeing her. When I finished telling him about Lisa, Sidney nodded his head in apparent understanding and sympathy.

"If she won't m-marry you at least get her to pose for the model head in your office. That way you can worship the image of her beautiful face and make a few extra bucks at the same time."

After he left I went to bed immediately so I could get plenty of sleep and be ready for the operation at eight the next morning. Just before I dozed off the phone rang and it was Snake. He had gotten confirmation that Sharon was at Norman's Cay in the Exumas and wanted to come over Monday night to my apartment to work out a plan. He didn't explain how he got the confirmation but of course I agreed to get together.

I spent most of the next day at the hospital performing an operation that required help from a neurosurgeon and couldn't be done at our clinic. When I got back, Lori came in to tell me about getting reservations for Norman's Cay. I had called her from the hospital and given her a number in Fort Lauderdale. We could cancel later if Snake disagreed.

"I made reservations for Dr. and Mrs. Devlin at the Norman's Cay Club for Friday night through Sunday night. There wasn't any problem. They said it was slow right now because it was summertime. They do have a dive shop there with a boat and everything. I tried to make a reservation for you to go diving but they couldn't do it. They said that a man named something or other ran the dive shop and school, but that he was leaving and a man named Ricky Norton was taking over. The person who I talked to in Fort Lauderdale said that they didn't know if Norton was already there or not. If he was there, he could probably take you out, but they haven't started making dive reservations yet.

"I also have you and Rocket booked on a flight from Miami International to Nassau Friday morning at eight thirty. They don't fly to Norman's, but they do have several pilots that they work with and they will set up a flight for you. You should be at Norman's Cay in time for lunch. I worked out the same thing for you coming back on Monday."

I didn't comment when she assumed I was going with Rocket. We had decided that Snake shouldn't fly the plane down to Norman's Cay. There was too great a risk of someone remembering him and thinking about it later.

I was halfway expecting Lori to make some remark about my going off with Rocket again right after our cruise, particularly since I had asked her to make the reservations as Dr. and Mrs. Devlin, but she made no comment. She also told me that Butch had called and asked if I wanted to go sailing on *Ojos Verdes* the Saturday after I was going to Norman's. There was also a message to call

Patricia Rivera. I kept waiting for Lori to make some clever remarks, but she surprised me.

I called Butch, thanked him again for the party, and told him that I would definitely like to go sailing. We talked for a while and decided to try to make it a weekend. We would go someplace on Friday night or Saturday, anchor and then come back on Sunday. I really liked Butch but I also wanted to go out on the big boat. Although I had sailed for many years and had gone on many boats, I had never sailed on anything larger than a 12 Meter. I knew I would be like a little kid.

I was really interested in the big ketch. They called her a motor-sailer, but that wasn't completely accurate. She had a very large and powerful engine, even for a boat her size, and she also had larger ports than usual for a sailboat. Other than these two things she was just a big cruising sailboat.

When I returned Patricia's call she was very direct.

"Dev," she said, "I would like to see you again. Will you take me out to dinner?"

"Of course. I'm going away this weekend but if you're free Wednesday night I would love to take you out."

I went through my routine of explaining how I would have to make it a very early night and that I would have only one glass of wine at dinner. I had learned the hard way that most women were at least a little offended if they got all dressed up and then were taken home at nine thirty. She said she understood completely and that she worked strange hours and had to arrange her own social life around the broadcasting schedule. We talked for a while longer and she said she had a funny story to tell me about the mouth twisting when we met for dinner.

After everyone else had left I went in to see my partner. I told Bill that a very important person I knew had a drug problem and had to be dried out so I needed to use the clinic for a few days. Bill listened carefully and then, to my surprise, immediately came up with a plan.

"As soon as you find out when you're going to need to use the clinic come into my office and close the door. The two of us can fake an argument. We can yell at each other and call each other names and that will upset all the women in the place since we've never done it before. After a few minutes, we can get everyone together and tell them we've decided to close the clinic for a few days for a vacation because the two of us are under a lot of pressure and need a rest. We can tell them that we've never had an argument before and don't want to start. We'll pay the ladies for the days that we are closed so they'll be happy to get the time off. Do you think it will work?"

"I think it's a bullshit plan and I don't think the girls will believe it. I just came back from a three-week vacation."

"Dev, it is bullshit, but so is your story. You want to use the clinic for a few days with nobody else around. That's O.K. with me. Even though it's your building it's *our* practice. I'm sure that if I told you I wanted to use the clinic for a few days you would agree without needing an explanation. My guess is that you want to do something slightly illegal."

"I can't think of any better story to tell the girls. They will probably be so happy to get a few days off they won't really care. I just don't want any of them to come around. The person we are going to detox just possibly might die. I don't want them or you involved in any way."

"I'm not going to ask you if there is any other way to do what you're planning. I assume there isn't."

"There isn't any better way. The person is a close friend of mine and he cannot go to a hospital, even a private one." I lied to Bill because I thought it was best if he knew nothing at all in case there was trouble.

"Unless you come up with a better plan, I think we should handle the girls the way I suggested." I couldn't come up with anything better that day, or later.

That night when Snake got to my apartment I had a chart spread out on my dining room table. It covered a section of the Exumas which included Norman's Cay. I also had some sketch charts which were hand drawn and show some details that the government charts do not. Snake came in with a bag full of cheeseburgers from Burger King and we sat at the table and ate and looked at the charts.

"How do you know she's on the island?"

"I don't know for sure, but I have to gamble. She could be moved again or she could be killed. It's a little easier to kill people and get rid of bodies in the Out Islands than it is in downtown Miami, but not much. That's probably why they took her there in the first place. There's a man who has a brother in one of the federal penitentiaries. The man works for a drug dealer. Once in a while he supplies information in exchange for small privileges for the brother. The Billy Goat told me the name of the man and I exchanged some favors with an F.B.I. man. I don't know if she's still there, but at one time not long ago she was on Norman's Cay."

"Do you have a plan?"

"I've got a rough idea but I've got to go there and actually see what the place is like. I think I'm going to charter a boat in Nassau and go anchor at Norman's Cay. Then I'll go ashore and take a look around. Maybe stay in the hotel for a night. I've got to learn the layout."

"I've got one suggestion we might think about."

"What the fuck do you know about kidnaping people?" He started laughing.

"I don't mean for the actual snitch, or snatch, or whatever you hardened criminal types call it, I mean a way of finding out what's going on around the island before we actually try to get her off."

"What's your plan?"

"Look at this advertisement in the Yachtsman's Guide to the Bahamas. It's the latest addition, too."

I showed him an advertisement for Norman's Cay Club that listed all of the services available on the island and called it the "Jewel of the Exumas". In addition to all of the usual things for cruising sailors, the ad listed air-conditioned villas, small car rentals, a restaurant, a bar and scuba diving equipment for rent. I suggested to Snake that I make a reservation for two people by calling the phone number listed. The ad showed an address for the Norman's Cay Club on Sunrise Boulevard in Fort Lauderdale and a phone number. After we argued for a while, I convinced him that Rocket and I could go over there for a long weekend of scuba diving. I didn't tell him that Lori had already made reservations. The two of us wouldn't arouse any suspicion. Hopefully, we could look around and find the house where his sister, Sharon, was being kept. The advertisement also showed Sunfish and Hobie Cats as available for all guests. We could sail around after we located the house and try to figure out the best way to go in after her. We were probably going to have to use both boats and airplanes but we couldn't risk trying to use the airstrip. We would have to get her back to Miami in a hurry because she would start the drug withdrawal process as soon as we took her away.

If the person in Fort Lauderdale who Lori talked to was supposed to screen people, we certainly wouldn't seem suspicious. I would tell Rocket what we were doing or what we wanted to do. Our plan for actually rescuing Sharon would be to bring a small boat right in to the beach some place near the dealer's house if it was close enough to the water. Snake would go into the house alone. He said he didn't want any inexperienced people going ashore. He would either come from the boat or from a rented villa. We even talked about taking some other boat and anchoring in the harbor. We talked about having some sort of distraction take place while Snake went after Sharon, maybe like a fire or explosion. I suggested we might blow up the clubhouse or light it on fire, but Snake rejected anything like that because he didn't want to hurt any innocent people.

He got a little annoyed at me and kept pointing out that we were going there to get his sister and nothing else. For all we knew, nobody on the island, except the drug dealer and his crowd, had anything to do with drugs or crime.

While Snake was there, I telephoned Rocket and asked if we could meet after work the next night. I would tell her what we were going to do but leave out the details about Sharon and, of course, tell her nothing about what Snake did for a profession. I wouldn't tell her about the Billy Goat either. She asked me if I would come by her apartment for an early dinner and look at some of the sketches she had done of sportswear designs. I said I would be there.

Snake and I talked for a long time and came up with the framework of a plan. I would go over with Rocket on a Friday morning for a long weekend if we could get reservations. Snake would charter a plane and fly us over. We would stop off at Chub Cay and talk to Jimmy Lightbourne and see if he had been back to Norman's recently. We would see what Jimmy had to say and how he felt about the drug smuggling. If he said the right things we might include him in the operation.

After Snake dropped us off at Norman's Cay he would take the plane down to Staniel Cay and see what the airstrip was like. On the night we went after Sharon, we might be able to put her in a small fast boat and go from Norman's down to Staniel in a hurry. By going down the east side of the Island Chain we could be in deep water and go down fast. When they built the airstrip on Staniel Cay they had done it by partly filling in a small lagoon which left a narrow strip of water on one side of the landing strip itself. We might be able to bring the boat in there and transfer Sharon to an airplane. I asked Snake where he was going to get a pilot he could trust and he just pointed to himself.

"Where the hell did you learn to fly?" I asked.

"I used to be a pilot in the Israeli Air Force."

"Are you serious?"

"Yes, I'm a very good pilot. It may have been the Saudi Arabian Air Force, though, now that I think about it. It was several years ago and I can't remember too well. It was one of those countries where it's hot all of the time." He said it with a straight face.

"Snake, why can't you be serious. Why do you always have to act like an asshole?"

"Habit, I guess."

Sometimes Snake could drive me crazy. I wondered if he was going to dress up like the Red Baron to fly us over to Norman's Cay. We talked some more about how many people we would need and decided we would need three. I'm not sure exactly when it was determined that I would actually go to Norman's with him. I guess I had just assumed that I would go from the time he found out she was in the islands. One person would be with Snake in the small boat the whole time. This person would meet Snake and me at Staniel and then bring us back to the plane and take the boat back to Miami. This couldn't be me because I would always have to be with Sharon. We also would probably need somebody ashore pretending to be guests. Another idea we talked about was having somebody else there who could set off the explosives or start a fire. Snake felt that if the drug dealer was away from the house at the time we went after Sharon, it would be easier.

We talked about having someone go to the house and give Hogge a message to come to the club house. We also discussed having a person actually in the club house. Finally, at about eleven o'clock we decided to wait until I got back from the island before we went any further in making plans.

On Tuesday night I arrived at Rocket's apartment a little after seven. She looked great in a pair of toreador pants and a Spanish blouse. She got some iced tea for me and a beer for herself. I told her the story about what we were going to do and explained there was no danger in going over to the Norman's Cay Club for a weekend. I showed her the advertisement in the Yachtsman's Guide and told her that Ricky Norton was setting up a dive shop there. The name didn't register until I reminded her that we had met him at the Treasure Cay Hotel at the same time we met Carlos Lehder, and that he had been looking for a location for a dive shop then. She remembered Lehder and also that he liked to be called Joe.

I told Rocket that our trip to Norman's Cay was strictly for making a plan to come back later and get the friend of Snake's. I made it clear that we were going to rescue a man and not kidnap a person. Rocket listened very attentively while I talked, without interrupting and without asking questions. I told her nothing about the friend, only that he was being held prisoner by a drug dealer. I felt that the less she knew about what we were doing, the better.

I also told her we would have to be careful about what we said and how we acted, even in the privacy of our cottage, or villa, as they had called it when Lori made the reservation. The idea of having a bug seemed pretty remote, but I did know that maids in hotels and motels knew a great deal about people who stayed in their rooms. I decided not to wait to bring up sleeping in the same bed. I told Rocket I thought we should if there was a double bed but that I would not attempt any lovemaking. She said it would be fine, but I wasn't sure how she really felt about our relationship. On our cruise in the Abacos six weeks ago, we had managed to keep our hands off each other, but somehow things had changed since the last night at Chub Cay and I knew it would be a problem. What happened at Butch's beach party could be written off as just an accident caused by plain frustration for both of us, but it would be really a mess if one of us wanted to get serious again. Rocket asked only two questions after I outlined the trip.

"Had Snake been at Norman's Cay when we met him at the Pilot House Bar in Nassau?"

"I don't think so. He's pretty vague sometimes but he didn't know where his friend was until last week. He told me about Norman's Cay at the party at Butch's." I said it carefully.

"Do you want me to do anything to help you make a plan?"

"I don't want us to talk about it at all during the trip. We should act like two people going to the Bahamas for a weekend of diving and fun. If we get into conversations with other people, tell the truth about everything except, of course, why we are there. Try to remember all that you can about the island and where things are. When we get back I'm going to try to put different buildings on a map. I've got a sketch chart of the Island and the H.O. chart," I explained.

"Anything else?"

"If I suggest something that seems strange just go along with it."

"Gimme a for instance. You always suggest strange things."

"If I suggest a moonlight walk on the beach, I'll do it because I want to see how the place looks at night and I'll be looking for a place to bring a boat in close to shore without trouble. I won't be looking for a place to get your pants off."

"Why would you look for a place to get my pants off? We're going to be sleeping in the same room, aren't we?"

"I was just kidding. There won't be any sex on the trip."

"Suppose you see me in my underwear? You know how crazy that makes you. Remember what happened at the party. One little kiss and you went insane with lust."

"To be safe then, you better not wear any underwear."

"Do you know which house Snake's friend is in?"

"That's why we're going over, or at least part of it. We can't finalize a plan until we know which house."

"Why don't you find out before we go?" she asked.

"How would we do that?"

"I don't know but if you have the name of the guy who owns the house, and he's an American, you might be able to find the record of the sale somewhere. Do you know anybody who works for Dade County? Somebody who would know where records like that are kept?"

"I thought about that and couldn't come up with anybody so I called this afternoon and asked for help. A woman who answered gave me the address of the building where all records of real estate transfers are kept. She told me where it was and said I would have to go in person to find out anything. All sales of real estate are a matter of public record but they make you look up what you want and charge you to use a copy machine."

After we had finished talking about the trip, Rocket fixed dinner and told me about what she was doing in her job. She had never talked much about it before, but now she seemed to want to. Maybe since she now knew what I did in my work, she felt she could talk about her own career. We had a brief dinner of antipasto and ravioli and then she showed me some sketches of sportswear designs she had done. I didn't know anything about women's clothes but I could tell that she had some artistic talent. Quite a bit.

She also showed me some cartoon drawings. I thought they were good but the characters looked very much like people from Lil' Abner dressed up in Miami clothes. She said she had started out by tracing enlargements of the characters from comic books when she was a kid and eventually learned how to do it. The sportswear designs were for business and the cartoons were for fun.

I was able to make a few suggestions. I'd gotten many years of formal art training while Rocket had learned what she was doing all on her own. I took a few of her sketches and copied them, making changes to demonstrate points I was trying to make. She listened carefully and then did some new ones the way I suggested.

After a while I got an idea. I suggested she give the models or mannequins in her drawings some real faces. The whole purpose of a designer's drawing is to show the dress, or the outfit, or whatever, so the women don't have faces, not real ones anyway. In order to be a little bit different, I thought she could give the faces a little more character. Not enough to detract from the designs but enough to be a tiny bit different from all the other people who submitted designs. A tiny bit different. She seemed to think it was a good idea but wasn't sure how to do it so I showed her. The results were good.

"Winfield Devlin, that's a fabulous idea," she said. "I'm so excited I could kiss you! I would do just that except that I know you would get excited and loose control and attack me."

"Are you actually going to try it?"

"I certainly am. I'm going to do over all of my sketches using the stuff you suggested and I'm going to do each one with the old type face and the new type face. How did you come up with an idea like that? Because you paint faces or because you do surgery on faces?"

"Actually, neither one. Did you ever look through the design sections of yachting magazines? There's a designer named William Garden who does a lot of character boats. He has little men on the boats he designed. Tiny little guys steering the boat and smoking a pipe or something. It makes him a little bit different and the little men didn't detract a bit from the designs."

We talked for a while about her next step. She would do a complete portfolio of designs and prepare a resumé and then start looking for a job as a designer. When I asked about available jobs in South Florida she told me that most sportswear designer jobs were either in New York or Los Angeles. Later on when I kissed her goodnight it was a tiny bit longer, and a little bit wetter than it should have been for just friends.

On Wednesday night I met Patricia Rivera at a restaurant in Coral Gables called *La Patata*. She had picked it out because it was close to the clinic, gotten there a few minutes before I did, and found a corner table. As soon as she saw me she started making funny expressions with her mouth and I was laughing when I sat down. She looked terrific. As with all beautiful women, I studied her face for a few seconds even as we were talking. Excellent bone structure. Dimples. Beautiful mocha-colored skin a little bit dark. A tiny curve to her nose that looked a little Hispanic, sparkling dark eyes and hair. Her hair was very dark red and wavy but in places it had been bleached blonde by the sun. She could have been a popular television commentator on looks alone but she had the extra ingredient, the animated mouth. That and a low, sultry, almost naughty-sounding voice.

"I've been looking forward to seeing you again," she said.

"I can see *you* any time I want," I said, trying to be clever and knowing immediately that it was a mistake. It just wasn't my personality to make clever remarks.

Patricia told me about holding a meeting with the people she worked for at the television station. She told them she had consulted with a famous doctor who was an expert on speaking and especially the use of facial muscles. She actually convinced them that her use of her mouth had been developed with great effort and that it was deliberate. The enthusiastic way that she talked on television, even in describing unimportant things, was the same way she talked in person. It was completely natural and very charming.

I was an extremely good listener. Both of my parents had been talkers, especially my mother, and they both had intelligent things to say. As a boy, I realized when I was very young that most people liked to talk and that if I listened and asked questions they were happy. Patricia was a professional talker and a very good one. She was so nice to look at that you had to pay attention to every word. I didn't like to talk and I did like to listen. The conversation was pretty one-sided. She talked for the entire time we were together, stopping occasionally to ask me questions about me and my work. She surprised me with one of them.

"Did Carl and Lisa Winter drop their lawsuit because of what Dr. Montgomery said at the preliminary meeting?"

"Yes."

"What would have happened if he had testified against you?"

"I don't know. I probably would have won eventually but the insurance company would have killed me by raising the rates on my malpractice coverage."

"Do you still work on accident victims without permission?"

"If it's necessary. Since I worked on Bobby Winter I've been getting requests for help from other doctors, but they always make it legal."

"I think what you did for Bobby Winter was very courageous."

"It wasn't courage. It was just habit. In New York I did it all the time and most of the people I worked on didn't have enough money to hire any lawyers. After a while a habit like that becomes almost an instinct. Anyway, how did you know about Carl and Lisa and the lawyers?"

"The accident was on all the local news programs. I don't suppose you noticed the T.V. cameras at the Sailing Club, but they were there. After that my boss wanted to do a follow-up story on the six o'clock news so we interviewed

Carl Winter and tried to interview his wife. Don't you remember when the station called your office and tried to set up an interview with you?"

"I don't remember anyone calling the clinic."

"I called there myself and talked to someone named Lori who sounded very professional."

"What did she tell you?" I asked, not remembering the call.

"She told me to go shit in my hat."

I had been listening carefully to what the television reporter was telling me, not remembering any news coverage at all. When she told me what Lori had said I started laughing so hard I couldn't talk for a while. Patricia started laughing, too, and we didn't talk for a few minutes.

"Did you tell her to say that?"

"I don't remember her telling me that a television station had called. I don't watch television very much."

"Doesn't it bother you that she would tell me that and not even ask you about it or ask you what to say? What would you have told her to say if she had asked?"

"I would have told her to say the same thing without the four letter words. Or maybe to say the word in Spanish. *Mierda en el sombrero.*"

"You just said you don't watch television. I thought you told me at the party that you had watched me on television and thought I had an interesting mouth."

"I do watch you sometimes when I get home early enough but I just watch, I don't really listen." After I said it I knew I might have been rude but she didn't seem upset.

"I think I would be mad if somebody else said they watched but didn't listen. With you I guess it's a compliment."

I didn't answer. The night went quickly and pleasantly. She was such a skilled conversationalist she actually got me talking. When we were walking out she made it easy for me to ask for another date.

"I hope you'll call me again."

"I'll call you on Monday. I'm going away for the weekend to do some scuba diving in the Bahamas and the following weekend I'm sailing with Butch on his father's boat. During the week I don't go out very much but if you don't mind an early dinner like this, we can do it again next week."

I made no attempt to kiss her goodnight and we left in our own cars. Driving home I thought about the weekend that I was going to spend with Butch on *Ojos Verdes* and decided I would invite Pat. I hadn't asked about her schedule and I knew it was a hectic one with telecasts at strange hours, but it wouldn't hurt to ask her and find out. I knew I wanted to see her again, but she was too unusual for me to know exactly why.

At lunchtime on Thursday I got out the Yellow Pages and found a gun store near the office. In Florida there are as many gun stores as there are drug stores so it wasn't difficult. I made a call and found out they would be open that night. After work I drove down to the AA Lock and Gun and found a crowded place. There seemed to be guns there of every type made in the world. When I found a free salesman I told him that I wanted to buy a pistol to keep around the house in case of a burglar. After telling me I shouldn't even own a gun unless I was willing to spend the necessary time to take care of it and learn how to shoot it, he started describing guns.

He showed me several different revolvers and explained that a .38 caliber revolver with no safety was probably the least likely weapon to malfunction or to be a problem. I looked at several different types of revolvers and became confused by the variety. He confused me even more when he started telling me the differences between an automatic and a revolver.

I asked him how long it would take for the application to clear and he explained that there was no waiting period and that I could take the gun home with me that night. After I had seen what seemed like a hundred different guns, the salesman, whose name was Clint, showed me some automatics. I liked the automatics much better. It was obvious that he did, too.

When he started going into the various types of automatics I felt like I was listening to Sidney Fontaine explain why he liked models of steam engines better than diesel engines on his H.O. railroad layout. The old six-shooters have some romance about them, he explained, because of the romance of the period itself. Some of them are beautiful and interesting but mostly revolvers are ugly. On the other hand, guns like the Walther P-38 and the German Luger have an interesting look to them. Some boats look special and some don't. Some women look special and some don't. Guns seemed to be the same. I mentioned this thought to Clint and he agreed.

"You got it. I don't know too much about boats but I know something about women. Ugly ones can function but the good looking ones function better." He was a good looking young guy and I suspected he knew something about women.

After listening to Clint explain the history of the Colt .45, and how it was developed specifically to stop a charging man, I decided to buy a particular Luger. It was not the best choice for what I needed but I liked the looks of it. Clint then took the gun apart and showed me how the serial number #2630, was the same on all of the parts. This he said was very important since it meant they were all the original parts.

I bought a few boxes of 9mm ammunition and Clint took me into the range, a large room divided into lanes. He gave me some ear protectors, set up a target, and showed me how to load and fire the weapon. I found that my hands were steady, since I used them so much in surgery, and that my eye was good. I took the Luger home with me that night.

I talked to Rocket on the telephone just before I went to bed. Everything was all set for our weekend trip to Norman's Cay. She would have to take some unpaid leave because she had used up her vacation time on our cruise but the plans were set. I was going to pick her up early and she would be packed.

About three o'clock in the morning the telephone rang and it was Rocket in tears. Her mother had just called with the tragic news that her father had died unexpectedly from a coronary. She would go home immediately. I told her I'd drive her to the airport if she was going to leave in the next few hours. She hung up and I got dressed. Before I had finished a cup of coffee, she called back and said she could get a flight to Dulles if she could get there in an hour so I got the ugly green car and took her to the terminal. There was no traffic so we got there in plenty of time and didn't talk on the way. She did ask who I was going to get to replace her on the trip to Bimini, but I had no idea at all, and had just about decided to go alone. I knew that a lone man wouldn't look as innocent as a couple, but I had to go, and I had no idea what things were like on the island.

I offered to park the car and go into the terminal with her to wait for the flight, but she pointed out that there wouldn't be any wait if the plane left on time. I dropped her at the Delta entrance and got her suitcase out of the trunk. I kissed her quickly but made sure that I let her be the one to pull away first. Her mind was too preoccupied with catching the plane to be worried about the length of a kiss, but I wanted to make sure she felt at least a little warmth from me. At a time like this I wished I wasn't such a cold person and could demonstrate my concern if not my feelings.

Driving back toward Coconut Grove I started to try to put Rocket out of my mind and think about the trip to Norman's Cay. After a few minutes of this I realized that the only thing that made any sense was to call Snake immediately and tell him about Rocket. I turned off the main highway at the first exit and looked for a coin telephone. It was a almost five o'clock in the morning and still dark when I spotted a 7-11 with a telephone booth in front. I pulled out my address book and started to flip the pages from the back and got the page with "W". Winter, Carl and Lisa. I had crossed out Carl when he died, but I had three numbers still listed for Lisa. I suddenly remembered the last time I had seen her and what she said.

It was at lunch one day at the Café Europa. I had finally persuaded her to see me again. Carl had been dead for almost a year and except for conversations at the Church, she wouldn't see me or go out with me. I had told her how I felt about her and insisted she explain why she changed so suddenly when Carl died.

"Winfield, I don't want to see you any more. I love you but I'm not in love with you. At this point in my life I can't afford a relationship that would be that intense. I couldn't handle it. If I kept seeing you I might fall in love and I can't take that chance. I do love you, though, and if there is ever a time when you need help from me please ask. I will do anything to help you. Anything."

She had gone on to tell me that she knew I was independent and would not want to ask for help, but that Carl had left her a lot of money. The part that I remembered when I flipped through my book was her saying she would do anything to help me. I skipped over the numbers for Bar Harbor and Sun Valley and dialed the number in Coral Gables. After three rings she answered. I had rehearsed what I wanted to say so I could be as clear as possible.

"Lisa, this is Devlin. I have an emergency and I need your help very, very badly. I need you to go some place with me for four days. I need you to leave with me on an airplane at eight thirty this morning, three hours from now. We'll be back on Monday around noon. It's very complicated and I would have to explain it in person, not over the telephone. It's very important. Can you do it?"

She hesitated for only a few seconds.

"Yes. I can do it. Do I meet you someplace or will you pick me up or what?"

"I'm not at home. I'll go home and get my things and pick you up around seven. The plane leaves from Miami International at eight thirty."

"Tell me what to bring, what kind of clothes should I pack?"

"We'll probably be eating dinner in the restaurant two or three times and they used to require a coat and tie. Other than that just bring bathing suits and casual clothes. A dress or two."

"I'll be ready. I'll meet you in the kitchen. Just walk in when you get here."

We hung up and I called Snake. There was no answer. We had decided it was too risky for him to fly in to Norman's Cay with us, but he had probably gone over to Staniel Cay to check it out for what he called a staging base. It was getting light when I went into my apartment and got my things. I had packed the night before so I was there for only a few minutes. It was another twenty minutes more before I pulled into the gate at Lisa's house. I drove around the circular driveway and got out of the car. The front door was open so I walked back through the house to where I saw a light in the kitchen.

"Do we have time for a quick cup of coffee?" she said, as she handed me a cup.

"Yes. We have a couple of minutes."

"I'm all ready to go except for waking up. My body is moving around but my brain is still upstairs asleep. I guess you're used to getting up at strange hours for medical emergencies but I'm not. We can talk in the car. Let me sleep until then."

We finished our coffee without talking. I couldn't help staring at her. It had been a long time since I had talked to her and it was a shock. I had tried to convince myself since then that the impact of her physical beauty had been mostly in my imagination. Only a few days ago I had been staring at the Spanish girl Antonia and wondering if anyone could be more beautiful. Antonia's beauty seemed perfect to me as both an artist and as a cosmetic surgeon. It also seemed perfect to me as a man and I couldn't help making a comparison as I looked at Lisa.

They both seemed equally beautiful until Lisa saw me staring and said something. As soon as she started moving her eyes and lips the facial movements made her into a different person, even more beautiful. I thought for a moment that her face was like a diamond with a different face or facet being revealed each time it was turned. As soon as I had the thought another one passed through. I realized I was full of shit. It would take a poet to describe the extra dimensions of her face. I helped her with her two small bags and we went out to the car. The sun had come up, revealing my dirty ugly green car.

"Whose car did you borrow?"

"It belongs to a friend of mine," I lied.

"Where are we going? This sounds important."

I told her the story I had told Bill Gaines, except I didn't tell her who the friend was. I also didn't tell her anything about Snake's sister and how she had been used. I showed her the advertisement for Norman's Cay in the Yachtsman's Guide which I had brought with me. I was careful to explain that we were going as tourists only and that we wouldn't do anything but look around.

"We have to pretend that we are just a couple that came over for the weekend to have some fun. Don't even say anything when we're alone that would be suspicious. If you have to tell me something or ask me something, say you want to go for a walk on the beach. When we are absolutely sure we can't be overheard then we can talk."

"What about when we're alone in the cottage. Is it separate from the other buildings?"

"I don't know. Probably. I think we should act like lovers even when we're alone, except of course we won't be making love. I don't know anything about this kind of thing. If the villas are bugged it would not be because of us, but later we could be tied to the rescue. On this trip we don't actually do anything but try to find out where the man lives."

"What's the drug dealer's name?"

"Wouldn't it be better if you didn't know?"

"You mean because I might act funny if I met him?"

"Yes. You're not trained to do this sort of thing. Neither am I. If you hear anybody's name try to remember it and mention it to me as soon as you can."

I told her to act completely normal the whole time even if I did something strange like wanting to go for a walk on the beach in the middle of the night. She was to just act normal and I would do the same.

"Why don't we really just be ourselves. Talk about what you've been doing and how you have been and that kind of thing?"

"Would that be easier for you than making small talk?" I asked, remembering how painful it had been for me to find out she wouldn't see me after her husband died.

"It wouldn't be easier but it would be more realistic. I don't think I would know how to act in a situation like this. I have never gone away for a weekend with an unmarried man."

I had to be flip and try to make a cute remark.

"You mean you always go away with married men."

I knew I shouldn't have said it, but being with her made me act like a jerk sometimes. She didn't respond and we drove in silence the rest of the way to the airport. It was a beautiful day with no clouds in the sky. A perfect day for flying. It was power-boat weather. No wind at all. We checked in at the terminal and waited for about a half hour until the plane arrived then went aboard and got seats together. The big jet took off within ten minutes after we fastened our belts, circled once over the Everglades and then turned east for Nassau. I was off to the Bahamas again. This time I was going with Lisa Winter and we were going to look for a girl named Sharon Heather Moran, the sister of a man called the Snake.

Chapter Eleven

Friday, 9 June
The flight to Nassau was only a little over an hour and we both slept most of the way. When we landed at the International Airport and cleared customs, I pulled out the directions and instructions that Lori had gotten for me. The Norman's Cay Club had made arrangements for us to be flown down to the island in a small plane which charged people about twice what it would have cost on a regular airline. It operated on a non-scheduled basis around the islands and went everywhere. We carried our bags to the hangar described to us by the people in Fort Lauderdale and asked for a pilot named Charley Murphy. He turned out to be a tall, tanned man in faded khaki shirt and slacks.

We introduced ourselves and Charley told us it was about forty five miles to Norman's and would take only a short time. I paid him in advance as I had been told to do. When he accepted my traveler's checks, I noticed that he had whiskey on his breath and I wondered if he was sober enough to fly.

We loaded our baggage into his plane, a Cessna, and climbed aboard. When he saw my fins and mask he told me the diving was good at Norman's but sometimes there were a lot of hammerhead sharks around the harbor there. Minutes later we taxied into position and were cleared for takeoff. I sat in the seat next to him and watched him carefully. I didn't know anything about flying but I thought I could tell if he was drunk or not. He opened up the throttle and nursed the plane up off the asphalt. I relaxed a little and looked out the window. He seemed to be O.K.

Lisa, in the seat behind us, was also looking out. We could see tops of pine trees and then a white beach. After a few minutes we could see the water, first a translucent shade of green and then suddenly deep blue. We turned slowly and headed southeast toward the Exumas across what is called the Yellow Bank. It's fairly shallow water, only ten to fifteen feet in most places, with coral heads that sometimes come within three or four feet of the surface. Yachts crossing the bank are told by the books to proceed with caution, but unless you cross at night there's no problem spotting the heads. I've seen them but I never had any trouble.

The Exuma Cays sweep in a chain from Beacon Cay in the north to the islands of Great and Little Exuma in the south. Many sailors who have cruised all over the world claim it's the most beautiful cruising area in the Western Hemisphere. Personally, I felt it lacked only the spectacular views of nearby land that you find in Maine and Nova Scotia, or in the Pacific Northwest. Since I was born in Nova Scotia and spent my early years in that part of the world I remembered it vividly.

Supposedly there are three hundred and sixty five islands in the Exuma chain, one for each day. I think somebody just made that up, but there are some of the most beautiful anchorages and harbors you can find anywhere. Towns and marinas are few and far between so you're pretty much on your own. The little towns are picturesque and very primitive. You can cruise for days on end and not see many other boats except maybe local smacks fishing or gathering conch. The northern tip of the Exumas are only a one day sail from Nassau but they seem remote and far away from the fast pace of a city. The Bahamas all over, and especially the Exumas, are spectacular from the air at a low level. I had gone across the Yellow Bank a few times but never flew over it, and I looked out during most of the short flight, trying to identify the various islands. We flew pretty much the same course a boat would sail, over to Highborne Cay and then down the chain.

Norman's Cay is the most westerly island of the chain. As we flew down the string of islands it looked like a paradise. It's a hook-shaped coral island in the middle of a turquoise sea with a white sand beach four miles long. It's a favorite anchorage of many of my sailing friends because it's sheltered on three sides by land and is ideal for sitting out the Northers that sometimes come through. I remembered that the island store sold excellent wine and that the restaurant at the Norman's Cay Yacht Club and Hotel served a fabulous dinner. I wondered if they still required men to wear coats and ties, a practice which was really unusual in the Bahamas.

Soon I could make out Saddle Cay, which was north of Norman's Cay and then a little later the long white beach on the western side and the airstrip. Charley Murphy circled around and came in for a smooth landing. We taxied up to one end of the runway and he turned off the engine. There was a jeep there and a tall, handsome Bahamian woman came over to us and introduced herself as Cecelia Cotten, the manager of the hotel. After saying goodbye to Charley, we got in the jeep with her and drove down a short road that was lined with palm trees, past some well-kept tennis courts and a few buildings. The courts were clay and looked like they were well constructed but there was not a person in sight and it was too hot for tennis.

We parked the jeep and walked up a few steps to the hotel building, which was on top of a small hill with the dock and yacht club not far away. There was a sign over the entrance that said "Norman's Cay Club." The manager held the door open and we entered the lobby. It was a small square room with a glassed-in bar and dining room to the left and a reception counter to the right.

Cecelia pulled out the book and I signed as Dr. and Mrs. Devlin from Miami. Lisa was watching me closely, probably to see how I signed. We hadn't had much time to rehearse and I hadn't told her who she was supposed to be. Times were changing and unmarried couples were allowed in most hotels without any real pretense. I had thought about it before and decided to sign this way but not to pretend we were married if we met anybody who asked. Cecelia wasn't paying any attention.

"We are booked up solid for several months in advance," she told us. "You were lucky to be able to get a villa on such short notice."

I was puzzled by this statement since Lori had told me she didn't have any trouble getting the reservation, but Cecelia didn't seem to expect an answer, so I said nothing.

"I'll drop you off at your villa. It's not far from here but you don't need to carry your bags on a hot day like this. We will be serving lunch in about an hour but you will have to tell us in advance what you want. Let me show you a menu," Cecelia said, and walked over toward the restaurant section. I followed her over. Lisa was still looking at the guest register. She came over after a minute or two and looked at the menu with me.

There were only a few things to choose from but they all looked good. We picked out what we wanted and Cecelia wrote it down. She spent a few minutes showing us a small diagram of the island and gave us directions to the Yacht Club and dock. I asked about renting a car and said I'd seen the advertisement for small car rentals in the Yachtsman's Guide. She said she would try to arrange for one by the time we came back for lunch. We went outside and she took us to our villa, which was an easy walk from the club. The villa was very nice but it was simply furnished, with a living room, bedroom and bath. Both the big rooms had sliding glass doors that opened out toward the beach about fifty feet away. There was a sort of kitchenette off one end of the living room. It was much nicer than a rental beach house you would find in most places along the east coast of the U.S. but not as plush as one of the better motel chains. Palm trees surrounded it and would have made it romantic under other circumstances.

I had gone over the plan with Snake a number of times and knew my primary objective was finding out which house the drug dealer owned. If I were able to find the house I might be able work out a plan to approach it at night and from the water. If that was something that made no sense we had a bigger problem. There weren't any houses on the island that were very far from the water because the whole thing was small and the land surrounded the pond and the harbor. The pond was shallow and north of the harbor. If you flipped a capital letter **J** upside down, with the long side on the left and the hook at the top you can picture Norman's on a map. The pond is to the north in the curve and the harbor is south of that and separated by sandbanks. A small shallow draft boat could come right up to the beach almost any place on either the pond or the harbor. Facing west was the four-mile white beach that looked out on the banks. Boats could approach the island only from east or west. From the west you come around the south end and go a little way north right into the deeper harbor where the dock is. From the east you come in from Exuma Sound, which is really the ocean, through an unmarked passage, directly into the harbor. You can get into the pond only from the east and only with a shoal draft boat. All this would be important later.

Finding out which house belonged to Emile Hogge would be a matter of asking questions of people we met. Asking at the hotel desk would be a last resort and one I would not do until perhaps Sunday. Snake had told me about several ways to ask for names without raising suspicion, but I couldn't ask questions until I actually met some people. We had planned that I eat all my meals at the restaurant, spend a lot of time at the bar, and talk to as many people as possible. I would have to learn as much about the island as I could even before I found out which house Sharon was in. We knew we might have to come after her without knowing for sure that she was even on Norman's Cay. Snake had said he would never tell me any more than was absolutely necessary because he had to use some of the sources or informants that he used in his job with Interpol. It was clear to me after several talks with him, that his life depended on absolute secrecy, and I wondered which of his eccentric characteristics were part of the job and which were part of him.

After Lisa and I had unpacked our bags and hung a few things in the single small closet, I suggested we go for a swim before going back to the club for lunch. I took my shorts into the bathroom and changed quickly, then hung up my clothes and sat on the couch with a copy of the Yachtsman's Guide. I had thought about bringing a chart over and marking it, but Snake said no. He pointed out that somebody would be coming in to clean up the villa and make the bed. There was absolutely no reason to be cautious since we had no connection to anybody on the island, but after we got Sean's sister there would be a lot of questions asked of a lot of people, and we didn't want anything to tie us into a kidnaping. Somebody might remember a map seen in a bedroom.

When Lisa came out of the bathroom in her bathing suit there was an awkward moment. The swim suit was modest enough, a one piece red and white striped thing, but there was no way to hide her body. It wasn't startling but everything was in the right place. I did notice that her legs were fairly long for a woman of average height. I was in pretty good shape from jogging and spending a few nights a week at a health club so I didn't feel awkward about the way I looked.

We went down to the beach and waded out into the water until we were about waist-deep and until I felt absolutely safe from anybody hearing what we said. I was being a little ridiculous by being overly cautious but I wasn't used to this sort of thing and I knew that Lisa wasn't either.

She looked around and started to smile at me.

"Do you think anybody can hear us?"

"Didn't you ever watch a James Bond movie? The bad guys have special binoculars that actually hear what people say a long distance away. They might be watching and listening now."

"I was asleep when you called me," Lisa said. "I still haven't woken up. Let me see if I understand why we're here. You have a friend, who has a friend. The friend got kidnaped by a drug dealer who lives on this island and you want to kidnap him back. I'm here as part of your cover so you can try to find out which house he is in so you can plan your kidnap. Is that all correct?"

"Yes. That's about it. The friend is a man. His sister got kidnaped. Having a woman with me makes it less suspicious looking, both now and later. Especially later. If we get the girl out, the drug people are going to want to know where she went and I don't want them to come looking for me. Or you. It also means that we can talk to women without looking funny. If I started talking to every woman on the island it could look like I'm on the make. I don't want some guy coming after me because I talked to his wife or his girlfriend."

"Why would a drug dealer live in a place like this? There's nobody here to sell drugs to."

"He doesn't live here. He lives in Miami in a big house. This is probably just a vacation place. I'm sure the people in his neighborhood in Miami don't know that he's involved in drugs and probably the people here don't know it either. He's not the kind of dealer who sells to people who use the drugs. He's got a lot of people who work for him who sell drugs to other people who sell it to users. He's pretty high up in the whole thing."

"Like Marlon Brando in the *Godfather* movie?"

"Something like that."

"Is it dangerous? Our being here?"

"No. Not this weekend. Not at all. I wouldn't have asked you to come if it was dangerous. We have to be careful, though, not to do anything that would be recalled later. Even innocuous questions could be remembered. Get everyone's name that you meet and make sure you get it right. Find out if they live here. When we have a chance to talk privately you can tell me the names you have. If we don't get the name and location of the house after a while, I'll start asking if there are any for sale. If you talk to anyone who lives on the island ask where he lives, and if it isn't awkward, ask who his neighbors are."

Standing there talking I was very much aware of her body. The water was crystal clear and we could see small fish swimming around, and wisps of seagrass on the bottom. We were forty feet or more from shore but standing close together and talking almost in a whisper. I had never been so close to her.

Most of the time I had been with her in the past we had been in a restaurant, or in a church, or in my office at the clinic. I had been separated from her by a table in a restaurant or by the desk in my office. My attraction to her was almost overpowering and I had never had another woman make me feel this way. While she asked questions I tried for the hundredth time to examine her face as an artist or as a cosmetic surgeon would. It was difficult because my feelings as a man were so strong.

She was so beautiful it was hard to be objective and my whole process of looking at faces got mixed up. Up close as we were, I could see how perfect her skin was and how even and white her teeth were. As always, though, the thing that amazed me was how her face changed as she turned her head or changed expression. It wasn't that she was so animated, the changes were small and subtle. The thing that was so amazing to me was how she could look so different with each expression.

"Is your friend named Joe, or is that none of my business?"

"My friend is not named Joe. I'd tell you his name if it made any difference, but there's no reason why you need to know it. I doubt if you will ever meet him or hear about him again. After this weekend you should just forget the whole trip and anything about it."

"Like they do in the movies?"

"This whole thing does seem like a cheap detective story, doesn't it?"

"Actually it's kind of exciting. I've never done anything even slightly adventurous in my entire life. I promise I won't ask any more questions than I need to."

The dark, almost purple blue of her eyes was brilliant. I wished we were there for a different reason and that I could take her in my arms and kiss her. Her mouth was not wide but the lips were slightly full and they looked like they had been designed especially for that purpose. Even without any lipstick they looked pink.

"Why did you think my friend was named Joe? Was that just an expression like *G.I.* Joe or *John Doe*?"

"Because of the guest register," she said. "Didn't you notice me looking at it while you went to look at the menu?"

"No. My mind was on Cecelia. I was wondering where she came from and how she got her job."

"In the guest register there was a column that had the name of the person who recommended each guest. After you signed for us, she had written Joe L. beside our names."

"I looked up Norman's Cay in the *Yachtsman's Guide to the Bahamas* and found an advertisement for the club and hotel with a telephone number in Fort Lauderdale to call for reservations. I don't know anybody named Joe L. I have no idea who it could be. When we go to lunch I can ask Cecelia Cotten."

"What are we going to do this afternoon?"

"We're going to find the dive shop and see if there's anybody operating it. A couple of months ago I was cruising on my sailboat in the Abacos, in the northern part of the Bahamas, and one night in the bar at the Treasure Cay Hotel we met a guy named Rick Norton. He was looking for a place to set up a dive shop. He bailed out of the Florida Keys because it had gotten so crowded. When Lori called to make reservations, she asked about the dive shop because the advertisement mentioned scuba diving. They told her that Rick Norton was going to set up a shop on Norman's and that if he was on the island he might be able to take us for a dive. I don't really know him since I just met him that one time. I don't much care about going diving but I do want to find reasons to talk to as many people as possible so I can ask questions."

We went back to the cottage and changed clothes to go to lunch. Just as before, we took turns using the bathroom to change. When she came out in a pair of pink shorts and sleeveless blouse I tried to act as if she had no effect on me. I didn't say anything but I suddenly got an idea and decided to mention it at lunch. I had brought along a small kit of water colors and if we found out which house Hogge lived in, I was going to paint a water color scene that included the house. I didn't think it would look suspicious and even thought people might come up to watch, as they often do when artists are painting on the street. It would give me a chance to ask more questions.

We walked the short distance to the club and found that the restaurant was in business. There was another couple standing at the bar and I introduced us as Winfield Devlin and Lisa Winter. The other couple said they had a villa on the island in a section called Smuggler's Cove and that they were from Georgia. They had been leasing their cottage for five years and spent several of the winter months down here. Since it was summer, I asked what they were doing out of season. They told us that they had come down because they had heard from some friends, who also owned a villa, that a lot of the old owners were leaving and new people were moving in. They said they hadn't found much going on, though, and were going back to Savannah in a couple of days. Lisa did most of the talking, asking all kinds of questions that could have provided information but didn't. The couple, whose name was Harbaugh, told us a lot about the island. They were middle-aged people who spent their time mostly reading and occasionally fishing. They did say that they usually had both lunch and dinner at the restaurant and that they knew most of the people who had been there a long time, but not many of the new ones.

"I do a little painting as a hobby. I thought I might do a scene on the beach, maybe something with the water on one side and the beach and some palm trees on the other. Do you have any suggestions of places that would be good for a picture?" I wanted to have as many reasons as I could for walking all over the island and I wanted as many people as possible to know about it. Snake had suggested I have reasons for moving around. We talked for nearly half an hour with the Harbaughs and asked them to join us for lunch. They declined and said they were going to lunch at the house of some friends. They did tell me where the dive shop used to be.

After lunch we found the dive shop, but the door was locked and there didn't seem to be anybody on the inside. I wrote a note on a piece of paper that I tore out of a little notebook and wedged it into the door.

The note said, "*Rick Norton. I met you at Treasure Cay in May. Would like to go for a dive if you are in business. Will look for you at the Club tonight. Winfield Devlin*".

We walked back to the Club and found Cecelia Cotten. I told her about wanting to do a watercolor scene and asked about the car. She said that it would be no problem and that they had one there I could use. I signed some papers and used a credit card then we went outside and got in the car.

"Go that way for I-95," Lisa said, pointing north.

"I've got enough friends who are smartasses. I don't need any more." I laughed at her anyway.

We spent nearly an hour driving around the small island and I began to realize that it was fairly unique. It was really like no other island in the Bahamas. The pond and the harbor were both only a ten-minute walk from the airstrip. You could be scuba diving or snorkeling on the reef within twenty minutes of landing in a plane. Because of the shape of the island almost every house had a private beach. The houses were very private and surrounded by pine trees. On the beach side they all had a stretch of beach and were partially hidden from the water by palm trees. Several times I drove right up long sand driveways looking for people, but all of the houses seemed to be empty. A few times we got out of the car and walked down to the beach. Although the island was small, I realized that it would take a long time to cover it. I didn't know what else to do. I decided that I would see about renting a small sailboat the next day and sail up and down the beaches until I had a good feel for the island up close from the water.

We drove back to the villa and went out on the beach. There was one spot where a huge tree had some branches sticking out to one side and it provided a shaded area within fifteen feet of the water. I didn't have an easel to work with but I found a card board box and set it up so I could prop my watercolor paper up against it. Our villa was on the western side of the island looking out over the banks. There was nothing beyond us except miles and miles of shallow water and eventually the ocean and Gulfstream. I started sketching a scene looking north up the beach. The sun was off to my left out over the banks. Palm trees came down close to the water in some places and there were a few villas that I could see.

It was a typical Bahama scene, beautiful but actually a little boring. I decided to add a little drama to the picture by adding a huge mass of very threatening looking storm clouds to the left, out over the water. The clouds were a little phony looking but they did add excitement or tension or something.

Around three thirty or four, Lisa went up to the cottage and said she was going to get a drink. I asked for a rum and tonic. A few minutes later a man came walking down the beach toward me. He was an older man, perhaps about fifty, and dressed in old, but not ragged clothes. He walked up and introduced himself as John Campbell and said he was from Tampa. He owned a cottage about a mile up the beach and spent as much time there as he could. I stopped working on my watercolor and asked him questions about the island.

After a few minutes Lisa came back with our drinks and offered one to John Campbell. He accepted her offer and asked for a rum and water. When she came back, we all three sat in the sand under the branches of the tree and talked. I directed the conversation toward Norman's Cay and the people living on it. Lisa asked him to tell her the names of some people living there. She said she thought she knew some people who had just bought a small house but that she had heard the story from a third party and couldn't remember which of her friends it was supposed to be. The story seemed plausible and John Campbell came up with ten or twelve names of people that had bought houses within the last five years, but there was no mention of an Emile Hogge. He told us quite a bit about the island, and it was interesting, but not really what we came there to learn.

Back in the early sixties a lot of the land on Norman's was bought by an American businessman named Bill Smith who then sold what he owned to a guy named Perrine. Perrine was a guy who had made his money by digging artificial lakes in the Midwest and selling waterfront property. Since the island already had most of its land right on the water it was a natural for that kind of development. Perrine spent about two million dollars trying to start a combination resort and housing development. He built the marina, the hotel, the tennis courts and a few model homes. His planning was good but his timing was bad because the Bahamas got their independence from Great Britain in 1967. Lynden Pindling and his Progressive Labor Party formed an all black government for a population that was ninety percent black. This scared investors away and Perrine went bankrupt. He sold his property to the Meridian Corporation, a division of a Canadian company. They sold to the company that held the mortgages and that company still owns most of the property.

Since John Campbell didn't seem to know anything about Emile Hogge, I eventually changed the subject. We talked some about other things and after awhile he left and we went back to the cottage.

We dressed for dinner pretty informally but I did wear a coat in case they still had the old rule. Lisa put on a simple dress but she was so beautiful that she would have looked good dressed like a bag lady. She acted perfectly natural about being in the cottage alone together. There was a sexual tension on my part because just being with her was exciting but I think it was all one-sided. She did all her dressing and undressing in the bathroom and also put on her makeup there. When she said she was ready she had put on a tiny bit of eye shadow and a dab of perfume.

"How do I look?" she asked. I stared at her for a few seconds. She had on some small gold earrings. Her sandy blonde hair had been bleached by the sun. Her dark blue eyes looked violet in the light of the cottage.

"Better."

"Better than what?"

"Better than anybody else I've ever seen."

"Thank you," she said, as if slightly surprised.

Although we had been alone before, I had never felt that it was appropriate to compliment her. She knew how she looked and I'm sure she knew the effect she had on men. I had wanted many times to find out why she had married a man so much older than herself. I'm sure that men had been chasing her for most of her life. Although I had gotten to like Carl, and to admire him when he was alive, he was not so special that a woman like her should have married him. All I knew was that she had been his secretary at one time.

When we walked up the little hill and in to the club I was surprised to see how crowded it was. Since we had not seen many people driving around, I figured the island was empty. The bar was almost crowded but we found one seat for Lisa and I stood up behind her. I knew immediately that it was worth having a woman with me, especially one like Lisa Winter. It seemed as though everybody there wanted to meet her. The men outnumbered the women about two to one and there were a lot of Latin Americans there. Much of the conversation around the bar was in Spanish. I knew what they were saying, but I made a point of not speaking any Spanish myself.

We met a number of people and Lisa always managed to work the conversation in such a way that new names kept being mentioned. We made a point of staying at the bar for a long time before we went over to sit down for dinner. I had told them when we came in that we would eat as late as they served, which was nine o'clock. I didn't invite anyone to sit with us.

When we did go to our table, I tried to forget why we were there and to just enjoy being with her. I could concentrate on Lisa, but with her there it was hard to concentrate on other things.

"Are you a good painter?" she asked.

"I'm a good one, but I never would have been a great one. I was studying art in college when I decided to become a surgeon."

"What made you decide to change your career?"

I told her the whole story about getting suspended from school and going to Paris. I even told her about throwing Milo Carter out the window, and about Laufenberg and his warning. I don't know why I told her so much, but I wanted her to know.

"Are you always looking for some kind of higher justice when you're not satisfied with how things work out?"

"Maybe. The shrink used those words. Higher justice."

"When I first met you in the lawyer's office you gave me a strange look, a kind I had never seen before."

"That was pure admiration. I thought you were the most beautiful woman I had ever seen. Maybe a little lust, too."

"I don't mean that. I know when I'm being admired. I mean later, when the lawyers were talking. It was the coldest look I've ever seen. It wasn't evil or mean looking, it was just ice cold. I knew when I saw you looking at me that we would drop the case no matter what the lawyers said. It wasn't fear or anything like that. You just looked so objective, like you wouldn't do anything based on emotion. You looked as if you didn't even feel any."

I didn't say anything for a few minutes.

"Is that why you wouldn't see me after Carl died? Why you wouldn't go out on dates with me?"

"No. That had nothing to do with it. I learned very soon that you were a good person. The problem was me. It still is. I just don't want to get emotionally involved. I just can't, and I don't want to talk about it. I care a great deal about you and I decided the minute you asked me to come over here, that I would. We just can't get involved."

"Is there another man in your life?"

"Of course not. Let's see if we can get some dessert and coffee." That was the end of the conversation.

We went back to the bar after paying the check, in hopes of meeting more people and hearing more names, but there were only the same ones that had been there before dinner, so we left after one drink. Walking back to the villa we didn't talk but I kept wondering why she had said "of course not" when I asked about other men in her life. I didn't understand it.

After Carl had been dead for a period of time there must have been many men, besides me, who came looking and hoping. Extremely rich and incredibly beautiful is an attractive combination. I knew that she had been very devoted to Carl and Bobby, but she was only a little over thirty. The way that Bobby got along with me made me think he would not resent another man in Lisa's life. It didn't make sense.

In the cottage there were twin beds pushed together and each one had it's own set of sheets. Lisa went in to the bathroom and came out a few minutes later in pajamas. They were functional type pajamas but they looked funny because they were much too big for her. I started to laugh.

"Those are the funniest looking pajamas I've ever seen. Did you expect them to shrink to half size?"

"They were Carl's. I don't have any pajamas of my own."

"Don't you have any nightgowns?" I said, as I started into the bathroom to change.

"None that I want you to see me wearing."

I had a very modest pair of brand new pajamas that I had bought specifically for the trip, when I thought Rocket was going to be with me, but she made no comment when I came out of the bathroom. She was half asleep but just before I turned off the light she mumbled.

"At home I sleep in my underwear."

I stayed awake for a few minutes thinking about that and wondering if she meant her underpants and a brassiere or just her underpants. A few seconds thought and I realized a brassiere would be too uncomfortable to sleep in. Just before I fell asleep I made a solemn vow to go out and find myself a new girlfriend when I got back to Miami. I tended to idealize women and having sex with a woman just to satisfy lust had never worked very well for me. During the three weeks on the boat cruising with Rocket, who was always in various stages of being partially dressed, I thought I would die of terminal tumescence or over-stimulation. I fell asleep wondering what kind of panties Lisa wore and decided for some reason that they were Belgian lace. Probably pale gold.

I woke up in the middle of the night because of some noise that I didn't recognize. I listened for a few minutes and realized that it was the sound of some kind of engine. The room we were sleeping in faced out on the water and the sliding glass doors were wide open to let in the soft breeze. I could hear the waves washing against the beach but there was another sound and I was sure it was an engine. I had gotten used to waking up in the middle of the night when I was a Surgical Resident in Manhattan and still was able to come out of a deep sleep and focus fairly quickly. The airfield was less than a mile away and the sound was coming from that direction. I sat up and thought for a minute. The airstrip on Norman's Cay was a long one and a good one for the Out Islands but it was not equipped with lights for night flying nor did it have the navigational aids that would be required.

All of a sudden the thought hit me that nobody would be flying at night unless they were doing something they didn't want other people to see. Like smuggling drugs. Jesus Christ, Hogge was a drug dealer. Maybe that's why he had a house here. Both Snake and I had assumed that his cottage on Norman's was just a vacation house. Or a hideout. I wondered for a minute if Snake knew something about Hogge being here that he hadn't told me. I decided quickly that there would be no point in not telling me especially since it was my idea for me and Rocket to come here instead of him. I decided that if people wanted to fly airplanes at night and smuggle dope there was nothing I could do about it. The purpose of my trip was to find out which house belonged to Emile Hogge and the best way to get Sharon away. The engine noises stopped and I rolled over to try to go back to sleep. I couldn't.

If Hogge actually used this place for flying in drugs to the U.S., then Snake needed to know about it. He hadn't told me what he did for Interpol. Maybe he could arrange to get somebody to arrest Hogge and free his sister without doing anything as crazy as kidnaping her. I got out of bed as quietly as I could, trying not to wake up Lisa, and put on some shorts and a knit shirt. As I walked over to the door I could hear the sound of somebody slamming the door of a car off in the distance. I put on my Topsiders with no socks and walked out the front door of the cottage closing it quietly behind me. I stood on the porch for a few seconds thinking about what to do next. I wanted to get close enough to the airstrip to see if something was being loaded on a plane. If there was an emergency, and a sick or injured person was being taken to Nassau, they could use the help of a doctor, but Cecelia knew I was a doctor.

I hesitated and tried to think clearly. If I walked over to the airstrip I might be able to guess what was going on but I wouldn't know if it was drugs. I knew that the only thing I could do anyway was to tell Snake what had happened. If I stumbled into somebody who was actually moving drugs, or watching out for people who were loading the plane, he would have to find out who I was. If that wasn't a problem on this trip, it still might be after we came for Sharon. Most of all I couldn't do anything that would cause people to remember me. It wasn't fear that made me decide to go back to bed. Unconsciously I reached down and took my pulse. I had gotten into a habit of doing that when I was a resident at Bellview in Manhattan and chasing ambulances. My pulse was normal. I always wondered why, at moments of the greatest excitement, my pulse never increased.

I went back inside the cottage, took off my clothes and got back in bed. Lisa, in the next bed, made a few noises but she didn't wake up. As I fell asleep I thought about it and wondered what it would do to my pulse if I ever made love to her. My last thought before I drifted off was a curious one. When I thought about other women, even ones I cared about, I thought about getting in their pants. With Lisa I thought about making love.

When I woke up around seven she was already awake and had fixed some coffee in the small kitchenette. The smell of the coffee was nice and I laid there for a few minutes staring at the ceiling and thinking how nice it would be if we didn't have to worry about Sharon Moran and were just there on vacation. Lisa noticed that I was awake and came over and sat on the edge of the bed.

"What are we going to do today?" she asked.

"Well, we're going sailing and fishing and diving and then I'm going to paint a picture."

"That sounds good. Can we eat breakfast first?" She handed me a cup of coffee and I sat up in bed.

"Let's go down to the restaurant and I'll check out the dive shop before we eat. I'd like to find out if Ricky Norton is on the island before we go off on our own today. If he's here I'll schedule a trip on his boat and then plan around that."

I stopped by the dive shop on the way to the restaurant. Lisa went on to get a table and order. I found the door open and there was someone inside.

"Rick Norton," I called out. "Is that you?"

"Are you looking for me?"

He was about five feet ten and well muscled. It was the man I had met a few months ago in the Abacos on Treasure Cay.

"My name is Winfield Devlin. I met you a few months ago at the Treasure Cay Hotel. You were looking for a place to set up a new dive shop. I guess you found it here."

He looked at me and seemed to remember our meeting.

"You're the plastic surgeon, right?"

"That's right. You have a very good memory. It looks like you've found your place. Is there any chance we could set up a dive? Are you in business yet?"

"I'm just starting to get set up and really don't have any boat here. I'm sorry. I hope you didn't come over here just for the diving. I've got to bring my boat over from Florida before I can really get in business."

"That's O.K. I understand. The people in Fort Lauderdale told me that you weren't really set up yet."

"What people?" he asked, looking at me sharply.

"I saw an advertisement in the *Yachtsman's Guide To The Bahamas*, with a telephone number in Fort Lauderdale. We called there to make a reservation for the weekend. The girl who signed us up said she thought that you weren't really set up yet but that you might be able to arrange a dive. Don't worry about it. I was just hoping."

"I've got tanks but I don't have a boat. Sorry."

"If you're around at dinner time I'd like to buy you a drink. I'll look for you at the bar. Good luck with your new venture. I hope it works out."

I left him and went back to the restaurant where Lisa was having coffee. They brought the food as soon as I sat down. I told her about my conversation with Rick Norton. It was not a big disappointment, but I was feeling a little frustrated about the lack of progress in finding out about where Hogge lived. As I was finishing my eggs and toast, Cecelia Cotten came over.

"I have a message for you, Dr. Devlin," she said. She handed me a scrap of paper. The message written on the paper was "Dr. Winfield Devlin. The patient in J-41 is doing fine. Lori."

I looked up at Cecelia.

"Was this a telegram or what?" I asked.

"It was the overseas operator. I took the message myself. It was a woman whose name was Lori. She said she didn't need to talk to you and that you would understand the message."

"Thanks a lot, Cecelia. I do understand."

"Good news?" Lisa asked.

"Very good news. One of my patients is going to be O.K. and I was a little worried."

We sat for a while having a third cup of coffee and I tried to think of some way I could find out which house Emile Hogge lived in. Just before we got up to leave I saw Rick Norton come walking in the door. He looked around and then came over to our table.

"If you're still interested in making a dive, I've got a boat lined up. One of the guys who lives on the island here has agreed to let me use his Boston Whaler for a few hours. Do you want to do it?"

"Sure," I said. "Sit down and have a cup of coffee."

I introduced him to Lisa and we talked for a while. It was obvious that he was a little uncomfortable with her looks. She was just too beautiful for an ordinary man to talk to without becoming a little self-conscious. She had never been diving with a scuba tank before and didn't want to try it now but she did want to go along in the boat with us and perhaps do a little snorkeling. We agreed to meet at the dock at ten o'clock. I liked Rick. He seemed to be a straightforward kind of person. Walking back to the cottage Lisa asked me if I had been very worried about the patient mentioned in the message. There was no one around who could hear me so I told her the truth.

"I don't have any patient in a room numbered J-41. In fact I don't have any patients in any hospital right now. I operate at my own clinic and two hospitals. Both hospitals have the same numbering system which has only numbers and no letters. Room 41 on the second floor would be 241. Room forty one on the third floor would be 341. Most office buildings use the same system. I don't know what J-41 means.

Lisa looked a little startled.

"Does Lori know why you're here?" she asked. Lisa knew who Lori was because of all the visits she made to the clinic when I was treating Bobby.

"Nobody knows why I'm here except you and my friend whose sister we're looking for. Somebody had to tell her to send the message or make the phone call."

"Do you think it was a real message that got mixed up or do you think it was a fake message that was supposed to mean something?"

"I think it was a fake message, and that my friend told Lori to send it, and what to say. I think the message means that the person we're looking for is located in J-41, but I don't know what J-41 is. Maybe the villas have numbers."

"Does Lori know her?"

"Does Lori know whom?" I asked.

"The person who asked her to make the call. She's a little bit immature but I don't believe she would make a call and send a message to you for someone she didn't know and trust."

"Lori knows my friend well enough to trust him. The friend is a him, not a her. The person on the island is a woman."

"Do you ever read detective stories?" she asked.

"No."

"Well if you had read the Nancy Drew Mysteries or the Hardy Boys Adventures you would know that J-41 is the number of the house we're looking for. All we have to do is look for J-41," she said.

"I'll tell people I'm looking for a vacation house and see if I can find somebody here who knows something about real estate on the island. J-41 has *got* to be a plot number.

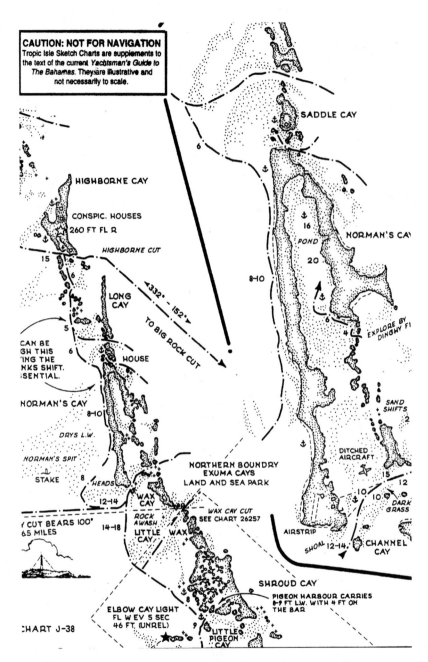

Copyright© 2001 by Tropical Island Publishers Inc., PO Box 8010 Red Bank, NJ 07701-8010 – All rights reserved. Reproduction in any form, including office copy machines, in whole or part, without written permission is prohibited by law.

Chapter Twelve

Saturday, 10 June
By the time we had finished the conversation we were back at the cottage and had almost an hour before we were to meet Rick. Lisa said she wanted to read, so I pulled out a book and we sat out on a screened-in porch. After a while Lisa wanted to know what I was reading and I showed her the book, a biography of George Gordon, Lord Byron written by Andre Maurois in 1930.

"That's a pretty unusual thing for you to be reading, isn't it? Do you know a lot about poetry?"

"I know a lot about Lord Byron. He's the only poet I ever read."

"Do you like him that much better than the others?"

"I've never read poetry written by anyone else."

"That's strange, not just to prefer one poet or one writer, but to read only that person."

"I don't have time for two poets. I only have time for one so I only read about Lord Byron and I only read his poems."

"Why don't you read any other poets? Maybe you would like someone else better."

"A friend of mine told me once about a system they have at Worcester Polytechnic Institute for teaching Literature and History and things like that to engineering students. They believe that depth is better than breadth so they don't have survey courses. They concentrate on a few things, and go into them very deeply. I probably have the system all mixed up but anyway that's the way I started with Lord Byron. I have too many other things that I'm doing to have much time for poetry. Like going sailing and painting pictures."

Later on we took the little car that I had rented and drove down to the dock. Rick had loaded the tanks aboard the Boston Whaler that was really an open launch with a canopy over the area where the steering wheel was set up. We motored out to the reef through water that changed from crystal clear, through various shades of aqua to a deep but not dark blue. *Ton Bleu Cerulean verit.* There was little or no wind, and when Rick cut the engine, almost no sound. A perfect day for a dive. I put on my mask and fins and the tank he had given me, then rolled backwards over the side. I waited for him and then we swam down to the bottom together. After awhile I came back up and told Lisa to follow me on the surface. We swam along together with our faces turned toward the bottom. My plan was to let her see what it was like on a reef and then later on if she wanted to, I would ask Rick if I could show her how to use the scuba gear in shallow water. We were anchored in about ten feet of water and swam toward an even shallower area. Sometimes I would dive all the way to the bottom and pick up something to show her. I had explained my plan of staying with Lisa and told

Rick to go off and do whatever he wanted. Although Lisa had not used a snorkel before she was a good swimmer and had no trouble swimming and floating along the surface.

After doing this for close to an hour, we swam back to the boat where Rick was already climbing aboard. When we had gotten back on the small launch and were headed in, I asked if there were any people from Miami who lived on the island, people who I might know. He said he didn't know many people because he had just gotten there, but suggested I check with a man named Paul Knudsen who was involved in real estate and owned some of the houses. He thought that Knudsen was on the island right now and that I might find him in the clubhouse at lunchtime or later at dinner.

After we tied the boat to the dock we waded out off the beach and I showed Lisa how the regulator worked. Like most people who have seen a reef up close for the first time, she was very enthusiastic about what she had seen and wanted to do it again. She was laughing and even giggling a little while we messed around in the waist-deep water. She was so comfortable with me, and laughed so easily, I could not understand why she would not even go out on a date. I had asked, but her answer that she didn't want to get involved with anyone just didn't seem to make sense.

When we got back to the dock, I pulled out some traveler's checks from my wallet and paid Rick. I told him we would like to go back to the reef the following day if he could get the boat again. He said that was fine with him and that he would see about the boat.

We drove back to the cottage and took turns using the shower, then got dressed and went to the restaurant for lunch, where we found a bigger crowd than before. There was a group of people standing around the bar so we went over and ordered two Pauli Girl beers in hopes of asking about Paul Knudsen. Lisa was sitting next to a plump little old lady wearing what seemed a lot of makeup for lunchtime and she introduced herself. The woman and her cousin were from a small town in Kentucky and had recently bought a cottage. When I asked who handled the deal for them, she said it was Knudsen and that he was sitting over at one of the tables having lunch. I walked over and introduced myself. He was alone and asked me to sit down. He was a sort of rugged-looking man with blonde hair turning grey, probably a Scandinavian. I explained that I was with someone who wanted to see some of the villas on the island. We had decided to have Lisa be the one who was going to pretend to be looking for a place. Knudsen suggested that we both join him and he could describe the real estate situation on the island.

Lisa came over when she saw me wave and sat down with us. She introduced herself and told Knudsen that she was a widow and was interested in finding some place where she could have a lot of privacy. He said he would have made arrangements if he had known she was coming. She answered that our weekend here was just for fun but if he knew of anything interesting she would like to see it. He told us that he had several houses for sale that we could look at and he could start looking for others. He also said that there were a few lots for sale.

We ordered lunch and ate while Knudsen talked. He was full of enthusiasm and stressed the island's privacy combined with its close proximity to Nassau and Florida. He suggested we take a look around that afternoon and explained some of the changes that had taken place in real estate laws. He didn't seem interested in anything other than real estate and did no fishing or diving but it was interesting listening to him talk.

When we finished lunch, Knudsen told the waitress to put the bill on his account and we went out to his car which was a small jeep-type car that looked foreign. He told us that we would start with the smallest cottage and then look at the other two. The first place we looked at was the furthest from the clubhouse and marina, right on the water facing the pond, and was really very nice with a large paneled living room. It had a kitchen area at one end and a huge screened porch.

Lisa really did an acting job, commenting on everything and picking out things she disliked as well as things she liked. I stayed completely out of the conversation, responding only when she asked my opinion. She didn't need any help and was really very convincing. Several times she asked questions that made me wonder if she wasn't really serious about getting a place on Norman's. After about fifteen minutes of checking out the first place, and even making notes in a small note book she had brought along, she told Knudsen that she had decided that she wanted a place that had more than one bedroom.

"I think I'm going to want a place with two bedrooms," she told Knudsen. "I really like this place, though. What's the number of the property?"

"It doesn't have a number. We're pretty informal here on the Island. Just call it the Jameson property."

"Mr. Knudsen, I am planning to have my attorney take care of the purchase, if I decide to make a purchase, and I have no intention of telling him to check out something called the "Jameson place". Every piece of property in every civilized country in the world has a plot number of some kind unless it is considered wilderness or some other classification. The Bahamas were part of the British Empire for many years and the British are not informal about such things. If you cannot provide me with some sort of document or map showing the plot number of each of the cottages we're looking at, I believe I have lost interest in buying a house here."

Lisa was smiling when she made her request, but it was clear from the way she looked at him, that if he didn't come up with plot numbers, she would consider him something much worse than an imbecile. The impact was startling.

"Why don't I drop you off at your cottage and go back to my office. If I can't find what we need there I'll call Nassau. If it's acceptable to you, Mrs. Winter, I'll be back in two hours. There aren't any telephones in any of the cottages, of course, or I would call you."

"Thank you very much, Mr. Knudsen," Lisa said. "My attorney would laugh at me if I asked him to purchase another property and did not give him precise information. If you can be back at three o'clock I would appreciate it very much. We may go out on the beach for a while but we will be ready to look at the other two places at three."

I had seen it before but I was still amazed at how a really beautiful woman could intimidate a man with one or two sentences and a look. Knudsen dropped us off at the clubhouse where we had left our little car and we went back to the cottage.

"You were terrific!" I said. "For a few minutes there I was actually wondering if you were going to buy the place."

She turned toward me and smiled like Mona Lisa. Standing there in the cottage that day, I wanted to put my arms around her so bad it nearly killed me not to do it. My desire for her was so great that I knew it would overwhelm me if I didn't get out of the cottage.

"Let's go for a swim. I'll change first."

I went into the bathroom and changed quickly into my bathing suit as I had to get away from her while I could still control myself. I was already beyond being able to talk normally so I ran down to the beach and jumped into the water. I waded out until the water was nearly up to my shoulders and then swam out a way. I treaded water for a few minutes and then swam back in. As I walked up out of the water and onto the beach I realized I had forgotten my towel. I knew Lisa would be in the bathroom if she hadn't already put on her swim suit so I walked into the cottage without announcing myself. It was like some contrived scene in a movie. She was standing there in the middle of the main room with her bathing suit in one hand and her brassiere in the other. She had nothing on but her panties which were a light ice blue color. We were both startled.

"I'm sorry," I said. "I forgot my towel."

I got a towel and my copy of the Byron book I was reading and walked back down to the spot where I could sit under the overhanging tree by the edge of the water. I sat down on the towel and put the book in front of me as if I were reading and tried to deal with my feelings. After I had calmed down I tried to think.

Rocket had told me one time, when we were about to stop being lovers and start trying to become friends, that getting laid by me was like "getting screwed by a mummy." She was probably not too unfair. I simply did not feel pain or happiness or anything else the way most people seemed to. Rocket was a passionate lover and a very good one. Part of it was because she was very female and simply liked making love and part because she got so excited she completely lost control. When this happened she did and said everything that came into her mind, which could at times be startling. She said that I was actually skillful as a lover but sort of boring.

I had been in love with Lisa Winter ever since I saw her in the lawyer's office, and had known it for sure the first time she laughed in the restaurant. I had probably been in love since our confrontation at the hospital because I couldn't think of anything else but her incredible face while I was riding in the taxi on the way back to the Yacht Club. Unfortunately for me it had been kind of an ethereal or poetic type of love. During the period of time when I was doing operations on her son I had seen a lot of her, much more than I needed to for just keeping her informed. I had explained in detail what each operation would accomplish and I had also kept Bobby up to date. I faked it some, and made numerous lunch dates with Lisa that were more like romantic rendezvous. We both knew those lunches were not necessary but we did it anyway.

We were having some sort of affair but it never went beyond lunch. She always seemed pleased when I called and I knew she really enjoyed seeing me. She let me know that, but she never once gave me any indication that she wanted it to go any further or that she would ever allow it to. I had been confused about her feelings for me, but not about her actions.

I had gotten to know her husband when he came to the clinic with her several times and I was invited to parties at their home on a few occasions. She was always pleasant and charming at those times, but not quite the same as when we were alone. Her husband had died suddenly about a month after we took the bandages off Bobby for the last time. Bobby had looked good, really good. I had changed his appearance slightly and he looked perhaps a little bit tougher or more rugged.

After the funeral, I had waited for several months before I asked her to go out to dinner with me. I made sure she saw me at the Catholic Church services and waved at her several times but I didn't want her to know I was there just to see her.

One day when we were talking at the coffee hour after one of the services, I had casually asked her if she would like to have dinner with me the next weekend. She had refused and told me that since Bobby was all right she didn't think we needed to keep on seeing each other. She told me in a nice way but it was very definite. I was too disappointed to even ask why. I had been devastated, but I kept on going to the Catholic Church to see her even though I probably would never have her as anything but a casual friend.

My fascination with her had not involved lust or physical desire. That part was always there, of course. She was too much of a physical beauty for it not to be, but it had never been very important. I had known that I would keep on trying to see her, even when she was married. When Carl died, and she would not even see me any more, I was really hurt. I did not get over it and I could not get over her.

I had learned to live with the ache but this weekend was just about all I could stand. Strong emotions were unfamiliar to me and I didn't know how to handle my feelings. I wondered if other people went through this sort of thing on a regular basis. Now, physical desire had been added to my other feelings and confusion as well. When I walked in she had made no attempt to cover up her breasts. She just stood there with her swim suit in one hand and her bra in the other. She didn't even look startled or surprised. She didn't say anything. Although I had quickly apologized and left I had stared at her long enough to remember every detail. Her breasts were splendid. When she was dressed they were very attractive and added to the package of her figure but naked they were startling in the way they stood up. It may have been my imagination but the nipples seemed very erect and almost cherry red.

Her light icy blue panties were almost transparent and the triangle of blonde clearly visible. The smallness of her waist accentuated both her hips and breasts. Lisa was a little over thirty but her body looked nineteen and incredibly ripe.

I decided after cooling off for a few minutes that I wasn't going to say or do anything about my feelings for her. She had agreed in the middle of the night to come with me for a pretty strange weekend and I was not going to forget that. If she were paying me back for what she felt was an obligation because of Bobby, then I would let her do it without letting my feelings spoil anything.

I thought for a few minutes about how I had been teased over the last few months. Three weeks on the boat with Rocket with her walking around in a tee shirt and underpants in the cabin, not teasing me on purpose, but driving me crazy all the same. Then the beautiful Spanish Antonia gets her heel caught on the steps and I spend twenty or thirty seconds with my eyes a foot away from her panties. She follows it up with comments that confuse and excite me. Then Lisa gets caught half naked and doesn't even cover her nipples.

I made a silent vow to myself that I was going to find me someone and screw her brains out. Soon. But not this weekend. Lisa came down a few minutes later and went into the water. She had put a book down on a towel near where I was sitting. As she came out of the water and walked up to where I was pretending to read, I realized that I was looking at her body and not her face. She sat down on her towel and picked up her book.

"Are you still reading about Byron?" she asked. We did not mention that I had walked in when she had no clothes on. While we sat there we didn't talk much, but not because I had seen her naked or almost naked. We both knew that Knudsen might come back with the information we needed. That is what I tried to think about.

When he did come back at three o'clock, we were ready. He came up to the door of the cottage and told us he had a map of the island that showed plot numbers for each of the parcels of land. It was a map made by the British and was more than ten years old but it showed what we wanted. Since we had to go ahead with the charade, I let Lisa do all of the talking again. She took a quick look at the map and ignored it.

"Thank you so much, Mr. Knudsen. That's exactly what I was expecting. You are terribly efficient. Let's look at the other houses. Surely there are more than two available."

The next three hours were amazing. Lisa flirted with him and bossed him around and assured him that she wanted him to be her real estate agent on the island, even if she bought a house he didn't show us that day. As a spectator I kept pretty much silent. The act that she was putting on wasn't really too hard for her since she was very wealthy and had obviously bought some property before. Actually, she was far more businesslike than I would have been, asking questions that amazed me and sometimes baffled Paul Knudsen. We went all over the island, covering some of it two or three times. While we were driving between the first and second house, Lisa turned to me in the back of the car and asked if I had made notes as to the plot number of the house, the number of rooms and other things. When I said I hadn't she pretended to be annoyed.

"Paul, give him the map so he can take care of the details," she said. It was the first time she had called him by his name and the way she said it implied that I was only the note taker and of no real importance in what they were doing. I'm sure that I would have been lighting her cigarettes if she smoked. After we had seen the three houses that Knudsen represented, she insisted that we see anything else that even might be for sale. At one point she actually asked to see only the nicest houses on the island.

There was no trouble in finding J-41 on the map and then figuring out which house it was. It was on the west side of the island, right on the beach, with the houses on each side of it nearly fifty yards away. Of course, I didn't know if J-41 meant anything anyway. I didn't know what Snake's resources were. He could have gotten the information from anywhere. If the message that Lori sent didn't come from Snake then she would have some explaining to do. Maybe J-41 was the apartment number of Lori's latest boy friend.

After one last look at the one-bedroom cottage where we started out, Paul Knudsen dropped us off back at our place. Lisa told him that she didn't think we would be going to the club for dinner because she was too tired, but that she wanted to meet him for lunch the next day. He said he would be looking forward to it.

As soon as we got inside the cottage I motioned for her to come out back on the beach. There was no reason in the world to think that someone had bugged the cottage because of us, but I had never been involved in planning a kidnap. I'd never worried before about anything I said. When we had gotten seated in the sand under the tree I said, "You were fantastic."

"Did you figure out which house you are looking for? Did you get what you wanted?"

"The house is on the west side of the island. We won't learn anything about it when we go out with Rick Norton because the reefs are on the east side, but I want to make the dive anyway. After lunch tomorrow we'll rent a Hobie Cat from the club and sail up that stretch of the beach. I want to see if I can find the house coming in from the water. I'm also going to try to go out on the beach from one of the houses on either side and pretend I'm doing a watercolor. If J-41 is the plot number then we've accomplished most of what I wanted."

"So far though we haven't heard anyone mention the name Hogge and I've been afraid to ask. If J-41 is not the plot number then we haven't accomplished anything. When we go to dinner we have to work harder at getting some names. Are you really too tired to go there for dinner?"

"No. I just said that so he wouldn't ask us to sit with him. If he shows up there tonight, we might have to be polite and have dinner with him, but we need to meet more people so we can ask more questions and hear more names."

We talked for a few more minutes and then Lisa said she wanted to take a shower. After standing up she said, "I'm sorry I let you catch me undressed today. I shouldn't have been so careless. Maybe you thought I did it on purpose but I didn't. I hope you didn't think that."

While she was in the shower I wondered about what she said.

A woman like Lisa would be admired constantly by all men, but perhaps she had never been admired for her naked beauty before. I didn't understand it, but I knew she was a tremendously complex woman.

We did the same thing at the clubhouse as the night before. We found a place where Lisa could sit on a stool and I could stand behind her, ordered rum swizzles, and looked over the crowd. I left Lisa for a minute to make sure they had made a reservation for us with the cook. Many places in the Out Islands operate that way. You tell them a few hours ahead of time, or you don't eat. When I came back, Lisa had started a conversation with another couple, some people from Texas. She introduced me to them and we heard all about the fish he caught that afternoon. Lisa was pumping them for names of people, under some pretext, and actually getting a lot of them.

At one point she described some of the houses near and including J-41 and asked if they knew who owned the houses. She told them she was planning to buy a house but wanted to know who her neighbors were going to be. It was a good ploy and worked well. The couple, whose name was Barnes or Burns, mentioned more than twenty people, but not Emile Hogge.

After awhile I figured we had gotten all we could from the Barnes and I started a conversation with the man next to me at the bar on the other side. His name was Felderman and he was the professional captain of a boat called

Valkyrie anchored out in the harbor. It was a fifty-foot Hatteras, and I was a sailor, so we talked about boats, but there was no reason to try to get names from him since he had just come in that afternoon and knew nobody. I was polite but I didn't waste much time talking to him.

"Excuse me, you are Dr. Devlin, I believe."

I turned and looked into the eyes of a dark-haired man I had seen at Treasure Cay the same night I met Rick Norton. I recognized him immediately, partly because I'm so conscious of faces, and partly because of the man's presence. His eyes were alert and intelligent, and he had a wide friendly grin on his face. He seemed to be proud of remembering my name and genuinely glad to see me again.

"We met at the Treasure Cay Hotel a couple of months ago," I said. "It's good to see you again. Was it Joe?"

"Yes, Joe Lehder."

He looked to be about thirty, perhaps a little younger. He had a trim and muscular body and his face was unlined and fairly handsome. With his long hair and boyish looks he seemed to be just about right for Lori and her generation. It was obvious, though, that he was far more self-assured than most men of twenty or thirty. He was poised and very friendly and he had the eyes of a much, much older man.

After a few minutes Lisa turned around and I introduced them, explaining to her that I had met Joe the same night I had met Ricky Norton, and at the same place. Joe asked questions about plastic surgery. I didn't like to talk about my work in social settings, but he seemed very interested, so I told him about Joan Pegram and the gondola crash. Lisa listened intently. When I finished my brief description of what I was going to do to Joan, Lisa told Joe about the accident with the outboard motor, and what I had done with Bobby. I was amazed at how objectively she could describe the experience and how much technical knowledge she had acquired.

"How long will you be on the island?" Joe asked.

"We're going back Monday morning."

"I'm having a small dinner party at my house tomorrow night at six o'clock," he said. "I would be very honored if you could be my guests. Your presence would add a great deal to my party."

I started to accept immediately because I thought it would be a chance to talk to a lot of people, then I realized that it would be more natural if I hesitated and let Lisa make the decision. I looked at her.

"Oh, Devlin, that sounds wonderful," Lisa gushed, sounding very natural, but not at all like herself. "Please say we can go."

"Sure. That sounds great," I said. "Tell us how to find the house and what time to be there."

Joe Lehder described the house with the cone-shaped roof that we had seen driving around the island and told us to be there at six o'clock the next night. I didn't ask what to wear because I figured I would dress like he was, with a sport coat and tie.

"Enjoy yourselves, Mrs. Winter, Dr. Devlin," Lehder said and pointed to the huge buffet. Then he moved off.

"Interesting person," Lisa said. "He acts so much older than he looks. I didn't have a chance to ask him about houses. Could Joe Lehder be the Joe L. on the registration?"

"I don't know."

We talked to everyone at the bar including a very, very old man who was very drunk and seemed completely out of place. After introducing myself and saying that I was over for the weekend from Miami, he stared at me very intently for a few seconds and then spoke very clearly and distinctly.

"The situation is old and useless."

"I'm sorry sir, I don't understand."

"The situation is old and useless," he repeated clearly. I agreed with him and moved on to talk to someone else at the bar. I spoke to several other people but nobody who I thought might be of help. After awhile we went over and sat down at our table and had dinner. We were both very tired and didn't talk much while we were eating. During dessert, Lisa did ask me a question that made me wonder what she had been thinking about since I picked her up Friday morning.

"Do you ever eat at the Café Europa anymore?"

This was a question that could mean a lot of things. It had been a new restaurant in Coconut Grove and had opened up a few months after Carl Winter died. I had taken Lisa there for dinner, planning to tell her that I was in love with her, and that I wanted to see her as much as possible. Instead she had told me that she didn't want to get involved with another man and didn't think we should go out together again. It had been a very painful night for me. Bringing up the Café Europa could have meant a lot of things, or nothing.

"I didn't go there for a long time until some friends went as a group and I didn't have much choice," I said. "The night that you and I went there wasn't the highlight of my social season. It was painful for me and I didn't understand. Do you want to talk about it?"

"I don't really want to talk about it but I do want you to know that I still feel the same way. I love you, Devlin, but I'm not in love with you. I can't afford to get involved with another man. Emotionally, I couldn't handle it. I'm not in love with anyone else, of course. I'm not even seeing anyone else. There's an old friend of Carl's and mine who takes me to the theater and sometimes to social things, but he's just a good friend."

There wasn't anything more to say and we started talking about what kind of season the Dolphins might have. To my surprise she told me she had kept the season tickets that Carl and she used for many years. She tried to take Bobby to every home game. She knew quite a bit about both the team and the game. We talked about football until we left the restaurant and went back to the cottage.

Neither of us was drunk, but we had consumed enough food and alcohol to want to go right to bed. We took turns changing in the bathroom and then went to sleep. I woke up in the middle of the night and realized it was raining, then I fell back to sleep.

When I woke up the next morning there was bright sunlight outside. I looked over at the other bed and it was empty. I went into the bathroom, shaved and brushed my teeth, and then walked into the tiny kitchen. I fixed a drink that was half orange juice and half Myers rum. It was my vacation special, and I enjoyed it even more than a drink at the happy hour. Sometimes on a long ocean race I would have rum and orange juice before breakfast. When I was working, I usually started surgery at eight A.M., so I didn't drink at all during the week. I think the rum was sort of symbolic of being on a vacation. Something like that. Lisa was sitting down by the water with a cup of coffee and a book, so I walked down and sat beside her.

"Have you been awake long?" I asked.

"A little over an hour. Can we go down to the club and get some breakfast? I'm starving."

"Let's eat now and then go right up to Hogge's house. I've decided to do a sketch of you on the top page rather than doing a watercolor of the house. I can use a big pad that I brought with me. Underneath, somewhere in the middle of the pad, I'm going to draw a map with a few things that can be identified in the dark. It's going to be very difficult to find that particular house after the sun goes down."

"Can't you have somebody find the house from the shore and guide the boat in. I don't see how you can ever pick out the right one. All of the houses along that part of the beach are set back in the trees. You probably can't see any of them from the water."

"You may be right. I'll try to figure out something we can pick out to guide us in."

Lisa changed quickly and we went to the club for breakfast. There was nobody else around when we got there and I think they weren't happy to have to cook more breakfast. It was well worth it, though, because they fixed a great seafood crepe, with kippered herring. For an Out Island Club the meals were pretty amazing.

Afterwards, I found Cecelia Cotten and arranged to rent a Hobie Cat 14 for two o'clock that afternoon. I was tempted to ask about the note that said "Joe L." on the registration but I didn't. We drove the little car through the palm trees and up the road where Hogge's house was located. We found a road that cut through to the beach about a quarter of a mile south of the house. I parked the car at the end of the road. I took out my pad and my easel and we walked north along the beach. The sun was still low in the eastern sky so there were huge shadows from the trees that came almost down to the edge of the water. We found a spot and sat down.

I positioned Lisa so that she was comfortable, facing me but looking out toward the water. I first sketched her head, blocking out the proportions the way I wanted them because I was planning to do the sketch as I always did, and not just fake it. To complete an oil painting I would have to get her to sit for me a few more times, and I wasn't sure she would do it. I could worry about that later. I got the sketch about half done and then flipped the huge pad over to somewhere in the middle. After making sure there was nobody walking along the beach in either direction, I drew a map of this section of the beach. There was a large water tower about a mile inland that I could get a bearing on that afternoon when I had the Hobie 14. We could use it to aim for when we came to get Sharon. I noticed several other things and sketched them on the map. Lisa was right. The beach itself was straight and the houses were set back in the palm trees and Australian pines. It was going to be very hard to pick out the right house and come in when it was dark. I suddenly had visions of Snake grabbing some woman out of her bed, and finding out when we got her to the boat, that she was just a fat lady from Topeka, Kansas.

I switched back and forth from the sketch of Lisa on the top sheet to the map underneath. After about thirty minutes of doing this I had finished the map. There was a lot more to do on the sketch but I thought we needed a rest.

"Let's take a break and go for a quick swim," I said. "I'm getting a little tired doing two things at once."

I had actually completed a sketch of the target house, as well as the map, and wanted to jump in the water for a few minutes before I started to concentrate again on the portrait.

"Can I see what you've done so far?"

"Sure. This is only the beginning of a sketch. Don't expect too much."

She stood with her hands on her hips and stared at the lines I had drawn. She looked perplexed.

"It doesn't look like anything, but at the same time it looks like me. How does an artist know where to draw the lines? You've got lines all over the place that aren't part of my face. I know a fair amount about art, the famous paintings and stuff like that, but I've never understood how an artist knows where to draw the lines or where to put the paint. I understand how you mix colors by putting two or three of them together to get exactly what you want, but how do you know where to draw all the lines. Are you born that way?"

"Natural talent is the big part of it, but art school of some kind is important. Most of the early masters were apprentices to established artists. I had both private lessons and classes. You have to learn the tools of the trade. Right now I'm using a piece of charcoal and a chamois. What I am doing is called blocking. I learned most of this part from an instructor in college named Jeremy Rose who taught beginning art students some valuable rules for beginning a face. His class was called 'Rose's Noses 101', by the students. He emphasized the importance of first deciding how long the nose was to be, and how all the other stuff like ears, eyes, eyebrows, and chin, could be blocked in proportionately. He showed us how to extend the nose length back in parallel lines from the eyes. This gives you the ear line.

"A vertical line drawn here gives you the center of the head. Two nose lengths from the center of the head gives you the chin and the top of the head. The head should be about four nose lengths high. The mouth is one third of the distance between the nose and the chin. It's all geometry."

"This is pretty basic stuff but it always works well for me. I have friends who can draw great female heads but not male ones. The initial blocking is the same but the finished eyes, nose, and especially the mouth are very different. For example, the female nose is usually more refined, being narrower and shorter with smaller nostrils.

"Blocking in your face was easy once I decided on the angle I wanted. I know my problem with you will be a harder one. With your face I'll find it hard to keep the finished work from looking like a glossy advertisement featuring Breck shampoo. It's going to be hard to keep from adding a few bogus lines or imperfections to make the painting look realistic. Maybe I'll put a wart on your nose or maybe some pimples."

With a different woman, one who was not so beautiful, I couldn't kid around like that.

"I have an unusual problem with you. Usually an artist tries to keep his integrity without hurting his model's feelings when the flaws appear on canvas. I've got to make sure you don't look too perfect." Lisa smiled and I guess she felt flattered.

We left everything as it was for a few minutes and waded out into the clear water until we were about waist deep. I ducked under to get wet and cool off.

"I feel like a character in a spy novel," Lisa said. "Do you think it's safe to talk out here? Do you think maybe there's a fish or two working for the drug dealers?" We both laughed.

"I know it seems silly but we don't know what's happening on this crazy island. I've been cruising in these waters for a lot of years and it's not exactly Smalltown, U.S.A. There are a lot of very rich people and many more very poor people. Nobody seems to know exactly where the money comes from and there is no income tax. The government is now black Bahamian when it used to be white British. Naturally there are rumors of corruption everywhere. There are thousands of little islands and very few policemen. The main thing for us is to avoid doing anything or saying anything that would make people think of us or remember us."

"Did I do all right yesterday with Knudsen? I felt it would be more realistic if I acted like I really wanted to buy a house. I've done that before, when Carl was alive, bought houses I mean. We had them in several places, and a beach cottage as well."

"You were terrific. I think you're a natural actress. Did you ever think of doing it professionally?"

"I have enough trouble acting out the part I play in my own life," she said, with a strange look on her face.

"What do you mean by that?" I asked.

"It's still very early Devlin. Is there a church on the island? Do you think we might be able to find a service? I just don't feel the same without going to Mass on Sunday, even in a beautiful place like this."

She didn't explain what she meant when she said she was an actress in her own life and I was really curious. I thought it was a very strange thing to say and wondered if it had anything to do with her refusing to go out with me, and saying she couldn't get involved with a man again.

"We could go looking for a church and I'm sure there's one on the island. Of course we could use my emergency portable church high service that I carry around in my suitcase."

"What do you mean?" Lisa said, laughing. "How can you have your own church service that you carry around with you?"

"I spend a lot of time cruising and racing on sailboats and out on the water someplace. A friend of mine, who's a priest, helped me design my own service. I picked out my favorite hymns and my favorite psalms. I have a bunch of sermons that I put on cassettes. I have the words of songs on paper that I can give other people. I've got the Lord's Prayer in Greek and a lot of Latin stuff. I even tried using incense once but the wind was blowing too hard. There was a boat anchored downwind of us and when they smelled the incense they pulled up the anchor. They probably thought we were the Hare Krishna and wanted money."

Lisa kept on asking questions and laughing. The sun was warm and the waist-deep water felt good. She was as beautiful as I could imagine a woman ever being and I was enjoying that, too. In the past I had been so entranced with her face that I had never paid any attention to her body, but being startled the day before, when she had nothing on but her panties, changed that permanently. Now lust was a part of my feelings.

While we talked and laughed in the shallow water we regained, for a short while, the feeling of closeness that we had felt so often during the period when we had met every week for lunch. We had talked then about Bobby mostly, about his last operation and his next one, and what he would look like at the end.

We didn't talk about ourselves very much but we had both known that there was no need for the meetings. We met because we had a special feeling about each other. That Sunday morning the feelings were back again. We were walking back, through the water toward the beach and the easel, when she asked about the hymns I had included.

"I've got all my own favorites, each one for a special reason. I've got the *Battle Hymn of the Republic,* of course. That's my favorite. And *Amazing Grace.* Naturally I have the Naval Academy Hymn. You know the one - *For Those in Peril on the Sea.*" I sang a few lines that were recognizable, but just barely.

"I have a few Gregorian Chants and *Jerusalem* for England. I also have *Onward Christian Soldiers.*"

"I don't know *Jerusalem*. What's that."

I sang the song for her just as we were sitting down again at the easel. As I sang I realized that I had forgotten about my being an Episcopalian and not a Catholic.

"Why do you have a song about England. What's that got to do with the Roman Catholic Church?" she asked curiously.

"I'm not a Catholic, Lisa."

"I don't understand. You were at Mass almost every time I was. I talked to you after the services and I saw you talking to Father Murphy and Father Torretta lots of times. If you aren't a Catholic then what were you doing there?"

She was sitting there in the sand staring at me with a funny look on her face, a kind of look of amazement.

"I went to the Catholic Church so I could see you. When Bobby had his last operation there was no longer any excuse to be with you again. I didn't want to stop seeing you, though. I didn't want you to just go completely out of my life. The Catholic liturgy is very similar to the Anglican and I lied to the priests. I'm an Episcopalian but it didn't bother me any to worship in a different church. It never has. It's the same God."

Sitting there on the beach with Lisa, and telling her about chasing her by going to her church was an emotional moment for me. I was very uncomfortable with it. I had cared a great deal about a few girls and women in my life but never with such intensity, never to the point of it hurting so much.

Lisa stared at me for a few minutes. Her beautiful purple eyes were bright and glistening. I guess I hoped she would tell me she didn't know how much I cared, and that she felt the same way. I wasn't prepared for what came next.

"I think that's the funniest thing I've ever heard. It's nice, I guess, but it's like a little boy having a crush on an older girl and following her around. Weren't you embarrassed at all? I don't see how you could have kept a straight face when you talked to the priests."

Lisa was laughing hard now at the idea of my following her around. I didn't feel any sense of humiliation, although I guess a normal person might have, but I was truly pissed off.

My rage disappeared quickly, but not my feelings of annoyance. I listened to her for a while and realized that she really thought it was funny, and didn't understand at all how I felt.

"Lisa, you arranged most of those meetings in restaurants. You knew it wasn't necessary. I never see patients or patients' parents outside the clinic. I went when you asked me and I did it because I wanted to see you. I thought you wanted to see me as well. When he was having the operations you wanted to see me often, but I don't know why."

Lisa was still laughing but she realized that I wasn't.

"It is funny," I said. "All those times I went to Mass just to spend a few minutes with you. There was one thing that I didn't know at the time, though, something that really changes things. I didn't know until just now that you were a total asshole."

For the first time since I met Lisa Winter she had filled me with anger but as real and strong as it was I knew that my words were just covering up the pain that I felt. I knew now how little I really meant to her.

I folded up the easel and put the rest of the artist things in my carrying bag and started back down the beach toward the car. I didn't look back until I was twenty yards down the beach so I didn't see her reaction. If she wanted to find a church, this was one time she would be there without me.

I decided to concentrate on the rescue and put Lisa out of my mind. I thought about what we had learned about the house where Emile Hogge lived. I decided that I would drive to the airstrip and see if we could find someone with a plane who could get us to Nassau. From there we could get a commercial flight back to Miami. I had seen enough of Lisa Winter.

There was no way to guess what I might learn if we had dinner with Joe Lehder and stayed on Norman's Cay another night, but the whole thing depended on finding the house in the dark and on Sharon being there. We didn't need to stay another night for me to realize that I was going to have to come ashore to guide Snake and the boat. I didn't want to be with Lisa any longer and I wasn't going to trust her to act the same role at Lehder's house that she had before I got pissed off.

When I reached the road where the car was, I turned and looked back before I went through the trees. She was walking along behind, carrying her things.

I waited in the car and a few minutes later she opened the door. Neither of us said anything and we drove off. I thought it over carefully and decided that leaving today wouldn't look any more suspicious than leaving tomorrow.

I drove down to the airstrip and parked the car. I got out and walked over to the small building near the fuel pumps and found two men sitting in the shade. I talked to them and told them I wanted to see if I could make arrangements to get a plane to Nassau. They told me they didn't think so, and because it was Sunday there was nobody around. They suggested I talk to Cecelia at the hotel. I thanked them and started to walk away. One of the men called after me.

"Why don't you check with Joe. He might be able to help you."

I started to turn back and ask about Joe, then changed my mind. I could ask Cecelia who Joe was, and ask how he could help. If he meant Joe Lehder I could do it myself. I got back in the car and drove to the cottage. Lisa was looking at me the whole time but saying nothing. Just before we got to the cottage I spoke to her.

"I stopped at the airstrip because I wanted to see if we could get a plane to Nassau today and go on back to Miami. The men at the airport said there wasn't much chance, but then they suggested that I talk to Joe. They probably mean Joe Lehder, since he's in the airplane business. I could drive over to his house and ask him right now, but that would mean giving him an explanation for why we are leaving early. We're supposed to go to his dinner party tonight. I want people to forget that we were ever here. Nobody walked by while I was doing the sketch so nobody saw us up close, but after we come back for the rescue anything could happen. The police could get involved unless the drug people decide to take care of it themselves. Anybody with half a brain is going to figure out that a boat had to be used and nobody could find that house in the dark without knowing exactly where it was." We were both still sitting there in the car.

"Do you want to leave today because of me?"

"Yes."

"I guess I can understand that, but I don't think you should change your plans because of it."

"I can go to the dinner at Joe Lehder's house alone and say that you didn't feel well."

"Are you saying that because you don't trust me or because you just don't want to be with me?"

"I really don't want to be around you right now. Trust has nothing to do with it."

"I think we should go ahead with everything just as you have it planned. When we get back to Miami there is no reason why we have to see each other again, but right now you need to help your friend. We wouldn't be here at all except for that. I'm just here for decoration. I can go out with Ricky and go to the dinner just as if nothing has happened. I don't think we should go home today. Helping your friend is too important."

I sat there in the car for a few minutes thinking about what Lisa had said and realized that she was right. I got out of the car and went into the cottage. She followed me in and we sat for a few minutes without saying anything.

"We're supposed to meet Ricky Norton at eleven thirty," I said. "If he can get a boat we're supposed to go for a dive. The reefs are on the east side of the island and Emile Hogge's house is on the west side. I didn't know that when I made the plans. We will probably learn nothing going out with him so the only reason to go is because there is nothing else planned. You can come with me or stay here."

Lisa said she wanted to go.

We got ready and drove down to the dock. When we got there I didn't see a boat at the pier so I went to the dive shop. I found Ricky in the shop working on some equipment.

"Hello Dr. Devlin," he said. "I'm sorry but I haven't been able to get a boat. The one we used yesterday is being used by the owner to go up to Highborne Cay to visit friends. I really can't do much until I bring my own boat over here."

"That's fine. I understand completely. Why don't you come up and join us for lunch. I'd like to hear about your experience in setting up the dive shop here."

"Please come, Ricky," Lisa said. "I would love to hear about your adventures." She had followed me into the shop.

He probably would have accepted anyway but he had been on the island without his wife for a few weeks. An invitation from a woman as beautiful as Lisa was hard to turn down. He agreed and we walked up together to the dining room. It was almost empty and I picked out a table where we could talk freely.

All three of us ordered Grouper which had just been caught that morning. It was excellent. Rick Norton told us all about why he liked Norman's Cay so much.

"The first time I came here I was fascinated," he said. "It was only a few days after I met you at the Treasure Cay Hotel. I went out for a dive with a guy who named Forbes. I liked what I had seen above the water but I wanted to get a look at the reef. I hadn't been on a dive for a long time and it felt good. I was in a great spot when I went down the first time. There were huge strands of Elkhorn coral, huge round brain coral, some radiant gorgonians, everything. When I got down deeper I realized that the reef was actually teeming with life. After diving for years in the Florida Keys, where the reefs are pretty much fished out, I was really excited. You know what it's like.

"Then when I was on my way up from down around a hundred feet, I saw four hammerheads come gliding by only about twenty feet away. One of them was about twelve feet long and the others a little shorter. I was fascinated. I just stopped there and watched them. I wasn't particularly afraid of them but I could see the little eyes looking around. A hammerhead is a real killing machine but it's so sleek and powerful that you could almost call it beautiful."

We got another cup of coffee and listened to him. It was obvious that he was an expert on hammerhead sharks.

"On the way in to shore, I learned that schools of them had been migrating to the island to mate in the pond as far back as anybody could remember. I'm opening a dive shop here, but what I'm really interested in is the sharks. I have a degree in marine biology and I'm sure I can get a grant from some foundation. I can do research when I'm not taking out dive groups."

Lisa started asking him questions and I was a little amazed at the pattern of her questions. I realized fairly quickly that she would use one question to set up another. She was a little bit like a television lawyer but with no intent except to make herself a mental picture of what the sharks did. I had never seen this facet of her personality before.

Rick told us all about his plans for raising capital, getting leases and finding a house on the island. His excitement about the hammerhead sharks mating in the lagoon was contagious. Rocket was with me when I met Rick the first time up at Treasure Cay. Obviously he knew I was with a different woman this time, so he avoided any questions. Lisa didn't know this but she started talking about buying a house on Norman's and started asking him questions about the island. While it had been obvious to me that she considered Knudsen to be a total fool, it was just as apparent that she liked Rick Norton and respected what he was doing. After our plates had been cleared away and the dining room had cleared out, he looked around to make sure nobody could hear what he said and then told us in a quiet voice.

"There's something I'm concerned about. Something strange is happening here on this island and I think it may be drug smuggling."

"What's happened that makes you think so?" I said.

"I don't know if you noticed or not but there are airplanes flying in and out of this place all night. That airstrip is not equipped for night landings but there are plenty of planes that land here. There is far too much traffic for just the people who have homes here and tourists."

As soon as Rick brought up the planes taking off at night I remembered waking up the first night and hearing engine noises.

"I heard planes taking off Friday night. There could always be an emergency that would require a takeoff. If somebody had appendicitis, for instance, they would need to get to a hospital in Nassau, but that strip isn't set up for regular night flights. Is there anything else? Do you suspect anyone in particular?"

"Yeah, there's a guy named Bob Word. Wife named Frannie. He used to work at Westinghouse and he claims to have been an executive. I don't know if he's a smuggler or not, but I do know he isn't what he claims to be. Seems to have a lot of money but he doesn't even have a good explanation for where it came from."

"Do you think I should stop looking for a villa here?" Lisa said. "I don't want to own a house on an island where the people are doing illegal things. I think you've scared me away!"

"It's only a suspicion, Lisa," Rick said. "By the time you get finished with the red tape involved in buying a house it will probably be cleared up. If I get something more specific than airplanes in the night, I'll go to the government in Nassau. If I were you I would go ahead with your plans, but you might check with me again before you finalize the deal."

We talked for a while longer and then he left to go back to the dive shop. Lisa said she wanted to go with me on the catamaran even though it would be a long sail, so I found Cecelia Cotten and told her I was ready to use the catamaran. She told me that one of them was down by the beach on the west side and another one was on the lagoon side near the Yacht Club. There were also two or three Sunfish with the catamarans.

I made a comment that there didn't seem to be much wind in the lagoon so we would go the other way. She told me she couldn't remember what the rental was, but it was off-season so she would charge me twenty dollars for as long as we wanted. I thanked her and said we would be about three hours. Just as we were walking away I turned and said to her, "Have you seen Joe L. around today? We're supposed to go to his house tonight and I can't remember what time we're supposed to be there."

"Our people are preparing the food for him and he wants it served at eight o'clock. He's probably expecting you around six thirty but I will try to find out while you are out sailing."

I knew the time we were supposed to be there but I wanted to use the name Joe L. and see how she responded. Now I knew that it was probably his name on the registration, written down beside our names. This meant that he knew somehow that I was coming over here this weekend, but I couldn't figure out how he knew, or what difference it made. Maybe he just remembered me and wanted to say hello.

We walked through some pine trees and down a path to the beach on the west side of the island. There was a small shed with four Sunfish sitting on racks outside. The Hobie 14 was sitting at the edge of the water. Although the masts and sails for the Sunfish were under a roof that had been built to protect them from the sun and rain, the Hobie 14 was rigged.

We pushed it out into water that was deep enough and hoisted the sails. There was a good breeze in the right direction so we could reach along the beach and hopefully reach back again later. Lisa knew nothing about boats or sailing so I steered. We went out about thirty yards off-shore to get out of the wind shadow of the trees and sailed north along the beach. I started to watch the silhouette of the shoreline to try to find some sort of landmark that I could find when I was coming in at twilight from the west side of the island.

If you start at the south end of Norman's Cay and go north, the island is mostly straight for a couple of miles in a west- northwest direction until you come to a point. One end of the airstrip is close to this point and a plane taking off in this direction is airborne only a few seconds before it's over the water. After you round the point and pass the end of the airstrip the shore curves in and then out again and then goes in in a long sweeping curve almost due north. The deepest part of the curve is about even with the other end of the airstrip, which is roughly parallel to the beach, but inland a little way. The house we were looking for was about a mile and a half to two miles beyond the end of the airstrip. Fortunately the breeze was strong enough so we were able to sail very fast, even with two of us on board. It was still a long sail, though, and took more than an hour.

Chapter Thirteen

Sunday, 11 June
When we got close to the house I thought belonged to Emile Hogge, we came in close to the beach. I sailed the cat back and forth for a few minutes, trying to find some way that I could identify the place where I had done the sketch. The water tower would be a good landmark when we were further out but close in it was impossible to see. I sailed the boat into shallow water and asked Lisa to hold it while I waded to shore. I found the spot where we had been sitting that morning while I did the sketch and I could see the house without any trouble. It was set back among the Australian pine trees and palm trees, about a hundred feet from the beach. There was actually some grass behind the house and a small low deck with some tables and chairs. There was even a barbecue grill. I walked a little closer, without getting off the beach, and saw there was a door leading into the house. If Snake did what he was planning, he would go through that door and then come out again with Sharon.

I walked back down again to the edge of the water and turned to look at the house. I stared at it and realized I was going to have to come ashore, find the house, and guide Snake in with some kind of light. In the dark, there was no possible way I could find my way back to this place from out on the water. I knew that Snake was going to have to drop me off somewhere and that I'd have to find the house walking around on shore. I waded back out to where Lisa was holding the Hobie Cat and got aboard. I trimmed the sails and we started back toward the south end of the island. We opened cold cans of beer and for a while we just sailed. Fortunately the wind was still strong so we could make good speed. On a normal afternoon sail I wouldn't have gone so far because of the problem of getting home if you get becalmed. There was no danger but it could be a long slow sail if the wind quit so I sailed the little Hobie the way I would in a race. The wind was strong and we were on a close reach. We had too much weight to plane consistently but we could do it part of the time.

Lisa didn't bitch even though it was a long sail. Rocket wouldn't have bitched either but she would have been having fun. I started thinking that maybe the quality I most admired in a woman was just not bitching too much. I thought I would try the idea on Gus and Sidney when I got back to Miami.

Sometimes I think best about the past and the future when I'm on a boat. When I'm working at being a doctor, I concentrate only on surgery. When I'm racing, I concentrate only on that. When I'm sailing a boat, but not in a race I can think about anything. I can even daydream about ladies' underpants.

We sailed on without any signs of the wind decreasing and I started to relax a little about getting back. I didn't want to be late for the dinner party at Joe's house. I had no particular hopes of learning anything helpful, but I did believe we should go.

I looked at Lisa. She smiled but she didn't say anything. I realized that she hadn't asked when we were going to get there, or why it was taking so long or anything. I couldn't think of any woman I knew who wouldn't have bitched at least a tiny little bit. I was still mad at Lisa for laughing at me because I had followed her to church. I guess it was pretty strange, but it seemed like a good idea to me. It had worked, and I was still seeing her, but I was pissed off that Lisa had invited me to have lunch so many times and arranged to see me so much. I didn't understand how she could do that and make fun of my efforts to see her. I had gone along with her plans because I was in love with her, or at least thought I was.

We reached the southwest point of the island just as a plane was taking off. It seemed to be only a few feet above the top of the mast and made a tremendous noise, scaring us both. The last leg after we rounded the point was wet and uncomfortable. We had been in the lee of the island before and protected from the chop. When we reached the section of the beach where the boats were kept we were both happy to be finished and to get dry. We put the little catamaran away and walked up to the car.

The long wet sail had accomplished little except to convince me completely that I would have to come ashore, find the house, and guide Snake in with a light. I knew I could find the road. It was not paved and it ran from the main road, through the trees and down to the beach. From there I could walk the fifty yards to the place where I had done the sketch of Lisa. That spot was right behind the house.

We drove back to the villa and took turns with a very noisy shower. The heavy sound of raindrops was starting to hit on the roof and it sounded like we were under a waterfall. I fixed myself two shots of rum with water and no ice. It was still a few hours before we were due at Joe Lehder's house so I pulled out Byron and settled down to read while Lisa took a nap. I guess I picked the wrong poem, *She Walks in Beauty*, because it reminded me of the woman on the bed in the next room.

I deliberately concentrated my thoughts on the night I had taken her out to dinner at the Café Europa. That had been just seven months ago but it seemed like longer. I had continued to show up at the Catholic Church even though Lisa always turned down invitations for lunch or dinner. But one Sunday, a few days before Christmas, I decided to force the situation. I told Lisa that I had to see her and that it was extremely important. I had not done this before and had always made my invitations casual and never urgent. I had deliberately made them seem unimportant. She had agreed to meet me for dinner so I told her to pick a night and she decided on a Tuesday, three days before Christmas. I asked her to meet me at the Horny Frog at five o'clock and to allow enough time for some serious talk.

I left the clinic a few minutes early and was sitting there at a sidewalk table when she arrived. Coconut Grove was decorated for Christmas with lights and wreaths all over the place. It was an exceptionally warm night so all of the sidewalk café tables were filled as crowds of people were having a drink after doing last-minute shopping. There was a store on the corner that sold nothing but bikini bathing suits. A woman at the next table had just come from there with what she described as the most exciting thing she had ever seen. Apparently she had bought it so that her boyfriend of the moment could give it to her for Christmas. She was a little pudgy for a bikini to my way of thinking, but she thought she would look wonderful and described to the woman at the table with her exactly what was going to stick out, and what was going to show, and how it would affect her boyfriend. Lisa and I listened while we sipped our drinks and tried to keep from laughing while our neighbor anticipated the reaction of her man. I was sure I heard more than one man's name but I couldn't tell if there was more than one, or if she just had trouble remembering his name. We sat for a while enjoying the strange combination of the festive feeling of Christmas with the slightly degenerate gaiety of Coconut Grove on a warm pleasant night. It started getting dark while we sat there and the lights were turned on. The music in the background was a combination of traditional Christmas songs mixed with Caribbean and Bahamian.

Eventually we walked down the street to the Café Europa. It had been open only a few months and had gotten a reputation for excellent food as well as atmosphere. The decor was European and deliberate, but not limited to one country or one period. I had made a reservation for six o'clock so we didn't have to wait. We were hungry, so we sat down and decided to order and have them bring wine right away, instead of getting another drink. I chose a good *Beaujolais* after we both picked out meat dishes. When the waiter left with our orders, I got to the point of why I had insisted on having her meet me.

"Lisa, I want to talk for a few minutes and I want you to listen. Then I want you to answer a few questions as honestly as you can. Will you agree to that?"

She nodded.

"I'm in love with you and I probably have been for a long time. After Dr. Montgomery explained at the lawyer's office that I was legitimate, you invited me to lunch and apologized for taking me off the case and planning the lawsuit. Of course, it wasn't necessary, but it was nice and I appreciated it. After that you made appointments for lunch, appointments in the office, and even meetings for dinner. You knew we didn't need to talk about Bobby that much or away from the office. I don't believe I have ever met with a patient or a patient's parent outside the clinic. I made myself available and helped you make plans because I knew I was falling in love and I wanted to be with you as much as I possibly could."

Lisa was listening carefully and saying nothing. I had never been able to concentrate completely on anything when I was with her. This night was no exception. Even as I talked, I couldn't help being aware of the perfection of her bone structure. Her dark blue, almost purple eyes with the long lashes were staring expectantly at me.

"When I did the last operation on Bobby, and got all the bandages off, there was no longer any real excuse to keep seeing each other. Even though you had given me every reason to believe that you had some sort of strong feelings for me, you never led me to believe that you wanted to go to bed. I think I might have tried that, but you never acted like that was what you wanted. After Carl died I didn't suggest we even see each other for a number of months. When I finally asked you to have lunch with me you made polite excuses, never cutting me off completely but never really encouraging me. When Carl was alive you had every reason to stop seeing me. You were a married woman then and Bobby's operations were finished. After Carl's death, you had no logical reason or excuse not to see me, so I stopped trying."

"I asked you to have dinner with me tonight," I had said, "because I want to understand what happened. I told you it was important and it is still very important to me. I want to know why you pursued me when Carl was alive but won't even see me now that he's gone. You acted as if you were falling in love with me. We had a lot of three-hour lunches that you arranged. I was in love with you, and I knew it at the time, but I also knew that you were married. If you had suggested that we go back to my apartment one day instead of having lunch I would have been happy to screw your brains out. You never asked for that and I didn't because you were married. I waited until six months after Carl died before I even tried to see you again. I hoped we could pick up where we had left off before the operations were finished and we were still seeing each other. I was still in love with you and I still am now. I want to know what happened. If you were never in love with me then why did you act like you were? If you were in love with me then why won't you see me now. I really feel that you owe me an explanation."

I stopped then, feeling that I had stated my case as well as I could. I poured both of us another glass of wine and waited for Lisa to tell me what had happened between us. She didn't speak right away and I realized she was trying to be careful.

"If I could fall in love with another man, Devlin, it would probably be you. The problem is with me and not you. I do love you, but not in the way that you want, not in the getting married kind of way, or in the go-off-to-your-apartment way. There is something about you that attracts me tremendously but you also scare the hell out of me. When we were in the lawyer's office, and your career might have been in jeopardy, you looked as if you weren't even interested in what the lawyers had to say. I don't mean that you looked like you didn't care, I mean that you looked like you knew that anything the lawyers said would be nonsense anyway so you weren't even going to listen. Even when your lawyer was talking you weren't paying any attention. Then you started staring at me. At first I thought it was anger or bitterness toward me and then I realized that you weren't even thinking about the legal proceedings – you were just examining my face. You looked at me as if you were far more interested in my underwear than in your medical career. It was frightening, but also terribly exciting."

"When Dr. Montgomery testified so favorably for you I was more relieved than you can imagine. I knew then that I had been wrong but I knew even before his testimony that you wouldn't lose. When Montgomery was talking you seemed a little surprised that he was so strongly on your side but you didn't seem relieved. When he was finished I just collapsed. I was ashamed of what I had tried to do."

The waiter brought us our appetizers, which were *escargots* for both of us, but Lisa kept on talking and I listened carefully and tried to understand.

"Afterwards, when we got home, I thought about you and I was fascinated. I wanted to see you and find out about you. I knew that a written apology would have been enough, even though I wanted you to help Bobby. I invited you to the restaurant because I wanted to see you and get to know you. When I kept on making plans, I did it because I wanted to be with you. There is something about you that is both frightening and attractive. Until today you never seemed to feel strongly about anything, but your eyes are like an anger meter or something. They turn this bright shade of green when you're mad. I learned that quickly but after awhile I learned that they also got very green when your feelings about me were strong. I guess there were some times when you wanted to take me back to your apartment and I thought I could tell by your eyes. When your eyes got really green, and I knew you weren't angry, I got scared because I knew it was lust. I wanted you to feel that way but I was scared when you did."

She paused to eat snails for a minute or two and then she continued.

"I realized that our feelings for each other were getting confused but I couldn't wait to see you each time. I knew you wanted me in bed, but I also knew that you wouldn't do it unless I asked you to. I knew that it wasn't fair to you, but I couldn't help myself, so I kept on finding excuses to see you. As time passed we didn't even pretend to talk about Bobby. Those were exciting times for me. After nine months and seventeen days, when Bobby was finished with his operations, I simply had to stop seeing you. I felt very badly about stopping it but I knew I had misled you. When I first called to apologize, I didn't realize my feelings and yours would become so strong."

We stopped talking to eat our dinner then, even though we both knew we weren't finished. I had Beef Wellington which was cooked to perfection, and

Lisa had lamb chops. When we finished and ordered coffee I asked her what happened when Carl died, but I told her my part first.

"When Carl died I waited for a long time before I tried to see you again. I was tempted often, particularly when I talked to you at church. When I did finally invite you to have dinner with me you acted as if we had never had those romantic lunches, as if we hardly knew each other. You seemed like a totally different person, as if I meant absolutely nothing to you, or even worse. You have been almost cold and I want to know why. I believe you owe me an explanation."

She tried to give me one.

"When I had my marriage as protection I could have a make-believe affair with you, one without any sex, without any real danger. I knew you were not the type of man that a woman could safely flirt with but I was a patient, or at least the mother of a patient, and that kept me safe. I could enjoy being with you without any real risk. Carl was more than just a husband to me. He was much older, of course, and in many ways he was like a father to me. We were well suited to each other. He loved me very much and took care of me. He protected me. I've learned how to act cool and sophisticated. People sometimes think I'm cold and aloof, the stereotype of the ice maiden. Above it all. You don't really know me well, but I'm really very weak and dependent. I have very little strength. I can act the part but that's all it is. Carl knew me and understood me.

"If I allowed myself to be in love I would be devoured. I would be overwhelmed. You're too strong a person for someone like me. I don't mean that you are not kind and gentle. I've seen you with Bobby and other kids, but there is something frightening about you. When I say you scare me, I'm not afraid that you would ever harm me. I don't mean that at all. I think you are the kind of person people would want as a friend because you would take care of them and they could trust you. I can't see you any more because I can't be in love with you. After a time you would destroy me. I don't plan to marry again and I have to protect myself. You would love me for a while and then you would despise my weakness. I told you before that the problem is me and not you."

I knew she was finished but I didn't say anything. We started making light conversation about other things and finished our coffee and dessert. I was glad I had invited her and forced her to say what she did. I was disappointed but I was glad to know there was not another man. I thought about what she said while we sat with a brandy, but I couldn't think of anything to say to her.

After I paid the check I walked down the street to her car with her and opened the door. I kissed her quickly on the cheek and then stood there for a minute. She sat in the driver's seat and looked up at me.

"Lisa, I listened carefully to everything you said in the restaurant and I think it's total bullshit."

I stood there for a few minutes and then said goodnight and walked away. That was just before Christmas. I hadn't seen her since then until I picked her up two days ago to come to the Bahamas and Norman's Cay.

I had not believed what she said that night in the Café Europa, but I didn't know what to do about her except to try to put her out of my life. Whatever there was or wasn't between us, she had come with me to this island and had done a fabulous job of helping me play detective.

I tried to force Lisa out of my mind but it was very hard with her sleeping in the next room. I tried to concentrate on planning the rescue. I knew I was going to have to get ashore to find the house and I was sure I could find it, even in the dark, but I'd have to figure out where Snake could drop me off the boat. I decided I would practice some more with the gun when I got back.

When I couldn't think of anything else I read a little more of Byron's poetry and dozed off. I woke up a few minutes later and Lisa was already getting dressed. She came out of the bathroom and for the first time ever I looked at all of her and not just her face. She was radiant and still slightly flushed from her shower, with wisps of blonde hair curly and damp. There was nothing soggy about her crisp cotton dress, with aqua and yellow stripes on a white background. One shoulder was bare and the top was molded fairly tightly around her breasts. The dress was fairly tight and accentuated her slender waist. Now, having seen her in a bathing suit, and then accidently with only her panties, I was aware of the whole package. Her skirt was short and flared and showed her knees. Even these were cute and I couldn't help staring at her bare tanned legs.

I apologized for falling asleep and not being ready but she said she had let me sleep so she could use the bathroom. I shaved again then put on my slacks and blue blazer. I decided to wear a sport-shirt instead of a dress shirt but I put a necktie in my pocket in case the other men were wearing them.

The rain had ended and the sky was clearing. We drove to Joe Lehder's house without saying much. The long sail on the Hobie Cat had tired us both and I knew we would have to work hard to stay awake and learn something at the party.

We had driven past the house with the conical roof several times the day before, so we had no trouble finding it. We parked the car and walked up to the door. It was open so we went in. As soon as we entered the first room, an attractive woman came out and introduced herself.

"My name is Marianne," she said. "Come in and make yourselves comfortable. Carlos is getting dressed and will be in shortly. Do you call him Carlos or Joe? What can I get you to drink?"

She was a tall woman with blonde hair, large breasts and a nice smile. She walked with us over to a bar, where I fixed drinks for Lisa and myself, and then offered to show us the rest of the house.

"Carlos has only owned the house for a few months," she told us. "It was built by a very wealthy minister who was planning to use it as a religious retreat. That's why it is so big. Carlos doesn't need a house with seven rooms, of course, but he really liked it so he bought it anyway. Isn't the fireplace nice?"

The fireplace was huge and looked like it belonged in a ski lodge or a Swiss chalet. The house was well decorated but I was more curious than impressed. I couldn't see why anyone would want a huge house on a small island like Norman's Cay. Marianne showed us around and introduced us to several people. I recognized a few of them from dinner the night before. We met a man who looked to be about forty with a small goatee and a pretty Bahamian girl named Chocolata with a very ripe body. Also two men who didn't speak English, named Juan and Pedro. When we got back to the living room, there were about ten more people.

"Do you ever go to Sea World in Fort Lauderdale?" Marianne asked. "Carlos bought the house from a man who was part owner of that place. I have always wanted to go there."

When we got back to the living room Joe was there and came over to greet us.

"Dr. Devlin and Mrs. Winter, it is so nice of you to come. Let me introduce you to my guests."

Joe took us around and introduced us to everyone we had not already met. There was a fat man named Bob Word from St. Louis and his wife Frannie, obviously the same couple Rick Norton had mentioned. We talked with them a few minutes. Bob said that he had worked for Westinghouse for a number of years and implied that it was an important executive position.

Another man he introduced us to was named F. Nigel Bowe. He was a black Bahamian with a mustache and a pleasant smile. Joe told me he was an attorney and close friend of Prime Minister Lynden Pindling. He seemed like a nice guy and spoke excellent English. Another man we were introduced to was named Pepe Cabron. Everybody we spoke with was fascinated by Lisa. She started gathering names as soon as we met the first person. I thought of writing down the names of all the people we met so I could go over them with Snake when we got back to Miami but decided against putting them on paper.

The group that Joe had invited seemed to be made up mostly of Americans who owned homes on the island, and some other people who worked for him. Nigel and Pepe did not work for Joe, but I got the feeling they were business associates and not personal friends.

I made a point of introducing myself to people, talking to them long enough to see if they could be of any value, and then moving on to someone else. Lisa seemed to always be surrounded by men. I introduced myself to a man named John Durant who said he owned a small commuter airline in Miami. When I asked him if he knew Charley Murphy, he said that Charley worked for him and we had flown over in one of his planes. I didn't ask him if his pilot always drank while he was flying passengers.

Although I tried to keep moving and asking questions that would lead people to mention names, I found it hard to separate myself from one of the women. Her name was Violeta Mercado and she was apparently related in some way to either somebody's cousin or to his mistress, I couldn't figure out which. She appeared to be about twenty five and could best be described as voluptuous.

She was a good looking woman whose body had so many bumps and curves that a dress one size too small made it look better. For some reason I couldn't shake her and she seemed to stay with me as I moved around the huge living room. She told me she was from Cuba and she seemed to be a mixture of a lot of different races and colors. She had incredibly sensuous lips and beautiful dark eyes. At one point I was only half listening to her while I tried to overhear another conversation.

"When the party is over, it would be nice if you invited me back to your villa," she said in a low voice that nobody else could hear.

"I'm here on the island with a lady just for the weekend," I told her. "I'm sure she will want to go to sleep as soon as we return."

I was sure that Violeta meant she wanted to get laid, but I thought I would respond as if she meant just a social visit, or that I didn't understand.

"When the lady goes to sleep you can have me," she said. "You can have as much of me as you want. In any way that you want. As many times as you want." She was smiling at me and still talking in a low voice.

"Thank you, Violeta," I said. "I think I understand your offer and I am very flattered, but I'm very attached to the lady I'm with. Perhaps you could give me a call if you are ever in Miami. Possibly we could get together sometime there. Do you ever visit Miami? Marianne told me she had always wanted to go to Sea World. Have you ever been there?"

"I'm interested in men, not fish," she said. "I'll be in Miami next month. I'll call you there."

I looked at her as she said it and wondered what I would do if she did call. She was obviously a whore, either amateur or professional, but she looked like she would be a holy terror in bed. After the cruise with Rocket and the last two days with Lisa I was so overheated I might just take her up on it.

People were moving around and I saw they were setting up a huge buffet. Lisa was already in line and I decided to make no attempt to sit together. I had begun to come to the conclusion that Emile Hogge was not on the island and didn't spend much time here. I felt certain he did own the house, but I had no way of finding out if Sharon was there. If Lisa and I were with different people we would have a better chance of finding out something that would be helpful. I told Lisa this and assured her I wasn't doing it because she had laughed at me.

There were several tables set up in the dining room and I saw Joe Lehder waving me over to where he was sitting. When I had filled up a plate at the buffet table, I went over and sat down with him. Violeta followed me and sat down beside me. Another woman sat on the other side. There were now four other men at the table and four women. The two on each side were both attractive in a coarse sort of way. Gradually, as time passed during dinner, I figured they were both probably prostitutes. I was seated between Violeta and a woman named Conchita Diaz and the two of them carried on a conversation in crude Spanish throughout the meal. Sometimes they talked in almost a whisper so that nobody could hear except me. I had told them I didn't understand Spanish so they talked the way they might have in the women's room. Their conversation was almost exclusively about sex and clothes.

Joe Lehder was tastefully dressed compared to the other men at the table who wore flashy jackets and a lot of gold jewelry. Lehder had on a silk suit and of course I had a Brooks Brothers navy blazer and tan slacks. The whole dinner was loud and the place was filled with smoke. The men with Joe were drinking a lot and after asking me some questions when we first sat down, they pretty much ignored me. Joe never really criticized any of the people with him, but he did manage to convey the impression that they were somehow lackeys of his and they did what he told them. Joe and the man named Pedro did most of the talking that every one could hear, and the others talked among themselves.

I mainly listened. Joe told us that the pond was a breeding place for hammerhead sharks and that Rick Norton was going to study them as well as taking diving parties. He said that he was going to support Rick Norton and set up some kind of scientific research institute. Lehder also told us that he was in the aviation business, buying used aircraft and fixing them up, then reselling them. Joe Lehder was a very pleasant and charming guy. He told us that he had bought the house because he liked it, even though he didn't need it. People called it "Volcano" because of the cone shaped roof.

I had noticed that he never took a drink even though all of his companions drank a lot. Because he was seated across the table from me, he could not hear what Violeta and Conchita were saying. By the time we finished eating and the waiters had brought coffee, the conversation between Conchita and Violeta had gotten very raunchy. I had a terrible time pretending that I didn't understand, particularly when Conchita told Violeta in a conversational tone that she was going to put her hand on my leg and play with me. I was talking to Joe Lehder at the time she said it, and tried not to act startled. I felt her hand on my left knee and a few minutes later I felt Violeta's hand on my right knee. I wasn't sure what to do so I just sat there and let the two sluts work their hands up toward my crotch. I kept on talking to Joe while they teased me and didn't even stop them when they started feeling and squeezing me. Violeta looked me in the eye and said in a very serious voice, *"Yo necesitar chupar su pinga."*

When I just looked puzzled they broke up laughing. What she said was very dirty. In Spanish *chupar* means to suck but I had to guess at *pinga*. When I sensed that one of them was about to unzip my fly, I stood up. I looked back and forth from one face to another and they kept on laughing and giggling.

I noticed a big commotion over at the table where Lisa was sitting, but it quieted down very quickly. Everyone seemed to get up from the tables about the same time. Almost immediately people started thanking Carlos Lehder for the party and leaving. People seem to leave early on Sunday nights no matter where they are or who is having the party. I found Lisa and we were about to start out when John Durant came over. He told us he was going to be flying back directly to Miami the next morning and that he could get in touch with Charley Murphy and tell him not to come down to pick us up. I accepted his offer immediately since it meant we wouldn't have to stop and get on a commercial airline in Nassau. He just waved a hand and laughed when I said he was hurting his own charter business. He arranged to meet us at the restaurant where we would return the rented car. He was planning to leave the island at nine o'clock. The new plan would get us back to Miami two or three hours earlier.

We thanked Joe Lehder for the dinner and I told him to look me up in Miami. We drove back to the villa without saying very much except that both of us had heard a lot of names but none that seemed to be of any value. We stopped talking about things involving the coming rescue as soon as we got inside the villa. It had turned out to be a beautiful night so I opened the sliding glass doors to let the breeze come in. To make conversation I asked Lisa what the commotion was at her table.

"The man who was sitting beside me put his hand up my dress and I had to get him to stop."

I started laughing and told her about Violeta and Conchita putting their hands on me. I still wanted to be as careful as possible, on the remote possibility that the villa was bugged, so I didn't mention the conversation in Spanish. I did tell her what they had done.

"Did you just let them do what they wanted?" she said, laughing as if it were the funniest thing she had ever heard of. "Why didn't you stop them? I think that's terrible. Two of them at the same time! I'll bet you enjoyed it! Why didn't you stop them?"

"What about you?" I said. "Who was the guy?"

"It was Bob Word," she told me. "The fat guy from Westinghouse who claims he was a big executive. His wife was sitting across the table from us. What a jerk!" She was laughing hard.

"What did you do?" I said. "How far did he get?"

"He got his fat hand under my dress and almost up to my underpants. I needed a minute to think about what I wanted to do."

"What did you do?"

"I took out a small bottle of perfume and showed it to him. I took the top off and told him it was sulfuric acid. I said I was going to throw it in his face in five seconds. He took his hand away and jumped up so fast I started laughing."

By this time we were laughing hard at the fact that both of us had gotten groped under the table. Lisa said she had been frightened and revolted but now it seemed ridiculous. We started inventing some possibilities of what other people had been doing to each other. It was a really funny conversation but it was also a very erotic one. At one point she started to describe how awkward it would have been if I had tried to take off both girls' panties at the same time. To make things worse for me Lisa took off her dress. It seemed that she did it without thinking, just to get comfortable. There was no air-conditioning and like many women in hot climates she seemed to feel it wasn't immodest to be clothed in only a slip indoors. Watching her slither and wiggle out of the tight little dress while we talked about an imaginary sex orgy taking place under dining tables was almost too much for me. I think that I would have simply raped her if I hadn't been laughing so hard. In an R-rated movie, our erotic conversation would have led gradually to a point of sexual tension where the man and the woman couldn't control themselves. The camera would have shifted to various close-ups of Lisa's face and body. Many retakes would have been necessary because the guys operating the cameras would have gone crazy watching her. At one point, when she was describing how far up her leg the man had put his hand before she threatened him with the pretend acid, I thought I was going to go crazy. She held her fingers about two inches apart and said, "He had his hand this far away from my panties!"

We were having an extremely sexy conversation. The sliding glass door was partially open and we could hear the small waves on the beach and the rustling of the palm fronds. There was a three quarter moon and it was like the movie. I knew that she was either teasing me deliberately and sadistically, or she really didn't know the effect that all of this was having on me. It seemed inconceivable that she wouldn't know exactly what was happening.

I couldn't handle it. Without saying anything I walked out of the open sliding glass doors and down to the water. I did take off my slacks so I wouldn't get my wallet wet, but I went right into the water. I either had to cool off or fuck Lisa and going into the water seemed like the best thing. I waded out to where I could sit down on the sand with just my head above water. I decided that women either had to legalize rape or invent some kind of signal like a big green earring for go and a big red one for no.

I don't know if Lisa realized what she had done to me or not but she stayed in the villa and didn't follow me to the water. I stayed there in the water until I had regained control over my feelings. As I cooled off I asked myself why I hadn't just fucked her and the answer came quickly – she just wasn't hot. The whole business would have excited a normal woman but she just wasn't hot. That thought upset me and I put it out of my mind. I walked back up to the villa and found Lisa asleep so I hung up my wet clothes where they could dry, put on some clean underwear and went to sleep.

I woke up Monday morning early, while it was still dark. I looked at my watch and realized it would be more than two hours before they started serving breakfast at the hotel. I got up and went into the living room without turning on any lights so that Lisa wouldn't wake up, and started reading Byron again. I dozed off and when I woke again Lisa had already packed and was fully dressed waiting for me. We drove to the restaurant without saying much but just before we got there Lisa finally said something.
"Did it upset you when I took off my dress last night? I'm terribly sorry and I apologize. I really didn't think. I really didn't do it to tease you."
"You almost got raped."
"My God. I really didn't think it would bother you. The dress was just uncomfortable."
As we walked into the restaurant I realized that she really didn't understand the effect she had on me and I thought that was very strange. I was a little apprehensive at breakfast, wondering if John Durant would remember that he had invited us to ride back in his plane to Miami. He showed up, though, when we were about half finished and sat down with us. He told us that we could leave when we finished. We talked about the party the night before and I noticed Lisa trying hard not to laugh. I was sure she was thinking of our conversation about what was going on under the table. When we finished breakfast I found Cecelia and paid for the weekend in cash. I usually use credit cards for hotel bills but for some reason I didn't this time.
Cecelia drove us the short distance to the air strip and we got aboard John's plane. It was a six-passenger Cessna and there was plenty of room with just three of us. It was a beautiful morning and we could see for miles around us. When we took off at the end of the runway by the point, where we had sailed in the little Hobie Cat, I looked down and back at the island. I still hadn't figured out where I wanted Snake to drop me off. It had to be someplace easy to find and still close enough to walk quickly to the house where we hoped Sharon would be.
We circled around and then straightened out on a course of 273° straight for Miami. We would fly directly over Andros and nowhere near the Island of New Providence. I tried to put together everything we had seen and done on the island, but I had been over it so many times I couldn't think of anything new or different. After awhile I fell asleep. When I woke up we were approaching Miami International and John Durant had already gotten clearance to land.

Chapter Fourteen

Monday, 12 June
After dropping Lisa off at her house, I drove straight to the clinic. I felt guilty because I had taken so much time off from work, and I thought I could at least get some paper work done. It was after two when I sat down in my office, and, as usual, Lori came in with my messages instead of leaving them on my desk. She did this so she could keep track of my personal life, and give me advice.

"You were very popular today," she said. "You got one call from a sinister person, five calls from patients, and one call from a famous television personality. She said she worked out things at the T.V. station so she could spend the whole weekend with you and that she was very excited. Snake didn't tell me what he was calling about. I'm sure it was something sinister, though. I could tell by his voice."

For some reason Lori had seemed slightly different to me since she had dinner on Gus and Paulette's boat. She still felt compelled to make cute remarks but somehow they didn't seem as impertinent.

"Sit down for a minute, Lori." I had never noticed it before, but I suddenly realized that she always stood up in my office and never sat down unless I asked her.

"Who told you to send the message to me about the patient in room J-41? You know I don't have any patient in a room number J-41 or any other room right now."

"Sean Moran called and he said to get a secret message to you that had the number J-41. I figured it was part of some sinister plot that you were involved in with him and that I needed to be really sneaky about the message. Actually I thought that it was probably the number of the box that you and Snake smuggled into the United States. I thought up the message. Can you tell me what it meant? I feel like I'm a part of the plot. Did I hide the number well enough?"

Lori had what I call a cartoon face. Every feature of her face was well shaped and in the right place. She was actually very pretty. Her nose, however, was just a tiny bit smaller, and her mouth a little bigger, than the rest of her face suggested it should be. When cartoonists draw characters, they exaggerate some features and minimize others, producing a caricature. Normal people would simply look at her and see a very pretty girl. I saw things in faces that other people didn't.

"You did a good job with the code. I really appreciate the skill you displayed in helping me cover up my criminal smuggling activities," I said, deciding to kid around about it. "The number was just part of a joke that Snake was playing on me. I'm sorry to disappoint you about the smuggling. The box was just some letters that came from Sean's sister. The number has nothing to do with the box. Thanks anyway, though. Close the door on your way out so I can call all of these people."

Lori looked a little crestfallen so I told her again that I appreciated her cleverness. As soon as she closed the door, I realized I had said the letters were from Snake's sister and nobody was supposed to know that he had a sister. I had to be more careful about secrecy. I called Snake at the three different numbers he had given me and got no answer at any of them. I was talking to one of my patients, returning a call, when Butch called me. It was a strange conversation.

"Are we all set for the weekend? Will you be able to leave Friday night after work?" Butch asked.

"I can leave here at six o'clock and be at the dock at seven. Is that early enough?"

"My parents will be coming along. I hope that's O.K. with you. When I invited you for the weekend on *Ojos Verdes,* I didn't know they would be coming. It's because of Antonia."

"Fine," I said. "Whatever we do is good with me."

I was confused and didn't know what else to say. When he invited me to go sailing, and do it for a weekend, I was just excited about the sailing part and never even wondered who else was coming.

"I've invited Patricia Rivera with me for the weekend. She was with Sean Moran at the party. Do you remember her?"

"Sure, that's great, but I've got to explain something to you about my parents being there. If there were only four of us and one or two crew we could do whatever we wanted. Sleep whatever way we wanted. I don't know if you wanted to share a cabin with Patricia or not. I don't know if you are screwing her or not and it's none of my business, but with my parents along you are going to have to sleep in separate cabins. My parents are coming because of Antonia. She is my little sister's best friend and they went to convent school together. She's not my girlfriend and I'm not screwing her. I don't kiss her or anything. When she comes to visit, I escort her everywhere but that's it. As far as I am concerned she is untouchable. If my parents weren't coming you could do whatever you wanted to. You could sleep in a cabin with Patricia or you could sleep separately and it wouldn't matter. With my parents along you sleep by yourself. Period."

"It doesn't make any difference at all to me. Remember, I had your father aboard my boat in Chub Cay for dinner. That was when I thought he was the professional captain of the boat. He's a great guy and I'm looking forward to the whole thing," I assured him.

"The older Spanish families are very old fashioned, particularly about virgin daughters. When my parents are around Americans they act like Americans but among themselves the old rules of behavior apply."

"Butch, I understand," I interrupted. "Don't worry about it."

"What I'm trying to say is that strict rules of old fashioned Spanish culture dictate that you ain't going to get any pussy on *Ojos Verdes* this weekend. No *chocha* whatsoever. I'm not either but I wasn't planning on it and you might be."

We both started laughing and we hung up after agreeing that we would have dinner at his house around seven and then go aboard the boat. If the weather was favorable, we would leave the dock while there was still some light and go down to the Miami Beach Marina. We would tie up at the fuel dock, which would be closed down, and then leave around midnight and go over to Bimini. If the weather wasn't as good as we hoped, we could go down Hawk Channel the next morning to the Keys. If the weather was really terrible, we could go down Biscayne Bay through Featherbed Shoals, and stay inside, protected from the weather.

After finishing up my list of calls to patients, I got Pat at her studio and told her the plans for the weekend. She was very enthusiastic and agreed that meeting me at the Salazar's house would be the easiest since she would be leaving from her studio in downtown Miami.

After everyone else had left the clinic, I went into Bill Gaines' office and talked to him for a while. I covered my trip to Norman's Cay, telling him everything that happened and not leaving out anything, except the identity of the person we were going to snatch off the island. I was still trying to make him believe that we were going to rescue a man who was both a friend of mine and of Snake's.

I told Bill that I had decided to take Joan Pegram to New York for craniofacial surgery. Although South Florida was loaded with talented plastic surgeons, I felt I needed to get her into a place where this type of surgery was routine. It would involve five different types of doctors and nurses and fantastic teamwork. Bill agreed with me and actually seemed a little flattered when I insisted he come along and participate. He had no experience with operations involving so many people, but I hoped that one day craniofacial surgery would become routine in Miami and that Bill would be part of it.

Bill surprised me a little by asking me if I was screwing Lori. I started laughing because I knew he was kidding but I couldn't resist the chance to be a wise guy.

"Of course I'm screwing her. Aren't you?"

"Seriously, Winfield Scott. Something has changed. She suddenly seems more grown up. She was never really sloppy, but all of a sudden she's really well-groomed. She still works hard thinking up cute remarks but her comments aren't raunchy recently. I could always count on at least one or two really funny, dirty jokes every week but she's stopped that, too, and I can't figure out why. I miss the jokes. Do you suppose she's in love? Has she got a special boyfriend?"

"Why don't you just ask her?" I suggested. "You're closer to the girls than I am."

When I got to my apartment that night, I opened all three locks on my front door and let myself in. Sitting there in my living room was Sean Shannon Moran. I looked closely at him to make sure it was really Snake. He didn't have on a false beard or mustache, he wasn't wearing glasses and he wasn't dressed in any strange clothes. There was only one change. His hair, which was very black and slightly wavy, was now very blonde and slightly wavy. His eyes also had changed from black to blue. I hardly noticed the difference.

"How did you get into my apartment?"

"I picked the locks. They aren't very good."

"Lori told me you got her to send the message with J-41 in it. I hope that's the plot number of the house where your sister is being held. I did confirm that the place is owned by a man named Armando Sepulveda and not by Emile Hogge. Does that make any sense?"

"The house is in Sepulveda's name but it's the right one. Emile Hogge is an American citizen now but he is a Boer, South African from Dutch descent. Hates blacks. When he isn't working on drug deals he is beating up on black people. Sepulveda is a Colombian national. Tell me about the house," he said.

"Where did you get the information about J-41?"

"Don't ask questions or I'll give you a bullshit answer."

Sitting there talking to Snake I realized that I would never really know much about him. Someone once described him as being like a drunken chameleon walking across a Scotch plaid. He had many facets and faces and changed from one to another rapidly and without prior notice. His eyes were normally sort of a pale blue-green, *bleu azur,* but I knew that he wore contact lenses of various colors when he wanted to change his looks.

Snake did not act evasive. He would happily tell you anything you wanted to know about his family or his job or his past. He would tell you anything and everything, but if you asked him the same questions a month later he would tell you a completely different story. If you pointed out the differences he would tell you he had mental problems. I always had the feeling that, down underneath his strange weird actions, he really was crazy. As strange as he was, however, he became the soul of integrity when he made a promise. If he said he would do something it got done. Always on time and exactly as he promised.

We sat and talked for nearly two hours and started seriously planning. Snake said he needed two weeks to be ready. I told him I was going to spend the weekend with Butch and that Patricia was going to be my date. I offered to cancel it but he said to go ahead because he wouldn't be ready, anyway. I asked him about Patricia Rivera and if he had any feelings about my going out with her. He shook his head no and moved right on with the planning. Snake seemed to know an incredible number of people but I could never recall seeing him with the same woman twice. The girls he went out with were always attractive but I guessed he didn't get too close to any particular one because of his job.

We argued quite a bit about who would do what but not about the people we would get to help us. I had to do the recruiting because Snake was frequently watched. He knew people were there but he never knew exactly who they were. Sometimes they were bad guys and sometimes they were good guys who thought Snake was a bad guy. He told me he had one person lined up to help us and that it was someone I didn't know.

I have trouble working with anybody else on an equal basis. My partnership with Bill works well because we each understand who's responsible for what. I can take orders or I can give orders but I'm too impatient to decide anything together with anyone else. Bill runs the office. He's courteous and he tells me about billing systems and cost control and things, but I'm really not interested. I trust him and I would probably agree to almost anything he suggested even if I didn't understand it. Without any formal agreement, Bill defers to my judgement when it comes to surgical techniques.

Since I had just come back from Chub Cay, I knew that we wouldn't find the house if I didn't go ashore that night. I described how we could bring a small boat right into the beach, drop me off, and wait for me to locate the house. The only alternative was for Snake to make a trip to Norman's Cay himself and that would take time. Snake let me talk for a while and then he jumped on me. He was always kidding around and I had never seen him nasty before.

"How are you going to kill the guards? Do you think we should garrote them or use stilettos? Have you got the guns we need? The explosives? The poison?"

"I thought we were just going to grab your sister and take off. I thought you were going to get your revenge later? What's this shit about killing guards?"

Snake finished a pastrami sandwich he was eating and washed it down with some Pauli Girl Dark.

"Dr. Devlin, you sound like some real ass-hole in a movie. The guy agrees to help rob a bank and then gets upset when his buddy blows the brains out of a few security guards. As they haul his butt off to prison, he sadly claims he never thought it would come to this. Bullshit. I don't even want you to come ashore. I need you alive when she comes off the drugs."

He looked me in the eye and I saw something really cold and deadly there. He stared for a few seconds and then started blinking rapidly.

"I'm trying a new type of contact lens," he said. "They don't feel comfortable. Think I'll go back to my old ones."

He got out a small mirror and changed his lenses.

"I'm going to go ashore alone and I'll try not to kill anybody if it won't help us get her out. If it's necessary, however, I will eliminate everybody in the house. There's no point in getting revenge that night because things will be moving fast and I wouldn't have time to enjoy it. I will do it out of necessity only, but I will kill as many of them as I need to. I will do it quickly and I will do it silently but if I have time I will castrate each one. You will not be with me. You will stay in the boat and you will not go ashore. I want somebody in that boat who can handle it. An experienced seaman."

"Then I don't go at all. I'll wait for you at the clinic and you can conduct your own rescue operation. You won't find the house without me. Sharon might be on the island but you can't find the house coming in from the water in the dark. You won't even come close. The house is right on the beach on the west side of the island. Coming in from the water is the best way to do it, but the houses along that shore are hidden back in the trees. It's not possible to find it from the water. To try to get Sharon out of the house and over to the airstrip would be impossible. That would be suicide, but a small boat could be brought in twenty feet from the beach."

I told him about sitting there sketching Lisa and coming back with the catamaran. I told him everything we did while we were on the island. I showed him the map I had drawn while I was doing the sketch. Then I went over a list of names with him and he asked to keep the list. When I had finished everything, he asked me about Lisa.

"I thought you were going to take Rocket with you. Why did you take Lisa Winter? What did she think you were there for?" He was really pissed off that I had included another person.

"Rocket's father died suddenly. She had to go home. I had to get somebody else in the middle of the night or go by myself. I told her the captive was a man that I knew and I didn't mention your name. I didn't tell her when we were going to do it. We didn't even know at the time. I know you have to be paranoid in your work but it was the best thing I could do. You have to trust somebody and I trust her. Have you forgotten? It was her kid who got his face fucked up by the outboard motor. It was the accident that happened when we were sailing in from the Star boat regatta. Don't you remember Whittaker? Don't you remember stuffing him in the dumpster and filling up his convertible with shit?"

"Yeah. I remember Whittaker." Snake suddenly got a big smile on his face. "Did you ever tell Lisa Winter about what we did to him?"

"No. You remember what happened. She was going to sic the lawyers on me because I didn't have legal authority. Then a four-foot doctor named Montgomery testified that I was magnificent and that working on the kid quickly made a big difference. Lisa and I became really close friends. She was a tremendous help. I don't think I would have found the house without her. I can tell you for damn sure that we won't find the house unless I go ashore."

"I knew she was the woman you were sniffing after when you started going to the Catholic Church," Snake said. "She's about the most beautiful woman I've ever seen. Are you fucking her?"

"It's none of your business what I'm doing with Lisa Winter. Screw you!"

"You're involved in planning an action with me that might result in people getting killed. It might be in the newspapers or on television. It is my business who you bring into it and what your relation is with them. Particularly women. If you're in love with her, you shouldn't have gotten her in it."

"She's not really part of it. She just helped for one weekend and she can be trusted. I'm not screwing her. We're just friends. Besides, why would you trust Rocket and not Lisa Winter?"

"Because Rocket is in love with you and Lisa Winter isn't."

I didn't say anything. After a while he explained how his secret work for Interpol was related only to thefts of art. He seldom had to kill anybody, but that he was trained to do it when necessary. He said he had been on a few missions to capture or kill prisoners when he was in MI5, the British Intelligence. He said he had been in a lot of other jobs. He also said it might be necessary to kill somebody if we were kidnapping a person who was being held by drug dealers. He then went on to explain several of the more effective ways to do it silently. I agreed that he was the boss completely and that everyone else would have to do exactly as he said. This was fine with me, so I listened to his rough outline of a plan that was based on what I had told him about the house.

The plan we talked about was to have someone bring a boat in and anchor it near the dock and clubhouse in Norman's Cay harbor. At a specified time they could cause an explosion of some kind out in the harbor or at the dock. This was to be a diversion since it is a small island with few telephones, and everybody would want to find out what happened. Hopefully some of the people in Hogge's house will get in their cars and drive down to the dock, leaving Sharon behind. A few hours before that Snake and I would go close into the beach in a small boat. I said that Snake should drop me and I would swim in to the beach and find the house. When I found it I would signal him and he would come ashore. As soon as we heard the explosion, he would approach the house but give them time to get in the cars and leave. He was going to go into the house no matter what. If we were lucky there would be just one man or possibly nobody. Snake would disable the guard. I took this to mean he'd hit him with a blackjack, or something, but kill him only if absolutely necessary.

Meanwhile, somebody would bring the boat in close. Snake assumed that Sharon would be in the house, but unconscious, and that he would have to carry her. We had to be able to get her in the boat without swimming. I would wait on the beach to help him get her aboard. The plan made sense but Snake still didn't want me to go ashore before he did.

After we got Sharon in the boat we would head west in case anybody saw us. Then, when we were out of sight, go north up past Highborne Cay, Allan's Cay, Ship Channel Cay and take a turn to 118° through Ship Channel and out into Exuma Sound. If somebody were chasing us they should think we were headed north to Nassau. When we were out in the Sound we would go south at full speed to Staniel Cay.

When they built the airstrip on Staniel Cay, it was done by filling in a shallow lagoon and leaving narrow strips of water right alongside the airstrip. We could bring the boat in there and have a plane waiting. We would take off and fly to a tiny little air strip far west of Miami in the Everglades then drive Sharon to my clinic and try to keep her alive while we dried her out. Timing was critical for the detoxification.

"The plan for getting her away from the island is good. It will work," Snake said. "The problem is we need another person in the boat. We also need more information. We also need some periscopes."

"What do you mean by periscopes?"

"It's a nickname for somebody who just watches. An insider's term for somebody who just observes and reports. We need people on the island to help keep us informed, people who can watch the house that day to see if there is any sign of Sharon. Maybe warn us off if they see something. If we could figure out how to do it, we could have somebody in the clubhouse. People will be running around all over the place as soon as the explosion is set off and the clubhouse will be the place where people will be drinking and talking. If there is any excitement after I get Sharon, somebody might talk about it in the bar. It would be good to know what people think actually happened.

"In the sneaky craft that I practice, we call these people scopes. They pop up unexpectedly, look around and then submerge again. We need one on the island. Try to think of someone you trust. We won't tell them what is really going to happen."

We decided we would go in after her on Saturday night, the eighth of July. It wasn't much time to get the airplane and the offshore racing boat lined up. I offered again to cancel my plans for the weekend on *Ojos Verdes* but Snake said he couldn't move any faster. Almost anywhere in the world you can figure Saturday night as the one when more people are going to be drinking and partying. We both agreed that I would try to get Gus Draper to be the guy who set off the explosion in the harbor. We also thought we should get somebody else to be in the bar when the explosion went off. Just before Snake left, I called Gus and he said he would meet me at Monty Trainer's Tuesday night. When I hung up, I decided to get things resolved about my going ashore and finding the house.

"Snake, you've got to drop me off a few miles up the beach from the south corner of the island, near the airstrip and the clubhouse. I can walk up the beach or a road if necessary. I can find the house on foot very easily. I know all the landmarks and I can go straight to the road that cuts through to the beach just south of the house. It goes through the trees and runs right down to the beach. I can signal you with a flashlight or something, and then you can bring the boat in with the light as a guide."

"If we do it that way, you're in danger. Who stays with the boat?"

"We might be able to get Rocket. She knows boats. She could do it."

"O.K., but don't tell her it's my sister. Tell her he's a friend of ours."

"If she goes with us she's going to find out. If she agrees to go we've got to trust her completely."

"You're right. What happened to Sharon was not her fault but it was so disgusting I just don't want anybody to know about it."

"If we've finished talking about the rescue operation, I want to hear about Emile Hogge. Tell me what you know about him."

"You don't need to know about Hogge. We're not going there to get him. We're going to get Sharon."

"I *want* to know about him. I'll never see the man, and I'm sure as hell not going to help you get revenge, but I still want to know about him. You should understand that."

"Hogge has nothing to do with the things I'm involved in, so I had never heard of him until I found out about Sharon."

Snake sat down on the couch and stared at me for a few minutes.

"I have sources in the F.B.I., the C.I.A., the D.E.A. and several police forces. I've had to work hard at setting them up because I am not openly working for Interpol. I can't, and don't, let anybody make the connection. Actually I have more connections and friends in the underworld than with the ones who are supposed to be legitimate. I want you to realize that when I say that someone is a connection or a source or a friend I do not mean that I go sailing with them or have Sunday dinner with them. I know some of the sickest people on earth.

"I first learned about Emile Hogge from a man named Caruso who was a real artist at making motion pictures. He was fantastic at the use of lighting in unusual places and ways, and was becoming an important person in Hollywood, when he got into trouble for moonlighting. He was making a film on the set, using equipment that belonged to the producers. He would have been fired, or even thrown in jail, but the studio didn't want anything known about what happened. They got some thugs to beat the hell out of Caruso and told him not to ever go west of the Mississippi again. The producers were legitimate producers of motion pictures and didn't think the public would tolerate the knowledge that their set was used to film a pornographic sex movie featuring an eight-year-old girl and a German Shepherd dog. Caruso lives and operates in Fort Lauderdale now, devoting all of his time to making pornographic movies with boys and girls. He loves his work."

"Jesus Christ, Snake. Doesn't that disgust you! How could you even stand to talk to a man like Caruso? Don't you despise him too much to even pretend to want to do business with him?"

"Caruso is sick. He makes very sick movies for very sick people. But they are also very, very rich and there are not many of them. The people I hate and despise are the corrupt elected officials and mealy mouthed pastors who pretend that South Florida is not a paradise for perverts. Compared to Hogge Caruso is harmless.

"Anyway, when I talked to the college kid and found out for sure that Emile Hogge was the man who had taken my sister, I went to Caruso. I talked to many others using a slightly different story each time. I told Caruso that I had knowledge of some erotic art that had been produced by the Nazis and smuggled into the Netherlands. As everyone knows, the Netherlands is a world leader in pedophilia. I told him I needed to find a buyer with a few million dollars who had a taste for pornographic art. I tailored my story to fit a drug dealer. The porno art was to be paid for *specifically* with unlaundered money.

"After a few days, I met with Caruso in Fort Lauderdale. He asked me to leave my car at a convenience store and meet him in the parking lot of an elementary school. We sat in his car and talked while he watched the little girls and boys walking by. He came up with the name of four potential buyers, but made it clear that he wanted me to try Hogge first because he was a good customer of his and he wanted him to have first refusal. I got a great deal of information from Caruso, then went from there to get a real picture of him. I used a lot of different sources. Hogge isn't the kind of person you'd want for a neighbor.

"He's a strange looking person, almost like a cartoon. His profile is not too strange, but his head is kind of squeezed together. From a front view he looks like his entire head was put in a vise. The distance from one ear to another looked like only six or seven inches.

"Emile Hogge was born in South Africa. He lived there until he was sixteen when his family moved to Belgium. He was a racist and there is a story that when he was twelve he killed a few black people after torturing them. I did not pursue that part of his character.

"There are other stories about him. Supposedly he killed his own father, who was a banker. A drug dealer from Tampa told me that Hogge had learned all about banking and exchange rates and stuff from his father. When he thought he had learned all he could from him, Emile got his father to rewrite the will leaving everything to him. He convinced his father that his wife was having affairs so he would do this. After arranging an accident for his father, he collected his inheritance and left."

"What happened to Emile Hogge's mother?" I wanted to know.

"What difference does it make?"

"I am extremely curious about a man who would do what Hogge did to your sister."

"I was told that he used his mother sexually for a while, and then left her with no money. It doesn't matter what he did. People like Emile Hogge are beyond the comprehension of the most skilled psychiatrists. What he did to my sister was hideous. I have to get Sharon back and then kill Hogge and the other people who used her. Before he kidnaped her he could have led an exemplary life. It wouldn't matter to me. He used Sharon so he dies. Are you trying to work up a feeling of hatred for him to justify what we have to do? To justify the rescue?"

"I don't know, but it's more than just curiosity. For some reason I need to know." I really did need to know and Snake continued. "Hogge banged his mother for a few months and then moved to Amsterdam. He apparently developed his pedophilia in the Netherlands and then went to Switzerland to learn more about banking and money. He became an expert at laundering money.

"Hogge came into the drug trade backwards. He became such an expert at laundering money that he had to find huge sources of unlaundered money. Like many people who are very good at making money, he did not have expensive tastes. His great interest is sex, pornography, erotic art, pedophilia, anything and everything that is filthy and rotten. He's extremely intelligent but some of his brain was wired wrong.

"The people who work for Hogge all share his perverted sexual interests. It's what holds them together, maybe. Hogge is an easy guy to hate. Just think of everything evil and shitty and you got his character down pat."

The next morning I worked in the operating room from eight until almost one. Bill was also operating all morning and I didn't have a chance to talk to him until one thirty. I told him we were going to try the rescue in twelve days and that I wanted to use the clinic for a few days starting sometime late that Saturday night. I told him the complete truth about everything except whom we were bringing back. I was one of those guys who had been brought up on King Arthur and the Knights of the Round Table. I believed that women were somehow special and that they were to be revered and protected. What had happened to Snake's sister was more than I could even talk about. It was too vile.

I had closed the door to Bill's office when I came in. After my speech, he opened his desk drawer and pulled out some notes. I started shaking my head and laughing when I saw what he had done. He had actually written a script. On the Thursday morning before we needed the clinic, he was going to come in my office and start a conversation with the door open. That was to lead to an argument about how everyone was working too hard and how everybody had become a pain in the ass. He and I were to start being nasty to the women in a subtle way that very day, as soon as we finished talking. That would give us two weeks to get them ready. We also were not going to speak to each other until after the girls had gone home each night. There was some risk of permanently hurting someone's feelings but we could be careful.

We always closed the clinic for a week at Christmas and six months later we closed again for a week in May. Also each person took a third week at different times. Our type of practice didn't have many emergencies so we could make plans, but we did need some explanation for closing an additional week.

Except for the fake argument, it was very subtle. He wanted to give the women as little time as possible to talk after we announced the sudden closing. We would both make appointments that could be easily canceled for the week I expected to be drying out Sharon. Bill's plan called for us to follow up the argument by calling in everyone and telling them to spend the rest of the day getting ready, and then to go somewhere away from the clinic for a week of extra paid vacation. I told him the plan looked good and that I would take the script home and study my lines. The fake argument and the announcement would take place on Thursday morning, July 1 – in nine days.

That night I met Gus at Monty Trainer's. I got there first and found a table far enough away from the others that we could talk without being overheard. It was very busy for a Tuesday night in the summer. I always felt good there. I had been to Monty's for the first time as a teenager when I came down from the cold weather up north for the Southern Circuit. The Circuit was a series of long and short ocean races that started on the west coast at St. Petersburg, and then had several races on the East coast including the longer Miami-to-Nassau Race.

I ordered some nachos to nibble on and waited for Gus. As soon as I saw him, I realized that he had Paulette with him. I was annoyed because I had told him specifically to come alone. After they ordered, I reminded him that I had asked him to come alone. He shrugged his shoulders and Paulette jumped in.

"After you two guys sobered me up I decided there were not going to be any secrets between Gus and me. Alcoholics have a lot of secrets and I spent a lot of years trying to hide the fact that I was a drunk. No more. When Gus said you wanted him to come alone, and wouldn't tell me why, I told him I was going to come with him. If you can't let me in on what you're doing then count Gus out. I mean it."

I knew Paulette well enough to know that she *did* mean it, so I didn't waste any time arguing. We needed Gus badly. I told both of them that Snake and I had a mutual friend and that he was being held captive in a house on Norman's Cay by some criminals. I saw no point in going into any further details about the person we were going to rescue. I was not capable of describing to a woman the things that the Boer and the Billy Goat had done to Sharon.

I explained that what we wanted him to do was anchor in the harbor on Saturday, July 3, or even a day or so early. He would take an extra dinghy or a small inflatable. Snake would provide him with a package of explosives and a timer. He would row the dinghy in and tie it to the dock. The dock was used for unloading freight and boats do not stay there for very long. The explosion would damage the dock a little but not destroy it. If there were boats at the dock, he could drop an anchor nearby. He would set off the timer and swim back to his own boat and watch. I explained that the explosion was strictly a kind of diversion and not intended to harm people or do any damage. From the time he started the timer he would have one hour and could leave the harbor before the blow-up if he thought it would be best.

I told him we were going to try to have somebody on shore but there would be no contact. He and Paulette could even go ashore for lunch or dinner if they wanted to. I told them that I was going to ask Sidney to go to Norman's as a tourist with a date for the weekend. If they saw each other they would not act as if they were acquainted. The only thing that was *really* important was that he set off the timer at eleven fifteen.

When I finished, I looked at them both and asked, "Can you do it? Can you go over there?"

"How soon can you get the explosives aboard?" Gus asked.

"Thursday night. They'll be in a cardboard box and look like cans of soup." I turned to Paulette.

"Paulette, why don't you have Gus leave you in Nassau?"

"Get serious, Dev. I wouldn't miss it for anything. I just wish we were using the dynamite to blow up kidnappers. There's nothing I would like better than to blow the asses off those bastards," she said, looking very determined.

I looked at her for a few seconds and wondered how her millions of movie fans would have felt. They had watched her on the screen and didn't even like it when a leading man kissed her too passionately. She was too sweet and innocent for anything that wasn't really nice. She still looked sweet and innocent even when she said she wanted to use dynamite to blow the asses off the bad guys.

I knew a great deal about Paulette and her history, including her childhood and the Hollywood part, but I knew nothing about Gus and his past. I *did* know what both of them were like now. I knew that we could depend on them no matter what happened. We set it up so that Snake and I would come down to their boat and bring the explosives with us. We would arrange things so that Gus could call from Highborne on Wednesday or Thursday just before he went to Norman's. If something had changed and the rescue was off, we would let him know by a code message. We had some coffee and dessert and I drove back to my place. Gus and Paulette left on the motorcycle.

It turned out to be a fairly busy week for the middle of the summer, but nothing out of the ordinary. We did seem to get a number of cases that were going to be complex and would require a series of operations. I got one call from a writer from the Miami Herald who wanted to do a series of articles on craniofacial surgery. I agreed to work with him but told him we could not do anything for three or four weeks.

I thought it would be easy for me to be a little short with the women in the clinic and that it would be hard for Bill, but it turned out the other way. Because he talked all the time and was such a friendly person he didn't need to do anything but stop talking and all the ladies got upset. I never talked much even when I was in a good mood, so I had to start talking to make any impression on the girls. I had to work hard to find critical things to say that didn't just sound stupid. I found a few but what really did get the women concerned was the fact that Bill and I stopped talking to each other. We had to really work hard at it because we normally got along so well, but we did it and everybody started getting jumpy.

Chapter Fifteen

Wednesday, 14 June

Wednesday night I left work and drove into Coconut Grove to meet Sidney. He only needed to walk out of the back gate of the church yard and across the street to meet me at a place called the Taurus. It was mostly a stand-up bar with only a few tables. It had been in the Grove a long time and since they didn't serve food, it was a hangout for people who wanted only to drink and talk. The walls were filled with memorabilia, some of which had been there many years. Right outside the bar a guy named Martin had set up a grill and cooked hamburgers. When nobody wanted hamburgers, he fixed shoes and became known as the village cobbler. His special hamburgers became known as Martinburgers and since there was no place close that served hot dogs and hamburgers, he did a pretty good business. Sidney was consistent at being late but this particular night he was almost on time.

"It's g-good to see you, Dr. Winfield. Have you thought about my idea of using credit cards and model heads to increase the take in your glamour emporium? Actually you could even use model b-breasts as well as heads. I can see it now. This one is the Jane Russell model and the other one is the Katherine Hepburn style, a trifle smaller but much less expensive."

Sidney ordered a vodka gimlet and I asked for a glass of iced tea.

"Sidney, I need your help in kidnaping someone."

"Will the r-r-r-r-ransom money be large enough to b-build the new wing on St. Stephen's?" he asked with a straight face. Sidney had great aplomb.

"This is very serious, Sidney. Snake and I have a friend who has become a prisoner of a drug dealer. This person is being held on an island in the Bahamas and we're planning a rescue. If we are successful it will be called kidnaping. What we want you to do is to go to the island for the weekend as a tourist. You'll be in the restaurant drinking and talking when the rescue takes place. There will be a harmless explosion, which we hope will cause distraction. The person we want to rescue is being held in a house on the beach and we're going to come in with a boat and do the snatch right after we hear the explosion. Hopefully some of the people in the house will go down to the clubhouse to see what happened. You won't be involved in the actual rescue at all. The friend we're going after will be loaded with all kinds of drugs. I'm going to try to take him back to the clinic for a few days to dry him out. If you help us, you'll be at the bar exactly when it's happening and right after. We need to know if anybody there knows what happened. There's no reason for anyone to suspect Snake or me since there's no known connection to the person who is being held but we want to know what's happening and what's being said in the bar right after we set off the dynamite. We also want to know if there's anything being said about the person we're taking."

"Have you exhausted all legal means of getting the person b-back?" he asked.

"There are no legal means. The government of the Bahamas might even be involved in the drug trade. I know that sounds ridiculous but it might be true."

"It's not ridiculous at all. You may have heard of the Opium Wars when England was involved in the drug trade. I would be startled if the Government of the Bahamas or s-s-some of the people in it were n-not involved. In the United States the Federal Government does not participate – it simply facilitates. Am I to assume that you feel no need to give me any more information about your planned kidnaping or snatch or whatever?"

"Sidney, I've already told you the whole thing except for who the other people are that are going to help. You don't need to know any more. Everybody involved is a close friend of mine or of Snake's. They are people that can be trusted. All you have to do is go to the island and have a good time."

"How good a time can I have?"

"Seriously, Sidney, will you go to Norman's Cay and spend one or two nights?"

"I am sure you have considered the fact that I will seem much more like a tourist if I bring along a lady friend," he said, looking as if he had just thought of it. "The r-r-r-r-rector at my church has, at the moment, ceased to be p-pissed off at me. I recruited more than twenty new members for the church this month and some of them even have haircuts. Of course I will do it. A weekend of real debauchery would be exciting. I have been scoring well in the evangelical area for a number of months and deserve a little sin."

"Call Lori in the morning and ask her to make reservations for you. She has the number of the Norman's Cay Club and she knows how to set up a special flight from Nassau. Have a good time and enjoy the weekend. The only thing you need to do is to be in the clubhouse at the bar between nine thirty and twelve, or whenever they stop talking about the explosion."

I thought about offering to pay for Sidney's expenses but decided he would be insulted. Sidney was worth several million dollars and could afford it. As always, when we were in the Taurus, many people came over to talk to Sidney. Although only a few belonged to Saint Stephens, it seemed that everybody had some kind of problem they expected Sidney to solve. I told him about my trip to Norman's Cay and what I had done to locate the house where our friend was being kept. He asked a lot of questions and eventually wanted to know about the lady friend who had gone with me. I told him it was Lisa Winter. He knew the whole story about Lisa and Bobby Winter and how I had gone to the Catholic Church so often to try to see her.

"I noticed that you started coming back to Saint Stephens a few months ago. Did you give up on any future progress? Are you still in love with her?"

"I'm still in love with her. Spending a weekend with her on Norman's Cay was about all I could handle. We slept in the same bedroom, and we were together all the time, but I made no attempt to touch her. I accidently revealed that I wasn't a Catholic and she laughed at me. I got really pissed off."

"Sometimes unconsummated love is the most painful and the hardest to understand. Unrequited love is even worse. Perhaps in your mind she's too much of a goddess. Maybe you believe you have found the perfectly beautiful face that is superior to all others, the one you will never grow tired of looking at."

"I know that my love for a beautiful face is superficial but I can't help it. Perhaps it's an occupational risk. Maybe the fact that I paint portraits is part of the problem, I just don't know. She's the first truly beautiful woman I've ever met who didn't act like an asshole most of the time. She does not seem to be in love with herself."

"I will pray for the wisdom to guide you."

In whatever role he wanted to act, whether it was clown, gourmet, or raconteur, he was essentially a serious priest. Sidney could stop for a prayer in the middle of a dirty story and it would not seem strange to people who knew him.

We talked for a while there in the Taurus about other things, like the Dolphins' chances for next season, and the growing national debt, and then left and walked up to the Café Europa. Since it was new that year and offered a very sophisticated menu, it had become an immediate favorite of Sidney's. I also liked the food there, but I always remembered it as the place where Lisa had told me she didn't want to continue seeing me.

The Café Europa was near the Taurus, at 3159 Commodore Plaza and had the lettering *Bistro/Creperie* in the window. The canopy outside had multicolored stripes with artificial silk flowers in window boxes. Inside there were a lot of shiny copper cooking utensils hanging from the walls and ceiling as well as baskets of plants.

The café advertised French Gourmet Cuisine but actually there were a number of things on the menu that were Algerian. We both ordered the *bouillabaisse* and talked for a while with Maria and Bernard, the couple who owned and operated the place. They had been in business only a few months but already they had an enthusiastic following. The bread there was especially good, crusty outside and soft inside, more like the bread found in New York than in South Florida. I kidded Sidney about owning an interest in the place, since he went there so often.

After he learned all he needed to know about the Norman's Cay kidnap snatch, Sidney spent most of the dinner telling me about the latest developments in the Green Mountain Express which was an H.O. scale model railroad he was building. He lived in a big, three bedroom apartment, and had knocked out walls and connected two of them. A huge spread of miniature towns, chasms, bridges, and mountains filled the two rooms. Once when Sidney was having a formal dinner he started describing his layout to his guests and then showing it to them. The rest of the evening was spent with gentlemen in tuxedos throwing tiny switches so that ladies in formal gowns could drive tiny locomotives through dark tunnels and across perilous bridges. That night he described building a new bridge as if it were real. He was the engineer and I was the builder. I went home that night wondering if we should use four spans or five for the bridge and whether we should try to anchor it to rock or concrete. If Snake was crazy, Sidney was at least half way there.

I had started calling Rocket as soon as I got back from Norman's on Monday, but there was no answer at her apartment. On Thursday I called her office and found out she had gotten back that afternoon. I talked to her only long enough to arrange to come to her place that night.

When I arrived about six, I just hugged her for a few minutes and then we sat down on the couch and talked. The sudden loss of her father had really upset her. She wanted to talk so I listened while she told me about him. Most of it was about sailing on the Chesapeake when she was a little girl. Apparently, her dad was a guy who could really enjoy being on a boat no matter what the weather was like or whom he was with. I think I would have liked him a lot.

Rocket looked great even with her eyes a little sore from crying. The soft brown of her eyes was like butterscotch and her lashes seemed extra long. I was a really good listener and I didn't mention the rescue until she had stopped talking about her dad. After hearing how things were at her job, I said I had something important but it could wait for a few days. She was never any good at being kept in suspense so she insisted on hearing about it now.

"We're fairly certain that our friend is on the island. When you went home for the funeral, I got someone else to come. We went there and spent the weekend and I located the house. We're going to go back on Saturday night, July eighth, and try to make a rescue. We need somebody who knows boats to help out and it has to be somebody we can trust."

"You want me to help you kidnap somebody from a drug dealer?"

"We want you to stay in a boat while Snake and I go ashore and try to make the rescue. The house is close to the water. He'll go into the house. You'll bring the boat in to where the water is shallow enough to wade out. We will jump in the boat and take off. I'm going to provide some medical assistance to help detox our friend. If there's a problem ashore, you will leave as fast as you can and go straight to Nassau."

"And you want me to help because I can run a boat, and you can trust me, and because I'm a friend?"

"Yeah, that's about it."

"The last time you asked me to do you a favor because we were good friends, you took me to Ricardo's party and banged on me forty-seven times. Is that what you have in mind this time?"

"There won't be any time for that kind of thing."

"Can I do it without taking any more time off from my job? I realize you're talking about something really important but I would like to stay employed."

"We'll probably fly over to some place in the Exumas on Saturday morning and pick up the boat. Snake is working it out. He thinks he can borrow a Cigarette-type boat. We'll go in around eleven. If things work out right, we should be back in Florida Sunday morning before noon. You can sleep all afternoon if you want to."

"O.K., I'll do it. You can tell me the details later. Can we go get a pizza or something?

"I really don't want you to be involved in this and I wish I weren't myself. Trying to get the person out legally, though, is impossible. They might already be destroyed by the drug addiction."

We left and went out to a local place. I told her about my trip to Norman's Cay and taking Lisa Winter with me. The accident with Bobby had happened before I met Rocket and I had never told her much about it. I didn't tell her anything about my relationship with Lisa except to mention that she was grateful about Bobby and that her husband had died.

"Did you screw her on Norman's Cay?"

"She's just a friend. I hadn't even seen her for several months before I called that night."

"I'm just a friend, too, but remember what you did to me after Ricardo's party? It was obscene."

"There was nothing obscene about it."

"If we had been lovers it would have been a normal night but for just good friends it was not at all proper."

"I spent three weeks in the Bahamas with you flaunting your hooters and wiggling your behind and never even grabbed."

"You know what that makes you, don't you?"

"It makes me stupid."

After we finished the pizza we drove down to Dinner Key and went aboard *Pauletta*. We talked for a while before Snake came with the explosives. He had two cardboard boxes labeled Campbell Soup. He opened one of them and it looked like cans of soup. It would pass an inspection unless they opened the wrong cans and tried to eat them. Most of the cans actually were soup. It was a terrorist type of explosive package. After explaining how to use the explosives Snake gave them their final instructions.

"You show up and anchor in Norman's Cay on either Friday or Saturday. You tow your wooden dinghy and leave it tied to the stern while you're anchored so people can see it. Go ashore if you want, but don't spend too much time there. As soon as it gets dark, you inflate this little two-man boat I brought. Gus, you row the inflatable into the dock. You have a timer on the explosives that will give you thirty minutes to row back to your boat. You decide whether to stay there and leave the next day or pull out that night. You should anchor in a place where you can get out to Exuma Sound in the dark. You could use the restaurant as a bearing because it will be lit up at night. Once you set the timer on the explosives, you're finished and whether you go or stay is up to you. Don't stay any longer than daylight Sunday, though. Nobody knows what's going to happen."

"What do I do if there are boats tied to the dock?"

"Two choices. You either anchor the inflatable thirty or forty feet from the dock with the explosives in it and go back to your boat or you leave the explosives on the beach forty feet from the dock. The package is set up to make noise and not do much damage. Up close though it could do serious damage."

Gus nodded and Snake continued.

"Paulette, you will listen to channel sixteen from eight o'clock on, even if you decide to pull up the anchor and take off. We want to know what's going on after the explosion. If we cancel, we will *not* attempt to contact you. If we postpone, we'll try to call you with the message written here. If you miss this and blow off the explosives, we'll just make the attempt later but without the diversion. If you get the 'postpone' message before Gus goes in, you sit in the harbor all day Sunday and we'll find a way to contact you."

After Gus and Paulette said they understood everything, we told them how much we appreciated their taking two weeks to sail over to the Exumas and set off some explosives. At one point in the conversation Sean offered them some money. Gus just shook his head and glared. Snake was good at lurking in the shadows, but Gus could glare a hole through a stone wall. Snake didn't offer but once. Actually, I can glare as well as Gus but he's really mean looking and I'm only semi-mean looking. After everything was covered, we got off the boat and helped them with the dock lines. They motored out of Dinner Key and started across Biscayne Bay toward Cape Florida and the ocean. I drove Rocket home to her apartment and made a promise to myself that I would stop seeing her completely when this was over. I was beginning to believe she was in love with me and, if she were, then seeing me had to be painful. I knew I wasn't in love with her. At least not yet. At least not quite.

On Friday night, as I was driving across the Julia Tuttle Causeway to Miami Beach and the little private island, I realized I had lied to Butch. When I told him I didn't care about the sleeping plans I was mistaken. Patricia Rivera had been fairly aggressive in calling and asking me to take her to dinner. She had obviously been enthusiastic about spending the weekend with me and I had a feeling I could get in her pants. I was really looking forward to sailing on the *Ojos Verdes,* but I might as well spend a little effort chasing Pat, too.

I drove past the gatehouse, telling the guard who I was, and being waved on, crossed the bridge to the island. It was just as impressive as it had been the night of the party. I put my car behind a large white Cadillac convertible. The bilious green color looked even worse next to the gleaming white car. I noticed the convertible had the initials "B.S." in little silver letters on the door.

I went up to the front door and was shown through the house by a servant, then out to a screened-in porch which overlooked the large terrace where the party was held. Antonia was there dressed in jeans and a plaid shirt with no sleeves.

"Good evening, Dr. Devlin," she said. "It's very nice to see you again."

I was a little startled at her appearance since she looked about sixteen years old. I couldn't figure it out, but I kept on staring at her while I asked questions about what she had been doing with her time while she visited the Salazars. She had on absolutely no makeup but this didn't seem to make any difference. Her eyes and eyelashes looked the same. I could see her unusual grey eyes with the tint of green now, better in the light on the porch than in the darkness at the party. They were exquisite. She had her black hair pulled back in a pony tail and this accentuated the contours of her face. Just as before, I was impressed with the beautiful shape of her un-plucked eyebrows.

She offered to fix me a drink. When I told her what I wanted she went over to a rolling type bar and fixed it for me. When she raised an arm, the sleeveless blouse allowed me to see that her armpits were not shaved. Antonia did not arouse me sexually, in spite of her great beauty, but for some reason I found this to be erotic. Once again I thought about painting her portrait and decided to mention it.

"Toni, I have a hobby of painting portraits and I wonder if you would let me paint a picture of you?"

"Of course, Dr. Devlin, I would be very flattered. When Don Ricardo comes I will ask his permission."

She said this without changing expression and I couldn't tell if she was being polite or whether she really wanted me to do it. A few minutes later Ricardo and Carmela came out on the porch with Pat Rivera. She had arrived a little before I did and they were showing her the house. Apparently she had missed the "tour" at Ricardo's birthday party. He was very warm and friendly as he had been at his party, but I was a little bit surprised at Carmela. She called me "Dr. Devlin" instead of Dev, but she talked as if we were old friends and wanted to know if I had done any interesting operations this week. She was also curious about Pat and wanted to know all about her and her job at the local television station.

When the others were listening to a story that Ricardo was telling, Carmela whispered to me.

"Why didn't you bring Rocket?"

I was a little startled at her question. It was none of her business, of course, but somehow she made it seem perfectly natural and I was reminded of my mother. It was the kind of thing she used to ask me and my friends all the time when we were growing up. Women like her assumed that their approval of your girls was important, and somehow it was.

"Rocket and I are just friends, Mrs. Salazar. At one time we thought we might be in love but it didn't work out. I think it might be honest to say that we love each other but more like friends than anything else."

"I think you are making a mistake, Dr. Devlin. There's something very special about her. Of course it is none of my business but Butch is about your age and I shudder sometimes at the girls he goes out with. I wish he could find someone like Sylvia and get married. Ricardo told me about having dinner aboard your boat, and he told me all about Rocket and how she got her nickname. What do you think of our Antonia?"

I was amazed at how much Carmela seemed like my mother. I was past thirty but she treated me like I was a college kid. I remembered how my mother had treated Gus when she came to visit and suddenly realized that both these women probably treated all men as if they were still boys. I wonder why we don't mind.

While I was talking to Carmela, Butch came in with a man that I didn't recognize. He introduced the man to Patricia and me as Senator Harvey Morton. His wife was named Alicia and she looked much younger than he did. Butch explained that Harvey and Alicia were going to have a quick dinner with us and leave. We would be wanting to sleep for a few hours before we left at midnight for Bimini or the Keys. Nobody had mentioned where we were going, but the weather forecast was good, so I assumed we would leave that night for the Bahamas.

Butch started telling his father about how he had been on the overseas telephone most of the day to Spain about a problem they had with bulls. It seemed that a mistake had been made and two bulls had been switched. One bull, who was supposed to go into the ring in Seville, had been put with a cow that was set apart for breeding. The female was in heat and the fighting bull went slightly crazy. Just as he was about to mount the female, the mistake was discovered and he was separated from the cow without completing the act. The next day when the frustrated bull was released at the *Corrida* he had no interest in fighting anybody and tried instead to mount one of the horses. The people who had paid a very high price for a fighting bull naturally wanted their money back since a lover bull was of no use to them.

Butch told the story so well that everyone was laughing out loud. When he described it from the bull's point of view, he was really funny. He could have gone on stage as a professional.

"Can you imagine the feelings of the poor bull? Think of what happened to him. After weeks of running around with no companionship except for other males he was suddenly taken over to the ranch and introduced to this beautiful lady cow. He smells her perfume. It is love at first sight. She tells him she is ready and then, just at the moment when he is about to begin making love to his lady, they come and take him away. They put him in a truck and take him to Seville, which he doesn't like because it has far too many tourists, and put him out in a big *Plaza de Toros* where everyone seems mad at him.

"What would you do if you were a bull in such circumstances? He sees a horse, which is not to his taste but is nevertheless a four legged female, so he tries to make love and everyone laughs at him. What embarrassment! What frustration! By now this bull needs a psychiatrist. They put him back in the truck and take him away. The only consolation he has is that he didn't really like Seville, anyway. You know – the tourists." As a story teller Butch had learned well from Ricardo.

The cocktail hour was very short since we would be sailing all night and when Butch finished the story we went into the dining room and sat down. When we were all seated at one end of a huge table Ricardo said grace. I guessed that the family was devout Catholic. It seemed a little strange because the room was so beautiful and we were all in casual clothes. The food was good but very basic with nothing spicy, and no wine was served. Experienced sailors are careful what they eat before going offshore.

I was seated next to Senator Morton and talked mostly to him. I didn't like congressmen in general, but Harvey seemed like a nice guy. The only interesting thing I learned about the Senator was that he was a member of a committee, or a subcommittee, that had something to do with assassinations. While I was talking with him, I heard Patricia, who was talking to Ricardo, mention Sean Moran. I listened and heard Ricardo say he knew Sean's father. I asked Ricardo how he knew him.

"I knew Shannon Moran years ago in Marseilles. He was one of the strangest men I have ever met, and I did business with him for many years. He was in the same business that young Sean is in."

"Excuse me, Ricardo," I said. "Sean is a good friend of mine and sails with me a lot, but I've never actually known what he does for a living. What is he?"

"Are you with the police? Or the government?" He winked at Harvey Morton and spoke with a big smile on his face.

"Sean is primarily a dealer in art and artifacts. Sometimes he buys and sells pieces on his own and sometimes he works for museums or individual buyers. I met his father many years ago when I was looking for a particular piece of art that I had only read about. I went to *El Prado* and talked to all the experts there. I told them of my interest in the piece and showed them some of the references to it. They were helpful in every way, except they couldn't tell me how to find it. They did lead me to books that described the piece and introduced me to some people that knew about it. They showed me similar pieces but they were no help in telling me where to look for it, or even how to start. They did put out the 'word' that I was in the market."

We were all listening carefully now, really interested.

"One day an old man came to my hotel. I recognized him as a clerk, or record keeper, from the museum. He said he had heard me talking with the curators about the piece I was looking for and that he had a suggestion. He gave me a piece of paper and on it was written Shannon Moran and a telephone number. He asked me not to tell the people he worked for about his visit because they were not friendly toward the Moran. I asked why, but he wouldn't tell me, and begged me not to get him in trouble. I was dubious, but the man did not ask for money. He actually refused my offer when I extended it, but reluctantly accepted a small amount."

By this time everyone was listening as Ricardo continued the story. "I called Shannon Moran and arranged to meet him. I told him what I was looking for and he said he was familiar with the piece and could find it. He said I could either pay him to look for it or I could pay only if he found it. Naturally he charged more if he went after it without a guarantee of reimbursement, but I didn't know him so I named a specific amount. He agreed on the amount without argument and we shook hands.

"The next morning he called me and said he had located the piece. I was astonished that he had found it so quickly. We flew together to Algiers and met with the man who had the piece and was willing to sell it. He wanted too much money – not more than I could afford, of course, but more than the piece was actually worth. I refused to pay and we flew together back to Madrid. On the flight back I wrote out a check for the amount we had agreed on, but he refused and said that I had not been able to buy the piece. I tried in vain to pay him.

"Just before we landed in Madrid he asked me what I *would* pay and I gave him a figure. He said he would try again. About a month later he showed up at my office in Toledo with the piece. He told me what I owed him, which was far less than what I had said I would pay. This puzzled me since he could have asked for the amount I originally said I would pay.

"He told me that sometimes he had to deal with people who are criminals. In that world he said that a man's word was the thing that was valued most. When laws and contracts are not part of the system, there has to be some basis for trust. Lying to the police or the government was, of course, acceptable, but a man's word must be good or he can't function. I've never forgotten what he said."

"What about Sean? When did you meet him?" I asked.

"I saw Shannon Moran from time to time. He worked as I do in many different countries. Sometimes I bumped into him by accident. Occasionally I needed him to do a search for me, for some rare work of art that I couldn't find on my own. Once he did a search for me on a particular piece and failed. Five years later he turned up with the piece."

"It sounds like he was really honest," Patricia commented.

"Extremely ethical would be more like it. He was in a very rare profession. I do not know of anyone else who operated as he did. You cannot go to the yellow pages and look up 'searcher for rare and stolen art work'. His was a one-person union and he wrote the rules and ethics. I did business with him for many years and he never lied or attempted to cheat me, but I do not know that he was an honest man. There were some who said that Shannon also was a thief and that he sometimes stole works of art from his enemies and sold them to his friends. It was also said that he had many other occupations."

By this part of the story we had finished our dinner and were having coffee. Pat had complimented Carmela on her choice of food, because it was simple but very interesting. She had provided some long pieces of baked bread, sliced in an unusual way, with a variety of things such as black olives, peppers, lettuce, sliced pickles, tomatoes, salami, chicken slices, pepperoni and oil and vinegar. Pat had asked Carmela if the sandwiches were a specialty of Spain or perhaps Algiers. She said she had picked them up at a new place in Miami called the Subway which made all types of submarine sandwiches or hoagies. When Pat looked a little crestfallen, Carmela winked at her and smiled so we all could see. Pat laughed at herself and Ricardo continued to tell us about Shannon Moran.

"I've never met Sean Moran," Senator Morton said. "But his father sounds like an interesting person. What were his other occupations?"

"Once I chartered an airplane to fly down to Capetown to look at a rare piece. Shannon was with me. When we came home a few days later, we had a long flight over the whole continent of Africa. We left late in the afternoon so we could sleep all night. It was a nice plane with two couches that made up into beds and we talked for a while before going to sleep. We talked about personal things for the first and only time I knew him. He told me he had a son, Sean Shannon, who was going to come to live with him and that he was going to train him to be a curator at a museum. I also asked a very personal question. I had been told that he had another occupation, working undercover, or under assumed identities, and asked if it was true. He swore me to secrecy then claimed he worked as an agent for British Intelligence in MI5. I told him that I would never reveal what he had said but I was totally surprised. I didn't believe him, of course. No agent of MI5 would confide in me unless there was a reason."

"Why were you so surprised?" Pat Rivera asked. "Didn't you already know that he worked under cover?"

"I had been told by usually impeccable sources that Shannon worked for the Irish Republican Army as a gun runner."

"Do you think he was a double agent or whatever they call people like that?" Pat asked.

"Probably."

"What about Sean? When did you meet him?" I wanted to know.

"Sean simply showed up in my hotel room one day in Paris when I was expecting his father. He brought with him a very rare painting that he had been searching for, a Botticelli. He was about fourteen at the time but looked and acted older. He spoke French that first meeting, very fluently. I asked about his father and Sean said he had gone to Japan to buy an object for himself."

"Did you ever meet his wife or any other children besides Sean?" Pat asked.

"There are no other children. Sean has no brothers or sisters. Of that I am certain," Ricardo said, and stood up. "I think we need to go aboard the boat and sleep for a couple of hours if we are going to leave at midnight."

"It's only eight fifteen," said Butch. "Why don't we go down now and tie up at Miami Beach Marina. We can probably use the gas dock since it will be closed. Then we can go through Government Cut around one o'clock. What do you think? How about you, Dev? Should we go down now while we are still wide awake?"

"Fine with me," I said.

"Let's do it that way," Ricardo said. "Let's go."

Pat asked me if I could walk out to her car with her and help carry her duffle bags while Butch said he would take my single bag and hanger. The Salazars and Toni had put their things aboard earlier in the day. The Senator and his wife knew what we were doing, so they said goodbye and left.

As we walked out to Pat's car I thought I needed to bring up the sleeping arrangements, since I had no idea what she expected.

"Butch told me when he invited me that his parents would be coming along. He said that they would want you to share a cabin with Antonia. Is that O.K.?" I said, feeling a little awkward.

"Were you planning to have me share a cabin with you?"

I couldn't see Pat's face in the dark, so I couldn't tell if she was mocking me.

"It's their boat and we're the guests, so I just figured I'd let them worry about it."

"Suppose there had been only the four of us. What would you and Butch have done?"

"Antonia is a friend of the family, not Butch's girlfriend."

"I know that. Sean told me before we went to Ricardo's birthday party. Why did you want me to come away with you for the weekend? Why didn't you bring the girl that was with you at the party? Why did you invite me?"

I've never been good at clever remarks but I knew she was needling me so I had to give it a shot.

"You seemed very sexually aggressive and I thought I could get in your pants."

Because of the darkness I couldn't tell if she thought my comment was smart-ass or funny but she didn't say anything and I didn't hear any laughing.

When we got down to the dock and aboard *Ojos Verdes* I noticed that there was still an armed guard. The boat was ready to go with the sail covers off both the main and the mizzen. The big diesel was idling slowly, making that deep throaty growling noise that sounds so powerful. I carried Pat's bright red duffel bag below and put it in the forward cabin. They had decided not to take any of the paid crew and there would be just the six of us.

Ricardo took the wheel and Butch cast off the dock lines. We moved slowly away from the dock. There was a tiny strip of land with a few bushes and some palm trees that protected the dock from the chop in Biscayne Bay and we went north about two hundred feet around that and then turned west toward the main channel of the Intra-coastal Waterway. There was a nice breeze out of the south, about fifteen, Ricardo told me after looking at the dials on the instrument by the wheel. There was a three-quarter moon starting to appear. Butch took the wheel and we all sat in the cockpit enjoying the evening. Although my own boat was a little over forty feet, it would have bounced around a little in the moderate chop. The much bigger and heavier boat seemed almost unaffected.

I had been out on Biscayne Bay at night many times but I never stopped appreciating how beautiful it was. For the first few miles we were headed west away from Miami Beach toward the city. All the lights were on in the buildings as it grew dark. The Intra-coastal Waterway runs down Biscayne Bay at this point, but it is way over toward the mainland side away from the beach and not in the middle of the bay. I was curious as to how they could cross most of the shallow bay and not run aground. Butch told me how they did it as we motored west.

"If you look back you see the outline of that tall palm tree on the north end of the small strip of land that forms the little harbor. With that on our stern we head directly toward that building. Even at night you can see the outline." He pointed out a large building over on the Miami shore. "You can always see that building. It looks white in daylight and they light it up as soon as it starts to get dark. Going out we hold a course of exactly 275°. We line up with the tree astern and the building ahead as marks. We hold this course until we come between the markers of the Intra-coastal which runs almost directly north and south at the point when we turn. When the black port marker is about a hundred feet away and due north, we make a 95° turn to the left and go due south until we pick up the next set of Intra-coastal markers about a hundred yards away. We have to be careful because the *Brilliant* is not there to rescue us."

Ricardo came up and sat down. He lit up a cigar.

"When did you first come to Miami, Dev?" he asked.

"I first came down here when I was in high school. I used to crew for a guy from my yacht club who decided to bring his boat down for the Southern Circuit races. I lived in New York at the time and it was a cold winter. Coming down here where it's warm was really exciting. I did the whole thing with him, Saint Pete to Lauderdale, Lipton Cup and everything. I also came down when I was a kid to crew in the Bacardi Cup."

"Where did you sail in New York?" Butch asked.

By this time we had reached the imaginary mark and turned left, which was south on the Intra-coastal.

"I lived in a place called Rye, New York and sailed out of Larchmont Yacht Club, about five miles away."

"Hey, I've been to Larchmont Yacht Club," Butch said. "I was there for the World Championship of the 5-O-5 class. Did you ever sail a 5-0-5?"

"I had my own Star and raced it most of the time, but I liked the boats and crewed for a friend of mine in the Nationals and the Worlds that summer. We must have raced against each other! Did you bring a boat from Spain?"

"No, I borrowed an American boat and the kid who owned it crewed for me. We finished in the middle. Remember the two guys from Australia? Chris and Bryan? Weren't they something? As soon as the breeze started to blow they just took off and left everybody."

"Where did you stay when you were there?" I asked.

"With Bill and Nancy Burroughs. They had four Englishmen and a guy from Bermuda as well as me. They were all older, in their thirties and I was about twenty but they were all great. I can still remember James Bridge-Butler and David Court-Hampton. Mac Lightbourne from Bermuda was another one. Bill had a 5-O-5, U.S. 1003, light blue boat."

We talked all the way down to where we turned east and went out Government Cut toward the beach. We turned into Miami Beach Marina a few miles later and tied up at the gas dock. There was no dock-master and nobody tied up there so we set an alarm for 2:00 a.m. and went to sleep.

Chapter Sixteen

Late Friday Night, 16 June
    I have been jangled awake in the middle of the night by an alarm clock many times but I have never lost the desire to smash the clock. When I lived on the *Vanitie,* docked in the East River, and rode a motorcycle around Manhattan chasing ambulances, I got startled by the telephone as well as the alarm clock, but I never got used to that, either. This time was no different.
    When it went off I looked across the cabin to the other pilot berth and saw that Butch had already gotten up. I looked at my watch and saw that it was three minutes after two, so I rolled out of the bunk and put on my clothes. By the time I got to the galley, I was beginning to wake up. Carmela was there fixing coffee.
    I accepted a sandwich and a mug of coffee, and went up on deck. Ricardo and Butch were already there and had the engine running, so I just sat down in the cockpit. They cast off the dock lines and we started out of the marina. The moon was still there but it was very dark. Government Cut is the entrance for the port of Miami. Miami Beach Marina has a huge wooden barrier around it to protect the boats from chop caused by several channels running together, and the wake from large ships coming in and out. The covers were off but the sails would not be hoisted until we were outside of the jetties. Everything else was set up and ready to go.
    On my own boat I always liked to be at the wheel going in or out of a harbor, but as a guest I sat down in the cockpit and enjoyed my coffee and sandwich while I waited for instructions. In a few minutes Pat came and sat down beside me with a mug of coffee.
    "What am I supposed to do?" she whispered.
    "Just enjoy yourself. It's a beautiful night and it should be a magnificent sail. Have you ever been out on a sailboat this large before?"
    "I've never been on any sailboat before."
    "Well, just relax and have a good time."
    "I'm sure we're safe," Pat whispered. "Right?"
    As we left the rock jetties and started out between the buoys and into the ocean, Toni came on deck. To my surprise she took the wheel. Butch asked me to take the main sheet while he and Ricardo went forward and started cranking up the main. The breeze had enough south in it so that we might be able to go hard on the wind and hold a course that would fetch Cat Cay on one long starboard tack. Butch and Ricardo cranked, the main slatted and banged, and the headboard worked it's way up the mast. Toni slowed the speed to bare steerageway and held the bow exactly into the wind until Ricardo yelled, "Fall Off!"

She turned the wheel just enough, and the big powerful boat fell off on a starboard tack, and started moving slowly under sail power. I had trimmed the main sheet in tight when they had it up into the wind before we started to fall off. I eased it a little as we fell off and cleated it.

Butch and Ricardo moved back to the mizzen mast. I eased the mizzen sheet way out since the bow was not directly into the wind and the boom needed to be free. Toni had kept the engine running in neutral, ready if a quick correction was necessary.

Ricardo and Butch were both strong men and it was easy work cranking the big wire reel winches. The headboard on the mizzen went up the mast smoothly and quickly just like the main. When it reached the top Ricardo said, "Trim!"

I trimmed the mizzen and *Ojos Verdes* picked up additional speed. Since the boat had a roller furling jib both men came back to the cockpit. Ricardo eased the furling line, Butch cranked a huge Barient and I trimmed. As soon as he had released the furling line Ricardo put both hands on the top section of the double winch handle. With both of them cranking, the jib came in smoothly.

"Let's see how she goes without the staysail," said Ricardo. The big Rhodes was starting to move now with tremendous power, totally unaffected by waves that would have slowed down my smaller boat or bounced it around a little. The wind was perfect and we had the full main, mizzen and genoa. I guessed we could have handled another five miles of breeze without any sail reduction. The motion of the boat through the water was something I had never experienced before. I had crewed on Twelve Meters and occasionally steered one, but this boat was not only much heavier than a twelve, it had additional power from its beam. I was hoping Ricardo would offer me a chance to steer.

"Toni, go below with Dev and go over the course with him." Ricardo took the wheel and I went below with Antonia. Butch was talking to Pat and asked me to bring him up another sandwich when I came back. Since we came aboard the *Ojos Verdes,* I had been impressed with the lack of commotion. Experienced sailors always operate that way, but moving a boat this size anywhere requires skill and knowledge. And discipline.

The navigation station was huge, with a table almost large enough to spread out a full-sized chart. *Ojos Verdes* seemed to have every electronic aid to navigation currently invented. There were three separate radios that were way out of the yachting class. When I asked about them Toni told me Ricardo had offices all over the world and that he liked to keep track of what they were doing by short-wave radio. I was very impressed.

H.O. 4123 was spread out on the navigation table held down by some small leather bags filled with shot. Toni told me that she was assuming an average speed through the water of eight knots. With the wind out of the south, she was assuming the Gulfstream would set us north at two and a half knots. She had set a course of 120° degrees and estimated that the set of the stream would carry us up to Gun Key Passage. When we were sure of our position, we would ease the sheets and reach up to Bimini.

The only light was the dim red one over the navigation table and it cast a strange light on Antonia as we talked. Her face was so perfectly shaped that even the soft red light was flattering. The only light I could imagine that would not flatter her would be total darkness. She had her black hair pulled back in a pony tail and she looked very young. She had on a long sleeved knit shirt that was tight on her slender body and accentuated her plump breasts. She was speaking in Spanish quietly and in a very serious way. I tried to think of when I had ever seen her smile, and could remember only at Ricardo's party in the receiving line. When she realized that he was about to reveal that he was not the paid captain, she had gotten a real grin on her face. It was strange standing there so close to her in the weird red light. She was magnificent and I should have felt an urge to kiss her but I didn't. I did appreciate her beauty, though, and I was close enough to smell a hint of something very nice, a faint trace of perfume.

I was very impressed with her knowledge of navigation and also that Ricardo had left the task to her. She had turned on the Loran C, made a notation in a notebook, and marked a small note on the chart.

"Do you have any suggestions, Dr. Devlin?"

"None at all, Toni. You could charge Ricardo a fee for your services as a navigator, though."

"Thank you very much, Dr. Devlin. Your approval means a great deal to me." Even in the dim red light I could see that she was very serious. She was a nice polite kid and a gorgeous female, but I couldn't see why she would care very much what I thought of her. I noticed a trace of lipstick on her lips.

Toni finished off the navigation, turned off the red light, and showed me where to get a sandwich for Butch. I got another one for myself and a mug of coffee. She got some things for Ricardo and Pat and we started back up to the cockpit. Toni went up the companionway stairs first. She was wearing jeans and it was dark, and there was no reason why I should pay any attention to her behind, but I did. When I got back up in the cockpit and sat down I realized that something was sticking in my mind about her bottom or her legs or something, but I couldn't figure out what it was. I sat down beside Pat in the cockpit and asked how she was enjoying the sail.

"I think I'm going to puke," she whispered.

"Did you take a seasick pill?"

"I didn't know I was supposed to."

"I should have told you. If you're not used to sailing it sometimes helps."

"Some fucking doctor you are."

I went below and found some crackers and persuaded her to have a few. Sometimes that helps. By now we were well out in the stream and the waves were fairly large. *Ojos Verdes* was almost hard on the wind but not quite. She was sliding through the waves with enormous power, perfectly balanced and well sailed. Ricardo was steering and it felt like he was using his finger tips to do it.

It was what I called a "Brilliant night." On overnight races or cruises I used the expression to describe a night when the sailing conditions were good or perfect and the stars were putting on a show. People who sailed with me had gotten used to using the word as both an adjective and also to sort of pretend that the splendour of the night was there especially for my boat the *Brilliant*, and the people on it. On a night when we were racing and overtaking boats, with a lot of stars as a background, the term would be used over and over again, with the emphasis on our boat's performance. Rocket teased me about it but she used the expression more than anybody and probably enjoyed those times more than anyone. If you think you are about to vomit, however, the beauty of almost anything can get lost.

Ten or fifteen minutes after Toni and I came back up Ricardo finished a sandwich and announced that he was going to go below and get some sleep. He offered me the wheel but I said I would take it later. Butch suggested that Toni steer so that he could lay up against the cabin and take a siesta. I wanted to be with Pat to see if I couldn't prevent her sickness or at least be there with a bucket if she threw up.

She and I were sitting on the port side of the cockpit which was the leeward side. I got her to turn a little so that I could point to a freighter way off in the distance. We could see the red running light as the ship passed across our bow and then went on up north using the northward set of the gulfstream to get a few extra free miles. There was a lot of traffic that night and I started pointing things out to her. I explained the gulfstream and how it was formed and flowed like a river until it affected Europe. There were all sorts of ships and a few of them came very close. For everyone except Pat it was a magnificent night.

After awhile she started asking questions and I thought she was going to be all right but then suddenly she wanted the bucket and managed to get her head into it before she vomited. I held her and the bucket while she retched into it. After a few minutes there didn't seem to be anything left. She looked up.

"What the hell do I do now?"

"Just sit still for a few minutes. You may feel better now but wait a few minutes."

Butch went below and came back with a small paper cup. "Try to swallow this, Pat. It's *creme de menthe* and it should make you feel better. The syrup soothes your stomach and the little bit of alcohol will help your morale. If it doesn't work you will just puke it up and you won't be any worse off than you are now."

She accepted the cup and swallowed it in tiny sips while I held the bucket in the ready position and waited. After awhile she seemed to relax. Toni suggested that I take the wheel and that she take Pat below and put her in a bunk. She would probably be O.K. now and would feel better if she got some sleep.

I sat down on the comfortable helmsman's seat and took the wheel from Antonia. We were steering by instruments, mast-head fly and feel. *Ojos Verdes* seemed to be in a groove that required very little pressure on the wheel and the power was impressive. If you have enough experience to steer a boat that size and to steer it well, the thrill is tremendous. We were heeled over about twelve degrees according to the gauge and doing just under nine knots. I was wondering if the extra speed would force Toni to make adjustments.

"According to both my dead reckoning and the Loran C we are moving faster than I planned, so we are further south. I would like to ease off a very tiny little bit."

Toni moved over to the winch where the genoa was trimmed and uncleated the sheet. She put one small hand on the coils around the winch and eased the sheet a very tiny little bit. Then she moved to the mainsheet and eased it a tiny bit and then the mizzen. I realized that Butch was awake and that he didn't seem to think that Toni needed any help in easing the sheets. It did not require any physical strength, of course, but the tension on the genoa sheet was several tons and a little slip could have been a mess. Maybe lost fingers. I was amazed that Ricardo and Butch would let this little girl navigate the boat, steer the boat, and go around in the middle of the night doing pretty much whatever she wanted.

After the sheets were eased, and we had settled on a slightly different course, I was a little surprised at how I could actually differentiate between the old and the new. I had a fairly large compass on my boat but any small course change was an estimation because the compass itself did not have every degree marked. The motion of the boat itself made it hard to hold it steady. On the *Ojos Verdes* the compass was larger and broken down further, and the motion of the boat made it easier. We were two degrees to the left of where we had been steering before. Toni came over and asked about the course and seemed to be satisfied with the two degrees.

I liked the idea that Ricardo and Carmela treated her in a very old fashioned way. When a woman or girl is as beautiful as Antonia you usually expect them to act a certain way. The only really truly beautiful woman I had ever met who wasn't a pain in the ass was Lisa Winter and she was a kind of mystery. Maybe Toni was another exception.

She made herself comfortable with some cushions in the corner of the cockpit, very close to me, but not touching me. She sat there quietly and I couldn't tell if she was trying to sleep. I was enjoying the magnificent sailing. *Ojos Verdes* required my attention, but she didn't wander like short-keeled racing boats usually do. Like all experienced racing sailors I tried to steer "quick and small", meaning constant tiny adjustments but no big swings or course changes.

When I'm racing, day or night, my concentration is total and I never think of anything but the speed of the boat, the tactics or strategy, and sometimes the weather. On a night like this, with no race to worry about, I found my mind wandering all over the place. I thought deliberately about Sean and Sharon and the kidnap but I couldn't think of anything else I could do to get prepared. I thought for the thousandth time that I hoped Snake knew what he was doing, although I didn't feel any apprehension or nervousness about it. I was worried, though, about Sharon and whether or not they had destroyed her brain. The ugliness of what they had done to her was unbearable to think about. I thought about Lisa, but only for a few seconds because I was always thinking about her, and the image of her telling me she wouldn't go out on dates with me still hurt.

I was very conscious of the stars and how bright they were in the clear black sky and of the phosphorus in the water and how it made the wake sparkle. I thought, as I always did at times like this, that one day I would make a deal with Bill and a new partner that would allow me to take a year off so I could go on a long ocean cruise. Maybe to the Mediterranean. Or the South Pacific.

As soon as I dreamed of a long ocean cruise I thought about Rocket and wondered if I would take her with me. Then I thought about it a little more and realized that I couldn't and that I really shouldn't see her any more. I had been insane. I spent three weeks cruising with her and never touched her. I spent nine or ten hours every day staring at her luscious little body in shorts and things. Sometimes in one-piece bathing suits that covered everything and hid nothing. Sometimes in the sexiest outfit of all, a long tee shirt and pink panties. Always pink. No bra. Nipples poking out at me. Sometimes I'm pretty sure she didn't even have panties under the tee shirt.

For the first time that night steering the boat, and nothing else on my mind, I realized how stupid I had been about Rocket. We had made a deal that we would be friends and not lovers. We agreed that we would go cruising without any screwing, and we had both stuck to the deal. I had come back so horny I could have been put in charge of the rape department for Ghengis Kahn and his army. I should have gone out and found myself a cooperative young lady and satisfied myself with her. Instead, I take Rocket to a party, screw her in the bathhouse and then fifty or sixty times back at her apartment. I must have been insane. I must still be insane. Anybody with half a brain would have known that Rocket wanted me to do it to her on the cruise. All over the Abacos maybe. Maybe in Nassau and Chub. Maybe every night. Maybe every day.

I tried to concentrate on steering the boat and took a look around the horizon for ships or other boats but there was nothing and my mind went back to Rocket. When we were dancing at the party at Ricardo's house she had teased me about staring at her face instead of her behind. She must have been wiggling her behind at me the whole trip and wanting me to break the agreement and ravish her. She must have been horny as hell herself and I didn't figure it out. She must have been mad as hell and felt some sort of rejection.

I was about to write myself off as the dumbest guy in the world when I thought about Chub Cay. Suddenly she had started acting funny, almost shy. A little bit of lipstick and perfume and soft music. She was all dressed up for dinner that night with a full set of underwear. She could have worn her tee shirt with the nipples staring at me and panties or no panties underneath. She had worn that for dinner plenty of times. As the big ketch moved along smoothly and powerfully through the dark warm water of the Gulfstream, my imagination told me that Sylvia Brzinski had fallen in love with me because I had kept my hands off of her during the whole cruise. This possible insight into the psychology of the female mind was more than I could handle. I had to ask a question and Toni was the only female around. I startled her with the question.

"Toni, you're a woman and I've got to ask you a question. Does a woman always know, when they tell a man something, whether it is the truth or not? Do they sometimes not even know themselves how they feel?"

"*Yo no se, Senor Winfield. Yo todavia soy senorita.*" I do not know, Mr. Winfield. I am not yet a woman.

I did not know what to say to that, and I did not even know what she was talking about, so I stopped talking and concentrated on sailing the boat. Toni went below to check her navigation and I tried to figure out what she meant. In America girls seemed to think they were grown up adults when they were about twelve and I was sure that Antonia was at least nineteen or twenty. She might have meant that she was still a virgin but that didn't make much sense. I decided to stop thinking about women. It always gave me a headache whenever I thought about the psychology of women. Just when I had it figured out, that they said the opposite of what they meant, some young lady would talk straight and confuse me.

I looked around the horizon and it was all clear. I could see the lights of a few ships in the distance and a few stars that moved and then turned out to be airplanes. There was something almost hypnotic about a boat sailing for a long time on one tack. In the 1964 Bermuda Race we had started off close hauled on starboard tack and sailed that way for five days, reefing the main or changing jibs a few times but never setting a spinnaker. When we finally tacked about five miles from the finish it seemed like every loose item aboard the boat had found its way into a leeward bunk and came flying across the cabin with the tack.

Suddenly I remembered Toni coming down the companionway ladder the night of Ricardo's birthday. When she slipped and her dress came up, I probably stared at her underpants for a full thirty seconds. She had paused without moving, almost as if she were giving me a brief permission to look. When she said, "Now that you have examined the details of my panties would you like to see the boat?" she had been right. I had examined the details and from only a foot away and now several weeks later I remembered that she had on plain white full cut cotton underpants of the type that little girls wear. They were definitely not the kind that ladies wear to parties. Not bikini cut, and not tap pants, and not a panty girdle. She did not have on a garter belt and her stockings seemed to just hold themselves up. No woman would wear that kind of panties to a party and she had said that she was not yet a woman. I realized that Antonia was a *virgin*. No wonder Ricardo and Butch were so protective of her.

Sometimes at sea in the middle of the night, men see visions of strange things but I had never heard of anybody having visions of virgins' underpants. I had experienced things like this before, though, having my brain make connections and develop insights that I never would have come up with on land in the daylight. Maybe if I had not gone for several months without a woman I would not be thinking about such things. I didn't count Ricardo's party and the thing that started in the bathhouse as significant, since there was just too much that happened too fast.

Ojos Verdes kept moving along, powerfully and smoothly, sailing up one long swell and gradually down and then up and down another swell. According to the instruments, the wind had not gone over eighteen or under fourteen for several hours and it had not changed directions more than a few degrees. Our angle of heel had not varied more than a few degrees all night. The sensation that I felt steering the big ketch through the dark was one of power as much as speed. It was exhilarating, but at the same time it was gradually putting me to sleep, and I was having my visions get mixed up. I was seeing Toni's white underpants in detail and then the vision blurred and it was Lisa coming down the companionway steps with nothing on but her ice blue panties. I was half dreaming and saw Antonia standing there in the cottage in nothing but her panties, holding a bathing suit in one hand and staring at me as I examined the details. I shook my head to try to wake up and decided that I must be a panty fetishist or something. Maybe I was nuts. Maybe just very horny.

"I'm falling asleep, Toni. Are you still awake?"

"I will get Butch to steer, Dr. Devlin," she said.

"I'm awake," Butch said. "I'll take the wheel."

Antonia said she was going below to check our position and offered to bring up coffee. Butch accepted but I refused and moved over to where Butch had been. It was a comfortable spot in the corner where the cabin and the cockpit came together on the leeward side. I got a couple of cushions and got myself in a position to sleep.

I focused my mind on Patricia Rivera. She was going to be my next piece of ass. I was going to find some way to get her alone on Bimini and get her pants off. She was pretty aggressive and had made it clear that she wanted me to take her out on dates. I also liked her a lot and thought she was fun. As I fell asleep I thought about what I was going to do to her.

I slept for a couple of hours and when I woke up it was starting to get light in the east. I went below and went into the head. I shaved and washed my face. If I went twenty four hours without shaving I looked like the wolf man. I went into the galley and found Carmela fixing fresh coffee.

"Good morning, Dr. Devlin. Did Toni let you steer the boat at all last night? She is very possessive about *Ojos Verdes* and sometimes she wants to do everything."

"I sailed for nearly three hours and enjoyed it tremendously. She's a magnificent boat but I'm curious about Antonia. She really seems to know what she's doing. How'd she learn so much about sailing and navigation?"

"She and my daughter, Carlotta, practically grew up on the boat together. Carlotta was supposed to spend the summer in Miami with us also, but she did so poorly on her examinations that she had to go to summer school in order to enter the university in September. Although she was bitterly disappointed there was no choice."

"At Ricardo's birthday party, Walker Griffeth mentioned that the two girls were friends. He said that they had occasionally gotten into mischief together."

"Frequently is a better description than occasionally. I would never have left Carlotta alone except that she is living with Toni's parents. Dr. Enrique, Toni's father, is far more strict with the girls than Ricardo and I. He will keep her out of trouble this summer."

"Toni's father is a doctor?"

"Yes, he is a cardiac surgeon. A very good one, I believe."

"Did the girls learn to sail together?"

"We always took both of them on the boat with us to keep them out of trouble. Ricardo taught them both as much as he could to keep them occupied. Toni practically grew up on the boat. She can do anything Butch can do except where a man's physical strength is required."

"She's a very beautiful girl, Mrs. Salazar. How old is she?"

"She will be twenty one on Saturday, September 2. I am sure we will have some kind of party for her over the long weekend. I don't know which day, though. Butch will call you. It would mean a lot to Toni if you could be there."

"I'll certainly try. Why is Toni so serious? She really doesn't smile or laugh very much."

"I think she is like that when you are around, Dr. Devlin. I think she is a little bit intimidated by you. It's nothing you do, so don't worry about it. Tell them on deck that I will serve breakfast at exactly six o'clock."

When I got on deck, Ricardo was at the wheel. It seemed as though nobody had touched a sheet all night except the one adjustment when we were closer to nine knots instead of eight. Antonia was sitting down at the leeward side of the cockpit with a pair of binoculars. A few minutes later she saw something.

"I see the radio tower on Bimini."

"Are you sure?" Ricardo asked.

"Yes, I'm sure."

"Will our present course take us to Gun Cay?"

"Yes, but I won't be able to see it for a while."

"Does the Loran C check out with your dead reckoning?"

"Yes."

"Let's continue on this course until we pick up Gun Cay Light. The stream is still pretty strong and we don't want to have to come back against it," Ricardo decided.

There is a two hundred and eighty foot LF radio tower on South Bimini that's visible for more than twenty miles at night and about half that distance in daylight. The code letter "B" is flashed from the summit three times per minute in all directions. It's painted orange and white and carries red fixed lights at the lower levels. This was what Toni had seen with the binoculars. A few minutes later Pat Rivera came up and sat down in the cockpit. I asked her if she felt any better.

"I feel a lot better now. I'm very sorry, Senor Salazar. I'm very embarrassed."

"Did you have a little seasickness?" he laughed. "Don't worry about it. I once sailed in a three-hundred-mile ocean race with a very famous European yacht designer who spent the whole time with his head in a bucket. Besides that, you look very beautiful this morning."

She did look good, really good. She was wearing a white blouse with a lot of lace. It was far too dressy for wearing around a sailboat but I knew enough about women to know that they were totally inconsistent in the way that they dressed. She had worn that blouse because she felt like looking good right then. It was probably because she felt a little embarrassed at having been sick. So to her it was appropriate. She also had on just a trace of lipstick and some earrings.

I was not surprised at the earrings even though the sun was just coming up because I had never seen her without them. With her dark red hair, the silver rings, large or small, always seemed right. Her face was very pretty but there was something else. She always looked like she was about to start laughing. Even though it was very early in the morning, I started looking at her well-tanned legs and white shorts and started thinking about how I could get the shorts off.

Patricia had spent some very careful time in the sun and her complexion was a little lighter and rosier than *cafe au lait*. It was remarkable for its nearly-perfect satiny finish. Because of my profession, I examined faces inside or outside the practice. If you examine many beautiful women you realize that excellent nostrils are essential. Pat's face had the high cheekbones which are so much admired in Western culture and also the long enough nose for great beauty. She also an upper lip that was a tiny millimeter short. Her nostrils were perfect except a tiny fraction long. This gave her a trace of a sneer. It was a tiny, tiny trace but it made her face exotic as well as beautiful and unusual.

Although her hair was dark, the sunshine had bleached some of the ends blonde. The early rays of the sun seemed to light up these ends. I glanced at Toni and she seemed to be watching me while I stared at Pat. The sun was also reflecting off her black shiny hair. With a gorgeous Puerto Rican woman and a beautiful young Spanish girl together this weekend I would have to work hard not to stare too much.

After a few minutes I asked Ricardo if he had any rum aboard and any orange juice. I went below and fixed myself a glass that was about half of each and came back up to watch the sunrise. It was a drink that I called a Sunriser.

Everybody came up to the cockpit for a few minutes, even Carmela, and watched the magic moments when the sun seems to suddenly pop up over the horizon. We had picked up Gun Cay Light earlier in the dark and now we could see traces of Cat Cay and Gun Cay before the sun got too bright. After awhile we went below in shifts for a breakfast that seemed like a brunch or breakfast buffet at some country club or fancy resort.

When Antonia identified the Gun Cay Light to her satisfaction, we eased the sheets and reached off towards the end of South Bimini. As we came off in a northeast direction, we started to make out Holm Cay, Piquet Rock and then after awhile Turtle Rocks and the concrete ship, which is sunk just south of Bimini.

The sands that border South Bimini's western shore are always shifting, so the entrance channel is unreliable. Prolonged high winds and strong tides sometimes rearrange the shallow bars so you have to be careful. When we started to approach the two islands I offered to go up to the bow to watch the bottom. The water is so clear that you can actually see when it's getting too shallow. When we were about two miles from the beach Ricardo took the wheel and started the engine. He headed *Ojos Verdes* up into the wind and we dropped the sails.

We came in toward South Bimini on a course of 82° with both a water tower and the radio tower lined up. This took us across the bar into the deeper blue channel that parallels the beach. When we got near the beach and into the deeper channel we turned north and headed for the harbor. Inside there is plenty of room to anchor but Ricardo had decided to stay at the Bimini Big Game Fishing Club and had called ahead. It was off-season but there was a fishing tournament. We motored slowly through the harbor passing the docks, Browns, and Weechs, and Bimini Blue Water on our port side. We tied up at the Club and put up the big quarantine flag. Ricardo sent Butch off to clear customs, explaining to us that he had gotten Butch listed as the boat's captain so that he would have to do the walking and waiting when they went to different countries.

We had a kind of conference in the cockpit to decide how we would spend our time in Bimini. Carmela said that she wanted to attend mass at the Catholic

Church on the hill the next day and I got the feeling that everyone was expected to go. Ricardo and Toni immediately said they would be going with her and I knew that Butch would do what his mother wanted. I was a little bit surprised when Pat said that she was hoping she wouldn't have to miss going to mass. As a guest I knew I could go, or not go, as I chose.

"Are you a Christian, Dr. Devlin?" Carmela asked me in a tone that was pure polite curiosity with no implication.

"Mrs. Salazar," I said with a smile, intentionally trying to be humorous, "not only am I a Christian, I am in fact a double Christian, since I attend services of both the Roman Catholic Church and the Church of England. Sometimes I go to both services on a single day."

"Well I think that's just wonderful, Dr. Devlin. I will certainly send a telegram to your mother and tell her what a good boy you are."

I realized that Carmela was teasing and I laughed with her. She suggested that I take Pat for a walk and show her Bimini and I said it was a good idea. We all decided to meet later at the bar on the second floor of the restaurant. Even though it was summer, the main dining room was open because of the fishing tournament. For dinner we would go to the restaurant up on the hill, facing the ocean. It's owned and run by the Bimini Blue Water Company and is a great place to watch the sunset.

Pat went below and grabbed a hat, and we started out toward the south end of the island. North Bimini is seven miles long and is extremely narrow and flat. Nowhere is the elevation more than twenty feet above sea level. We walked down past the docks, the small hotel and the ramp where the Chalk's seaplane comes in. When we got to the end of the island, I showed Pat where we had come in, and told her about South Bimini and the airstrip there.

Then we turned around and headed back north past the straw market and the Red Lion on up toward the custom house. We stopped off at Weech's to see an old friend of mine. Jerry was a black Bahamian who had been the dock-master there for many years. Since I usually tied up there when I had *Brilliant* in Bimini, we had become friends. He told me about his family and a new baby girl grandchild and I told him about a couple of operations I had done. He was fascinated by plastic surgery and loved to hear me describe operations. I had brought him a six-pack so we had one, even though it was only a little after nine.

The little island has a special charm for those who like it. It's part Bahamas, part deep-sea-fishing mecca and a little bit like a border town with plenty of bars. The Compleat Angler Hotel, which was built in the thirties, was the first fishing club in the Bahamas. It was more or less copied from the Charles Dickens Compleat Angler in England, and is full of mementoes. It was also one of Ernest Hemingway's hangouts and there are a lot of pictures of him. I liked Bimini, but many people I knew thought it was just scruffy.

When we got back to the boat we found a note saying that all the others had gone over to the beach, so we decided to walk over. We went below and changed to our swim suits and I grabbed my camera. We found them easily, since there were very few people on the beach and sat down with them.

I was a little surprised at Pat's bathing suit. She obviously had a splendid body, but she wore a one-piece suit that had so many ruffles and folds and flaps that a nun could have worn it and felt comfortable. It was so modest it was a shock, but it was several shades of blue and white and very pretty.

We sat around talking for a while and then I fell asleep. I had started reading some poetry and dozed off. I didn't sleep very long and when I woke up Patricia and Ricardo were talking. I didn't hear much of what they were saying, but I did hear a few words that got my attention. Interpol, paintings, and robbery. I listened for a minute and the next thing I heard was the mention of a valuable Rembrandt painting. I raised up and yawned, letting them know that I was awake. I didn't want to butt into a private conversation.

"Good morning, Dev," Ricardo said. "I hope you slept well. Since you young people sailed the boat all night, while I was in the bunk below, I am feeling wide awake. Move over here with us and listen to my story. Here is some wine that was made in one of our vineyards. It is very much like a Rhine wine and tastes best chilled. Please excuse the Styrofoam cup.

"My story is one about the International Police and a stolen Rembrandt. Pat was asking me about my collection of paintings and artifacts, and I was starting to tell her a story about a famous robbery."

I decided to just keep my mouth shut and listen. Butch and Carmela must have heard the story before, but Toni apparently had not. The two girls and I listened while Ricardo told us a very strange story. He started by asking if we had been to Tours, in France. We all three said that we had not and so he started.

"Tours is a very, very old city, a staging post on the trade routes that crossed ancient France a thousand years before the Romans came. They came, left their monumental imprint, and went away. The dark ages of Europe passed and Tours emerged as a bustling, prosperous city. The French people have always had a passionate love for beauty and an unerring appreciation of monetary value. When Marie Antoinette got her head sliced off in 1793 and the forces of revolution were sweeping the land, the people of France kept their cool, as Butch would say. Instead of just destroying the great abbeys and chateaus that symbolized the oppression of several hundred years, they made them into public buildings. All of the furniture, paintings, tapestries, and porcelain were carefully gathered together from all of the now-dead dukes, duchesses, bishops and friends, and put in the archbishop's palace right in the middle of Tours. The plunder from the surrounding estates of the ancient regime was neither wantonly destroyed in vengeance nor stolen for private profit. The archbishop's palace became known as Tours' principal school, library and museum. The wonderful old seventeenth-century palace with its triumphal arch under the shadow of the cathedral, its spacious, high-ceilinged rooms, its leafy gardens full of giant elms, of shimmering ash and tulip trees and sweet-scented magnolias, became eventually the great Museum of Tours."

We were sitting there on towels, on the beach in Bimini, sweating a little and drinking wine, but Ricardo was taking us, in our own imaginations, over to France. His English was superb, and the slight Spanish accent added something. He sounded a little like a travelogue, with his complete sentences and perfect grammar, but he was a splendid and colorful story teller.

"By December 1971, Tours had become the cultural center for that section of the great Loire countryside and its museum was world famous. Naturally, it was *ripe* for a robbery and since it was known throughout the art world, the robbery couldn't be a little one. Imagine how upset the director of that museum must have been when one fine day she found out they had been *ripped off big time!*"

When Ricardo slipped American slang words into his scholarly descriptions, he liked to say the words slowly and dramatically. He seemed to really enjoy it, and got a big grin on his face as he rolled out the words "ripped off big time."

"Mademoiselle Marie-Noelle Pinot de Villechenon was the French National Museum's curator assigned to the Tours collection. Early in the morning of December 22, 1971, a guard named Jackie Joubert came charging into her office, waving a hook that had replaced an arm amputated in the war, and yelling that the museum had been robbed. They rushed to the Salle Hollandaise, and found that the museum's prize painting, an irreplaceable Rembrandt, was gone. Salle Hollandaise means Holland room. It is not a *salad dressing*." He laughed hard and we laughed with him.

"The missing painting had been given to the museum by Mademoiselle Benjamin Chaussemiche, widow of the French National architect for palaces and gardens. It was executed in oils on wood, and depicted the flight of the Holy Family into Egypt to escape King Herod's massacre of the innocents. This was a favorite subject for artists from the Renaissance onward and this magnificent version was on a wood panel only nine by ten inches.

"When the gift was received in January, 1950, it was thought to be possibly a work of one of Rembrandt's students. Later, to everyone's great pleasure, the initials R.H. were found after careful cleaning and examination. Rembrandt Harmenzoon van Rijn, the great master, used these initials to sign his work."

Ricardo said the words "Rembrandt Harmenzoon van Rijn" as if he were announcing the king of the world.

"The painting at the time of the robbery was worth about one million, three hundred thousand dollars. To put this into some perspective, consider that ten years earlier, the Metropolitan Museum of Art in New York paid two million, three hundred thousand for Rembrandt's *Aristotle Contemplating the Bust of Homer*."

I was really enjoying listening to Ricardo. He told a story well. Even in a bathing suit, sitting there on the beach, there was an aura about the man. His huge head kept reminding me of a Roman Senator or Emperor. He poured us each another Styrofoam cup of wine and continued.

"Poor Mademoiselle Pinot nearly *went bananas*, of course, but she was not the only one. It was a great loss to the whole region. At once all of Europe was notified and the word *Rembrandt* got everyone's attention. Actually there was another painting stolen, a seascape by the seventeenth-century Dutch artist Jan van Goyen. It was a pleasing modest picture done with considerable skill but worth far less than the Rembrandt. There was also a statue which was mounted on an intricately carved box made of lignum vitae. The statue and its stand were considered to be worth less than a thousand dollars and were not even reported with the paintings."

"When the local police arrived it was embarrassingly obvious how the break-in was accomplished. The thieves had taken a small ladder from across the street where workmen were repairing the southern face of the cathedral. The company entrusted with the work was in the process of erecting scaffolding against the lofty buttresses. The robbers simply borrowed a ladder.

"They had put the ladder against the wall that encircled the Tours Museum and climbed over it. On the inside of the wall was a hut-like structure that was the covering of the transformer that supplied the electrical power to the museum. They apparently had pulled the ladder over and used it again to get into the museum itself. Although the window that had been entered was almost fifteen feet above the ground, the top rung of the ladder was high enough to let a man climb in. So careful had the expert planning been that only the window nearest the Rembrandt had been broken. The paintings were stripped from the wall and the thief or thieves had gone back the same way. The van Goyen was considered to be an afterthought, as was the statue.

"Since valuable stolen art is generally disposed of in a different country, the International Police headquarters at St. Cloud just outside Paris became involved. It took nearly two and a half years to close the case but Interpol accomplished it and retrieved the paintings. I will not bore you with all the details of how Interpol tracked down and arrested the people involved now, but I will give you a quick description if you want to hear about it later on."

Pat insisted that he finish the story while we were in Bimini. She wanted to know how Interpol recovered the paintings. I thought it was interesting but I didn't have much interest in detective stories and didn't care much one way or the other. Toni had been listening to every word but didn't say anything. Ricardo stopped talking and looked at his watch.

"Why don't we finish this story tomorrow," he said. "We had breakfast at sunrise and I'm beginning to get hungry."

"Finish the part about recovering the pictures before we go back to Miami," Pat pleaded. "I think it's a wonderful story and I can't wait to hear what happened. I thought people who stole great works of art were clever and sophisticated like Cary Grant or someone like that. Tell us the rest of the story, Senor Salazar. I want to hear what happened," Patricia persisted.

"Later this weekend I will tell you the rest of the story. Right now I am going for a quick swim. Then I am going to get something to eat. A lot of something to eat. Even if it spoils my lunch later on I am going to have a big second breakfast."

Ricardo stood up to his full height. A magnificent man – six feet four and two hundred sixty pounds. He had a beautiful smile on his face and I knew he loved telling stories. I wondered how a man as rich and powerful as Salazar, who owned and controlled enterprises all over the world, could get so much pleasure out of drinking wine from Styrofoam cups and telling a story on the beach. I remembered Chub Cay and how easily he got along with Jimmy Lightbourne. I really liked the guy.

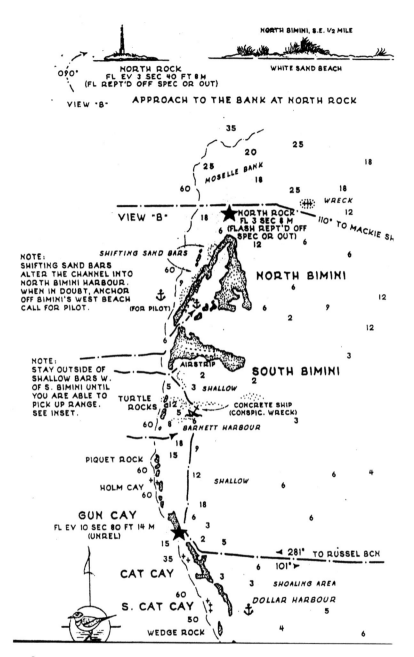

Chapter Seventeen

Saturday, 17 June
After he finished talking about the stolen Rembrandt, Ricardo went into the water. After a short swim Ricardo and Carmela left. The four of us stayed at the beach for a while and then walked back to the Big Game Fishing Club. When we got there we found that Ricardo had rented a suite. He and Carmela were there and left a note suggesting we meet them for a second breakfast.

We decided to join them and changed into fresh clothes back at *Ojos Verdes*. Pat and Toni both looked terrific and it was obvious that Pat had gone shopping for some resort-type things. She had on a white skirt with an aqua blouse and black and white kerchief. During the summer the main dining room would have been closed for lunch, but because of the fishing tournament it was open and even crowded. The upstairs room, where the bar was located, was serving a big buffet with both breakfast and lunch food. Ricardo and Carmela were already there and seated when the four of us came from the boat.

As soon as we sat down and ordered a drink, Carmela excused herself. When she left she had on shorts and when she returned she was wearing a skirt. It was obvious to me that she had changed so that Pat would not feel overdressed. It was also obvious to Pat.

"That was nice of you, Sra. Salazar, but it wasn't really necessary. I'm afraid that everything I've got will seem like I'm a tourist. I've never been cruising on a yacht before and I thought we would wear cruise clothes. I hope you don't mind."

"Now I look like a little girl with two grown up ladies!" said Toni, who had on shorts. She smiled for the first time since the receiving line at the party.

"You *are* a little girl with two grown up ladies," Carmela said, teasing her.

Ricardo, Butch and I all wore slacks and monogrammed knit shirts with collars. They had on green shirts with *Ojos Verdes* in dark green block print letters above the pocket. I had on my Carolina blue with *Brilliant* in dark blue script. I laughed at all three of us when I saw that they had the same kind of shirt that I did. I guess men aren't very original.

The brunch buffet was excellent. It was actually set up for the people who came for the fishing tournament but was open to everybody. Everyone talked a lot except Toni and me. We both just listened and enjoyed the stories. We took a long time and did not get back to the boat until nearly one o'clock.

When we got back I took out my camera and started taking pictures of *Ojos Verdes*. Butch went below and Toni decided to take a little siesta in the cockpit where the Bimini top provided a shady spot. Pat and I started taking more pictures.

I'm not a very good photographer but Rocket had spent hours teaching me the fundamentals of my camera. She had also told me how professionals shoot the same thing over and over in slightly different ways and then select the best results. I love boats and pictures of boats. I wasn't exactly sure of what I wanted, but *Ojos Verdes* was a majestic boat and I hoped to get one picture that I could have enlarged and framed as a gift for Ricardo. After I had enough for that purpose, I took some pictures with Pat aboard for myself. She was very patient and posed all over the boat in every possible place.

I took pictures of her up close with the boat as background and other pictures where Pat was merely part of the background. Finally, after I had photographed the boat from every possible angle, I got a kid in a Boston Whaler to take me forty or fifty feet away from the dock so I could get a picture of the full length of the boat. Because of her size we had tied up on the outside of the dock. The current was strong in Bimini harbor so the Whaler had a little trouble staying in one place long enough for me to take pictures, but I finally got enough so that a few had to be good.

When I got back to the dock, I thanked the kid and gave him five dollars for helping me. Pat had stayed aboard sitting in the cockpit watching while I took pictures from the skiff. I asked her if she wanted to go for a walk and she agreed enthusiastically. Her smile was wonderful and she used it a lot. The more time I spent with her the more I liked her.

Bimini is a small island and there are not many places that are very private. I knew of a place, though, that was a little bit private and I decided to go there because I wanted to kiss Pat and I couldn't do it on the boat or around the Big Game Fishing Club. At the south end of the island, past the seaplane landing and the old hotel, there is a place where there is some grass and a few trees. It is down beyond the old deserted swimming pool and almost to the tip of the land. As we started walking Pat could tell that I had something in mind.

"Where are we going?"

"There's a place at the end of the island that's kind of secluded. I want to go there."

"What do you want to go there for?"

"Because I want to kiss you and I want a little privacy." She didn't say anything and I suddenly stopped walking.

"Would you rather go back to the boat?" I asked. "We don't have to go there."

"Let's hurry up and get to the kissing place," she said.

When we got to the little grassy hill we started laughing while we looked around for other people. There are lots of small brown children all over Bimini and you can expect to find them looking at you almost any time, laughing and giggling, just curious like kids anywhere. We could hear some men working over by the old hotel but nobody was near us. It was actually very quiet there with the wind making a soft noise in the pine trees and the waves breaking on the beach in the distance.

When we were sure of our privacy we moved closer together, still laughing a little at ourselves. Pat may have been overdressed for lunch, but the aqua blouse was perfect with her dark wavy hair, and the black kerchief accentuated the colors. It may have been my imagination or it may have been because she was about to be kissed, but Pat Rivera's eyes actually sparkled. Her dark hair seemed to glisten in the sun. I pulled her close and kissed her hard. We both knew that a few kisses would be all for that day and it seemed that we wanted to put everything into the few. Pat knew how to kiss as well as any woman I had ever touched, wet and passionate but with something held back. Her mouth tasted sweet and she knew how to use it. Her lips were parted but only slightly. Her tongue was only a teasing flicker, touching and disappearing.

We kissed for a long time and then pulled apart and stared at each other. Then she closed her eyes and we kissed some more. With her thin aqua blouse and my knit shirt I could feel her breasts against my chest. They felt hard and pointed. I made no attempt to touch them. After one more long passionate kiss I dropped my hand to her behind and squeezed it then pulled away.

"Pat, I think we had better go back to the boat. This is not the time or the place for anything more than kissing and I can't handle any more kissing. I think you burned my mouth."

She started laughing. Her lipstick was all messed up. She was breathing hard and her delicate nostrils were flaring. Her lips were still wet and glistening from the kissing and slightly parted. Her dark skin kind of glowed. Her shiny black eyes were slowly opening and closing with the long eyelashes fluttering as she tried to regain her composure and cool off.

"I was starting to look around for soft spots to lie down in the grass, Dr. Devlin," she said with a huge grin. "I am *caliente. Muy ardiente.* You better stop kissing me and give me some cooling off pills or something. Let me clean up my face and put on some lipstick and calm down. We better go back to the boat before we get in trouble."

Caliente means hot and *muy ardiente* means passionately hot. Pat wasn't the only one. She pulled some kind of pre-moistened tissue out of her purse and wiped the smudged lipstick off of her face. Then she had me hold a little mirror for her while she put on fresh lipstick. When she was finished she asked me if she looked all right.

"You look terrific. Absolutely gorgeous. Nobody will even know you've been kissed unless you grin. Why don't I take a few pictures of you here. I've only got several hundred that I took on the boat and I've got plenty of film left."

"You must like my looks, Devlin. You've already used up a small fortune in film. Tell me where to stand and how to pose."

I really tried to get some good pictures of Pat, trying to get the lighting and distance and everything. Rocket had done a good job teaching me photography basics and practice with lots of boat pictures helped. After I had taken about thirty exposures I tried to make a clever remark. I never learn, though.

"Why don't you pose in the nude and I'll do a painting from the best picture," I said, trying to be funny. "I've got every other pose I can think of." I was just kidding.

Pat stared at me really hard and I expected her to burst out laughing and make some smart remark. She kept on staring at me for a few minutes and then she took off the black kerchief that she had around her neck and put it down beside her purse on the grass. She looked around to make sure that we were still alone and that the trees would hide what she was doing. Then she took off the aqua blouse and put it with the kerchief. Her brassiere was the same shade of aqua and it was full. She stood facing me with her shoulders thrown back, not saying anything. I thought of stopping her but I couldn't say anything. I couldn't tell her I was just kidding. It was too late for that.

She stared at me for a while without smiling or laughing and then she took off the white skirt. She didn't have on a slip or any stockings. Her panties were the same shade of aqua as her brassiere. She stared at me, watching my eyes as they moved around looking at her body. She just stood there in her panties and bra for a while letting me look. Her breasts were plump and the nipples obvious. Her waist was tiny and her hips flared and turned into long shapely legs. She kept on standing there and I kept on staring and then she took off her brassiere.

Her breasts were not overly large but they were powerful. To describe them as perfectly shaped isn't enough. Powerful is the best word. I watched them move a little as she breathed in and out. The nipples were dark and pointed.

"I'm not gonna take my panties off. You'll have to use your imagination. Start taking pictures and tell me how to pose before I get scared and chicken out."

I couldn't think of anything to say that made any sense so I kept my mouth shut, moving her around in the same places as I had when she had clothes on. I just waved my hand to move her. Her body was so lush that it didn't matter what pose she assumed and her poses were far more erotic with her panties on, than if she were completely naked. Although her pants were full cut they were very thin and were more of a decoration than anything else. They didn't really hide much and seemed more like a colored ribbon on a package. Her startling breasts were brown all over and she had obviously been in the sun with no top on.

She made funny faces with the first few poses, and then started using different facial expressions for different emotions. In spite of her wonderful body I couldn't keep my eyes off her face. It was obvious that she was getting very excited. I took close to fifty shots, taking three or four exposures in each pose and putting in new film twice. When we finished I just watched while she got dressed. We didn't say anything to each other until we had left the kissing place on the grass, where the trees hide what you do. We had passed the old hotel and the seaplane landing before I calmed down enough to say anything.

"Thank you, Pat. That was very beautiful."

She suddenly came up with a big dazzling smile.

"If you ever let anybody see those pictures of me dancing around in my *choninos*, I will cut off your hands and make sure you never practice medicine again. I will also cut off your *cojónes* and make you pray for death."

"I'll pick out the best picture and do a painting," I told her, wondering what I'd do with the picture when I finished it.

"Will the painting be with panties or without?" she asked, laughing.

"I don't know. I don't have a very good imagination."

"You don't need any imagination. Even with my *choninos* on you could see my *chocha*."

"That's true. The pants are like aqua-colored cellophane."

"Maybe you better paint me in a full girdle. I was flopping around pretty bad."

"I'm gonna paint you just like I saw you."

As we walked back to the boat I realized that we were holding hands. She was humming a song quietly that sounded familiar but I couldn't seem to place it. Just before we got to the Big Game Fishing Club I asked her what it was.

"It's an old Irish song. I'll sing the first few lines and you'll recognize it." She sang a little.

"Black, black, black is the color of my true love's hair. Her lips are something wondrous fair."

I was sitting at dinner that night with the song running through my mind before I realized what it meant.

When we got back to the boat, both Toni and Butch were reading in the cockpit. They told us that the plan for that night was to get together for cocktails at six o'clock at the upstairs bar in the Big Game Fishing Club and then go up to Bimini Blue Water on the hill. Since the picture windows there faced west, it was a perfect place to watch the sunset while you enjoyed your dinner.

We sat around the boat for a while and then a few of the fishing boats started coming in with the day's catch. Toni was sitting there in the cockpit looking serenely beautiful. Her pale grey eyes, with the touch of green, were looking at us and then suddenly she saw the boats and turned into a little kid in her excitement. Her face was almost always without expression but when she saw the first big fish get hauled off a boat she jumped up out of the cockpit and ran down the dock. She had a big smile on her face. Pat and I followed her but Butch said he had seen enough fish to last a lifetime.

Because of the fishing tournament there was an enormous number of boats for that time of year and they just kept on coming in. We had come into Bimini

Harbor after most of the boats had already gone out fishing so we hadn't realized what was going on. We were too far up the harbor to see all the boats come parading by. Brown's was the place for that, since it was the first dock as you came in, but there were enough boats staying at the Big Game Fishing Club to see plenty of fish. We followed Toni all over the dock, from boat to boat, while she gave us a running commentary on each species of fish.

"That's a blue marlin. It should weigh about two hundred fifty pounds. Not a record, but good." She explained all about blue marlins and what kind of bait you use to catch them. At every boat she knew what kind of fish had been caught and its approximate weight. Several times she had me or Pat ask the people in English what kind of bait they had used.

After awhile we went up off the dock to the weighing station and watched them check each fish. There was a similarity between this scene and the one after a sailboat regatta with excited people coming in after a day of competition on the water. I had tried big game fishing a few times and found that I was bored, but then I had never actually caught anything exciting.

Later on we went back to the boat to get dressed and found Carmela there. She said she felt like dressing up for dinner and that she wanted to see what Pat was going to wear. I had never had a sister or wife so I had never experienced what happened next. They got out Pat's dress and then Toni's dress and figured out they had to make some changes so they would look good together. Carmela and Pat kind of dominated the discussion with Toni not saying much but after awhile they concentrated on what Toni was going to wear. Butch and I opened a couple of cold Coronas and sat in the main cabin laughing at the three of them and clapping each time one of them came out of the after cabin with a new dress on. They were laughing, too, but they were very serious about finding the right combination of dresses for all three of them. Carmela seemed to have an unlimited supply of dresses in her hanging locker in the after cabin. All three of them were about the same size except for behinds. Toni's hips were more slender than Pat's with Carmela in between. All of a sudden they had the right combination and started yelling at Butch and me to take our showers and get dressed. I thought the whole scene was really funny.

The restaurant that Bimini Blue Water owns up on the hill is very nice but it's not fancy. If we all showed up in shorts we would have been served. It was obvious that the ladies wanted to dress up just because they wanted to dress up, and that Butch and I better look presentable.

I took my shaving kit and a towel up to the showers and came back quickly. I put on a pair of clean pressed slacks that were bone colored and a green cowboy shirt with black trim. The string necktie made me look dressed up without looking too fancy. I got another Corona and waited in the cockpit.

Carmela had gone back to her room, after all the decisions had been made on clothes, so the four of us walked together up the dock to the restaurant. Butch and I spent the whole walk telling Toni and Pat how wonderful they looked. Although we were acting a little silly, both girls just smiled and acted as if we were supposed to say what we did.

I had gotten used to being around Butch by this time but I was always aware of his looks. Both Toni and Pat were beautiful women but there were a lot of beautiful women in the world. I had never seen another man before I met Butch that I would actually call beautiful.

We had one drink at the Big Game Fishing Club and the story-telling began. Butch started it with a story about being left with no money in the middle of the night in Springfield, Massachusetts when he was pledging for a fraternity at Amherst. We kept on telling stories all night, even while walking up the hill to the restaurant. We did stop talking for about fifteen minutes just as the sun was setting. We had asked for a table on the west side of the room near the windows.

The sun goes down every night and nobody pays much attention, but there is something special about watching a sunset on the ocean. I always looked for the green flash but I had only seen it once. Just as the sun dipped below the horizon Ricardo made a toast to the sunset. It was in Spanish and had several words in it that I had to have explained. It was very beautiful and I wrote it down.

I watched the faces of the others as we told stories. Since I had wanted to be a portrait artist it had become a habit. I had wanted to paint faces, but not in repose. I wanted to paint faces with expressions, faces that were animated. I had seen Antonia enough times that I knew her face pretty well, but I had never seen eyes exactly her shade, the unusual grey with the tint of green. The black unplucked eyebrows were a perfect frame.

Toni was a quiet person. At first I thought she was quiet because she spoke only Spanish and the conversations had been in English. Later, when I learned that she was only twenty, I thought she was quiet because everyone else was older than she was. As I watched her listening to each story I noticed something that I had not seen before. Although the rest of her face seemed to be expressionless, her eyebrows seemed to be able to describe exactly what she thought. The contrast between her face and Pat's was extreme. Both were very lovely but Pat was all animation, with everything moving. When she started talking her mouth seemed to move a different way with each word. Even though I had teased her about it, and she had told her bosses it was acquired by practice, she had never been self-conscious about it. It was fun to watch her talk.

Antonia was exactly the opposite in that her face never seemed to move at all. Her eyebrows were able to express almost anything. She could even laugh with her eyebrows and not move her mouth. It was fascinating. It sort of flashed through my mind that if Toni and I ever went any place alone, neither of us would have anything to say. We could get Gus and the three of us could have a contest to see who could say nothing for the longest time.

Since I don't like to talk I didn't tell any stories until we had finished dessert and were having some brandy. Everyone insisted I tell a story about medical school so I described my one and only experience in cardiac surgery. It took place when I was an intern.

"When I was at Bellevue I was in training for general surgery in the beginning and we did all kinds of things. For a while I worked at Triboro Hospital and got a little bit involved in heart surgery. Not open heart surgery like it's done now but an earlier version. The guy who was my nominal boss was really into it and wanted every case he could get. One day there was an opportunity for him to work on a guy who had something called a coarctation of the aorta. This is a congenital condition where the aorta, which is the main arterial trunk of the body, has a narrow area in it about five or six inches from the point where the aorta rises from the heart."

"Anyway, Jack Spurrier, my boss at the time, got permission to do the operation and he wanted to practice first. This meant dogs. I didn't realize it at the time, but suddenly I was into a mess because Bobby started spending a lot of time in the dog lab which was back in the morgue. One day it was my turn to go to the dog pound in downtown Queens to pick up a dog. Usually I would get one of the ambulance drivers to take me. They would complain like crazy but they would always do it. That particular day there was a war on in Queens or a mafia shootout or something because all of them were in use. I waited around for nearly an hour but when two or three came back and then went out again I got impatient and took my own car. My parents had always given me a new car every three or four years and the one I had at the time was almost brand new. When I got to the pound I picked out the biggest dog available. We always did this since we were practicing for an operation on a human. The dog was quiet while I drove back to the hospital and I drove pretty fast. When I got there I pulled the dog out of the car."

When I got to this part I had to get help from Butch. The dog had defecated all over the back seat of my car. I knew how to say it in Spanish but I wanted to use polite language in front of the ladies. When Butch explained to Antonia she burst out laughing along with the others.

"*Mierda*," he said. There is no other way to put it.

"What a mess it was," I continued. "What a stink! I had a leash on the dog but when I was pulling him out of the car he got loose and took off. I chased him for a while but I couldn't catch him and he got away. I went back to the morgue and found Bobby operating on a corpse. He could smell me from a long distance away, even with a mask on his face. I told him what had happened and that I wasn't going back to the dog pound again that day no matter how badly he needed a dog. I said I was going home to clean up my car. Jack was laughing so hard he messed up his practice operation and killed the corpse."

"Did the patient live?" Toni asked. "The real patient?"

"Yes, the operation on the aorta was successful."

After Ricardo paid the check we started back to the boat. On the way down the hill I asked Pat if she'd like to take a look at some of the local bars. Butch and Toni wanted to go with us but Ricardo and Carmela decided to go to bed. We started out at the Compleat Angler, which Pat and Toni liked because of the pictures and memorabilia, and then stopped for one drink at almost every bar along the street. We ran into two couples that I knew from the Yacht Club in Coconut Grove. We met them at the Red Lion and all eight of us ended up at the End of the World where we danced on the sand floor. It was a fun evening but nothing much happened. We got back to the boat around two and immediately went to sleep.

I woke up in the middle of the night when I heard the radio in the navigation area. I was startled awake and heard Butch talking to somebody on one of the single side band radios. I couldn't make out what he was saying because he turned down the volume just as I woke up. I looked at my watch and it said it was four a.m. I went back to sleep.

I'm used to waking up at exactly six thirty every morning because I always operate at eight o'clock. Since I don't drink on Sunday nights, or during the week, I'm usually at my best in the morning. I usually go to sleep early, even on weekends, but an occasional late Friday or Saturday night doesn't keep me from waking up at the same time. After I opened my eyes and realized that I was in a pilot berth in the main cabin of the *Ojos Verdes,* I heard somebody moving around in the galley. I looked over across the cabin to the other pilot berth and saw Butch sleeping soundly. Since I sleep in my underwear I found a pair of khaki shorts and put them on before getting out of the bunk.

I pulled on a knit shirt and tip-toed into the galley where I found Antonia pouring a cup of coffee. She asked me by raising an eyebrow and holding up a cup if I wanted some, and I nodded that I did. She whispered that she was going to walk over to the beach for a quick swim before breakfast.

"Yo voy a ir a la playa por un rato a nadar antes del desayuno."

She simply stated that she was going and didn't ask me if I wanted to go with her. I took a sip of coffee and noticed that she had on a bathing suit under her knit shirt. I thought for a minute and decided that jumping in the water would feel good. My head didn't hurt but I could feel the effects of drinking a lot of beer the night before.

"Would you mind if I joined you for a swim?"

"I would be very happy for your company. Pat is still sound asleep. Do you think we should wake her?" Antonia asked.

I thought for a minute before I answered. I felt sure that Pat would want to sleep but I wasn't sure what she would think of my going off with Toni. Even though she was only twenty she was simply too beautiful for anybody to ignore.

I didn't want Pat to feel any jealousy about me and Toni. I found a pencil and paper in the navigation area and wrote a note saying that we had gone for a quick swim and would be back no later than eight o'clock, probably sooner. I gave the note to Toni and told her to put it where Pat would see it as soon as she woke up. Butch was still sound asleep.

As we walked up the dock we could see boats all over the marina going out and getting ready to go out for what was probably the last day of the tournament. I thought to myself that I was glad that I was a sailor and not a fisherman. One design races don't start at six o'clock in the morning. We walked toward the south end of the island until we found a street that went up to the top of the hill where there was a sidewalk. We walked down the sidewalk for a way until we found a path leading through the bushes and down to the beach.

"I woke up in the middle of the night and thought I heard Butch on the radio. Was that my imagination or was he really talking to somebody?"

"He was talking to the office in Madrid. Because of the time difference, he sometimes calls in the middle of the night. Ricardo and Butch have the very powerful radios so they can always be in touch with the main office. It is easier sometimes to use the radios instead of an overseas telephone call. When we are at breakfast Ricardo will ask many questions and Butch will not have all the answers so he will have to call again. Ricardo used to call always himself but now he makes Butch do it. He likes to sleep. Butch will run the business in a few years and he is learning."

"What about you? When will you go back to Spain?"

"I will fly back on the Tuesday after your Labor Day Holiday and start classes at the University of Madrid immediately. I will actually start a few days late but I am going to have a birthday and the Salazars are going to have a party for me. Not a huge, big party like when Ricardo was sixty, but a small, big party. I will be twenty one."

It is impossible to be alone with a girl or woman in a bathing suit and not be aware of her body. I suppose it's the same with a woman, but perhaps not. Maybe a woman is mostly aware of her own body and not so much the body of the man. Toni was very slender but there was enough flesh in the right places to give her soft curves. She wasn't voluptuous like Patricia, perhaps that would come with a few more years, but she stuck out in all the right places. She had on a one piece maillot swim suit that covered a lot of flesh but didn't hide her shape.

"I would be very honored if you could come to my birthday party, Dr. Devlin. Do you think you could?"

"Certainly, Toni. I would be delighted to help you celebrate your twenty-first birthday."

When we got down to the beach we went right in to the water and waded out until we were waist deep. The water felt good but it was warm. This was partly the Gulfstream and partly the fact that it was summertime. I wanted to find cooler water so I swam out a little further and then dove down near the bottom in some deeper water. The colder water seemed to wake me up.

After swimming around for a short while we went back to the boat where we found Butch in the galley making more coffee. Patricia was still sound asleep so we whispered. Butch said he had to go up and see his father, even before breakfast, because he had talked to the office in Madrid and they needed to talk to Ricardo right away. Butch apologized for talking on the radio in the middle of the night. He explained that they had radios in the office and that it was easier than using the telephone. We had already checked on the time for Mass so we decided that the three of us would meet Butch and his parents at Blue Water on the hill for breakfast and then go directly to the church. Butch fixed himself a large Styrofoam cup of coffee and left to go to his parents' room at the hotel.

Toni and I sat in the main cabin talking quietly to keep from waking Pat. She told me that she was taking courses in International Relations and English. She wanted to get a job with either the Spanish Government or the United Nations. She said that her parents, who were close friends of Ricardo and Carmela, did not want her to work at all, and wanted to arrange a marriage with someone of their social class from Madrid. I tried to avoid asking any questions about Toni's family or the Salazars since I really didn't know what was polite and what wasn't. After a while Pat came into the cabin and joined us. She got herself some coffee from the galley and sat down at the cabin table. She listened for a while and then started asking questions. I guess her job as a T.V. news lady had accustomed her to asking questions of anybody about anything. In the short time before we started getting dressed for breakfast and church, I learned that the scope of Ricardo's operations was larger than I had imagined. He owned businesses all over the world as well as a soccer team in Spain. I also learned that he had cousins in Canada and Argentina with whom he had business dealings. The more I learned about his business operations the more I was impressed with what a down-to-earth person he seemed to be. I had met many important people through my family and friends but I had never known anyone with his scope of international operations.

When we got to the restaurant Butch and his parents were already seated and Ricardo immediately told us what the radio call was about. He said there had been a problem between his company in Argentina and the Canadian bank he used in Nassau. He told us that he and Butch would have to leave early the next morning and take the *Ojos Verdes* across the bank and down to Nassau. There he would have to meet with his people from Argentina and the Canadian Bank people. He explained that he was going back to the boat while we went to church, and then he would go down to the little building that Chalks used at the seaplane ramp and arrange for the four of us to fly back to Miami. If Chalks was booked up he would arrange a charter flight for the four of us. He was very apologetic about it and Pat and I assured him that it was not a problem. Our plan had been to leave Bimini at first light Monday morning and sail back to Miami. It really didn't make much difference to me.

For some reason, perhaps the change in plans, everyone seemed a little distracted at breakfast. Although Ricardo acted his usual jovial self, his mind seemed to be elsewhere. He teased Butch and told us that the crisis in Argentina and Nassau was probably caused by him and that he would probably be arrested by the United Nations for personally setting off world inflation. I had gotten used to his teasing Butch and had realized that the humor made it easier for Butch to work with his father in a high-pressure situation. A father and son working together had to be difficult, particularly with the size and scope of their operations. Butch liked to make himself out to be a sort of good-natured clown who stumbled around in the business world, saved from disaster only by the patience of his father. In every story he told about business, he had made some huge mistake and his father had to rescue him. I had figured out fairly quickly that Butch was very intelligent and probably very capable. I wasn't sure if he used the good-natured clown act to offset his beautiful looks or just to make it easy to work with his father. It was probably both.

Toni didn't say much, but that wasn't unusual. Carmela was also quiet. She and Ricardo teased the four of us a little about staying out late and drinking too much. She included Toni even though she had not had any alcohol the night before. I noticed Pat's distraction and I couldn't figure it out. Since she had gotten sick coming over, I was sure she wouldn't mind flying back to Miami.

When we finished breakfast, Ricardo went back to *Ojos Verdes* while the five of us walked down to the Catholic Church and attended the Mass. Both the Catholic and the Church of England buildings were built on top of the hill that runs down the west side of North Bimini. I usually went to Anglican Churches when I was in the Bahamas, but I had gone to services of different religions many times. Pat suggested that I sit beside Toni and help her, since she had the two problems of not speaking English and the unfamiliar form of the Mass. I was fairly sure that Antonia understood far more English than she admitted, but she was so shy that I guess she didn't like to risk making mistakes in front of people.

The people of Bimini really dressed up for the services and looked very nice, especially the children. The singing was good. Afterwards we talked with the priest and a few other people then went back to the Big Game Fishing Club where we sat around the swimming pool for a few hours before we felt hungry enough for lunch.

We were sitting at a table at one end of the pool. It was very pleasant under the shade of some palm trees and we ordered rum swizzles. As soon as the drinks arrived, Patricia started to push Ricardo for more of the story. He teased her for a few minutes, and then agreed to tell more of it. Neither Butch nor Carmela were listening this time.

"Yesterday on the beach I stopped the little story at the point where Interpol tracked down and arrested the people involved. I will now explain the details of how they did it. I will tell you how the pictures were stolen, then I will tell you how they were recovered.

"Listen carefully," he said with a smile and humorous glint in his eye. "The robbery, which was supposedly planned by some master criminals, was actually the work of a single person. He was a young, hippie from Czechoslovakia named Karel Whitman. He was twenty-two years old and had been drinking cheap red wine in a nearby bar. The bartender didn't like *les hippies* and had asked him to leave. He started walking home in the bitterly cold night and stopped between the cathedral and the museum. While he was taking off his mittens to urinate, he saw the scaffolding and the ladder. On an impulse he decided to use the ladder to climb the fence and then to get in to the museum where he figured he could steal something of value that he could sell for traveling money. When he broke the window and got inside, he just happened to be in the Salle Hollandaise. He heard a guard moving around and got scared. He took the nearest items, which were the paintings.

"He climbed back out the same window and back over the electrical shed and wall and down to the rue Fleury. From there he walked back to the Hotel Zola, which was a sleazy dump, and got in bed with his girlfriend who was named Anne-Marie Frank.

"The next day Karel Whitman and Anne-Marie checked out of the hotel and hitchhiked to Paris. They moved into an apartment on the Boulevard St.-Michel, the "Boul Mich" as it is known to so many students.

"Finding the two of them and getting the paintings back was unusual only in who they were. Whitman was not a professional thief and knew nothing about art. The amazing thing was that he actually did it on an impulse. If he hadn't stopped to pee-pee, the Rembrandt would never have been stolen. The International Criminal Police Organization known as Interpol did a wonderful job but that's nothing special. They always do a good job when the politicians leave them alone."

"That's really wild, Sr. Salazar," Pat said. "How did Interpol do it?"

"Immediately after discovering the robbery, a call was made to the Police Commissioner, a man named Roger Millet, who conducted the survey of the crime scene. When he got back to his office he concerned himself with the recovery and not the crime itself. During the next two hours, messages containing information about the robbery were sent out to fourteen different destinations. These included the mayor's office in Tours, the local customs bureau, the national customs headquarters, the national police and, of course, Interpol headquarters at Saint Cloud, just outside Paris.

"One of the messages was sent to the divisional commissioner of police in Orleans, seventy miles northeast of Tours. Two very experienced men were sent to assist Millet.

"A second, more meticulous search of the museum area yielded nothing, absolutely nothing. Extensive checks were made of hotel registrations, employee records at the museum, and of the laborers involved in the cathedral's restoration. For a month there were plainclothes police everywhere, in bars and hotels, businesses and railroad stations. Nothing.

"On January 17, 1972, Roger Millet wrote a formal account of the investigation stating that it was meticulously planned by a group of experts who were probably responsible for several other recent art thefts. He called them a ruthlessly efficient and highly organized gang.

"The first break came in February when a man named Hans Deter got a telephone call from a stranger. Deter was a hefty, smiling-type man with graying hair and horn rimmed glasses. He was the Kriminalhauptkommissar and chief of the robbery division of the Interpol office in West Berlin. The stranger claimed to be a lawyer and said that a client of his had been offered a Rembrandt painting for one hundred thousand deutsche marks. He also said there was a van Goyen available. He told Deter that if the sale took place the paintings would go to South America. He said his client thought the paintings might have been stolen from a museum in Amsterdam and wanted to know about a reward.

"Deter was puzzled because he had not heard of a Rembrandt being stolen. He wired Interpol and found out that by mistake several of the branches had not even been notified. When he got the call, Deter figured it was phony but he decided to act anyway. He issued instructions to the men in Berlin's plainclothes unit. His message said 'We seem to have two hot paintings in the manor. One of them is a Rembrandt. Get out on the streets and push your sources. I want the name of the thief'.

"Within a few days a name crossed his desk. Nobody recognized it, but a quick check of the files showed that the thief was a Czech named Karel Whitman, who had a previous conviction for a petty theft.

"Here's what happened. Karel Whitman and Anne-Marie Frank had gone to Paris and hung out around the Boul Mich for a while. Whitman tried to get a job and couldn't find one, so he took off for Berlin carrying the paintings. The trip took three days. At every border post his papers were carefully examined. Several times he was questioned at length before he was allowed through. Yet, not once did it occur to any of the border officials to look inside the scruffy little guy's suitcase. He went from France to Belgium to Luxembourg and then to Germany without even being searched.

"Anne-Marie followed him a few days later. When she got to Berlin she went to live with a family named Gormann, where she resumed a former job of teaching French to their children. Whitman got a small place on

Schleiermacherstrasse, a dingy street in a run-down area of West Berlin. A few days after she got there Karel Whitman came for a visit and met Herr Klaus Leo Gormann, the head of the family. Leo was thirty five, dapper, educated, charming and also ambitious. He described himself as a sculptor and musician but his money came from dealing in antiques.

"After visiting Anne-Marie a number of times, Whitman got to know Gormann fairly well and realized he might be a way to sell the paintings. He decided he didn't know enough about art to try to fool Gormann, so he told him the truth about how he had stolen the paintings. Gormann said he would try to find a buyer. They invented a story in which Whitman was a Sudeten German who was trying to sell the pictures for an old Czech lady because under Czech law it would go to the state when the old lady died."

At this point in the story Patricia interrupted and asked Ricardo to repeat some of what he had just told us. When she was satisfied, he went on. I had lost interest but Pat seemed fascinated by the story.

"Using the fake story, they were able to sell the van Goyen to an antique dealer named Wilhelm Braun of 49 Bayerischestrasse for 5000 deutsche marks. For some unexplainable reason Herr Braun had not gotten his copy of the 'wanted' circular that had been sent out by Interpol. It had been published by the art-theft section and carried black and white reproductions of the paintings. It was routinely sent to all art and antique dealers, art magazines, museums, galleries, and any other organization or individual that might learn of the stolen goods.

"Karel Whitman was thrilled with the money. He gave Gormann a commission of DM500 and told him about the other painting. Two weeks later Whitman was arrested in Charlottenberg because he had gotten into a violent argument with a whore in the Hotel-Pension Juno. Within an hour of his arrest the police had matched his name with the Interpol report on the stolen Rembrandt and they were asking questions about it. Can you imagine what happened next?"

Pat interrupted, "I can tell you what would have happened in Miami." Pat pretended she was on television and holding an imaginary microphone.

"In the cold light of dawn, Karel Whitman, a young poet from Europe, was dragged screaming from the Hotel Juno after a vicious attack on a cute little lady who was an employee of the hotel. The Hotel-Pension is reported to be a house of commercial romance. Whitman also reportedly stole a Rembrandt painting worth several tons of cocaine. Karel Whitman was released after questioning because he seemed like a nice boy. When asked about the Rembrandt, Whitman said 'no comment'. When asked about Whitman's no comment comment the police said 'no comment'."

We all laughed so hard at Pat's little comedy act that we had to take a few minutes to calm down. Pat had done her mouth twisting thing and it was first class comedy. After awhile we started again. Ricardo was laughing so hard he had to struggle to start talking again.

"Karel Whitman was released. There was a long interrogation during which he changed his story several times. The police were sure he was involved but had no proof at all. Telegrams to Interpol in Wiesbaden and Saint Cloud brought every office up to date on the arrest but there was no *habeas corpus*, no charge that would stick. Whitman walked out, literally giving the finger to the police.

"He was scared, though, and called Gormann. They agreed that Gormann would keep the painting until things cooled off. Whitman disappeared into the underground and nothing happened until that summer. Actually he left Berlin with a new girl named Hilda Bauer. They went to Holland where Hilda got sick. Then they came back to Germany where she was treated in a clinic and went to stay with her parents in the Black Forest. After awhile he got the urge to travel again and went to Italy. Later, when Hilda was completely well, she joined him and they went to England. She got sick again and went back home while he went to Heidelberg where he got a job as a waiter. He started getting drunk every night with a new friend named von Arndt who claimed to be a big time thief. Whitman told him about the painting and von Arndt claimed he could find a buyer. He got a guy named Fritz who said he had a Swiss buyer but when Whitman called Gormann he was told that the painting had been put in a safe place and that he could not get it for three weeks. Whitman got mad or impatient or something and went to Berlin. He probably wanted to go see his friend Gormann and see what he was trying to do and where the painting was hidden.

"Unfortunately for him, some other crooks in Heidelberg were robbing paintings from museums while he was there, and there was a lot of bragging in bars about who stole what and who was the best thief. Somebody heard something Karel Whitman said and reported it. When he landed at Tempelhof airport he was arrested for suspicion of stealing paintings back in Heidelberg, which, of course, he didn't do. He was arrested for stealing the wrong paintings."

When we stopped laughing Ricardo said he would have to finish the story some other time but Pat persisted.

"Please tell us the rest of the story, Sr. Salazar. I want to hear what happened."

"Some other time I will finish the story. Perhaps you and Devlin can come over for dinner one night in Miami. Right now I am going for a quick swim. Then I am going to go pack the things I moved to the room and check out. I will come back to the boat in a little while. The hotel car will take you to Chalks."

We thanked Ricardo for lunch and walked back down the dock to *Ojos Verdes*. He had arranged for us to take a Chalks' seaplane at three thirty so the four of us said goodbye to Butch and Ricardo later in front of the Club. Carmela did not seem concerned about the change in plans. She had told them that she would fly over to Nassau and join them if they were going to be there until the following weekend, and she asked him to make reservations for her and Toni for that Friday at the Pilot House by radio in case the meetings took longer than expected. She told him this in front of me and then winked and made a comment that she kept him on a short leash now that he was over sixty.

Later on, the Big Game Fishing Club had two small cars ready to take us down to the south end of the island where the seaplane ramp went out into the harbor. We said goodbye to the two men when we got in the cars and thanked them for the weekend. I had talked to Butch privately and asked him if I should offer to pay for the plane tickets. As I expected he said no, but thanked me for the offer.

I had learned from years of crewing for, and sailing with people who were very wealthy, to make the offer and be prepared to pay. My father had drilled this into me when I came down to Florida as a teenager for the first Southern Circuit. I came down to crew for a very wealthy man. I offered to pay for everything everywhere we went including my plane tickets. He wouldn't let me pay for anything until the last night in Nassau when the whole crew went to dinner with the crew from a rival boat. There were eighteen people in an informal seafood restaurant. He gave me a check for twenty one hundred dollars in a place that didn't take credit cards or traveler's checks. Everyone stared at me when the waiter gave me the check and I realized the owner of my boat had taken me up on my offer. After a few minutes of terror for me, everybody started laughing. He had already paid the check and was just having some fun. Everybody was in on it. Later he told me that he appreciated my offers to pay my way. He said he always paid the tab for his crew but that he didn't like it to be taken for granted.

The flight from Bimini to Miami was a short one and there was a limousine waiting for us. On the ride up to the northern part of Miami Beach and the Salazar home, Carmela invited us to stay for dinner with her and Toni. As soon as Ricardo had told us they were going to go to Nassau, I had started thinking about a plan to ravish Patricia Rivera. The last six months had been almost total sexual frustration and now I figured Pat was going to be the object of my frustration. I had suggested to Pat that she come over to my place after we got back. I said that I would cook a special kind of steak on the barbecue by the swimming pool at my apartment. My plan, of course, was to go upstairs after we had dinner and do all sorts of things to her. She said she would like to come for dinner.

When Carmela made the offer in the limousine, Pat immediately declined, saying she had to get home. She came up with such a plausible-sounding excuse that I knew she had expected my invitation, and planned the refusal. I guess she was as horny as I was. The image of her in her *choninos* in the glade on Bimini was enough to raise my temperature ten degrees.

When we left the limo at Carmela's house, we thanked them again and said goodbye. For the entire weekend we had mixed up English with Spanish, sometimes in the same sentence but saying farewell was all in Spanish. Pat got in her car, and I followed her off the island past the gatekeeper. She pulled over and let me pass. After that she followed me all the way to my apartment in Coconut Grove.

When we got to my apartment, I defrosted a sirloin and cooked it Thai-style. I also fixed a curried rice dish to go with it. She was a little perplexed as I explained that I could cook only a few special recipes that had been changed to make all the measurements in grams or cubic centimeters. I had prepared the same things many times before and they were excellent. I had also brought down a portable cassette player with some of my old favorites like *Blueberry Hill* and *The Old Lamplighter*. It was a perfect night for romance. We were sitting under the palm trees in the twilight. There was a gentle breeze softly rustling the palm fronds and a three-quarter moon. It was perfect for falling in love or getting laid or both. To make conversation I asked about the *Rembrandt* story and why she was so persistent in getting Ricardo to talk about it.

"You were asleep when I started talking to Ricardo. I was asking about his art collection and if he bought everything at auctions. He said that most of it was acquired that way but that Sean Moran sometimes found things for him. Other people too, but mostly Sean. I asked him what would happen if Sean, or someone like him, found an item worth far more than the piece he was searching for. Something that was not part of the deal. Something they both wanted very much. Something really unusual. Who would get it?"

"Were you asking about Sean and Ricardo specifically?"

"No. Of course not. I made it a hypothetical question."

"Did he give you an answer?" I asked. I was really thinking about getting into Pat's *choninos* and not interested in the story but I had to carry on the conversation until we finished dinner.

"No. He started talking about Tours and the Rembrandt."

"Then why not forget it? Who cares anyway?"

"Because I'm a TV journalist with an instinct for a story. I think Ricardo is teasing me. I think he personally has had the experience I described. Maybe with Sean. Maybe with somebody else. He could have answered my question directly and given me an example in two minutes. My investigative reporter instincts tell me there's a real story. Probably nothing for me or TV but nevertheless a story of some kind that isn't public knowledge."

We changed the subject to politics or something for the rest of the meal but my mind was on something else. I got up and put some water on what was left of the coals and then kissed Pat. She was sitting down and I was standing up but it wasn't awkward. After the first kiss she stood up and I wrapped my arms around her. It was a long passionate kiss and it was just like in Bimini. Except that it wasn't like in Bimini. It wasn't at all like Bimini. We did the same thing but she was not the same."

"I'm going home, Devlin. I would like to go upstairs with you, but it wouldn't be any good. I admit I am *muy ardiente* but it still wouldn't be good."

"I don't understand, Pat. I got the feeling on Bimini under the trees that we both wanted each other."

"I will be blunt about it. And crude. I don't think you would be any good at fucking just for fun."

"It wouldn't be just that."

"For me it wouldn't. I actually like you a lot. Maybe more than like. I'm not sure exactly why. You talk as if every word cost a thousand dollars and you never seem to have any expression on your face. If you and I appeared side by side on a television show the audience would think you were dead after a few minutes. You're kind of mean looking and you need a shave most of the time, but I've still got the hots for you. The problem is your other women."

"That's bullshit, Pat. I don't even have a girlfriend. You met Rocket at Ricardo's birthday. Sylvia Brzinski. She and I were almost in love for a while, but that was a long time ago. We are very good friends now. Nothing else. We cruised for three weeks in the Bahamas and never even kissed each other."

"I've got a feeling it's not over. There's also Lisa Winter who just happens to be about the most beautiful woman I've ever seen. She's out of my league. A lot of people think I'm pretty gorgeous, but not compared to her."

"There's never been anything between Lisa Winter and me," I said, a little startled. "How did you get that idea?"

"Bobby Winter's accident was in the Herald and on T.V. There were a lot of pictures of her. I talked to you about it. Don't you remember? The story had potential. Heroic doctor and beautiful mother. I'm a professional news snoop so I followed it up. I found out the two of you went out to lunch a hell of lot of times."

"What else did you find out?"

"Nothing. I don't believe you ever zonked the lady."

"There was never anything between us."

"Nobody could go out with that woman so many times and not get either his head or his heart messed up. Probably both. She's just too beautiful."

"Rocket and Lisa are both just good friends."

"Then there's the little Spanish beauty. Toni is a very nice girl and a really good kid. When we were alone together she talked a lot. She speaks pure Castilian Spanish and I speak Puerto Rican Spanish but it's close enough and we understood each other. I even taught her some Spanish dirty words. She really blushed and giggled. I don't think she ever heard any words like that before and I'll bet she doesn't forget the words or what they mean. When you're around, though, she's quiet. She clams up and gets a sort of reverent look on her face.

Didn't you ever notice how serious she is when you're there? She's probably trying to act grownup."

"She's only twenty and she's going back to Spain. There is nothing there for me. She's very beautiful, though, and so are you."

"Anyway, Dr. Devlin, there's already too many ladies in your head. I don't want to be added to the group. Give me a big juicy kiss and squeeze *mis nalgas* a little. Then walk me out to my car. It was a wonderful weekend and I like you a lot. I wish you would fall in love with me."

I did what she said and even used both hands on her behind. It was a long, juicy kiss without anything to it. We walked out to her car together. When she was seated she had one more thing to say. I leaned over to the car window.

"When you were taking pictures of me *en mis choninos* I figured you were doing it for the excitement. I didn't mind. But if you ever really do an oil painting I would like to see it. If you ever get the other ladies out of your brain and want to pursue a gorgeous Puerto Rican T.V. lady exclusively for love and romance, just call me on the phone. If you want me to be just a good friend, or just a piece of ass, I'm not available."

I went up to my apartment and went to sleep.

Chapter Eighteen

Saturday, 24 June

We got out early and practiced setting the spinnaker a few times. I hadn't raced the Bermuda 40 for quite a while and we needed experience in working together. Sidney, Gus, Paulette and Rocket were my crew. They had all raced with me many times before so it was just a matter of assigning jobs and positions. Sidney brought along a young Oriental woman named Lea Kahn. I remembered her from the dinner party.

She was medium height, almost as tall as Sidney, who's about five ten. She was Oriental but she looked somehow different from any I had ever seen before. I just stopped what I was doing and stared. The skin around her eyes was tight and part of her was clearly Oriental. The rest of her features were simply excellent but not of any special race. Her eyebrows had a graceful arch and above them, a well-shaped forehead up to her hair. Her nose was straight with delicate nostrils. It was her mouth that was truly amazing. Her upper lip was an exaggerated cupid's bow that might have looked funny if it were not so perfectly shaped. Her lower lip was very full but her mouth was narrow. All the parts were put together correctly.

Although she would just be a passenger, I gave her several jobs to make her feel part of the race. The two men would crank the winches and trim the sheets and guys. Rocket would be my bowman and do the foredeck. Sidney would handle the halyards and help Rocket forward. All of them had done these things before.

It was a sparkling day, cooler than most of June. White puffy cumulonimbus clouds, blue sky, shiny water and a sailboat race. For a sailor this is as good as it gets. There was a big fleet out and it looked like our class would have twelve boats. Before the race we had turkey sandwiches, steak sandwiches and some strange ones made of curried shrimp in grinder rolls contributed by Sidney and heated in my Force 10 oven. Stowed on ice below was two gallons of "Beach Bombs" for after the race.

The starting line was about a mile south of the outer marks of Dinner Key Channel. It was set up there to clear the channel and to give us a little extra distance to the windward mark since the Bay got wider south of Key Biscayne. The wind was coming from the southeast and the first leg was a 2 ½ mile beat to a special race committee mark set up near twelve-foot marker "B". The course was almost directly southeast toward Biscayne Flats and Stiltsville, the group of houses built on stilts on the flats.

Rocket was a superb crew and never wasted time talking after a race started but she did have a few quirks. One was analyzing the other boats and giving me advice. She was looking over the fleet with binoculars.

"The two Block Island 40s are out," she said. "Krieger has a 300-pound blonde woman aboard with a bikini that would fit in his ear. A bimbo like that will slow *Artemis* down half a knot at least." Block Island 40s are much like Bermuda 40s, beamy centerboard boats designed by Bill Tripp. The Hinckley boats are built with unexcelled craftsmanship, though, and I get a little extra pleasure in beating these two. Also in our class was a Northeast 38 called *Actress*.

"The gorillas on *Renegade* are already drunk," Rocket said. "I can see the beer cans flashing. They won't even be able to find the first mark." She was very competitive and literally hated every person on the other boats until the race was over. Ashore she forgot all her antagonism and became normal. Maybe not really normal but her usual self.

There were some wooden boats also, well maintained and still fast. There was a Concordia, a New York 32 named *Ace* and a *Loki* class yawl. There were also several fairly new custom boats designed to the International Offshore Rule. The owners had gotten tired of changes and elected to race with us. With a little over ten minutes to go, Rocket came back to the cockpit and gave me my instructions.

"I think you should just concentrate on getting clear air at the start and try to get to the first mark without too many tacks. It's a short leg and we can win on the reaches if you don't screw up the start." She left the binoculars in the rack and went up to the bow with a huge grin. She wouldn't give me any more advice unless I asked for it.

Lea Kahn called out the time with the stopwatch and Sidney trimmed the genoa. Rocket was right on the bow telling me how close I was to the line. We hit it five or six seconds late but with real good speed and clear air. The sloop-rigged *Artemis* was more aggressive and pulled off an excellent start with clear wind at the north end of the line.

The fleet split right after the start with most of the I.O.R. boats going to the right along with *Vamp*, the *Loki* and the Concordia. There were four of us that went off to the left and we settled down quickly. The first leg was too short for a lot of tacking and clear air was essential. The were only four boats that went left and we all had air. *Ace*, the New York Thirty Two, was the furthest to leeward and moving out fast. Because of her age and rating she seldom won any races unless there was a long windward leg and very little reaching but she could still move. When I looked at her sliding along and pointing just a little bit better than the other three I was impressed by her beauty and reminded again of Rod Stephen's *Mustang* that I remembered from so many races on Long Island Sound when I was a boy. *Renegade* was also to leeward and moving well. *Actress*, the Northeast 38, was to windward of us. We all stayed on a starboard tack until we were just about on the lay line. *Ace* tacked first and closely crossed all three of us. The Thirty Eight, which was usually not quite as fast as we were and rated a little lower, held her tack until a little past the lay line and forced *Renegade* and *Brilliant* to go a little too far. Good move for her.

When we got close to the mark Rocket went to work. She set up the spinnaker pole and attached the sheet, after-guy, fore-guy and halyard. We approached on port and she had the chute in stops up under the genoa. The first leg had been short and without any major wind shifts so the fleet was very close together. Four of the larger I.O.R. boats had gone around first and then *Ace*. Two more I.O.R. and then *Vamp* came from the right. *Renegade* was right behind *Actress* and then us.

The rounding was wild with nine boats turning at almost the same time and barely avoiding collision. As I turned the wheel the chute popped open and filled. Gus was on the sheet, Sidney on the after-guy and Paulette on the topping lift and fore-guy. They had the chute full and trimmed within ten seconds. Ten more and the spinnaker staysail was up and trimmed. None of the boats we rounded with were nearly as fast we were. After rounding the mark, we were lined up as close as husky dogs behind a sled, with bows almost bumping sterns.

All of the I.O.R. boats were very fast to windward but they didn't reach particularly well and they rated high. They had a habit of racing each other and ignoring the older boats. As usual they all started heading way up trying to roll over the boat ahead by passing to windward or luffing-up to defend. Our real competition was the yawl-rigged Block Island Forty *Vamp* who had rounded three boats ahead of us. The next leg was a long reach down toward Featherbed Shoals with another reach back home. The four boats that we had to sail against were lined up on a beam reach right behind each other with spinnaker poles on the head-stays. Krieger on *Renegade*, just ahead of us, was a good sailor and also very aggressive but he got frustrated easily. I noticed Rocket, who was standing at the port shrouds trimming the spinnaker, whisper to Sidney and Sidney to Paulette and she to Gus who laughed at the message.

"Rocket says to use old play number KF79 to pass Krieger. The fat bimbo will get excited and explode her bikini. *Renegade* will stop dead in the water."

I started laughing but I nodded to the crew that we would do it and they got ready. KF79 was a famous football play that Columbia had used in the '30s. We used the number for a sneaky tactic in this kind of situation. First we made a big ceremony of bringing the mizzen staysail on deck and setting it up. Then Rocket started her act.

"Ease the sheet. Trim the guy. Ease the mainsheet. Trim the spinnaker," she yelled. "Lower the centerboard. Sit on the rail."

I knew that if I set the mizzen staysail and tried to pass *Renegade* to windward she would luff me up. There was no question that my yawl rig with the mizzen staysail was a tiny bit faster than he was on this point of sail. He knew it as well and would not let me pass him without a fight. Paulette was trimming the mizzen staysail well and we started moving to windward of him.

Krieger didn't hesitate and immediately started steering a higher course into the wind so that he could prevent me from passing him. Rocket was yelling so loud that his whole crew was watching her.

"You're catching him!" she yelled at the top of her voice. "Trim the chute! Trim the main! Head way up you stupid bastard!" She yelled at me.

We steered both boats higher and higher into the wind until the spinnakers were about to collapse. I knew that I couldn't wait any longer.

"Shut your mouth you crazy little bimbo!!!"

That was the signal to the crew. I turned the wheel over. The bow of my boat swung to the right and directly at *Renegade*. It looked as if we were going to ram his stern. Because my maneuver had been planned ahead all of the sheets were eased at the same time, quickly but smoothly. We had practiced.

Krieger saw my bow swing sharply and aim at his stern. He was startled and just stared, standing straight up at the wheel. He didn't realize what was happening until the bow swung by, missing him by only about two feet. Then he turned sharply, as if to cover and blanket me but his crew wasn't ready and the sheets weren't eased. His main, trimmed way in, was stalled completely. His spinnaker, with the pole on the head-stay and the sheet way in, collapsed immediately. His boat didn't stop dead in the water but it seemed that way. We sailed through his lee and into clear air. It was a pretty vicious tactic for this level of racing but I knew I couldn't roll over him. After the maneuver we were laughing so hard we almost lost all our concentration. When we settled down after passing Krieger, Paulette got the binoculars from the box and looked back at the fat blonde. I could hear the sweet voice from her old movies.

"Oh my goodness, a terrible thing has happened. There is a lady in distress. She is somewhat heavy and the top of her swim suit has come to pieces. What a terrible thing as her bosoms are completely exposed. She is so embarrassed and they are *so* huge. Really huge! Actually gigantic and everybody can see them!"

Actress was the next boat right ahead of us. On a long reach she didn't have a chance against us so she played it smart. She stayed right on a direct course to the mark while Krieger was luffing us up. Now they let us by. They could follow us closely and maybe beat us on corrected time. I sailed by her to windward and we went after *Vamp*.

For the next forty minutes we concentrated on nothing but boat speed. I let Rocket steer most of the leg and Sidney trimmed the spinnaker. I adjusted the centerboard a tiny bit every time the wind picked up or eased off. The balance was so good Rocket could steer with her fingertips. When we passed *Renegade*, *Vamp* was about five boat-lengths ahead of us. Now we just aimed at her stern and tried to sail faster. I wasn't too strict about what a crew did on a race but I did have one firm rule – only one person moved at a time. If somebody had to pee, nobody could go for food or do anything else until they were finished. Now we took turns eating the sandwiches and shrimp curry grinders. Biscayne Bay was sparkling and the smell of suntan oil was mixed in with the salt air. What a day!

We caught up to *Vamp* a tiny bit at a time and when we came to the second mark we were right behind them. We dropped our stay-sails to prepare for rounding about the same time they did. *Vamp* rounded the mark with a quick sharp turn intended to keep us from getting the inside. They did a lousy jibe and collapsed the spinnaker. We did a wide turn and kept our chute drawing all the time. We did a dip-pole jibe as smooth as you could ask for while the beer gorillas did an end for end and lost control. We sailed around and through her and got clear air. Both the stay-sails were up and drawing in seconds and we sailed the last seven miles to the finish without incident. We passed two of the I.O.R. boats who gave us time and finished ahead of all the older boats except *Ace*. She was forty-four feet overall and we finished fifteen seconds after she did so we had her beaten on corrected time. I figured we would get at least a third for the day.

Rocket started jumping up and down as soon as we crossed the line. She went below immediately for the Beach Bombs. We put all the sails away and cruised back down the Dinner Key Channel with the engine.

There was the usual parade of boats going in the Dinner Key Channel, splitting when they passed between the little palm-covered islands and coming to the outermost docks. Some turned left to go to the Sailing Club and some turned right to go to the other yacht clubs and docks. Most of the smaller boats sailed across the shallow water outside of the channel. I always liked the sailing-home part of a day and I usually let the person with the least experience steer for fun. Today Lea Kahn was at the wheel.

The minute we crossed the line, Rocket started running around the boat cleaning up and putting things away. She was giving out instructions and directions to everybody. Rocket had decided it was time to celebrate and her enthusiasm was always contagious. Most of the time she was pretty normal and ladylike but sometimes she got excited. When I made love to her she would go completely nuts. She would say and do really wild things. At times like this she could get so excited about doing well in a race she could even get a stodgy old guy like Gus to start jumping up and down. Paulette loved her like a kid sister.

We got the jibs, spinnakers and staysails in bags and the mainsail down and furled with the cover on it. Rocket left the spinnaker sheets and guys in place for tomorrow's race. When the boat was completely organized she came back to the cockpit. I was sitting there giving Lea Kahn directions on how to steer. Rocket pretended to be formal and nautical.

"Sir, the crew requests permission to celebrate."

She saluted with a big grin.

"Permission to party is granted."

We started in on the Beach Bombs immediately. I decided to get a little bit drunk and enjoy myself. I had a lot of things on my mind but I couldn't do anything until Snake learned more and made some decisions. I might as well try to enjoy it. I had a deep-down feeling that Snake would find out something really bad and knew that the thing with Sharon would not be over until he killed some people.

Gus and Paulette were good party people even without booze and Rocket seemed to turn them on. Sidney and Rocket were just getting to know each other but they both kind of sparkled. Lea Kahn kept glancing at me as if she thought we were all a little nuts.

At the inner end of Dinner Key Channel there are two little islands covered with palm trees and underbrush. By the time we passed between them and turned right for the yacht club Rocket and Sidney started singing. She had a terrible voice but she could remember every school song since first grade as well as all the ones her mother taught her. Sidney had both an excellent voice and a prodigious memory and claimed he knew more songs than she did. They agreed that a song counted if the person knew all the words of at least one verse. Pretty soon they were demanding that each of us come up with some songs. Lea Kahn sang a couple of songs in Japanese or maybe Chinese. Gus claimed he grew up in an orphanage that didn't have any songs but Paulette sang a couple from an old MGM musical.

As we went past the end of the long pier at Monty Trainer's, people could hear us and were even pointing. Occasionally the singing sounded good but mostly it was just noise. We stopped singing long enough to bring the boat into my slip at the yacht club and tie it up. While we were adjusting the lines Bill and Anne came down the dock with drinks in their hands. Early in our partnership I had taken them out sailing and I had been invited to play golf. We found out pretty quickly that he hated sailing and I hated golf. We both liked parties, though, so we each used the other guy's club a lot. They came aboard and joined the party.

After a few more drinks and songs the girls went up to the club to change clothes and put on makeup. The guys changed aboard the boat, using the cockpit shower to clean up. By six o'clock we were all ready to go up on the lawn for more drinks and food.

Rocket came back in a really nice outfit that she had designed herself. The cloth was a homespun, rough cotton canvas in white with two shades of green. The skirt was very short, kind of cute short or regatta-type short. It was just right and Rocket had such nice legs it looked great. Anything shorter would have attracted too much attention. The top was like a shapeless bathing suit that covered her stomach but not her shoulders and had a tiny short-sleeved jacket. She was not much good at acting cool and sophisticated. When she realized how much I liked it she sort of lit up.

"I thought it would look good with your silly-looking green eyes," she teased.

A big party after a regatta is something special. Probably half of the people there had been out on Biscayne Bay racing in the afternoon with all the tension and excitement. Even those who didn't do well had the fun of a good sail and the promise of another chance tomorrow. Nearly half of the crews were women or kids. Some of the smaller one-design classes were all kids. I think it's fun to have a few drinks and talk to people you have just competed against. Even though some yacht racing has reached a state of professionalism that's no longer sport, this level is still amateur with good sportsmanship as part of it. It's still competitive but not usually cutthroat. There is a camaraderie in yacht racing seldom found in any competitive sport. At the end of a racing day, everyone, young or old, has experienced racing a sailboat in the same wind and weather conditions.

The bar was set up near the swimming pool and the buffet tables were being worked on. Rocket and I left the others and got some rum swizzles. Then we made a tour of the lawn, trying to find our competitors from the afternoon who belonged to the club.

"Hello, Charley," Rocket said, giving a big hug to Charley Krieger from *Renegade*.

"Hello, Rocket, you little bilge rat." Charley was a plump guy with a great sense of humor. He thought Rocket was wonderful. I shook hands with Charley and asked him where the lady was. "She got mad and went home. When you fooled us with that dirty, sneaky trick she exploded the top of her bathing suit and my crew went crazy laughing. She didn't have anything to cover up with and I started laughing, too. She got really pissed off at me. She went below and didn't come back up until I got to the dock and then she took off. I don't think she wants to go steady with me."

"I'm sorry, Charley," Rocket said. "What was her name?"

"I can't remember," he said. "I *really* can't remember. She was too fat anyway. Think she slowed the boat down?"

"Definitely," said Rocket.

"Definitely," I agreed.

Some of Charley Krieger's crew came up and we talked with them for a while. They were happy to learn that I had caught the *Vamp*. Norton Strange, the guy who owned *Vamp* was very serious about racing. He always had a crew of huge men who sometimes ran into each other. He kept his boat at the marina and never came to parties at any club. Rocket had a way of saying Norton that sounded like a frog.

"Nor-r-ton didn't wave at us before the start. He's not very friendly," she said.

"I think Norton Strange is a jerk," Charley said.

"Nor-r-ton is strange," said Rocket.

"He is a little different," I said.

"Nor-r-ton is a frog with huge beer-guzzling toads for a crew," Rocket croaked.

Charley then told Rocket how wonderful she was and asked her to leave me and marry him. He always did this and Rocket was used to it. After awhile we left Charley and his crew and found Clay Shiver, the owner of the Northeast 38, *Actress*. I told him I thought he was smart to just let me pass and not waste time with a luffing match. He agreed and said he thought he had come in third on corrected time just behind us. The Concordia and *Ace* were both kept at Dinner Key and none of them were at the party. After wandering around for a while we checked the bulletin board and found we were second, *Actress* third and a 37 foot I.O.R. boat named *Flicker* was first.

We were having fun.

Like most women, Rocket sometimes had subtle mood changes. With her it usually wasn't too subtle. There had been lots of different ways that she acted when we started going out together but much of that had changed after Chub Cay when she said that I became like a real person. She was somehow different tonight. I hadn't actually asked her to be my date but it seemed that way. What was different was the lack of tension between us. It was as if we had gone through some bad times and gotten them behind us. It felt like we were just naturally supposed to be together.

I enjoyed eating food, particularly seafood, but that was it. She enjoyed even *thinking* about it. She would spend hours with the Thursday edition of the *Miami Herald* and its food section. The Yacht Club always put out a special effort for certain parties and tonight was one of them. It was the once-a-year time when they brought in real Down East lobsters with claws as well as tails.

"Look at them, Devlin, look at those claws," she said, almost jumping up and down. "Let's get one extra just in case."

"You mean one for me and two for you."

"Right," she said with a big smile.

Snake could sneer better than anyone I had ever seen but nobody could smile like Rocket. Watching her tease Charley and get excited about the food and the race brought back the memory of the first time I met her. It had been here at the Yacht Club at a party just like this. There were Japanese lanterns then and soft romantic music that night, too.

It was Labor Day, three years ago, and she came with a couple who raced a Lightning, people she knew from the Oxford Yacht Club on the Eastern Shore. Sylvia Brzinski had been working at a department store in Washington, D.C. and had recently moved to Coral Gables so she could sail year-round. I noticed her just as they were playing an old favorite of mine, a song called *Oh, What It*

Seemed To Be. She was with her friends sitting at a table eating a barbecue sandwich and getting it all over herself. She was totally involved in what she was doing. I had never seen anybody eat with such concentration and I kept looking at her. She noticed me and looked up then went back to the sandwich. I kept staring. She would ignore me and eat for a while and then look up. It was twilight but I could see clearly and she looked pretty. Excellent bone structure and a smooth tanned face. All of her features in the right proportion. When she finished eating she put on some glasses and looked directly at me. Eventually I looked away. Then she left the table and I lost track of her. A few minutes later I walked over to the temporary outside bar to get a drink when she walked up to me.

"I noticed that you were looking at me. Do I look like somebody you think you know or was it because I was making a pig of myself and getting barbecue all over everything?"

"I was staring because I thought you looked pretty and I was trying to figure out if you were with a date or by yourself."

"I'm with Joanie and Frank McMillan. I was crewing for them today on their Lightning. Nice talking to you." She walked away.

Up close she looked even better than before. White, even teeth with that very pale pink lipstick that looks so nice with a tan. She must have gone to the ladies room before talking to me and put on the lipstick. I was usually confused by things that women did so I wasn't too surprised that she would be forward enough to approach me and then walk away without giving her name or asking mine. I guess that meant I was supposed to do something next.

I really didn't like courtships and flirtations and that sort of thing. It wasn't that I minded the indirectness, it was just that I didn't know how to do it. I think women are pretty wonderful and I get along with most of them but I never knew how to act or what to say. I don't get flustered or embarrassed or ever feel uncomfortable but I never quite understand the system.

The girl wasn't quite beautiful but close enough that it shouldn't matter. Too close to be called just cute. I could see enough to know this even in the semi-darkness. I could also tell from what she did and said that I would never out-guess her in whatever game she was playing. I did the only thing I could think of at the moment. I watched her and when she sat back down at the table I walked over and asked her for a date.

"Would you like to have dinner with me?" I said.

"I'm not really hungry right now but maybe in an hour or so I'll be ready."

"I didn't mean tonight. I meant some other time." I'm not good at clever remarks and I responded before I realized she was just teasing and then I felt silly.

"O.K." She looked at me for a minute with a beautiful smile. "Any particular night or just dinner in general?" she asked.

"Tomorrow night O.K.?"

"I live in Coral Gables. I'll write down my address unless you'd rather meet me here after the races tomorrow." She started writing on a piece of paper without waiting for an answer.

"Why don't I pick you up at eight o'clock? Even if there's a slow race it should give us plenty of time."

"Were you racing today?"

"Yeah. I was racing in the Star class."

"What boat?"

"*Starfire*."

"W. Devlin. Right? You got a third. You gotta cover Ding Schoonmaker and Herb Christie tomorrow to win the series. You've got to decide which one to cover if they split. Have you decided or will you wait?"

Our date actually started that night. She introduced me to Joanie and Frank McMillan. We talked to them for a while and then when they were ready to leave I offered to give her a ride home. We stayed at the Yacht Club until the bar closed and then managed to find an all-night diner.

I found out her name and why she was called Rocket. It wasn't love at first sight. There was plenty of physical attraction but there was something even stronger. I really liked her. I had never really liked a girl before. If they were good looking the physical attraction always overshadowed any other feelings.

We always had a lot of sailing stuff to talk about but there was a lot more than talking. I don't like smart-ass women but her comments never seemed caustic even when she was making fun of me. She never asked me what I did to earn money and somehow I figured that it didn't matter much. She did want to know about every boat I ever owned or sailed.

Watching her, and thinking back to that first night, I wondered if somehow my feelings of being friends with her had obscured the realization that I was in love. I had never thought about it that way before but maybe that was my problem. Maybe Paulette could explain it.

When we left the food table we were carrying two plates each but three of the four were ones she had piled up. When we found the table where the other part of the crew was sitting we made a mess. We had clams, oysters, conch chowder, cold shrimp, cracked conch, spicy Cajun shrimp, conch salad, corn on the cob and garlic bread. Conversation ceased for a while. Rocket managed to get butter and cocktail sauce all over her hands and face but somehow she never got anything on her clothes.

At the end I had about as much to eat as Rocket since her appetite was always larger than her capacity. She volunteered to go up and get coffee. When she left I was sitting alone with Paulette for a few minutes. We were very close and she was like a big sister to me but on the subject of Rocket she was relentless.

"I understand Rocket has a new boyfriend. Do you think it could be serious?" she asked. I stared at her, suddenly feeling very funny.

"She didn't mention it to me."

"You better get used to the idea, Devlin. Rocket never told anybody that the two of you were *just friends*. If she puts out the word that she wants to go out with other men there's going to be quite a crowd. While you were mooning and moaning over Lisa Winter and sniffing after Pat Rivera, Rocket was sitting home watching television. I think that's over. I think you are about to become a thing of the past."

"Who is her new boyfriend? Does she really have one?"

"She doesn't have one yet. I was just teasing you. You may still have time but you have a real mental problem. Do you want me to explain it to you?"

"Go ahead."

"I don't know how the two of you ever decided to be *just friends* but I do know it's total bullshit. Rocket is clearly in love with you and she knows it. You are far more in love with her but you don't even know it or you are too immature to do anything about it. Women think about being in love and getting married from the time they are little. Men don't think about anything. If she left Miami right now she would hurt a lot because she loves you. You would wake up and realize what you had lost. Then you would die. I think you are brain dead already."

Rocket came back with the coffee and ended our conversation. Around eight o'clock the band started playing and we all started dancing. I danced with Rocket first and then each of the other ladies. Anne Gaines tried to talk me into going up to Hilton Head with them for a week to play golf. Paulette talked about how great it was to be married. Lea Kahn made it clear she wanted to go sailing again, with or without Sidney. I told her she was welcome to come with us the next day when Sidney was preaching. When I mentioned it to Sidney later he seemed pleased. Sidney had more girlfriends than anyone I knew but they all seemed to be just friends who happened to be female.

At one point the band played a lot of old tunes including the Charleston. Sidney and Lea Kahn were far better than anyone else and gradually people stopped dancing to watch them. Sidney had on his clerical collar and Lea had on a fairly tight oriental outfit. They looked strange together but they danced very well. After they finished there was huge applause.

It was a great party. I had gotten a little drunk with the Beach Bombs on the boat and rum swizzles on the lawn but the huge pile of seafood and two cups of coffee sobered me up. By the time we left I was fine. I walked with Rocket to her car and kissed her goodnight. I was hoping I could get her to come home with me. It was a serious kiss with my intentions obvious and she responded.

We both got pretty warmed up and then she whispered, "Please don't take me home with you. I'm really hot now but I want to go home by myself and sleep alone. I'm really worried about trying to make the rescue."

We talked for a minute about who would be crewing the next day and then she drove off. I went back into the Yacht Club and sat at the bar until it closed. I was sure of two things. I wanted Rocket very badly. I knew that. But I also knew that my mind was pretty mixed up and I was also worried about the attempt to rescue Sharon Moran. I wondered for a while, sitting there at the bar, if I would ever understand women. Or even one woman. I thought about that for a while. When I started thinking about the idea that I didn't even understand myself I decided it was time to go home and go to bed.

Monday morning I met Truman Montgomery at the Miami International Airport and we flew to New York. I had decided to become friends with Truman after he stood up so dramatically for me in the law office. It was hard, though, because he was basically an unlikable prick. I had invited him to lunch a few times and found that he couldn't talk about anything except plastic surgery. I took him out sailing and he got seasick. I brought him along with me one night when we had a serious running session on the Green Mountain Express. I was the main engineer for section number one with an elderly lady from the Baptist Church as my switchman. Tess McCarthy had section two, with another old Baptist lady as her switchman. Sidney was trying to recruit the two old ladies for our church. Tess was a hooker from Miami Beach he was trying to reform.

Sidney had section three with Truman Montgomery as his switchman. Things did not go well. Sidney's layout is extremely sophisticated and, like all good H.O. railroads, it's capable of some things which require skill from the operators. The two old ladies and the hooker picked up the H.O. skills quickly but Truman couldn't do the simple timing things.

There was one beautiful but complex sequence where six trains of eight to ten cars each passed and crossed each other. They appear to be on the verge of crashing repeatedly. Sidney was the most pleasant man there was except when running his railroad. Sometimes he became a Vince Lombardi. Sidney rehearsed us all carefully. Sections one and two went through the sequence separately and then together. When a third section of track, operated by Truman and Sidney, rehearsed their sequence Truman kept hitting the wrong switch. Sidney modified the whole scheme so that the little man only had to do auxiliary switches that didn't effect the timing, except for one critical flip. Truman had to move one switch that had three positions, right, neutral and left. He had to flip the switch within a few seconds after a ten-car freight train entered a tunnel high in the mountains. This was at the fifth and highest operating level, high in the mountains and hundreds of scale feet above the valley below.

There was a full ten seconds when this train was in the tunnel, and the flip had to go to the *right* between the first and fifth seconds after it entered the tunnel. This was the most dramatic part of the sequence but when we got to it Truman froze. After the train went in the tunnel he waited almost ten seconds and then flipped *left*.

Another tiny train, fully loaded with passengers, came roaring out of the tunnel, went left instead of right where the tracks split and then instead of passing close to a Tess-controlled freight train they *crashed horribly*. Both trains went tumbling into a gorge where they landed on and crushed a delicate wooden bridge with two other trains passing. All six trains, with more than fifty cars, crashed into the hard fake surface of the White River. Hundreds of passengers were killed. Truman had caused the worst disaster in the history of H.O. railroads.

Sidney almost turned white. He was livid and speechless and then pointed his finger and glared at Truman.

"You f-f-f-fucking f-f-ferret!" he screamed. "You have killed all the f-f-fucking passengers!"

Tess, the whore, broke up laughing. She pointed at Truman.

"You f-f-f-fucking f-f-ferret!" she screamed.

The two old Baptist ladies looked apoplectic and I thought they would faint or die. Then they both turned and pointed at Truman at the same time.

"You f-f-f-fucking f-f-ferret," they yelled. It was probably the only time either old lady ever said a bad word.

After that night, things were different. Truman was a strange little creature. As a boy he had been such a miserable little shit that nobody would play with him and so little he wasn't worth beating up. Now he had a nickname. Having a real nickname made him one of the boys or something. He didn't care if we called him a fucking ferret as long as we called him something and didn't throw him out.

After the crash Sidney cooled off and let him run the slightly damaged train by himself through the tunnel a few times until he could flip the switch to the *right* a few seconds after the train entered the tunnel. We then added trains and more trains until shortly after midnight we added sound effects and lighting and got it all on video tape. It was fantastic.

My parents met us at LaGuardia airport to drive us back to Rye where they still lived and we talked all the way. I introduced him as Ferret Montgomery. In Miami we had called him the f-f-fucking f-f-ferret for a while and then just ferret. I doubt if he ever realized that a ferret was a small domesticated European polecat with pink eyes and yellowish fur.

We stopped for lunch at the Larchmont Yacht Club. The Club itself looked beautiful with everything painted and mowed and clipped but the grass was a little beat up from being trampled on all summer. We had lunch on the

"Quarterdeck" which is the name that is used for the formal dining room. It is completely open in the summer on the side that opens out to Long Island Sound. The floor has two levels so that all tables have a good view of the water. My mother managed to keep Truman in the conversation and facial surgery out. She also managed to keep my dad and me from talking about boats. Both were major feats that only a woman like her could pull off.

After lunch we drove up the Boston Post Road, past the Sloan-Kettering Cancer Research Center and the Rye Golf Club. We drove down Oakland Beach Avenue and out to the famous old Playland Amusement Park that has been there for years. My dad pointed out the ice hockey rink and explained to Truman how it had been one of the reasons they had decided to live in Rye when they left Nova Scotia. We barbecued out on the terrace that night for dinner and both my parents treated the Ferret as if he was a normal person.

The next morning I borrowed a car and we drove into the city and met with all the doctors who would be involved in the surgery. After planning the operation, we talked with Joan Pegram and her mother and then hung around the hospital for a couple of hours.

The morning of the operation we rode into the city with my father. He usually took the train but we were going directly to LaGuardia airport after the operation so he dropped us off at the hospital and went on downtown. We went inside and met Gene Stallings, who would be the major surgeon, and the rest of the team. We all got scrubbed up and waited in the operating room for Joan Pegram to be rolled in.

The operation was not dramatic and there was no point where Joan's life was in danger. When Bob Mickatavage examined and freed the optic nerve there was some question of the outcome but not much. Joan's eyesight would either improve a tiny bit or a lot. The anesthesiologist for this type of surgery has to be very careful since the area operated on is so close to the breathing passages. As the assisting surgeon it was my job to take the bone from her hip that would be used as a building material to re-sculpt her eye socket. If the need for bone had been small we might have used rib or the inside of the skull. While I was doing it Gene explained to the Ferret what we did with the bone while we were waiting to use it. The pieces that we took were, of course, alive and since they were part of Joan's body they would not be rejected later.

The line for the coroneal incision was marked in blue just inside the hairline. Gene made the incision by the left ear, up across the front of the head and down to the right ear. After tying off the necessary blood vessels he separated her upper face from the bone. He then pulled it down so that he could work. Because of the nature of the surgery, and the care taken, there would be minimum blood loss. Only about two pints would have to be replaced. We all wore head pieces with special lights.

Seeing a person's face pulled off can be disconcerting and takes a little getting used to. It's like special effects in a horror movie. Specially designed tools called elevators are used to separate the flesh from the bone. The plastic plate that had been put in for an eye socket was removed and Bob Mickatavage examined the optic nerve. I don't know exactly what he did but when he finished he felt that the optic nerve was free and clear. The plastic plate had touched it and affected her vision.

Because a small portion of her brain was exposed during the operation a neurosurgeon would examine it to make sure no damage had been done. Gene took the pieces of bone that I had carved out earlier and shaped them with some special tools. Although the tools he used were specially designed for this purpose they would have worked well in building model airplanes. The things that Gene did with his hands and his own brain when he first visualized, then cut, then pieced together a new eye socket were art, not science. There was no textbook that told him which shapes and combinations of shapes would form the perfect curves. He used four small separate pieces of hip bone. Each had four sides. Each one was different and each asymmetrical.

Gene wired the four pieces of bone to her skull and to each other in such a way that they formed the eye socket. The edges of the bone would grow together forming a new eye socket that would be much better than the plastic piece. When the pieces of Joan's new face were together, Bob examined her eye again. He knew it would look slightly crooked when the bandages were removed but it would eventually settle and match the other eye. The plastic socket was no longer affecting the optic nerve so her vision, which had been slightly impaired, should now clear up.

After her skull had been re-sculpted Gene put her face back on and "zipped it up." He pulled the whole face back up and I very carefully stitched back the incision he had made inside the hair line. The anesthesiologist stopped all anesthesia and allowed her to wake up. We stayed with her until she was fully conscious. Gene liked to have his patients wake up right there in the operating room and moved to a recovery room after he was sure everything was all right. We stayed around long enough to talk to Joan and Mrs. Pegram and then took a cab to the airport. The Ferret was thrilled with the whole thing and wouldn't shut up until I left him at Miami Airport.

Chapter Nineteen

Monday, 3 July

We were scheduled for some minor surgery early on Monday and again in the afternoon. Bill and I had planned surgery in both the mornings and afternoons of the first three days so I could get some operations finished before the week of the rescue. I made a point of being very abrupt with all of the women in the office. I was not actually rude but close to it. I knew that our plan of explaining why we were closing the clinic was not very good but I wanted to make it seem as real as possible. The surgery went well, without any complications and I left to go to the gun shop before noon.

There was no crowd there so I bought four boxes of 9mm Luger rounds. They were 115 grain with full metal jackets. Clint, the guy who sold me the gun when I first came there, told me the extra clips that I had ordered had come in. I paid for the clips, bullets and a set of earmuffs and found a lane to shoot in. I used all three of the new clips and moved the target to various distances. After firing the first box of sixty I went back to the front of the gun shop and got some new targets. I had been using the bulls-eye type target before and now I got some of the ones shaped like a man. It was a lot more realistic.

When I told Snake about deciding to buy a gun he said that if I brought a gun with me I'd better know how to use it. He also said that if I shot him by mistake he would shoot me on purpose. For some reason I found it awkward using two hands the way Clint had shown me. Because I used my hands and forearms so much, almost every day in surgery, they were both very strong and steady. The Luger pistol wasn't heavy and I felt that I didn't need to use my left hand as support. The more I practiced, however, the more I realized the importance of the bracing hand for sideways control as well as up and down.

Clint came in while I was using the second box of rounds and made some suggestions about where I placed my feet and how to bend my knees. The shooting posture seemed a little like what I used to use as a defensive back when I played college football. The idea then was to get in a position where you could move in any direction without losing your balance, including backwards. The way Clint explained the stance to me was that everything you did was for the purpose of having a steady base to aim and fire and using two hands on the gun was also part of this. He kept telling me to look at what I wanted to shoot and point my finger.

After I had finished firing the second box of rounds, I took a holster out of my brief case and put it on my belt. I practiced a quick draw like the cowboys did in the movies. After awhile I decided to cut away part of the leather when I got home so I could draw faster. I guess I looked pretty silly drawing and shooting like a cowboy, particularly with a Luger pistol. By the time I finished the third box I was getting pretty accurate. I felt sure that I would never need to use the gun and sure as hell I wouldn't be using a quick draw, but it was interesting learning and practicing.

I had more surgery scheduled for the afternoon but, like the morning's, it was not complicated and went well. At five o'clock I drove down to Watkins Island and picked up Jimmy Lightbourne. He had flown in on the Chalk's seaplane and was planning to stay for a couple of days to work out the details of his new sails with the sailmaker and to visit a few marine hardware stores. Like many other Bahamians who were involved in marinas, boatyards or sailboat racing, Jimmy came over to Florida every two or three months to make purchases or order equipment. Because of the heavy duties charged for imports it was sometimes cheaper to fly over to the States to buy things than to get them in the Bahamas. Jimmy had been the dockmaster for a long time and the people who owned the club trusted him to make trips like this.

I had arranged with Charley Fowler to meet us at his loft at six o'clock so we drove straight there. Charley was an old friend and I bought most of my sails from him. Jimmy spent most of the drive telling me how ugly my green car was and how I had to trade it in or ruin my reputation.

Like most sailors, I enjoyed buying sails. I liked the discussions about the shape and the weight of the cloth and all of the things you talked to a sailmaker about. When I lived in Rye and sailed on Long Island Sound I used to make a whole day out of it. It started with my father and his boat. He used to take a day off from work when he wanted to buy sails for his Owens Cutter. We would drive down to City Island, which is an island in the Sound, connected by a bridge to the Bronx. For many years it was a boat-building center but had gradually changed. The building of boats had moved elsewhere but there were were still some sailmakers and a lot of great seafood restaurants. My father and I would go to Charlie Ulmer's and order the new sails and then have lobster at Thwaits. Later on, when I started buying sails for my own boats, I would get my father to come down with me. It was our version of a father-son day.

When we first started going to City Island, there was a beautiful smell in the lofts from the cloth and the ropes and the resins but that had been replaced by a new one. In the boat-building yards there used to be a wonderful smell of cedar but that had long since changed to the synthetic smells of fiberglass and epoxy.

At Fowler's the three of us argued gently about all aspects of the new sails but in the end Jimmy got exactly what he wanted. We asked Charley to join us for dinner at Monty Trainer's but he was tied up so Jimmy and I went together. While we were driving, I asked him if there was much drug smuggling going on in the Bahamas but he didn't seem to want to talk about it.

We drove down to Bayshore and parked in the lot next to Monty's. It was almost dark by the time we sat down and ordered. I got some iced tea and Jimmy had a rum swizzle. We got a big plate of Mexican stuff for a start and then I switched over to some shrimp and steamed clams. Jimmy wanted red meat since he ate seafood so often in the islands. After we started eating I asked him if he remembered the captain from the *Ojos Verdes*.

"Yes, I remember him well. He was a magnificent mon. As big as a house. He knew boats, too. He knew a lot about boats. I liked him very much."

"Rocket and I got invited to his sixtieth birthday party. It turned out that he wasn't the captain, he was the owner of the boat. He lives in a huge house on an island in Biscayne Bay and owns about half of Spain."

Jimmy stared at me very seriously for a couple of minutes. "Which half does he own?"

"The half where the money is, of course," I said, laughing. I told Jimmy the whole story about Ricardo and the party and meeting Butch and Antonia when we were at Chub. His eyes got big as I was telling the story, especially when I described the huge buffet tables and the items that I had picked out. Fortunately for us, the waitress brought our food at just the right time as we had both gotten hungry thinking about the Spanish food. The trip to the sailmaker had made me think of my father so I told Jimmy a little about him while we ate.

"The memory that's most vivid about my dad was when he bought the *Owens Cutter*. The war had been over for a few years and we were living in Rye. One time he took a few days off from work and we drove to the Owens plant. Our boat was near completion and my father spent more than four hours checking things and making notes. Afterwards we sat in the foreman's office and while my dad pointed out changes he wanted made. He started with the box that holds the battery. Dad pointed out that the battery itself would become dislodged if the boat were rolled over. The man started to argue but my father explained that *all* the new boats should have a better way of securing the batteries and not just our boat. We were there for hours but the man realized that the suggestions were good ones. Most of them added no substantial cost to manufacturing the boats. I learned that being paid to do something did not make a man a professional.

"Driving home the next day I asked a lot of questions and learned a lot about boats. The main thing I remember, though, is him telling me that the skipper of a boat, large or small, is responsible for *everything*." Jimmy nodded his head in emphatic agreement, his mouth being full of steak at the time. Eventually we got back to Bahamian racing boats and the time I had crewed for him in the Out Island Regatta down in Elizabeth Harbor. That had been the second year after I came to Florida and Jimmy and I had been good friends ever since. I wanted to bring up the subject of drugs again, but I wanted to be careful. I asked Jimmy a lot of questions about his family and about Norman's Cay. I asked him if he was from Norman's Cay and he said that he was born there and still had some family living there. Neither of us mentioned drugs.

After dinner we drove back to my apartment and went for a swim. Later, when we were getting ready for bed, Jimmy unexpectedly brought up the subject of drugs. We were in the living room in our pajamas.

"Why did you ask me about drugs in the islands?"

I decided to seem direct but not to tell the whole story.

"I spent the weekend on Norman's Cay with a girlfriend a few weeks ago. People were talking. I got the feeling that the island is being used somehow for smuggling. Airplanes were taking off in the middle of the night and that airstrip doesn't have the right navigational aids for night landings or takeoffs. I could hear the fucking planes taking off all night long. I don't give a shit if people are doing something illegal but I'm a physician and I know what drugs can do to people. I would hate to see the Bahamian people get involved."

Jimmy sat there for a few minutes thinking and then started talking.

"My people are already involved. My cousin Sammy got a great job in Nassau. He was working for Clement T. Maynard, the Minister of Tourism. Real good job with a necktie and briefcase and everything. Chance to move up and be important. His aunt, who is my mother's youngest sister, is very proud of him. Then he met some bad people and started smoking marijuana cigarettes. Soon he started using other stuff. Pretty quick he is stealing money and shooting drugs in his arm with a needle. One day he is showing up at the hospital. His friends dump him off at the door to the emergency room and leave him. He stays alive for one hour and then he is dead from too much overdose. My aunt is now very sad but there is nothing she can do. I know about drugs in the Bahamas but I didn't know that Norman's Cay was involved in any special way." Jimmy seemed very sad.

"I'm sorry about your cousin Sammy. Since I'm a cosmetic surgeon I don't get involved directly but I do know how devastating a drug addiction can be."

We went to bed after that and I started thinking about how I might get Jimmy to visit Norman's on the weekend. I was sure the people there had some sort of grapevine for information that they did not share with outsiders. Jimmy could probably find out what the local story was the night we took Sharon. I decided to call Snake in the morning.

The next morning Jimmy dropped me off at the clinic and took my car. I told him he could hitch-hike or take a bus if he didn't like the color. He was going to drive up to Fort Lauderdale and go to a place called Sailorman. It's a unique store that advertises itself as "the world's largest used and new marine emporium." A friend of mine, Chuck Fitzgerald, owns the place. He's a happy-go-lucky guy who loves people and prefers working with customers over doing paperwork. There is a huge selection of used marine equipment which is truly amazing. There is also a wide selection of new stuff. It's a very colorful and informal place. Most of the people who work there live on sailboats and know boats and boat equipment. They all dress very casually and sometimes the men don't even shave. Sailorman gives away free beer every other Saturday. Shopping there is a real social event.

Before I did anything else, I called Snake on the private line and told him about Jimmy and his cousin. We decided that it could be very valuable to us to have someone on the island at the time of the rescue and the next day. We decided that I would ask Jimmy to make a trip to see his relatives on Saturday and to try to listen to gossip. I would tell him that something was going to happen but not tell him anything else. Sidney would be able to tell us what was said by the people in the restaurant and bar and Jimmy could tell us what the black Bahamians had to say. I gave Lori a check for five hundred dollars and asked her to go to the bank and cash it for me. I wanted to have money to give to Jimmy if things worked out and he went to Norman's.

I had surgery again in both the morning and afternoon. In the work I did that morning I tried to be critical of Maggie Lindsey but I couldn't find anything that I could complain about. I settled for saying only what was absolutely necessary.

We were finished and cleaned up a little after eleven so I went to my office and went through my mail. There was a long letter from Otto Laufenberg with some suggestions about how we might try to rehabilitate Sharon. Otto was very clear on one point. She *might* need extensive psychotherapy no matter what her physical condition was. He said to be prepared for the worst. She might possibly be O.K. but probably not. Even with therapy she might relapse and also could be brain damaged. He also raised the terrible prospect that she might want to go back to the drug people later. He gave some examples of how this could happen and explained that it was similar to the things that happened in cults. I wondered if Otto looked at people and decided if they were crazy or not. If he ever met Snake Moran and tried to figure him out he would probably get a short circuit in his own brain.

After I read the letter, I wrote out a reply in longhand with all of the details of our planned rescue. I said I would call him on Monday or Tuesday when we got back. I told him I'd say that my mother was coming to visit if the rescue had been successful. If she decided not to come, it meant the raid was not successful. I made a photocopy of the letter and sent it to his office with the original to his home. I marked both copies "Personal and Confidential." I was glad I had become a doctor instead of a secret agent or whatever. All the plotting and secret codes were a pain in the ass.

After I finished the letters I closed the door to my office and got out my Luger and the holster. I cut away a little bit of leather to make it easier to pull the pistol out quickly. I used a surgical scalpel and trimmed it neatly. Then I went to the gun store and found the range almost empty again. I bought five more boxes and shot four of them in quick succession, all at targets shaped like a man. It took awhile to get used to pulling the gun out like an old-time cowboy and then using two hands to aim the damn thing. I had never seen a cowboy in the movies use both hands. Of course I had never seen a cowboy with a Luger pistol, either. I used the quick draw for two boxes and took time to aim with the other two. I was getting better. Dead-eye Devlin.

When I finished surgery that afternoon Jimmy Lightbourne was waiting for me in the reception room where he seemed to be entertaining Lori and Polly Pitino. He had his hands spread apart and I assumed he was talking about a fish. He said goodbye to the ladies and we drove down to Watkins Island. I asked him about his conversation with the girls.

"Were you telling the ladies about a fish you caught? It must have been very small. Your hands were only a foot apart."

"I was describing the length of my tally-whacker," he said with a grin. "They both seemed quite interested. Of course I have never in my life caught a fish so small except maybe a bonefish."

While we were driving along I brought up Norman's Cay. On the spur of the moment I made up a totally bullshit story. I wanted to give him some reason for my wanting to ask him to go there. I told him that I was asking about Norman's because I knew a friend in the Drug Enforcement Agency and there was going to be an arrest or something on Saturday, the eighth of July or Sunday the ninth. I told him that I could probably get the D.E.A. to pay for a trip to Norman's that weekend if he would just listen to whatever the black Bahamian people had to say about the arrest. I explained that he would not actually have to do anything but listen and ask questions of his own people about drug dealing. His response was prompt.

"If I understand you correctly, they will pay for my airplane and expenses if I will go back to Norman's Cay this weekend to simply stand around and bullshit. Is that correct?"

"That's right. I'll have to clear it with my friend but he told me that a lot of Bahamians are against the use of drugs and provide the D.E.A. with much helpful information."

"With my good looks and superior intelligence I will make an excellent detective. I will, of course, expect to eat well."

"You will fly down Friday morning and come back Sunday or Monday. While you are there you will do nothing but visit your friends and family. You will ask a few questions about drugs and drug smuggling but nothing more. When you get back to Chub I will contact you. You will not try to get in touch with me. Do you understand?"

"Suppose I uncover a drug smuggler. Can I arrest him?"

"Cut out the bullshit, Jimmy. You go to Norman's Cay for a visit next Saturday and Sunday and the D.E.A. pays for it. You just listen and nothing more. No detective stuff and no mention of the D.E.A. to anybody."

"I am agreed. You have a deal but remember I will eat well while I am undercover."

When we got to Watkins Island I found a telephone and dialed my empty apartment. Jimmy could see me so I pretended to talk to someone. When I finished the fake call I told Jimmy that I had talked to the Drug Enforcement Agency and that they gave me the O.K. to go ahead. I gave him five hundred dollars in twenties and a check for another five hundred. I told him that the money was his only if he made it to Norman's Cay by noon on Friday and stayed until noon Sunday. I emphasized that he was not to do *anything* except talk and remember what he heard. I even cautioned him not to ask too many questions about drugs or drug smuggling. I said I'd get in touch with him within a week or two afterwards. Jimmy thanked me again for everything and went aboard the plane.

I still had almost two hours before I was supposed to be at Sidney Fontaine's apartment for the final meeting to plan our attempt at getting Sharon Moran back.

My Luger pistol was in the trunk of the car so I went by the A.A. Lock and Gun to use the target range. I fired away at targets for nearly an hour, alternating again between bulls-eye targets and ones shaped like a man. There was a device that allowed you to move the targets out to various distances so I practiced at everything from 10 feet to 50 and then fired 30 rounds using the quick-draw like a cowboy. A guy came in and watched me doing it for a while, like I was crazy. He started laughing so I turned and stared at him as if I was ready to draw and shoot him. He giggled nervously and left. It was the end of the day and I needed a shave pretty badly. My eyes probably turned green, too, like they usually do when I get pissed off.

When I got to Sidney's apartment, Rocket was already there. We had to wait for Snake, so Sidney showed us his orchids. He had a huge porch which ran the full length of his eighth-story apartment. It was a lavish place, almost ridiculous for a young priest. The porch was nearly fifty feet long, part screened-in and part open, and nearly filled with flowers. Mostly orchids. I had seen them enough times that I actually recognized each one and could tell which were new. Rocket seemed fascinated as he showed her the different groups of plants and described them.

"This group of p-plants is called *Dendrobium.* They are native to the high Himalayas and mountainsides in Japan, through the hot areas of Southeast Asia and the entire east side of Australia. Since some of the species are native at s-s-sea level and some at high elevations, they have varying habits. As a general rule, the *Dendrobiums* grow during the summer or wet season and flower during the dry or cool season. If the plants take a rest, less water and lower temperatures are necessary."

I listened carefully. Sidney had given me three different types of plants which I had at the clinic. I didn't have much interest in plants or flowers but the orchids were beautiful and Sidney was so enthusiastic that it was hard not to appreciate them. After showing and describing each group, Sidney cut a beautiful

Cattleya orchid and pinned it on Rocket. The *Cattleya* is the type sold by florists for corsages and looked great on her. She managed to smile and blush and giggle, all at the same time. Sometimes she was so appealing it drove me crazy and I couldn't understand why I wasn't in love with her.

"What are these squiggly looking plants? Are they orchids, too?" Rocket pointed at some plants that were growing in empty wooden baskets with no potting material such as charcoal or tree fern. The roots were growing right out of the basket and down several feet in just air.

"Those are *Vandas*. They are a type called *monopodial* and grow differently than the others over there which are called *sympodial*. They have what is called aerial roots. That's why they look so squiggly."

Snake came in while Sidney was putting on his orchid show but he didn't interrupt. After pinning the flower and describing the *Vandas*, Sidney suggested that we eat dinner and talk at the same time. The table had already been set with plates, real silver and napkins. Sidney went into his kitchen and started bringing out things and Snake helped him. Rocket and I sat down. I had been to dinner many times at his apartment but I could never figure out whether he cooked the food himself or had a caterer prepare it for him in advance. I had asked him several times but he never gave me an answer.

We had asked him to get some sandwiches because the meeting was at seven and it was convenient to eat while we talked, but I'm not sure Sidney had ever eaten a sandwich from a brown bag or ever been to Burger King. He served us jellied consommé and Beef Wellington with an excellent Beaujolais. For dessert we had Tiramisu, which turned out to be small lady fingers, espresso and Mascarpone cheese with bits of chocolate.

Rocket was very quiet during dinner. At first I thought she was in a rare somber mood, but then I realized that she was concentrating totally on her food. I watched in amusement as she carefully cut through the layers of the Wellington. She seemed to be memorizing the different layers. I decided that she wasn't planning to ever actually make it, but that she wanted to remember all the details of an excellent meal. I nearly laughed out loud when she made the same quiet inspection of the Tiramisu, which was obviously new to her. When she finally put down her fork and gravely announced that it was a "jazzed up Italian version of an English trifle. Delicious." Sydney looked relieved.

While we were eating, a call came in for Mr. Shannon which meant it was Gus calling from somewhere in the Exumas. Sidney carried on a meaningless conversation about sailing and fishing and then put Snake on. Gus was calling through the overseas operator and was anchored at Highborne Cay, an easy one-day hop to Norman's. Gus said he was going on down there on Thursday or Friday. His call simply meant that they were getting close and would go into the harbor at Norman's Cay and anchor Friday afternoon unless a bad weather forecast pushed them into going sooner. When we finished our Tiramisu, Snake reviewed the plan again for what seemed like the hundredth time.

"Sidney, you and the girlfriend fly to the island on Friday. You do whatever you want while you're there but you make a point of being in the restaurant and bar from about eight o'clock until it closes. Gus is going to go in to the dock that night in a small inflatable. It will have the identification numbers removed. He will row it or tow it in and tie it to the end of the dock. He will row back to the *Pauletta*. Under some old canvas in the inflatable will be a time bomb. It will explode at *exactly eleven fifteen*. It will make a hell of a lot of noise but will not damage anything except the dock because there will be nothing near it." Snake was very serious in telling Sidney what to do and what not to do.

"When the explosion comes you will run down to the dock with the other people from the restaurant. Then you will go back and stay at the bar talking and listening until closing time. Do you have a lady friend lined up for the weekend who will be cooperative?"

"Cooperative in what r-respect?" Sidney asked with a smile.

"Somebody who will hang around the restaurant with you from eight o'clock until closing time. What you do before and after is of no concern unless you call attention to yourself. I'm sure the explosion will bring a lot of people out of the cottages and down to the dock. I'm hoping that those people will go into the bar for a few drinks before they go back home."

"Shall I register at the desk as a p-priest or a layman?" Snake paused for a few seconds before answering. That night he was a blonde with slightly wavy hair and blue contact lenses. He was shaved close.

"If you're going to get laid you register as a layman. If you're going to behave then you sign in as a priest." I think it was the only time since I met him that Sidney was stuck without a clever reply.

"If you run into Gus and Paulette on the island, introduce your friend to them but don't try to make any plans to meet again or do anything together. Gus is going to decide after the explosion whether to go out that night or leave the next morning. If there are too many people running around the dock they might see him leave so waiting could be necessary. If there's anything that would make us abort the attempt then get your ass out to the *Pauletta* and tell Gus. You might have to swim or steal a dinghy but you have to warn us if there's trouble. We'll have a radio on the rescue boat and Gus has signals in code."

"Rocket, you and Dev will be at his apartment Saturday morning and I'll pick you up at six a.m. We'll take my car. I don't want to be seen in that green thing. We'll drive to an airstrip out in the Everglades and then fly to Staniel Cay. There's a Cigarette boat there which I borrowed from a friend. We'll go up to Norman's on Saturday night. Dev will go ashore and find the house. Then he will signal and Rocket and I'll bring the boat in close to shore. Rocket will stay with the boat. I'll go ashore and into the house where I think I'll find Sharon. As of this afternoon she was there. My information comes from an F.B.I. man who gets his information from a guy in jail who is in touch with somebody else who works for Emile Hogge. The information is good, but sometimes there is a time lag."

"Dev will wait outside the house and then help me get her out to the boat. If it's calm we can bring the boat in close. If it's blowing so hard we can't bring the boat in close we'll postpone and go in Sunday night. The long-range weather forecast says there is a good chance of some rain but since it is the middle of the summer there shouldn't be too much wind. The rain is bad for visibility but it could be useful and make a cover for us.

"If we get Sharon, we go back to Staniel and leave in the plane as soon as the sun comes up. We land at the airstrip in the Everglades and then drive her to Devlin's clinic where he's going to detox her. After that I don't know what I'll do. If she's O.K. at the end of the week I'll take her someplace and try to get her head straightened out."

Snake answered a few questions and then Sidney asked if the meeting was over. Nobody had anything else to say so Sidney said he had a question. Snake nodded.

"If we have completely c-covered the details of our little excursion I would like to give young Rocket a chance to drive the Green Mountain Express through the beautiful mountains of Vermont. It is Autumn now and the f-f-foliage is magnificent." Snake and I knew that he was asking if she would like to drive his H.O. model railroad trains around his layout. Sidney had a huge four-bedroom apartment and had torn down the wall between two rooms. He had a model railroad that was very large and extremely well done. Like many other people addicted to the tiny trains, he referred to his railroad as if it were real. It was called the *Green Mountain Express* and had the Green Mountains of Vermont as scenery. Sidney had decided that the foliage season was the prettiest so he had hundreds of tiny trees with all of the beautiful orange and gold and red colored leaves that attract so many people to New England in the Fall. It was so realistic it made me homesick when I saw it.

Sidney did not treat his hobbies like other people. He didn't even treat them like other fanatics. Once when he was having a dinner party, one of the guests was Russ Larson, the editor of Model Railroader Magazine. Sidney had invited him to come to Miami for a few days of sunshine when Milwaukee was snowed in. They spent four days talking about railroads and playing with Sidney's little trains. While talking about orchids he referred frequently to his friend, Tom. "Tom" was Thomas Anderson Fennell, the fourth generation of a family that had helped move the hobby of orchid growing from nothing, to a point today where thousands of people now grow the beautiful and exotic flowers. The Fennell guys actually went down to the Amazon and climbed up trees to get the plants.

It was not enough for Sidney to simply participate in one of his hobbies. He had to meet and get to know all the people in whatever he was currently interested in. If Sidney's hobby had been professional football I would expect to meet Tom Landry at one of his dinner parties.

After he explained to Rocket that the *Green Mountain Express* was the name of his model railroad, we followed him through a door to what had once been a fairly large bedroom. The layout was now over fifty feet in length. Sidney had set up the switches and things so that it could be controlled or driven by either one or more people. The transformers were set on opposite sides of the whole thing. He put Rocket in one of the seats and stood behind her giving instructions. Snake sat down at the other control panel and I assisted him. Both of us had played with Sidney's trains before and knew how to operate them.

Before starting the operation Sidney handed out engineers' hats to each of us. He insisted on the hats with a straight face. An entire wall had been removed between the two rooms and each complete set of controls could handle the room they were in or both rooms.

Rocket started with a beautiful Rivarossi-built engine, an FEF3 #841 Northern that was first used on the Union Pacific in the early forties. Rivarossi is probably Europe's premier model railroading manufacturer and the little model of the huge steam engine was a work of art. Rocket moved it slowly out of its place in the marshaling yard, across a small bridge over a large culvert and up to an industrial yard where it picked up a loading car with a tiny crane. From there she went to the warehouse of a company called the Morgan Machine Company. She picked up two empty flat- cars there and then moved to the Spencer Oil Company and got three tanker cars. Since she was new to train driving, Sidney limited Rocket's train to the six cars and a caboose. With the small caboose it left the town and went through a tunnel, up a steep grade where the red and gold leaves of the trees almost hid the passing trains. At the top of the grade she went through another short tunnel, across a short trestle bridge, over a deep gorge and through some more trees.

Rocket was much more animated than at dinner. Except for short periods, when she was completely concentrating – frowning, with her tongue part way out of her mouth – she chattered to the train, talking it around each corner. It reminded me of how she talked to the boats she sailed.

While it passed through the trees, the little train of cars crossed the invisible line into the territory that Snake controlled. Snake knew how to flip the switches that allowed him to assume control of the little engine.

While Snake drove the train around his part of the layout, Rocket started putting together another train of cars using a Pennsylvania 2-8-0 engine 9976 with a large outside dry steam pipe on the fireman's side and a high side tender. Pretty soon they had four separate trains moving around on six different levels of track and passing back and forth from one territory to the other. Both Rocket and Snake were fascinated by the H.O. railroad. It was not too surprising.

Bill Russell, the great Boston Celtics center, used to have his arch rival, Wilt Chamberlain, over for dinner when his team came to Boston. After dinner Russell would invite Wilt to play with his trains. Wilt would lose track of time, stay too late and perhaps not play as well the next day. That's the story, anyway. It was nearly midnight when we put the little trains away.

Before we left the apartment we set it up so that Rocket would come over to my place after work on Friday. We would have dinner and she would stay there. This worried me because of our unsettled relationship, but it was the practical thing to do. Snake would pick us up early the next morning. When I got home that night I spent a few more minutes studying drug detoxification. It was complicated.

The next afternoon I got a call from Snake. He said he was in Miami Beach in a place called Thunderboat Row, a section of town where the offshore racing powerboats were built. He said he had borrowed a boat from a friend and was going fishing down in the Florida Keys. This meant that he was leaving to take the boat over to Nassau. He was going to meet a friend of his at Yacht Haven and either he or they were going to take it down to Staniel. I wouldn't see him or talk to him again until he picked us up at my apartment a week from now. I felt like I should say something in code, but I couldn't think of anything. I thought about the trip to Norman's driving home and wondered how I had gotten mixed up in so much shit that had nothing to do with my profession.

The following Thursday I nearly choked on a mouthful of *Crab Armand* when Bill asked if anybody was going to get killed in the Norman's Cay rescue. We were eating our monthly lunch at Bill's country club to make last-minute plans for the fake fight at the clinic. Afterwards we would announce closing for a week. We had set up the ladies in advance and Bill had pretty much stopped talking. This was totally against his nature and seemed to upset them. It was harder for me to be different. I didn't talk much anyway, and they were used to it, so I had tried not to smile or laugh at Lori. Impossible.

Lori monitored my personal life very closely and kept the other ladies informed. She knew I had spent the weekend on Norman's Cay with Lisa Winter and she also knew I had spent a weekend on Bimini with Pat Rivera. She was younger than the others, brash and very funny. She asked me personal questions constantly and she also kept suggesting that we should have dinner with Gus and Paulette again. I assumed she wanted me to take her out to dinner there or anywhere. I worked very hard at showing no humor at all when I responded to her impertinent questions and ribald suggestions, and thought I made an impression that everything was not quite right. All day Wednesday she kept completely silent and I thought I had finally gotten to Lori.

Thursday morning she had arrived at the clinic wearing a tee-shirt with N.A.N. in block across the front. I knew I had to ask what they meant, so she told me it was National Association of Nymphomaniacs. I managed not to laugh but Lori kept on and told me that they had meetings and discussed things like what kind of man made the best lover. I couldn't resist it and asked the next question. I knew it was part of the game. She told me that American Indians were the best lovers and Jewish men second. I didn't know what I was supposed to ask next so I didn't say anything. A little later Lori told me she had a new boyfriend and I bit and asked his name. She said it was Tonto Goldberg. I managed to keep from laughing and asked if she was planning to do any work that day and she was impressed that something really was wrong.

After I finished chewing and swallowing the *Crab Armand* I told Bill that there was a possibility of someone being hurt but that I didn't expect it. I had told him every detail of the plan except the fact that it was Snake's sister who we were going after. Bill had offered repeatedly to help in some way but I kept telling him that he couldn't be involved. I told him I thought the biggest danger was really at the clinic and not at the island. We spent a few minutes talking about his kids and then went back to work.

By the time we got back we were ready for the phony stuff and started as soon as we walked in the door. Our topic for the fake argument was about adding a third partner to our clinic. We had flipped a coin and I had to take the position that we didn't need a third doctor and that he would get in the way. Bill would argue that we had plenty of work for three people and that we also had plenty of room.

We talked loudly even though we had two patients who had shown up early. When we finished with them we called all the ladies together and Bill made a speech. He did a great job and actually made it seem spontaneous. He told them we would cancel all appointments for the following week and that they would get an extra week of paid vacation. He apologized for both of us for being short-tempered the last few days and told them that things would get back to normal. He attempted a little humor by saying that I was still exhausted from chasing Sylvia Brzinski all over the Bahamas. Since Lori kept everyone posted on my personal life this got a laugh. He said the clinic would be closed for a week and that our excuse to the patients was that both doctors had to go out of town unexpectedly. I don't know if any of the ladies actually believed what he said, but the idea of an extra week of paid vacation was appealing to them.

When we finished, Bill talked to Lori and asked her to organize the cancellation calls so that the other ladies could help make them. He also told her we would have to have appointments on at least one Saturday some time in the future to catch up. He said that we would be back on a regular schedule by Monday, July 17. Bill did not ask them if there were any questions.

We spent the rest of the afternoon and all day Friday trying to get ready for closing down. A few patients were able to come in on Friday and the whole problem of rescheduling went as well as expected. Both Bill and I had worked on it by stacking the deck with appointments that were easily postponed. We both worked through lunch on Friday and by six o'clock I felt I could be gone for a week without any major problems. We set up an answering service to handle calls.

Rocket showed up at my apartment around seven. Being able to leave the next morning and go straight to the airport made sense, but it meant that we would be under some sexual strain. Rocket was a little bit of a flirt and a tease and she could drive me crazy without any effort. We decided to go down to Monty Trainer's for dinner and took my car.

"Why don't you leave the keys in the ignition?" she said. "Maybe somebody will steal it."

"Nobody would ever steal it. The police could identify it before they had a chance to paint it." Sometimes I get tired of smart-ass comments about my green car.

We sat down at one of the thatched roof tables at the Monty's and ordered *nachos* along with raw clams and steamed shrimp. We talked about Rocket's career for a while and I learned that there was a chance she would move to New York. I realized that I had missed her. I had been with two very beautiful women on two different weekends but I still missed Rocket and now sitting there with her I was very conscious of just how bonny she was. Her expressions were so animated that even a simple question about the *nachos* could light up her whole face. Her huge gold brown eyes could express excitement over the anticipation of shrimp with Mexican sauce. She had her hair cut short but it always looked good, kind of soft brown and a little wavy.

She asked questions about cosmetic surgery while we were eating and I told her that I hoped one day to develop a team of people that could do craniofacial surgery. She had never heard the term so I explained the history, going back to Tessier and describing my plan with Joan Pegram. She kept asking questions until we got back to my apartment.

Six months earlier when we thought we were in love, Rocket had stayed in my apartment many times and slept in my double bed with me but this night was different. I had put clean sheets on the beds in what I called my guest room and put her there. We said goodnight and I brushed my teeth and crawled into bed. I laid there for a while trying to visualize what I would see when I went ashore on Norman's. I knew I would be totally confused in the dark until I found some key landmarks and the airstrip would be the big one. If I could find that I would be able to locate the house. I was just about to fall asleep when Rocket came into my bedroom and sat on the edge of my bed.

"Do you think you could behave yourself if I got in bed with you for a few minutes? I'm really scared about tomorrow and I just want you to hold me a little."

I pulled back the sheet and made a place for her. She crawled in with me and I put my arm around her.

"Do you like my new underwear?" she asked.

"What the hell are you talking about? I can't see your underwear in the dark."

"I don't mean now. I mean when I was taking off my clothes. Weren't you peeking through the keyhole to watch me undress and try to see me naked? I know the sight of my body makes you crazy so I wiggled a little when I took off my panties. Weren't you peeking?"

"Come on, Rocket. You're not being fair. Can't you ever stop making smart-ass remarks and kidding around. Now's not a good time for bullshit. I thought you said you were scared."

"I *am* scared, Dev. I'm *really* scared. That's why I said what I did. I was trying to be funny just because I'm so scared. Hold me tight and tell me it's going to be O.K."

I put both arms around her. She was actually shaking and I realized she really was upset.

"I'm not worried about the boat part, Dev. I've been around all kinds of boats all my life and that part doesn't scare me. What does scare me is when you and Snake go ashore. I'm scared you won't come back. I'm not in love with you or anything but I do like you a lot and I don't want you to die. I have this horrible vision of the sun coming up and I'm still there waiting in the boat and the two of you never come back. It scares the hell out of me."

Rocket was such a feisty girl I had a hard time getting used to the idea that she was scared. She was, though.

"Baby, just relax. Snake has done this sort of thing before. He's planned it carefully. If there are more people in the house than he can handle he'll just back off and we'll try again some other time. He's not going to get us killed or captured or anything."

"Suppose he goes in the house and doesn't come back. What will you do? How long will you wait?"

"I'll wait exactly twenty minutes and then come back to the boat. Those are his instructions."

"When you were brushing your teeth I came in here for a minute and I saw the gun on top of your dresser. If you're going to bring that, I'm really scared."

"The gun is my idea, not Snake's. He thinks it's unnecessary and says there's no need for it."

"It's a really funny looking gun. I've seen old World War movies and that's what the Nazis use. Are you sure it won't blow up if you try to use it?"

"It's called a Luger. The Germans used them in World War One and Two. I've fired the gun lots of times. It's safe and won't blow up."

"I'm not going to let you kiss me goodnight because the last time I did that you went crazy and attacked me. I'm going to go to sleep now. Thanks for hugging me."

Rocket dozed off. When I was sure she was asleep I went into the guest room. I had to because it would have been impossible for me to get through the night without taking off Rocket's pajama pants.

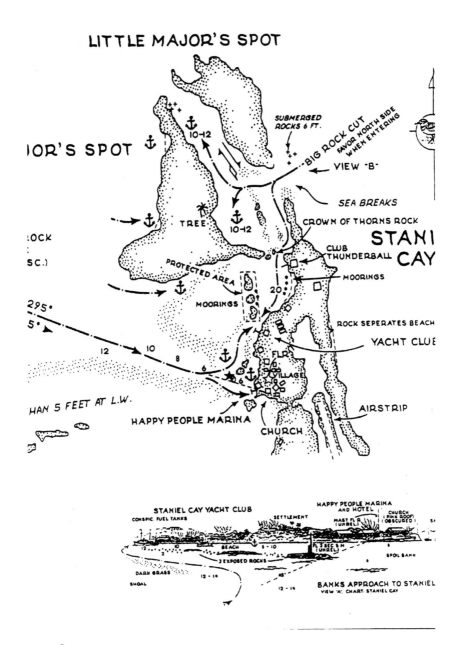

Copyright© 2001 by Tropical Island Publishers Inc., PO Box 8010 Red Bank, NJ 07701-8010 – All rights reserved. Reproduction in any form, including office copy machines, in whole or part, without written permission is prohibited by law.

Chapter Twenty

Saturday Morning, 8 July

Early the next morning Snake picked us up and we drove in silence to an airport where we would fly out and then bring Sharon back. Snake told us that the little airport on the edge of the Everglades was not actually legal for night take-offs or landings but that it was equipped with lights. Planes bringing in drugs always dropped them off somewhere before landing there. We had taken Snake's car, a nondescript-looking thing that would not call attention to itself anywhere. Using my car had never been an option.

As soon as we got in the car I noticed a difference in Snake and I became concerned. He was nervous. I had been around him in a few tense situations in offshore races and he had always been very cool. Today he was definitely shook up. He even lit up several cigarettes while he was driving and I had never seen him smoke before. I couldn't blame him, of course. Going into a strange house in the middle of the night to get your sister when she might be dead or crazy was scary, and of course the drug people might kill him, but I was sure Snake would function like a phantom and get it done. A guy we both knew once made a comment about Sean that I remembered. "Snake Moran is slicker than greased eel shit." I think he was right. Since I wasn't going into the house I didn't think I would be in any danger.

Snake had taken the Cigarette boat over to Nassau on Tuesday with a man named Pluto. Pluto had taken it on down to the commercial yacht club at Staniel Cay and set himself up in a cottage. He would take care of the boat until we got there and then watch the airplane while we went up to Norman's. After we came back with Sharon he would take the Cigarette back to Nassau or directly to Chub Cay, depending on the weather.

Snake told us that we would never see Pluto again and that we shouldn't ask any questions about him. We wouldn't know who he was or what he did, only that Pluto didn't work for Interpol or know of Snake's connection, although he was aware that Snake was involved in some way with rare art pieces. Pluto had no idea why we were going to Staniel and didn't know where we were going with the boat when we left.

The plane was a six-passenger Cessna with two engines and it had enough fuel capacity for us to fly to Staniel with no stops for refueling. Rocket said she wanted to sleep some more so she stretched out on the two middle seats and I sat in the co-pilot's seat. I was interested in the instruments since I had never flown in a private plane this large or complex. It seemed to have every type of navigational device that I had ever heard of and a few that were completely new to me.

We left the airport, climbed up to altitude and flew down along the Keys for a while. Snake explained that he had some sort of complicated plan for filing a different flight plan and then changing it. He didn't want any record that we had ever gone to the Bahamas in case somebody checked it out later. I didn't really understand *what* he was doing but I could understand why.

Snake was a little better when we got in the airplane but he was still very nervous and uptight. He was always talking when he was normal. What he said was always bullshit unless he was doing something important, but when he stopped talking I knew there was something wrong. When he started smoking cigarettes it was really bad. Although I knew that smoking in the plane was safe, it wasn't cool for a guy who didn't normally smoke at all. I thought the fact that his sister was involved had him worried. The idea that he might be scared never entered my mind but I knew he was worried about her.

After a short time we were over Sombrero Light and turned left toward the Bahamas. Our course would take us over the south end of Andros and then across the banks to the chain of Exuma Islands and to Staniel Cay. It was a fine day for flying, with unlimited visibility, and it wasn't long before I could see Andros. There were tiny whitecaps on the ocean but no real waves. From the height we were flying it was easy to make out the deep, dark blue of the Gulfstream. I usually enjoyed looking at the Bahamas from the air but this time my mind was on our mission.

Rocket slept the whole way and I had to wake her up as we started to circle for a landing on Staniel Cay. The airstrip is not hard to recognize from the air because it is built in a shallow lagoon and actually has some water on both sides. There was no other traffic so Snake brought the plane right in with no delay. We taxied over to the fuel pumps and filled the tanks. Snake wanted to make sure that they were full so we could leave later in the dark without wasting time. An old black man helped us and accepted cash payment. We told him we were going to be leaving early the next morning and that we'd be staying in one of the cottages near the Staniel Cay Yacht Club. He offered to give us a ride down there after we paid so we threw our gear in his car and listened to him describe the life of Staniel Cay while he drove.

When we got to the yacht club dock, Snake found Pluto inside the small clubhouse shooting pool with one of the local guys. We sat down at the bar and inquired about the chances of getting lunch. Staniel Cay has a very small village and two docks and marinas. The Staniel Cay Yacht Club is a commercial dock, bar and restaurant with all the marine services. It is owned by a guy named Bob Chamberlain and his partner, Joe Hocher. The clubhouse itself is fairly large by Out Island standards and has a cool interior with a lanai dining area. The food is Bahamian-American and is served only on certain nights and by reservation only. The pool table inside is very popular and the walls are covered with yacht club burgees from all over, as well as many other nick-nacks and pictures.

Up the street and also out of the tidal current is Ken Rolle's Happy People Marina and Hotel. A few steps away is the Royal Entertainers Lounge, a really fun place to party. Not this trip, though. I enjoyed one cold Pauli Girl, but only one. It was going to be a long afternoon and night.

The Yacht Club agreed to fix lunch for us in about an hour so Pluto took us to the cottage he had rented. It was plain but it would be a place to wait until we left. I was hoping we could take Sharon directly from the Cigarette to the airplane and get her right back to the clinic before she started suffering any serious withdrawal symptoms. My big problem would be convulsions. If she could talk and knew what drugs she had been using it would be a lot easier.

The lunch they prepared for us was excellent. A boat was bringing in fresh lobsters and fish at the same time we ordered, so we had a lot of choices. Snake had grouper, I had snapper and Pluto and Rocket both had a lobster salad. Another time it would have been more fun. Snake was practically silent during the whole meal. This was not surprising since the danger was obvious, and not knowing what condition Sharon would be in had to be terrible for him. I suspected that situations involving danger were not new. He had made it clear to me that he didn't want questions about his job with Interpol, so I'd never asked about any of his work.

After Ricardo talked about him, and what he and his father did in the art world, I wasn't completely convinced that he actually was employed by the International Police. Perhaps everything he did was in the underworld of art.

There wasn't a lot of conversation at the table. Pluto was an average-sized man with no special characteristics except that he had hair which seemed to stand up straight. His job had been to get the boat from Nassau, where Snake had turned it over to him, and deliver it to Staniel. He would watch the airplane until we got back in the middle of the night and then deliver the boat back to Miami. I had the impression that Snake had used him for various things in the Bahamas before. He looked to be about half black and half white.

After lunch we went back to the cottage and rested until a little after four o'clock when the four of us went down to the dock and went aboard the Cigarette. A part of the rear seating compartment was taken up with big pieces of plywood wrapped in canvas. I didn't ask what they were because Pluto was there. We also took along a lot of fishing gear with us, which we would use as a little bit of a disguise.

There was always current running at Staniel, coming from the banks through to Exuma Sound and back again. Pluto knew the boat very well and he and Snake did the work while Rocket and I just watched. We started out west toward the shallow banks at only about five knots then turned north. After we turned we put out two big fishing rods but we didn't bait them or put the lines in the water. We went a mile or two north and then turned back slowly south. We kept the fishing rods out and slowly worked our way around the south end of the island, stopping occasionally just to look around.

All the way around from the marina we talked about the problem of being able to find our way back in the dark and decided we would have to wait until there was some daylight. This could mean waiting a few miles off-shore when we returned, but we would have to take that chance. We were careful not to mention that we would have an extra passenger coming back.

Both Rocket and I spent some time at the wheel, getting used to the overpowered Cigarette. The gear shifts were smooth and easy but I had never driven anything with such immense power and had trouble with the throttles. Rocket seemed completely at ease and handled the boat at slow speeds with no trouble.

Gradually we worked our way through the shallow banks and small cays until we found a way to the airstrip. We took the boat into the lagoon on the eastern side of the strip and looked for a place to bring it in against the bank. There wasn't any dock in the lagoon that we could use but there was a place where we could bring the boat right against the shore.

We walked from the boat up to the airplane as if we were rehearsing. Snake told Pluto that he should stay away from the airstrip until midnight. After that he was to come back over and wait for us on the bank. Snake still never mentioned to Pluto that there might be a fourth person with us when we came back. I guess he thought we were going to steal something or perhaps buy some drugs. Pluto knew we might not come in until daylight but Snake wanted him there to take the boat out again as soon as we got there or at least when the sun came up. Pluto was being paid to help. Snake made it clear that he wanted him to leave with the boat as soon as possible when we returned.

After he had finished checking the plane, Snake gave some final instructions to Pluto and we got back in the Cigarette. On the way out we went slowly, trying to familiarize ourselves as much as possible with what we would see coming back. The church with the red roof, the settlement itself and the fuel tanks would all be helpful once there was daylight, but nothing would really help in the dark. We would have to wait.

We headed away from Staniel Cay going east out into Exuma Sound, which is really the ocean, until we got a few miles out then we turned north. Snake pushed both throttles and the big powerful engines quickly moved the boat up onto a plane. Rocket was the navigator and Snake was the driver and on the return trip I would be taking care of Sharon. By doing the navigation up, as well as coming back, Rocket would have a feel for what we were doing and where we were going. There wasn't too much of a chop but it seemed like it because we were going so fast. It didn't take much imagination to get an idea what it would be like in rough weather. We headed north past Shroud Cay, Norman's Cay, Highborne Cay and Ship Channel Cay to a point where Rocket figured that Beacon Cay Light would bear 298° and about five miles. We turned left on that course and slowed down. Snake eased off the big engines and put the gears in idle. We slowed down and came to a complete stop. He then got me to help him with the plywood pieces that were taking up most of the rear seats. He told me we were going to put a "mustache" on the boat.

When you're looking at one of the Cigarette boats sitting still in the water and not moving at all it looks like it's going about a hundred miles an hour. It's long, very long and low and sleek. It has a distinctive look to it and Snake wanted to change the look by putting some plywood pieces up around the cockpit that made it look like a cabin cruiser. A boat with a big oversized cabin does not look fast at all. The plywood panels had been cut and painted so that we could bolt them in place very quickly. If somebody came aboard, like the Bahamian police or the United States Coast Guard, or even total strangers, Snake planned to tell them that the boards were a disguise so that we wouldn't look like drug smugglers. We had all the panels in place in less than ten minutes and started west again, toward Beacon Cay Light.

After awhile we could make out Ship Channel Cay to the south and then some fairly conspicuous houses on the high points of land. Bluff Cay appeared when it was supposed to and then we picked up Beacon Cay. This would be an important light for us coming back since it was one of the relatively few real lights that operated in the Bahamas. Coming back north again we would be able to pick up the light in the dark and then cut through to Exuma Sound on a course of 118° where the water was deep and we could go back south to Staniel at high speed. Finding this light would be critical later that night.

From Beacon Cay we started south, avoiding the little Bush Cays that were really more like rocks, and holding a course of 195° to avoid the long shallow sandbank that extended out several miles from the south end of Allan's Cay. Navigation was actually easy because there was plenty of daylight left and the boat was so fast that the tidal currents that sweep on and off the banks could almost be ignored. In a sailboat moving at four or five knots those currents were a big factor.

We changed course to 185° when we were cleared of the sand banks and continued down past the west side of Highborne. Our plan was simple but we knew it wasn't very good. We just couldn't come up with a better one. We kept on until Wax Cut was bearing 100° and then turned and approached Norman's Cay on that course at a relatively slow ten knots. When we got in close to the end of the island where the airstrip was, we circled around some shallow heads and started up the same side of the island where I had sailed with Lisa in the Hobie, except that I had cut inside the heads back then. We slowed down to almost nothing so I could try to identify the various things I had seen two weeks earlier. Even at slow speed it seemed like we got to the place opposite the water tower quickly. We went a little further then slowed down and turned. We went to a point about fifty feet off the beach and just sat there for a few minutes while we adjusted the fishing rods, then actually put bait on the lines. I felt silly as hell going through this charade but Snake insisted that every detail was important. If someone was watching us with a pair of binoculars at least we wouldn't look too strange. The plywood disguise was done well enough that even binoculars would not reveal anything unusual.

After we did the little show with the rods for about half an hour, we headed back west away from the island for two miles and anchored. We were far enough north to be clear of the shallow water over Norman's Spit so the depth was eight to ten feet. We had some sandwiches and coffee and waited for the dark. I couldn't think of anything else to do so I told Snake about the story that Ricardo had told us on the beach at Bimini about the stolen Rembrandt and the silver statue. I asked him if he was still looking for it. He seemed a little irritated that Ricardo had told us the story but I couldn't tell if it was just nerves and tension. He said the story was true and he was still looking. When Sharon was safe, and Emile Hogge was dead, he was going back to Europe and put all his efforts into finding the statue.

It was a beautiful evening with an incredible sunset out over the banks accentuated by some dramatic looking clouds. The various shades of orange were almost startling against what was left of the blue sky. *Jaune de cadmium fonce verit et bleu de cobalt verit.* I thought about colors with their French names.

I stared at the clouds for a while and gradually realized that our beautiful evening was changing and a squall was coming fast. The first drops of rain started down just as the darkness closed in. Snake and Rocket immediately put on foul-weather suits. I stripped to my bathing suit first and then put on the rain gear.

The phony plywood cabin provided some shelter so we sat under it and reviewed again the various possibilities. If I got ashore and found something that would make us cancel the rescue I was to go to the harbor and get out to where Gus and Paulette would be anchored. I was supposed to call in code on channel sixteen and Snake and Rocket would bring the Cigarette boat into the harbor and pick me up off Gus's boat. If I found the house and everything looked all right I was to start signaling with a light at nine thirty, nine forty-five or ten. They would know that I was fifty yards south of the house. My first signal was to be made as soon as I got there and then I'd flash additional signals according to a schedule.

At exactly eight we started to monitor channel sixteen. We heard a few conversations between boats in the Exumas and then silence. Around Miami or Fort Lauderdale the calls were almost constant but out here it was quiet. We listened for a while and then heard Gus calling.

He said it was the yacht *Serenity* calling and gave out some fake numbers. Gus had used the fake name *Serenity* because A.A. used a prayer called the

Serenity Prayer. He pretended to be trying to reach a boat named the *Jolly Green Giant*. The name he used, with green in it, meant go ahead with the rescue. It meant that Sidney had not contacted him with any potential problems and that neither he nor Paulette had noticed anything that would make us want to cancel. Even though the call really just meant that they were anchored in the harbor ready to fire off the dynamite, it was reassuring. If there was something serious enough to just leave in a hurry, Gus would have tried to call the yacht *Exit*. If something had happened that called for us to cancel the rescue and he wanted us to come around to his boat he would call for the yacht *Rendezvous*. All of these were fake names. Gus would repeat the call every fifteen minutes until he left his boat to go into the dock and set off the explosives.

I was taking two powerful waterproof flashlights with extra batteries so I would be able to signal back to them when I found the house. I asked Snake what I should do if I couldn't find it. He said that not finding it was not an option and asked me if I remembered the Billy Goat. I think he was kidding just to make the point but then again I wasn't completely sure. I did remember the Billy Goat with his feet burned off and his testicles thrown in the garbage can.

After waiting twenty minutes we turned on the engine and went almost due east on the opposite course of what we had steered coming out and for exactly the same time. Rocket had kept track of the current when we were coming away from the beach as well as when we were anchored and we knew it was flowing south. She took a course of 100° to offset the current and we steered in the dark toward the beach. After exactly thirty minutes we dropped the hook again and waited a little longer. The squall had passed through with very little rain and the sea was still pretty calm. The plan was timed carefully and I was wearing two waterproof watches. They always make a big thing in the movies about checking watches but nobody ever has more than one. In timing starts for a sailboat race everybody has a backup watch. Arthur Knapp probably had a spare for the backup and a backup for the spare.

I went over the side at exactly eight fifty. Two hours and forty-five minutes until Gus would blow up the dynamite. Rocket kissed me goodbye without saying anything. Snake just wished me good luck. The water was warm and not at all uncomfortable. I felt for the bottom with my feet even though I knew it was about eight feet deep. My waterproof bag had the two waterproof search lights, my Luger pistol, a small whistle and a tiny medical kit with nothing in it except a syringe and a drug called Dilantin in case I had to give Sharon a shot to prevent convulsions. I left my regular bag of medical things aboard the Cigarette. I also had two sandwiches in the bag. There was no reason to bring them but I had never been anywhere on a boat or near the water when I didn't wish I had a sandwich. I also had a set of dry clothes, socks and sneakers.

We were still getting small squalls and the visibility was sometimes bad, but I had no trouble aiming for the beach. I had a small waterproof compass strapped to my wrist along with my two watches. I swam slowly kicking with the fins and looking at the scattered lights. Something big and slimy brushed against my leg but it didn't bite. Occasionally, between short periods of rain, I could see the outline of the trees against the sky. It was impossible for me to tell anything about the houses since they were all hidden by the trees and the darkness. When I reached a point where I could stand up, I realized how much the current had pushed me. I buried the flippers in the sand. I wouldn't need them again and didn't want to be bothered carrying them. I kept on swimming under water trying not to make any commotion that could be seen from the shore.

When I reached a point about ten feet from the water's edge, I stopped to listen and look around. I didn't recognize anything from where I was and standing up didn't help any. Ahead was thirty or forty feet of sand beach and then bushes and trees with no house in sight. I couldn't see any open spaces between the trees so I decided to go up to the edge of the underbrush and put on my clothes and shoes. I thought carefully for a minute about whether to walk or run because Snake had stressed that I shouldn't do anything that would look suspicious.

I stood up out of the water, walked onto the dry sand and up the beach to the edge of the trees. The sand ended abruptly and I found a place between palm trees where I was hidden from sight if anyone appeared on the beach. I stripped and opened the waterproof bag. Then I dried myself with some paper towels. I put on the underwear, slacks and a knit shirt. I had a wallet with me that had money and a false identification. The Luger pistol was wrapped in waterproof plastic and I left it that way. I put on the shoulder holster that Snake had given me and stuck the gun in it. Then I put on a waterproof windbreaker that would hide it and protect it from the rain.

I pulled on the heavy socks and running shoes and tried to figure out what to do. I had three choices. I could walk north on the beach, I could walk south, or I could try to get through the trees and bushes to the road that ran up that side of the island. I knew the current had carried the boat one way or the other coming in but I didn't know which. I also didn't know for sure that I had identified the correct place when we first came up the beach in the Cigarette. I felt fairly certain I had seen the place where I had sketched Lisa, and I even thought I had seen Emile Hogge's house among the trees, but I didn't recognize anything now.

I looked at my watches – nine fifteen – and decided to walk south on the beach. If I went that way I would eventually come to something I recognized. If I was too far to the south from where I had intended to be I would come to the airstrip. I didn't think I was that far down but I wasn't sure. If I walked north I wouldn't recognize anything because I had never been to that part of the beach. If I tried to cut through the bushes and the trees to the road, I could get lost or stuck where the underbrush was thick.

I had just started walking along the beach at the edge of the trees when another squall passed through. The rain pounded down furiously making a roar as it hit the water. The waterproof windbreaker kept the top of me fairly dry but my pants got soaked. I couldn't see much anyway but when the squalls came it was even worse. I walked south at a fairly rapid pace for five or ten minutes and stopped to rest. While I was standing there in the rain I heard a tremendous clap of thunder, and then another one and suddenly above the thunder and the rain I heard the roar of an airplane taking off. The noise was loud and I knew immediately that I was close to the airstrip. Very close. It was time to leave the beach.

I couldn't find a path or anything resembling one so I just pushed into the underbrush. I got scratched quickly and the bushes were hard as hell to get through in the rain and the dark, but I knew I didn't have far to go. Suddenly I came out onto the brush grass where the land was cleared beside the airstrip. I looked both ways and figured out that I was somewhere in the middle. The runway was a single concrete strip running almost north and south. I was afraid I might be seen crossing it even though it was not lighted so I stayed close to the trees and walked all the way to the north end. I thought I could see some men in the distance where the fuel tanks were so I tried to avoid making noise. I went to the end of the strip and crossed over to the east side where I easily found the road. I knew I could walk north on the road for one or two miles and find the house where we thought Sharon was being held.

I had brought a pint of whiskey with me. I took a mouthful, swished it around and swallowed it. I knew I might run into somebody walking up the road but I would look even more suspicious if I tried to sneak around. I decided that if somebody stopped me, friendly or otherwise, I would act a little drunk and offer them a drink. I knew it was a strange plan but I thought it would give me a minute or two to figure out what to do.

I was on familiar territory now. Lisa and I had driven up this road several times, including a few trips with Knudsen. After about ten minutes I heard a car in the distance and found a place to hide. I could hear people in the car and they sounded very drunk. It was Saturday night.

As soon as the car passed it started to rain again. The squalls were short but heavy, though visibility was not much of a problem and after about thirty minutes I found the road we used when I did the sketch of Lisa. I walked down it until I came to the beach. I looked at my watches. Nine forty-two and I had made it on time. I was supposed to give my first signal at nine thirty, nine forty-five or ten o'clock from this exact spot. The rain had mostly stopped again so I ate the first sandwich while I waited. It was one of my favorites, corned beef on rye with cole slaw and Russian dressing. And two pickles.

At exactly nine forty-five, according to both my watches, I started signaling with one of my lights. Both of them had been set up with special lenses so that

Snake and Rocket could see them but they would not give off a beam that could be seen from behind. In Morse code I blinked out the letters S-H-I-T.

I thought Snake was being silly but he said that if anybody out on the water saw it and knew Morse code they would think it was someone just fooling around. I waited five minutes and then sent out the same signal again. When Snake saw the lights he would know that I was about fifty yards south of where he could bring the boat in. We had talked about bringing it in down here but we knew there was a good possibility that we would be carrying Sharon when we got her out of the house. We would need to get her and ourselves into the boat as fast as possible. As soon as we were at the right place we would signal Rocket to move the boat in. When Snake went into the house the boat would have to right at the water's edge.

I found myself a spot under some trees that provided shelter from the rain and sat down to wait. Between rain squalls there was a fairly bright moon with clouds racing by and it seemed like a dramatic background for what we were doing. While I sat there I wondered about Sharon and her condition. I had warned Snake over and over that she might be so bad that we would have to get her into a hospital immediately to save her life. I knew Snake was getting information from some source that he wasn't revealing to me and he seemed to think her condition was not too bad. I couldn't think of anything else to do while I waited, so between squalls I ate my second sandwich – roast beef on white bread with barbecue dressing. I also drank some water from a small flask I had brought and buried the foil wrappers.

After my third signal at ten fifteen I started up the beach toward the place where I had sketched Lisa. I stayed away from the open sand and tried to move along the edge of the trees and bushes, staying in the shadows. When I got to the place I was searching for, it looked completely different in the dark and it made me uncomfortable. I had a few minutes before the next signal so I went cautiously up toward the house. I wanted to be sure I was at the edge of the grass in the back yard but I avoided the path that led from the yard through the trees and down to the beach. When I got close I could see some lights between the shutters on the windows. I couldn't hear any sound until I got fairly close when I thought I heard guitar music that sounded like a tape being played on low volume. As soon as I was certain I had the right house I went back to the beach. It was the same house that Lisa and I had confirmed as being on plot J-41, listed as being owned by Sepulveda but actually the property of the South African drug dealer. This was it.

At exactly ten thirty I started signals again but this time from the spot where Rocket would bring the boat in. Just as I started, a rain squall swept through and the visibility went down to practically nothing. I was supposed to use the "SHIT" signal only at the end of the road so when I signaled "F-U-N" they knew I was at the house fifty yards up the beach.

Snake and Rocket would get a compass bearing on the light and start in slowly with one engine running. After I finished the signal I walked back down to the road, staying in the edge of the shadows, next to the sand beach but not on it. Going back and forth from total darkness during the rain squalls to almost bright moonlight when they passed was spectacular, but it was not going to help us any.

When I got back to where the road came down to the beach I found my sheltered spot again under the trees and sat down to wait. I wished I had brought another sandwich but I concentrated on listening and looking for Snake. If he came in where he was supposed to, and took a right turn down to the edge where the beach came up to the trees, he couldn't miss the road or me. I listened as carefully as I could but the only sound when the rain slowed was the small wavelets breaking on the beach. During the squalls, the sound of the rain drowned out all other noises. Again I signalled "S-H-I-T" at ten forty-five in the middle of a squall and then the rain stopped completely. There was complete silence and suddenly I felt my arm being squeezed and Snake whispered "Dev" in my ear. It startled the hell out of me. He motioned for me to go so I led him back to the spot where I had done the sketch of Lisa. He found a spot right at the edge of the trees and we paused. He asked me if I was sure it was the right house and I told him it was J-41 for sure. I told him if he found a fat lady from Akron it was the wrong house but he didn't appreciate my humor.

I was aware as soon as he appeared that he was as calm as I had ever seen him. He didn't talk except when necessary but he didn't have a trace of the nervousness that was so obvious during the trip over in the plane. He was dressed in street clothes but they were black and he was almost invisible in the dark. A little bit after eleven he squeezed my arm again and we started toward the house. He was able to move without making a sound and I tried to do the same but couldn't. As we approached, the rain became constant for the first time that night and that helped hide the noise of my footsteps. It wasn't coming down as hard as during the squalls but it was steady.

On the back of the house was a patio that had been terraced with something similar to flagstones. A permanent-type barbecue grill had been built with huge grills and a big smoke stack. We crouched behind the grill and waited. About half of the rooms in the house seemed to have lights on and the other half were dark. A little after eleven Snake moved up close and looked through a window and then another. He came back but he didn't say anything about what he saw. He had told me before we left the boat that I was to wait outside the back door of the house when he went in. He said he expected to come out again with his sister and that he might be leading her by the hand or he might be carrying her. She might be unconscious. I knew all this but he repeated it.

I was to wait for a minute and then follow him up to the house. He had wanted me to wait on the beach but I had convinced him that he might need me to help carry her. He had been pissed off when I told him I was bringing the Luger. He told me not to shoot at anyone and that if killing had to be done he would do it himself.

At eleven fifteen we were both looking at our watches when we heard the explosions. Three of them – so close together they sounded almost like one. Even this far away they made a tremendous noise. It sounded like Gus had blown up the whole damn island. As soon as it happened all the lights went on in the house and we could hear people yelling. I couldn't make out the words except one man's voice saying it was down at the harbor and to get moving. We could hear people running out the front of the house and a lot of yelling and then several cars starting.

I don't know how Snake decided when to go inside but it was right after the cars pulled away and the sound of their engines moved off. He walked silently up to the back door of the house and let himself inside. I don't know what he would have done if the door had been locked but apparently it wasn't. I could hear voices in the house as soon as he entered but they were not clear and they all seemed to be women.

I took the Luger out of the shoulder holster and pulled the plastic wrapper off. I switched the safety off and waited with the gun in my hand. I listened carefully and heard all of the voices stop. Then there was silence.

Suddenly a lot of lights went on around the terrace. I was startled by the light but nothing else happened for a few seconds and then the back door snapped open and Snake came out leading someone by the hand. I felt a tremendous sense of relief. They were half running and went right by me toward the beach. I waited for a second and started to follow them when suddenly two women came yelling and running out the door right toward me. I could see their faces clearly in the light and they saw me at the same time. I recognized them.

I raised the Luger pistol and aimed at the first woman and fired. She was close and I hit her in the face. The bullet seemed to tear her face apart and exploded her head into a lot of pieces. The other woman had stopped abruptly when I fired the first shot and just stood there screaming. I shot her twice in the chest and she fell on top of the first one in a bloody heap. I stared at them for a few seconds and waited to see if anyone else came out. Nobody did. The house was silent now. I was almost numb with shock.

For a few seconds I waited in an eerie silence with my Luger aimed at the open doorway. Suddenly the huge body of a man came hurtling through the open doorway straight at me. I fired once but it didn't slow him down and a massive body threw me on my back and landed on top of me. I was as close to him as any woman I had ever been with and he stunk like rotten food and old garbage. I tried to struggle but he had me pinned and I couldn't move. Neither could he. The smelly body on top of me was dead. I squirmed and worked my way out from underneath him and stood up aiming again at the open doorway. For two or three very long minutes there wasn't a sound from inside the house.

I turned away and ran through the trees and down to the beach. Rocket had brought the boat in close but it was still in knee-deep water. Snake had waded out with Sharon and they were climbing into the boat. Rocket was standing up in the bow holding the anchor line. She was making sure the wind didn't blow it out of position. She had started the engines as soon as she heard the explosion. I helped Snake push Sharon up and over the high gunwale and Rocket helped lay her on the cockpit sole. Snake took the wheel as I climbed over the side. Rocket threw the anchor line over the side. I rolled and fell into the cockpit and we started away from the beach.

We went slowly. Anyone who might possibly be watching would think we were a small, slow cabin cruiser. We did not have any lights turned on and just as we started moving away from the shore another heavy rain squall came, concealing us completely.

I crawled into the rear seating compartment where Snake had put Sharon and tried to examine her. She was conscious but just barely, and obviously full of some kind of drugs. I felt her pulse and found it was fast. I put a stethoscope against her chest and her heart sounded all right. I asked her what she had been taking and she just stared at me. I kept asking, even shouting at her but she didn't answer. She probably didn't even know. Maybe they had given her something to knock her out for the night.

After we had gotten far enough from the shore to turn north, Snake had Rocket take the wheel and I helped him unfasten the wing nuts from the bolts that held the fake plywood cabin in place. He had waited until there was a very heavy rain squall so nobody could see us from shore in the rain and the dark. We just let the plywood pieces fall in the water. As soon as Snake went back to steering he opened the throttles on both engines and we took off at almost the maximum speed of the boat. It was very dangerous for a while since we couldn't see anything, but after about ten minutes the rain stopped again and we had some moonlight and good visibility.

I sat in the stern and tried to calm down. We had Sharon with us now but the realization of what I had done hit me quick. I had agreed only to supervise the detoxification of a young girl in my clinic. Then I had gotten in deeper. In the first plan I was going to wait in the boat and not even go ashore. Then I learned that I had go ashore to find the house. It was my idea to buy the gun and learn how to use it. What if I didn't have it? I knew I couldn't have killed the two women with my hands. I might have just run down to the boat after they recognized me. I couldn't do that. And there was no way I could have handled the man except to shoot him. Without the gun I would be his prisoner now.

I had murdered three people. I was now a killer. Laufenberg had warned me and I had done what he was afraid I would do. I didn't know enough about this sort of thing to estimate our chances of getting away cleanly. I couldn't guess at that, but I knew I would never be the same. My life might not change but I would never be the same person. I had killed three people. I tried to stop thinking about it.

From a point opposite the south end of Norman's to Beacon Cay Light is only 16 miles and we covered the distance in just a few minutes. At the light we slowed down to less than ten knots and even slower as we passed north of little Bluff Cay. Rocket had done an excellent job of navigating. We had been very lucky that the rain had stopped long enough to let us find Beacon Cay Light and then to go through the ship channel between Dog Rocks and Bluff Cay. After we were sure we were out in Exuma Sound and in deep water with no obstacles, Snake opened up the two powerful engines again and we took off.

Sharon was laid out on the seat in the rear compartment. I found the cloth cover that was used for that compartment and fixed it up so it protected her a little bit from the rain. The squalls kept coming. Ten or fifteen minutes of what seemed like solid water then stopping for an eerie period of bright moonlight. The bouncing around at that high speed was terrible but the heavy rain gradually reduced the size of the waves.

Sharon's pulse was fast but her heartbeat sounded good. Once I had Snake bring the boat to a complete stop while I gave her a shot of Dilantin. Dilantin Sodium is something used to prevent epileptic seizures and convulsions in addicts. I didn't want to break off a needle and we were pounding like crazy. For about an hour we went back and forth from complete darkness and blinding rain to a few minutes of beautiful bright moonlight with dramatic clouds racing across the sky. Then back to pounding rain again. From time to time Sharon opened her eyes but she didn't say anything and I didn't know if she realized what was happening or where she was.

When we reached a point where we thought we were due east of Staniel Cay, we took a sweeping right turn and headed for what we hoped was the tip of the airstrip. We continued at high speed for a few minutes and then slowed almost to a stop. We kept going, slowly waiting for a break in the rain. When it came it was only for a minute or two, but when we couldn't see anything ahead on the horizon we knew we had three or four miles with nothing to run into. Snake opened up and we got in what distance we could before the next squall and darkness. We did this several times. On the fourth try it was getting light and we could see Staniel Cay. We were fairly close and could actually make out the red roof of the church and what we thought was the Happy People Marina.

After that we inched our way in very slowly, moving by the fathometer more than anything else. Navigation in the Bahamas is almost impossible at night since there are few lights and no marked channels. The last two miles when we were approaching Staniel took longer than the whole leg going south. The last mile was very tedious as we worked our way into shallow water. Snake had only one engine running and this was in neutral most of the time. We could see the airstrip long before we reached it.

We pulled the Cigarette into the narrow, shallow strip of water beside the airstrip and found a place where we could pull it against the bank. Snake told us to wait while he found Pluto. The Cessna was sitting where we had left it about fifty yards from where we tied up the boat.

It was a little after four o'clock and still very dark. The rain had almost completely stopped but the moon had disappeared. Rocket moved back to the rear compartment and asked about Sharon. I told her she was alive and that I could tell more when we got her in the airplane and better light. The darkness, the rain and the boat pounding had made it impossible for more than a superficial examination.

Snake came back after a few minutes and told us that he couldn't find Pluto. He said he was going to go to the cabin that Pluto had rented and see if he was there. This was a big problem since we couldn't leave the boat where it was and go off in the plane. Snake wanted us to make sure the boat was secured and then wait in the airplane.

Snake and Rocket helped me, and we carried Sharon off the boat, up the bank and down the concrete strip to the airplane. When we got into the plane I put Sharon in the back seat where she could lay down almost full length. It was a fairly luxurious airplane and the middle and rear seats had armrests that were removable. Rocket held a light for me while I took off all of Sharon's clothes and examined her completely. I did not put them back on because I knew she might lose control of her bodily functions and cleaning up would be easier without them.

The first hours of drug withdrawal aren't the most dangerous. The addict still has the chemicals in his blood and is not yet feeling their absence. I did not know what she had or how much or even when. I was hoping she was still juiced up, hoping that she had enough to get her through the night. Some drugs are fast to act and fast to stop acting but I had expected her not to know what she had been using. I gave her another shot of Dilantin and tried to wake her up but I had no luck. It was probably just as well and she could be unconscious on the flight back to Miami.

When I finished, I covered her with a blanket and spread her out on the rear seat with a pillow elevating her head. I moved up to the middle seat where Rocket was taking off her own wet clothes. We had been wearing foul weather suits on the boat but the heavy rain had soaked us anyway. Although it was dark I was very much aware of Rocket taking off her jeans and then her underwear. When she had stripped and dried herself she wrapped up in a blanket and I realized that she was shivering.

I knew that she was just cold and not in shock so I gave her the bottle of whiskey. After a few minutes and a few swigs she seemed to be all right. I got myself dried off and put on some dry clothes that I had brought along in a duffel bag. I told Rocket I had extra clothes, even underpants, but no brassieres.

Snake had told us that he would be back in an hour. He said to wait exactly two hours and no more. If he didn't come back we were supposed to take the Cigarette down to Georgetown and do whatever was necessary to keep Sharon alive.

It was still dark and the cabin of the airplane was comfortable and warm. Rocket said she wanted to use my dry clothes but she didn't think she would know how to put on a pair of men's underpants and that I would have to do it for her. I started to explain that there was no difference except for the fly which she wouldn't need anyway. Then I realized that Rocket was teasing me.

Since we always had the erotic joke about her having to take off her own panties, I knew she was teasing me to put my shorts on her. In the situation we were in it was startling – but Rocket was like that sometimes. Hot and saucy and teasing even when she was scared.

I told her to quit fooling around and that some crazy drug dealers might suddenly come charging out of the dark and blow up the airplane. Even if that didn't happen, Snake would probably come back any minute. He had been gone only ten minutes but it made no sense to start fooling around in a small plane sitting on a runway waiting for a quick takeoff in the rain.

The rain had started again and the sky, which was beginning to lighten up, turned dark again. The sound of the rain on the metal roof of the plane was similar to the sound on the cabin top of a boat. The feeling of being inside, dry and warm, while it came down outside was very nice. It was a little like being anchored in a safe harbor but there was no motion. It was more like being in the back seat of a car with even a tiny smell of leather.

I had given Rocket the duffel bag while it was still light. I had watched her put on a tee shirt and thought as she did it that she didn't need a brassiere. She had put on a cotton shirt and pulled out a pair of cotton boxer shorts and handed them to me. She had just told me to put them on for her when the rain and darkness came.

I tried to but it was hard in the dark. She wasn't much help, moving around and making it impossible not to touch a lot of places. I knew it was what she wanted – to be touched in a special place where she was already wet. I got her left leg into the shorts and got them pulled up but when she raised her right leg to try to get her foot through the opening, my hand slipped down between her legs. As I felt the slippery softness and wetness I thought to myself that I better get it over with. I pulled the men's boxer shorts completely away and told her that she had won and that I was taking her pants off.

It should have been short and quick but it wasn't. After I put my hand between her legs I started kissing her and playing with everything. Although I was very conscious of the time and kept looking at my watch, the pleasure of feeling all those female things was so nice I didn't want to stop. We didn't stop when Rocket exploded with an orgasm. When she was excited, that only slowed her down for a few seconds at a time. We *did* stop our lovemaking suddenly, though, because I could hear Snake banging around the airplane doing a pre-flight check. Rocket somehow managed to put on a pair of my cotton slacks without the boxer shorts. The shorts were pretty messy by then anyway and she stuffed them in the duffel bag.

I moved up to the co-pilot's seat and Snake climbed into the plane. He started the engines one at a time and waited for them to warm up. While we were waiting I kept silent, knowing that he would tell me about Pluto when he was ready. After timing the warm-up with his watch he told me we were ready. Just before we started to taxi he pulled out a white scarf and wrapped it around his neck. He turned, looked at me with a straight face and asked me if he looked like the Red Baron. He taxied to the north end of the strip, ran up the engines and took off onto a southeast wind that was just beginning to fill in. We climbed up through some nasty-looking clouds into brilliant sunshine and headed back to Florida. As the engine settled down to a steady drone and things got quiet in the cabin I began to calm down. A feeling of reality settled in. We had rescued Sharon Moran and I had killed three people. I knew I would never be the same.

Chapter Twenty One

Sunday Morning, July 9
Sharon Moran woke up several times during the flight back to Florida. I tried to get her to talk but she seemed only to be able to stare. At one point I sat in the front seat with my hands lightly touching the wheel while Snake put the plane on auto-pilot and came back to the rear seat to talk to her. She never said anything but she did seem to recognize him and started crying.

Any old-timer from A.A. or N.A. can testify that the first few hours of detoxification can be a very smelly proposition. I had kept Sharon naked under the blanket knowing we would have to deal with this. I brought several blankets since I figured it was easier to throw a soiled blanket out of an airplane than to try to keep it and stink up the whole cabin. Fortunately, she lost control of her bowels only once on the entire flight. This happened right after we had climbed up to cruising altitude and turned west. It was a stinking mess. Her eyes were open and I think she knew what she was doing but she couldn't stop it. I used some diapers that I had brought along for this purpose and wiped the excrement off of her with the cloths and put them in a bucket. Then I tried to clean her up as best I could with some of those pads that contain chemicals instead of water. The chemical evaporates quickly and they work well but I needed several boxes of them to clean her up. I took the shit-covered blanket and towels and put them in a large plastic garbage bag then we threw it out the window. Snake had to slow the plane down almost to a stall but we got it out and the cabin started to smell a little better. I put a diaper on Sharon and after that she didn't foul herself again, although she did pee in the diaper several times. That wasn't nearly so bad, but she was shaking and sweating and that concerned me.

Despite our efforts, the cabin of the plane smelled a little for most of the trip. Other than that the flight was not too bad. Snake tried to explain to me what kind of course he was flying but I didn't understand much about aviation regulations so I didn't really get it. We flew west across the Gulfstream until we got to the Florida Keys and then turned south almost to Key West before turning northwest. After a few minutes, this course took us out over Florida Bay then we headed northeast and continued on that course for a while.

Breakfast is my favorite meal but if I can't have the real thing I like to skip all the way to lunch. I had brought along a huge plastic cooler. I had filled the cooler with dry ice and packed some delicatessen sandwiches in insulated bags. I offered them around. I ate a club sandwich with some pickles, and rare roast beef with horseradish sauce. While I was looking at the ocean from five thousand feet up, I found it almost impossible to think of anything except the people I had killed.

I thought for a few minutes about Violeta and Conchita. Violeta had been so specific when she offered me all of her body that I knew she meant it. I wasn't flattered by the offer but I knew she wasn't just teasing. Later on when the two of them started feeling me up and playing with me under the table, I knew *that* stuff wasn't just kidding, either. I could have taken either one of them into a bedroom right from the table and if I had suggested it they both would have come with me at the same time. Two very coarse and dirty women.

I had been able to see their faces clearly when they came running out of Emile Hogge's house last night, but I had the names mixed up. I didn't know whether I had blown off Conchita's head and shot Violeta in the chest or the other way around. I searched my brain – and my soul, for that matter – to find out how I felt about murdering the two women. I wanted to understand the emotion of having killed them and realized there just wasn't much. Maybe some fear of getting caught. That would come later.

I tried to tell myself that the women and the man were evil and that they had helped hold and degrade Sharon. I tried to get a real feeling of revenge. I tried to feel guilt and I tried to feel hatred, but the only real feeling I had about shooting the two women was amazement at the fact that I had been so accurate with the Luger pistol. In a split second I had recognized them and shot Conchita's head off. Maybe it was Violeta. I tried to remember and decided that it was Violeta who had propositioned me before dinner. She was the one who was coming to Miami to go to Sea World.

I had shot the other one twice in the chest and I thought it was really amazing that I had become so accurate after holding a gun in my hand for the first time a few weeks ago. When I watched movie gunfighters draw and shoot each other, I figured their speed was exaggerated. For a while I thought about what I might have been like if I had been a gunfighter and I decided that I would have been very fast because I had good hands from the surgery and didn't get too nervous.

I probably slept for close to an hour and Rocket woke me up to tell me that we were getting ready to land. The first thing I did was check Sharon. She had peed all over herself again and she was starting to shiver. I cleaned her up and gave her one more shot of Dilantin. I checked her heart with the stethoscope. It sounded all right but I didn't like the shivering.

I looked out the window and thought we were over the Everglades since all I could see was saw-grass and water. After a while we circled around and started coming down in what seemed to be nothing but trees and swamp. At the last minute an airstrip appeared and we came down for a landing.

It was the airstrip we had left on Saturday morning and Snake's car was still parked in the same place. There were three airplanes parked under the big trees but there was nobody around. Because we had left in the dark, I hadn't noticed much about the place, but now I could see planes that were invisible from the air. The airstrip was narrow and the cleared area right beside the concrete was narrow, too. Trees were very tall there and hung over so far they almost came out to the strip itself. The only use I could think of for such a place would be for smuggling in drugs or people.

We took Sharon out of the airplane and half-carried her to the car. Snake and Rocket got in the front seat and I sat in back with the girl. We drove down a dirt road that turned into a dirt road and then another dirt road. The fourth road that we got on was a real one with a black top and finally we got on the Tamiami Trail going east to Miami and Coral Gables.

We stopped at a gas station so Rocket could use the bathroom and just as we started off again Sharon started to have convulsions. Rocket crawled over the seat and helped me hold her down. I was expecting it and got a padded tongue depressor in her mouth so she couldn't swallow her tongue. The padding was for her teeth. When I felt that Rocket could hold her still I gave her another shot. Finally she stopped thrashing and slumped into unconsciousness.

An hour later we pulled into the parking lot of the clinic. I had Snake pull the car right up close to the back door. I opened the door and we got Sharon inside quickly with a minimum of commotion. Since our clinic is in a residential area I have neighbors that are nosy – like neighbors anywhere. I didn't want them to notice our bringing her inside.

The back door of the clinic opens into the reception area because patients come in from the parking lot. As soon as Snake and I got her through the door I *sensed* that there was someone else in the building. The clinic was so familiar to me that I could just tell. We had been talking little and saying nothing since we got inside. I put my finger to my lips and had Snake hold Sharon while I started down the hall toward my office. Because we have carpets on all the floors except the operating rooms, I could walk without making a sound.

I moved slowly. When I came to Bill's office the door was open and there was nothing inside. My office and the examining rooms were also empty. I couldn't check the operating rooms that were at the other end of the building. I was near the end of hall on the left side of the building where there's a large room that we use as a combination meeting room and social room. The long-range plan is for this to become two rooms to accommodate a third doctor. Until then, it's a luxury recreation room with T.V. I could hear that there was someone there and I walked up to the door to see inside.

There were two men seated in the room. Bill Gaines and Otto Laufenberg were watching a baseball game on the T.V. with the sound down low.

"What's the score?" I asked.

"Boston three and New York two. Bottom of the sixth," Bill said. "What took you so long?"

I shook hands with Otto. "What are *you* doing here in Miami?"

Otto has an unusual sense of humor and didn't usually make wisecracks, but I guess he thought it was dramatic to be there and surprise me, so he tried to be funny.

"I'm a Red Sox fan and I came down to watch the game. It wasn't on T.V. in Boston."

I went back immediately to where the others were and told them it was all right. We took Sharon down to my office. When I originally bought furniture for the office I got a convertible couch that folded into a bed. Although we had examining tables, we didn't have any beds in the clinic. My convertible and one just like it in Bill's office were the only ones in the clinic. We made up the one in my office and put Sharon in it.

After introducing Snake and Rocket to Otto Laufenberg, we asked them to wait in the conference room while the three doctors examined Sharon. I felt relieved to have Otto with me since he was an M.D. and an expert in addiction. We drew blood and I prepared it for the lab. The chances of her having a sexually transmitted disease were overwhelming. It had to be a question of which ones she had gotten and whether or not they were curable. I prayed that she had nothing serious.

Sharon had lapsed into a semi-conscious state and was almost limp. I now had bathroom facilities and could completely wash her. She was pretty stinky before I cleaned her up but not too bad afterwards. I had always had nurses to do this sort of thing and felt awkward doing it. I didn't feel that it was degrading for me, even when I was cleaning excrement from her body and wiping her genitals, but it would have been for her and it was better that she was unconscious and not aware of being treated like an infant.

After she was cleaned up, we examined Sharon completely. None of us had been trained in proctology, but we agreed without doubt that Sharon would have to have major rectal surgery. Repeated acts of sodomy had torn her up pretty badly. The physical damage was severe but it could be repaired. The mental damage might be irreversible. It now seemed appropriate that Sean had cut off the Billy Goat's testicles and penis while he burned him up. When we finished, Otto tried to wake her but she didn't respond.

"I'm concerned," he said, "about not knowing what drugs she has been given. I know you are, too. You've been with her for more than twelve hours and she hasn't died. It would be during this period that a person would most likely die from overdose. I'm pleased with that but I am not happy with the fact that she hasn't been awake. We could try to wake her and to ask what she was using, but she probably doesn't know."

We decided to take shifts and have one doctor sitting with her constantly. We could do it for two hours at a time. There was nothing else now. After reviewing the equipment on hand, there was nothing that a hospital would have that was not available in our clinic. Bill Gaines took the first shift. I had not asked Bill why he was at the clinic. He was a friend and he knew what I was doing. I could have reminded him that we would be in trouble if Sharon died, but it would have made no difference.

As we planned, I had Rocket drive me to my apartment and switch cars. If neighbors or a police car saw my puke-green car sitting outside the clinic they would recognize it and not really think too much about why it was there on a Sunday. A strange car might have aroused curiosity. Leaving Snake's car in my space at my apartment was no problem.

When we got back to the clinic we ordered several pizzas and started to get into a routine that would last for several days. In my letters I had told Otto about Sharon's seduction into the drug situation. Now he wanted to quiz Snake about every detail of what happened, hoping to pick up some answers as to exactly what drugs she had been using. He needed to know more than just about the drugs, though, and asked Snake for every detail of what had happened to her.

The four of us were sitting in the conference room with the empty pizza boxes and crusts on the table. Otto asked Snake if he would mind talking about his sister before she used the drugs. He wanted to know things about when she was a young girl. He told us that Sharon was going to need intense psychotherapy to be able to adjust to what had happened to her. He said that if her brain had not been damaged by the drugs, then the things that had happened to her would be stored away in her memory. As she regained physical health, these memories would appear and would have to be dealt with. He said he had a long-range plan for taking care of Sharon which he would discuss later, but since there was time now while Sharon went through detoxification, we should use the time well.

The next few hours were very strange. Otto had never explained why he was there in my clinic. I had written him in detail what my plans were so he knew I would be bringing Sharon there. From his actions he made it clear that he was taking responsibility for her psychological rehabilitation if she lived. Rocket stayed in the room and heard the whole discussion. Any of the three of us might have asked her to leave. What Sean told Dr. Laufenberg was intensely personal and painful for him, but somehow it seemed that Rocket had a right to know everything. Actually it seemed she had a responsibility to learn. She had risked her life to get Sharon off the island and now she was like a sister or cousin or something in a weird relationship that the fucking Chinese would think up. In some way, Sylvia Brzinski and Winfield Scott Devlin were both now linked to Sharon Moran in a way that I recognized but did not understand.

Later when I asked Otto about this and tried to explain it in my own terms, he nodded his head to signify that he understood. When I asked him to put it in *his* terms he said that it wouldn't be accurate to put it in his terms. He said that he was a psychiatrist and not a mystic.

That Sunday afternoon in the conference room at the clinic, Dr. Otto Laufenberg got Sean to tell us about Sharon. Rocket and I were drinking cold Heinekens and eating pizza when he started the story. Rocket had taken a shower and changed to a very pretty white dress.

For some reason it's a memory of Rocket that will always be with me. I think it was because of both the situation and the contrast. The remembrance of a strange, almost incredible story that went from the Hebrides of Scotland, through parts of Europe, to Coral Gables over to Norman's Cay and back was almost mystical. The fresh vivid memory of the high-powered Cigarette smashing through waves at fifty miles an hour in the dark and the rain and the moonlight, was in stark contrast to the relative luxury of the thick carpets and oil paintings of the room we were in.

It did not seem inappropriate in that setting for Bill Gaines to come in from the lab and sadly inform us that Sharon had syphilis. For a few moments, just before Snake started telling his story, I was watching Rocket. She had just taken a big bite of pizza, which had burned her, and cooled it off with cold beer. She wiped off her mouth with the back of her hand and then, as if she wanted to be lady-like, she used a napkin. Her big gold-brown eyes had little lines of fatigue around them but her soft brown curls looked like she was ready for a party to start. It was the kind of hair that always looked nice even when it was plastered down with salt water during a race. When she realized I was staring at her she grinned and took another bite of pizza. What a gorgeous, gutsy woman she was.

"Are you O.K.?" I asked.

"My behind is sore from all the bouncing around in that macho boat," she whispered. "Getting attacked and ravished in the airplane didn't help it any either. Everything else is O.K."

I opened another cold Heineken while Otto was asking Snake if he minded being taped. Snake said no and started telling about his sister. In the beginning, Laufenberg did not interrupt to ask questions.

Snake's mother was not a French whore as he had told me once or twice. She was also not a Gypsy and she was not a circus trapeze artist from Brazil. That Sunday afternoon, at least, she was a delicate, very beautiful girl from the Hebrides Islands on the west coast of Scotland. Shannon Moran, Sean and Sharon's father, was a romantic man who had one day sailed into the harbor of a fishing village named Portree on the Isle of Skye. Snake explained to us that Portree is the chief town on the island and about twenty miles north of Kyle on the mainland. There is not much else on the island, which is only about fifty miles long and thirty miles wide, although it does attract a fair amount of tourists.

Shannon was big and powerful and beautiful with black hair and pale eyes that looked at Annie Laurie Campbell as if to say "you belong to me." The courtship was short and she sailed away with him on his ketch which was named the *Artifact*.

Shannon was an Irish Catholic and Annie Laurie was a Scotch Presbyterian. His world was art, and art-dealing, and gun-running and traveling all over the world in search of adventure. Shannon claimed that money was his goal, but when he got it he always gave it to Annie Laurie to put in the bank and then forgot about it. At first she traveled all over the world with him – to the South Seas for a while in the boat and all over France and Spain looking for rare pieces of art. When she became pregnant with Sean she went back to the Isle of Skye in the Hebrides and never left again for very long. She never tried to hold on tight to Shannon because she knew she couldn't.

Soon after Sean was born he left for a year. After that he would come to the house and stay for a month or two and leave again. When Annie Laurie became pregnant with Sharon, he stayed for the full term. After she was born he left again, but this time he was gone two weeks and came back. He opened an antique shop in Portree and stayed home a lot with the baby. By then Sean was seven and Shannon started taking him on trips and teaching him things. He learned a great deal about the world at an early age.

Occasionally Shannon would take the family on one of his trips. Both children saw much of Europe as they were growing up. Sharon saw only the nice part, the museums, the cathedrals and parks and gardens. On his trips with just the boy, his father showed him the seedy underside of Europe. Sharon grew up and was a favorite of everyone in the town of Portree. They were a popular family in the little seaport.

There were a fair amount of tourists and he sold some things but Shannon's little shop was really the base for his international business in artifacts or whatever else he did. Sean did not mention that his father was involved with the I.R.A. Maybe he wasn't.

When Annie Laurie died at age thirty-nine, Sean was old enough to take care of Sharon when his father was away. Soon after her death, Shannon started making trips to Stornoway, a small town on the Isle of Lewis in the Outer Hebrides. It was a trip he made by boat. When he sailed for Stornoway he told them where he was going but they never learned why he went or what he did when he was there.

The children missed their mother tremendously and when their father went on trips they were lonely and grew even closer together. Sharon got more beautiful each year, but growing up as she did, with a sweet and innocent mother and a doting and protective father, she was very naive about many things. If any man or boy ever used language that Sean didn't like in front of Sharon, he got injured quickly and sometimes seriously. The local Magistrate knew Sharon and he lectured, but never penalized Sean for doing it.

The years passed. Sean went into the business of art and art dealing with his father. When they left town, Sharon stayed with her aunt. By the time Shannon died, Sean had learned the business and could continue on his own. He wanted

Sharon to stay in the village of Portree where she could remain innocent, but Sharon wanted very much to leave, so Sean set up an art and antique shop in Coconut Grove. He told Otto that he had, at that point, decided to concentrate on pre-Columbian art and that Miami was the gateway to South America and the Caribbean. I guessed that he had been told by Interpol to establish a base in Miami but, of course, he never told Otto about Interpol. It was the first time I learned that he had a shop in Miami.

They decided that Sharon would enroll at the University of Miami. Snake described the move in a way that I couldn't forget.

"I couldn't think of any other way to try to protect her and have her close by than to let her sign up for the University. I had moved around so much myself that I didn't see the danger. She went from the quiet and quaint little town of Portree in Scotland to Miami, U.S.A. Everything is different."

His eyes got a far-away look when he described the islands.

"The Isle of Skye is the largest of the Inner Hebrides of Inverness. It's separated from the mainland by the Sound of Sleat, Loch Alsh, the Inner Sound and the Sound of Raasay. It's separated from the Outer Hebrides by the Little Minch and the Sea of the Hebrides. The sea is all around and the smell is of clean salt air. It's completely different from Miami.

"Out there you are always aware of the smell. It's clean and clear. It comes from the hills as well as the sea and it's sweet and damp and sometimes you can smell the heather. My sister is called Sharon Heather." He paused as if he were trying to remember his home.

"And what is the smell of Miami?" Laufenberg asked.

"Marijuana," Snake said. "Rum and pizza and cocaine and garbage and many things that are sick and rotten."

The four of us were sitting around one end of the conference table. The table itself is a beauty. Actually, it's a dining room table for ten people that was made by the great craftsman George Nakashima. It was one of my indulgences and would someday be my dining room table when I bought a house. There were two pizza boxes and a bunch of empty beer bottles on the table. Sean kept talking.

"South Florida is a giant outdoor fornicatorium. Starting at Palm Beach and going south to Key West. South Florida has more gay homosexuals than any place outside of San Francisco but there is never any controversy because everyone is so busy just 'getting' that nobody notices or cares. Getting is the main function of South Florida. Getting laid, getting drunk, getting drugged, getting killed, getting raped, getting rich, getting robbed.

"I was the dumbest man in the world to bring Sharon into this crazy town but I did insist that she live in a dormitory that was for women only. A co-ed dorm is just a university-sponsored whore house. I also had a private detective check out the two women that were her roommates and they seemed to be decent girls.

"I saw her as often as I could and tried to keep track of whom she was seeing and what she was doing. I tried to warn her about everything – drugs, booze, sex – everything I could think of. She went to church two or three times a week. When she started seeing the kid who got her hooked on the drugs I had him checked out. I couldn't find out much about the kid, but he seemed O.K."

Snake told Otto the whole story about Sharon going to the parties and down for a weekend in the Keys. He related the story in every detail, except what he did to the Billy Goat in the swamp. He mentioned blackjacking the Billy Goat and taking him some place to question him. He never told Otto what he did with him and Otto didn't ask. He told the whole story about what the drug people had done to Sharon, making her a sex slave and loading her up with exotic drugs.

I glanced at Rocket from time to time as Snake told the story and I watched her face. When I look at a face I look for the surface beauty, the skin, the eyes, the bone structure. I look first as a painter. If I see imperfections and flaws I think as a surgeon. When I look at a face, I don't look for the soul. That's for poets and psychiatrists and priests. I simply look for the outside.

That Sunday afternoon at the clinic I could see deeper into Rocket than I wanted. She listened intently as Snake described the degradation. He could have asked her to leave but he didn't and she didn't go on her own. It was not curiosity. At one point she got up without saying anything and went into the small bathroom that's attached to the conference room. I could hear the sound of her vomiting. Snake had been describing how the Billy Goat sodomized Sharon while other people watched the show. I wondered if Conchita and Violeta had watched and I felt sure that they had.

Otto Laufenberg was magnificent. Even though it was summer he had the white around his eyes and looked like an owl. I had never seen a shrink in action before except when he was trying to figure out why I had thrown Milo Carter out the window. He knew when to ask Sean questions and when to let him talk. After Snake had finished the whole story, Otto went back and asked him all sorts of questions about Sharon, including some that puzzled me. He told us that her chance of recovery was greater because she was a Scotch Presbyterian and not a Roman Catholic. Guilt is such a part of Catholicism that it would add to her psychological burdens.

When Otto finished talking to Sean I still had time to drive Rocket home before my shift. She had taken a taxi Friday night so we wouldn't have to worry about her car. She was obviously exhausted.

"I heard a lot of shots when I was waiting in the boat," she said while I drove. "Did you hit anybody or were you just shooting at beer cans?"

"I shot two women. They were both whores that I met when I went to Norman's Cay the first time. I also shot a man."

"Did you have to shoot them?"

"The women recognized me. I sat between them at a party. Do you remember when we were at Treasure Cay with *Brilliant*? We were at the bar in the Treasure Cay Hotel and met two guys the same night while we were sitting there. One was Ricky Norton and the other was Joe Lehder. Do you remember them?"

"Yeah, I remember. Ricky was the guy who was fed up with Florida and was looking for a place to set up a dive shop. Joe Lehder was the guy about my age who seemed like the boss of the guys he was with. I remember the others because they wore suits and looked funny. They had on neckties when everybody else had on sport shirts. They looked like gangsters."

"I met both Ricky and Joe again on Norman's. Ricky took us on a dive. Later, he told me he thought there was some drug smuggling going on there. I met Joe in the restaurant. He has a house there on Norman's and invited us to dinner. I met two women at the party and ended up sitting between them. They were the two who came running out the door right after Snake came out with Sharon. There was plenty of light and I recognized both of them." After a long pause she asked, "How do you feel?"

"I feel hungry. You and Otto ate most of the pizza."

"I don't mean that, you ass-hole. I mean how do you feel about shooting the women? And the man?"

I thought about it for a while and tried to figure out how I really did feel. I had killed three people last night and I knew I should feel something, some remorse or some sense of regret, but I didn't.

"I'll talk to Otto when I get back to the clinic. I don't know how I feel. They were with Sharon and they probably watched the Billy Goat do things to her. I guess I'm glad I shot them."

We drove for a while without saying anything and then she said, "Are you in love with Lisa Winter?"

"I don't know," I said, startled at the question.

We didn't talk anymore until I dropped her off. I walked up to the door of her apartment.

"I really appreciate what you did and I know Sean does, too. You were magnificent navigating in the rain squalls. I can't tell you how much we appreciate your help. I was pretty dumb not to realize it would be so dangerous for you. I'm really sorry about that."

"It's the only time I ever got screwed in a Cessna with twin engines," she said with a grin.

I gave her a brotherly kiss and left.

When I got back to the clinic it was my turn to watch over Sharon and it did not go well. A few minutes after I sat down beside her she started having convulsions, a *grand mal* seizure. I got a padded wooden tongue depressor in her mouth so she wouldn't swallow her own tongue and shouted for Bill and Otto. They came quickly and Otto gave her a shot of *Dilantin* while we held her down.

A massive seizure like that is a horrible thing to watch, even for a doctor, and she was thrashing around as though an electrical current was being passed through her body. Her face was ghostly pale and she was sweating profusely. Otto had insisted that Sean stay in the conference room. If he had seen her it would have scared the hell out of him. Gradually the injection started to work and her thrashing slowed down. Bill and Otto stayed for ten minutes and then went back to the conference room. My mind wandered a little while I watched her and I found myself wishing I had gone inside the house on Norman's Cay and shot some more people. I hoped that I would be able to help Snake find and kill Emile Hogge some day.

When I finished my shift, I went into the conference room and sacked out on a couch. Six hours later they woke me and I took another shift watching her. Bill stayed at the clinic all night. He called Anne several times with feeble excuses but he said that she understood.

Early Monday morning Sharon woke up enough to talk a little. Otto had been watching her and got Snake to come in. She was awake for only a few minutes but long enough for Otto to ask her what drugs she had been using. As we expected, she hadn't the slightest idea. She recognized Sean and nodded her head when he said everything was going to be O.K. She went back to sleep very quickly.

A little after eight o'clock, Lori Young unlocked the back door and walked into the clinic. I was in the conference room at the time and I saw her come in. The first person she saw was Otto Laufenberg.

"Who the fuck are you?" she demanded.

"Dr. Otto Laufenberg. I'm a personal friend of Devlin's."

I could hear them talking and came out. I took Lori into my office and asked her to sit and wait for a few minutes. I woke up Snake who was asleep on the rug in the conference room. We talked and agreed to tell Lori that Sharon was here and was his sister but to say nothing about what happened, except that she had been on drugs. I went back in my office and talked to Lori.

"Why are you here?" I asked.

"I thought your fight with Bill was phony. You guys never fight about anything and I didn't believe what you said at the meeting. I didn't know what else to do, so I thought I would come over here and find out what was going on. I saw your car and Bill's car and let myself in. *What the hell is going on?*"

I told her everything about Sharon that she needed to know. When I finished, she asked what she could do. She made it clear that she was planning to stay and help, so I asked her if she would mind giving Sharon a sponge bath. I had washed her the night before but I didn't want her to wake up and find a man bathing her. Lori stayed all day and helped us tremendously and at one point late in the afternoon, after being with Sharon for nearly eight hours, she made a comment to me.

"I ain't never gonna smoke another marijuana joint," she said. "Not ever again." I made no comment.

During the day it appeared that Sharon was getting better. The three of us who were doctors spent less and less time with Sharon and Snake went out for food and newspapers. There had been nothing in the Miami or Fort Lauderdale papers on Sunday because it was too soon, but the Monday *Miami Herald* had an article. The headline said "Brutal Double Murder". It went on to say that two tourists from Colombia were brutally murdered on Saturday night just outside their bungalow on Norman's Cay. There was also some jewelry stolen and the murders were apparently committed by a thief who was caught in the act and arrested. I had no feelings about the article except to wonder who was arrested. That part was a shock and I was really curious.

Around five o'clock Monday afternoon Snake came back to the clinic with a bottle of Meyer's rum and announced that it was happy hour. Rocket came in from work around five thirty and we got together in the conference room. It was not a victory party or celebration, it was far too early for that, but it was a little bit of a relief. We were having a second round when Sidney Fontaine came walking in.

I introduced him to Otto, and explained that he had been in the restaurant on Norman's Cay when we went in for the girl. After bringing him up to date on Sharon's condition, we all looked to Sidney to tell us what happened. Sidney realized he was on stage with all of us waiting for his story so he gave us a performance.

"For my traveling companion I selected a lovely Oriental girl named Lea Kahn. Since my handsome bone structure and perfect s-sun tan attract attention wherever I go, I needed a b-b-beautiful woman for b-balance." I thought Otto, who had never met Sidney before, would fall on the floor laughing. Sidney was dressed in his priest uniform. He had a rum collins in his left hand and used his right to help his descriptions. Sidney was a very handsome man and his light brown skin looked like a perfect tan.

"We came down in a plane flown by a whiskey-soaked p-pilot named Charley Murphy. After checking in with Miss Cecelia Cotten we played two sets of tennis in which Leah Kahn defeated me 6-4, 6-3. The courts were in very poor condition. This is a fact you should note for any future trips to Norman's Cay.

"Miss Kahn and I shared a bungalow with separate bedrooms and enjoyed ourselves tremendously. We ate all of our meals at the restaurant, went snorkeling twice and played b-b-bridge with a couple from Tucson. The highlight of our weekend was lunch on Saturday. We walked into the bar shortly before noon in order to enjoy a cocktail before lunch. There was a man at the bar and we started talking. I introduced Miss Kahn and myself. When I mentioned that I was a priest and the Curate of Saint Stephens in Coconut Grove he asked if I knew his friend, Dr. Winfield Scott Devlin. I told him that I was in fact a close friend and that I worked constantly to keep you from the ways of the devil.

"He said his name was J-Jimmy Lightbourne and he worked as the d-dockmaster at the Chub Cay Club. He said he was on the island for the weekend and was visiting friends and relatives. He invited us to a wonderful lunch and insisted on paying the check f-f-for all three of us.

"When he first mentioned your name I was caught off guard. I may have been wrong, but I guessed that his being there was a coincidence and meant nothing. But I also knew that he might be there as a favor to you. P-possibly on a similar mission as my own. What *was* he doing there?"

"The lunch that Jimmy so generously paid for came out of my pocketbook," I said, laughing. "Jimmy was there as a favor to me although he did not know anything about what was going to happen. He believes he was there to gather information about drugs and whether or not Norman's is involved in smuggling. His bumping into you was just a coincidence. Keep on going."

"B-because of the beauty of Lea Kahn many people wanted to talk to us. Saturday night we had finished dinner and were standing at the bar talking to the couple from Tucson. Hutchison, I believe their name was, and we heard the explosion. Boom, boom, boom. There were three separate explosions and they were all very loud. The restaurant and bar were very crowded and everyone, including Lea Kahn and myself, ran out and down to the dock where it seemed to come from. There was a big boat at the dock but it was apparently unharmed. The dock itself was undamaged. There was no debris or anything else to indicate what had been blown up and nothing looked damaged. A lot of people who were not in the restaurant showed up. There were some policemen who came a few minutes later. After awhile everyone moved inside. The bar was full of people talking about the explosions but nobody seemed to know what happened. Eventually people lost interest.

"The next day we had breakfast and lunch in the restaurant. By then everybody was talking about the man and two women who had been shot. The p-police came around and asked questions of everybody. They wanted to see identification and wanted to know where we were when the shooting took place. Since we were in the b-bar and restaurant for several hours before and after, with plenty of witnesses, they didn't spend much time on us. We flew back to Miami Sunday afternoon. It was an excellent weekend. I have n-n-nothing else to report."

We all clapped a little and laughed at Sidney's recital. I thought it was really funny that he had bumped into Jimmy, and that they had lunch together, even though I expected to get a bill from Jimmy for the meals. After another hour or so I went out for some Chinese food. The feeling that we all had was one of cautious relief. I stopped at what I call the out-of-town newspaper store to get a copy of the *Nassau Guardian* but they didn't have it. Sitting around a clinic waiting to see if a drug addict lives or dies is not an ordinary social event so nobody knew what to do. We spent Monday night watching television.

Tuesday morning Lori Young came back with a sleeping bag and made it clear that she was going to help out with Sharon until she was ready to go someplace else. I took her to my office and made a speech about how she should use the days for vacation. When I finished the speech she told me to go shit in my hat.

Late Tuesday afternoon a car pulled into the parking lot and Gus and Paulette got out of a rental they had picked up at Miami airport. They had left *Pauletta* at the Yacht Haven Marina in Nassau temporarily and come back. By this time Sharon had improved enough so that people other than the three doctors could watch her, and everyone but Lori came into the conference room. She had taken charge of Sharon and pointed out that it would be bad for her to have a bunch of strange men around while she was sweating and shaking.

Both Rocket and Sidney had come in after work. We had another small happy hour and while we had drinks Gus told his story about the night of the raid. As usual he didn't use many words.

"Everything went exactly as planned. I waited until after it got dark and inflated the rubber dinghy. I towed it with my fiberglass dinghy in to the pier. There was a big boat tied up there so I anchored the inflatable in the shallow water about fifty feet from the pier and about thirty feet from the edge of the beach. I set the timer and rowed back to our boat. It was a long row for an old fart like me but I made it O.K.

"We had anchored very carefully in a place where we could go out the cut on a compass course without making any turns. In the dark if necessary. When the three explosions took place we watched with binoculars and saw all the people come running out of the hotel and restaurant. About ten minutes later there was a tremendous rain squall so I decided to haul ass. We upped the anchor and went out the cut. We went straight out for five miles with the engine at high speed and then turned north and set the sails. Nothing happened and nobody chased us. We got very wet."

When Gus finished his recital of events, Sidney stood up, raised his glass, and proposed a toast.

"To Gus and Paulette. To m-m-more and better explosions!" Everyone but Gus laughed at Sidney and people started talking about what to do about dinner. Gus quietly came over to me and said he thought I might be interested in taking a look at a copy of the *Nassau Guardian*.

"I think this may be about your friend. I hope not," he said, and walked away.

It was on the front page. Not headlines but still the front page. The title of the article was "Man Arrested in Norman's Cay Double Murder." The story described how Jimmy Lightbourne had been arrested in connection with the murder of the two women tourists because he had been seen by several people in the neighborhood of the house where the murders took place. He was the dockmaster at Chub Cay and claimed to be visiting relatives. He had been taken to Nassau and was being held subject to further investigation.

I felt like I had been kicked by a horse. I wondered if Jimmy had actually learned something and gone near the house on purpose or if it was just a horrible coincidence. I was sure that Gus knew that either Snake or I had done the killing. A couple of minutes later I got Snake and we went into my office. He read the article and thought for a minute.

"I've got to get him out, of course," he said. "My obligation to him is the same as it would be to you or Rocket or Gus. I see it this way. We work on two plans at the same time. You work through a lawyer. You get a really good criminal lawyer who has connections in Nassau. It will probably take a lot of money for bribes as well as the legal fees. You can do this out in the open without connecting yourself to the shooting. Charley Fowler and the people at your clinic are witnesses that Jimmy was here buying sails and that he said he was going to visit relatives on Norman's. Your buddy, Fitzgerald, can be a witness that he came to Sailorman to buy marine parts. I know a lot about the legal system in the Bahamas and I really believe we can get him off. I'll provide the money, of course."

"Where the hell will you get the money?"

"I'll probably steal it from drug dealers. I'm going after them for the things they did to Sharon and if I'm going to kill them, anyway, I might as well steal some money first."

"What if we can't get him off?"

"Then I get him out. That will be a separate thing and will not involve you. I'll have to recruit a professional team if I'm going to rescue Jimmy from the prison. I may have to leave my job with Interpol or take a leave of absence. I feel sure that this problem with Jimmy has nothing to do with the rescue. It's just an accident. If Emile Hogge can connect me in any way to Sharon's disappearance then I've got a problem. If he's coming after me I won't know where he's coming from or who his allies are. If he can't connect me, then he is the one who doesn't know what's coming. I'm going to kill him but I want to be the one sneaking up. I will plan it carefully and do it at my leisure. I want to torture him for a while and hear him scream. Something imaginative. Something creative. I'll know in a few weeks if they've made any connection."

"What will you do until then?"

"I'll assume that somehow, sometime, he's going to find out about me and I'll try to find him and do him before he does me."

"What should I do?"

"Nothing different. Worry a little and pray a little. Don't worry about the Bahamian police, though. The two Colombian whores won't be of much interest to them. There has been no mention of the man. Hogge's people must have gotten rid of the body. I have to worry about Hogge. I assume they're in business together and I need to know more about both of them."

"How long do you think it will take? How long will we have to wait before we know Emile Hogge is not after you?"

"Labor Day should be enough time."

"Why Labor Day? What the hell has that got to do with anything?"

"The patience of criminals is greatly overestimated. If Emile Hogge hasn't come after me by Labor Day, it means he's made no connection. I know about these things. I'm going to bet my life on it and be very visible for the next few weeks even though I'll also be looking for him. I might even go for several days without a disguise. If they haven't come after me by Labor Day, I'll go after them. If I disappear you have to assume they have me and will connect you somehow. I'm sorry. Without the shooting, Hogge would have just figured that Sharon got away from the people guarding her. I'm sorry you got so deeply involved. I didn't want it that way. Let's go get a drink and see what people are talking about for dinner."

When we got back to the conference room we found out that Otto Laufenberg had gone out for Italian food and German beer. We spent another night talking, eating and watching television.

The next morning I called Bellamy Craddock, my personal lawyer, and asked him to find me a good criminal lawyer who could handle a case in the Bahamas. I told him that Jimmy Lightbourne was a good friend of mine who had stayed with me and mentioned he was going to visit his mother and old friends on Norman's Cay the weekend of the 8th and 9th of July. I knew I might eventually have to tell him the truth, but that could come later. Craddock said he'd get back to me the following week.

On Friday morning I talked to Sharon for the first time. I'd gotten in the habit of going in to check on her frequently, even when it was someone else's turn. Somehow, seeing her alive had made the whole thing seem more real. Even in her condition she was an attractive girl.

"You're Devlin, aren't you? Sean told me about you and what you did. I don't know exactly what happened to me but I'm glad you came and got me."

"I'm glad too, Sharon. I hope you're feeling better. You look much improved to me."

"I'm beginning to feel better physically, but I'm afraid to even think about what happened. Sean said that Dr. Laufenberg was going to take me up to Vermont and that he would help me try to get over what happened. Sean said he was a friend of yours."

"I needed a psychiatrist in college, and went to him. We've been friends ever since."

"Did he help you?" she asked very seriously.

"He helped me understand some things about myself. I think he'll be a wonderful person for you to be with right now."

Every time I looked at Sharon I felt a sense of shame that human beings could do anything as repulsive as what was done to her. I didn't blame Snake one bit for his desire to get revenge.

By the end of the week things started getting straightened out. Gus and Paulette flew back to Nassau to get their boat and bring it back to Miami. Before they left I thanked them again and offered to pay them something because of all the expenses. Gus refused with one of his more eloquent speeches.

"Stick it," he said. Paulette laughed and rolled her eyes.

Sharon became a little bit better each day. By Wednesday Bill was playing eighteen holes of golf every day. Otto started playing with him.

On Sunday morning Snake and I drove Otto and Sharon to Miami International Airport. Lori Young had stayed all week and didn't say goodbye until we left the clinic. She and Sharon hugged and I saw tears in her eyes. I had fixed up Sharon with a blonde wig and some bandages on her face. Nobody could even see her face, much less recognize her. They would fly to Boston non-stop and then to Brattleboro. From there they would drive up to Stratton. Otto's ski lodge seemed like a perfect place to spend a month or two. Otto was an expert on ancient Greece and was writing a book about what he called the "Longest War." He would work on his book and work with Sharon every day. It seemed like an ideal way for her to try to get well.

Chapter Twenty Two

Monday, 17 July
When I got to the clinic I noticed a letter addressed to *Mr.* Winfield Devlin at the clinic address. It was a personal letter from Cecelia Cotten, the manager at Norman's Cay. It said that some things had been left behind in the bungalow that I had rented and would I please contact her about what I was missing. I thought it was a peculiar letter because I had reserved the room and registered as *Dr.* Winfield Devlin using the clinic address. I decided to talk to Snake before I did anything.

I called Butch to invite them for dinner at the Yacht Club. I had tried to figure out the best way to entertain people who owned businesses and houses all over the world but I wasn't too clever at that sort of thing so I called my mother. I explained to her how I had met them, about the party at *Casa del Malecón* and the trip to Bimini on *Ojos Verdes*. I also told her I was going to the Salazar's house again. I was going for dinner with Pat Rivera that Saturday night.

She understood and said it wasn't important *what* I did as long as I invited them to do *something* as my guests. She pointed out that even the richest people in the world can get hurt feelings and they also like to eat. She emphasized that I should extend the invitation to Butch personally and let him help me figure out what to do and when to do it.

Butch laughed when I told him my predicament about not knowing how to entertain his family. He said that all four of them would be happy to come to dinner at the Yacht Club, that he'd like to bring a girl and would I mind if Antonia was my date for the evening. I couldn't exactly refuse. I asked him to crew for me in a Star boat race that same Saturday afternoon. We decided on Saturday night, August 19th.

The more I thought about it, the better I liked having Toni as my date for the evening. She'd arrive with them and leave with them and it would be simple. She was also very beautiful. I also wanted Butch to crew for me on the Star. After the adventures of the early summer it would be nice to go out for a simple afternoon race.

I spent the next Saturday afternoon hanging around the Yacht Club, washing the Bermuda 40 and then sitting around the swimming pool. I left the Yacht Club at five o'clock and picked up Pat at the studio. We had light traffic all the way to Miami Beach. I was curious as to why Pat had been so insistent on hearing the rest of the story about the stolen Rembrandt, and I wondered if she had called Butch to prompt the invitation. It had been more than a month since Ricardo told us the story on Bimini and I didn't even remember the names of most of the people in the story. I really didn't care what happened to Karel

Whitman or Anne-Marie Frank or even Leo Gormann. I wasn't curious about what happened to the paintings either, but I did want to know how the thieves got caught. Pat admitted she had wangled the dinner invitation from Butch. She also admitted she had used some of her T.V. sources to learn more about the Rembrandt robbery. So far everything Ricardo had told us was straight out of the Interpol files.

"What is it you expect to find out from hearing the rest of the story?" I asked, as we were driving over the causeway. We already know who did it and how."

"I want to find out the *real* story. T.V. journalists think that way. We're always looking for a story. I want to find out what happens if a guy like Sean finds something so valuable that he wants to keep it himself or sell it to somebody else. Something he wasn't hired to search for."

"Ricardo explained that he did business with Sean's father and now Sean because they could be trusted."

"If something has enough value or importance," she answered, "nobody can be trusted. Nobody."

The guard at the gate recognized us and we drove across the short bridge. We went to the front door and a servant sent us back to the huge screened-in porch where we found Carmela and Butch. I was now very much aware of the construction details that Rocket told me about. I guess if I owned millions of dollars worth of art and artifacts I would want to keep them in a house that was built like a bank vault. And in addition to being burglar-proof it had to be hurricane-proof. The tidal surge in a major hurricane would sweep right over Miami Beach and Biscayne Bay. It would hit the city of Miami at the same height it hit the beach. That's why everything of any real value was above the first floor.

Pat asked Butch if she could see a few of Ricardo's paintings and they went upstairs leaving me with Carmela. She immediately started asking questions about Rocket. I felt the same as before. Because of my mother and her friends it seemed perfectly natural even though it was really none of her business. I did feel like I could talk to her so I got myself a rum and tonic and sat down.

"Have you seen Rocket since you were in Bimini with Pat?"

"No, Sra. Salazar. I think Rocket is a wonderful girl but I'm not in love with her. I think Pat is also terrific but I'm not in love with her, either. By the way, neither one of them is in love with me, so I'm not breaking anybody's heart."

"Mothers worry about such things, Devlin, especially when the men are now over thirty. Like you and my son. No doubt you were too busy learning medicine for several years to think about selecting a wife. Now you have time. I worry about Butch and Carlotta. Butch seems to be attracted to girls for about six months each and then he gets a new one. I worry even more about Carlotta. She is the same age as Antonia. They even look alike but Toni is quiet and

Carlotta is not. She wants to get her own apartment in Madrid when we return. We will not let her, of course, but we cannot keep her at home forever."

We talked alone for a while and then Butch came back with Pat. Ricardo and Toni came in soon afterwards. We moved in to the dining room and Pat wasted no time in urging Ricardo to tell us more about the Rembrandt robbery. As soon as a servant had poured us each a glass of wine, he started. If he was reluctant to continue the story, and was doing so only because of Pat, he gave no sign of it.

"When we were having lunch on Bimini I stopped when they had just arrested Karel Whitman at Tempelhof Airport for something he did *not* do. O.K.? Karel Whitman was the thief who stole the paintings in the first place. Remember? Am I starting again at the right place?" We all nodded.

"This is a complicated story with a cast of thousands as they say in Hollywood but only a few people are important. Karel Whitman stole the paintings, of course, and Klaus Leo Gormann was the guy trying to sell the Rembrandt. Whitman had met him when Anne-Marie Frank was teaching French to his children. Leo Gormann was thirty five, dapper, educated, charming and also ambitious. He described himself as a sculptor and musician but his money came from dealing in antiques. In America you would call him the fence.

"A man named Hans Deter was also involved at the end. He was the Kriminalhauptkommissar and chief of the robbery division of the Interpol office in West Berlin. He was a hefty man with horn-rimmed glasses who got the first phone call with an offer to sell the Rembrandt and the Van Goyen back in February. Marie-Noelle Pinot de Villechenon was, of course, the French National Museum's curator assigned to the Tours collection. So now let me finish the story.

"Whitman has been arrested but for a different robbery. Marie-Noelle gets a phone call from a German woman who says she has a friend with access to some paintings which the museum might be interested in. The caller says that a collector in the United States will pay DM100,000 for one of the paintings but that she would like to see them stay in Tours. The caller is actually the wife of Klaus Leo Gormann who will later use the fake name Garten in trying to sell the painting.

"A meeting is set up at the Saarbrucken railroad station for five o'clock the next day with the woman. Marie-Noelle, of course, alerts the police. The woman says she is thirty-five, small and brunette and will wear a raincoat. She says she will be carrying a copy of the French newspaper *L'Aurore*. O.K., now use your imagination. They have a whole day to set up the Saarbrucken railroad station for the meeting. By late afternoon when the express from Mainz arrives right on schedule, the station is filled with cops dressed as passengers, janitors and cleaning ladies. Everybody has guns.

"Nobody shows up at 5:00 but at five thirty a woman in a brown coat comes to the newsstand, and asks for a copy of *L'Aurore*. The sales-clerk reaches down and finds she is sold out of the magazine that is to be the secret signal! Can you imagine the stupidity? *What planning!*"

Ricardo had obviously told the story many times, and he had it down perfectly. He was having fun.

"The customer waited. The salesclerk apologized. Finally the customer bought a copy of another magazine and left. The sales-clerk was confused and eager to notify the police about having no copies of *L'Aurore* so she left her stand quickly. In the middle of the concourse she was certain she saw the plainclothes policeman she had been instructed to report to. He really looked like a cop so she approached him and rattled off her story. The man listened gravely, nodded sympathetically and then turned and left. The man she had approached was actually Klaus Leo Gormann. He walked quickly across the station to the brown-coated woman, who had been watching the entire scene, and together the pair hurried from the station. In a room filled with cops the saleslady picks out the *woman's accomplice!*"

We were laughing hard at both the story and Ricardo.

"Outside the station Leo and his wife separated. The police tried to follow each of them but managed to lose both."

"At six forty that night, a little over an hour after the railroad station fiasco, a call came in to the Saarbrucken police station and was taken by an Inspector Vogel. The man on the phone said he was named Garten and that he and his wife had arranged the meeting at the railroad station. He said he had gotten mixed up. The meeting should have been at six o'clock instead of five because the lady was actually on the five fifty-one train from Paris. He also said he hadn't planned on the station being full of cops. He said that he had not planned to call the police until the next day. Inspector Vogel and Garten agreed to an immediate meeting at a nearby parking lot. Imagine calling the police to sell a stolen painting!

"An hour later, Inspector Vogel pulled up outside the parking lot. Beyond the gate he saw a man smoking a cigarette and knew it must be the man called Garten. They introduced themselves.

"Garten, who was really Klaus Leo Gormann, described himself as a salesman. He claimed he'd seen the painting at a friend's house in Essen. He'd read about the theft from the Tours Museum and knew the painting's history. According to his story, some people were blackmailing him and forcing him to sell the picture for them. They insisted he find a buyer for it. He didn't explain why he was being blackmailed and Vogel didn't ask. Garten said he had become suspicious at the station when the clerk from the newsstand asked if he was a policeman and told him what had just happened.

"After a long conversation, Vogel reminded him that nothing could be done without the painting itself. Garten agreed and they parted. The next day Garten called Vogel and said he had made the necessary arrangements and proposed a meeting Saturday, December 9, at guess where? *Tempelhof Airport*, of course! That's where Karel Whitman was arrested by mistake. Remember?"

Ricardo was really into it now, having a hard time not laughing while he talked. I kept thinking he looked like a Roman senator with his massive head, slightly beaked nose and coal-black eyes. I had taken some close-up pictures of him before we left Bimini and started doing an oil painting from it.

"As soon as Vogel hung up on this call, he placed one to Detective Superintendent Siegfried Rupp at West Germany's Federal Criminal Investigation Office in Wiesbaden. Remember Rupp? He was the specialist in art thefts and had followed the case since he got the first message from Berlin six months before.

"The case now fell within the specific jurisdiction of the Saarbrucken police, so Rupp said he would gather the 100,000 deutsche marks asked for and bring it to Vogel in Saarbrucken. There was too much at stake for any chances to be taken. At the critical meeting at Tempelhof, the buyer would have to appear genuine beyond any shadow of doubt, even to the extent of having the purchase price in cash with him.

"On December 8, Superintendent Rupp flew to Berlin. Chief Deter and Vogel met him at the airport and the three police officers went over the arrangements for the next morning's operation. They were determined to avoid a repeat of the fiasco at the railroad station. But again, there were cops everywhere. Almost to the minute, Vogel and Deter, who would pretend to be the prospective buyer, walked into the main hall. They hesitated. A man approached them. Instantly the news was relayed by radio to all the armed detectives in the building and the cars outside. As the hidden observers watched the scene, they saw Vogel introduce Deter to Garten. Then the three men hurried out of the airport and left in a bright yellow Volkswagen owned by Garten.

"Following it were seven unmarked police cars and vans, each with a complement of armed officers. Half a mile from the airport the Volkswagen pulled to the side of the road. Garten reached behind him and produced a slim oblong parcel wrapped in brown paper. He removed the paper and handed the object to Deter. He inspected it with a great show of care and interest. He held it up to the light, turned it on its side, examined the tiny signature at the corner, and ran his finger delicately over the thick paint.

"Deter, under Rupp's tutelage, had been studying reproductions of the work for a week. After the examination, he said he was satisfied and gave Garten a plastic bag bulging with money. Everyone agreed. They all nodded and smiled. The seller had his money and the buyer had his Rembrandt and everybody was happy. And then, as Butch would say, they *nailed his ass!*

"Deter and Vogel got out of the car with the painting. Vogel very slowly he raised his hat. It was a signal to the two thousand, four hundred and sixty three cops that had been following them. Instantly seven vehicles surrounded the

Volkswagen and a wave of armed detectives surged forward, and there in the misty light of an early December evening, a startled and amazed Herr Klaus Leo Gormann alias Garten found himself under arrest. In his hands were 100,000 deutsche marks which he had just gotten for the painting that Karel Whitman had stolen from the Tours Museum on an impulse that cold winter night when he had stopped to pee!"

"*Incredible*," said Toni, who had been silent.

There was a pause in the story for a couple of minutes while a servant put a roast beef dinner in front of us. Then Ricardo smiled broadly before he continued.

"As you know I have made fun of Interpol a little bit, especially about the crazy mixup in the Saarbrucken railroad station. Do not take that too seriously. They did make a few small errors but they did recover both paintings. They actually do a remarkable job, with many countries communicating and cooperating in an extremely thorough manner."

"Wait, Ricardo," Pat protested. "You didn't finish about the robbery. What happened to Karel Whitman and Gormann?"

"What happened to them is not important, but you are right, Patricia. I did not really finish the story of the robbery. O.K. Whitman was extradited and came to trial on March 4, 1974 in Tours. The judge sentenced him to two years in prison, not counting the time he had already served. Karel Whitman served his time in the jail at St. Martin on the Isle de Re, three miles off La Rochelle on France's southwest coast. He was released early and returned to West Germany in the spring of 1975. Interpol kept track of him for a while. He moved into a commune briefly and then he started wandering again.

"Leo Gormann confessed everything and helped the police find the van Goyen. No charges were brought against Braun, the dealer who had sold the Van Goyen, or his customer. Gormann was in prison for a while and then was given a suspended sentence of six months. He went back to dealing in antiques and to his artistic activities in art and music. Ann-Marie Frank resumed her studies in German, pursuing her original aim of becoming a fully-qualified teacher of the language."

One of the servants brought in more food and we all listened as Ricardo continued. I had enjoyed the story. It was interesting and Ricardo was a superb story teller but I couldn't see why Pat thought there was some big story in it.

"Now let me go back to the day after the robbery. When the theft was reported by Marie-Noelle Pinot de Villechenon, the museum listed the two paintings as having been stolen but they did not include the small statuette or its lignum vitae stand. The little statue was about nine inches high. The wooden stand was nearly three. It had eight sides and was intricately carved. I heard rumors that the statue, which was not supposed to be very valuable, and its carved lignum vitae stand, were actually the objects of the robbery, and not the paintings."

"Months later I heard a strange story from a man in Rio de Janeiro. It was at a large party and the news of the arrests of Whitman and Gormann had just made its way across the ocean. I thought nothing of it. Stories like that accompany every robbery. I forgot about it until I heard it again from a museum director in Brussels. He added a little bit to the story that I did find intriguing. He mentioned that the lignum vitae stand really was the object of the robbery, not the paintings or even the statue. There was supposed to be something inside the stand, something more valuable than all of the other things. Supposedly the stand weighed exactly what a piece of solid lignum vitae would weigh. Museums always check and record things like that. The stand had been hollowed and enough wood removed, so that whatever was inside didn't change the weight. The stand seemed to be a solid piece but it really wasn't."

"Had the museum director seen what was inside?" Pat asked.

"No. The museum director in Brussels had not seen the statue or the stand. He had only heard the story. I thought it was a wonderful story, myself, better than most of the rumors that circulate around the art world. I forgot about it until one day when I heard that the Interpol record was available. When a case has been solved, and the records closed, the information is available to the public. I was able to obtain a copy of the report and it was supposed to be complete and accurate. I read it carefully and there was no mention of anything being stolen other than the paintings. I was amazed. In the articles that I had read in the newspapers and museum periodicals, the statuette was usually reported as being stolen, but unimportant. When the police report was taken, the little statue was perhaps verbally reported by the museum but not written down by the police.

"This was very unusual because the French police are very meticulous about details. Another strange thing. When Karel Whitman climbed down the ladder, he had the two paintings under one arm and the statue in that same hand so he could climb with the other hand on the ladder. This was described in detail in most of the periodicals.

"After reading the Interpol report I called around looking for Sean Moran and found him in New York. We arranged to meet later that month in Miami. He came out for lunch and I told him the story. He said that he had not heard it before, and that he would check it out. A few weeks later he got back to me and told me that the story was widely believed by men who usually know these things. Nobody, however, seemed to really know, or even pretend to know, exactly what was inside the lignum vitae stand. There were stories that the hollow space was filled with diamonds or rubies. Sean felt strongly that the story was true about the stand being the real object of the robbery. I paid him a fee to find out as much as he could but not to do an actual search. He has completed that but now I have lost interest. Although I am intrigued and love to collect things that are unusual, I did not know enough to ask Sean to continue. Perhaps soon we will read about it in a newspaper."

After he finished the story we went into the huge living room and talked about other things for a while. I mentioned the portrait to Antonia and we set a tentative time to get started. After brandy and dessert we thanked them again and headed for home. The minute we crossed the little bridge Pat started talking about the Tours robbery again.

"I don't believe Ricardo even a little bit. Even a tiny bit," she said. "Remember the conversation that I had with him on the beach at Bimini before you woke up? I asked him *what if Sean, or someone like him, found something that wasn't part of the deal.* Instead of answering the question he started telling the story about the Rembrandt robbery. Later on that weekend I overheard him talking to Butch and he mentioned the statue and Bodyguards of the Christ in the same sentence. I believe Ricardo is still looking for that statue. Maybe he's looking for it without Sean knowing because he's afraid Sean will keep the statue. Maybe Sean is looking for it himself. Something has changed since Bimini. I think they both want that Goddamn statue really bad. My instincts as an investigative reporter are so strong I can feel vibrations!"

I suddenly remembered the story that Snake had told to me and Rocket that morning at Chub Cay. I repeated the story to Pat and she laughed hysterically.

"Was he just making up a story or was he actually talking about the statue that was stolen with the Rembrandt?"

"At the time I thought he was just making up a story to explain how complicated the market is for valuable art. Now I'm not too sure. Anything Snake says could be real or imagined."

"Can you imagine telling a story like that on the 6:00 o'clock news. It has just been learned that a statue originally worth ten billion dollars was recovered today in the Iberian Peninsula. It was discovered and offered for sale by the French fry specialist at the local Burger King. Unfortunately his penis was broken off. The statue that is – not the French fry specialist – which makes the statue worthless!" We both laughed all the way to Pat's apartment.

I tried to invite myself in but got nowhere.

"Devlin, if you come inside you'll start kissing me. I'll get *choninos caliente*. You'll try to get inside. I'll say no. You'll get upset. Call me next week and let's have dinner. Give me one big wet kiss."

I woke up in the middle of the night and realized that something was bothering me. I stayed awake for a long time and then it dawned on me what it was. Snake had told me on the trip to Norman's Cay that when Sharon was safe he was going to go back to Europe on a search for something very important – something that Ricardo wanted badly. I wondered why they told different stories.

On Friday I had a lunch meeting with Sylvester Salmon, the Bahamian lawyer, at a place near the clinic. It was the first time I had talked to him in private since we had been introduced. We found a table where we could talk quietly.

"I'm going to get Jimmy out," was the first thing that Sylvester said. "I couldn't get him out before on bail because of the publicity but now I'm sure I can get him off completely. Now that the Nassau Guardian isn't writing about it nobody gives a shit."

We stopped talking for a few minutes to eat our lunches and when I finished my sandwich I started asking questions again. "I'm surprised you're so sure since the charge is murder. Isn't that unusual?"

"There are several factors involved. The most important one eventually is money. All the evidence against Jimmy is circumstantial. He happened to be on the island that weekend and be seen near the house an hour or so before the murders. Purely circumstantial. Another thing is the two women. They both appear to have been whores. Real ones. Professionals. When there is a murder or murders the prominence of the victims is a big factor. If a well-known person is killed or tried for a crime, it's a big thing in the Bahamas. Worse in the U.S. The other people who were staying in the house left the island after the Bahamian police had talked to them. The actual owner of record is a man named Sepulveda, who lives in Colombia. Nobody seems to care much that the two women were shot. They haven't even identified the man."

"How is Jimmy doing? Is he bitter? Is there any way I can see him and talk to him?"

"It could be arranged but I don't know if it's a good idea."

"What did Jimmy tell you about his part in the shooting?"

"He says he had no part in the shooting. He says he was on the island to visit his mother. Period."

"Did he ask you who was paying? Where the money was coming from?"

"No. He seemed to take it for granted that someone would be taking care of him and footing the bills."

Jimmy probably thought the D.E.A. was taking care of him. I hoped he *did* think so, and hoped he wasn't too worried. Sylvester Salmon was an unusual man, both in appearance and in background. He looked like a Jewish lawyer except that he had very dark skin. I would have bet money that he had a white father and a black mother or vice versa. He'd gotten his law degree from the University of Florida.

"I have a check for you. It's made out in the amount that Bellamy told me. Let me know what your charges are as we go along." I gave him the check.

"I think I ought to go over to the Bahamas and talk to Jimmy about what happened. Can you arrange it?"

"I don't know what your part is in this thing but unless you have a compelling reason to see him you should not go. Nobody knows that you're involved. Jimmy did not mention you at all. I can advise you better if you tell me what your involvement is but I don't really need to know. A trip could just confuse things. You can get over there in a few hours if it becomes necessary. I don't think you should go, otherwise."

We didn't talk much more. I thanked him for coming to see me and he left promising to call if there were any developments.

On Sunday morning I had scrambled eggs and bacon at the Rat. The name *Café de Rat Mort* is French for Café of the Dead Rat and it's run by an old woman who has sailed all over the world. It's really a nightclub that serves a basic breakfast starting at two a.m. Sidney calls it the "Rat" but with real affection. Bronco, the lady who owns it, is an experienced engineer on Sidney's miniature railroad.

Afterwards I went to the eight o'clock service at Saint Stephens. Sidney wasn't preaching and wasn't there. I listened intently to a sermon called "Choices." I thought about the choices I had made in my own life and realized that most of them had been made already except for the woman choice. I had been in a kind of limbo since the trip to Norman's and hadn't gone out on very many dates. I made myself a promise that I was going to conduct a search for a new girlfriend after the Labor Day weekend was over and Toni had gone back to Spain. Maybe I would chase after Pat Rivera. Thinking about Pat made me a little horny so I stopped daydreaming and concentrated on the sermon.

My mind was still wandering when I went up to the alter rail to receive Communion. I was kneeling at the rail between the wafers and the wine when I glanced over and saw Lisa Winter looking at me. I was startled and wondered what she was doing in the Episcopal Church. I kept on kneeling for a bit after the silver goblet was passed and waited for her to get up. I watched as she got up and walked back to her pew. She sat down about halfway back, a few rows behind where I had been sitting. She seemed to be alone. I went back to my previous place and sat down. For what was left of the service I kept glancing back at her. Each time she was looking at me. At the close of the last hymn I turned quickly, afraid perhaps that she would disappear like some of my dreams about her. She was waiting for me as I turned to go down the aisle at the end of the service.

"Can we go someplace and talk?" she asked.

"Let's go down to the Yacht Club and have some coffee," I suggested. "Do you have time for that?"

"Yes, I have time but I would rather not go to the Yacht Club. Can we go to some other place?"

I asked her to follow me so we walked through the parking lot and came out the driveway near the Taurus. We went over to the Green Street restaurant and took one of the sidewalk tables. We both ordered coffee and Danish. Lisa ate very quickly and then waited for me to finish. I told her how nice it was to see her and how surprised I was at her being in the Episcopal Church.

"Coming to your church was an impulse. I'm not sure why I did it. I suppose I wanted to see what it was like for you coming to my church. I don't know why coming today was important either but I do have something I want to tell you. It will be very awkward for me and I hope you'll be patient."

"Take your time. I'm going to race my boat today but not for about three hours."

"When you talked about the English song called *Jerusalem* on the beach at Norman's Cay and you let it slip out that you had come to the Catholic Church just to see me I didn't know what to do. I acted like a fool and I was very rude to you. I was very cruel and I'm sorry."

"It doesn't matter. I was hurt and I was pissed off, but only for a short time. Coming to your church was really kind of stupid. It was the kind of thing a kid would do, a kid with a schoolboy crush. It was not surprising that you reacted like a grown woman and told me how silly it was."

"I didn't react like a grown woman, Dev, or even like a girl. I reacted strangely because I'm a little different."

"You're exceptionally beautiful, Lisa. – that in itself is very different."

"It's not only my looks that are different, Devlin, there is something else."

I didn't know what to say so I just listened.

"I have to explain it to you in Greek. Not in the Greek language, I don't speak any. But in the classical way that they think. I will explain things to you the way they were explained to me by a psychiatrist."

I sat quietly without interrupting while she explained to me what made her different. It was strange, indeed.

"In the English language we have only one word for love. It is supposed to cover all the different feelings we have. You love your boat and your family and the New York Jets. The word love defined broadly may be understood as any strong affection, closeness to things or persons. The Greeks distinguished four types of love. They are *storge, philia, eros* and *agape*. *Storge* is the word for familial love. It's a word for the bond that exists between one who loves and the persons, animals and things that surround him or her. It is compatible with quite a bit of taken-for-grantedness or even hatred at times." She paused for a few seconds and then continued.

"I'm sorry I sound like a dictionary but I need to be very accurate. The word *philia* pertains to friends, freely chosen because of mutual compatibility and common values. The word *eros* is for passion, not only of a sexual nature, but also of an aesthetic or spiritual nature, for what is conceived as supremely beautiful and desirable. *Agapic* love is manifested when one person has much to give to another more needy. It is generous self donation without concern for reward.

"Such distinctions as the Greeks make become very important in discernments about marriage, because the strength of *eros* may blind one to the absence of other types of love that are needed to experience a good Christian bond. One that can endure till death us do part. Do you understand what I'm saying?"

"I studied that stuff back in college but I didn't remember the words. I know what you're talking about."

"Devlin, I can experience all of these types of love except *eros*. I'm not capable of *erotic* love. I never have been."

I was sitting there at a sidewalk café staring at a woman who was so beautiful she could make most men feel powerful *erotic* love just by smiling or saying hello. She was telling me something I could hardly believe. Something I didn't believe.

"Are you a lesbian?"

"No. Homosexuals feel erotic love, or think they do, for their own sex. I don't have those kinds of feelings for either men or women. I am capable of feeling the other kinds very strongly. *Philia* best describes my feelings for you. I love you, Devlin, but not in an *erotic* way. I have never felt any *erotic* love for any person, man or woman."

I was stunned. "Lisa, it's none of my business and I don't want to get too personal but have you been to a gynecologist to make sure there is nothing physically wrong?"

"It is very personal, but it is your business. I've hurt you a lot and I should have told you these things before. I've had some men who were very persistent in trying to make me love them but those men always gave up. I never had a man come to my church. I never had a man pursue me relentlessly the way you have. I know I should have told you these things before. I've been to a lot of gynecologists and there's nothing at all wrong with me physically. I am capable of orgasm."

"With another person?"

"No."

"Is your situation or condition very common?"

"It's extremely uncommon. It takes three long complicated words to describe it and the last one is *raris* which means rare. I'm still seeing a psychiatrist but I'm resigned to my situation. Let me tell you about myself."

We were there for almost two hours while she told me her story. She had grown up in a very small town north of Montreal. Her father was French Canadian and her mother American. Her father worked for the railroad. Both her parents were extremely religious. There were no feelings between them except duty. No affection, but no cruelty either. They both treated her the same way. At night when her father was there he read aloud from the Bible. When he was gone the mother did the reading. When Lisa was eighteen and had finished convent school she decided to leave home and go to Toronto. She got a job as a waitress in a grubby café and found a room. One day a man offered her a job as a secretary. She couldn't type but he didn't seem to care being mostly interested in looking at her and occasionally trying to pinch her. He gave her very little work to do and he was out of the office a lot. She spent hours just learning to type and to take dictation. Eventually she found a job in a much larger office. She refused offers of dates because none of the men appealed to her. This got her the reputation of being cold and unfriendly, but it helped her in the business because she was perceived as being very efficient.

"Eventually I started going out on dates but only with men from other companies. I never went out socially with anyone from Winter Limited, which was Carl's company. People there knew me only as an attractive girl who was very friendly to everybody but not close to anybody. At first the men thought I was a lesbian but the women at Winter Ltd. assured them I was not. Because I was totally unpolitical I didn't make enemies but I didn't make friends either. Women who were envious of my looks always found out that I never used them to manipulate people. Eventually I moved up and became an executive secretary to Carl Winter, who owned the company. I was worried about sex and I deliberately tried it with several men before I got married. I also tried it with two different women but I never felt the excitement of *erotic* love with anyone."

"Did you feel a sense of revulsion?"

"No. Not really. It just seemed strange. Like a funny thing to do."

"How about guilt?"

"I felt some guilt, naturally. How could I feel otherwise growing up the way I did? Afterwards I confessed to a priest each time. They were too shocked and confused to know what to say."

I just sat silently and listened. Like the priests, I was totally shocked and confused.

"Eventually I married Carl Winter and Bobby was our child. I was honest with Carl about everything and I have been seeing psychiatrists off and on ever since."

By the time she finished her story both her eyes and mine were a little wet.

"What I told you before was true, Devlin, about how you were too strong a person for me. Carl was much older than I was. He was a tough businessman and strict with his employees, but he treated me like a daughter. He wanted sex, of course, but he was not unreasonable about it. He knew that I was indifferent. He never made me pretend. I became pregnant with Bobby the third month we were married. After that Carl did not use me very often. I made myself available any time he wanted but he became wrapped up with Bobby. I'm seeing a psychiatrist now but he has pretty much given up. I'm not unhappy. I would probably become a nun except that I enjoy worldly things too much."

"What kind of things, Lisa?"

"Dolphin games when they win. Opera when the performances are good. Skiing in Canada. I go up there for a few weeks every year. Usually Mont Tremblant, the area were I grew up. It's fun being a rich lady even if I'm no good in bed. As a rich widow it's probably better that way."

"What happened when Bobby got hurt? Why did you make so many lunch dates?"

"When Bobby was injured and we were seeing each other I think I wanted something to happen. If it had, I would have gone to bed with you. I almost did many times but it would have been false. It appears that I will never experience erotic love or even erotic feelings. I'm deeply sorry that I hurt you so much when you told me about coming to the Catholic Church just to see me. Either an immature school girl or a mature woman would have handled it better because they would have understood *your erotic* feelings for me. They would have known and experienced the feelings themselves but I just never have.

"I had never felt intensely for anyone so I didn't know how you felt. I acted like a real jerk and it could have messed up your chances of finding the house. I really was sad that it ruined the weekend. I was having such a good time even though our reason for being there was unusual."

It was a typical Sunday at the sidewalk cafés in Coconut Grove. There was a soft breeze blowing and a few wispy clouds in the sky. The streets were crowded and as usual every person walking along the street had an ice cream cone or a drink in their hands. I had to talk about something else just then, since I was too overwhelmed with what she had told me. I thought back to the time on Norman's Cay when we were having the conversation about the man putting his hand up her dress. She was teasing me about the two women playing with me under the table when she wiggled out of her dress. I had gotten so horny I had to run out of the bungalow and jump in the water to avoid raping her. When I cooled off I realized that she wasn't even a little bit excited.

I would ask a few of my psychiatrist friends about her condition. Maybe claim I had read about it or something. I would ask Otto Laufenberg about it. I felt such pity for Lisa Winter at that moment that I couldn't even talk.

"Thank you for telling me, Lisa. I'm not sure whether I should feel better or worse, but thank you anyway. I guess I should have called you first. After spending the weekend locating that house I should have told you what happened later. I told myself that you didn't need to know but I think it was more that I didn't want to talk to you."

"Devlin, please tell me everything you can about rescuing the man. I've been worried about you ever since we came back from Norman's Cay. When I got home I felt sick about making fun of you for watching me in church. I called you every week to see if you were at the office. I always hung up when Lori answered because I just wanted to know if you were all right. Tell me what happened."

I told Lisa the entire story, leaving out none of the details except the part where I shot the two women. I told her it was the sister of a friend and not a man we rescued. She listened intently.

"What about the girl? Where is she now? Is she going to be all right psychologically?"

"I think so. She's with a psychiatrist up in Vermont who's a personal friend of mine. He will see to it that she gets the best counseling and treatment possible."

"I'll pray for her," Lisa said.

"I'm having a party on Friday of Labor Day weekend at my place. I do it every year. Almost everyone who's going to be there helped out in some way with the rescue except for a few people who know nothing. Nobody will talk openly about it but privately we will all be congratulating each other. You belong there, too. Your help was really important. Can you make it?" I hesitated and then added, "Bring along another person if you want to."

"I would like to come. I think I can be there."

We talked for a while about Bobby, who was at a summer camp in Canada for two weeks, and about other things. I told her I had become friends with Dr. Montgomery. She understood and appreciated what he had done at the lawyer's. We talked about all sorts of things but not again about her or her feelings. I knew that my own feelings for Lisa Winter would be even more painful to live with in the future than her rejection of me had been in the past.

I spent the rest of that day thinking about women. Even during the race. About how wonderful they were but how strange. Everything that ever happened with Lisa Winter now seemed unreal. Although I had seen her once in just her panties I had never even kissed her and now she was like a dream that disappeared because I woke up. That night I went to the canvas I was working on for the portrait of Pat Rivera.

I have a third bedroom that I use for just about everything but sleeping. I didn't even have a bed in the room. When I rented the apartment, I chose a place with three bedrooms so I could have one to mess around in. I tried to keep the rest of the place fairly neat and clean but I had a habit of throwing things in the extra bedroom and not cleaning it up. The room had a desk and a big stuffed chair with a good reading light. This room was where I painted. There were shelves for paint, an easel, a storage cabinet and a place where I kept canvasses. Some of them were blank, some were partially finished and some I had started, didn't like and would never finish. I had worked on this canvas before.

When I'm doing a serious painting I always take a great deal of care in preparing my canvas. I had gotten an excellent grade and stretched it over Masonite which was cut to the size that I wanted. I had prepared two of these, each one exactly the same size, twenty four inches wide and thirty six inches high. About a week ago I had primed it with gesso, a mixture of chalk and glue. It's like a thick white paint and easy to use. I had taken a large varnish brush and put it on with huge sweeping strokes, brushing from side to side and then from top to bottom. I let each coat dry, then rubbed it with very fine sandpaper. I had done this four times. It was time-consuming but I only did it for paintings that were something special.

I had started on the painting itself. Over the years I had consciously gotten into the habit of using two types of backgrounds. When I was doing a picture of a person doing something, or with a particular expression, I tried to find a background which would relate to that person. A picture of a priest like Sidney might have a church in the background and a sailor would have the sea or a ship. When I was doing a formal portrait I usually used a plain cloud background. Sometimes a dramatic one.

The canvas was ready now with a big blank open space in the middle for Pat to be painted in. I roughed in some foliage on the extreme left of the canvas. Regardless of which photograph of her I chose, or what the exact background was, I wanted a tiny bit of the sea to be visible, and enough flowers and palm fronds to place it in a secluded part of a nature setting. The type of paintings that I did of faces was not at all the style of Gauguin, but I wanted some of that outdoors feeling.

Shortly after the trip to Bimini I had gotten back all of the photographs I had taken. I separated the two rolls of *Ojos Verdes* from the four of Pat. I marked Pat's as "before and after," meaning before she took her clothes off and after. I studied the pictures carefully and separated out all the ones that had no possibility of use from the ones that did. Then I took the rest and separated the ones that showed Pat's face up close from the ones that showed more of her body. I had then taken several from each group and had them enlarged. They were spectacular and the color was excellent. I decided to combine the two kinds. I was not sure how I wanted to set it up so I started with a drawing. I sketched in a body and then enlarged it and shrunk it until I had what I wanted. I had painted nudes before, every serious art student does at some time, but it wasn't my real interest. Faces were what intrigued me.

I sketched the head in as large as I could get it and still leave room for a lot of body. I reluctantly decided to cut off Pat's body just above the knees. I thought about cutting it off at the waist to make the face larger but I couldn't do it. This wasn't an artistic decision, it was just lust or lechery. The memory of her transparent aqua-colored panties was too vivid for me to leave them out. *Choninos bleu de cerulean verit.*

I went back to the easel and sketched out the whole picture with everything the size I wanted. The green foliage on the left side would make it appear that a voyeur was watching a woman in a secluded glade, wiggling around in her underpants. It would look like she was posing for a lover or just dancing around to tease. I had picked out seven pictures to use, three of Pat's face and three of her body and one that was a little of both. The painting was a composite of something I got from each picture.

I had done paintings from photographs many times. I had also painted attractive nude women. During the time I was in Paris I had made love to two of my models. The first time I had done it because it seemed that I was expected to. I didn't enjoy it much and I don't think the girl did, either. The second time I did it because the model made it clear that she expected it and also to be paid extra for it. She seemed to enjoy it but maybe she was just acting. I wished Pat was here in person. The feeling was strong.

As usual I worked erratically, sometimes very fast and sometimes slowly. I had started right after I got home and I worked well into the night. As I painted the picture I realized it was going to be very erotic. It wasn't just the body, although I tried to capture some of what I felt that day, it was her face. In the picture that I chose to copy, her expression was intense. Her face was turned up and her eyes partly closed. Her lips were slightly parted with her teeth showing a little and her look was one of sheer ecstacy, pure pleasure. It was not surprising that I had gotten so excited watching her wiggle and then stop and pose. As I painted I thought about how she had reacted when I suggested she pose in the nude. I was too startled at the time to realize it, but I think she enjoyed the stripping and the posing as much as I did. I knew she was terribly hot when she did it. *Muy ardiente*. The following night, when she had refused to go to my apartment with me, now seemed like a major tragedy.

I had a hard time painting her panties. I had to mix the yellow and the green and blue several times to get the exact shade of *bleu de cerulean verit* in the photograph. Then I had to paint the full color in just a few places where the sheer cloth was bunched since the material was so transparent. The pose in the picture that I used for her body, had her hip thrown out on one side like a hula dancer. Belly buttons are not supposed to be very sexy, but when I started making tiny circles with the brush just above the dark aqua line that was the elastic of Pat's panties, I realized I was very, very horny. I went in the living room and dialed her telephone number.

"Hi, Pat. This is Devlin. I've been doing an oil painting of you from the pictures I took at Bimini. I've been staring at color pictures of you for three hours now and I'm as horny as a three-ball tomcat. You look incredibly beautiful and I have decided to come over to your apartment and fuck your brains out. It is now eleven o'clock. If you get this message before one o'clock please call me. Sooner or later I'm going to get into your *choninos*."

I left the message on her answering machine and went back to the painting. I worked for another two hours before I ran out of steam. Pat didn't call and I didn't finish the picture but it was going to be one hell of a sexy painting when I did.

Chapter Twenty Three

Friday, 11 August

At the beginning of August I felt I needed to confess something to a priest. The problem was I didn't know exactly *what* to confess. The Rite of Confession has become very rare in the Anglican Church but it is still part of the religion. Today it has been pretty much replaced by counseling. I had talked to Sidney on many occasions when I wanted his advice on a point of morality or ethics but we also had a way of separating a truly "c-c-confessional discussion," as he described it with his stutter, from a regular conversation. If I wanted to have a serious talk with Sidney about some personal sin I told him I wanted to talk to him "as a priest." He would put on his "lily white necktie" as he referred to the clerical collar and talked like a priest. Sidney had been well trained in counseling and psychotherapy and he could also mix in religion with no trouble. I called him and said I wanted to talk to him "as a priest." We agreed to meet at his apartment in Coconut Grove to talk and then go out to dinner. Leaving for dinner would be the cut off point between pastoral counseling and a social evening. We had picked Friday night because St. Stephens was usually closed on Saturday.

I took the elevator up to the seventh floor and rang the bell. Just as I realized that the front door was partially open I heard him yell at me to come in. I walked in and saw Sydney lying on the rug. He had on a pair of boxer shorts and a pair of sandals on his feet. He also had on his clerical shirt and collar. He sat up.

"L-l-look at this incredible airplane," he said, waving a picture of a little two-wing beauty that looked like a stunt plane or an aerobatic plane or whatever they called them.

"Isn't it beautiful? It's called a *Pitts Special*. Now look at this. It's a photograph of the actual airplane and this is a photograph of a painting done by a friend of mine. The painting was done by Bob Jenny and it's displayed in the Smithsonian. Isn't it fabulous? Have you ever s-seen a s-sweeter airplane?"

"Who is Bob Jenny?"

"Bob's an artist who paints things the way they actually look. Nothing abstract. Nothing fake. No symbols, just real paintings and he does a lot of airplanes. He really knows a lot about them and gets the details right. Does a lot of flying himself. For some strange reason he never got credit for the painting of the *Pitts* in the Smithsonian, though."

"It looks like an airplane that Gus showed me in a magazine. I think he said he was going to buy one in kit form and actually build it himself. Is it the same airplane?" Sidney looked ridiculous sitting there on the carpet in his underpants and clerical collar but I assumed that the collar was because of me.

"Not the same airplane b-but you are right about the similarity. L-let me explain."

Sidney told me that Gus had mentioned he was going to buy and build a kit model airplane named the *Aviat Eagle*. Sidney had never heard of it but he was familiar with a plane called the *Pitts Special*. Although Sidney did not know how to fly he had always wanted to learn and had become interested in sport flying. He looked at the brochure that Gus gave him and realized that it was very much like a plane called the *Pitts Special* that he had flown in and knew about.

"This plane, the *Pitts Special*," Sidney said, pointing to a color photograph of a painting, "has been number one in world aerobatics for years. W-world championships and everything. Fantastic airplane. A guy named Frank Christenson tried to buy the business but Curtis P-pitts wouldn't sell. Frank designed a new plane and called it the *Eagle*. You can buy it in a kit like a model airplane and build it yourself."

He showed me a picture of the two flying side by side and there was little to choose between them. The *Pitts* was yellow with black trim. The *Eagle* was mostly white with an eagle emblem on the side. They were both so pretty I was amazed. I wondered whether or not I would have become a sailor if my dad had bought a *Pitts Special* instead of an Owens Cutter.

"I have decided to be Gus's partner and we're going to buy the kit and build it together," Sidney proclaimed.

"How will you find time to work on the plane? You're already involved in all sorts of stuff for the church. And what about the model railroad?"

"The model railroad is actually complete now except scenery in the valley and a few buildings. The track layout is complete with switches that work and turntables that turn. I've decided that I will solicit more help from my friends. You've built a few bridges and buildings yourself. I'll keep things going by getting some help. I also expect to pay for much more than half the cost of the plane. Paulette will get involved, of course. I'm sure of that. The two of them will do most of the work but I will handle my share by working as much as I can and paying more than they do. I might even hire somebody."

"I'll come up and watch you work. I always enjoy watching other people work."

"Let's get down to business," Sidney said, as he stood up. I assume you are here to confess to something. Before we get started I think I'll make some martinis. The gin has been on ice for several hours. It is now ready."

I flipped through the pictures of the aerobatic planes while Sidney fixed the drinks. They were truly beautiful.

"I hope you don't let the m-martinis detract from this confession, Dev. I also hope it doesn't bother you that I am listening to your c-confession in my underwear. Before we start I want to say a prayer. Let's sit down at the table."

Whatever Sidney said was in Greek and I didn't understand a word of it. He would sometimes do this when he wanted to get serious in a hurry. The effect was instantaneous and powerful. It changed the tone of our conversation from enthusiasm over the airplanes to one that was much more serious. I had never heard of any priest or minister who clowned around the way he did but underneath it he was deadly serious.

I told him about the night of the rescue. I also told him about buying the gun and learning how to shoot it before we ever went to the island. He asked a lot of questions about the pistol and the gun range.

"Sidney, I wasn't *planning* to shoot anybody when I went to the gun store. I bought it to defend myself if it became necessary. Do you think I had some sort of plan or compulsion back then?"

"No."

"Sidney, what the hell kind of priest are you anyway? I came here to confess to three murders and not to talk about guns and airplanes."

"Tell me about the shooting," he said as he poured gin from the carafe and added some vermouth.

I described how I had waited outside the door and how Snake had suddenly come out leading and half carrying Sharon. I told him the details about how I recognized the two women and decided instantly that I had to shoot them. I explained how I had shot one in the face and then shot the other one twice in the chest. Then I told him about the man.

"How did you feel when you had gotten back into the boat and had a few minutes to think about what happened? Did you feel any sense of remorse?"

"No."

"Because they were sluts or whores?"

"I don't think that was it. Those women had been holding Sharon prisoner. At least they were with the men who had. They had probably watched her being abused. The man had probably used Sharon himself."

"Did you feel any sense of triumph? Of revenge perhaps?"

"Sidney, I felt nothing. Absolutely nothing."

He didn't say anything, giving me time to think of anything else that I might have felt or thought about.

"I was amazed at how accurate I was with the Luger."

"That's all?"

"That's the only feeling I had at the time or later." Sidney took a sip of his martini.

"Dev, I think that's why you want to confess."

"What do you mean?"

"You know you killed three people and you know you should feel something but you don't. You feel guilty because you don't feel any remorse or emotion and you think you should."

"So what do I do about it?"

"We will pray and I will give you absolution for not being sorry you shot the two girls and the man."

"If you had been there would you have shot them?"

"I don't know. I truly do not know."

"What do you think you would have done?"

"To be honest, Dev, I think I would have j-j-just shit in my p-pants." We sat there looking at each other for a few minutes and then Sidney said the prayers and asked God to forgive us for what we had done. He then asked me if I was worried that the Bahamian police might somehow connect Sean with the murders. I told him that Snake was more worried about the drug people than the police. I also told him that I had gotten a few telephone calls when there was nobody on the line. I didn't think they meant anything but it was strange.

Sidney then got a letter and showed it to me. It was addressed to Mr. Sidney Fontaine and sent to his apartment. It was from Cecilia Cotten, the manager at Norman's Cay. It said that several personal items had been left in the room where they stayed and would he please contact her.

"Do you think it means anything?"

"I doubt it but I know we didn't leave anything in the room."

"I got a letter just like that addressed to Mr. Winfield Devlin but sent to the clinic. I got mine several weeks ago."

"What did you do?"

"I talked to Snake and then wrote back using stationary from the clinic. I actually had Lori send it. The letter said that Dr. Devlin had lost a pair of expensive sunglasses but that he didn't believe he had left them at Norman's Cay. How did you respond to your letter?"

"I didn't respond. I just got the letter two days ago. What do you think I should do?"

"Snake said that a lot of people go to resorts like Norman's with women and use fake addresses. I used the clinic address but you used your address in England. There is probably only one Sidney Fontaine in the whole State of Florida. If something expensive was really left in a room they would probably make a serious attempt to track you down. Why don't you write back and say that the only thing you are missing is a copy of the King James Bible?"

"Are you serious?"

"I believe that an answer like that would seem perfectly real and normal. Have you gotten any phone calls when there was nobody on the line?"

"A few but no more than I was getting before we went to Norman's Cay."

"I think we should just forget about it. Let's go eat."

After that we went out and got a sidewalk table at the Green Street. I introduced Sidney to Caroline Lancaster and he immediately invited her to come up some time to be an engineer on his H.O. railroad. She looked at me and asked if he has just escaped from some place. I explained to her that his railroad was indeed real and a marvelous thing. I also explained that the invitation was just a trick to recruit her for our church. She shook her head to indicate that she thought we were both crazy but she asked for Sidney's phone number.

We had dinner and didn't talk much while we ate. Then we went bar hopping and pub crawling all over Coconut Grove. After the second bar, I realized that Sidney was recruiting. It was an unusual way to get new members but it seemed to work. I decided to help him and before the night was over several new prospects promised to be at the service on Sunday morning. We went home late and feeling good because we were a little drunk and we had eleven new potential members.

The next Saturday morning Butch arrived at the Yacht Club at the same time I did and parked near me. We walked through the palm trees that lined the parking lot and through the clubhouse to the front lawn. We went down to the area for the boats that are dry sailed and pulled the cover off of my boat. I got a hose and washed a little dirt off and we rolled it over to the hoist. My Star was the same colors as the Hinckley, pale blue topsides, a dark blue water line and a white bottom. I called it *Starfire*. Butch seemed to know what he was doing as well as I did so we got the boat in the water with a minimum of effort.

We paddled over to one of the docks and checked out the race circulars, binoculars and other stuff and went back up to the club to use the bathroom. After that we hoisted the sail and left the club. We sailed over past the docks at Monty Trainer's and the Merrill Stevens hangar buildings and around the end of the Dinner Key dock. There was a lot of traffic going out between the two tiny islands that provided shelter from the wind at the big marina.

Dinner Key Channel is fairly long and extends pretty far out into Biscayne Bay. The Bay itself is a fabulous place for small boats. Where we race, between Key Biscayne and the mainland, was somewhat protected, but with plenty of room for one design racing.

Dinner Key Marina got its name back in the twenties when people used to bring picnic dinners down to the area. It has its place in history because Pan American Airlines built some huge hangars and a seaplane ramp for the first clippers. What is now the City Hall was originally an administration building.

The starting line that day was just to the east of the entrance to Dinner Key Channel, so we sailed back and forth near the Race Committee Boat for a while. Butch had crewed and steered Star boats enough that he didn't need any instructions and asked only a few questions about the boat. We talked about the weather and our strategy for the race. The wind was southeast, and seemed to be fairly steady around twelve to fifteen. Most of the better guys in the class were out that day and we had thirteen other boats to compete against. Two of the best, Ding Schoonmaker and John Boyer, were there.

We chose the left-hand side of the starting line although the right was slightly favored. We got clear wind at the start and moved out quickly from several boats around us. Although we experimented some before the start, we didn't have the other boats to compare with our boat-speed. Butch weighed 213 pounds and I weighed 185. We were both in good shape and had no trouble holding the boat down and getting maximum speed. Over on the right side, John Boyer, Ding Schoonmaker and Pete Cooper had moved out and seemed to be clearly in the lead. Butch suggested we move our weight aft a touch and altogether we seemed to have a little better boat-speed than the others in our area. It was a beautiful day and the bay was crowded. We held the starboard tack for a long time until I felt we were in some danger of getting to the lay line. Butch was superb. I usually encouraged my crews to hike out but he didn't need it. He wasn't as athletic as Snake but close enough. He didn't waste time talking about things other than the race. Several times after we had gone over to the port tack he offered comments when he thought we would clear the bows of boats on the starboard tack. We crossed the entire fleet except for Pete Cooper, John Boyer and Ding. All three rounded the windward mark ahead of us and we went around fourth. The wind had been very steady and a little stronger to the right since our boat-speed had been excellent.

We had a modified Gold Cup course that day and the next two legs were reaches. The wind was not quite strong enough to surf and all the positions at the front of the fleet were unchanged at the leeward mark. Cooper went around first, Ding second and John third. We were a close fourth and the rest of the fleet was behind us. Going up the second and last windward leg our speed really made a difference. Pete was sailing well but he was having a hard time holding his boat down. He had his wife aboard and she probably didn't weigh over one twenty or thirty. We passed him half way up the leg and closed up on John and Ding.

The second and last time we rounded the windward mark there was no real space between the first three boats as we were all overlapped. The leeward leg was exciting. The wind had picked up to maybe seventeen or eighteen. Broad-reaching across the bay toward the finish line, we had our booms all the way out. Although the course was dead down-wind, there was no need to jibe back and forth to increase speed. All three boats were moving at almost hull speed, nearly surfing but not quite. I was trying to steer and balance the boat as well as I could without making a mistake that would slow the boat down. With the finish only fifty yards away, Schoonmaker suddenly jibed over to starboard and changed course slightly, heading for the flag-end of the line. I hesitated for a few seconds and then jibed over myself. Even though I hadn't given any warning, Butch had no problems. John Boyer did not jibe and kept on course to the committee-boat end. When we crossed the line it was too close to know who finished first. The gun and two whistles all sounded simultaneously. Later we found out that John Boyer had gotten the gun.

We had to change course only a little to head for the marks at the end of Dinner Key Channel. Butch opened two cans of Coors and we speculated on who finished first.

"Why did we jibe over at the end?" Butch asked. "Did you see something?"

"I jibed over because Ding Schoonmaker did. I hate to admit it, but it was just a reaction to his jibing. I think I must have guessed that he saw something. I didn't think about it. I just reacted."

"Well, it was a great race, skipper, and you did a good job. I don't think we made any bad mistakes and the boat seemed to be as fast as anybody."

"You were really good, Butch. I felt sorry for Pete Cooper and his little wife. They just didn't have the weight."

"I'll bet you never feel sorry for them in a drifting match."

Butch then started clowning around and pretending he was me in a race against Pete and his lightweight wife when there was no wind and they would have the advantage. He did a real comedy act.

"Look, look. That crew doesn't weigh a hundred pounds. The boat's skimming across the water. It should be illegal. Put up a protest flag. They should have to carry ten cases of beer to make it even. I'm going to call my lawyer."

I started it too and we both acted silly for a while. There was no real reason, it had just been an excellent race and we were both exhilarated and feeling good. Butch had a wonderful and gentle sense of humor. He made fun of everything, including himself, but he never ridiculed other people. I wondered again, as I had before, whether he acted the clown to make it easier for him and Ricardo to work together. I didn't know him well enough yet to ask a personal question about his father but I did want to know more about the search for the statue so I decided to ask.

"Do you get involved in Ricardo's searches for paintings and statues and things?"

"No. I could never get interested in paintings or rare art or any of that sort of stuff, but my father spends hours reading books about it. I don't think he does it for profit even. He sells something once in a while but I think he just does it when he gets tired of a painting. Some of the stuff he collects is really beautiful, but some of it is ugly as hell. My mother thinks it's all kind of silly. Sometimes she will tell my father how beautiful a painting is and then wink at me. Personally I have no judgement. If I really like a painting or a vase or something it's usually worthless."

"What's so special about the statue? It didn't sound like the museum at Tours put a lot of value on it."

"I don't know. I think he believes there really is some kind of valuable thing inside the base of the statue."

"Like diamonds or something?"

"Maybe. I think more like information. Maybe like the Ark of the Covenant or the Dead Sea Scrolls. Some historical shit."

"It's really an interesting story."

"Every damn thing Ricardo comes up with has an interesting story. You hear one story you've heard them all. Once, a long time ago, he had Snake's father chasing all over the Far East for a frowning Buddha. Papa should have been a professor. Right now I think he's more interested in that sort of stuff than he is in the family business."

We had opened a second beer and passed through the two little islands that provide the shelter for Dinner Key Marina. As we sailed across the short distance past Merrill Stevens docks I was surprised at what Butch said next.

"When we were in Bimini you mentioned that someday you were going to try to open a clinic for craniofacial surgery. Do you have a plan?"

"I don't have any plan. I don't even remember mentioning it in Bimini. It's something I've thought about for a long time but at this point it's more of a daydream."

"What would you need to be able to do it?"

"It would require three things, two actually."

"Doctors and money. A third would be the patients, of course, but enough publicity would get the patients. Unfortunately, most of the people who are severely disfigured don't seem to have any money. There are plenty of women with money who want big tits but severe problems and being poor seem to go together."

"I'm mentioning this for a reason, Dev. My father is going to bring up the subject and I wanted you to know in advance."

"What do you mean by bringing up the subject?"

"He's going to offer to advance you some money for a clinic. I want you to be prepared so you don't hurt his feelings by refusing."

By this time we had gotten in to the dock and stopped the conversation to put the boat away. I had gotten a slip that was a little longer than I needed for my forty foot yawl so I would have some extra room to tie up the Star. On Saturday nights, when I would be racing again the next day, I left the boat in the water. When I came in on Sunday evening I would haul it out again. We tied it up between an outer piling and the stern of *Brilliant*. We put a cover over the cockpit in case it rained, and walked up on the lawn. It was a fast race so it was early. We got drinks from the bar and sat down on the grass. The lawn was crowded with people who had been racing or swimming in the pool. I could smell rum and salt air and suntan oil and perfume all at the same time. I loved the atmosphere. Butch brought up the clinic again.

"My father heard you mention a craniofacial clinic so he sent me to the library to do some research. I usually hate that sort of shit. I also hated it at Amherst but I do know how to do it. I read about Tessier and some of the others. It was interesting. I always think of plastic surgery as old women getting their wrinkles smoothed out or young women getting plastic boobs. I don't mean any disrespect for your profession but I just wasn't aware of what could be done. Tessier must have been a genius. Why did you get into that field instead of some other specialty?"

I told Butch the story about going to Paris and meeting the photographer and all about the "before and after" pictures. He listened to me carefully.

"You must get a great deal of satisfaction from some of the cases. I heard about the Winter kid who got cut up with the outboard motor. How's he doing today?"

"He looks good. Not quite the same but just as good. That was one of my best efforts." Butch had been serious since he first mentioned the clinic but the clown in him had to come out.

"Why don't you hire me as an assistant. I would like to specialize in examining women's breasts after they have been enlarged and completely healed. I can do a complete exam with both hands and assure the ladies that their new set is perfect. I can get a hat that says 'quality control inspector'."

"You're not the first guy to offer that service. I've had lots of volunteers for examining women."

"Seriously, Dev, I think Papa would like to put up some money for a clinic and I think he will mention it tonight. If you aren't serious let me tell him not to do it. He would be embarrassed to make the offer and have you refuse."

"Butch, I'm not in a position to accept or reject an offer like that. A craniofacial clinic is just an idea. It's not a plan or a project. I don't even know how much money it would cost."

"Bullshit, I'll bet you have a very good idea as to the size of a building and the number of doctors. I'll bet you think about a new clinic all the time."

"That's not true, Butch, I think about *chocha* all the time."

"I'm serious, Dev, he is going to bring it up."

"If your father brings it up I'll tell him as much as I can. I won't say no to it, of course, but I can't accept, either. I would have to do much more work before I even know that it's practical for Miami."

After that unexpected discussion we talked about sailboats and politics and football. He told me that they had a good trip to Nassau after they left Bimini. Carmela came over and they decided to buy a house there. I tried to think back to the Bimini trip but I could not remember ever talking about a craniofacial surgery clinic. We decided that we would shower at the club and put on clean clothes before Butch picked up his date for the night so I showed him to the men's locker room and we both changed. He suggested I ride with him when he went to pick her up.

After we were dressed we drove in Butch's white Cadillac out to Coral Gables to an apartment there. His date was an English girl in her late twenties who was a medical student. Her name was Alice Grey and I liked her immediately but I didn't know exactly why. She wanted to know about the race that day and where we were going to dinner. Butch explained that I was a cosmetic surgeon and that I was the host that night at the Yacht Club. I asked her a few questions about her training in England and we drove back to the Club. We got drinks and sat in some chairs on the porch. The others showed up a few minutes after we sat down.

It was a pleasant night with a lot of kidding and laughing. Although there were some conversations that included all six people, most of the talking was Carmela, Toni and myself while Butch and his father talked with Alice. Carmela immediately brought up the painting of Toni that I had asked to do and pinned me down to a time when I could start. She said that Toni would soon be returning to Spain. The three of us talked in Spanish although Toni mentioned that she had taken some lessons in English during the summer and said a few things for practice. After we discussed the painting, Carmela started asking questions about me and where I had grown up. I didn't like to talk about myself much but she made it pleasant. When we left the porch to go into the dining room I had a feeling that Carmela was giving Toni a lesson in how to flatter a man by asking him questions about himself. She was very good at it, and I was flattered.

At dinner we talked about all sorts of things. Carmela and Ricardo went out of their way to make Alice Grey feel comfortable but it was not obvious to her and I'm sure she was enjoying herself. Butch told a few stories that I had never heard and as always he was the clown. I found myself wishing that I could be a little more like him and I had my opportunity during dessert.

Alice had asked a lot of questions about sailing and boats. When someone mentioned the *Ojos Verdes* she asked what the words meant and why they called it that.

"It means green eyes and we named it after Dr. Devlin," Ricardo said, laughing and making fun of my green eyes. "Seriously Alice, *Green Eyes* is a very famous Spanish poem by one of our greatest poets. You English have the wonderful old madrigal, *Greensleeves*, and the Americans have *Brown Eyes*. Do you know that song?" Butch sang the first few lines and laughed.

"How about you, Dr. Devlin. Tell me the name of your boat and why you picked the name," Alice asked.

"My boat is called the *Brilliant*. I named it after a famous old schooner that was built in 1932 and donated to the Mystic Seaport Museum. It's fully commissioned and is tied up to a dock in Mystic, Connecticut."

"Why did you pick that particular name? Do you consider yourself to be particularly brilliant?" I think she was teasing.

"When I was at Yale I used to date a lot of girls from the Connecticut College for Women. One afternoon I went there with a date but the museum had just closed for the day. We came back after dark and found a way to get into the grounds. The *Brilliant* was tied to a dock and we went aboard. We sat in the cockpit drinking beer. After that I used to go there with girls on a regular basis. I never got caught."

"Did you ever make love on the boat?" Alice teased.

"Brilliantly," I said feeling very clever.

"You are lucky the Coast Guard didn't catch you," Ricardo said laughing. He then told Alice Grey about my adventure with the Coast Guard Academy. He obviously enjoyed telling the story.

We decided to have brandy on the porch so the ladies went to the bathroom while the waiter was bringing them. We stayed at the table and Ricardo brought up the clinic. He handed me an envelope.

"Dev, this is some information I have gathered about setting up a clinic for craniofacial surgery. I have approached it from a cynical point of view as I do anything that involves money. Do not be offended. Of course, you did not ask for any help but my people are used to evaluating things from a skeptical point of view. Look the papers over. The basic idea is that this clinic could become self-supporting, or almost self-supporting in ten years. I apologize for the personal things. My people do a check on anyone I am thinking of doing any business with. It is similar to the checks done by your F.B.I. in getting security clearance for military secrets. It is similar but much more thorough. I do not have the same ability to recover from and cover up mistakes that national governments seem to have."

Ricardo was smoking one of those black skinny cigars and he looked very serious. Again he reminded me of a general or an emperor. I was always aware of his physical presence.

"I have a great many things going on in various parts of the world. I find that I get better results by giving people freedom to make decisions themselves. The decisions that they make are ones that involve *my* money and, of course, *my* family. I place much trust in people, but I find that I sleep better if I check out the people before I have to trust them. Do you understand? Please do not be offended." He looked me in the eye and lowered his voice.

"I have an enormous budget for security. Can you guess what the largest expense is? Can you guess what costs the most security money?"

I silently moved my head sideways because I hadn't the slightest idea.

"Keeping track of Butch. It costs me millions just to make sure he doesn't destroy all of my businesses. I'll have a report in my hands tomorrow morning detailing exactly where he goes when he leaves here tonight with Miss Alice

Grey. It will tell everything. I already know everything about Alice Grey. I have the report here in my pocket."

I was confused for a few seconds and then realized that Ricardo had switched from being serious to teasing Butch. He pulled out a piece of paper and pretended to read. Butch rolled his eyes.

"'Extremely Confidential. Subject named Alice Grey. Born in Nottingham, England. Medical student. *Muy Guapa. Tiéne unas buenas nalgas!*'"

The ladies had come back from the bathroom and Alice heard the last sentence.

"I heard you mention my name," Alice said. "What does *muy guapa* mean? What are *tiéne unas buenas nalgas?*"

"Butch will explain later," Ricardo said, laughing.

Carmela and Toni looked at each other.

I was laughing at Ricardo and his fake security reports and planned to ask Butch later how he explained things to Alice. *Muy guapa* means real nice stuff and *tiéne unas buenas nalgas* means she has a splendid ass.

We sat on the porch for a while sipping brandy and talking. Ricardo started telling Alice and me about the ranch where he raised fighting bulls and about the *corrida de toros*. Having heard it all before, the others moved away. He was a splendid talker on many subjects but he seemed to relish talking about this more than anything I had heard before, even art. I knew very little about it and Alice seemed to know less. He described in detail how the *banderillas* were carefully placed to irritate the bull and not to hurt him. They were actually barbed darts that were placed two at a time in the back of the bull's neck. The bull tried to shake them loose, which tired him. Everything was done to wear down the massive neck muscles so that the matador could go in over the horns to place the tip of the sword in exactly the right spot. He said it was painless if it was done correctly.

"How about the guys on horses, the ones with the long lances? That must hurt like hell!" I said.

"The lance is called a *pica* and the tip is designed to penetrate only an inch or two. The picador is not supposed to wound the bull, only to irritate the neck muscle. However, the horses are occasionally gored," he conceded. "Sometimes a very poor *picador* will stick the lance into the bull's ribs. It is an ugly thing and not at all correct."

"How does the *matador* decide when to kill the bull?" I asked. I wasn't sure how I felt about bull fights but I did find it fascinating.

"There is a sequence of things that happens. All of it is designed to tire the neck muscle of the bull but there is a time limit. In about twenty minutes the bull realizes that it is the man he should be after and not the cape. Sometimes a very brave bull will be allowed to live."

I glanced at Alice while Ricardo was talking. I had heard someplace, probably a Hemingway novel, that women got very excited at watching bullfights. Many wanted to make love immediately after and some even had orgasms while watching. From the look on Alice's face, Ricardo's description was going to make things easy for Butch later on that night.

"Do the matadors ever get too scared to perform?" I asked.

"Occasionally. Not very often. That's what the whole thing is about. It is a test of the man's courage and is not a cruel spectacle or a sport. It is the man against himself. When it is done correctly it is a thing of beauty. Not cruel at all."

At this point Butch asked me to come over for a minute. Ricardo had heard him so I just excused myself and walked over. Alice Grey kept on listening to Ricardo, apparently fascinated. Butch said he had a suggestion about the tuning of my Star boat and started talking about the tension on my shrouds. We were out of earshot of the others but after about five minutes I suddenly heard Ricardo shouting.

"You know nothing of Spanish culture. You should have better sense than to make judgements when you are totally ignorant. How dare you question what I say!"

Just as I turned toward them Alice ran off the porch and inside the Yacht Club. Antonia and Carmela were just coming back from looking around the Club and they went after her. I had never heard Ricardo raise his voice before and I was startled. Butch whispered to me, "Oh, shit. Alice probably told him she thought bullfights were cruel. It has happened before. My father is very sensitive about our Spanish culture, especially the *corrida*. Actually, I think the bullfights are a little cruel myself but I would never say so."

Ricardo came over to where we were talking but he said nothing so we talked about Star boat racing. In a few minutes the ladies came back and we all acted as if nothing had happened. Around eleven Carmela suggested that it was time for them to leave and I walked out to their car with them to say goodnight. I was sleeping on my boat and wouldn't be going anywhere. I had been very nice to Toni all night, talking to her and treating her like a date. I enjoyed being with her. She hadn't said much but she did speak English, sometimes mixing in Spanish with it. I confirmed again the appointment to start painting her portrait and said I was looking forward to it.

When I got back to the porch Alice and Butch were having a drink. She asked if she could come by and see our clinic and I gave her the telephone number. She seemed to have recovered from the incident with Ricardo. We talked a little longer and Butch said he wanted to make a quick trip to the men's room. Alice and I talked while we waited for him.

"It's none of my business, Alice, but I can't help wondering what Ricardo was shouting about. I was part of the conversation until a few minutes before that. What the hell happened?"

"He asked me if I would like to see a bullfight sometime and I tried to be tactful and still honest. I said I thought it would be very exciting but I didn't understand it and I thought it was cruel to the animals. He went crazy and said that I understood nothing about Spanish history or culture. He said that the British were a bunch of faggots."

"I heard him say, 'you know nothing of Spanish culture. You should have better sense than to make judgements when you are totally ignorant. How dare you question what I say!' Was that the whole thing?"

"No. He called me a British *puta*. I *don't* want to know what that means."

After I walked up to the car with them and said goodnight, I went back to the boat to go to sleep. It was a beautiful night with a bright moon and a gentle breeze. I thought about Rocket and wished she was with me.

A few days later I picked up Otto at the airport. We went back to my apartment and sat around the pool for most of the afternoon talking. He went into great detail about Sharon and how well she was doing which made me glad I had chosen cosmetic surgery instead of psychiatry. What sounded like permanent psychological damage to me was quite different for him. I wondered if either Snake or I would have realized her need for extensive psychotherapy. Otto had a full schedule for the next few days, having convinced himself that a move to Miami made sense. He had appointments with old friends and acquaintances who he thought would be helpful and I had also set up some interviews.

Leaving New Haven quickly would hurt him financially because he couldn't get his full asking price for his practice. He seemed determined, however, and Bill and I decided to let him use office space in our clinic for about six months to make it easier.

It was a pleasant visit and we found we had a lot to talk about. We had breakfast every morning at one of my favorites and dinner each night at a different place. Otto drove around all day Monday in my green car then got a rental. He said there were so many comments he was getting an inferiority complex.

When he walked into the clinic, Lori Young greeted Otto like an old friend, with hugs and everything. When she learned that he was going to be with us for six months she immediately proclaimed herself his appointments secretary and started keeping a calendar for him. Lori had become very close to Sharon in the week we had her at the clinic and she knew that Otto had taken it on himself to take care of her.

I asked Otto about his house up at Stratton and found out he was going to keep it. He said that the value of the house was going up so fast that it made no sense to sell it. He would rent it for most of the year and use it himself for two or three weeks at Christmas. He suggested I come up then. He had already listed it with rental agents.

On Thursday night I took him to the Café Europa for what was the most interesting night of his visit. Otto had a *Bouillabaise* which he described with tears in his eyes as "simply sublime." I had *Coq au Vin*. I introduced him to Renee and Henri, the couple who owned and operated the restaurant, and they gave us special attention. I knew that Otto had been working on a book for quite awhile but I never knew what it was about, so I asked.

"It's about the longest war, Devlin. That's actually the title of the book. It's a complicated and confusing book but it's easy to describe. It starts out in Rome on the day that the Emperor Constantine made Christianity legal. Since that time there has been a war between Christians and their allies on one side and pagans and their allies on the other side."

I didn't understand what he was talking about so I asked him to elaborate.

"Western civilization has been built on two things, Greek culture, which the Romans adopted, and Christianity. Greek culture, that is the old Greek culture, is pagan. There are Christian countries that do pagan things and vice versa but the war goes on anyway. It has lasted for two thousand years."

"How do you draw the line? It's very confusing."

"Actually, you can draw the line between a contraceptive and an abortifacient but let me describe it in terms of a belief system. If you believe in God, then you believe in certain things. You believe that the visible world is part of a more spiritual world from which it draws its chief significance. You believe that union or harmonious relation with that higher universe is our true end. You also believe that prayer or inner communion with the spirit, who you call God, is a process wherein work is really done, and spiritual energy flows in and produces effects, psychological or material, within the phenomenal world. If you believe in prayer then you believe that somebody is listening. You believe that God is listening.

"What do you believe?"

"Let me finish. To believe in God, of course, does not make you a Christian. What Christians believe is stated and explained very well in your Nicene Creed. That's the one they wrote before the Romans split off from the main church.

"What position do you take in your book?"

"The book is neutral or at least tries to be. I'm a pagan, personally. People use words like atheist and agnostic because it sounds better but pagan is more accurate because pagans such as me have other gods like Bacchus and Midas.

While we're talking about religion, let me ask you something. Did you know that Sean Moran spent several years in a seminary studying for the priesthood?"

"I didn't know that. I thought he spent most of his time going around with his father learning the art business. It's hard for me to imagine him in a highly disciplined place like a seminary. Did he finish or drop out or what?"

"Apparently he dropped out just before ordination – just before he was to take his final vows. I've spent many hours talking to Sharon about her past and naturally I learned a lot about Sean. Let me tell you something. I'm speaking as both a psychiatrist and as a friend. I want to warn you about Sean.

"There's something about him and his past that worries me. I can't put my finger on it and I don't understand it. I can give you this advice, though. Don't get involved with Sean or any more of his adventures. You see things as black and white. You are somewhat predictable or at least consistent. Weird, of course, but consistent. Sean is a mystery and I believe there is a dangerous side to his personality. You can be his friend without getting involved. A person who sees things as you do would have no choice about helping him rescue Sharon. You had to do that. But stop there. Sean is in a very strange profession but there's more to it."

"Do you think he's crazy? Actually a little psychotic or something like that?"

"Maybe." Has he ever mentioned an organization called the *Prostates Tou Christu?*

Sean never did but Patricia Rivera thinks Ricardo Salazar and Sean are both looking for a statuette that has something to do with an organization by that name. It means Bodyguards of the Christ right?

Otto nodded his head yes but he changed the subject. We didn't mention Sean Moran again and finished the evening talking about the Dolphins and Patriots.

We didn't mention Sean Moran again and finished the evening talking about the Dolphins and Patriots. I was still a little in awe of Otto and thought he was a brilliant man. I also trusted him completely. Because of this I usually tried to kid around with him, to try perhaps to put us on the same level. I knew that Otto could be invaluable to me as a mentor or *rabbi* but I also wanted him to be a friend. I wasn't much interested in psychology but I did understand a few things.

"Otto, I've noticed the last few days that you never lose an opportunity to hug Lori Young. I believe that being together in the clinic when we were detoxing Sharon made us all feel close and I understand that. But is it possible that your affection for Lori might be caused by an unresolved Oedipus conflict or perhaps a Lolita-type obsession?"

I said it with a straight face.

"Certainly not. She has an incredible pair of hooters. I never lose an opportunity to squeeze them against me. Because I'm a pagan I never lose an opportunity for a little sensual pleasure." Otto was quite serious. At least I think he was.

Friday morning I drove to the clinic with Otto and went to work while Lori took him to the airport. I was very happy that he was going to be coming to Miami.

Chapter Twenty Four

Saturday Morning, 26 August
Saturday morning I went out jogging for a while and took a quick swim in the pool. After my swim I was unlocking the door to my apartment when I heard the phone start ringing. I got it in the middle of the fourth ring but when I said "Devlin here" there was no response. After almost a minute of repeating myself somebody at the other end hung up. This had been happening three or four times a week for almost a month. I knew it was probably coincidence but I couldn't help wondering if there was some guy like the Billy Goat on the other phone. Snake had said do nothing.

By nine o'clock I had taken a shower, finished breakfast, and put on a Hawaiian shirt and jeans. I stared at the completed painting of Pat Rivera in her panties. Just looking at it made me horny. I hid it and replaced it with a blank canvas carefully prepared for a portrait of Toni. She showed up a few minutes after nine and I offered her a cup of coffee. We sat down at the counter in my kitchen.

"Have I dressed properly for the painting?"

"You look terrific but you've got more makeup than usual. Why did you put on so much rouge?"

"I decided I wanted to look like Carmen in the opera. I have seen it many times and have gone backstage a few times with my parents in Madrid. Twice I have met the ladies who had the role of Carmen. I guess I wanted to look like them. Of course they had on lots of makeup. Do you want me to remove some of it?" Toni was speaking both English and Spanish, sometimes mixing the words in one sentence.

"No, leave it on this morning. After we finish today I can think about it and tell you what to do for the next sitting." Toni had on a white peasant blouse and black skirt. When I looked closely at her face I could see immediately where she had used different makeup. Her eyebrows were dark enough and heavy enough that she didn't need mascara but she had used eye shadow. Not much, but enough to make her look a little older and perhaps a little more sensuous. The color was a startling shade of burgundy which had been chosen carefully to blend with her dark lipstick and the rouge. All three were a wine color and produced a stunning effect that was both lewd and appealing.

Many of my patients had problems that required a series of operations so I had learned about makeup. I could advise them and suggest ways to improve their appearance between operations or prior to the final healing. For eyes that were grey or blue I knew that experts recommended such colors as blue, violet, beige, grey and also burgundy but for a Spanish girl of only twenty it seemed like an unusual choice.

The thing that surprised me was the rouge. Her complexion was tanned and a little lighter and rosier than *café au lait*. It was remarkable for it's nearly perfect satiny finish and the color and texture did not need any embellishments. The tiny dab of rouge on her cheeks made her look a little cheap but then maybe she wanted to look cheap. Maybe she wanted to look sexy. Women are very complicated.

"Let me just sit and stare at you for a few minutes, Toni. I want to think about how to ask you to pose. You don't have to sit still or anything. Have some coffee or some Danish pastry."

We sat there facing each other across the counter and I remembered the first time I met her at Chub Cay. I was preoccupied with Butch and his unusual looks but I had examined her features. Antonia was a classic beauty who usually had very little expression on her face. Her eyes were that unusual color, the grey with the tint of green. The black eyebrows were so well shaped they needed no plucking or defining.

I realized that her face was not a classic oval. In doing a preliminary sketch I would have to block out more of a triangle, almost a diamond shape. Her cheekbones were slightly high and wide, just enough to highlight her eyes, which were accented by very long lashes. I looked at people's faces and speculated on possible changes or improvements, but to even contemplate a change to Antonia's face would be a sacrilege.

When I looked at beautiful women I seldom, if ever, thought about surgery but I usually thought about painting them and about going to bed with them. With Toni I realized I had never thought about anything but a portrait. I wondered why and guessed it was a combination of her age, the protectiveness of the Salazars and perhaps the fact that she talked so little.

I decided to do a preliminary sketch before I asked her to pose so we went into the other room. I would use it to lay out the canvas. I got a pad and drew the vertical and horizontal lines to get the shape correct. While I was drawing her cheekbone I made an unconscious decision to paint the exact shade of burgundy she had on for the eye shadow, rouge and lipstick. My decision about the color was not because of the lines on the paper but because of the color of her brassiere.

The white peasant blouse was modest and the burgundy kerchief around her neck was also, but I could see through the thin cotton of the blouse and she had on a wine-colored bra. For a girl that wore plain white cotton schoolgirl underpants, a bra of any color but white was startling.

"I think I will paint you exactly as you are, Toni. You will sit with your body and shoulders half turned to your right. Then you will look directly at my eyes. As usual there will be little expression on your face except your eyes and eyebrows. You have beautiful eyebrows and they are very expressive. I want to try to get a certain look in your eyes. This is the angle I want to get. Is it all right with you?"

I showed her the small rough sketch I had done so she could see how to turn her head.

"You can do anything you want with me, Dr. Devlin." She did answer my question but the words she chose sounded like she meant something else.

"Finish your coffee and I'll be ready in just a minute. I want to set up the canvas."

After I got things ready I had her sit on the chair that I usually used for painting people and then got her body and head aimed in the right direction. I told her to just look straight ahead while I got started. I had her look at me a few times the way I wanted for the picture but it was too intense and too uncomfortable to hold for very long. When I did the eyes I would have her look at me. I finished the rough sketch and then looked at her and back at the sketch.

She *was* a classic beauty and the look was perfect. Her face was without expression except the eyes. It was the way she looked most of the time I had been with her. Kind of serene and calm and above it all. I knew I had what I wanted. And then I suddenly changed my mind. *I wanted something else. I wanted to paint a different kind of picture.* I started yelling at her.

"Goddammit Antonia, try to smile! Get some expression on your face and look like you're alive! Right now you look like a corpse!" I said it on an impulse.

Her grey eyes went almost white in anger and a flush came to her skin. Her delicate nostrils flared and for a second it looked as if she were going to snarl at me or jump up and attack me. I hadn't seen Toni really angry before and I was a little surprised at the change in her face. She was no less beautiful and perhaps even more so, but very different. I stood up and apologized.

"Forgive me, Toni. I did that for a reason but I hadn't planned it. It just happened spontaneously but I do know what made me do it."

I sat on the arm of the stuffed chair and tried to tell her how I had always wanted to paint faces with expression. At one time it was the thing I most wanted to do. I still liked to do it but in many ways it was harder to do than a picture of someone sitting still. I explained all this to Toni. I told her she would look very beautiful in a classic pose but I also tried to explain another kind of painting.

"Imagine you really are Carmen in the opera. Imagine how she would look dancing or fighting with someone or even laughing. I think a picture of you with some animated expression on your face would be superb. A wild look on your face would make an exceptional picture. You have a kind of serene beauty that doesn't need a lot of expression but I'll bet every photograph of you looks that way. Do you understand what I mean? Would you like a painting of yourself with a wild gypsy look on your face? Which do you think you prefer? We can do it either way. I don't know how we could get you to look wild but we could try. What do you think I should do?"

"I think you should make love to me, Devlin," she said in Spanish. "Find out for yourself what I look like when I am wild. I don't even know myself. I am a virgin and I have never had a man make love to me. I might be too wild to paint but I also might just cry."

I was speechless. All I could do was sit there and stare at her. My Spanish was good enough to know exactly what she had said. I wasn't at all surprised that she was a virgin but I was completely startled at what she suggested. And I didn't know what to do or say. I just sat and stared.

"I would love to have a painting of myself that you painted, because you would be the artist. My family can afford to have all the paintings I want done by the greatest artists in Europe. Pictures or portraits or whatever. I was excited about coming here today so I could have all day alone with you. I am a virgin and I want you to be the man who does it to me first."

I went over and got myself a cup of coffee and offered a cup to Toni. I was stalling because I hadn't the slightest idea what I would do or say. I came back and sat on the arm of the chair.

"Toni, sometimes young girls think they're in love with older men when they really aren't. I am very flattered that you feel that way about me. I really am. I can't tell you how much I'm flattered. But it's not really love, Toni. In America it's called a schoolgirl crush. I don't know what you would call it in Spanish. Maybe *capricho*. Crush means something else in English but if a young woman has a strong feeling for an older man that seems like love but really isn't, they call it a crush."

"I know about the schoolgirl crush, Devlin. Carmela told me all about it when I told her I was in love with you. Then she explained it all to me."

"Did Carmela have any idea what you came here for today?"

"She knew why I came. I did not tell her, but she knew anyway. Butch and Ricardo do not know, of course. She will not tell them."

"Didn't she try to talk you out of it?"

"No. I think she secretly approves of what I am doing."

"Toni, we've got to talk about this. I think you are a wonderful girl but I think of you as a girl. I am much older and I'm not in love with you. I think of you as a kid sister the way that Butch does. I don't think of you as someone to make love to. It would seem wrong. I like you too much."

"Do you not like some of the women that you go to bed with?"

"If I'm not in love with a woman, or at least think I might be, then I don't want to go to bed with them. I'm what is called a very old fashioned man. Liking and loving are not the same."

"Do you like Rocket as a friend or are you in love with her?"

"I like her now very much but at one time I thought I was in love with her."

"Did you like her very much the night of Ricardo's party or were you still in love with her?"

"It was over by that time, Toni. We were just very good friends. I invited her to the party because she had met you and Butch at Chub Cay."

"I think you did it to her at the party, Devlin. If she was just a good friend why did you do it to her?"

"Why do you think we did anything that night?"

"When we were at the sand beach by the swimming pool, after the party, I was watching you. I saw you kiss her. Then you both went around the corner of the rocks and you were gone a very long time. I think you did it to her in the bathhouse. After you came back to the beach I went to the bathhouse and there were some *choninos pink* on the floor. I think they belonged to Rocket and I think you did it to her there."

I didn't know how to handle this. I didn't know what to say but I knew I was starting to get in deep. If I didn't call it off quick I would be in too far.

"Toni, you're right. Rocket and I were in love once and we had made love to each other many times. That night was just an accident. We got careless. It was a mistake. I don't want to make another mistake."

"I want you to do it to me, Dev. It won't be a mistake."

"But I'm not in love with you, Toni. Not the way you want."

"I know that. It's one of the reasons why I want you to be the first one."

I was not used to analyzing my feelings and I didn't know what I felt. Lots of different things at one time. I didn't want to reject her and hurt her. I really did like her and I guess I liked her even more because of what she was doing. She had always seemed so quiet and shy. I was startled and I knew what she was doing had been planned so I tried a different approach.

"Antonia, in a few weeks you're going to be back in Madrid. You're going to forget me very quickly. You might regret what we did. You're not really in love with me."

"You are right, Devlin, I am not in love with you. It is only a schoolgirl crush. But I never had a real crush before, even a little one, and I didn't know what it was like until now. I don't think it could really feel any better than what I feel today. I am almost twenty-one and I am ready. In America girls start doing it when they are twelve. In my social class in Spain it is very different and I personally have been protected more than even my friends. I have been protected more than Carlotta and that is a lot. Think how exciting it will be for me to remember my first real crush and how you made love to me. I will remember everything for the rest of my life even if it hurts a little. I will remember every detail. I am very excited."

I realized it was going to happen in spite of what I was saying. It would be impossible for any man to talk about making love with a girl as beautiful as Antonia and not become excited. I had been too startled by what she was saying to be aware of it but the feeling had started long before the conversation. It might have even started that night on *Ojos Verdes* when she slipped on the companionway stairs. A man cannot think about what kind of underpants a girl wears without thinking about her. Even white cotton little girl underpants.

"Did you wear the burgundy-colored eye shadow and the rouge to look like Carmen or because of something else?"

"I wanted to look sexy so you would think about making love to me. Maybe I wanted to look a little bit wild, like an American bombo. My brassiere is also the same color." She paused for a few seconds. "My panties are the same color as the rouge. Would you like to see them."

She started pulling up the long skirt. Not slowly like in a strip-tease but almost. She was sitting in the straight wooden chair that I used for posing portraits and she pulled the long black skirt up above her waist. She did it with an innocent look on her face as if she were showing me a new pair of shoes but I glanced at her eyes and I knew she was teasing. It wasn't the teasing of an older woman who knew from experience what effect pulling up her dress would have. It was more like a kid trying something for the first time. Her panties were full cut with lace trim around the edges and the same burgundy shade as her lipstick and eyeshadow. I stared very hard and said nothing.

"*Bueno, ya que terminó de inspeccionar el encaje de mis pantaletas, le gustaría ver el yate?*" As soon as she said this we both started laughing. It was exactly the same thing she had said when she slipped on *Ojos Verdes* and I had stared at her panties when her dress came up. "Now that you have examined the details of my panties would you like to see the boat?"

"That was pretty funny. I thought you were very upset that I stared so long. I did apologize. Remember?"

"I was very embarrassed but I also thought it was exciting. Just like in the American movies. I thought you might start kissing me."

"What would you have done if I had?"

"Whatever you told me to do."

"Do you wish I had?"

"No, I was too scared then. I am not so frightened now. Just a little bit. Should I take my clothes off? Would you like to see me naked?"

"Yes, but not now. Pull your skirt down and let's go in the living room. If you have never done this before we have to talk about it a little."

I decided the best way to start was to sit on the couch and begin by kissing her. I think most girls lose it in the back seat of a car or on a couch but I didn't think my ugly green car would be appropriate. Just before I kissed her she started laughing.

"I don't know what to do with my mouth. I have been kissed a few times by boys at school and I always kept my lips together. I have seen American movies, though, and those people open their mouths very wide. Tell me what to do."

"Put your lips together when I first kiss you, then open them a little if you want. You'll know what to do."

I decided to move very slowly with Toni and not rush it. We had all day. I put my arm around her and started. I was very conscious and aware of everything. My senses were just as sharp as on mornings when I have surgery. I was determined to be as careful and precise as I was then. Rocket had told me I was a skillful lover but that I made love with no emotion or passion, like an undertaker or mortician. Sometimes when her excitement would get ahead of my actions she would say things like, "Hey Mortician, put your hands down here. I'm a hot lady not a corpse." Things like that.

Since I had kissed only three women in the past year I could not help making comparisons. Kissing Toni was like kissing a young girl, kissing Pat Rivera like kissing an excited woman and kissing Rocket was like kissing a Rocket.

I decided very consciously that I would try to determine Antonia's level of excitement and move carefully with her instead of getting ahead of her. I concentrated hard on trying to know what she was feeling. She kept her lips together but her arms were squeezing me hard. After awhile I noticed that she had not worn any perfume. Since she had planned to seduce me I was a little surprised. After kissing her for awhile I stopped.

"Open your lips a tiny bit," I said.

She did what I said and I realized she was really enjoying it. Since I had noticed the absence of perfume I was very much aware of her smell. If they put the fragrance in a bottle it would be called "Young Girl." All men would understand the name and would buy it and sniff it like glue.

After I had kissed her some more she parted her lips even more and I touched them with my tongue. She pulled away suddenly and looked at me.

"Don't you like what I am doing?"

"Yes, I like it very much. It feels very funny, almost like electricity. Do it some more. Should I do it to you?"

"Yes, if you think you would like it."

I kept on kissing her, not knowing exactly what to do first. I put my hand on her breast and squeezed and then changed my mind and put my hand on her knee. If she had on perfume I might not have noticed the smell so soon. It was exciting.

I moved my fingertips very slowly up the inside of her leg, up under her skirt. I have been told by some women that it is more exciting to have a man's hand under her dress than it is with no dress. I moved my hand very slowly so as not to frighten her but eventually my fingertips reached the thin strip of her nylon panties. I brushed lightly where the cloth was puffed out with the soft wetness inside. She pulled her mouth away from mine.

"Devlin," she asked intently, "is Rocket really good at doing it? I bet she is. I think she is wonderful and I think you should marry her as soon as possible. I wish I could be more like her. Is she good at making love?"

"Stop talking and let me take your skirt off."

She helped me while I unfastened it at the waist and then raised her hips while I took it off. She looked like something out of a magazine. Her beautiful face no longer had a classic look. I had licked and kissed the burgundy lipstick off but the rouge was still there as well as a little bit of a flush in her cheeks. Her lips were parted and very wet. I kissed her some more and then asked her to open her eyes.

"I want to watch your eyes when I do this, Toni. I want to watch your face. Just let your feelings show."

I unbuttoned the lacy white blouse and opened it up exposing the burgundy-colored brassiere. She still had her big silver earrings on and the burgundy scarf around her neck. I had my left arm around her neck and my right hand between her legs. I had been tickling the inside of her thigh and the outside of her panties with my fingertips. While I stared at her I put my whole hand between her legs and squeezed and rubbed the squishy wet nylon and soft flesh underneath. When I started squeezing she opened her eyes wide. The unusual grey color with the green tint grew brilliant. Her black eyelashes seemed to be even longer than before. She squirmed while I played with her *chucha* and then she stopped me.

"Stop, Devlin. I want you to make love to my breasts before you do anything else. I want you to see them and kiss them before you do the other things. Nobody has ever seen them before."

I kissed her some more and squeezed each breast with my right hand then stopped and took off her blouse. She watched my eyes as I reached around and unhooked her brassiere. I took it off and looked at her.

"Pose for me a second, Toni. Put your hands like this, behind your head."

As she raised her arms and elbows it thrust her breasts out and exposed her armpits. I reached up and touched the soft black hair with my finger tips. I found it very erotic and realized immediately that its similarity to a woman's pubic hair patch was the reason. I looked at her and tried to visualize a painting. She watched me as I examined her body and then I watched her eyes as I put my hand between her legs. The burgundy eye shadow set off her grey iris to perfection. It would have looked lewd in public with the rouge on her cheeks but here with nothing but panties of the same color it was perfect. It looked lewd. Her *choninos* were very wet now and she was very hot. While I was squeezing we were staring at each other and I was watching the excitement in her face. She pushed the elastic waistband of her panties down about an inch as if to signal that she was ready for me to do something. For the first time I realized that she had a thin silver chain around her hips. I looked down at my hand. She was laying back on the couch with her legs spread. I had never watched a woman just this way before. My eyes went all over, from her painted eyes to her breasts then to the soft black curls in her armpits. I looked down at her navel and the tiny wisps of black that were escaping the strip of nylon on each side of my hand and showing at the edge of the elastic. There was a tiny strip of hair that went from her navel down to the triangle. I glanced up for a second and realized that she was watching my hand and her panties. She had thought about this a long time and didn't want to miss anything I was doing down there.

"*Bueno, ya que terminó de inspeccionar el encaje de mis pantaletas, le gustaría ver mi chucha?*"

I looked up and she had a big grin on her face. It was the same thing she had said before with two words changed. Now that you have examined the details of my panties would you like to see *mi chucha*? *Mi chucha* means my pussy.

This was the first time I had ever heard Toni use a word like that. It must have been the first time she ever said it out loud to a man. A girl from Puerto Rico or Cuba would have called it chocha.

"*Si, señorita.* What would you like me to do to you?"

"*Quítame los choninos y chíngame con tu dedo del corazón.*" Take off my panties and fuck me with your finger.

She lifted her hips and I took off the burgundy panties. I did examine the details. She laid back on the couch with her legs spread wide and I got down on my knees. I kissed her stomach and the insides of her thighs up close with the soft black hair touching my face. I did not kiss her *chucha,* though. That would come later. I teased her and myself this way until I couldn't stand it any longer. I got back up and sat beside her.

I started kissing her and put my hand between her legs. I put my finger between the soft slippery wet lips and up inside her. I licked her mouth and made her come with my finger. Toni didn't become a woman until later that afternoon when I had taken her to my bed and done everything I could think of and kissed and felt her everywhere. Except for the one night with Rocket I hadn't had any *chucha* for months. Or *chocha.* I couldn't seem to get enough. She had been waiting all her life to give it to someone.

Although we stopped for lunch we spent most of the day on my bed talking and making love. We both stayed naked except that each time, after she had reached a climax, she would put the wet burgundy panties back on. She would even put on some of the burgundy lipstick again. Then we would lay on the bed and talk for a while. Eventually I would start feeling her legs again or kissing her nipples or nuzzling her armpits or something. After some of this she would use what became her signal words.

"*Bueno, ya que terminó de inspeccionar el encaje de mis pantaletas, le gustaría ver mi chucha? Està muy ardiente otra vez.*"

Està muy ardiente otra vez means it is very hot again.

Then we would go at it some more. At one point I found some champagne and chilled it and we toasted the loss of her virginity until we finished the bottle.

"To the bopping of my grape," Toni said.

"Popping of your cherry is the expression in America."

"Why do they call it a cherry?"

"Because virgins sometimes bleed when the hymen is ruptured and the blood is red like a cherry. What is it in Spanish?" I asked.

"In some countries they call it *argolla*. There is the bolt and the nut and the washer which is the *argolla*." She giggled then asked, "Did I bleed?"

"You were very, very tight but you were also very, very wet and slippery. I don't think you bled any."

"I wish I had bled all over the place. Then you would know I was pure."

"I know I was the first, Toni, and I feel very honored."

"Don't be crazy, Devlin. The whole day was my special day."

"Toni, I'm curious about something. You came over here today with exotic makeup and carefully chosen underwear that you put on just to excite me. I'm surprised that you didn't have on any perfume. I've noticed your perfume before. It's very subtle and very nice. Why didn't you put some on this morning?"

"Carmela told me not to wear it. She said that perfume was for flirting and teasing and for everybody to smell. She said that you would want to smell me today without the perfume."

"She was right. You said she actually knew what you were coming here for. Did the two of you talk about it openly?"

"We talked about it but we always pretended I was getting ready for the painting and not for the lovemaking. We talked as if it was only for the portrait. Even not wearing perfume."

"What about the *choninos y el sosten*. Did you pretend that you had special underwear just for the painting."

"Yes, we pretended. She helped me put the makeup on. We did it when I was in my underwear. She said that my panties were very pretty and would make me feel special when I posed for the picture even though I would be fully dressed. She didn't tell me that *mis choninos y el sosten vino* would get you very excited but that's what she meant."

"Do you really believe she knew?"

"Of course she knew but she would never admit it, even to me. Not to anybody ever."

"I hope you will never tell Butch," I said. "I would be very embarrassed."

"I think he does it to lots of girls but he is such a gentleman that he pretends he never does anything. Of course I will not tell him. But I will tell Carlotta. She is my best friend and she will want to know everything. I can't wait to tell her. She will be with my parents when they meet me at the airport in Madrid."

"Is she a virgin, too?"

"She was when I left Madrid."

"What is she like? Is she at all like Butch?"

"She looks very much like me," Toni explained. "People think we are sisters. But she is very different in one way, she talks all the time. As you know I am quiet. She is not like her brother very much. Butch likes everybody he meets. He is very friendly but Carlotta is more detached. She is very independent and sometimes thinks up things that get us in trouble. My parents probably went *loco* trying to guard her this summer."

"Why do you say guard?"

"Because that's what it really is. Ricardo probably has lots of private detectives guarding her *and* my parents. Any man who marries Carlotta with Ricardo's approval will become very, very wealthy. Let's not talk about Carlotta any more. Do that thing that feels so good. The thing with your fingers. *Chingame otra vez con tu dedo.* Do it some more."

Once, when I was slipping her panties off, I noticed a small silver cross on the chain around her hips. It had probably been around behind her before but when I noticed it the cross was right in the middle of the small strip of tiny hair that went from her navel to the pubic triangle. Even though we had been at it for hours the little chain and cross were incredibly erotic. I was instantly excited again. I put her hand on me and told her the effect of the cross. I asked her what it was.

"It is my *chucha* cross. It is to remind me that my *chucha* is very sacred and that nobody can touch it. Nobody except you and someday my husband. You can examine the details as much as you like. Do it now. Kiss me where the cross is and teach me how to *lamerte tu pinga. Esta muy dura y lista.*"

Late in the afternoon I fell asleep. When I woke up Toni was lying there crying quietly."

"What's wrong, Toni? Are you alright? Are you sorry you lost your virginity."

"Devlin, it was the most beautiful day I have ever spent. I am so happy that I waited for somebody like you. Everything you did to me was so wonderful. I don't know if my underwear and my makeup excited you but you acted like it and it was so much fun. When you took off everything but my *choninos* and just devoured me with your eyes while you fingered my *chucha* I thought I would go crazy. You even seemed be excited by the scarf around my neck and my silver earrings. If you were acting today, even a little bit, I don't ever want to know about it. I've got to drive back to the Salazar's for dinner now. They have a bunch of guests that are coming. A Senator Morton or something and I don't want to be late. There is one last thing I want you to do to make my day perfect."

"I'll do anything you want, Toni."

"I want you to sit in a chair and let me sit on you. When you are inside me I want you to say some wild things to me. They won't be true but I want you to pretend."

We went back in the room where I paint. I got the straight chair that I use for poses. I sat in the chair and she took off her panties. It was the first time she had taken them off herself and she did it standing up. I was instantly hard again. She straddled my legs and sat on top of it facing me. She used her hand and guided my *pinga* up into her very wet *chucha*. When I was inside her as far as possible she whispered in my ear and told me what she wanted me to do and to say to her.

"*Te amo con todo mi corazon, eres lo mas lindo en mi vida.*" I love you with all my heart. You are the most precious thing in my life. I said it to her, very much affected that she wanted to hear these particular words.

Then we did it one more time, squirming and wiggling and kissing and finally climaxing together. As I had promised I said one more thing when we finished. I said it looking deep into her grey-green eyes. She really wanted to act naughty.

"*Antonia, te mueves y me chingas como una puta de Arabia!*"

"Toni baby, you fuck like a wild Arab whore." She giggled when I said it.

She kissed me one more time and got off. She took a shower and I watched as she put her clothes back on. From a large leather pocketbook she pulled out some plain white cotton schoolgirl underpants and a white brassiere. She looked at me and smiled when she saw how intently I was watching. Then she put on some fresh lipstick. This time it was a pale pink shade with no eyeshadow. I put on some shorts and walked outside with her, a little surprised to find it was still very light.

"Who are you going to bring as your date to my birthday party?" Toni asked. "Do you have a girl yet?"

"I haven't asked anyone. I don't know who I will ask. Maybe I won't bring a date. Would that be alright?"

"It would be very nice if you could come by yourself and sort of pretend that you are my escort."

"If you will mention it to Carmela and she says it's O.K. and Ricardo and Butch don't mind, then I would be very flattered to be your date for the evening. I think that would be very nice. I will even bring you a corsage. I have a friend who grows orchids and I will get a *Cattleya* and a few *Dendrobiums* and have a florist do something special."

"How do you know the names of those flowers?" she asked.

"The man who grows orchids is a priest. He also builds tiny model railroads and full-size model airplanes. He is a little strange, but very nice."

"Sean Moran is a little strange too, isn't he?"

"Snake is indeed very strange but he's a good friend."

"I think Butch is also becoming a good friend to you. He likes you very much. Carmela, does too. She thinks you are a very old fashioned gentleman."

"What does Ricardo think of me?"

"He thinks you are very independent and completely honest. He likes you, too. He has a very high opinion of you."

We had reached the car. She was driving Butch's white Cadillac with the silver initials B.S. and we stood beside it for a minute.

"I will see you on Saturday night, September the second. I will be there early and I will bring some orchids for you. I can bring a corsage for Carmela, too, if she wants me to. Ask her."

Toni got in the car and closed the door. She looked at me.

"How can you take so many orchids from this priest who is your friend?"

"I build a lot of bridges and tunnels for him in the Green Mountains of New Hampshire," I answered.

She looked puzzled as she drove away. I went back upstairs and got myself a scotch and water. I sat on my couch thinking for a long time about what had happened. The smell of Toni's *chucha* was all over me and I knew I needed a shower but I didn't want to wash it away for a while. I stared at the wall and wrestled with my conscious. I did not know if I had given in to my lust for a delicious young woman or made a decision to make her first time what she wanted. Finally, I realized that my feelings and thoughts did not matter at all. How she remembered her first time was all that really mattered.

Chapter Twenty Five

Friday night, 1 September
After the Norman's Cay rescue I had tried to live and think as normally as possible. Driving home from the clinic on Friday night before Labor Day I realized that I hadn't been very successful. But Snake might be right. Fifty five days had gone uneventfully by since the Sunday morning we brought Sharon into the clinic. Nothing had happened. She had disappeared "without a trace" and nobody cared about the dead people, so I tried to make myself start feeling safe. My party tonight was going to be a quiet celebration about saving Sharon's life and not losing ours. It would be fun. A regatta was always fun. Saturday night was Toni's birthday and I felt like a college sophomore just before Homecoming Weekend. I was actually very excited. In the back of my mind I guess I was hoping Toni would want to do it again on her birthday.

I unloaded my trunk and took a lot of booze and mixers and cups and things out by the pool. I set up the bar there and then went back to the car to get some bags of groceries. I had gone up to the second floor on the elevator when I heard a telephone ringing and realized it was mine. I rushed into my apartment and dropped the groceries on the floor.

"*Buenos noches*, Dev," a woman's voice said in Spanish. "*Yo soy Violeta*. Do you remember me from the party at Joe Lehder's house? I am in Miami for a few days and I would like to see you. Can you have dinner with me at the Fontainebleau?"

I was stunned and couldn't speak. Violeta was dead. If the voice had stopped talking after the first sentence I wouldn't have been able to say a word. I had a few seconds to think and I would have to pretend.

"I'm sorry, Violeta. I'm confused. I remember the party, of course, but I was a little bit drunk. I met so many people that night and I'm really bad with names. Were we at the same table for dinner?" I tried to sound calm.

"I sat beside you at dinner. Don't you remember?"

"Just vaguely. I remember sitting between two pretty women. Were you one of those?"

"Conchita sat on one side of you and I sat on the other. We played with your *pinga* under the table. Don't you remember?" She giggled and waited for my answer.

"Of course, Violeta. I could never forget that night. What are you doing in Miami?"

"I am here for only a few days to perform some services for my boss and to have a vacation. Can you have dinner with me tomorrow night?"

I stumbled through some explanations of what my schedule was and we settled on Sunday instead of Saturday. She asked me to meet her at eight o'clock at the bar just off the lobby at the Fontainebleau on Miami Beach. As we talked I realized I had to see her and find out who she was. If I didn't I would go crazy from curiosity. Maybe if I went there I would die of gunshot wounds. The thought of some kind of trick or ambush occurred to me, but it made no sense. On television the criminals always want you to go alone to the old deserted warehouse, especially if you are a good looking young woman. Nobody ever says, "meet me at the Fontainebleau for dinner."

When I hung up the telephone I asked myself if I had sounded natural and concluded that I really didn't know. I didn't even know what natural would have been. I had talked as if I didn't know about Violeta and Conchita being shot. I couldn't remember if the newspaper accounts used their names or even names at all. *Mierda!*

While I was staring at the telephone and trying to clear my thoughts I heard the doorbell ring. Gus and Paulette had come over early to help me get ready for the party. The bar was set up outside by the pool but the food wasn't ready yet.

"Paulette, you look great. I would put a flower lei around your neck before I kiss you but Sidney hasn't gotten here yet so I don't have the flowers."

"Thanks, Dev. I guess this party is a kind of celebration because we got away with the kidnaping. Is that right? What significance does Labor Day have? It sounds like something Sean Moran just made up."

"He told me that if nothing happened after this much time, it was very likely that nothing ever would. The date is something he made up but I think he has some connections in Nassau who are keeping a close watch on the investigation. The people who were inside Hogge's house know that it wasn't Jimmy Lightbourne. Snake learned that all of them left the Bahamas almost immediately. The house has not been used since that weekend and the owner seems to have disappeared. When Snake gets here we can ask him."

Paulette looked terrific. She never wore any makeup except at a party or something special, but her years as an actress had trained her to get the most out of it when she did. As a close friend and cosmetic surgeon there might be a time in the future when I suggested a little bit of tightening up, but not soon. I wondered, as I always did, exactly what it was about her face that made her look like such a nice person. I never figured it out. Maybe it was because she was a really nice person.

"Is there anybody coming tonight who wasn't involved in the rescue?"

"Sidney is bringing Lea Kahn. Remember when she sailed with us? She's either a friend or girlfriend of his. I don't know which. Snake is bringing a lady named Pat Rivera. She is the pretty Puerto Rican girl on the six o'clock news. I've taken her out to dinner several times myself and she's a lot of fun. I think you both will like her. You know Lori from the clinic. She'll be here. She was there with Sharon at the clinic. Remember? Her date doesn't know anything. Lisa Winter will be here. She came with me when I went to Norman's and found the house. You remember her. If there is anyone with her he won't know about it. Bill Gaines knows, of course, but Anne doesn't."

While we were talking I showed them where the party stuff was. Gus and Paulette got some soft drinks and carried things out to the pool. There was a huge round table surrounded by palm trees. Off to one side was a barbecue grill and a table. The overhanging trees and the surrounding shrubs were placed and trimmed in such a way that the area around the table seemed like a room. Four *Dendrobiums* and four *Cattleyas* hang from the trees. A *Cattleya* is a corsage-type orchid and a *Dendrobium* is a species of orchid with smaller and more numerous flowers. I had gardenias, hibiscus and birds of paradise all around the area. The swimming pool was about fifteen feet away and was a large irregular-shaped affair. It wasn't exactly a jungle lagoon like Ricardo had down near his docks but it was a beautiful place to have a party for a small group.

Rocket showed up next. I hadn't seen her for a few weeks. She had come straight to the barbecue area and slipped in through the trees. Gus and Paulette greeted her with hugs and kisses. Both of them had made it obvious to me many times that they considered me a total fool for not asking Rocket to marry me. When Rocket and I looked at each other it was painful. The first thing each of us said to the other was, "I've missed you," and we both said it at the same time and then laughed.

"Sit down and have a drink," I said. "I've got most everything to drink including Beach Bombs. Remember when we had them on the boat? The bar is set up on the table. When Sidney gets here he'll have some genuine South Florida flower leis. Similar to the Hawaiian ones except Sidney's are much better looking."

"It's nice to see that none of you have been arrested for kidnaping," Rocket said, "or murdered by avenging drug-dealer-perverts. Do you think we got away with it?"

Everybody laughed a little at Rocket's comment and then we talked seriously for a few minutes. We all admitted we had been looking at the calendar and counting the days. I told them about how many times people had asked why I looked at my watch so much. I didn't say anything about tonight's phone call because I wanted to tell Snake about it first. I left the three of them at the table and went back upstairs to get more stuff.

While I was in the kitchen, Sidney came in with his arms full of cardboard boxes. Following him was Lea Kahn carrying a huge box full of the flower leis. I was standing at the counter cutting up some things for the salad. Her face was so unusual that I was always a little startled even though she had sailed with me several times. I had stared at her many times and realized that it was her mouth that was so amazing. I had never seen a face like hers. The exaggerated cupid's bow of her upper lip and her full lower lip were narrow and I had never seen one quite like it. The flowers in her lei were red and white and framed her face perfectly.

"Please excuse m-my friend, Dr. Devlin, for staring so hard. As you know from sailing with him he is a plastic surgeon and is now p-probably contemplating a small operation on your f-face such as moving your ears down beside your mouth. Lea Kahn is indeed the lady who inspired my suggestion for a deluxe-model head for your office, Dr. Devlin."

We nodded and smiled and I made a nice comment. Sidney went back out to his car and brought in some more food. He had been stubborn and insisted on bringing things to the party. We had argued and I finally told him it was my damn party and he could bring only one thing. We had settled on a shrimp curry dish from a Thai restaurant. It was one of the few things I knew how to make myself and a big favorite of people who had cruised with me. I suggested making it myself but Sidney wouldn't hear of it. I found room in the refrigerator for some containers of the shrimp Thai curry that we were going to serve in a heated casserole pan. The three of us then carried everything down to the barbecue area and set them on the table.

Sidney and Lea Kahn went around kissing everyone and putting flower leis on them. It was a nice touch and the leis were something special. They were made from fresh cut gardenias, roses and white orchids and thicker than conventional ones.

When I left to go back upstairs everyone was talking and laughing. The holiday feeling was part of it, I'm sure, but we had the extra excitement of feeling the raid on Norman's Cay was over and nothing would happen. I wasn't sure how I felt after getting the telephone call from Violeta. I couldn't help wondering if her call earlier tonight was made by the same person or people who had called so many times before and hung up when I answered. I tried to postpone even thinking about the call or the rescue until after I talked to Snake.

I was standing alone in the kitchen when Pat Rivera came in. She was dressed exactly as she had been at Bimini when I took the pictures of her in her underpants. She had on the white skirt, the aqua blouse and a black kerchief. She looked gorgeous.

"I'm sorry I'm late," she said wiggling her mouth. "I came directly from the studio. Sean is my date tonight. He's going to be late, too. He asked me to tell you."

"You look terrific, Pat," I said. She had a new hairstyle and the dark red hair with blonde streaks was very attractive. "Isn't that the same outfit you had on at Bimini?" After I said it I realized I shouldn't have. I knew women didn't like people to think they ever wore the same thing twice. Pat looked around as if to make sure nobody else was there. Then she came over close to me. She pulled the tail of her blouse out on one side. Then she pulled the waistband of her skirt down a little and the edge of her panties up a little so I could see the color. It was aqua.

"I wore the same outfit including the underwear because I knew it would drive you completely insane with lust. I want to punish you for not being in love with me. Eat your heart out."

"You've been successful. I'm mad with lust."

"How are you doing on my pornographic portrait? Did you ever do a real painting from the pictures?"

"Come on, I'll show you." I took Pat in the room where I painted pictures. The painting was covered with cloth and I pulled it back all the way. Pat stared for a while and said nothing. We went back in the kitchen.

"I don't know what to say, Devlin. That's *some* picture. The expression on my face is amazing. Did I really look like that?"

"Almost like that. I used my imagination. I fantasized about what you would look like if I ever made love to you."

"What are you going to do with it?"

"Give it to you, I guess. Do you want it?"

"What would I do with it? Send it to Penthouse magazine?"

"You could hide it. When you get married you could give it to your husband for a birthday present."

"Looking at that damn picture makes me horny and I'm the one in the picture! How in hell did you mix the paint to do those transparent panties? *Choninos tranparente.*"

"It took me hours of hard work. It was a labor of love."

"Labor of lust you mean. How could you control yourself while you worked?'

"I called you lots of times when I was trying to paint the picture. If you had answered the phone even once I would have hung up quietly and then raced over. I did leave a message one Friday night. Didn't you listen to the message?"

"I didn't get it. The machine must have been screwed up. What did you say?" I told her what the message had been.

"Let me know when you're going to be working on it again and I'll arrange to be home. You can lie to both of us and pretend you're in love with me. Let's go down to the party before we lose control."

"O.K. Let me go in the kitchen and finish the salad. Have you been seeing a lot of Sean? Maybe he's in love with you?"

"Sean is a wonderful guy to go out on a date with regardless of which version shows up. He's attractive, he has a terrific personality and he's considerate and courteous. The next time you see him, though, he has different colored eyes and hair. Maybe a beard and glasses. He has a different occupation, a different background and a brand new history. I do like him a lot, though, at least the versions I've seen. Who's your date tonight?"

"Rocket. She's racing with us this weekend." I couldn't tell Pat about the Norman's Cay rescue and that Rocket was part of it.

"Are you back with her now? I think that's great."

"Just for tonight. We're still just friends. I'm ready now. Let's go downstairs."

When we got back to the party, Lisa Winter had arrived with a man named Haven Yates. He was talking with Lea Kahn at the table in the palms while Sidney was with Lisa over by the swimming pool. I introduced Pat to Lea Kahn and Haven Yates then moved out to see Lisa.

The setting sun was shining on Lisa's hair and she was just as beautiful as ever but to me she looked somehow entirely different. I knew it was just in my mind but she appeared somehow tragic, as if she had some kind of hidden disease. In a way I guess she did. It was my imagination, of course – that and the knowledge that she could never really love anyone erotically. At that moment I felt so sorry for her that I could hardly speak. Sidney saved me.

"I've been trying to p-persuade Lisa to consider giving up the Catholic faith and signing up with us. I've been quite successful in getting Madam Butterfly to turn her back on the Shinto crowd and I f-f-feel I'm on a hot recruiting streak."

Lisa looked at him as if he were slightly demented but she had a pleasant smile. I had to comment.

"A few weeks ago I went with Sidney on a recruiting tour of the bars and bistros of Coconut Grove. I didn't realize that was what we were doing until I heard him lining them up for Mass. By the way, you look terrific. I'm really glad you could come tonight."

She kissed me briefly and held my hand for a few seconds.

"Think about this," Sidney continued. "We line up the five young ladies that are here tonight. Pat, Rocket, Lea Kahn, Paulette and Mrs. Winter. We start with a warm-up communion at Saint Stephens and then strike at the Taurus, grabbing sinners left and right and having a few vodka gimlets as we go. If these five ladies sang one or two verses of "Amazing Grace" at even one sidewalk café the people would think that Jesus was near and sign up in droves."

"Is he serious?" Lisa asked, looking at me.

"Look at it this way, Mrs. Winter. Young Devlin almost became a Catholic simply for the privilege of staring at your ethereal beauty on Sunday mornings. If I had met you at the time I might have joined him. M-m-might have even become a P-papist myself. I'm going to propose to the other ladies that they help me try this system next week. Devlin can lurk in the background with his threatening-looking friends Gus and Sean Moran. They look mean enough to deter any kind of interference." Sidney left us by the pool and went back to the rest of the party.

"He's got the most incredible grin," Lisa said. "I can easily imagine him going anywhere to recruit for his church. Why isn't he wearing his clerical collar? Aren't they supposed to do that at social events?" Sidney had on a Hawaiian flower print.

"He's very close to almost everyone here. He doesn't need the collar. Besides you have to remember that he is an Episcopal priest and not Catholic."

"Devlin, please tell me everything you can about the person you rescued."

"Physically she's great, mentally she still has a lot of problems. She's coming out of it very slowly – a little better each day with a lot of setbacks. Two steps better and one step worse, but mostly in the right direction. I'd better get over to the table and start broiling steaks. Come on and help me."

"Devlin, before we go I have to ask you something. I've been getting the *Nassau Guardian* every day since I went with you that weekend. They reported the murder of three people on the night of the eighth of July. Did that have anything to do with the girl? You told me that you got her that weekend."

"It had nothing to do with our rescue."

"Dev, the article described the house and named the owner. I was the one who found the place, remember?"

"Lisa, please don't ask me any more questions about that weekend. We went there to get a girl, nothing else. Anything that happened was an accident and unintentional."

"Dev, there were pictures of the three people. The pictures were old and not very clear but they were the two women that sat beside you at dinner. I was there and I remember. They were the two women that were fooling with you under the table. Didn't you see the pictures in the *Guardian*?"

"I was hoping you wouldn't find out. I did see the pictures. It was the same two. I shot them both because they could identify me. I was standing outside when Sean went in and got his sister. They came running out and saw me in the light. I had no choice. Did the article mention their names?"

"No, but the paper said that a man named Jimmy Lightbourne had been arrested for the murders. Was he part of your rescue?"

"He was supposed to be what Sean calls a 'scope' which is short for periscope. He was there that weekend just to observe what happened and let us know. That's what Sidney was doing there. He and Lea Kahn were in the bar when Gus set off the explosives. She didn't know anything about it. I think that Jimmy learned something and went near the house on purpose. He wasn't supposed to. His getting arrested was just an accident. I hired a Nassau attorney through Bellamy Craddock, the guy who represented me when you were going to get me for malpractice and Truman Montgomery made his speech. We are going to get him off because nobody in the government over there cares about two dead Colombian whores. We'll take care of Jimmy and make it up to him somehow."

"Dev, I can't love you the way you want me to but I *do* love you and I don't want anything to happen to you. I'll pray for you every night."

Bill and Anne had arrived while Lisa and I were talking. Lori Young also came with a boy about her age whose name I didn't get. I couldn't leave her out of this after what she had done to help Sharon at the clinic.

Snake had also come while Lisa and I were talking. He was looking almost normal with no beard or makeup or anything. The only difference I could tell was that his hair was silver instead of black or brown. I think one of those was his actual color.

"I'm sorry I'm late," he said. I was down at the police station getting beat up by some guys with rubber hoses."

"What happened?" Paulette asked. "What did they arrest you for?"

"They arrested me for stealing diamonds up in Palm Beach. I confessed and my lawyer got me out on bail."

"Can I call the T.V. station and tell them?" Pat asked.

"Why did you confess?" Rocket asked. "Did you do it?"

"Confessing was the fastest way to get out and I didn't want to be late for the party. I haven't even been to Palm Beach recently. I don't like Palm Beach."

Between Sidney and Snake there was no shortage of entertaining stories. A little after Snake arrived I was standing up by the barbecue grill getting things ready and I happened to look over at Rocket. She was sitting between Lisa and Lea Kahn. Rays of the setting sun were coming from behind me through the palm trees and foliage and shining on the three women. Behind them were the orchids, gardenias and unlit Japanese lanterns. Rocket was sitting between two of the most beautiful women I had ever seen. Lisa's blonde perfection and violet eyes were in striking contrast to the dark haired Oriental beauty with the incredible mouth, and Rocket was sitting between them. In my mind I had always thought of Rocket as not quite beautiful and yet there was something about her that they didn't have. Where Lisa and Lea Kahn had the aura of unapproachability that great beauties often have, Rocket was like a magnet drawing all types toward her. Rocket had something that gave her a girl-next-door appeal. When her sexuality showed through the sweetness, it was startling, and seemed spicier because it seemed a little illicit. Not exactly sex with your little sister, but maybe your best friend.

All three women noticed me looking at them. All three knew how I stared at faces. Lea blushed a little and looked down in a charming Oriental way, almost like a bow. Lisa looked back at me, serenely comfortable at being admired. Rocket crossed her eyes and stuck out her tongue. I laughed at her and rejoined the conversation.

The luau barbecue party was working out well. Sidney had convinced every one to eat slowly, spreading things out into all kinds of courses and combinations with drinks in between. The Thai curry shrimp was served without rice so as not to be too filling and used as an appetizer. One course was a lobster for each person then later, after some time and conversation, I would serve a small filet mignon. The barbecue grill was actually natural gas and I could usually manage to cook steaks without burning them. It was a little weird but everybody seemed to like it.

When we were between the lobster and the steaks, Sidney began telling everyone about the *Aviat Eagle* that he and Gus were going to build. Gus, Paulette and Sidney had flown out to Afton, Wyoming and gone through the *Aviat Eagle* factory with Malcolm White, the owner. They had each gone up for a flight. Even Paulette was excited about the arrival of the first section. They had taken their own pictures of the little airplane in each stage of development and seemed to have endless color pictures of the beautiful little biplane. Knowing both Sidney and Gus so well, I realized I would also get involved in building it and I got a little excited, too.

I slipped away for a few minutes and went upstairs to get some of my photographs I wanted to show the others. I had been trying to get two great blown up pictures of *Ojos Verdes* from the ones I had taken at Bimini the same day I took the shots of Pat in her underpants, and I had several options. I wanted to give Ricardo and Butch each a large framed picture of the boat, with two different shots. A boat-lover never gets enough good pictures of his boat. I also brought down some pictures of Rocket from our cruise. I had taken lots of pictures of her and some were really great. In addition I brought some of Pat with her clothes on. I took out one small three-by-five of Pat in her panties. I put it in my pocket and planned to tease her with it privately and threaten to show it to everyone.

When I got back to the table it was covered with photographs. Everybody seemed to have pictures they wanted to show. Bill and Anne Gaines had brought pictures of the kids. Lisa had pictures of Bobby. Rocket had some snapshots of models wearing sportswear outfits she had designed. I postponed cooking the steaks so that everyone could look at the pictures. It was still very light out but I turned on some electric lights that were hidden in the shrubbery. I had just started to put the first steak on the grill when I heard Lea Kahn commenting about one of my boat pictures.

"This is a magnificent picture, Devlin. I'm not much of a sailor yet but I can recognize a great picture. It just looks so powerful. Look at this picture, everybody. Isn't it dramatic? Look at it, Sidney. It's the boat that was at the dock at Norman's Cay when we were there. Don't you remember meeting the owners at lunch that Saturday?"

It didn't register at first as I was watching the steaks very carefully trying not to burn them. *Ojos Verdes was at the dock at Norman's Cay that same Saturday when Sidney was there?* It was the day we rescued Sharon. I remembered Gus telling us that there was a big boat tied up to the dock that night when he planted the explosives. He might have said "big sailboat" but he didn't describe it.

Because the explosion was just a diversion he had to leave the explosives in the anchored dinghy so as not to damage the boat.

Ricardo had cut short our weekend at Bimini so that he and Butch could take the boat to Nassau. He said he had to do it so that he could have an emergency meeting about a Canadian company he owned. Butch had told me they were in Nassau and buying a house. I had talked to him after he sailed with me on the Star and he told me they stayed at Nassau the whole time and that the meetings were successful. I suddenly got a strange feeling. We gathered up all the pictures and each person took theirs back. I put mine in some big envelopes.

The steaks were superb. It was one of the nicest parties I can remember but there was a buzzing going on in my brain. When everybody had finished their dessert I asked Rocket to help me with the grill. I steered her over near the pool and asked her if she had heard the conversation about *Ojos Verdes* being at Norman's. She had heard it but she didn't know what was wrong. I asked her to stick around for a while. I had to get the people involved in the rescue together to talk about *Ojos Verdes* being at Norman's Cay.

Without being too obvious about it, I managed to set up a meeting for later that night. Around midnight Sidney took Lea Kahn home and came back. Bill took Anne home and didn't come back. Lisa and Lori both left with their dates not knowing anything. Pat left in her own car. Paulette, Gus, Rocket, Sidney and Snake stayed and we went upstairs to my dining room.

I explained to everyone about the picture of *Ojos Verdes* and then Snake took charge. First, Sidney confirmed that it was there and that he and Lea Kahn had met Butch and Ricardo at the restaurant bar just before lunch. Gus was certain that it was the *Ojos Verdes* tied to the dock when he tried to plant the explosives. Neither he nor Paulette had ever seen the boat before. Sidney, Gus and Paulette were all experienced sailors and knew boats. There was no doubt. Then I told everyone about what had happened in Bimini when I took the pictures of the boat. I also told them about the powerful radios. When we all stopped talking Snake started asking questions.

I stopped him when I felt it was time to mention the phone call from the dead whore. I told the whole story about dinner and the two women feeling me up and trying to get me to go to bed with both of them. Sidney knew about my shooting them but until then Gus and Paulette didn't. I told them all about the phone call from the woman but not about my dinner date. When I was finished there was complete silence until Sidney spoke.

"Being a p-p-priest I have read much about life after death but I have n-never heard of a woman who came back to this earthly life just to get laid. She must be v-v-very horny."

In spite of the tension we broke up laughing at Sidney's comment. Rocket asked if I was going to see her. I said I had only promised to call. Snake then started picking away at Sidney, asking about his meeting Butch and Ricardo and trying to get details.

"We were walking around before lunch and we saw them bring the boat in. We went down on the dock and helped them with the lines. There was a big problem with the dock because it was very high up and they n-needed a ladder to get from the deck of the boat to the level of the dock. As soon as they got the ladder set up the two of them climbed up on the dock. They thanked us and we complimented them on the boat. All four of us went into the c-clubhouse together. When we got in the c-clubhouse I offered to buy them a drink. While we were waiting for the drinks we introduced ourselves."

"How did they introduce themselves?"

"I'm Ricardo Salazar. This is my son, Butch."

"Where did they say they were from?" Snake asked.

"Spain."

"Where did you say you were from?"

"Henley on Thames. In England."

"Why did you say England?"

"I do in fact have a home in Henley on Thames. I'm also a priest and I was traveling with an unmarried lady. I wasn't wearing clerical clothes and I had listed my occupation as salesman."

"Did you have clerical underwear?" Rocket asked.

"What happened after that?" Snake laughed and then gave Rocket a dirty look.

"We had lunch."

"What else was said?" Snake asked. "Did you ask them any questions?"

"I didn't ask any questions. I didn't even ask where they were from. All he said was 'I'm Ricardo Salazar and this is my son, Butch.'"

"I said I was Sidney Fontaine from Henley on T-t-thames in England and this is my friend, Lea Kahn. I didn't say where she was from. I know that I made my introduction in those exact words because we decided before the trip to do it that way. Would you expect me to tell them I was an Episcopal priest from Saint Stephens in Coconut Grove and I was there with the beautiful Oriental squish so my congregation wouldn't know I was shacking up."

"Does squish mean you're in love with her? Or is that a British word for bimbo?" Rocket asked.

"Let me ask the questions. "What else did you talk about?"

"We talked about the boat and the island. Nothing else. They were both very interested in Lea Kahn but they didn't ask where she was from."

"Did the two of you eat lunch alone?" Snake said.

"No. We had lunch with Jimmy. Don't you remember? I told you that at the clinic right after we got back. We met Jimmy the night before. Friday night.

At the Pink Pussy Cat. At the place where Bahamians who work on the island all hang out. He came in a few minutes after the Salazars sat down."

"Neither of you knew that the other was a friend of Devlin's or that you were on the island for a reason. Is that right?"

"That is correct. Nothing that was said at lunch was of any importance."

"What about Ricardo and Butch. What did they do after they talked to you?"

"Two men came into the restaurant and went directly to a table. Ricardo and Butch excused themselves and went over and sat down with them. They thanked us for the drinks and explained that they were meeting the two men. It wasn't awkward."

"Tell me everything you can about the two men and what they did."

Sidney concentrated very hard and tried to recall what they did and how they acted at lunch.

"There was a very tall, very thin man. His head was thin from side to side, sharp like a razor. He looked to be about forty. He was with another man, a younger man about thirty. He was fairly normal looking. The tall sharp-faced man was talking with Ricardo and Butch. Later when we were leaving we walked by their table. The younger man was explaining something to the others. I heard the words 'tropical paradise' here." Sidney paused, thinking hard. "I also heard 'airstrip at night' and something that sounded like *volcano*."

"Does any of this make sense, Dev?" Snake turned to me.

"*Volcano* is what they call the house that Carlos Lehder lives in. It has a cone-shaped roof. Lisa and I went there for a party. That's where I sat between the two women who tried to feel me up."

"Does it have sentimental memories for you?" Rocket asked.

"Describe the young guy, Sidney."

"He looked to be between twenty-five and thirty. Slightly curly dark hair. Big smile. Animated. Confident looking. He seemed to be leading the conversation. He seemed to be very comfortable with Ricardo and the razor-faced man even though he was even younger looking than Butch. That's all I can remember. If you ask me anything else about that meeting I think I might confuse it with other things."

"That sounds like Joe Lehder," I said. "But it could be anybody. I think it's very strange that Butch and Ricardo would take the *Ojos Verdes* to Nassau for what was supposed to be a meeting and then continue down to Norman's Cay."

"Tell us what happened at Bimini, Dev. When Ricardo decided to take the boat to Nassau," Snake said.

"Butch got up in the middle of the night, early Sunday morning actually, and called Madrid on his radio. Toni explained to me that it's a regular thing. Ricardo used to call and now he makes Butch do it since the best time to talk to Madrid is early in the morning and Ricardo likes to sleep. The *Ojos Verdes* has some incredible radios that reach anywhere in the world. Before we even went to breakfast Butch went up to Ricardo's room. He said he had to tell him something that seemed to be important."

"When we were eating breakfast Ricardo said he had to change plans because there was a problem between a company he owned in Argentina and the Canadian bank he used in Nassau. He said that he and Butch would take the boat to Cat Cay that day. Then they would leave very early the next morning and take the *Ojos Verdes* across the banks and down to Nassau where he would meet with his people from Argentina and the Canadians. I wondered at the time why he didn't just fly to Nassau and leave the boat at Bluewater but I didn't ask him about it. I didn't think it was any of my business."

"How did you meet Carlos Lehder? The guy you call Joe Lehder?" Snake asked.

"I met him at Treasure Cay Hotel when Rocket and I were cruising in the Abacos. Do you remember him, Rocket?"

"The name sounds a little familiar but I don't remember a face."

"Joe Lehder remembered me when he saw Lisa and me at the bar at Norman's Cay. He introduced himself and I remembered him. He asked us to come to dinner the next night at his house. It was a fairly big party. He seemed to be a pretty nice guy but the group was mixed-up with a few women who looked and acted cheap and some guys who looked and acted like thugs. There were also some very nice people."

"Why don't you tell us everything you can remember from the party that might help us figure out what Lehder's relation is to Butch and Ricardo?" Snake suggested. "What we've got to figure out is whether Emile Hogge or anybody involved with him can tie the rescue and the shooting to us. Razor face could be Emile Hogge. The women were at the party and probably knew Joe Lehder but that doesn't mean anything. You and Lisa were also invited to the party. Who else was there that night? Can you remember any names?"

"We were met at the door by a woman named Marianne Meyers. She was a blonde with a nice smile and large breasts. She introduced us to an American couple from St. Louis named Bob and Frannie Word. I had been told by a guy named Rick Norton, who took us diving, that they might be mixed up in drugs. Then Lehder came in and introduced us to some people. There was a man named Nigel Bowe. He was a nice looking black Bahamian with a mustache and a very pleasant smile. Someone told me he was an attorney and a close friend of Prime Minister Lynden Pindling. He spoke excellent English. Another man we met was named Pepe Cabrera-Sarmiento. Something like that. People there seemed to be mostly Americans who owned homes on the island and other people who worked for Joe Lehder. Bowe and Sarmiento did not work for Joe but I got the feeling that they might have been business associates and not personal friends."

"I can have Nigel Bowe checked out very easily. I don't know about the other guy," Snake said.

"How can you have anybody checked out? Aren't you an art dealer or something?" Rocket looked at Snake.

"I sometimes do projects for the Central Intelligence Agency and I have friends in Tallahassee," Snake said. I didn't believe what he said but I knew that he would check out the two men with some kind of agency.

"There was a pretty little Bahamian called Chocolata. There were two guys, Juan and Pedro, who looked like thugs. There was a woman named Helen something who asked a lot of questions about plastic surgery. She was a real slut."

"How do you know?" Rocket demanded.

"Because of her language. There was a guy named John Durant who owned the commuter airline we used coming over. He gave us a ride back to Miami. Then there was Violeta and Conchita. Violeta said 'hello, nice to meet you, let's go to bed' all in one sentence. She sat on one side of me and Conchita sat on the other. I told them *no hablo Espanol* when we met. I hoped I could hear something about Emile Hogge but what I got was a conversation in Spanish between Violeta and Conchita about the various things the three of us could do in bed. Then they started rubbing me under the table."

"I bet you gave them instructions," said Rocket.

"Lisa was having the same problem," I said, ignoring Rocket. I guess she was still upset that I went to Norman's Cay with Lisa.

"What happened to Lisa?" Snake asked.

I then told them the story of how we had gotten back to the bungalow where we were staying and compared notes. I explained how Bob Word had put his hand up Lisa's dress and how she had let him reach almost to her underpants and then scared him with the fake bottle of acid.

Snake looked funny with silver hair, like a young man made up to act the part of an old man in a play.

"We know that Butch and Ricardo took the *Ojos Verdes* all the way across the banks and down to Norman's when they said they were going to Nassau for a meeting with bank people. They could have chartered a plane but they didn't. They weren't just cruising because they sent the women home. Maybe they wanted *Ojos Verdes* there so they could use the radios to communicate with other countries. We know that they docked the boat Saturday morning which is unusual because the dock is there mainly for the island freight boats. The hotel people control the dock and they would not allow a boat there unless there was a special reason."

I looked over at Rocket while Snake was talking. Her bonny little face was so intense I almost laughed in spite of the seriousness of what we were doing. She could be totally serious one minute and then make a smart-ass remark two seconds later.

"When Butch and Ricardo came ashore they went to the restaurant and met the guy with the razor-face who introduced them to Joe Lehder. At least that's what we think happened." Snake turned to Gus and Paulette.

"When did *Ojos Verdes* come into the harbor?"

"She came into the harbor from the east side between ten and eleven o'clock Saturday morning," Paulette said. "She came from Exuma Sound and not the banks and she went straight to the dock. I can find out exactly when I go back to the boat. I wrote it down. Gus went ashore with the dinghy just before it came in. He went to the cistern and filled two jugs with fresh water. When he came back I asked him the name of the boat and wrote it down. I wrote down either the name or a description of every boat that was in the harbor when we got there. We rowed around in the dinghy and I checked the names. I made a list. After that I wrote down a description and the time every new boat arrived."

As Paulette talked I couldn't help but remember one of the movies she had made, playing the part of a super-efficient secretary. It wasn't a real drama because her parts were always too nice to have anything very serious happen but there was one where she was in a scene very much like what we were doing. When she finished talking about her records Gus nodded agreement to what she was saying.

"We know that Butch and Ricardo might be somehow involved in something with Joe Lehder and that a man with a very thin head is probably part of it. He could be Emile Hogge," Snake said. "It could be something that is completely legal or it could even be something like drugs. Does anybody have any ideas I haven't mentioned?"

"Yeah," Gus said. "Let's all go home and go to bed. We got a sailboat race tomorrow which I would like to win. We also got a lot of really good food left over. Let's do something with it so we can have it for lunch tomorrow on the boat. We are going to race, aren't we? Lobster sandwiches would be good. So would steak sandwiches and we got a lot of both."

"Anything else?" Snake asked.

"Yeah," Gus said. "Either you got to tell somebody about the Salazars or we got to kill them ourselves and we ain't going to do it tonight. Why don't we kill the sons of bitches and keep the boat. I really like that boat."

"Gus Draper! How can you say such a thing!"

"O.K., Honey, I'm sorry. I'll say it a different way. I think we should speak to the Salazars and reprimand them most seriously. I'm tired and sleepy and I want to go home and go to bed. Paulette and I will meet you guys on *Brilliant* tomorrow morning."

The meeting was over after that. Paulette and Rocket got the food organized so we could use the leftovers for lunch. Snake and Rocket stayed for a minute after everybody else left.

"When I was late for the party I was at the police station. I just made up the business about diamonds but I really was there. A guy named Veltsin pulled me in and questioned me about everything possible. He mentioned a lot of names that I never heard of and he asked me about my connections with you. He also asked about what I was doing for Ricardo Salazar. I told him the complete truth in both cases. I also made up a few things about what I was doing with Ricardo. I'm still looking for that fucking little statue that got stolen in Tours with the Rembrandt. I've got a real lead and I planned to go to Europe on Wednesday to follow it up. Maybe I better cancel and stay here."

"Is that the statue with his penis broken off that you told Rocket and me about at Chub Cay?"

"That little statue might be worth millions, with or without his dick."

"Ricardo told us the whole story when we were on Bimini. I would like to hear about it from you sometime. Butch said you had some new leads. What are you going to do now? I've been assuming that you were still looking for Emile Hogge and that you would kill him when you found him. Have you been looking?"

"I've made some progress but I keep going off in different directions. Eventually I will go after him. I'm going to skip the boat races. I'm going to the party at Ricardo's tomorrow night, though, to Antonia's birthday party. I know you're going, too. I'll see you there. Don't ask any questions or do anything dumb."

"You mean like asking Ricardo why they went to Norman's to meet the guy with the razor-shaped head?" Rocket asked.

"I thought I was the wise-ass, Rocket. There is one thing, though, that I just thought of. Do you remember when I told you about taking that guy Billy Goat out to the cabin in the Everglades? When his brain got messed up by all the things I was doing and saying he confessed to everything he could think of so I would go ahead and kill him. He mentioned a lot of names and I got it all on tape. I checked out all the names right after but I didn't get anyplace. I'm going to listen to the tape again and see what I can come up with."

"Do you think there is a possibility that Ricardo could be involved in something to do with drugs?" I asked.

"Sure he could. His business is so big he could be involved and not even know about it. I *am* sure that he wouldn't ever tolerate anybody like Emile Hogge and the things he did to my sister. My guess is that he came to Norman's Cay to meet Joe Lehder and brought the boat because of those big radios. It doesn't make any difference to us or our situation. If Emile Hogge is connected to Ricardo in some way, Ricardo would kill him if he knew about Sharon. Not because he knows me and knew my father but because it wouldn't be acceptable to his ideas of right and wrong. I've known him a long time. Murder maybe, but not what they did to Sharon. There have been people in Hogge's house in Miami and in the Keys since we got her but not Hogge himself. He's been gone for a long time and I don't know where. Maybe I need to invite another one of his guys to visit me in the swamp. Perhaps I can fill in some blanks. Anyway, thanks for the party. I'm sorry I got here so late."

As Sean was walking out I asked him one last question.

"Do you really believe that Ricardo is involved in drugs?"

"Probably. I should be able to find out something. Maybe I'll learn from the Billy Goat tapes. Maybe the answer is up at Stratton Mountain."

"What do you mean?"

"Your buddy, Laufenberg, told me not to ever ask Sharon about what happened. I didn't want to hear it anyway and I already knew about Hogge but maybe he can ask her some questions about Lehder and even Ricardo. I may go up there."

"How the hell could Ricardo do something so inherently evil as dealing drugs?"

"You don't understand, Dev. In some cultures and countries it's not considered irresponsible to use drugs or to sell them. In much of South America, which has a slightly different form of Catholicism than the rest of the world, the United States is an evil country because we murder a million babies every year. I have known Ricardo Salazar for many years and my father knew him before me. We are not really friends, of course. I'm a socially acceptable agent or contractor. Not in his social class, but acceptable. In Spain where social class means much more than it does here the Salazars are close to the top. Ricardo and Butch certainly have a vast operation that would be capable of smuggling or selling drugs. Under certain circumstances I believe they would be capable of murder. Neither one, however, is capable of abortion or doing what they did to my sister. It is kind of a *macho* thing. Killing a man might be O.K. but hurting a child or a woman is not. There are millions and millions in South America who think that way. Don't worry too much about it. Good luck in the race tomorrow. I'll see you at Antonia's birthday party. I'll be wearing a goatee and mustache."

I was hoping that Rocket would leave when Snake did but she stayed. We were just friends but I didn't want to explain why I hadn't invited her to Antonia's birthday party.

"What do you think Snake will do about the Salazars? she asked as soon as he left.

"I haven't the slightest idea but I don't know why it is his responsibility. Just because he knows about the Salazars doesn't mean he has to do anything. Why is it up to him? Why not me? If we hadn't run into Snake that night at the Pilot House in Nassau we probably wouldn't have ever met the Salazars but that doesn't make it his responsibility. Or mine. In any possible way."

"Hasn't he known them for a long time."

"Yes, a very long time. I'm going to wait a few days and see what Sean does. It may not be his responsibility to do anything but I think he will."

"You've got to tell me as soon as you know something. I've got to know what is happening!"

"You don't have any reason to be involved, Rocket. Just forget about the whole thing. I don't see that it's my responsibility much less yours."

"I'm not talking about responsibility. I'm talking about me getting killed or put in prison or something worse. I was with you at Norman's Cay when you killed those people, remember?"

"We know you were there but nobody else does. Don't worry about it."

"Do you remember at the bar in Nassau when I showed you how fast I could draw a pistol?"

"Yeah, I remember. You pretended to have a gun. So what?"

"Look at this!" She made a quick motion as if she was drawing a pistol and then opened her hand. There was a card in it.

"What the hell is that?"

"It's a concealed weapons permit. I've got a gun and I knew how to use it!"

"I thought you were afraid of guns?"

"I was and I still am but after Norman's Cay I went to the AA Lock and gun. I bought a pistol and I know how to use it. I've been going to the range one day every week to practice. Guns still scare me but not as much as those guys who did things to Sharon."

It was all very serious but I couldn't help laughing at Rocket and I couldn't help getting a little excited when we were alone like this. With all of the beautiful women at the party she excited me the most.

"Why don't we have a contest next week to see who can shoot better. Tonight let's have a contest to see who can get your pants off the fastest." I made a motion as if I were going to grab her.

"No way, Devlin. Almost all the women at the party tonight were gorgeous so you are probably in a state of overwhelming lust for any female handy. You probably won't cool off for a month. Besides, we're just friends. I'll see you at the boat in the morning."

Chapter Twenty Six

Saturday Morning, 2 September

Because we were racing I went out early and got an outside table at Green Street. Caroline Lancaster waved from a distance to signal that she had seen me. Without asking she soon brought me Belgian waffles with pecans, Canadian bacon and coffee with chicory. I always had coffee with chicory when I had breakfast there. As usual I complimented Caroline on her beautiful skin and asked when she was going to be old enough to go out on dates with me. She told me how nice I looked and how she couldn't wait to grow up and maybe on her next birthday we could go someplace. Then she wanted to know when I was going to teach her how to sail. I gave her my telephone number at the clinic and told her to call me in four weeks.

It was a beautiful day with small white clouds drifting around way up high. Over in the west, out over the Everglades, it looked black. *Real black.* I had my newspapers and since it was the first week of the football season I concentrated on the sports section. According to the *New York Times* the Giants and Jets would both do better than last year and Ed Pope in the *Herald* said that the Dolphins would go all the way to the Super Bowl. I was engrossed in a short article about the Regatta when I looked up and realized that Rocket had sat down at my table.

"Hi, Rocket. What are you doing here?"

She gave me a frown and a cold stare.

"Eat," she said. "I didn't come here to talk."

I was a little startled at her rudeness and then realized that she was mimicking me. I laughed at her and went back to my newspaper. I did notice, however, that she had on a sleeveless pink blouse that looked very pretty with her light brown hair and smooth tanned skin. Rocket didn't stick out really far in any place but she stuck out just enough in all the right places. The pink blouse made her chest look really nice. When all this business with Butch and Ricardo was finished I was going to have to do something about her. She was too great to waste as just a friend. After a cup of coffee she did talk.

"Dev, I did come here to talk and I want you to listen. O.K.?"

I nodded.

"When Sean Moran asked you to use the clinic and detox his sister I don't think you had a choice. I don't think you could have lived with yourself if you had refused and I would have done the same thing. When you found out she was being held in the Bahamas and asked me to help I understood that, too. I've been in the Bahamas enough to know that Sharon had to be rescued in some illegal way. Trying to go through the corruption of the government would probably mean getting her killed. Going on the rescue scared me to death. Maybe I did that because of you but after the week at the clinic I really understood why you had to do what you did. Even killing the people was something I understood. I was actually sort of proud of my part in the rescue.

"Last night when we learned about the Salazars it really scared me. I hope that you and Snake will tell somebody in the government and not try to do something yourselves."

"Wait a minute, Rocket. We don't know for sure that there isn't some explanation for what happened. We don't know that they are drug dealers or anything else bad about why they went to Norman's."

"Yes, you do. Inside you know and I do, too. I was watching you and Sean Moran after Lea Kahn told us they had seen *Ojos Verdes*. Watching your faces. I also know something else. Sean is more than what he seems to be. I don't know what he is but I believe you do. An art expert or collector does not organize a dangerous raid like he did. He does not go into a dark house full of drug dealers and just take somebody away. What the hell is he anyway? Don't lie!"

"At one time in the past Sean was a professional law enforcement officer. I know that because he told me when he said he was going to get Sharon off the island. But that's all I know."

"Then he should go to the Drug Enforcement Agency or whoever and let them worry about the Salazars. Things didn't work out with you and me the way I hoped but I still love you. I don't want you dead. You're a surgeon and an artist and not a professional lawman."

"Why did you buy the gun?"

"To protect myself ass-hole. Nothing more. I had no idea Ricardo and Butch were bad."

We took separate cars to the club and found Gus and Paulette already aboard. Sidney was there with Lea Kahn. He would preach on Sunday and sail again Monday. I got everybody in the cockpit and reminded them that we might have some squalls before the day was over and that we would have to respond quickly and make quick sail changes.

On an ocean race people have a tendency to wait too long to reef down when the wind is getting stronger. It also seems that people will wait too long to go back to full sail when a blow is over. I had most of the wind-speed stuff written down with the best sail to use. In a short race you didn't have much time to think.

When everything was ready we motored away from the dock and over to Dinner Key and out the channel. I talked to Rocket and asked her to keep an eye on the black clouds in the west. I knew they were thunderstorms and we would probably get hit with a squall or two before the afternoon was over. I have a tendency to concentrate so hard on boat speed and tactics that I forget about the weather.

We motored around for a while congratulating people on some boats and insulting people on others. With a few we exchanged cold stares. When I was sailing against people I knew I thought of them as boats with characteristics and habits. I didn't think of the people much and never developed any special rivalries except with a few real ass-holes. I was usually interested in which boats I could beat and not which people. When there were about twelve or thirteen minutes left before the start Rocket went below and got her foul-weather jacket. She had asked around and nobody else wanted theirs.

"Are you expecting imminent rain?" I teased as she came up.

"A squall is going to hit us sometime soon. Get your mind off other things and concentrate on the start. I'll take care of everything else."

As she was pulling the jacket over her head I stared at her body and thought for a second about the crazy lovemaking in the Cessna at Norman's Cay. I still laughed at her comment back at the clinic when she said she had never been screwed in a twin engine plane. She put on the jacket but not the trousers and I stared at her cute little behind as she left the cockpit and went forward.

We sailed around, reaching up and down the line. The same boats were out in our class as usual. There were the two Block Island 40s, the Loki, the Concordia, the New York 32, and the Northeast 38. These and about ten of the I.O.R. boats.

I decided that the committee boat end of the line was going to be favored but knew it would be crowded. The course to the first mark was 105° and almost directly to windward. From there we had a long leg south toward Featherbed. The first turning mark was a little further to the east than usual but not much.

Lea had the stopwatch and she would give me the time left before the start. At ten minutes she began and gave me the time every thirty seconds until there was only five minutes. By that time I decided that the whole fleet was going to jam up at the committee boat. I wanted to be at that end but not to be mixed in with a crowd. I knew I would have to concentrate on the start and forget the squalls. I would worry about that after we got across the starting line. When Lea called out "five minutes" we were right in the middle of everybody, reaching along with both the main and genoa luffing. As time ran out we moved up toward the line. With just a little over two minutes things started happening.

"Two minutes and ten seconds."

There were six boats between us and the flag. We were moving at about two knots. Gus was trimming the jib and Paulette the main.

"Two minutes."

The Loki yawl jibed around and there were five boats now to leeward. We were still much closer to the committee boat than the flag.

"One minute fifty seconds."

We were doing about two and a half now, trying to be in a position to accelerate for the line. As the seconds passed we began to move faster. The

New York 32 was next to jibe around and go back up toward the committee boat. Four boats to leeward. When Lea Kahn got to one minute we were doing about four knots and still had room to start driving without being early.

"Fifty seconds."

We were up to four and a half.

"Forty seconds."

"Go for the line," Rocket yelled. She was lying down on the bow and could see both ends of the line. "Go for it, Dev."

"Thirty seconds."

We were up to nearly five knots, main and genoa both trimmed in all the way. The beamy little boat had settled into a groove and was moving well now. Soon we were up to five and a half. When Paulette had the main in she moved up to the windward rail.

"Twenty seconds."

"Go for it, Dev!" Rocket shouted. "Go, go, go!" Then a few seconds later, "Hoist the spinnaker! Big wind shift! Look out for the jibe! Look behind you, Dev! Move your ass!"

A lot of things happened at one time. The wind stopped so quickly it seemed like somebody had turned off the fan. We had been on a starboard tack heeled over almost ten degrees. Then both sails luffed, the mast stood straight up and we seemed to come to a complete stop. The wind suddenly came back but from a totally different direction. Somehow in the twenty or thirty seconds when there was no wind at all Rocket got Gus to hoist the spinnaker. He had already attached the pole to the mast and she had gotten the guy into the end of the pole just before she started yelling at everybody. Sidney was down to leeward on the port side of the cockpit trimming the jib. I had two Barient winches on each side of the cockpit and he just switched from one to the other.

"Trim the after-guy! Trim the after-guy!" she hollered. "Trim, trim, trim Sidney!"

Sidney got the after-guy trimmed back just before the wind hit. Gus got the fore-guy. When the chute filled it sounded like a cannon. Boom! Sidney quickly trimmed the spinnaker sheet and the chute was set perfectly.

When Paulette heard all the yelling and saw what was going to happen, she trimmed the main. As the new wind hit, she had already jibed the main. The power of it took some skin off her hands and left it on the main sheet. She couldn't hold it but she slowed it down enough and the boom didn't break. It did make a hell of a lot of noise.

The force of the wind was sudden and powerful. The boat rolled way over and the bow went down. The starboard rail went under and I thought the mast might come out. Even before the boat started righting itself it started to move and then to accelerate. With the sudden wind over twenty-five knots, the boat just took off like a scalded cat. Lea Kahn turned white.

The centerboard had been all the way down and I was glad of that because steering was a bitch. In less than three minutes we had gone from five and a half to nearly a dead stop and now were up to seven knots on a course of 105° headed right for the mark. The rain came right after the wind and it was like a wall of water. It was coming so hard I couldn't see the bow of the boat but I could see the wind speed and direction indicator instrument right behind my compass. I could barely see Rocket and Gus who were half under water and wrestling with the genoa on the foredeck. I never saw so much foam.

For three or four minutes there was confusion and chaos. It took me another minute to realize what had happened. We had hoisted the spinnaker and executed a jibe during the twenty or thirty seconds just before the squall hit. For the storm to hit just before our start was coincidence but to anticipate and execute the jibe was a fantastic piece of both seamanship and luck. I was amazed that Rocket had the nerve to do it.

In another minute or two the rain eased up from waterfall status to just hard pounding and I could see the other boats. I was startled to see that nobody else had a spinnaker up and then realized that only a few minutes had elapsed since the whole fleet got into a different wind. Everybody was to the right and behind. I could make out the New York 32 which was on course to the first mark but with no spinnaker and I could see several boats behind her with mains down and only jibs up. In spite of the noise of the rain I could hear Rocket yelling.

"Trim the foreguy! Ease the sheet! Square the pole!"

I was really startled when Gus stuck his head up in the companionway and asked me if I wanted to haul the centerboard up a little. I told him how much. Moving the center of lateral resistance aft a little would help the steering now. Rocket had the foredeck under control so quickly she had been able to send him down through the forward hatch. While other boats were still trying to get spinnakers up, Rocket was balancing the steering.

It was a short, fast first leg. From the starting line to the mark was nearly three miles. We had to be going hull speed or close to it so we got there in a hurry. Steering the boat was taking all my attention so I couldn't lay out a chart but I could figure out things in my head. We would jibe at the mark and then go down Biscayne Bay in a hurry. If the new wind stayed in the same direction we would have a broad reach to the second mark and then a long wet beat to windward and back up to the finish.

When we rounded the mark we were way out front. I didn't spend much time looking back but a glance told me that *Ace* was forty or fifty yards behind us and behind her a bunch of boats way back. Our jibe was slow and careful but poorly executed and I could hear Rocket cussing at herself. Nothing really bad happened, though, and we took off again for the second mark. It was five and a half miles and took us less than an hour. I couldn't figure out anything special to do so I just sailed for the mark. The wind did moderate some and then the rain let up. Rocket trimmed the spinnaker all the way down the leg and Paulette put some ointment on her hands. They were burned but not badly and I had all the stuff aboard that a hospital would use. The New York 32 never caught us and she gave us a lot of time anyway. We got the chute down well before the mark to avoid any problems and rounded in good shape. We switched to a number two genoa a few minutes before we got there and put a single reef in the main right after we rounded.

Since we had a huge lead my strategy was simple. Get to the finish as quickly as we can without doing anything stupid. The only strategic thing I could think of was the weather. If the new wind that came with the squall quit then the old weather would come back and the wind could go back to southeast. Since the course was almost directly north we would just have to make sure we stayed on the right hand side of the course. If the wind did shift and go back to its original direction we might be able to lay the finish line on one tack. I surely didn't want to have a bunch of boats beating us because I didn't protect our lead.

We rounded the mark leaving it to starboard and then went hard on the wind. After getting up to speed we tacked over to port and stayed there for a while. The New York 32 was even further behind than at the first mark. A whole bunch of boats were next with the two Block Island 40s and three of the I.O.R boats rounding about the same time.

Brilliant was well balanced with the reefed main and number two and everyone except me on the weather rail. The wind was varying between eighteen and twenty and the bay was very rough. We were taking a lot of spray but it wasn't too bad as it was still quite warm. We went on port tack for just long enough to be clear of the boats behind us and then tacked over to starboard. If the wind didn't shift again we could sail almost the whole leg on this tack. The rain stopped shortly after we tacked and the sun started to come out. The foul weather jackets, belatedly put on, all came off.

Rocket had gone below and climbed up on the rail just forward of the winches when she came back. Because she had the instincts and nerve to manage the foredeck so well at the start we now had a huge lead. I had been concentrating totally on steering the boat and getting position so I didn't see the wind shift and the squall coming. Weather and wind were part of her responsibilities but having the nerve to hoist the spinnaker was amazing. It was her race and I knew she would enjoy steering the last leg so I gave her the wheel.

"I've got the spinnaker set up so we can hoist it again if the wind goes back to southeast," she said.

"Good."

"If the wind comes right gradually we might be able to lay the finish line without tacking," Rocket added.

"Maybe," I said.

"Are you trying to stay to windward of the fleet?"

"Just steer the boat and enjoy yourself. The three boats we want to beat, *Ace*, *Renegade* and *Vamp*, went on port as soon as they rounded. They followed us. We tacked before they did and now they are behind and to leeward. Some of the boats down to leeward might beat us if the wind shifted suddenly and they got it as soon as we did. They might be able to lay the finish but it won't happen. Just concentrate on boat speed. I'll get the binoculars and worry about wind shifts."

Rocket steered the boat all the way to the finish, obviously enjoying it completely. Occasionally I would look at her and she would break into a big grin.

The sun was now shining, the water sparkled and the boat kept moving well. We changed to a number one genoa about halfway up and shook out the single reef. Our huge lead just kept getting bigger and bigger. The wind kept on coming around clockwise and we kept pointing more and more toward the finish. We were close to perfect, but not quite. We had to tack back on port once for about five minutes when we were about a mile from the finish. We crossed the line and got the gun with nobody close behind us. It was a brilliant afternoon.

Sailing in was pleasant when we did well since we always started celebrating when we crossed the line. Today was different. I had been concentrating so hard on the race that I had been able to put the Salazar problem out of my mind for a few hours. As soon as we got the whistle it overwhelmed me. I found myself wishing that I could spend the rest of the afternoon and night with Rocket, getting a little drunk and talking about the race. Maybe getting laid.

Rocket must have felt the same way since she mentioned sort of casually that she was reading a really good book and would try to finish it that night. I took this to mean that she had no plans and might be available if I wanted to do something. Then I remembered that it was Antonia's birthday and figured it was her way of letting me know that she was going to be sitting at home while I went to the party. I made a comment about how tired I was. I didn't lie and say I was going home after the race but I did lock up the boat and leave after one quick drink on the lawn. I told everyone I would see them at the same time on Sunday. We had a good start for the three-day series and I hoped we could stay ahead.

Chapter Twenty Seven

Later that day

I left the boat quickly after the race, drove home, took a shower and got dressed. I was tired and if there was a choice I would have rather been with Rocket. Instead I got all dressed up in my white dinner jacket and drove out to Miami Beach and Ricardo's island in a state of total confusion. I was going to a party at *Casa del Malecón* where two men, who were probably vicious criminals, were having a birthday party for an innocent young woman whose virginity I had recently taken. Maybe it was all just a mistake and they weren't really involved in drugs. Maybe Antonia wasn't really a virgin. Would she want me to screw her tonight? I guessed that she probably would if she could figure out when and how. I also knew that I would if she did and laughed at myself. In other circumstances I would be the one to worry about where and how. Butch or Ricardo must not suspect anything and I wondered if I was a good enough actor. Briefly I thought of calling in sick but decided against it. It was a strange feeling driving past the guard on the short bridge going out to the mansion. The old man, who had always been so friendly before, now seemed different, as if he were checking me out for a concealed weapon. He now seemed very sinister. I laughed at myself for thinking like Lori then realized that he probably always had some kind of weapon in the little guardhouse.

Because I was so early there were no cars parked on the lawn. I knew I would stay until the end as a courtesy to Toni since I was her escort for the night. I walked around the house and looked at the tents set up in back. It was very much like the setup for Ricardo's birthday except I counted fewer buffet tables. There were two bands again and an amazing number of bars. I walked up to the back of the house and went into the kitchen. I knew I would find Carmela in the kitchen because that's where my mother would have been. She had servants to do all the work but she would want to supervise and make sure everything was just right.

She greeted me with a hug and a big smile and I presented her with a beautiful orchid corsage. I lied and said they were grown in the garden of a priest. When I promised Toni that I would bring her a corsage grown by a friend I had forgotten that *Cattleya* orchids blossom only once a year. Although he had a tremendous number of plants we had used up all the flowers for the luau barbecue the night before. I had to go out and buy the damn corsages.

"Ricardo has told me about the possibility of the clinic for craniofacial surgery," Carmela said. "I surely hope that it can be done. We have a very famous clinic in Barcelona for the eyes. It is called *Instituto Barraquer* and is known all over the world. We donate money every year to this clinic. You have one here in Miami also, the Bascom-Palmer. Both Ricardo and I have a tremendous interest in such places. Neither of us has ever wanted for anything but there are so many who cannot afford even glasses."

We talked for a few minutes and she sent a message to Toni that I had arrived. I left her to supervise and went into the main living room to wait. Toni came in just a few minutes later. Her beautiful lavender dress had some silver threads in it and the orchid corsage I gave her was a perfect match. I told her that Sidney had blessed the flowers and said a prayer for her birthday. I just made it up.

I was curious about her dress. It was both modest and very sexy at the same time. It looked slightly Oriental with a high collar that showed no skin except the arms and then accented her breasts with a sculptured fit. Toni was so beautiful that she could dress modestly and still look special.

She was very excited about the party and insisted we go out and look at the bars and buffet tables and bands. We walked around and looked at everything. I wanted to sample a few of the things on the buffet tables but they were just getting set up. Although Toni was kind of like a little kid in the excitement about her party she never once mentioned presents. This might have been just good taste or maybe not wanting to embarrass me in case I hadn't brought her anything. I did have something and before too many people arrived I wanted to give it to her. I had it in the car but I wasn't sure what to do with it.

"Toni, I have a birthday present for you in my car. Can you open it later?"

She looked at me intently for a second.

"I want to see it now. Let's go get it. I bet I can guess what it is."

We walked around the house to my car and I opened the trunk. The present I had for Toni was the oil painting that I had done from sketches and memory and imagination. I followed her into the house and a room that seemed to be part library and part small living room. The shape of it made her guess an easy one.

The picture was unmistakably her but not exactly a portrait. It was deliberately much like the one of Patricia Rivera except Toni had some clothes on. She was a gypsy in the painting with flashing eyes and teeth. I had used up a whole tube of zinc white on the teeth and eyes. I had captured a look that was wild and very erotic. She had a white blouse, huge silver earrings and a burgundy-colored kerchief. The rouge on her cheeks was the same burgundy color. I had a hard time with the blouse and the breasts. The picture was from the waist up with her bare arms in a dancing position. There were castanets on the fingers. Even her fingers looked erotic.

I had started the picture of Pat Rivera before I did the one of Toni. I had worked on Pat's painting in a state of unsatisfied lust and liked the results. I told myself that I was painting with great feeling.

When Toni came over that day I had used her to satisfy the lust that I had for Lisa, Rocket and Pat all spring and summer. This showed in the painting of

Toni. The background for Pat was flowers and green foliage and a little bit of the sea, all of it in sunlight. The background for Toni was darkness and a campfire.

I had deliberately made Pat's picture look as if it were seen by a voyeur witnessing something he was not supposed to see. In Toni's picture there are many voyeurs. You have to look close but there are many grinning lecherous faces in the group that is watching her dance by firelight. They are almost hidden by the darkness but the looks are pure lust. Even the women in the crowd have an intense look. I do not believe that any of my paintings will ever hang in a famous art gallery but if I could pick my best they would have men's and women's faces showing emotions and feelings.

"Do you think people will know?" Toni asked me after staring at it for a while.

"Know what?"

"Do you think they will know you have gotten my *chucha*?"

"Maybe. I don't know."

"I hope so. I hope everyone will look at the painting and say to themselves, 'aha, the artist has feasted on the *panocha* of that woman many times. He is the one who put that wild look in her eyes. He has made her know the ecstacy.'"

"That's not exactly what I intended."

"Of course it is and you did it perfectly. Just looking at the painting makes me *muy caliente*, *muy ardiente*. I am going to wrap it up and have it shipped directly to Carlotta. I will write her a letter tomorrow and tell her everything about it. I'm not going to let anyone else see it until we are back in Spain."

The conversation made me horny and I was relieved when we went back outside to the party. In spite of the fact that I might soon be trying to kill the people who were putting on the party, I enjoyed being with Toni that night. She had a special sort of excitement that I remembered girls sometimes having at their coming-out parties. It was a very festive occasion and it was just for Toni.

I made a point of getting Butch aside early in the night and kidding him about Alice Grey. I knew now that he might be a drug dealer and I felt strange being with him. I didn't want it to show.

"Hey, Butch. Is she really *una guapa?*" I was surprised at his response.

"I might be serious about her, Dev, a little bit anyway. She is a very nice lady. Carmela and Ricardo think so, too, and it's a real possibility. Can you imagine me actually getting married?"

"Aren't you people some kind of royalty? Don't you have to marry in your own class or something like that?" I was teasing and Butch realized it.

"Royalty, my ass. The old man bought a title a few years back and had some crests and shit made up but nobody took it too seriously."

"When he dies will you become a count or a duke?"

"When Ricardo dies, I will sell the business and concentrate on playing golf and racing boats. We are basically riff-raff with a lot of money. Like that famous family in America."

"What family?"

"The Beverly Hillbillies. Don't we remind you of them?" Alice Grey walked up and joined the conversation.

"Alice," I said, "do Butch and his family remind you of the Beverly Hillbillies?"

"No," she said. "More like the Addams Family. Butch is definitely Lurch. He's the one who looks like Frankenstein."

It was actually a good party. I felt strange kidding around with Butch but I didn't know how else to act. Most of the night I moved around with Toni, introducing us to a few people but mainly being introduced. I realized pretty quickly that I was going to have to take a little initiative because Toni was shy and did not like to introduce herself. I worked out a little speech and used it over and over again.

"Good evening. I'm Winfield Devlin and, of course, this is the birthday lady, Antonia Lara Enrique. I can't say birthday girl because Toni is now twenty-one. Doesn't she look just wonderful?"

It was kind of a dumb speech but I had checked it out with Carmela in the kitchen before the party. I made a point of looking for Senator Harvey Morton but I didn't see him there at the early part. Carmela had explained to me that they didn't like to have a formal schedule for a party. They would serve drinks for a while before they started serving food at the buffet table and then Ricardo would make a brief speech about what a nice girl Toni was and propose a toast. After that the food would be served.

I asked Butch if he was going to have a party on the sand beach by the swimming pool later on. He said he was going to have a private party chasing Alice Grey around her apartment. Just then his father walked up and heard Butch say he was going to be chasing Alice.

"You heard him, Devlin. What am I going to do? I will have to alert my security forces to keep an eye on him."

"You're just jealous because you're too old to be chasing young girls around. I've heard some stories about you before you got married," Butch teased back.

"Don't worry, Sr. Salazar," I said. "Alice says he reminds her of Lurch in the Addams family. He doesn't have a chance of catching her." Butch wandered off and Ricardo put his arm around my shoulder.

"You've had enough time to look at the information on the clinic. Have you made up your mind? Do you want to go ahead with it?"

"The financial part of it is very complicated. I took the liberty of sending a lot of it to my father."

"Is there something I could explain?"

"If I understood your plan correctly, the doctors who worked there would be allowed to invest in the clinic. They would not be asked to sustain losses but would be able to profit in the future. They would have no risk but the potential for great profit. Do I get that part right?"

"Yes. I believe that would help you attract other doctors. Good ones who might not come otherwise."

"I'm concerned that profit could become too important. In order to become a great clinic we would have to take all sorts of people who couldn't pay. If we want to handle the hardest and most challenging cases the doctors would have to be on salary. It should be a generous salary but they shouldn't have to think about increasing profits."

"That's a good point. Change it if you wish. Listen to me, I've got a great idea. Why don't you invite your parents to come down and stay with us for a few days in Nassau. The house there is nothing like this place but there is plenty of room. Carmela would love it. Call them tomorrow. Any time your father can get free for a few days is fine with us. We can plan around it." He sure was a likable guy. Knowing that he might be involved in drugs made me feel very funny. When he walked away I looked around for Toni.

It was still very early when I saw Sean coming in with Patricia Rivera. They started walking toward us and when Pat and I looked at each other she started twisting her mouth in fifteen different directions and laughing. The mouth twisting should have gotten stale but it seemed to get funnier each time. Pat greeted Toni like a good friend, maybe like an older sister. I was impatient to talk to Snake alone and I didn't have to wait long. Patricia said that she just had to see some of Toni's birthday presents and the two of them left to go in the house for a few minutes. I wondered if Toni would show her the painting.

I followed Snake over to a place under a palm tree where we could talk without being overheard and there was no possibility of being bugged. He pulled out a group of photographs and told me to look through them quickly. They were pictures of paintings and vases and things that looked like ashtrays.

"This looks like a big bunch of junk to me. Does it have anything to do with Ricardo and the statue or drug dealing?"

"No. It's just a bunch of junk but if somebody walks over or the girls come back suddenly this is what we were talking about. We don't want to look suspicious. Now listen carefully. I went home Friday night and played the tapes that I made when I had the conversations with the Billy Goat. I had listened to them many times before but I'd never gotten much out of them. He admitted that he worked for Emile Hogge and that Hogge had taken Sharon but he never described him. I didn't think I would have any trouble finding him anyway so I concentrated on who Hogge worked for. Of course, at the time I was more interested in getting Sharon back than anything else. I will explain all this as soon as we can get together privately but the thing you need to know is that I have to do something about Butch and Ricardo immediately.

"I flew up to Vermont last night after I left the party. By taking a Learjet I was able to arrive at sunrise and land at a field that was only a few miles from Stratton Mountain. Otto picked me up. I spent a few hours with them and flew right back. He had Sharon in the car with him. She looks great but she still has severe periods of depression. Otto is there to talk to her as soon as they begin. He also has a psychiatric nurse living with them. They are treating the syphilis with some new types of penicillin. In about a month Otto will take her down to Boston and Massachusetts General for rectal surgery. Her sphincter was torn up very badly." Snake was pointing to the photographs of the painting while he talked. It seemed a little silly to me since nobody was within twenty feet of us but I guess it helped remind me not to look shocked or surprised.

"I had called Otto at three a.m. when I left to go up there so he knew why I was coming. When we got back to the house he told me that showing pictures to Sharon would upset her but to do it anyway. He said it might help in the long run. I showed her the pictures of Butch and Ricardo on *Ojos Verdes* that you took when you went to Bimini. She didn't remember the boat but she recognized Butch immediately."

I stared at Snake while he talked. He described how Butch used Sharon. He talked with the same expression on his face that he would have if he were talking about the photos in his hand. I tried to listen with no expression but something inside me changed. Rocket had been right. I had known but confirmation was something else.

"As soon as Emile Hogge got rid of the college kid and brought Sharon back from the Keys to his house in Bal Harbour he invited Butch over for a special treat. Hogge had used her in every way himself except anally. He saved that for Butch. Ricardo is the very top man in that drug empire and Butch is his son."

"Sharon's ass-hole was a present to the heir apparent. By the time she was handed down as far as the Billy Goat, Butch had torn her apart. Butch loves to inflict pain and likes to get a woman's blood all over himself. I don't think she got syphilis from Butch, though. I believe it was from one of the women. She said one of them was always complaining of infection but never went to a doctor.

"She said that Butch would sometimes withhold the drugs until she was going crazy then give her a syringe full. He would put on a show for the others. He would clown around and pretend he was a fighting bull and she was a cow. He would make her get on her knees while he mounted her from the rear. The rush of pleasure from the drugs was so intense that she loved both the physical pain and the degradation."

I nodded slowly and pointed to a landscape painting in one of the photographs.

"If you had to shoot a couple of whores at least you shot the right ones," Snake said.

"How do you know they were the ones?"

"She told me their names. They also made her perform for the two of them when the men weren't around. Sometimes with things like broomsticks and several times with a mangy dog. Hogge had used her just for himself in Bal Harbor and the Keys, then Butch, then everybody. Carlos Lehder was not involved in any of the sex but he is clearly involved in drugs. She had never heard of him. By the time they went to Norman's Cay Butch was finished with her so he let everybody do whatever they wanted. They would probably have killed her in a few days if we had not come to get her."

"What are we going to do?" I asked pleasantly.

"You aren't going to do anything. I have to do something about Ricardo and Butch as quickly as possible. I got back in the middle of the afternoon and spent several hours with some friends. I gave them a lot of information which they can't use but they gave me a lot of information that I needed. The drug people are operating out of a place called Medellin in Colombia. Nobody has *ever* had a chance to get anybody as high up in the business as Ricardo. He's the top. He may even be above the top. He is so insulated that he could never even be brought to trial in *any* country, much less convicted. I'm sure now that the big meeting at Norman's Cay was an important one and I'm sure that they brought *Ojos Verdes* down there for the big radios. I can kill Emile Hogge any time. I'm almost positive that he's the man with the razor-shaped head. He's a personal matter. So is Butch, now that I know. I have to stop Ricardo and then send some messages to Interpol. I think I'm going to try to get government professionals to kill them on the boat going to Nassau out in international waters.

"Drug enforcement people in every country have to start at the street level and try to work their way up. This time they can start at the top and work down, convicting and killing as they go."

When people committed crimes and the authorities didn't do anything about it, something happened to me. I knew that I was a little like those men in Attica Prison who killed people without feeling anything, but somehow this seemed different. I really wanted to see them captured.

We could see Pat and Toni coming from a distance so neither of us was surprised. Toni took my arm and said that I had to come with her so she could speak to the guests and thank them for coming. We went to the buffet table. I wanted to try something new and I picked something called *Solomillo con Frutas Secas*, a filet of beef tenderloin prepared with dry fruits, peppercorns, cream and Spanish Brandy. I also had *Tronzon de Tudanco al Tesviso* which is beefsteak with mushrooms in a Bleu cheese sauce made with white wine and garlic. I would probably never hear of any of these things again and I was sure I would never have another chance to try them. Everything was fabulous but I could eat only a few bites.

At one point, when Toni went over to speak to someone, I was standing alone at the end of one of the canopies that covered the buffet tables. I looked up at the clouds and the three-quarter moon. It was a beautiful night and I had to pretend to be enjoying myself. Inside I was seething. I watched Toni at a distance break away from the group that she was with and start back toward me. Before she got close enough to speak to me I calmed down.

A little after eleven o'clock people had finished eating but it was still too early for anyone to leave. I noticed Toni looking around. We had gone back to the buffet table for dessert and were standing together alone for the first time that night and nobody seemed to be paying any attention to us.

"Let's go down to *Ojos Verdes*," she whispered.

"What for?"

"Follow me and don't say anything."

We went up across the grass and into the house, through a living room, then a library and out a side door into a dark area where there were some trees. I followed her through a winding route that went past the swimming pool. I could see the white sand beaches and the waterfall that had been designed to look like it was coming from the base of a group of palm trees. The lights were turned on around the pool, accentuating the flowers. It was just as spectacular as the first time.

We walked down through the banyan trees and out onto the dock. I looked around and saw the same boats that had been there before. At the end of the concrete pier tied up to a floating dock was the offshore racing boat, a Donzi or Cigarette, as well as a launch. The Soling was up out of the water on a trailer beside the Star and some Lasers. The guard in the khaki uniform was there as before. He walked over close enough to recognize Toni but she ignored him. He said nothing and walked away.

I followed her aboard *Ojos Verdes* and went below first. After I found the light switch I turned and looked up at Toni. When she started down the companionway ladder I saw a huge smile on her face and realized what she was going to do. Her dress was very long with slits down both sides. She pulled the dress up and to the side and I was staring at the burgundy colored panties. She was laughing.

"*Bueno, ya que termino de inspeccionar el encaje en mi pantaletas, le gustaria ver la praline.*"

The Spanish meant 'now that you have examined the details of my panties would you like to see my *praline*?'

"What the hell is a *praline*. Is that Spanish?"

"It is French and means sugared almond. The French think it is a cute word because it looks like a clitoris. Do you think so?"

"Where did you ever learn so many dirty words?"

"Pat Rivera taught me most of them."

We stayed on the *Ojos Verdes* for only about thirty minutes but it was exciting. I didn't argue with Toni about whether we should or shouldn't or about getting caught. I concentrated on enjoying what we were doing. Walking back up to the party Toni was holding my hand.

"I go back to Spain next Friday and I will not be making love with another man until I am married." I didn't answer. A few minutes later when we were about to leave the banyan trees and go back into the side door she spoke again.

"Why don't you take a vacation and come visit me in Spain? The Salazars are going to Nassau in a few days but they will be coming back to Madrid in November. You could stay at their house in Madrid to make it seem proper. We could make love every night. You could pretend to talk about your clinic."

"I'll come back here again to say goodbye. Do you want me to take you to the airport?"

"Carmela will go with me. She will have the limousine take us to the airport. She is flying to Nassau herself an hour after my plane leaves. It would be nice if you could come here to kiss me goodbye. That would be very nice. I am sure Carmela would let us have a few minutes together. We will be leaving here at ten o'clock for the airport. Could you come at eight or eight thirty?"

"I'll be here a little after eight."

The rest of the night seemed to drag because I was so tired, but I stayed until the very end. By the time we said goodbye to the last guest I could barely keep my eyes open. I drove very slowly and carefully back to Coconut Grove. I was exhausted and fell asleep as soon as my head touched the pillow.

The jangle of the telephone woke me out of a deep sleep and my watch told me an accident had happened. Since I started my residency at New York Hospital several years ago a telephone call between two a.m. and six a.m. meant some kind of emergency and it was 4:53 a.m. As soon as I picked up the phone I heard the clipped English accent of Alice Grey.

"Dr. Devlin, there's been an accident. Butch was hit by a drunk driver just as he was pulling away from the curb at my flat in Coral Gables. It was about an hour ago. I heard the crash and ran outside. He isn't badly hurt but he did break an arm. I'm calling you because his face was cut up. I went with him in the ambulance and we're at Doctor's Hospital. I talked to the doctor in the E.R. and told him I would like to have a cosmetic surgeon look at his face. He's a young resident and very nervous. I think he was relieved that I wanted to get someone else. I called his father and he's on his way over here. He wants you to look at Butch and he'll sign the surgical release as soon as he gets here. Can you come?"

"Have them get an operating room ready. I'll be there in about twenty minutes. I'll try to get one of my own surgical nurses to meet me. I'll come directly to the E.R. but don't wait to get things started. Is there anything else I should know about his condition?"

"They've been checking for internal injuries but everything seems to be all right."

"Is he conscious?"

"Yes. He's awake and kidding around but I think he's scared to death about his face. He's such a good looking bastard it would be a shame if it's serious."

"Was he drunk?"

"No. He didn't have anything to drink after we left the party. I think he metabolized all the alcohol chasing me around my flat."

I laughed and said I would see her in a few minutes. If he didn't leave until four a.m. he must have caught her at some point. I called Maggie Lindsey at home and told her what had happened. She said she could probably beat me to the hospital.

"Sounds exciting. I'm tired of nose jobs and frontal boob balloons." That was her name for breast implants.

I was a little hung over from the party. Not too much but I was very tired. I put on slacks and a knit shirt and left without shaving. I needed a shave but I had done it just before I left for Toni's party. While I was driving from my apartment to Doctor's Hospital I started to wake up. I had two or three strong cups of coffee in a big insulated mug in the car with me and my head was starting to clear. I probably didn't need someone as skilled as Maggie for what sounded like a simple job but I suddenly realized that I was thinking about killing Butch. Then quickly the idea went away. It made no sense. What the thought did, though, was to make me realize how much I hated the man. Killing him at the hospital was just not an option.

By the time I pulled into the parking lot I had regained my composure. I knew that Sean was right. Killing two of the top people in what was a vast drug operation was a rare opportunity. The D.E.A. or C.I.A. would have to do it. Our criminal justice system was set up to give wealthy criminals every possible opportunity to avoid getting punished. He probably held some position like Secretary of Trade that gave him diplomatic immunity. But if somebody were able to kill Ricardo and Butch both on their way to Nassau it just might screw up the heads of a lot of drug dealers. If the F.B.I. or D.E.A. was blamed it would be even better. If people in the drug trade believed that the Federal Government was willing and capable of assassinating drug dealers without any trial it might slow them down a little.

When I got upstairs they had moved Butch from the emergency room to an operating room and I found Alice Grey with him. His head was completely covered with bandages but his eyes were open and he was sitting up on an examining table. I asked for the resident who had examined and bandaged him. As Alice had told me on the phone, he was very young and very nervous. He had handled things correctly, though. He described the wounds in detail and told me he thought they were flesh only. When he had learned that a cosmetic surgeon was coming he had not put in stitches. While I was talking to him Ricardo came in. I wanted to reassure him and explain what I was going to do. The resident had told Butch not to talk even though he was able to.

"The doctor says you have a hell of a lot of tiny cuts from the shattered glass in the windshield but he doesn't think any of them are very deep or serious. He stopped the bleeding but he didn't put in any stitches. I'm going to put you to sleep in a few minutes. I could use local anesthesia but it's going to take a long time and you would probably get bored. You will look pretty shitty for a few days after the bandages come off but after that you'll look just like you did before."

I was never any good at wise-ass remarks but I had learned how to kid around with patients and put them at ease before I did an operation. I tried to do it with Butch and his father.

"There's some good news and some bad news that I have to tell you. The good news is that you will recover very quickly and look exactly the same as before. The bad news is that you will have to pay me double overtime even though you're a friend. Also you can have absolutely no *panocha* for seven days."

Ricardo burst out laughing, realizing that I could kid around because it wasn't serious. *Panocha* is a Spanish word and it means unrefined brown sugar. In Mexico it also means sugar-sweet pussy.

While they were laughing I suddenly realized that this accident had given me the perfect opportunity. Not to kill him on the table, but to set them up to be killed by knowing the time the boat would leave. Snake had talked about killing them on the boat in international waters.

"I want you to stay here in the hospital today and tonight. Tomorrow you can go home. On Wednesday I want to take a look and I will probably change bandages. When were you guys going over to Nassau?"

"Next Friday. Butch and I are planning to take the boat over around noon Friday. We are taking several men with us and sailing or motoring non-stop. We are going up around Great Isaac Light, over to Great Stirrup Light and then down to New Providence. Should we change our plans?"

"It would be better if you could leave one day later. That will give Butch's face one more day to heal and I want to examine him before you go. Your arm is a simple fracture and not serious. You will have it in a cast for a while and wear a sling unless they tell you something else. I only do heads. Maybe you could go at noon on Saturday. That way I could drive over to your house and check you out Saturday morning just before you take off. I could be there at your house at eight, take a quick look and change bandages. I'll get the name of a cosmetic surgeon in Nassau and he can take the bandages off a few days after you get there. Can you do that?"

"We will depart at noon on Saturday as instructed," Ricardo said, laughing. "No problem." He was obviously relieved that Butch was no worse. After that I told Ricardo and Alice to go home. It was going to take me several hours to fix all of the tiny cuts the resident had described and there was no point in their waiting around.

"Would you mind if I observed?" Alice Grey asked.

I thought about it for a minute. There really wasn't any reason but I decided against it. I didn't feel it was fair to Butch to allow her to see him when he was such a mess. I apologized to Alice and promised to let her observe one day soon when I had a really interesting piece of surgery. After Ricardo and Alice left, I reviewed the situation with Maggie, then we put Butch to sleep.

The anesthetic we were using was a mild one. I was qualified to administer certain types under certain conditions. Having Maggie instead of strangers made it easier but I could have gotten along with any qualified people. When I got the bandages off I could see what the resident meant. There were a lot of cuts but fortunately they were superficial. The whole thing took several hours of work, picking out tiny pieces of glass and sewing up endless tiny cuts. The hospital had all the equipment for microsurgery and I used it extensively. When I finished I was exhausted. I thanked Maggie and said I would see her on Monday. She would get a bonus with her next paycheck. We always did it that way. I waited for Butch to wake up from the anesthesia and told him to come to the clinic on Wednesday. Since it was only a little after ten I had more than enough time to make it to the Yacht Club and get ready for the race.

While I worked on Butch I was pure surgeon with no thoughts except doing the best I could for my patient. Later, just as I was pulling out of the hospital parking lot, I got an idea about how the C.I.A and D.E.A could kill Butch and Ricardo. It hit me suddenly but I thought about it for a while driving down to the Yacht Club and realized it would work. I knew the C.I.A. was involved in assassinations all over the world, particularly in South and Central America. When Snake said he would kill them on their trip to Nassau, I visualized him working with the two groups and maybe the Coast Guard. With some fast boats and helicopters they could catch the *Ojos Verdes* while they were crossing the Grand Bahama Bank and shooting it out. Something like that. Some kind of James Bond bullshit. I hadn't had time to talk to Snake since then so I didn't know what he was thinking, but now I had a better plan for them.

When they left the island in North Miami they took the same route each time. Butch had explained this when we were leaving to go to Bimini with Pat Rivera. They lined up on a palm tree as they left the little harbor and crossed the shallow area on a compass course but also lined up on a big office building in Miami.

The C.I.A. could do it when the boat turned south on the Intra-coastal Waterway and kill them. They have to turn at exactly the same place each time to avoid running aground. The C.I.A. would know how to do it and they had the men and equipment. Knowing the exact time they would be leaving the dock would be critical and to some extent I could control it when I examined Butch. At least I could get the time.

I decided to tell Sean about the plan if I talked to him at the Fontainebleau that night. He was supposed to be lurking around in a disguise when I met the ghost of the dead whore at the bar. I thought about that dinner date for a while but it was hard to speculate. If a man showed up instead of a woman he would probably try to kill me. If a woman showed up and she was like the real Violeta she would surely want to get laid. It was too confusing so I decided to forget it and concentrate on the sailboat race later that day.

Chapter Twenty Eight

Sunday, 3 September

I got to the Yacht Club a few minutes earlier than I would on a normal day but the rest of the crew showed up right after I did. I think the chance of winning the series had us all pretty psyched up. Lea Kahn came but not Sidney. We went out early and sailed around for a while. The starting line was about the same as Saturday and the wind direction was similar but the wind speed was far less, only three or four knots. I had a light weather jib up and it seemed just right at the start. It was standard size for a number one genoa but very light weight and it would have to come down if the breeze went over ten knots. For the second day I tried to force myself to concentrate and stop thinking about killing people.

Winning races when the conditions are like this requires both skill and luck. Also enormous concentration. Our strategy was to try to beat *Ace*, the New York 32, and *Renegade*, the sloop-rigged Block Island 40. I really didn't enjoy light air when I was ahead because you don't sail to win, you just try not to lose. You try a 'prevent defense', using the football term. We could probably win the three-day regatta on points if we could beat them again. Our plan was to concentrate on these two and stay in the same wind pattern.

Right after the start, *Renegade* tacked over to port and we went with them and ignored *Ace*. When they tacked back we followed them again. At that point I think they decided to try to win the race and ignore us. We followed them all over Biscayne Bay it seemed, putting up a drifter-reacher four different times and using a small, very light spinnaker instead of a full-sized one.

It seemed as though Rocket was still excited from the day before so she never got bored with the drifting around. I thought she was going to wear out the binoculars looking for wind shifts and puffs. It was a long slow race but we did what we planned and finally worked out a lead over both boats. Four I.O.R. boats crossed the line before we did. *Artemis* sailed a good race and came in ten seconds after we did. This put us first for the boats rated by the C.C.A. rule. Rocket was so excited I thought she was going to jump overboard. We fixed drinks and started celebrating as soon as we crossed the finish line. For me it would be a short celebration, though, because the race had been so long and it was very late.

As soon as we got the sails down I started the engine and pushed up the throttle. I had been worried about this the whole afternoon. My dinner date with Violeta, the dead *puta*, was at eight o'clock at the Fontainebleau. I wanted to be a few minutes early and not a few minutes late so I had decided what to say to the crew.

"I'm sorry I can't stick around to celebrate. I've got a dinner date with a guy from New York who's going to help me put together some plans for a craniofacial clinic so I can't be late. Please explain to the other crews when you get ashore."

We were moving at five knots down Dinner Key Channel and pissing off everybody because of the wake. Normally I wouldn't do this but the woman had insisted that I be there on time so she wouldn't have to wait alone at the bar. We put the sails away while we were drinking and celebrating on the way in. Just before we got to the Yacht Club dock Rocket came over and whispered very quietly so nobody else could hear.

"I need to talk to you privately when the boat is tied up. Can you run the others off and stay aboard for a few minutes?"

My dad had told me once that when any of his employees ever asked to talk to him privately and closed the door it was going to be serious, quite often a resignation. I felt like that when Rocket asked to talk to me.

"I can't be late for the damned appointment. Can it wait until tomorrow? I don't have any choice."

"It can wait," she said quietly. Rocket knew about the phone call from Violeta but not the dinner date and I couldn't tell her. Snake and I had agreed to keep my meeting with the dead whore from the others. Since Rocket was worried that I would get involved with Snake in doing something about the Salazars it would really scare her. It only took a few minutes to tie up the boat and the sail cover was already on. I told everybody I had to go and shooed them off the boat.

I had changed clothes on the way in from the finish line, putting on pale blue slacks and a sport shirt. Some deodorant would have to get me through since the long slow race hadn't left time for a shower. I locked up the boat and walked quickly to the parking lot. There was no sign of Rocket.

Getting from Coconut Grove over to Miami Beach on Sunday night of the Labor Day Weekend was a bitch. My ugly green car would probably be remembered by irate motorists for a long time. I hadn't planned on the race being the longest and slowest in years. As Snake suggested, I finally found a parking place on the street so I wouldn't have parking attendants remembering me. I walked into the lobby and looked for the bar.

The Fontainebleau is spectacular and I suppose it's garish but I wasn't much at analyzing and I didn't see it often enough to feel critical. It was Labor Day and too early for the fall contingent of tourists but the lobby was still fairly crowded. Violeta's ghost had asked me to find two seats at the bar and save one for her. She said that it would not be appropriate for a lady to wait at the bar alone. Although I would be at the clinic at eight o'clock the next day there was no surgery scheduled, so I ordered a rum and tonic. I sat and looked around at the other customers and wondered if any of them were lining me up for something later. I had gone through every possible scenario in my mind and couldn't come up with anything. If they were setting me up for something, the Fontainebleau was as good a place as any to get killed.

The bartender was a man about forty who seemed to see everything and I had a very strong feeling he would be in total control even if the bar was crowded and the orders were coming fast.

It was a big bar, maybe fifty feet long, but there were only thirteen people when I sat down. I counted four couples and five single men. Since it wasn't too crowded I picked a spot where there was nobody around me. I was only ten minutes late so I was sure she hadn't come and gone. I had waited about ten minutes when a woman came and sat on the stool beside me. She was a beautiful blonde lady with a deep tan that looked like it had been acquired very carefully. She had on pale pink lipstick that accentuated her tan and her skin was flawless.

"Can I buy you a drink?" I asked.

"Yes, thank you."

The waiter came over and took her order and I waited to see what she would have to say. I was examining her face and finding something very delicate and very lovely even in the dim light.

"Are you Dr. Winfield Devlin?" she asked in a low sexy voice.

"Yes. What's your name?"

"Sean, Sean Shannon Moran. Call me Snake."

She said it in almost a whisper and I thought to myself, "That crazy bastard has gone and changed himself into a woman." I wondered for a few seconds how he did it and then realized that this was his smart-ass way of telling me that the woman was with him and that she was on our side. I hoped she was anyway.

"It was nice meeting you," she said. "Thanks for the drink."

I hadn't noticed that a man in a seersucker suit had sat down at a barstool about fifteen seats away. He had a neatly trimmed short beard, dark hair and horn-rimmed glasses. He didn't look toward me. The lady who called herself Snake took the drink and went down and sat next to the man. Neither of them looked at me again. I stared at my drink for a while. Snake said he would be lurking around someplace and that I might not know him. It was now eight thirty and the woman claiming to be Violeta said to meet her at eight. I decided to wait until nine or maybe nine fifteen and then go to the registration desk and leave a message. I could give the desk clerk twenty bucks and pretend that I was meeting a Miami hooker. I could ask him if he knew a woman by that name. I wanted to do something that would seem like I really thought Violeta was going to be there. While I was staring at my drink I felt small hands being put over my eyes and firm breasts being pressed against my back.

A woman's voice whispered in my ear. "Guess who I am?"

"Violeta," I said quickly. "Quit playing games and let's go get some dinner. You're late and I'm starved."

"It is not Violeta," she said. "It is me." She sat down beside me laughing.

"Chocolata!" I said. "What are you doing here? Where is Violeta?" I was a little surprised at being able to recognize her so quickly and even remember her name but I had discussed every person at the party over and over again with Snake and tried to put names with faces. Chocolata was the sexy Bahamian girl with the beautiful skin that looked about one-quarter black.

"When I called you I pretended to be Violeta because I knew you would remember her. You sat with her at Joe Lehder's house that night at dinner. My real name is Maria Rawlings. I was at the same table but you were with Violeta and Conchita. I could hear what they were saying. They were saying some very dirty things in Spanish. I hope you don't mind me pretending to be Violeta."

"It's nice to see you again. What are you doing in Miami?"

"I came here to take care of some very important business for my employer. I can't tell you what it is but it is finished. He told me I could stay in Miami for a few days."

"I'm really glad you called. I remember you from Joe's party. I thought you were very pretty."

I decided to treat Chocolata as if I couldn't wait to go to bed with her and pretending would not be hard. I had not really noticed her much at the party because there were so many people but she was *all sex*. I wouldn't ask anything more about Violeta until later, hoping she would bring it up. We sat at the bar for a while and talked. Her language was dirty and I tried to go along. I figured that she was planning on my taking her to dinner. That was O.K. It was certainly better than getting shot or something. I tried very hard to seem natural but I wasn't much good at describing what I was going do to her in bed. I tried, though, and I knew a few of the Spanish words. Just before we went in to the dining room I brought up something I had read in the newspaper about Pele, the great soccer player. This got her going and she kept it up all through dinner. She was a soccer fan and just as serious about it as an old Brooklyn Dodger fan was about baseball.

We went into the Crystal Room for dinner about nine thirty. When we got up to leave the bar I glanced at the blonde lady and she was still sitting with the man with the short beard and glasses. They weren't paying any attention and I wondered if it was Snake. The Crystal Room was beautiful and nearly full of people.

The Fontainebleau offered Maine lobsters and the waiter assured me that they were real and not the Florida version. I described the difference to Chocolata and talked her into having one. She had never tried the real thing. They seemed like they were close to three pounds each and the hotel had a little device that kept the butter hot. I finished every morsel, sucking the tiny bits from the feelers and getting butter all over myself. In the middle of dinner I glanced up and saw the beard and glasses man with the blonde lady. They were at a table near us talking quietly. I wondered what they would do if we went out to the beach.

The conversation we had while we were eating was really confusing. Chocolata mixed up Spanish and English words in the same sentence and sometimes she changed the subject from one thing to another without stopping to pause.

"I have seen the Colombian team play many times and they make me very excited. When I watch them *yo soy una señorita bellaca. Mi chocha està loca de remate.* Would you like to come up to my room after dinner? Something very bad happened to Violeta when the thieves came and stole the diamonds. Do you have a favorite football team? I think American football is *loco* and they just try to kill each other. Like Violeta. She got killed a few weeks after you were at Norman's Cay. I don't go there any more."

I tried to piece together as much as I could about what had happened after I shot the two women. According to Chocolata, who was in a different bungalow close by, nobody noticed the murders until about an hour after the explosion. Around two or three in the morning she and several other women were taken to the airstrip and put on a plane that flew directly to Colombia. She was told that thieves had broken into the cottage where *la anfitriona* stayed. *La anfitriona* means the entertainer. I assumed she meant Sharon. She said that the thieves murdered several people. The names used in the police report and newspapers were not true. Violeta Mercado and Conchita Diaz were their real names.

There were two other things that I learned as she babbled away during the meal. Someone they called *el monarca* was on the island that weekend. *Monarca* means monarch or king and I was sure that this was Ricardo. She did not meet him but she did meet his beautiful son and he made love to her. She didn't say it but I was fairly sure that she was one of the women who performed oral sex on Butch while he watched Sharon get sodomized.

While we were eating, a band started playing and Chocolata said she liked to dance. At first I was relieved because I didn't want to go upstairs and go to bed with her. Then I thought about it a minute and realized that she might want to dance for a few hours and *then* get laid. I was tired as hell, really just wanted to go home and get some sleep and it scared me when she suggested we go for a walk out by the beach. That sounded like a really bad idea to me. By the time she suggested it I was pretty sure that Chocolata was telling me the truth and just wanted sex. On the other hand she could be planning to get me out by the beach so someone could get an easy shot at me. Suddenly I realized that she could disappear by walking to the next beach and going out through the other hotel. She mentioned going up to her room several times and I had assumed she was registered, although I knew that she could have just walked in to the bar from the street. She could get me out to the beach where her buddies could slit my throat and then leave and be on a private plane to Colombia before anybody found my dead body in the surf. Fear of getting killed almost ruined my dinner but not quite.

When we finished dessert Chocolata made it clear that she wanted to see the beach in the moonlight and then go up to her room. During dinner she had referred to Violeta and Conchita as *putas, leonas, arañas, and garrapatas*. In English *puta* means whore, *leonas* means bitchy whore, *araña* means spider which is a Mexican term for whore and *garrapata* is a whore who grabs your paw. She said the two of them had been very vulgar to talk dirty like they had and feel my *pinga* under the table. I realized that she thought that both of them had their hands in my pants and that I had my hands in theirs.

During dessert it was obvious she was hot and trying to get me hot by talking dirty. I asked her if that was what she was trying to do and she admitted it. When I asked her what the difference was between what she was doing and what they had done, she explained that she was my date for the evening and that they had done it in front of everybody. She then described how much I would enjoy her *panocha* and how sweet it was. Under other circumstances, I might have responded to the conversation but I knew I might get knifed on the beach and would probably get germs if I got laid.

It was a crazy dinner but the lobster was superb. Several times I thought of making some excuse but I wanted to play out the hand, or whatever they call it. I didn't want to keep on wondering if somebody was after me. I wanted to be able to help catch Butch and Ricardo without worrying about anybody else. If all she wanted was to get laid then the phone call and her visit to Miami were just a coincidence.

The grounds of the Fontainebleau are beautiful. Between the hotel and the beach there's a small park with paths leading through well-trimmed grass and slanted palm trees. The pool was large and there was an outside bar at the south end of the trees. We walked down toward the bar and then she suggested we go up the other way where there weren't so many people. It was pretty dark and there were a lot of shadowy places since the moon was only a sliver. I hoped Snake was lurking in the shadows somewhere and remembered that he claimed to be very good at it.

When we reached a certain secluded spot, Chocolata stopped and pressed herself against me making it obvious that she wanted to get started. I squeezed her and then pulled away pulling her with me and moving toward the open sand of the beach. When we got out in the open I turned with my back to the water and kissed her. She was all over me. Since I didn't have my back to the shadows at least I couldn't get stabbed easily.

A few times in the past I had tried to put my hand on a girl's behind and had her move it above her waist. This was the same thing in reverse. When I put my hand on her waist she moved it down. After a couple of back and forths I decided to get on with it. I bunched up the back of her dress and put my hand underneath. As soon as I did that she started going crazy, using her tongue to describe what I was going to get and then sticking it in my mouth. In spite of the situation I started getting hot.

When she insisted that we go up to her room immediately, I began to believe the danger of getting syphilis was greater than the risk of getting stabbed. She didn't waste any time getting back into the hotel, through the lobby, into the elevator and down the hall to her room. I was relieved to find out she actually had a room. When we got inside she grabbed me and started kissing me and trying to take off my clothes. She was laughing and grabbing. My vocabulary of Spanish dirty words just about doubled in the next fifteen minutes. I learned that women's panties were called *calzones* and *bragas* as well as *choninos*.

She had a big bottle of vodka in her room and we both had a large drink. I offered her an 'ami' which is amyl nitrate. Amyl nitrate is a drug which enhances orgasm. She had used them before and knew what they did to you. She swallowed it quickly. She was spread out on a huge king-sized bed in just her *choninos*, when I gave her another 'ami'.

"*Venirse juntos con mi amigo ami*," I said, pulling down her black panties and using my finger. We will come together with my friend ami.

She was on her back with her legs spread telling me to do things like *darle de comer al chango* which means feed the monkey in Spanish. In Mexican slang it means fuck. She also wanted me to *echar un palo* and *medir su aceite*. Throw her the stick and check her oil. Just as I was about to *tomar medidas por dentro*, which means take inside measurements, she passed out. I kept on kissing her and playing with her *panocha* until I was sure she was unconscious. The second ami was really chloral hydrate, a powerful knockout pill. I found some Fontainebleau stationery and wrote a note then laid it on the bed where she would see it when she woke up. It said,

> "Darling Chocolata - It was a fantastic night. You are a beautiful woman and the best chocha I have ever had. Please call me the next time you come to Miami. It was unforgettable.
> Vaya con Dios,
> Dev

Between the drugs and the booze she would sleep for a long time and have a hell of a headache but she would be O.K. I put on my clothes, washed my hands several times, and quietly opened the door to the hall just as a man and a woman came walking by. I was startled and almost lost my composure since I was still zipping up my pants. I nodded politely and walked behind them to the elevator. I pushed the button for the lobby and glanced up at the woman. It was the beautiful blonde lady from the bar, the one who called herself Sean Moran. I looked at the man and nodded back. When the three of us were alone in the elevator going down the man spoke to me.

"I'll meet you for lunch on Tuesday at Monty Trainer's at twelve thirty. I hope you enjoyed having *panocha* for dessert."

I looked at him but I didn't answer. I didn't know what to say. I knew it was Snake but it was a hell of a disguise. He didn't speak again so I guessed he wanted to wait until the next day to decide what to do. The woman was probably somebody he didn't trust completely. I gave him plenty of opportunity to say something in the lobby but he and the gorgeous blonde headed for the bar.

I was exhilarated driving back to Coral Gables. I had hoped that the ghost of Violeta would turn out to be a woman who was interested in sex and not a man who wanted revenge. It was just a few minutes after midnight when I crossed over the Julia Tuttle Causeway. I was going almost as fast leaving Miami Beach as when I came over earlier.

The next morning Rocket was so late getting to the boat for the last race of the Labor Day Regatta that we almost had to leave the dock without her. Because I had a shallow draft boat and the tide was high I took a short-cut and didn't go out the usual way through the Dinner Key Channel. Rocket apologized but didn't explain. Except for Sidney's absence on Sunday we had the benefit of the same crew for all three days so we were well organized and got a good start.

The wind was steady, eighteen to twenty and far enough south that we had a long beat to windward. I was so confused and upset about the Salazars that it was a great relief to be forced to concentrate on racing the boat. We covered *Artemis* and though she crossed the line ahead of us I was sure we would either win the series or at least be the first C.C.A. boat.

The race was a fast one so the barbecue would be a good one with lots of food and drinking before prizes were awarded. We started celebrating as soon as we crossed the finish line. I remembered that Rocket had wanted to talk to me and asked her to help me with something below. She suggested we talk on the boat after everyone else had gone up to the lawn for the party.

When we were alone Rocket sat down in the cockpit with a beer in her hand.

"I've got some good news, Dev. I'm going to New York to make my fame and fortune as a sportswear designer. I know it'll break your heart to have me leave Miami but the opportunity is too good to pass up. I realize I'm irreplaceable as a crew but these guys will eventually learn what to do. I've got a fabulous job with Windom Wear as a junior designer. I sent out my drawings to a lot of companies and got several offers. I went up to New York three weeks ago for interviews and I was offered the job of my dreams. I'm going to miss you a lot, though."

I was stunned and just stared for a minute. I couldn't just let her go but I didn't know what to do.

"Why didn't you tell me sooner?"

"I was going to tell you yesterday morning. That was one of the reasons why I showed up when you were eating breakfast but I chickened out. Then last night I tried but you had to meet those people for dinner."

I was stunned – completely speechless. I knew that I would never see her again if she went to New York. Somehow that idea just seemed unacceptable. It gave me a stomach ache. But I wasn't ready to ask her to marry me. We were just friends. Or supposed to be.

"Did your decision have anything to do with us? With me?"

"Of course it did, ass-hole. At one time we thought we were in love. Then we decided we really just wanted to be friends. If we were actually in love, and planning to be married, I wouldn't be going to New York, would I? It just didn't work out. I realize that you will never meet anyone as exciting as I am but in ten or fifteen years you'll get over it. Maybe."

We sat without speaking for a little while. I couldn't think of anything to say. I wondered if the shock and hurt that I felt meant I was really in love with her. Marriage-type love. While we were sitting there Paulette came walking down the dock toward us.

"They're starting to give out the prizes, Devlin. The Commodore is making his usual speech and they'll start with the one-design classes but you've got to get up to the club. We did get first in our class. Hurry up!" Paulette said.

"We'd better go," Rocket said.

"Can we go somewhere and talk after the prizes?" I asked.

"I can't, Dev. I've too much to do to get ready. I'm moving out of my apartment and staying with a friend until I go north. I am planning to spend a week or two with my mother on the Eastern Shore but I'm not leaving Miami until I know what Snake is going to do about the Salazars. Whatever happens I want to know that you are not going to be a part of it. Do you understand?"

"I've got to talk to you. When do you actually leave?"

"I just told you. As soon as I know what Snake is going to do about Butch and Ricardo I am gone."

"I'll call you tomorrow or come over or something."

She stood up and kissed me goodbye. It would have been a nice kiss for a friend but it wasn't a lover's kiss. When she got up on the dock she turned and looked at me.

"It was a good race, Dev. All of it was good."

I didn't think she meant the sailboat race.

As I watched her little behind walking down the dock I decided I was going over to her apartment tomorrow morning before I went to the clinic. I didn't know what I was going to say but I knew we had to talk about us. I couldn't let her leave. I had to do something.

All of our crew stood on the lawn together watching while the prizes were handed out. Because of the strong breeze and early finishes there was a large crowd. When they called out *"Brilliant,* owned and sailed by Winfield Devlin" both Rocket and Paulette gave me a kiss and a hug before I went up to receive the prize. I shook the hand of the Commodore and thanked him. Then I made a quick two minute acceptance speech that I had used for first place since I was sixteen. When I went back to the crew Rocket was gone. I didn't say anything to them but I got a little drunk and went home early.

Because of the rum I went to sleep quickly and early but I woke up a little after 3:00 and couldn't sleep. I decided I had to go see Rocket. She was going to be pissed off when I woke her up, and I didn't know what I was going to say, but I had to see her and not just let her go. I couldn't let her go.

The streets were nearly deserted and it seemed like everybody wanted to get some rest after the long weekend. I found a parking place in front of Rocket's apartment and took the empty elevator to the third floor. I pushed the buzzer briefly. I waited and pushed again for a longer time. There was no response so I pushed the buzzer again and held it then banged on the door. Still no answer. *"Mierda,"* I said out loud. She's left the apartment. I'll call her in the morning.

I called at six thirty the next morning from my apartment and found out her phone had been disconnected. Later, at nine, I called the place where she worked. She said she was in the middle of a presentation and couldn't talk very long. She went into another room and closed the door.

"Call me here at work as soon as you know about the Salazars."

"Where are you sleeping?"

"You don't need to know. Just call me here at work when you know about the Salazars."

"Why can't you tell me where you're staying?"

"Because you'll come over to talk. Then you'll get excited and try to take my pants off."

"What's wrong with that?"

"You'll be saying things you don't mean. I'll end up taking my own pants off and we'll both regret it the next day. I've got to go back now and finish the presentation."

I spent the rest of the morning in a kind of daze and then remembered I had to meet Snake for lunch.

Chapter Twenty Nine

Tuesday, 5 September
I left the clinic early and got to Monty Trainer's about eleven thirty. Most of the tables were empty. Tuesday lunch after Labor Day weekend was always slow. I found a table where we could talk without being overheard. In a few minutes Sean showed up. Except for some bright red curly hair, which I'd never seen before, he looked like the Snake I usually saw. The skin of his real face was as smooth as a pool ball. Not a trace of hair.

"You look like you just ate a dog turd sandwich, Devlin. Why are you looking so gloomy?"

"Rocket is going to New York to be a sportswear designer."

"So what. You were just friends, anyway."

"That's what we both said, but I think we were in love and I just didn't know how to handle it."

"You ready to get married?"

"I don't know."

"If you don't know then you aren't in love. At least not enough. If you're ready to get married then go to New York and get her. If you're not ready to get married then leave her alone. It's that simple."

"She hasn't left yet. She moved out of her apartment. She says she isn't leaving until she knows what is going to happen with the Salazars. She's starting a new job and it's very important to her."

"Wait until she goes to New York. Then kidnap her. Don't shoot anybody this time. Just take a boat up the East River and grab her. I'll be glad to help out. I owe you a kidnap."

"Snake, did anybody ever tell you that you're a real asshole?"

"My father, mostly. He told me quite often and he was a man to be believed."

"Who are you to be giving marital advice anyway?"

"I've never been divorced."

"You've never been married."

"I have a perfect record."

"I can't do anything about Rocket until we've finished with Ricardo and Butch." I stared hard at him.

"Devlin, you're finished with Ricardo and Butch. I am, too, after this meeting today. Professionals have to do the job. I can find Emile Hogge and take care of him. That's personal. But the Salazars are too big and have too much power. In a few minutes two guys are meeting us here. One is from the C.I.A. and the other is from the D.E.A. I know them both and I trust them both. I've told them each the whole story separately. Usually government people are so busy filling out forms and covering themselves politically that nothing gets done. Either that or they get involved in some covert action and permanently fuck up some country like Cuba.

"These guys are different," he continued. They're straight and they will work with each other. Anyway, you and I are both out of it after today. I'll be grateful to you and Rocket and Sidney and Gus for the rest of my life but we can't get in any deeper. Ricardo's house is like a fortress. I could kill either him or Butch because they know me and trust me. I could get one of them alone but I would never get away alive. I want you to confirm what I have already told them and then answer any questions. After that you go back to your clinic and make beautiful women out of slobs and I deal with Hogge. I'm going to get that razor-headed bastard and take him on a picnic in the Everglades. Then I go back to the stolen art business."

After that we stopped talking and started eating. I started to order a drink then changed my mind since surgery was on the schedule for tomorrow at 8:00 a.m. I had a plate of something called Nachos that Monty's had just added to the menu. I had never tried them before but I had heard of them. There was a piece of melted cheese and a dab of refried beans on top of a corn chip with a piece of jalapeño pepper. They were delicious. Snake had a double order of oysters. After awhile, when we had finished eating, two men came up and sat down with us.

"Dev, this is Tony DiNardo and this is Tom Cooper. This is Dr. Winfield Devlin. Tell Dev what you know about Ricardo Salazar." DiNardo was a dark swarthy man who looked as if he'd just shaved. He never seemed to blink while he was talking. He seemed to know Snake fairly well but called him Moran. Tom Cooper was a little on the pudgy side but nice looking.

"We've been trying to pin something on Ricardo Salazar for a long time but not for drugs. We think he's been buying and selling works of art without paying taxes on the profits. A person who knows what he's doing can buy a painting at a public auction at a fair price where the sale is recorded. He holds the picture a few years then smuggles it into another country. He sells it at a profit and pays no taxes or duty. The art they are smuggling is damn near priceless. The profits run into the millions. It's done all the time but Salazar has the resources to do it with the really great works of art. A few years ago we found out Moran was searching and buying pieces for Salazar. We offered him a lot of money to help us catch him. Moran refused and said he wouldn't work against a client. Said it was unethical. Then he goes and investigates Salazar on his own and brings us records of a bunch of deals. The records show Salazar is clean on art deals. Or at least very smart.

"A week ago Moran contacts me and tells me Salazar is into dealing drugs. He says art is one thing and drugs is different. I talk to Tom, who is D.E.A., without revealing my source. Tom tells me they think Salazar is a cousin of some people in Medellin, Colombia. They know for sure that a guy named Carlos Lehder-Rivas is smuggling drugs. The D.E.A. is after him but he stays in the Bahamas or Colombia most of the time. We check a lot of sources and we know Salazar met with Lehder-Rivas in the Bahamas sometime in July. We had a guy on Lehder. They were both on Norman's Cay at the same time. Cooper calls Moran. They meet and he repeats the story."

DiNardo stared at me without moving his eyes or blinking while he talked.

"I believe Moran and my bosses might believe me. Cooper feels the same. We can put it all together but we can't do anything about it. The system is fucked up. The top guys in every agency are lawyers. Moran says you will confirm everything he told us. Is that true?"

"I don't know what he told you," I said, not knowing how far he had gone. Snake repeated the entire story exactly as it happened except the part about me shooting the two women and the garbage man. He told them that he did the shooting instead of me. I nodded frequently as he talked. When he finished I elaborated on the powerful radios and the fact that Ricardo lied about going to Nassau then lied again about it the next time I saw him.

"Dr. Devlin, we really appreciate the information," said Cooper. "We believe you and Sean. He says Salazar is going to help you build a medical clinic. We need you to keep your eyes and ears open. We know a lot of stuff we can't prove. We don't have enough to make a case against a guy that big. Here's an unlisted number. Ask for me and I'll call you back." DiNardo also gave me a number without saying anything.

"Can you tell me what you *are* going to do?" I asked.

"You want a an honest answer?"

"Yes."

"Nothing. Not a fucking thing. The Salazars are citizens of Spain with connections high up in the government. Both Ricardo and his son also have job titles in the Spanish foreign department. They don't actually do anything but it gives them diplomatic immunity. The information you gave us is very important but it is just one piece of the puzzle. Our people can't make a move without clearance from a lot of people. Even the Ambassador to Spain would have to be involved."

"I don't understand. You guys have been involved in all sorts of stuff over in Southeast Asia. Covert action to topple dictators and communist and things like that. I know the threat of communism is important but drugs are killing people right now, right here. Sharon Moran was in my clinic and I saw first hand what happened to her just because some ass-hole kid talked her into trying something. It seems to me that illegal drugs pouring into this country should be a higher priority than the threat of communism half way around the world. I know you guys don't run the government but I have a very distinct impression that nothing is ever going to happen to Ricardo or Butch Salazar."

"Dr. Devlin, you're a physician. You have a specialty and you're probably good at it. I don't blame you for lack of progress in finding a cure for something like Alzheimers. You're probably a member of the American Medical Association. But you're just one member. I don't even believe doctors have much to say about where money is spent on research. There are so many people involved in decisions about things like drugs that I couldn't even count them. The head of the C.I.A. is a political appointment. The Secretary of State has a lot to do with it. The straight story is that unfortunately you are right. We believe what you say and I think I can convince my boss but I think it will end there. I'm sorry but that's what I believe."

Cooper shrugged agreement and the two men thanked us again and left. I waited to see Sean's reaction. "I'm disappointed and actually surprised," Snake said.

"How high up is DiNardo?"

"There are two levels between him and the Director."

"How about Cooper?"

"About the same. They're good guys. I trust them both but they are right. There is really nothing that can be done. Ricardo Salazar has too much power. We see that as the main reason to do something but it is also the reason why he can't be touched. I can get Hogge myself because he is one man. He's not that important in the overall picture. He's local and it's just personal revenge. Period."

"Will you continue to work for Ricardo? Search for paintings and artifacts?"

"For a while, anyway. What about you? He's going to put up some money for a clinic you want to build. Are you going to take the money?"

"No."

"What are you going to tell him?"

"I'm not going to tell him anything. I'm going to kill him."

"Are you out of your fucking mind? You shot those whores and the guy because you had to. Why don't you kill the whole mafia or maybe the Chinese communist army. Taking on Ricardo is like declaring war against Cuba all by yourself."

"Do you know who Count von Stauffenberg is?"

"The guy who tried to kill Hitler, right?"

"He would have killed him if the bomb in the briefcase wasn't put behind a heavy table leg. The war could have ended sooner."

"He didn't get him though and they killed his ass for trying. They tortured him and hung him. They also forced Rommel to commit suicide because he was in on it."

"He had a chance, though, because he could get close to Hitler. I can get close to Ricardo."

"Devlin, I think you're fucking nuts. I'm supposed to be the crazy one. You get close and kill him and you're dead in two seconds. I know how to capture one guy. I'm good at it. I know how to assassinate somebody. One person. Maybe two or three if I'm on a hot streak. You don't know how to do that kind of thing. You must have had a few drinks before I got here. Are you sure you're not drunk?"

"Before you got here I was thinking about how the C.I.A. could get to Ricardo. They do a lot of killing in other countries and I thought they might be able to do it here. I figured out a way that they could kill him and Butch both. Now I can do it."

"How?"

"You don't need to know. If I succeed DiNardo and Cooper will think you were involved. You need to be somewhere else next Saturday that gives you a perfect alibi. Maybe up in Vermont with Sharon and Laufenberg. They won't suspect me for the reasons you just gave. You have the unlisted number. Use it if I get killed.

"Those guys just explained that the C.I.A. and D.E.A. will fuck around until they hold the Winter Olympics in Cuba. I wanted to know the government situation, how screwed up it is. I wanted to know and I'm glad I did. I had a part of a plan for them but I can do it myself."

"Devlin, you're crazy. You don't belong in this shit. You need to see a psychiatrist. Are you a fucking existentialist or something? Do you think you're responsible for everything?"

"No. I've read that philosophical stuff. I don't really understand it but that is not me. That's all abstract. Laufenberg said I had a lot of repressed anger left over from when I was a kid. He said that I might kill somebody some day. Maybe he was right."

"I hear what you're telling me but I don't understand it. You're not personally responsible for everything shitty that happens in this country. Explain why you think you personally have to kill Ricardo and Butch?

"O.K.," I said. "Let me try. One day there was this guy sitting in his office. His boss calls him in and fires him for no reason. He goes home and the fire trucks are there because his house has just burned down. A neighbor gives him a letter. It's from his wife. She's divorcing him. She's left with both kids and the car. He's really having a bad day. He sits down on the curb and starts crying and praying. Then he looks up to heaven and asks God what he has done to deserve what happened. 'Almighty God, what did I do wrong? What did I do to deserve this?' he asks. There is a loud rumble of thunder and the voice of God speaks to him. God says – 'You have done nothing wrong, my son. You *just piss me off!*'"

Snake stared at me with a strange look in his eyes.

"You have to kill the Salazars because you think you're God?"

"No, Snake. I'm not God. I'm just a doctor. I have to kill the Salazars because they piss me off."

Snake stared at me for a while. He was sitting with his back to the water and the sky. Past the thatched roof of the next tiki-hut-table I could see a big pile of cumulus clouds floating by, separate, distinctly shaped puffs and fleecy domed ones. They were towering clouds, brightly white in the sunlight.

Snake stared at me some more but he didn't say anything for a while.

"Let me get this straight. You're going to kill two of the most powerful criminals in the world just because they piss you off? No noble purpose or greater justice or belief in God or any of that. You're going to kill them just because they piss you off?"

"That's the best explanation I can give you."

Snake got a funny look on his face.

"Now I understand. You have to kill them because they piss you off. That makes sense. They piss me off too. You're right – we have to kill them. We have to kill them because they have pissed us off!"

We started laughing and then sat there without talking or eating. Then Snake said, "I've figured out what I'm going to do with Emile Hogge but exterminating him is strictly personal. I'll get revenge and I'll enjoy it immensely but it's purely me and him. I'm in the art department at Interpol, not the drug department. But killing Ricardo and Butch would be the single worst thing that ever happened to the drug business. Might even slow it down a little. I've killed a few people in the line of business but I never killed anybody before because they just pissed me off. Now I really understand."

"Sean, I was half asleep when I got dressed to go to the hospital but I knew I had an opportunity to kill Butch. I think subconsciously I planned to from the time I got the phone call. I even got Maggie Lindsay to come out and assist me on what was a minor case. Driving from home to the hospital I realized that I was actually trying to think of a way to kill them. I don't know anything about how the D.E.A. actually works on the drug problem but I already knew that it's almost impossible to catch the top people. DiNardo and Cooper confirmed it. I guess we have a 'once in a lifetime' opportunity."

"How the fuck can we do it and stay alive?" Snake said. "Why did you mention Saturday?"

"Because I know their schedule on Saturday. I think I know a time and place where they will be vulnerable."

"Tell me."

"I don't actually know *how* to do it but I do think I know where it can be done. Before you got here today I was making notes to try to clear up my thinking. Note number 3 says let Snake plan it." I showed him.

"Number 2 says control the schedule."

"How can you do that?" Snake asked.

I described how I was planning to examine Butch's face at *Casa del Malecón* on Saturday morning. I expected it to be O.K. and that they would leave around noon. To some extent I could control the time. We would know within a few hours. I told him how they take the *Ojos Verdes* across the shallow part of North Biscayne Bay and turn south on the Intra-coastal. Knowing the time they were leaving the dock we could predict when they would make the turn. He realized immediately that this could work. They would have no protection and no room to maneuver. They would be vulnerable.

If they went up around Great Isaac and Great Stirrup Lights we could predict about when they would pass each one but only within four or five hours. Out there would be much, much harder. Snake ordered another drink for himself.

"I believe we can kill them without any professional help at all. No C.I.A or D.E.A. I have three days to put together a plan but I think I can do it. I will have to get the right explosives. We will probably need some more people but only as a cover. Maybe the people who already know about Sharon and the Salazars. Maybe Gus, Paulette, and one or two more. That's all. It will be dangerous but just for you and me. No danger for them at all. Who else could we get?"

"Bill Gaines if there's no danger to him. Rocket if there's no danger to her. It wouldn't be right to involve either of them if there's any risk. Sidney would help, too."

"Sidney's a priest, Dev. How could you ask him to help in a killing, even indirectly?"

"Because I know how he feels about drug addiction and drug dealers."

Sean turned and stared out at Biscayne Bay for a while.

"You're right, Dev, at the exact moment when they turn south on the waterway *Ojos Verdes* will be extremely vulnerable. We can get them."

Chapter Thirty

Saturday, 9 September
I left my apartment at six thirty to drive over to Ricardo's house. I wanted to check Butch's progress and say goodbye to Toni. I also wanted to pin down the time they would leave the dock so we could catch them at the turning point and kill them. It was a still day, hot and completely windless with a perfect Carolina blue sky. Driving across the Julia Tuttle Causeway I looked out at the water and Biscayne Bay was like a huge pane of glass. Perfect for power boats or racing hydroplanes. It was early in the day and there was no traffic.

I drove past the guardhouse and across the low bridge out to the island. *Casa del Melecón* looked like a fairytale castle, zinc white and beautiful with the cerulean blue sky as a background. *Blanc de zinc. Bleu de Céruleun verit.* It really was like a fairy tale. Once upon a time there was a beautiful castle with cruel monsters lurking inside. The monsters were named Salazar. And of course there was a princess. Toni came down the stairs as soon as I walked in. A servant had let me in and when he left she kissed me on the mouth and whispered, "I'm so happy you came to say goodbye. I am already very sad that I am leaving. *Muy triste.* I know my love is only a crush but it hurts just as much to say farewell. I will miss you so much." She did look sad. And very beautiful.

She showed me to an upstairs room where Butch was reading the *Yachtsman's Guide to the Bahamas.* He was drinking coffee through a straw and looking at the Guide and some charts of the Bahamas he had spread out. I reminded myself that I had to act natural.

"Are you still planning on leaving for Nassau today?"

"Unless you screwed up my stitches, we're leaving around noon. We're going to sail and motor straight across. We're taking three men with us so we can go all the way without stopping. The weather report looks good. Mother is flying to Nassau about an hour after Toni leaves for Madrid."

"I wish I were coming with you."

"I wish we both were," Toni said. "I wish I was going over to Nassau instead of back to school in Spain. I'm tired of school. I would much prefer to stay here."

We talked for a while and then I asked Toni to leave the room so I could examine Butch's face. I took off all the bandages and checked every part of it that had been cut by the glass. I had brought along some instruments with me and was able to pick out a few almost microscopic bits of glass I had missed before. His face was red and raw, still covered with tiny scabs where the wounds were healing. I was satisfied with the progress so I put on some entirely new bandages which covered his whole head. I did not want adhesive tape to be touching his skin. He was like a mummy except that he had holes for his ears, eyes, nose and mouth. Because he was healing properly, the holes in the new bandages were bigger than in the old ones. While I was finishing up I told him about the doctor in Nassau.

"I have the name and address of a doctor in Nassau who is a plastic surgeon. I want you to see him as soon as you can after one more week. Monday, September 18 or soon after. I don't want you to take off the bandages until then but he should be able to do it for you. The cuts were mostly small and they're healing well. None of them are infected now but I want you to be really careful. A lot of tiny little infections would drive you nuts. You will recover completely."

As I put the last piece of tape on him I tried to be funny.

"After the bandages come off you can get *mucha panocha.*"

"In that case I am calling Alice Grey right now to invite her to fly over for the weekend after that. Why don't you come over, too. There's plenty of room at the new house. The two of you could fly over together. Call her on Monday and find out if she's coming. Bring Pat Rivera or somebody. If you come alone I'll fix you up with a girl over there."

We talked for a while and then shook hands and said goodbye. As we were walking down the huge stairs together Butch said, "I'm going down to the dock now and finish loading up the boat. My parents have gone to the grocery store. I'm going to leave you alone so you can say goodbye to Toni. You know, Dev, I think she's got a crush on you. She's never said anything to me but she gets a kind of goofy look when you're around. Be nice and kiss her goodbye. See you in Nassau."

Butch called out to Toni that he was going to the boat and that I would be leaving. She was in the library so I went in. After she made sure nobody was around she kissed me. It was a long kiss but sweet and sad. I suddenly realized that I was going to miss her very much. "I want you to keep on kissing me but Carmela will be back any second. She's taking me to the airport in her limousine in just a few minutes. Kiss me one last time and put your hand on my *chocha*. Then run out to your car before I get too excited and make you *chingar me otra vez.*"

The second kiss was sadder than the first and after several minutes we pulled apart and started out the door. Her parting words were specific. "I love you, Devlin. I want you to think of me all the time. Please come to see me in Madrid. I will write to you."

I thought about Toni all the way from Miami Beach back to the Yacht Club in Coconut Grove. Maybe I would go to Spain later in the Fall. After we killed Butch and Ricardo. What a mess!

I met Rocket and Bill Gaines on the Yacht Club porch and we made a point of wandering around for a few minutes and talking to people. We wanted them to remember seeing us. Doing that was one of Snake's ideas. He had told Paulette and Gus to do the same thing at Dinner Key Marina when they were leaving. I thought it seemed a little silly myself but I did what he suggested. I introduced Bill to several people and we said that we were going to anchor out and watch the Florida State game on a portable television. The swimming pool was crowded and we made a point of talking to some people as we walked by.

Neither Bill or Rocket asked a single question, even when we got aboard the boat. They knew that we were going to raft up and that Gus and I were going to leave the boat and go somewhere with Snake. We put some food and drinks and the television set aboard then started the engine. We waved at people as we moved out of the slip and started over toward Dinner Key Marina. We passed the docks at Monty Trainer's and Merrill-Stevens. I thought about the little airplane that Gus and Sidney were going to build up in the huge old Pan-Am hangars and wondered if it would ever get finished. I figured that Gus would finish most anything he started but I wasn't sure about Sidney.

We passed between the little islands and started out the long channel through the anchored boats. I always looked at them and wondered what was going on. Some were derelicts and some had odd characters living aboard. Most of them were just old boats with nice people who liked their freedom and didn't like to pay dockage. I looked around for *Pauletta*.

When we passed through the last two channel markers Gus was there. When he saw us he turned east over toward Key Biscayne. I fell into line behind him and we both increased our speed a little. It was such a hot and breathless day that moving through the air felt good. We crossed Biscayne Bay and found a spot just north of the entrance to Hurricane Harbor and the shoals around Southwest Point. We were about a mile west of where Richard Nixon and Bebe Rebozo used to hang out. It was a popular spot for anchoring and swimming or having a picnic because it was shallow enough for easy anchoring and far enough from Key Biscayne to get any little breeze that might come up.

Gus dropped his anchor and we came alongside. We both put out huge bumpers and tied up together. Gus then spent a few minutes telling me what a mess the *Brilliant* was and asking why I didn't clean it up. This was a ritual with us. Back when we both came to Coconut Grove I lived on my immaculate little schooner *Vanitie* and he lived on the *Nancy B* his almost derelict Tahiti ketch. I had made a point then of needling him about his boat. Now that we both had new ones which were in excellent shape he was getting back at me. It always ended the same way. I would remind him that only a fool would ride around on a motorcycle at his age and he would point out that my green car was the ugliest in history. We had the insults down pat, even the theatrics that went with them.

There were six of us. We all sat in the cockpit of *Pauletta* boat and talked. We talked about the weather and Bill talked about golf and Gus and Sidney talked about the *Aviat Eagle*. Rocket and Paulette talked about clothes. Nobody talked about what we were going to do when Snake got there. At ten o'clock we started looking around for him and spotted what looked like a huge tug boat in the distance coming our way. As it got within ten feet we could see that the boat was in fact a tiny little thing only about thirty feet long that had been made to look like a tug. It had a pilot house sticking straight up and there was a figure standing at the wheel inside behind the window. The boat came alongside and Snake was driving.

"I decided to come in a disguise," he said. "How do you like it?"

The little boat looked just like a miniature tug boat with a real looking pilot house and even small tires around the rail for bumpers and a big pad made from hemp rope on the bow where a real tug would push. It had big boards on the side with the name *Theodore Fremd* carved into them. The pilot house was red and white and black and very authentic looking. It was cute as hell. Gus and I climbed aboard. We did it in such a way that nobody from the distant shore or the three boats anchored in the same area could see us leave the two rafted boats. Snake stood up and waved then went inside the tiny wheelhouse while Gus and I crouched down so that nobody could see us. Then Rocket jumped aboard.

"You are supposed to stay here," I said.

"You needed me when we went to get Sharon and I'm going with you today. Don't waste time arguing."

I looked at Snake and he shrugged. We couldn't forget what a job she did navigating and driving the boat when we went to Norman's Cay. Rocket had gotten to know Sharon when she was in the clinic just as I had and I guessed that her desire for revenge was as great as mine. Nevertheless, she wasn't really needed and I didn't want her with us. When we were planning the rescue it seemed like a great adventure but now I knew what we were doing. I knew it was going to be very dangerous and if we were successful it was going to be murder. I tried to talk her out of coming with us.

"I am coming with you! And don't say you don't need me because you don't know what is going to happen and I can drive a boat as good as any of you!"

Snake and Gus stayed out of the argument but Rocket shut me up when she talked about leaving.

"I'm going to New York in a few weeks and I want to finish this thing with Sharon. You got me into it in the first place and now you can't tell me what to do!" I had to back down.

After I convinced Snake that we could destroy *Ojos Verdes* when she was turning south on the Intra-coastal he developed our plan. He knew that either the police or Ricardo's employees might eventually check out all of the family's friends and acquaintances. Rocket and I would be able to say we were rafting up with Gus, Paulette and Bill. Nobody else involved even knew Ricardo or Butch. If I was ever checked out I would have four witnesses to say I was there on the boat all afternoon. Snake planned to say he was in Nassau that day and I'm sure he can prove it. The people staying aboard said goodbye and good luck quietly and we left. Our plan had started with just Snake and me leaving the raft-up but Gus bitched so much we agreed to take him with us. Now we had Rocket as well. We stopped talking and the little tug boat pulled away from the two anchored sailboats.

Snake accelerated the little boat up onto a plane and headed for the Rickenbacker Causeway bridge going over to Virginia Key. The little tug was fast as hell so we got there quickly and passed under the huge expanse. Then we went up the channel going north past Claughton Island and the entrance to the Miami River, and under the bascule bridge going out to Dodge Island and the Port of Miami. Just before Watkins Island we turned right going out Government Cut. Going up the Cut we passed the big cruise ships on Dodge and all kinds of small boats going in both directions. When we got to the outer end of the cut we turned north again just before Miami Beach Marina. From there we went up past Star Island, under the fixed bridge at Belle Isle and after that I got confused. Snake was steering and he went through some waterways and canals that I didn't recognize at all. He took a sharp turn into a narrow strip of water with old buildings and sheds on both sides.

We went up the canal about halfway and turned left under one of the huge sheds. The slip we went into was empty but there were big work boats in all of the other sheds. It was a Saturday and there were no people around. We tied up to a dock at the far end and Snake took off our tug boat disguise. He and Gus unscrewed ten bolts that were holding the pilot house in place and the four of us lifted the whole thing up on the dock. Then we carried it into a shed where Snake covered it with a piece of canvas. After that he took off the little decorative tires that looked so realistic from a distance and the boards with the name on each side. We put them with the pilothouse. When we got back in the boat it was just a thirty foot fiberglass fishing boat with a small center console. There was no name on the boat.

Before we left the cover of the huge shed Snake said we had to put on disguises. He opened up a box that looked like it was full of furry animals but they turned out to be a wig and beard for Gus that was quite red and a wig and beard that was blonde for me. Snake had a black beard and suddenly a bald head. His hair which happened to be black that day was covered by some sort of latex cap. My beard was O.K. but I could have made a better one myself. The disguises wouldn't be any good up close. He handed a baseball cap to Rocket and told her to put her hair up inside. I guess he knew she might insist on coming. From a distance we would look like four men fishing.

"Jesus Christ, Sean," Gus complained. "Do we have to get all dressed up in these Halloween outfits just to blow somebody's ass off?"

"Fuck you, Gus," Snake said. "I'm an international expert at blowing up people. I know what I'm doing."

"Sometimes," I said. "I think you like to use disguises just because you think it's fun."

We were all nervous, I suppose, but somehow it seemed like we were just going fishing. We pulled out of the shed and retraced our route out to North Biscayne Bay, Then we went over to the Julia Tuttle Causeway and ran parallel to that going west away from Miami Beach until we had crossed the Bay and got into the Intra-coastal between the green thirty-nine marker and forty-one. From there we went north on the Intra-coastal until we got to the exact place where *Ojos Verdes* would turn south. We found the spot, sighting the large white building to the west in Miami and the tree on Ricardo's island to the east. The building and tree placed us north and south and the Intra-coastal markers lined us up east and west. This was where *Ojos Verdes* would make the turn and get blown up. After we pin-pointed the spot Snake took a canvas tarp off something in the stern. It was a big U.S. Navy undersea mine. All three men were needed to lift it. We put it on the rail, rolled it over and it went right to the bottom. Then Snake rolled over the side with some tools in his arms. Dropping the mine took less than two minutes.

Gus, Rocket and I motored straight southeast for about fifty yards, anchored the boat and waited for Sean. It was almost twenty minutes before he appeared and climbed up into the boat. The four of us sat down on the cockpit seats to wait.

"I think I got the wrong size mine," he said. "That fucker is big enough to handle a destroyer."

"What are we going to do now?" I asked.

"I don't want to join Ricardo for dinner in hell tonight so let's move the boat a little bit further away. There are going to be a lot of dead fish in Biscayne Bay and I don't want to be one of them."

We moved the boat a little and Snake went over the plan again.

"We're now about two hundred feet southeast of where they should make the turn. That funny looking thing on the console is the thing that sets off the explosion. I push a button and boom. If we go any further away the transmitter won't work. They're supposed to leave about twelve o'clock and Ricardo is always very exact about time. If their plans are changed and they don't leave today then it's just too bad. I'll have to think of another plan. We turn on channel sixteen now and start listening. Twenty or thirty seconds before we detonate the mine I start playing a recording of a Mayday call on channel sixteen. The call says there's a fire aboard the boat and the fire is spreading fast. About ten seconds before the explosion the caller will identify his boat as *Ojos Verdes*."

"We'll wait here for ten minutes just watching and doing nothing. If the explosives work as well as they are supposed to, there won't be anything much left of the boat or the people in it. The bullshit about a fire aboard is just to confuse people. Listen to Pat Rivera on the seven o'clock news. I've given Pat a couple of clues that something is going to happen to someone who's right at the top of the drug trade. She doesn't know who or what's going to happen but she does know it will be this afternoon and she'll be listening to channel sixteen and recording every call. She thinks her information came from the C.I.A and she thinks I am in Nassau."

"We'll leave here fairly slowly and then haul ass back to the other boats where I'll leave the three of you. Everybody will go back to the marina and the Yacht Club and find a few people who you can talk to about the raft-up. Just mention it, don't elaborate. Since there's no way to tie any of us to Ricardo except Dev and me, the subterfuge is probably unnecessary. We aren't really worried about the police. We're concerned about friends of Ricardo's – ones that we don't know about. Ones that know about us. I'm going to wait for a while before I take care of Emile Hogge. Probably more than a month."

"After I drop you off I'll disappear for a few weeks. You will eventually hear from me but don't worry because I'm really in the Bahamas right now eating lobster and I will leave Nassau tomorrow for Europe."

"What do we do if something happens and we get separated?" Rocket asked. "Like if this boat sinks or something."

"You mean before we get back to the other boats? If that happens you go back to Sidney's apartment. Gus you go there, too. The people on *Pauletta* and *Brilliant* will take the boats back in after dark. I left a note with instructions. I gave it to Sidney. They will wait until 8:00 o'clock and then leave."

There didn't seem to be much else to talk about so we got some fishing rods and pretended to fish. At least Gus did. He actually tried to catch something. Snake turned on the radio and started listening to the conversations on channel sixteen. We were too far away from Ricardo's house and dock to be able to see anything and the docks were hidden anyway by the trees on the little strip of land that formed the tiny harbor.

I got myself in a comfortable position and sat staring off in the distance at the trees on the island, occasionally using binoculars. The strip of land was less than ten feet wide but the Australian pines had been planted close together for protection from the wind so I couldn't see anything behind them. Snake told me to use the binoculars only at brief intervals because they could reflect the light and get somebody's attention.

I watched the other two men out of the corner of my eye. Snake was alert and listening carefully to the radio. He seemed aware of everything around us and stayed perfectly calm. I had read someplace once that one of the qualifications they wanted in an astronaut was the ability to do repetitious tasks or even nothing for long periods of time without becoming bored or upset. I had often wondered how they could sit quietly while there were delays and postponements for a launch. I knew I would go crazy or at least fall asleep. I wouldn't make it as an astronaut and I wouldn't be worth a damn as a secret agent or whatever it was that Sean claimed to be. He was always taking precautions on top of precautions or lurking around someplace. I didn't like the disguises much, either. The wig and the beard were hot as hell in the sun and very itchy. I got a hat and made myself comfortable on the seat. I started getting sleepy and my mind wandered all over, mostly daydreaming about women.

Half dozing, I thought about Lisa Winter for a few seconds, standing in the bungalow on Norman's Cay in her pale blue panties and watching me as I examined her. How incredibly painful it must have been for her to know how much desire I felt but also know she could never feel any of her own — for me or anybody.

I thought about little Rocket, too, and her farewell speech. I wondered what would happen after today. I liked having her here with me today but if anything happened to her I knew I would blame myself. For some reason a particular memory came back to me. Something that had happened when we first started making love and I was still trying to match her wildness and crazy remarks. We were rolling around on the double bunk in the forward cabin of *Brilliant* and she was naked except for pink panties. She was very hot and excited and very, very wet. I had my hand between her legs and I tried to tease her about the wetness.

"Good grief, Rocket," I had said. "What is this slippery, sticky stuff that's all over your underpants?"

"Rocket fuel," she said. "Pure high octane rocket fuel. Take off my pinkies. There's plenty more."

I looked over at her. She saw me and smiled.

"Think pink," she said. She knew I would understand. I did.

God, I was going to miss her. I knew when this business of killing Butch and Ricardo was over the pain of losing Rocket was going to be intense so I thought about Toni and her burgundy underwear and the little chain and cross on her stomach. Then I thought about Pat Rivera and how hard it had been to get blue and white and green oil paint mixed to do the aqua panties. After Pat I thought about Chocolata and how ugly that night in the room at the Fontainebleau had been and that rotten thought cooled me off completely. Almost anyway. I thought of the gorgeous blonde woman who approached me at the bar and said she was Sean Moran. If I could get her name I could call her.

"Hey, Snake," I said, breaking the silence. "How can I get in touch with the blonde lady who was with you at the Fontainebleau that night? I'm a little short of girlfriends right now and I would like to meet her. What's her real name?"

"His name is Bruce Watson. He just looks like a gorgeous blonde. He's really with the D.E.A. He goes where they would like to send a woman but consider it too dangerous. He's got a black belt in Karate and a black garter belt to hold up his socks. A very dangerous man."

"In that case forget the introduction."

Rocket didn't make any noise but I could see that she was laughing. Then there was silence again and the time passed slowly. There was a little break in the monotony when Gus actually caught two fish. He was enjoying himself as if we were really there to fish and nothing else. Snake never appeared to get bored or tired. He never missed anything that happened wherever he was. He was a clown sometimes but today he seemed to see and hear everything.

Butch told me this morning when I took off the bandages and examined his face that they would leave for Nassau at about twelve o'clock to catch the tide. When it got to be two o'clock I was beginning to think they had changed plans. It was not until almost two thirty when Sean said they were coming.

"*Ojos Verdes* is on the way. Get everything ready. Put away the fishing rod, Gus, and wake up Devlin."

Snake told me to put my binoculars on them for a second or two as they were coming out and then to start watching and counting constantly when I thought they were about three minutes from the turn. I was to say "turning now" as they went around and started south down the Intra-coastal.

The first time I took a quick look the cockpit was full of people. I watched the big boat coming without binoculars. She was so beautiful, so graceful and majestic. I didn't put the binoculars back on them until I guessed they were about two minutes from their turn.

"Two minutes," I said. Many years of counting off the minutes and seconds when I was timing the starts of sailboat races made this seem natural. "One minute thirty seconds." I paused. "One minute."

Snake started the taped recording and I could hear a strange excited voice going out on VHF channel sixteen. Every boat that was monitoring the stand-by channel would hear it.

"This is a Mayday call. This is a Mayday call. We have a fire aboard. We have a fire aboard. This is a Mayday call. This is a Mayday call. We have a fire aboard and it is out of control. We have a fire aboard and it is out of control."

"Thirty seconds," I said. The recorded voice continued.

"We have a fire that's out of control. Mayday."

"Twenty seconds. Ten seconds."

"This is the yacht *Ojos Verdes*. Yacht *Ojos Verdes*. Fire out of control. *Ojos Verdes*. Out of control," said the recording.

"Turning now!" I said.

"Fuck you, Butch. Fuck you Ricardo," Snake said and hit the button.

A split second before I heard any sound, the huge yacht seemed to lift about ten feet out of the water, and then as we heard the tremendous sound of the explosion the hull split apart in the middle. The bow and the stern pointed down. The main mast swung way forward and was almost parallel to the water just before it went under. The mizzen did the same thing the other way. It may have been my imagination, but I thought I saw some body parts flying around in the air, maybe even a head. It was over in just a few seconds, a huge explosion, startling in size. The waves created by the explosion reached us and bobbled our boat around and then in less than five minutes there was no sign of *Ojos Verdes* except debris in the water.

A baldheaded Snake Moran with a black beard turned and looked at Gus and Rocket and me.

"We killed him real good but now I've lost a client. He was a great art collector. I think we should leave here very slowly now. We don't want to attract attention."

Suddenly, just as we started the motor, I saw Gus point.

"Look over there! That boat is coming right at us and coming fast!"

All three of us looked in the direction of Ricardo's island. There was a boat, something that looked like a Cigarette coming right at us with the bow way up in the air and spray flying out to the sides. It had come out of Salazar's harbor and was only a mile away. The people on board must have seen the big explosion. It flashed through my mind that this had to be a bodyguard boat and that it must be the same boat that seemed to follow us over to Bimini that weekend.

"Go forward and pull up the anchor, Gus, and you take the wheel, Dev. Start the engine but don't put it in gear. We can't outrun them," Snake instructed. He moved to the stern, taking a canvas bag with him. He pulled out a machine pistol or AK47 or something, and a big machete and laid them on the seat. He stood up in the stern and started waving at the oncoming boat. He looked like he was trying to attract them or signal them. When the Cigarette got closer they slowed down and we could see there were about six men in the boat. Snake started yelling at them in some language that sounded like Chinese. They were startled and slowed almost to a stop as they tried to hear what he was saying. Snake waved them to come closer then reached into his canvas bag and pulled out a hand grenade. He pulled the pin with his hands down below the gunwales where they couldn't see and then tossed it the twenty feet right into the Cigarette boat. Perfect throw. Another big explosion. *Boom!!*

The hand grenade did not have nearly the explosive power of the mine but the Cigarette wasn't nearly as big as the ketch. We were so close that all sorts of debris landed on us, including some more body parts. A piece of a hand with a thumb and two fingers landed in our boat. Snake stared at where the Cigarette had been. "Fuck you, Butch's friends!" he said. "Wait for a second so we can see if they're all dead, then let's go."

Snake sat down on a seat in the stern and I stood up to look at some floating things. Gus was in the bow and I was back just forward of Snake. I looked east toward Ricardo's island and then glanced back at Snake. Suddenly something leaped up out of the water. A big man climbed up on the low stern of the boat and grabbed Snake. For a brief second I saw the nasty looking face of a man who had sat across from me at Joe Lehder's dinner party.

He clutched Snake's head with one hand, pulled it way back and slit his throat with a huge knife held in the other hand. The latex bald head came off and it looked like he was being scalped at the same time. There was blood everywhere. Rocket screamed. Without thinking I grabbed the machete off the seat and swung at the man's head. Because it was so close to Snake I couldn't swing sideways, so I swung straight down. The blade of the huge machete hit the top of his head and sliced it right down the middle like a watermelon. Apparently the machete was razor sharp because it went right through his skull and brains and right down through his face into his neck. Because he was turned slightly to one side his nose stayed intact and one eye went with each part as the head fell into two halves.

While I was using the machete another man came up out of the water and was trying to strangle Gus. Gus was choking and it looked like he was going to pass out. Then he put the fingers of his right hand in the man's mouth. He worked the fingers of his left hand into the mouth also and slowly pulled the man's jaw down until it ripped, making a terrible crunching noise. The guy tried to scream but he had no mouth so he just gurgled and slipped into the water. At the same time I watched as two other men started climbing over the side of our boat. Rocket shot each of them in the head. Up close. She didn't have to draw or aim.

I yelled at Rocket to leave in a hurry and grabbed Snake as he fell forward. Rocket gunned the engine and we made a wide circle bumping into a lot of bodies. There was blood everywhere. The fake beard that Snake had been wearing was soaked in it. I laid him out on the bottom of the cockpit and pulled the blood soaked beard away. He was still conscious and his eyes were moving but he was obviously in shock. His throat had been cut but because of all the blood I couldn't tell how deep the knife had gone. I took off my shirt and used it as a mop to get some of the blood away so I could make a closer examination. Then I got my medical bag and used gauze. I was able to stop the bleeding temporarily in several places and get a look. The cut was long and ugly but apparently not deep enough to cut the carotid artery. Very close, though. The thick black fake beard had protected his neck just enough to be the difference between life and death. The difference between a cut throat and a slit throat is the severing of the artery.

I stuck a breathing tube down his throat then packed gauze around his neck. By this time Rocket was doing about twenty knots down the Intra-coastal, passing boats and getting yelled at for the wake we made. When we passed under the Julia Tuttle Causeway bridge I had her turn and go out in the middle of the Bay between the Venetian Causeway and the Julia Tuttle. It's pretty shallow out there and I had Gus go over the side and hold the boat while he was standing up to his chest in water. Fortunately there was a minimum of chop and the boat was steady enough for me to sew up Sean's throat. Since I had done surgery on accident cases in some strange locations I was used to it. I had my medical bag with me and some extra things that were needed for rough plastic surgery. I injected Snake several times with a local anesthetic and started stitching. There were a few places where I had to do some repair work below the surface flesh but for the most part it was superficial. I did the tiny sutures as carefully as I would on an operating table. When I finished I bandaged his throat and laid him down on the cockpit floor. We took off again. He would be all right.

We went toward the beach and through the fixed bridge where the Collins Canal comes out near Belle Isle. Then down past the Miami Beach Marina and the Coast Guard Station. Snake pointed left without speaking so we went out Government Cut.

We went out through the rock jetties into the ocean and turned south. We stayed away from the beach but opened up the engines to full speed and steered in a broad curve down toward Cape Florida. We rounded it close and stayed near Key Biscayne past No Name Harbor and then around the point. We had nearly run out of daylight but both boats were still rafted up where we had left them.

Snake was not too talkative. I had threatened to inject him with a knockout drug if he said one word. He had to leave quickly so I decided to send Bill with Snake in the runabout in case he passed out or started bleeding again. I had a deck-wash pump that we used to pump salt water and clean up some of the blood in the little boat. When we finished there were still a lot of stains. Bill gave us several buckets of fish they had caught during the long afternoon wait. We dumped them right in the bottom of the boat and some of the fish blood partly covered up the bloodstains. Snake was still shaky but beginning to function again. He made signals with his hands that he wanted something to write with.

"What are you going to do?" I asked Snake after I had given him a pad and pencil from my nav station and handed him a chart. He pointed out a spot down south of Matheson Hammock and wrote the words "private dock, no people, car there."

Then he and Bill Gaines got back in the little boat and took off across Biscayne Bay. There wasn't much light left but it didn't matter. We decided that Paulette would come with me since there would be a lot of people at the Yacht Club. Rocket said she wanted to go with Gus. We would put both boats away and then meet at Sidney's apartment as planned.

Chapter Thirty One

Later that night
Snake suggested that Paulette go with me so that she could be seen at the yacht club. People always remembered seeing the former movie star. He still kept his boat at Dinner Kay and there might be nobody on the dock. Gus was going to get his motorcycle and meet us at Sidney's. Motoring back across the Bay was a short trip and I treated myself to a couple of cold beers. I sat in the cockpit while she steered. She insisted I tell her about what happened. When I got to the first explosion she asked me how I felt.

"I felt a tremendous sense of loss immediately."

"They were bad people. The government would never have been able to catch them or punish them. You had to do what you did."

"I don't mean the people. I mean the boat. It was a really magnificent boat."

"I was told you had become close friends with the whole family and saw them frequently."

"That's true. In a way I'll miss them, but I'm glad it's over."

"How about Rocket? Are you glad that's over, too? I understand she's going to New York to be a sportswear designer."

"I'll miss her a lot," I admitted.

"You screwed up, Dev," Paulette said as if to console me. "Lisa Winter is very beautiful. She would be very special even in Hollywood. She's also very, very nice but I don't think she's the right person for you." I had no answer for Paulette.

We were into Dinner Key channel now with Gus right behind us and the twilight almost turned into dark.

"Paulette, honey, I love you like a sister. But instead of giving me advice why don't you find me a brand new girlfriend."

"O.K., Dev, I'll shut up but I do feel like an older sister and I think you screwed up. Rocket is the greatest. Tell me what your requirements are for a new girlfriend. Exactly what are you looking for?"

"Face like Lisa Winter, body like Pat Rivera, personality like Rocket. Do you know any like that?"

"There aren't any like that. Nowhere in the world. Rocket comes the closest."

"I know, Paulette. That's the problem." I didn't say it but the thought passed through my mind that Antonia Lara Enrique was also close to the combination that I described. She had the face now and in a few years the voluptuousness. It seemed like she had some of the enthusiasm for making love that was so much a part of Rocket. Even some of the craziness, and she was also a good sailor. I had never thought of Toni that way before. I thought about it a little and realized I was just bull-shitting myself. Toni was great but there was nobody like Rocket. In a few days she would be gone.

We didn't talk any more about anything until we had tied up the boat in my slip at the Yacht Club. There were quite a few people around the club and at the bar. We stopped to talk to a few of them and mentioned that we had been rafted up with Gus all afternoon. Most of my friends knew that Paulette was a former movie star and that she and Gus were friends of mine. When several people asked where Gus was I said he was putting his boat away and that Paulette was with me so she wouldn't have to ride with Gus on his motorcycle. People laughed but nobody thought it was strange.

It was a beautiful night with a full moon. A soft breeze had finally come out of the southeast. We drove directly to Sidney's apartment and found a parking place. I knew the uniformed doorman whose name was Zeke and I made a few comments about the Florida State football game.

When we got inside Sidney's apartment the first person we saw was Lea Kahn. Sidney told us when we were at my cookout that he was going to get all the beautiful women together and go recruiting new members for our church but I hadn't really believed him until I saw the gorgeous Oriental woman standing there. He was really going to do it. A few minutes later Lisa Winter walked in by herself and I knew Sidney was serious. He had called them as soon as he got ashore.

Rocket had come with Sidney. Lisa and Lea knew they were there to help Sidney but they did not know we had blown up the *Ojos Verdes* that afternoon. Sidney asked for everyone's attention and made a short speech.

"We are gathered here tonight to serve the Lord's purpose and seek out some new members for his church in Coconut Grove. I have prepared a simple meal so we can eat before we go out. Patricia Rivera will be meeting us later but she called and said we might be interested in watching her on the seven o'clock news since she has gotten an inside tip on some special event which the other stations do not have. Grab a sandwich or something and I'll turn on the television. First, though, let us pray."

Sidney said a short prayer in which he asked God to forgive us all our sins, especially the really big ones. It was a really strange prayer unless you had just deliberately blown up a couple of boats and killed several miscellaneous hoodlums along with two particular people.

Rocket seemed to be enjoying herself. She was kidding around with Gus and Paulette. She had a huge grin on her face and I noticed she was drinking martinis. All of us were feeling relief because it was over. And because we didn't get caught. And because we had killed and didn't get killed. Several times I moved beside Rocket and started to talk but it wasn't the right time for talk about us. It was probably a good thing that we couldn't talk openly about what happened.

The simple meal that Sidney mentioned was a small buffet that consisted of some bacon, lettuce and tomato sandwiches with huge chunks of lobster in them. He also had a dish with angel hair pasta, lots of big shrimp and a spicy cheese sauce. I got myself a full plate and sat down beside Rocket to watch Pat. Sidney had two huge T.V. sets and we all sat on couches, in chairs or on the carpet. After a few commercials, Pat came on the screen and went right into her thing. She looked gorgeous and I watched her mouth moving in all different directions as she described a breaking story.

"Several days ago I was given secret information by a high level official in one of our most powerful and efficient government agencies. I was told that a major character in the illegal drug trade was going to be terminated by agents of the Sicilian mafia. The individual himself was alleged to be part of a group from Colombia who are supposed to have headquarters in a city called Medellin. My informant contacted me only by telephone and, in fact, he believed that I was a man when he made the first call. There were three telephone calls made to me. Each one was made at a specific time to a specific public telephone and I was not allowed to ask any questions. After convincing the man that I was, in fact, Pat Rivera, I was told that he represented a United States government agency and that they wanted the assassination to get a lot of public attention in order to increase awareness of the drug problem. I was told that the termination could not be stopped because they had no proof. I was told to be at the Coast Guard station near Belle Island and the Miami Beach marina. I was apparently chosen at random from a list of television newscasters."

I could only laugh and shake my head while I watched and listened to a most incredible bullshit story. Snake must have made up the whole thing. Pat was totally animated now. Watching her made me horny in spite of what she was saying.

"I went to the Coast Guard station at 12:15 p.m. and talked to the officer in charge. I told him I wanted to hang around for a while to get some background information on the Coast Guard for a story we were going to do on their part in the drug war. They were exceptionally helpful and it was a real pleasure spending the afternoon with all those *attractive* men. I was made aware of the fact that they monitor VHF radio channel 16 all the time, so I tried to keep track of what was going on. With the permission of the Coast Guard I set up a recorder so I could get things on tape."

"At exactly 2:37 this afternoon able seaman Cleve Benson yelled out the word *"Mayday"* and turned up the volume on the VHF radio. Fortunately I had brought along a camera crew and they got some of the action. What you are going to see took place just a few hours ago at the U.S. Coast Guard station on Miami Beach."

Pat's face disappeared and then came back standing beside a Coast Guard radio operator. There was a picture of Pat waving excitedly to her camera crew to start taping. Then the sound came on and you could see and hear everybody running around and then they stopped and listened to a *Mayday* call. After a few minutes we could see Pat with a microphone describing the call, and then after explaining it she played a tape of the channel 16 call. It was perfect. She played the entire tape and at the end for just a split second the sound of the explosion. Then the silence.

Pat had somehow gotten permission to take her camera crew aboard one of the Coast Guard boats and go up to the scene of the disaster. By the time they got there, the only signs of an explosion were pieces of debris that were still floating around. They had checked out the name of the boat and after circling the area a few times they sent scuba divers down. They found wreckage and some body parts. Then the whole group went into Salazar's dock and up to his mansion which is called *Casa del Malecón*. There were servants there and they confirmed that the boat had left for the Bahamas around two and that Sr. Salazar and his son were aboard, along with three paid crew members. The picture on the screen then went back to the studio and Pat's face. She continued talking.

"Ricardo Salazar is reported to have been one of the richest and most powerful men in the world. The idea that he could be involved in any way in the drug trade is almost unbelievable. In fact there is no proof whatsoever and that idea can only be called supposition. Our station's senior managers have been talking to the F.B.I. and the C.I.A. and those agencies deny knowledge or involvement of the event. There are many opinions being expressed. Some say the explosion was caused by a leak in the propane gas cooking system. The *"Mayday"* call from the yacht describing a fire would tend to bear that out. As of this moment nobody knows exactly what has happened. The C.I.A., the F.B.I. and the Drug Enforcement Agency are all involved now and all have men at *Casa del Malecón* as well as the Coast Guard Station. Tomorrow I will continue our up-to-the-minute coverage of the story. As always we have the news for you as soon as it happens live at the scene of the action. This is Patricia Rivera for Channel 6 saying goodnight."

With Lisa and Lea Kahn not knowing what had happened we couldn't talk openly about it but I was sure that the others were as amazed as I was at Pat's newscast. The phone rang a couple of minutes after we turned off the T.V. It was Bill Gaines. He was also astounded at the telecast but had his own story to tell.

He and Snake crossed Biscayne Bay and found the dock that Snake had planned to go to. It was up a canal and then further up a creek. They tied the boat to a small broken-down dock. From there a path led up to a dirt road where there was a rented car parked. Snake gave Bill the keys and rental papers and directions. The road led out to a paved street. Snake seemed to be in good shape when they got there, even with the almost-slit throat. He didn't talk at all coming across the Bay but when he left Bill at the car he thanked him for his help and said he was going to Nassau and then to Europe. He got back in the boat and took off again and Bill had no trouble getting home. Snake told him to watch Pat Rivera on T.V. Bill also said that Snake told him to have me meet Pat at the Taurus at exactly nine o'clock that night since she was going to leave the studio and come to Coconut Grove at that time unless there was more breaking news.

I had taken the call in Sidney's bedroom so nobody could hear what I said. When I came out, Sidney had three ladies practicing singing the hymn *Amazing Grace*. I looked around for Rocket and saw that she had left. Sidney told me that she had gone because she was too exhausted from the afternoon's work. I was supposed to call her at work the next day. I felt funny about her leaving. It was unlike Rocket to not want to be part of any celebration. I decided to show up where she worked at opening time the next morning. It was sinking in that I was going to lose her and I didn't like the feeling.

The ladies sounded great and after doing it several times Sidney said a prayer and we went out to the bars of Coconut Grove to recruit some new Christians. The first place we went was called the Hungry Sailor, a bar that looked like an English pub with a nautical motif. Maybe like a cockney bar on the London waterfront. Something like that. We walked in and Sidney talked briefly to the manager who simply nodded. The three ladies started singing *Amazing Grace* and the crowd was immediately quiet. Their voices were really good but what startled the crowd was simply how good looking they were. How incredibly beautiful. Spectacular. It would be hard to imagine three more beautiful women together but I wished Rocket was there. They would have looked even better. I was feeling disappointed that Rocket had left but I was on a real emotional high. When they finished all the verses they stopped singing and started recruiting. I learned later that Sidney had gone over his recruiting *shpiel* with Paulette earlier in the week and she had explained it to the others. Sidney did not seem concerned that Lisa Winter was a devout Catholic. I had heard him once in a conversation refer to the Roman Catholic Church as a branch of the Church of England. Nor did it bother him that Lea Kahn was probably a member of an Eastern religion, a Bhuddist or Shinto or one of those. Maybe he really did convert her.

Gus and I listened to Sidney talk to some people. It was hilarious hearing him, but startling to find out how well it worked. He asked people if they belonged to a church. If they did he invited them to come and listen to him preach and to hear the choir. He didn't lie but he did imply to the men that all the female members of the choir were all very beautiful. If they didn't have a church Sidney wrote down their names, addresses and phone numbers. Then he extended an invitation to come for a service and join him personally for coffee afterwards. Sidney acted as if recruiting in a bar was normal and people responded well. His approach was different but he was so charming and so sincere that it worked. I had seen him in action before and knew that when the people showed up Sidney would remember their names. I asked him once how he learned his recruiting techniques and he said he had studied the recruiting techniques of the great football coaches such as Bobby Bowden at Florida State and Joe Paterno at Penn State. By the time we left the Hungry Sailor, Sidney had seven people who promised to come to a service. The ladies had four or five each.

It was a beautiful night, warm but not hot, and every table at every sidewalk café was filled. We did the same thing at the Horny Frog, the Green Street, Le Café de Rat Mort, and all over Coconut Grove. When we got to the Café Europa, Lisa and I looked at each other since we had spent some time there. Lisa looked sad for the only time that night.

After we left Le Rat I realized I had to break away from the others and meet Pat Rivera at the Taurus. As I walked along the crowded street I thought about the future. It seemed to hit me that in addition to shooting the two women and the garbage man on Norman's Cay I had murdered a man that afternoon by slicing his entire head in half. It also occurred to me that I would be very happy to end all this adventuresome shit. It was necessary to perform rescues and get revenge and stuff but I really wanted to stop it and go back to basics. I wanted to concentrate on surgery and sailing, the two things that had been the most important in my life. Now that Ricardo and Butch were dead, Snake could get revenge on Emile Hogge himself.

During the next year I was going to concentrate on the simple things in my life. I was going to start racing my Star boat and compete in one-design competition for a few years. Surgery and sailing were my things, not shooting and slicing people. I would also start painting again seriously. First I would finish the picture of Pat Rivera. I would get the right combination of white and blue and green oil paints for the aqua-colored underwear. The thought of Pat wiggling around naked with nothing but the aqua panties as a decoration made me very horny and I was like that when I found her in the Taurus standing at the bar with a drink in her hand. It was five minutes until nine and I was on time. I got a cold Mexican Corona beer for myself.

Pat had on a white blouse and a short skirt. The skirt was one of those washed blue denim things made like jeans. It was very short. Cute short but very close to slut short. The blouse had a wide collar and was open at the neck but not open enough.

We stood there for a few minutes and talked about the recruiting for the church. I told her about what was happening and that we were going to join the recruiters at the Green Street at nine thirty or Le Café de Rat Mort at ten. I then suggested we step outside the bar for a minute to talk. We took our drinks with us and went out front where the Village Cobbler cooked hamburgers on the grill and fixed shoes when nobody was hungry. I had to ask about the news program and Ricardo and the explosion but I had no idea how much, if anything, Sean had told her.

"I was startled when I saw you on T.V. I couldn't believe what you were saying. Pat, do you actually believe that Ricardo and Butch were involved in drugs and that they were blown up on purpose? I just can't believe it. It must have been the fire and a leak in the propane gas system. I just don't believe the drug business at all. Do you? How did you get involved in the first place? How did you know that anything was going to happen? Was the story you told on television true or did you just make it up?"

"Sean Moran called me Wednesday at the studio and asked me to meet him for a drink after I finished work. He said he had something I might be interested in knowing about. I met him at a bar near the station and he told me a story. He told me to never tell anybody about the conversation. He told me he knew a guy who was with the Secret Service and that he wanted to get some publicity for a gang killing or mob murder or whatever. He said the Government wanted the country to know how big and dangerous the people were in the drug trade. He said his friend would call me personally and make the contact. If I wanted the story I could work with him and if not I could simply turn it down. So I said O.K. and tried to ask him some questions. That was all Sean said he knew. He said he thought the Sicilian mob was trying to move into the South American drug trade but that it was only a guess, just a guess. What the hell are you looking at?"

"I'm trying to look down your blouse. What happened after that?"

"I got a call at the studio the next day. A man's voice I never heard before. Said to call a certain number that night. I asked questions but got no answers. I checked the number and it was a pay phone in Hollywood. I called the number at the time the voice told me to. I got a recording that said to prepare myself to be in Miami Beach with a camera crew Saturday afternoon. It said to plan to leave the studio at eleven and to call another number just before we left. When I called this morning a different voice said to go to the Coast Guard Station at noon. Everything I said in the newscast was true. I'm not going to tell anybody about Sean making the first call. Stop looking down my blouse."

We were standing out in front of the bar but off to the side and in the shadows. There was light from the street lamp and I could see every detail of Pat's face. Her eyes were shining and bright and she was very excited as she talked.

"Is this a really big story for you?" I asked. "Is it the biggest you've ever been involved in?"

"It's a really big story, Dev, and nobody else knows anything about it. Naturally I'll ask for a raise on Monday or something. People in the news business will practically kill to get a story like this. The newspapers were actually interviewing me."

I was so fascinated watching Pat's excited face that I almost didn't notice her unbuttoning the two top buttons of her blouse. I glanced down and even in the dim light I could see that she was wearing the aqua-colored brassiere.

"I read in a story by Ernest Hemingway one time that a lot of ladies get very sexually excited watching bullfights. Many of them demand that their escorts make love to them immediately after they leave the *Plaza de Toros*. Do you think you would get excited watching a bull fight?"

"What's that got to do with what happened today?"

"Well I thought that all the excitement of the explosion and going on television with the story might have the same effect on you." I was moving closer to her and she wasn't backing away.

"Do you think that a big story like this would stimulate me so much in a sexual way that I would simply fall down and take off my *choninos*? Are you crazy or something? I'm a professional television reporter. My excitement is purely a response to a great opportunity. Surely you should understand that."

I didn't answer. I put both arms around her and kissed her long and hard. She responded with her mouth and her body. It was the best one since the hidden place on Bimini. She was putting everything into it. I dropped one hand and put it on her behind and squeezed. She pressed her breasts against me.

"I think you're right," she said, pulling back a little. "*Mis choninos muy estan mojados.* I've got squishy britches."

Mojados means wet.

"Is that why you wore the aqua-colored underwear?"

"Maybe it was. I don't know. Maybe you really piss me off because I want you to be in love with me and all you want is to bang on me a few times. Don't get me wrong. I'm not a virgin. I've done it a few times just for the fun of it. I think I could do it with you just for the fun of it but you aren't that kind of a guy. You gotta be in love with the woman. I think that's what I want, too, but you aren't in love with me."

"We've got to go meet Sidney and the others. When we finish going to the bars and recruiting we have to go back to Sidney's apartment for a few minutes to make sure he gets names and phone numbers. After that we can go to my apartment."

"So you can take advantage of my professional excitement and get an easy score."

"There's nothing easy about you. I've been chasing you since last summer. Actually, I've been chasing you since you stopped chasing me. Rocket is going to New York to become a sportswear designer. Toni has gone back to Madrid. You're the only woman I'm interested in right now."

"My phone hasn't exactly been ringing off the hook, Dev."

"Spend next weekend with me on the boat. We'll go down in the Keys and swim naked and stuff."

"Maybe. I'll try to work it out. A lot depends on the story about the Salazars. Call me Monday night at home."

"What about tonight? Will you come back to my apartment after we leave Sidney's? Will you stay all night?"

"I think so. I'm hot. Very hot. *Muy ardiente*. What about Lisa Winter?"

"She's with Sidney and the others right now. She's just a friend. I'll hold hands with you in the bars we go to so people can see us. How's that for romantic?"

"Let's go."

Pat and I found the others at Le Café de Rat Mort. They had added a few new people to the group. Some people were ready to join the church that night and some wanted to just join in the singing. Lisa Winter spoke to Pat as soon as she saw her and it was obviously very friendly. I did hold Pat's hand some of the time and she did become pretty affectionate. A few times during the moving from one bar to another we had slipped away into an alley for some serious kissing and squeezing.

Later on I was talking to Lisa while Pat took her place in the chorus for a while. We were at a place called the Perfumed Skunk. I was a little drunk by that time and I said something really stupid to her.

"Can I ask you a really personal question?"

"Nothing could be any more personal than what I've already told you. I think we're both a little drunk anyway. I am anyway. Go ahead. What do you want to know?"

"When you go flying solo what do you think about?"

She looked puzzled and then realized what I meant.

"I think about blue sky and white clouds and angels. I mostly think about angels and there is a wonderful heavenly orchestra at the climax."

"If you ever think about me instead of the angels will you let me know?"

"If I ever think about you at the climax I'll leave home immediately and move in with you. You'll find me naked on your bed when you come home that night. I guarantee it."

By midnight we had covered all the likely bars in Coconut Grove. Gus and Paulette had split off from the group to go back to Sidney's. When the rest of us got there the doorman at the apartment looked a little shocked when we paraded through the lobby with all of us that started out plus Pat and four people we had recruited in the bars.

When we got into the apartment Sidney asked us all to come into the extra rooms that he used for his model railroad. He gathered everyone around at one end of the rooms with all the lights turned off and said he had a new section that he wanted to show us. It was called *Folsom's Chasm*. He turned a lot of nobs and pushed some buttons and flipped a bunch of switches and something turned on a timed rheostat. A faint light came on at one end of the room and gradually we started to see what looked like a sunrise in the mountains of Vermont.

I hadn't worked with Sidney's trains for several months and I had not seen the new chasm section. There was a huge gorge with a river running through it. High up on one side there was a tunnel opening. While we watched, a tiny steam locomotive came out of the tunnel and ran slowly along a track which seemed to be carved out of the rocky face of a cliff. It ran along the precipitous edge of the mountain wall, through another very short tunnel and then curved onto a high trestle bridge that appeared to be thousands of feet above the chasm and the river below.

Suddenly we saw another train come out of another tunnel on the other side of the great gorge and start across the towering bridge in the opposite direction. A massive collision was imminent. For a few seconds the two tiny steam locomotives kept on at full speed toward each other and then just before they met head-on one of them switched tracks and they passed within a fraction of an inch of each other. While this was all happening the lights behind the artificial mountains had grown brighter and simulated the sunrise. The whole set-up was quite amazing. Really beautiful. I had spent some time working on the mountains and the bridge but I had never seen it complete with the sunrise effect. Pat was astounded.

"I always wanted my parents to get me an electric train when I was a girl but they said trains were just for boys," she said. "I've never seen anything like this!"

Sidney set up Pat as the engineer for one of the railroads with Lea Kahn as the switchman. Lisa Winter was the engineer of another entirely different railroad with a woman named Marjory who had joined us at the Rat as the switchman for that section. A third railroad was run by a couple from the Horny Frog restaurant. Friends, like Gus and myself, who had helped build the railroad and frequently ran the trains, were never drivers when there were strangers around. The guests who had never seen or played with an H.O. model layout like Sidney's always ran the railroads. I watched for a while. Pat was having a wonderful time, totally fascinated by the whole thing, laughing and giggling as tiny freight cars moved over bridges, through valleys and around mountains.

I went into the living room and sat down by myself on the couch. It had been a long day and I was very tired. The adrenaline that had been flowing since early morning was gone. I thought about Pat and realized that my desire to get her in bed was mostly a reaction to losing Rocket. Things had changed between us that night at Chub Cay. After that we both knew we could never be just friends. We had to get married or stop seeing each other. My summer should have been spent with Rocket. Instead I spent it worrying about Sharon Moran. Once I knew about her I could not have done anything differently. Now it was too late to stop Rocket from going to New York. I knew that. I also knew it would be wrong to get involved with Pat Rivera when I was in love with Rocket. I decided to go home and get some sleep. The laughter from the Green Mountain Express was loud enough that nobody heard me leave. Driving home I thought about Snake Moran and the Bodyguards of the Christ. I wondered if there really was such an organization and if Sean could be part of it.

As soon as I got inside my apartment I knew something was different. I sensed that someone was there. I would have immediately expected Snake but he said he was going to the Bahamas. If it was him he would announce himself quickly. Nothing happened. I pulled out my Luger. I was completely silent and listened carefully. I thought I could hear something in the bedroom so I stepped out of my shoes and moved slowly in that direction. At the door I stopped again. I heard soft breathing and saw what looked like a shape in one of my twin beds. I pointed the gun at the bed and switched on the light.

"Whose in my bed? What are you doing here?"

"It's me. Don't shoot!" It was Rocket. She was in her pajamas.

"What are you doing here? I thought I was supposed to call you at your office tomorrow!"

"You are. I just needed a place for tonight. Now go to sleep and leave me alone."

I took off my clothes and crawled into bed. My mind was in a real turmoil but I was too exhausted to think clearly. I was about to fall asleep when I felt Rocket move in beside me. "You have no initiative whatsoever, Dr. Devlin. I always end up taking off my own panties."

End

About the Author

Hank Burroughs — One day Hank Burroughs got a letter from his parents telling him that when he came home from Prep school that summer he would find that the family had moved to New York, owned a Lightning Class sailboat, belonged to Larchmont Yacht Club and lived across the street from Arthur Knapp Jr. who was the top sailboat racing skipper in the country at that time. He started sailing.

After Trinity College and three years active duty in the Strategic Air Command, Hank and his wife Nancy bought the Billy Atkins designed Dragon (built in 1926) and headed for the Bahamas to "practice" being retired.

Hank has owned and raced one design Lightnings, International 110s and Frostbite Dinghys. He was one of the original eight people who started the International 5-0-5 Class in the U.S.A. He raced his own boat *Foam* in the World Championship in 1969. He has owned and raced in the Midget Ocean Racing Club in an Excalibur 26 and Tartan 30. Add Four Bermuda Races, three Annapolis-Newport and the Westlawn School of Yacht Design.

At age 55 he sold his house and bought a Pacific Seacraft Crealock 34. Once again he and Nancy B. headed south for the Bahamas. They had practiced retirement 30 years earlier and knew the way. They have a son Tony and daughter Dana Klinges. They now live full time on Faber Cove in Fort Pierce, Florida and their Crealock 34 named *Brilliant* sits at the dock behind the house.